PLAN TO STAY™

PEACHTREE CITY LIBRARY
201 Willowbend Road
Peachtree City, GA 30269-1623
Phone: 770-631-2520
Fax: 770-631-2522

WINDWARD PASSAGE

WINDWARD PASSAGE

– JIM NISBET –

THE OVERLOOK PRESS
NEW YORK

This edition first published in hardcover in the United States in 2010 by

The Overlook Press, Peter Mayer Publishers, Inc.
141 Wooster Street
New York, NY 10012

Cataloging-in-Publication Data is available from the Library of Congress

Book design and typeformatting by Bernard Schleifer
Manufactured in the United States of America
FIRST EDITION
2 4 6 8 10 9 7 5 3 1
ISBN 978-1-59020-194-7

This one's for Riley, Peelhead, Joe Ellis
and Janwillem van de Wetering
. . . Four stone originals.

Acknowledgments

The passage from *The Story of a Life*, by Konstantin Paustovsky, translated from the Russian by Julian Barnes, was transcribed from pp. 102-104 of the Pantheon edition of 1964. Copyright 1964 by Random House, Inc.

Passages cited from *The Odyssey by Homer* arrive via Robert Fitzgerald's translation, Anchor Books Edition, 1963, pp. 205-206.

The four lines by Thom Gunn are from "Nights with the Speed Bros.," which can be found on p. 32 of *Boss Cupid* (Farrar, Straus and Giroux, 2000).

The citation from Apollonaire's "La Voyageur" is to be found on p. 75 of *Alcools*, University of California Press, 1965, translation by yr hmbl srvnt.

A stolen remark and a citation come from Tom Raworth; the latter may be found in "The Conscious of a Conservative," *Tottering State*, O Books, 2000, p. 105.

Twenty Small Sailboats to Take You Anywhere, John Vigor, Paradise Cay Publications, 1999.

Thanks to Gregg Gannon for his story about clocking the chief.

Thanks also to Brian Toss and *The Rigger's Apprentice* for the icicle hitch; Reeds' Nautical Almanacs; *Self-Steering for Sailing Craft* by John S. Letcher, Jr.; and *The American Heritage Dictionary*; to Klutch, for Rain Forest Crunch; to Dr. Scott Stryker for some provocative science; and to George Steiner for *Tolstoy or Dostoevsky*.

Please visit Colin Wilson's discussion of A.E. von Vogt's theory of the Right Man in the former's *The Criminal History of Mankind*, pp. 64-75.

The A.C. Swinburne poem via Jack London is "From Too Much Love For Living."

The strophe by Mikhail Lermontov is to be found on page 167 of *An Anthology of Russian Literature in the Soviet Period*, B.G. Gurney (ed. and trans.), Vintage Russian Library, 1960.

Readers! Do not pass up an opportunity to discover Leonard Clark's *The Rivers Ran East*, on pp. 64-66 of which is to be found the venomous snake citation herein.

Books and the sea, I discovered, had more
than a little in common; both were distilled
of silence and solitude.
—STERLING HAYDEN, *Wanderer*.

jerky people on the street
i have not thought myself
one of you for a long time
—TOM RAWORTH

A conspiracy wipes out all the titles conferred by social caprice. In those conditions, a man springs at once to the rank which his manner of facing death assigns to him. The mind loses some of its authority. . . .
—STENDHAL

There is something in a treasure that fastens upon a man's mind. He will pray and blaspheme and still persevere, and will curse the day he ever heard of it, and will let his last hour come upon him unawares, and still believing that he missed it only by a foot. He will see it again every time he closes his eyes. He will never forget it till he is dead—and even then—Doctor, did you ever hear of the miserable gringos on Azuera, that cannot die? Ha! Ha! Sailors like myself. There is no getting away from a treasure that once fastens upon your mind.
—JOSEPH CONRAD, *Nostromo*

Lonely and far a white sail soars . . . .
Beneath the azure current churns,
Above the golden sunlight glows;
Yet for a storm the sail still yearns—
As though in stores one found repose . . . .
—MIHAEL LERMONTOV

There remained the sea, which is free to all, and particularly alluring to those who feel themselves at war with humanity.
—RAFAEL SABATINI, *Captain Blood*.

Contents

PROLOGUE

"WINNER!" "DING DING DING. . . ." SPOTLIGHTS SWEPT THE ASSEMBLY.
"Second prize . . . The first civilian tour of the shrine since completion of
construction!" Desultory cheers and applause. A lune of light swept over
a projection of Officer Few's face and appeared to leave him temporarily
blinded. Speakers blared the inane and popular anthem of Condor Silversteed, "Mandate of Tripartism." It was too loud. It was in bad taste.
Members on the floor cheered. Members in committee skyboxes, despite
the double-glazing of their one-way picture windows, swiped down the
volume. The first-place winner was about to be announced, but it was pre-
ordained, the fix was in, some things just cannot be left to chance. The
audio discretely muted. In the skyboxes the loudest sounds to be heard
were the popping of champagne corks, coarse laughter, the especial groan
of an orgasm overwhelming a recalcitrant prostate, the smack of palms
over a sealed deal. Attending homunculi, cued by the latter, barked like
sea lions—not seals, but close enough—it is The True.

The winner was found eventually, her coccyx identichip scanned by
ceiling snurfs. The Announcer could have asked the snurfbase to pinpoint
her on the auditorium grid the moment her number was announced, but
why deprive the suspense of its artificiality? There was an argument that
she would have been just as surprised either way, but there was a counter-
argument to the effect that, the sensoria of audience members being so
damped as it was, her reaction time might have been sufficiently slow to
mitigate proceedings already protracted by ceremonial caparison. Though
unasked for its analysis, the snurfbase readily produced an inverse Fourier
transform comparing an average winner's reaction profile to a typical
audience-damping effect. Though programmed from square one to
encourage damping effects, management determined that this one went
too far.

Red Means glared down along the steep angle between the convention floor and the skybox—the latter which, for some reason, the Decorator
had lately lined with mohair. Long, coarse, orange mohair. Better it were
kelp stranded by a unusually high tide, left to fester in the sun, reeking
and hopping with sand fleas and flies, than synthetic mohair that reeked,
ever so slightly, of formaldehyde.

No sign of Tipsy. They'd arrived together; she'd left him almost immediately and hadn't reappeared.

He listlessly sipped his Kaliq. When a man has let his life get to where his beer doesn't taste right, matters have proceeded a lagoon too far.

This ceremony had happened only once before, some fourteen years ago, and he knew that a great deal if not all of what he was seeing was animatronic—edited reruns with computer-generated fills. He didn't trust what he was seeing, and he'd never trusted parades, pyrotechnics, conventions, and speeches, either.

So she was genuinely surprised. Not to worry. Her personal squirt patch micromanipulated her reaction, much as surrounding squirt patches coped their response. (In inverse proportion to the square of their distance away from her.) Her name was Melanie Hecatomb, she was seventeen years old, and she'd lived all her life on the 74th floor of the Transbay Tower in downtown San Francisco. What a coincidence. As it happened the shrine package included three days and two nights at the Disney Pier at the foot of Bryant Street, right under the Bay Bridge. So what if, right under the Bay Bridge, there were only five or six tides per annum of sufficient height to permit even the second-largest ship in Disney's cruise line, *Scrooge McPrincess*, from tying up there; each visit rang the gong to the tune of some two million Euroshells. Pressured by the Vendor Consortium informally known as *frijolistas*, Corporateers were working 24/7 on a series of locks, but the Bay, hydraulic manifesto that it is, was proving recalcitrant. Anyway, what a coincidence it would be, as the announcer pointed out, if the atmosphere were to be conducive to such productivity on her day of days, as it often was, in days of yore, in San Francisco, and will be again, especially after the code for the Transbay Environmental Machine Works, formerly known as Yerba Buena Island, is debugged, which will have to wait until this last bond issue is ninety percent Chineesiated; if all goes well, however, Melanie Hecatomb could walk to her Lying-in Suite! Then we'll have a parade! And fireworks!

The Telegates couldn't have cheered louder if they'd thought the propaganda actually meant something. Their response, piped in with the music, almost overwhelmed the old Condor Silversteed hit, "I Need a New Patch." The flesh-and-cartilaginous Delegates cheered because, heckadarn said and done, Melanie Hecatomb was one of their own. If it could happen to her it could happen to anybody.

Officer Oscar Few happened to be the ped image nearest her, and though he got to her quickly, it was not before Melanie had already dispensed three or four pubic endorsements. This Thrill Allotment, as wags in the know called them, were isolated from the Assembly by a Velum *cordon sanitaire* just as soon as they traversed the exit corona. A Member's patch could handle normal prophylaxis. But the Committee had yet to find a way to membranalize the inevitable endorphins released by this particular contact elation. They insisted on approaching the issue as if it were a mere hormonal imbalance, which in turn opened the door to a vast network of well-entrenched technologies and attendant no-bid contracts. Subject after subject, however, claimed that the experience eclipsed anything a synfuck had to offer, and so it was prized. The Committee caved and commissioned an entire city in India to work on the problem. Though the Velums worked well enough, they were expensive. The *frijolistas* whined about below-the-line shells. The Committee would issue a Report after they got back from Holidays, which kicked in right after the Party's big San Francisco Sedulity—in other words, months from now, which was then.

"Follow the money," Officer Few's image counseled Ms. Hecatomb. He pointed. A trail of glow-in-the-gloom thousand-Euroshell notes meandered away from her feet and through the crowd. "Only we can see it. Try not to stray. Even at this point, you could get tagged with Droid Under the Influence."

"I'm so, like, jacked up," Ms. Hecatomb told him, with a smile Few had seen all too often. "Do I have time for a couple more endorsements?"

Few shook a leg. "I'm afraid not."

Ms. Hecatomb pouted, then brightened. "What about you, big boy?"

Few, who was five foot nine, had learned the game. "That's possible," he mendacioed. "But first we must leave the holotorium."

"I'm all wet," Ms. Hecatomb enthused intimately. "Lead on."

The neural bundle known as Few had never gotten used to the New Sexuality—hell, he never gotten used to the Old Sexuality—, but he had become accustomed to ignoring its more louche manifestations, especially on the job. Still and all, what he was dealing with here was the future, which was rapidly becoming the present, and he did not like it. Within the circle of light they made their way through the crowd. The trail of lucre led them a triumviral chase, pollinating the vacuum of losers with the pheromones of her luck, wowing all rhinoported attendees post v.11, build 4. Though to any but the most cynical the path would appear as a Random Walk, the Committee had the dissemination down to parts per billion.

"And now," said the Announcer. "Let us preview what Ms. Hoax-at-home—."

A snurfcoder caught it in the delay loop and made the correction.

"Ah." Hearing it on his monitor, the Announcer adjusted his tie. "Hecatomb."

Amazing, Few thought to himself, and not for the first time, with a glance over his shoulder, they still wear ties.

"Ms. Hecatomb of course will arrive in Basra wearing only the finest Velum, custom tailored to the results of . . ."—a flourish of synthetic brass interrupted the old Condor Silversteed hit, "Pedestal Elevator" that had begun, almost subliminally, to percolate throughout the hall—". . . An all-expenses-paid, three-day trip to the Bird-in-egg Delight Suite high above Disney Pier." This program, as was well-known, costs thousands of Euroshells per hour, and the audience went proportionately nuts. "After which, this girl—," and here the Announcer threw a hand over his shoulder, palm up, toward the big screen tiling the darkness behind him, upon which cuerpometric assemblages of Ms. Hecatomb pole-danced the pixels. Anterior, posterior, lateral, there were even shots from above and below, all of which revealed, despite her tasteful pubic *couture*, extremely intimate details of her enhancements, many of which could be considered florid, even though scientifically derived by means of neural evaluations performed on what few celibate monks remained in captivity. ". . . will exhibit 99.9 percent of the physiognomy of the Three-Day It-Girl." Now tomography of Melanie Hecatomb's pelvic region appeared on the screen, and one of the most sophisticated programs ever developed by the Committee, the codebase of which required two cities in India just to maintain, began to systematically augment it. "A trim here, a tuck there, a blemish removed there, early scarring via adolescent sex there, and—wow! Ladies and gentlemen, we might just never let her mutate! Whaddya say!" The holotorium went nuts. For, after all, pheromones remained liberally distributed throughout the hall hinting to almost everybody that it could happen to anybody at any time at any place just so long as they didn't stray too far from the Party Voxel Projection.

"Ding ding ding ding," declaimed appropriately tinny audio randomly dispersed through the audio sensorium, "we have a winner!" Abruptly the applause decrescendoed through isolated hand claps and exuberant exclamations until it ceased altogether. It was as if somebody had thrown a switch.

The beer had become warm. Red dropped the unfinished bottle into the cooler and levered the cap off a cool one with his teeth. That's all I'm going to get out of this with, he muttered to himself, my fucking teeth. He sipped the beer. Maybe.

"After a mere three days' total immersion in the Zygote Continuum, Melanie Hecatomb will experience her tailored Velum like—like—you got it!" Here the Annoucer pointed into the darkness as if at some individual, "like a baby goat experiences the peristalsis of ana-CON-dadada. . . !"

As he took the second sip, Red snapped the crenelated cap between thumb and forefinger. It ticked against the glass and disappeared into an expanse of factory-extruded Angoralene with a slight hiss.

Male laughter erupted from the audience, riding a wave of feminized endorsement-enthusiasm pheromones. The Announcer blinked and held up a 3x5 card (of which anachronism Party Props [PP] still keeps a stash, subdivision Anachroprop). He appeared to read it again, at arm's length yet, squinting even, before he tossed it over his shoulder and out of the light (there to be caught, run through a hot mangler and refiled by a diligent propshadow). "Old technology," he said, leaning into the microphone, "only there for effect," and, despite having heard this tired synecdoche since the commencement of each of their individual axonal tracks, the audience roared their approval of this and, therefore, of all effects, special or not. Before the reaction had died down completely, the Announcer turned to contemplate a new image of Ms. Hecatomb on the screen. Now, for lack of a better term, she had been thoroughly fine-tuned. Cloaked in a chic skin indistinguishable from her designer Velum and vice versa, the program rotated her through various cuerpometric projections, X Y & Z, wooden, mechanical, and time-lapsed. Altogether, by the up-to-the-nanosecond algorithms, a four-dimensional babe. Gradually the image took on more and more posthuman characteristics, without losing entirely, however, certain animé qualities lately deemed fashionable and sexy, until she exhibited every popular salient of Committee-sanctioned Calabi-Yau Bardo humanoidism.

"Homologous hip resection and replacement. Breast augmentation of course, and vulval morphology. . . ." The projection was relentlessly specific. "And, get this ladies, and especially you gentlemen, the ultimate in personal luxury, perineal mink!"

"Shaving is so over," someone shouted. . . .

Though theoretically soundproofed, in fact Red could hear every tiresome fricative of fellation one booth over, let alone the "conversations" riding high and confident on their respective Vocative Makeovers.

"What's happening," inquired some Voice, its fricatives moistened by champagne.

"They're heckafucking ecstatic, Sir-Ma'am-Or-Thing-As-The-Case-May-Be," a Shadow9 recited, nearly redlining its Obsequiousness Asymptote. (The current beta takes care of that.)

"In future, you may indirectly address me as He/She/It. In direct address, Entity will do."

The Shadow9, shorn of an earlier generation of the inadvertently rude B-tree contraction to SHeIT, concaved toward this generous condescension. "Of course, Entity."

"It is more accurate," He/She/It said behind his hand to his astronomically recompensed Companion. He cleared his vox of petromucus and readdressed the Shadow9. "You're new here?"

"Fresh from the Unilaterally Referentiable Filesys in Eastern Sector Cold Boot Endocarp."

He/She/It considered this. "And how are things in Guang Dang?"

"Polluted." A second concavity. "Entity."

"And so what? All anybody does there is work—correct?"

"Twenty-eight-six, Entity."

"I like to get to know them a little bit," He/She/It stage-whispered, behind the hand, to the Companion. "Familiarity can randomly detect flaws in beta-write. Think on-the-fly Turing Test." He patted her rouged patella. "Why I get the big shells."

"Zut," cooed the Entity's by-the-second Companion. "Alors."

"Have you ever studied the Nazis?" the Entity asked. "No, really." He suctioned her labia with a reassuring appliance. "I'm interested."

"I could swot up instanter." Her laughter tinkled, very like a tray of chilled champagne glasses on the TGV to Luna, thought the Shadow9, despite never having been anywhere without getting there instantly, plus or minus the resistance inherent to vacuum twitter. No matter, the experience was on the Blear for all to visit. "Zut," the consort purred, "wouldn't you rather inject me with a Subject Capsule?"

"The very thought gives me wood."

"Get a load of that armature!"

Red closed his eyes and rolled the chilled bottle over his forehead as if it were the blade of a squeegee, temple to temple. It used to help.

". . . And what will she," rhetorically queried the Announcer, "our fully remodeled Ms. Hecatomb, witness during her tour of the shrine?" A montage slid over the screen behind him. A self-propelled hand slipped him a 5x7 card. "What's this?" The Announcer touched his lapel flybutton, currently asleep, with pronated fingertips. "I almost forgot!" He leaned into his light. He glanced a second time at the card. "And who do you think will give the lucky Ms . . . Heck . . . tome . . . her . . . tour?"

"Holo-Charley!" someone shouted.

The announcer fanned himself with the 5x7 card and rolled his eyes.

"Holo-Asche!" came an obvious rejoinder.

The Announcer folded his arms and shook his head with a sneer.

"No, no! HoloVirgil!"

"Of course!"

"Let it be HoloVirgil!"

Having pretended to listen to and consider these suggestions, and skating over the frown impulse generated by the classical reference, which as any apparatchik could tell you dangerously narrows the scope of audience comprehension, again the Announcer shook his head and suggested they give up.

"We give up!" shouted the *claquers*.

"Using the latest morphological and psychometric research . . ." The Announcer turned and indicated the screen behind him, whereon the image of Ms. Hecatomb reappeared, her body circumnavigated from cerebellum to toenail, from the two metatarsi to the seven chakras by diminutive animated comets of colored light. The image of the face of Oscar Few, or his guiding hand, or his thick-soled shoes, appeared, disappeared, and reappeared in the holographic shadows around the winner, much as they had another lucky girl, fourteen years before. "Nice," remarked a voice in the adjacent skybox. "That guy's the realest thing in the building. Except you, of course," it added unctuously, speaking to its Companion. All was choreographed to the famous composition for Hammond B-3 organ and glass harmonica, "Chromatic Evisceration," by Condor Rashid, from the only album he managed to release since his creative differences with Condor Silversteed caused them to separate until such time as cooler heads and economic necessity forced them to reunite, less than an hour later. Occasionally the animated Ms. Hecatomb squealed and twisted and favored one or another of the photonic entities with a bemused and censorious look, as if accusing it of a lascivious impropriety. Unbeknownst to almost everyone, only Few's steady presence kept her suborbital. A triumph of state-funded physics. Every woofer and sub-woofer in the hall rumbled tympani. Every small-to-midsize tweeter emitted ding ding dings. The midrange shrieked "Whoopee, Winner" and "Pow pow pow!"

". . . holostar, connoisseur of nightlife, and part-time woman who put the chick back in apparatchik, the one, the only, the metabodacious—Condor Silversteed!"

He drew out the syllable as women pseudosquealed and men pseudodeprecated. There were laughter and groans, guffaws and eructations, which evolved into a veneer of reluctant but good-natured applause instigated by *claquers* pinging cervical and prostatic identichips. No hint of anticlimax, forget foreordination, let alone the fix's being in, surfaced in so much as a single bandwidth—they applauded, au contraire, the textbook audacity of product placement.

"Ask her about Silversteed's *Party Endowment*," a male shouted to knowing laughter.

The announcer's mouth fell open. "Ah," said he. "Could it be that Ms. Hecatomb, aside from being the luckiest-girl-on-the-planet-today!—" applause and cheers, "knows exactly what she wants?" A roar of approval.

"But," said the Announcer abruptly, and the audience just as abruptly shut up. "What is it the lucky couple will witness, in the newly ionized Shrine to the Continuum? Eh?"

"Zygote Amour!" someone shouted.

"Political Awakening!" shouted another.

No one reacted. No one took up the cry.

"Anomalies happen," intoned the Announcer, "but, oh my, that was in extremely poor taste."

"I'm sorry." "I didn't mean it." "I'm sor—!" Two hisses and two pops, sounding like a pair of slightly out of sync bottle rockets firing backwards in time, truncated the apologia. Silence flared throughout the hall. A pair of minute sulfurous wraiths sieved through the nearest return grills of the pollution-conditioning system. The thought, *Lead By Example*, traversed every neural bundle attending the show.

Red pursed his lips. He'd never been quite certain as to whether such minor "corrections" were genuine or otherwise. Either way, however, they seemed somehow . . . touching.

"Moving right along," announced the Announcer, touching the knot in his tie with pronated fingers. "Here we have," he indicated the screen above and behind him, "the Grail of the Continuum."

Jesus Christ, Red growled, even I have it memorized!

In the adjacent skybox, He/She/It and his by-the-second consort leaned toward the insulated transparency. Even the Shadow9 concaved in interest. But, though they and the members of the audience expressed a certain awe, the Grail looked to Red exactly like a translucent lava lamp parked on a mesa in Golden, Colorado.

A paired infundibulum, the mouth of one amphora inverted over that of another like horizontally enantiomorphic zwiebelturm, the one tapering down into the up-turned taper of the other, not unlike like a large hourglass or a very small reactor cooling tower, contained a shimmering cocktail of blood serum and nutrients. One an artificial cobalt, the other a chromium yellow, strictly for effect, and each fluid seethed, indefatigably effervescent, like a cocktail on Venus.

"I'm thirsty," Red whispered. He looked at his bottle. Half empty, and tepid again.

Everything but the dry ice, the Shadow9 was about to opine, until it noticed the frosty fumes. Globules of gas spiraled upwards toward the surface, or clung to the transparent sides of the vessel, much like the three-sided kelp-bubble hotel rooms to be found in any Disney port of call. A bezel of gold, chosen because of its noble characteristics, encased the base of each vessel, and a ring of eight Torx shoulder screws affixed the display to its plinth.

Shit, Red whispered, the sibilance harsh with disgust.

"Live," the Announcer stage-barked, "from Hafiza min Zayt!"

The entire hall convulsed into reverent silence. "I must forewarn you that if you experience a slight itch in your transdermal patch, it is because, in anticipation of the next portion of our program, we are tweaking your metabolics ahead of time, inducing hypoesthesia, each according to the finest and latest prognostics based, of course, on your medical histories, what you had for breakfast this morning, and party affiliation."

Laughter. What affiliation? The party is the party!

A communal sigh wafted through the hall like a phero-modulated breeze over the afterdeck swimming pool adjacent the Dan O'Neil Hi-Roller Suite of any Disney cruise ship, bringing with it slight hints of chlorine, plumeria, blackberries, leather, freshly lasered chain mail, and the fumes peculiar to telegraphic plant decoders (*Desmodium motorium*).

"Behold the Alembic," the Announcer intoned reverently, as the dot of a laser pointer boxed it in, "which contains the protein site for the genetic . . . map of . . . Dynasty Kleagaaaan . . . !"

The sinuating shock wave addlepated the already adulatory audience. Cheers erupted and overwhelmed what applause the *claquers* had been intended to catalyze. In short, a cacophony.

"It was easy," the Announcer beamed. "All we had to do was ask!"

The reaction on the floor, two stories below the podium, and five below the skyboxes, in the spill of light beyond the lip of the stage, foretold that which was consuming the balance of the audience—the urge to mosh. Arms waved. Fingers pointed. Spittle flew. Plastic water bottles and the odd Saturday Night Merkin arched up into the lights and back down.

"On the right," the speaker insisted, his audio markedly louder. "On the right . . . " But the audience were not responding as hoped. It was beginning to sound like one of those old-time political conventions, the ones they used to have when the quantum condensate was harder to fake, the mid-twentieth century ones in which nobody was really sure who the candidates might be until an entire week had been consumed by argumentative debate, deal-making, tear gas, and payoffs. Tacky tacky tacky. Someone in Technical had the bright idea of re-cuing the timpani roll-out, which cleared the spatiotemporal sufficient for the repeat announcement: ". . . the protein . . . scaffold . . . Dynasty . . . Kleagan!"

This time it worked like ether in a diesel's injectors. Though chaos erupted, it flowed in the right direction: toward more chaos. Raw energy totaled the logic routines, with the result that transdermal patches spit narcotics and pharmaceuticals clean through rotator cuffs. Even the more gymnasium- and hormone-toned musculature couldn't U-turn the infusion outright. Bald domes spat sweat. The resultant aerosol confused sentient sensors, de-emofiers, climate diapers and, finally, outed the security circuits.

Catharsis, it says somewhere in some manual, keeps the lid on society.

On the big screen, Officer Few having inserted himself between the It Girl and the camera, backed her and himself into the shadows and out of the shot.

The hives released a ration of slogonated flybuttons. "Of course we could do it in a test tube," mottoed an inseparable pair of them—"But there's no place like home!" Others epoused, "In Vitro We Trust!" and "It Matters Not What We Say" Siamesed with "But How We Say It!" These and others attached themselves to the thoraxes of 'gates at random. Flybutton snake doctors monitored and picked off and recycled strays, mutants, orphans, and renegade units with expired credibility dates.

Despite enthusiastic crowdsurfing, fistfights broke out among Delegates. Even Telegates, visible on screens in the various organizational alcoves and hubs scattered throughout the Moscone Holodome, and thoroughly edited for content, erupted into punditry. And Hologates merged into choral static. The sound system erupted into Condor Silversteed's "Rational Anthem," which then segued into his sempiternal chestnut, "The Nucleotides Are With Us," shredding what paper cones remained in many a rented sound reinforcement cabinet.

The Announcer began to fragment into his holographic constituents, with a sound like an over-squelched VHF radio. Page keys, whose frequency normally exceeded the range of the human ear, but transposed by security algorithms into audible tones, rent the overemployed fuel/air mixture. Finally the Security Algorithms took over snurfing entirely, beginning with a global—meaning every 'gate inside or outside of the auditorium—transdermal infusion of a potent cocktail of Coke syrup, mescaline sulfate, and pentazocine.

Pandemonium, nonetheless.

He/She/It muttered as if to He/She/Itself, though there's no such thing as Privacy. "When the Security Snurf piggy-backs the Announcer's own voxcode, you know things are artificially intelligent," the Shadow9 interpreted sententiously.

The by-the-second Companion slathered baby oil on the Entity's smoking armature.

The very floor in the holotorium began to depixelate.

The screams were polemical.

"Now," roared the Apparatus. "How many people here stipulate the necessity of religion above that of a global marketplace?"

Nobody was stupid enough to show a hand for that one, but the floor opened up under the Believers anyway, for, as predetermined numbers of flybuttons retailed, "Privacy Compromises Truth."

A few flybuttons managed to attach themselves to some of these 'gates on their way down, their motto being "The Logic Is Hardwired." As if anyone needed to be reminded.

"What about the folks who surf party affiliation despite the True Vector of Capitalism?"

Static disorganized Holos and Teles.

The floor opened up under certain delegates whether they understood the question or not. . . .

And now Condors Rashid and Septum, triumphantly reunited with Condor Silversteed just in time to rib him about skimming the cream off the Honeymoon, invited every 'gate remaining to sing along on one of the band's Lawrencium chestnuts. And who could refuse an invitation like that?

It may not feel Immaculate, baby,
but it's certainly going to
Scan That Way
Scan That Way
Scan That Way . . .

"And how many of you fully intend to quaver by the light of every transmogrification of the sublime Melanie Hecatomb—" and here the fully remodeled image of Ms. Hecatomb, stripped of its prophylactic designer Velum, reasserted itself on the big screen and overrode every image on every screen on the Convovulum Hookup, and the *claquers* went nuts. In the background, the image of Officer Few stood stock still, visibly distressed. ". . . on her meta-haj to the Grail of Capital Continuum!"

Snurf-picked telegates, delegates, and hologates hammered the very rivets of the Mosconi Holotorium with a mighty roar. Spotlights envelummed each and every one, a lusty penumbra of pheromones overriding all rhinobuilds canceled every residual effluvium, left, right, and center, and the substrate re-congealed beneath them all.

"Winner! Ding ding ding: Winner! Pow pow, pow pow pow! We have a Winner. . . ."

Silence reigned in the mohair skybox. Anybody there might have heard a Kaliq cap drop to the fibers. But nobody was there. In the cupholder recently affixed to the recliner by Maintenance, little bubbles rose to the surface of a half-empty bottle of beer.

I

INCIDENT AT SEA

ONE

CHARLEY LAY BELOW, SOUND ASLEEP IN THE V-BIRTH, WHEN SHE STRUCK. The way on her sublimated into heat, splinters and noise until she came to a standstill. A floatstill. But afloat, still. The inertia of Charley's body, transposed into momentum, launched him headlong into the forepeak. There the stock of the 40-pound anchor attempted to sunder his left humerus from its glenoid, which mechanism rendered him inert again, his velocity sublimated into heat and pain.

But for various spare sails and the ditch bag, which cushioned the impact, the anchor might well have succeeded in dislocating his shoulder entirely. As this occurred early in the second continuous hour of sleep he'd had in four days, it wasn't the collision but the pain that woke him up. A few inches to port and the jolt might have been harmless; a few inches to starboard and he may not have lived to know it.

He'd once fallen ten feet off a dock onto a bollard on a Mississippi sand barge and inflicted pretty much the same injury on the same shoulder, an injury that had proven facile to repetition ever since. Facile or not, it hurt every time. And as he lay in the forepeak, rehearsing to himself the chronic routine—no left wing flapping for two or three weeks, no drug would completely kill the pain, even reading a book in the bunk would leave the shoulder throbbing, but for now it's breathe in and breathe out, let the pain swell like a pneumatic pylon right beside you, try and distinguish it from your inner self until it stabilizes sufficiently to permit coherent thought—he heard running water.

Water. Right below his head. Water, coming aboard.

Whereas a sailorman could sleep with one ear clapped to his ship's hull like a limpet to a rock as she made her way through almost any kind of sea, and rest there as soundly as a laborer might nap away an afternoon after a long hot morning of scything waist-high wheat, the least change in that watery tune would goad a sailor from his rest. By the time Charley disentangled himself from the anchor he was wide awake and the pain was almost forgotten, for, by the light of the foredeck skylight, mere inches above his head, seawater glinted among the links of 5/8" chain, the anchor's rode, which lay heaped on the sole. As he considered this a swell lifted her stern, her bow dipped, and warm

Caribbean brine rose through the links of chain to soak his knees.

"She's holed," Charley said aloud. "She's holed below the waterline."

Despite the wounded wing he might ship the storm jib over the hole, dive the hull, improvise some repair. . . . It's called fothering. Look it up. I'm busy. He watched the water. That hole's too big for fothering. Not to mention, he noted, I got no oakum, no yarn. He tried to lift the tingling arm. No dice. I'm sinking before my time. He touched the shoulder with his good hand. Better perhaps that first he move the anchor and some chain to get at the ditch bag, and ain't that seamanlike, he chastised himself, to have a 40-pound anchor and 200 feet of rode between the ditch-bag and the companionway? Downright salty. Yes. And as Charley thought this thought, she jibed.

He didn't have to see it. In fact, if he'd been on deck, it might have swept him overboard, or crippled him worse, or killed him outright. Her bow wallowing low, her stern lighter and faster, she came about sufficient to overwhelm the self-steering vane, her stern turned through the following wind, and the boom accelerated all the way to port from all the way to starboard, snapping the screws in its preventer block, and kept right on going. With a thoroughly loud crack, accompanied by a jangle of wire rope and shackles that shook the whole boat, the boom folded itself over the port shrouds, carrying away two until stopped by the third and last one forward.

I need, thought Charley, to be keeping up with events. He turned and scrambled aft through the cabin, the unstrung arm straight down and pendant as an unemployed halyard. Just as he gained the companionway she lurched and his shoulder banged the bulkhead. A searing pain concentrated all its heat in his shoulder joint, so sharp a protest that his stomach clenched. There's oxycodone in the ditch kit, he thought, as he stuck his head out of the companionway; it's there, that is, if Cedric Osawa didn't eat it all; it was to keep it away from Cedric that he'd stowed it there in the first place, some time back. He hadn't checked it since.

On deck things were much as he had foreseen, except that the auto-helm rotor floated in *Vellela Vellela*'s wake like the spoon of a giant bass lure, tethered to the vessel by one of its two stainless steel support stanchions; the other swayed above the transom like the stalk of a beheaded flower. And he realized with a start that it wasn't a reef he was seeing aft, beneath the galvanized vane, although, festooned as it was with barnacles, and sea fans streaming, it looked like one; but no, the reef was a shipping container, hovering half a fathom below the surface. The nearly 645 fathoms charted for these waters unreeled just below it—some 3,800 feet: two-thirds of a mile, and that's a datum adequate to clench the stomach for real. As he watched the thing it bumped the boat again, just a nudge this time, abaft the port quarter. He touched the tiller. So it wrecked the vane but missed the rudder. His presence of mind clamored for a pint draft of adrenalin, upon which resource amazement, fear, resignation, courage and his injury already disproportionately vied; while the monster iron box, nearly half again the length of *Vellela Vellela*'s twenty-eight feet, lumbered pornographically beneath the blue swell. All feathery edges concealing sharp corners, it languidly yawed five or six degrees as if enticing the little boat to mate again, perhaps fatally this time, stove you little stem, bash you little keel, the whole of its rectilinear bulk increased and obscured by streaming, rust-infused kelp, a giant pod ripe to be burst asunder by the implacable keel bulb preceding a thousand-foot tanker, disgorging a GI family's compact car, computers, clock-radio, kitchen appliances, TVs, bicycles, baseball bats, lawn furniture, arctic parkas, and parti-colored plastic yard toys into the aquasphere like some thalassic piñata. Sir, piped the bosun, resident in Charley's head lo these many years, make a note of that partially legible eleven-digit alphanumeric identification number and ring our solicitor, have her inform the freight-forwarding bastard what owns ten thousand of these things we'll have him up on charges, yank his chain, rattle his cage, bang his gong.

That's the bosun all over. Always angling for the female solicitor with wild underwear beneath the pinstriped suit, and here's the perfect opportunity. Her skills would be brought to bear, of course, on a contingency basis.

The Gulf Stream was carrying a pretty steep swell, though not too closely timed, but Charley needed to get this mess under control lest she broach or bury her stove nose in a trough. Even as he thought this thought, the next swell came along, inserted itself between the little ship and the container, and lifted her stern. Her nose dropped precipitously, awash. Charley waited. And *Vellela Vellela* labored up.

Atop the house he paid out the main halyard with his right hand while ineptly flaking the sail with his left. Back in the cockpit he snugged the main sheet in an attempt to get the boom off the remaining shroud, but it wouldn't come away. The aluminum had taken a bite of shroud, looking much like a tree limb grown up against and finally encapsulating a strand of fence wire. In fact, Charley thought, as he studied the situation, the stub of boom between mast and shroud seemed to be standing in as a sort of lower spreader. Which meant that at least some of the load was being thrown through the boom back to the mast, instead of to the remaining chain plate. Or some such structurally optimistic horseshit, glossed the bosun. Best leave it.

He turned his attention to the genoa, whose sheet had held through the jibe. It looked like the kite wasn't wrapped around the forestay, but when he released its halyard it wouldn't come down, and the downhaul wouldn't douse it either. Squinting aloft, his eyes shielded in the shadow of his raised right hand, for his left no longer lifted that high, he thought it likely the halyard had jumped the block and now lay pinched between the sheave and its cheek at the very top of the mast; thus to remain until somebody went aloft to fix it. Aloft on the main halyard with one arm and a single port shroud?

I don't think so, said the bosun.

He would have to sail with half a rig. So long as the wind didn't kick up he'd make lemonade with the lemon he'd been dealt. Genoa up regardless, he belayed its halyard at the foot of the mast and coaxed her round to a starboard tack, easing the sheet until she was on a beam reach to port, which threw the sail's strain onto the intact starboard shrouds.

And despite everything, she sailed like that.

So we're off to Texas by the compass, the bosun observed wryly. Better westward than downward, Charlie suggested. You must not have been to Texas, replied the bosun.

With a glance aft for assurance that they were putting sea room between themselves and the blundering artifact of commerce, Charley touched up helm and sail until, amazingly, despite her stern's moving through the water easier than her bow, she found a groove. Somewhere between a reach and foundering, it represented a new point of sail for Charley, who, despite a lifetime on the water, had never lost a vessel under his command, nor so much as crewed aboard one lost.

Sure, remarked his bosun, and every day at sea is a new adventure, ninety-five percent boredom and five percent terror, like a fuliginous green olive stuffed with habanero bobbing in ambush at the bottom of a perfectly gelid martini. I never thought of it that way, Charley admitted. Which is why I get the big money, skipper.

Charley retrieved a block from a bucket of gear in the starboard cockpit locker and gave it a becket to a starboard cleat, directly abeam the tiller. He routed the port genoa sheet around the port winch across the cockpit to and through the block, and made fast the bitter end to the tiller with a slipped clove hitch. He snubbed the tiller to a port cleat with a doubled length of bungee cord, fiddled around with it for a bit, et friggin in the riggin voilà, pronounced the bosun, sheet-to-helm self-steering. Not bad for a misanthrope who insists on bein' a purist boat bum to the extreme of sailing the bounding main without a friggin' engine.

A lot of good an engine would do us now, my salty Sancho Panza,

Charley pointed out. When's the last time we had a look at the chart?

Who needs a blasted chart? You know damn well where we are.

Uh, in the Gulf Stream?

Very good. And where we goin'?

Boca Chica, just north of Key West. Nominally, anyway.

The Gulf Stream will see to the literalization of that, the bosun agreed acidly.

That's likely true, Charley replied, with hooded eyes. Bermuda, here we come.

Maybe we should put up the radar reflector?

I don't think so.

Set off the EPRB?

Charley glanced behind him. Not to worry, the bosun reassured him. You disconnected the battery. And oh, added the bosun quietly, did you see that?

Charley saw it.

There's another.

Charley saw that one too. How do they know?

It's their job. At least somebody around here, the bosun added pointedly, is doing their job.

Charley could neither dismiss nor relish this truism but, informed by long experience, he had to admit them as altogether uncanny.

Say, said the bosun, ain't we someplace around where that jet went down in the eighties?

That could have been anywhere in these waters, Charley reminded him.

The bosun warmed to the story. The skipper did a good job of putting her down, see. Passenger and crew survived the impact. Not a single fatality. Everybody got out of the plane before she settled. Everybody had on a life jacket. Shipshape. Bristol, even. Then it got dark.

Are you going to—?

All night the survivors bobbed in the water, listening helplessly as one or another of them got picked off in the obscurity. First a scream off that way, then another off this way. Maybe distant, maybe right next to you, then silence. Maybe some whimpering. Then, over that way—

Stow it.

The sea hissed past the hull so that it almost appeared as if *Vellela Vellela* were really sailing. She lifted as the following swell passed under her and settled into the trough very like the seaworthy hull Charley knew hers to be. To have been. Though now she was clumsy. But there's nothing like setting to leeward, under the light of a rising sun to windward, with a following swell to pick up her hull as it passes and to let her gently down again, nothing like it for pelagic pulchritude. He'd never known seas like those to be found in the Caribbean.

She settles a little further into each trough, allowed the bosun, a little heavier, and heavier yet. And do we not descry the hour for raft and ditch kit, or will it be a stiff drink?

It is perhaps the former, agreed Charley, although they say that you should abandon your vessel only after she sinks out from under you because—. Because even if the deck's awash, the Bosun interrupted, as if bored, most vessels never really sink—especially if there's a watertight bulkhead or two aboard, and it's made out of fiberglass with a spade keel, he added sardonically.

She's holed, Charley admitted forlornly. He watched the tiller and the genoa for a while and it almost looked as if she could sail on indefinitely, or at least so long as conditions held.

But conditions wouldn't hold. There was a ton and a half of lead in the keel. Buoyancy will fail and gravity will prevail. And as he thought this he caught a glint of another fin, maybe two or three points and sixty yards off the port bow, just under the foot of the sail. It was time to get the ditch kit topside.

He left the helm and went below to find, as if he hadn't expected it, about two inches of water sidling over the cabin sole. A rubber glove and a red plastic lid bobbed back and forth, much as they might be expected to idle in a tidepool. There were several open-end wrenches in the water, too. Metric, as he happened to know, hastily and carelessly stored, and now Charley experienced a pulse of urgency. From a drawer next to the chart table he pulled a waterproof bag containing his wallet, passport, $2,500 cash Bahamian, the boat's papers and log, the marked-up type-script of an unfinished novel he'd been mostly not working on for almost two years, and six or eight business envelopes pre-addressed to his one correspondent, a sister he had seen once in twenty-five years.

Two hundred and seventy pages. Ah, them was fine 'n' idle days, mused the bosun, on the hook in Blue Hole Cove, layerin' up the narrative.

Two seventy-six, Charley corrected him mildly, as he folded NOAA chart 11013, *Straits of Florida And Approaches*, along its well-worn creases and added it to the pouch.

Not like today, the bosun observed.

Charley splashed into the forepeak to find that the anchor rode had draped several lengths of itself over the ditch kit. Sure and it's the amorous embrace of a foul and galvanized constrictor, glowered the bosun. Charley cleared the chain single-handed, for by now his overly exerted left arm was completely useless. He grabbed the grommets of the draw-stringed mouth of the ditch bag, sat down and, pushing with his heels, dragged it backwards over the flooded sole. The bag became heavier with each slog as its canvas sponged up seawater. He'd made the bag himself from an ancient sail. Shoulda been nylon, suggested the bosun. Maybe you should get a job, Charley replied. Got one, the bosun replied smugly. Charley paused to undo the reef knot in the drawstring and stuff the waterproof bag into the mouth of the ditch kit bag, so as to disencumber his teeth. Who's idea was it, the bosun asked, to give such employment to an old sail? A penny saved is a penny earned, Charley puffed. Penny wise, pound foolish, the bosun retorted. I don't want to spend my last day on earth thinking about money, Charley snapped. The bosun laughed out-right. And what demiurge donates to your charity the hubris to posit that your last day, of all your days, should be different from any other?

Passing the galley, his mind sorting through the boat's mostly invisible inventory, he yanked open a drawer and retrieved a thin Norwegian bon-ing knife, still in its sheath, and stuck it between his belt and the small of his back. He backed up the four teak steps of the companionway ladder and there, one foot outside on the cockpit sole and the other on the next to last step of the ladder, glanced aft to ascertain that the path was clear. His eye caught a movement beyond the transom, and he paused to behold a sight he'd never seen or imagined. The sea behind the boat displayed five or six dorsal fins, ranging in area from one to two square feet, each of them trailing a zigzag of little white bubbles. Charley bethought himself of the task at hand, and, though his eyes and mind remained abaft, gave a heave. One wet foot slipped on the cockpit floor. The other shot forward off the varnished top step of the companionway ladder. Seeking a pur-chase as he fell backwards, Charley's hand plucked a line that dangled from the mouth of the sea bag. It might have been the grommeted line that cinched shut the bag's mouth, but it wasn't. Instead, it was the infla-tion lanyard of the two-man life raft, and, as advertised, one good tug was all it took. The lanyard drove a stainless steel pin into the cap of a CO_2 cartridge and, lying on his back on the cockpit sole in several inches of water and nearly knocked senseless by the knob of the belayed tiller, which struck him square on the occiput, Charley watched helplessly as, inflating, the life raft split the hand-stitched seam in the old canvas from one end to the other. The raft popped and creaked like two clowns twist-ing up a pride of balloon animals, and kept right on inflating until, soon enough, the raft entirely filled all the space between the chart table and the roof of *Vellela Vellela*'s cabin.

Hm, said the bosun, reading a plastic tag that dangled off the lanyard, says right here that this thing can be easily deployed by almost anyone on board, even women and children.

Remind me to start a family, Charley muttered caustically, as he plucked the waterproof pouch out of the brine in the cockpit, into which the mouth of the ditchbag had spat it. For lack of a better place he stuffed the pouch between the waist of his shorts and the knife at the small of his back.

Best hurry up with that family, the bosun suggested.

Otherwise, they reminded each other in unison, we might die alone.

TWO

QUENTIN CAUGHT A RED LIGHT ON SECOND AT TOWNSEND, A BLOCK FROM the new ballpark and not thirty yards from the chandlery. "Oh my goodness," Tipsy said from the passenger seat.

"Yes." Quentin adjusted his shades. It was five twenty-five and they were facing directly into the setting sun. "Not many people stop for a red light any more."

Tipsy, her knuckles whitening around the in-dash grab bar, said to the windshield, "Such a nice man, preempting a girl's getting t-boned by two lanes of cross traffic."

"The real reason is that 1973 230SL passenger doors are hard to find."

"You should write a book on the steeds of chivalry."

"After I've cataloged the steeds of Folsom Street," Quentin sniffed under his shades, "I doubt I'll have any paper left."

Tipsy looked out the passenger window, looked again, and smiled in spite of herself. "Maybe you should take a frame out of this guy's movie."

Quentin looked. "All I see is an acre of burnt orange sheet metal."

"Up periscope," Tipsy suggested.

Quentin leaned forward and angled his glance up and through the windshield, about forty-five degrees above the plane of the hood. "It's a HumVee."

"You're the expert on steeds." Tipsy angled her own line of sight, up through the passenger window. "Can you see any of the video screens in that thing?"

"Why?"

"I can't tell you without embarrassing myself."

"Give me a hint."

"Wait till the light turns green."

Quentin glanced at her, then strained further over the dashboard. "Is it the governor?"

"I doubt it."

Quentin resumed his driving posture. "I'd like to have a word with him about same-sex marriage." After a moment he twisted both hands on the steering wheel as if it were a pair of motorcycle throttles. "So what's the big deal?"

"You'll see."

"This is the second longest light in town," Quentin pointed out. "Only that time warp at South Van Ness and Mission is longer."

The HumVee lurched ahead.

"It's green."

"So?"

"So follow him. Aren't you gonna—?"

The car behind them honked.

"Oh," said Tipsy. "I get it."

Two cars back, a driver honked twice. "No, you don't get it." Quentin drummed his fingernails on the rim of the steering wheel.

"I do too get it."

"It's rush hour, after all," Quentin observed. "If I get shot by an irate commuter, it'll be your fault."

A chamber arrangement of car horns.

"I declare," said Quentin. "This is worthy of George Antheil."

"Look, stupid—"

"Stupid, is it. And who is not behind the wheel because she racked up a DUI?"

Tipsy slapped the dashboard. "I try to bring you up to date on pop culture and all you can do is throw my past into my face." Vehicles streamed past on the right, honking.

"Your past? You got that DUI two months ago."

Tipsy sat back against her seat and folded her arms. "I should have been a lesbian."

Despite a prominent pair of No Left Turn signs on the other side of the intersection, Quentin turned on his left hand turn signal. The horns became continuous. "Face it, girlfriend, for one solid year, you're going to need me like a junky needs laxative."

"Only ten months remain, and that's disgusting."

"I couldn't agree more."

"Will you please catch that HumVee?"

"The ultimate transitive verb, used as an adverb." Quentin floored it, and a plume of blue smoke seemed to propel them forward. "This could be expensive," he added, glancing at the rearview mirror. "Crankcase oil is up to eight dollars a quart."

They caught the Hummer at Fifth, just as it was making an illegal left onto the 280 on-ramp. "Follow him," Tipsy instructed.

With a glance at his rearview mirror, Quentin followed. "We keep this up, we'll both be walking."

"Close to about twenty yards and stay behind him."

Quentin did so.

"Now." Tipsy pointed with one hand, still clinging to the grab bar with the other. "Note the video display in the back of each headrest?"

"Land sakes alive, it's a TeeVee in a horseless carriage."

"It's been an option for twenty years."

"So what? There isn't even anybody in the back to watch it. Clearly, the ostentatious swine has no friends or family."

"Can you see the program that's playing?"

The sunlight was at right angles to their direction of travel now, barely topping a thick fog that poured over Twin Peaks, about three miles to their right.

Quentin closed to within ten yards of the HumVee and squinted. "Caramba," he exclaimed, "it's a pornographic movie." He peered over the lenses of his sunglasses. "Tant pis, however, it would appear to involve straight people."

"There's a screen in the dashboard, too," Tipsy noted helpfully, "for a total of three." At seventy miles an hour, they watched for a moment. "Another page for the book of steeds?"

"Well," Quentin prevaricated, "perhaps, rather than waste his commute by marinating his brain in sports-talk radio, this Hummer-owning individual is pursuing a close study of heterosexual mating rituals, mores, and techniques in hopes of finishing that long-stalled masters degree in anthropology and entertainment." A quarter mile elapsed before Quentin added, "Which may well lead to tenure, bulletproof health care, and early retirement at eighty percent of full salary."

"I'll bet you a dollar," Tipsy retorted crisply, "he's got the sound off on the movie and the sound up on sports-talk radio."

"Plus, he's on the phone," Quentin noted.

"If he's masturbating with the spare hand," Tipsy reasoned, "who's driving?"

"Cruise control," Quentin suggested. "Hey, a close-up."

After a moment of silence: "That's one big dick," Tipsy observed reverently.

"Oh," Quentin responded mildly, centering the frame of his sunglasses on the bridge of his nose with the tip of a forefinger, "I don't know about that."

Tipsy shot him an annoyed look. "What do you mean, you don't know? You could kill somebody with that thing."

"People are lining up to get killed by such things," Quentin reminded her. "They call it phallicide."

"They have a name for—Look out!" Tipsy hands converted into talons, the better to reassert their purchase on the dashboard grab bar.

Quentin abruptly corrected the wheel. The tires on the Mercedes protested with a screech, but a looming guardrail receded.

"Whew." Tipsy relaxed her grip. "Until today, I never believed that pornography could kill."

Quentin allowed the two-seater to slow a bit. "So," he said, with a glance at their surroundings, "You brought us all the way out here to Portrero Hill to show me a guy with a porn tape on every screen in his HumVee?"

A black BMW dropped into the slot opened by the difference in speed between the HumVee and the Mercedes. "Is all you can think about," Tipsy said to the windshield, "you you you? What if some kid saw that? What's he or she supposed to think? Wait. If it were a little boy, I know what he would think. But what if it were a little girl? What if it was your little girl, Quentin, strapped into the back seat of your Volvo?"

"I don't do breeding," Quentin held up a hand, "and I don't do Volvos."

"Countenance the theoretical. You've purchased an adorable little girl from some catalog and you're driving her to daycare. She's in the passenger seat, right where I'm sitting, in her pinafore and saddle shoes, holding her book bag and lunch box—"

"What are we in, here, a Billy Collins poem?"

"—and she can see exactly what I'm seeing. What would you do? Huh? I'll tell you. You'd sit there and take it and take it and take it, just like everybody else in this shipwrecked culture." She slapped the dash. "That's what you'd do! This is a question of *moral rigor*," she added savagely, her mouth mere inches from Quentin's right ear.

Quentin cringed against the driver's door on his left. "Don't let that seat harness dent your mammillae." He checked his side mirror. "I hear what you're saying. You think that setup has a remote control?"

"I would think it mandatory."

"In that case, let us come to the rescue of my little girl's delicate sensibilities." Quentin accelerated into the left lane, passed the black Beemer, drew even with the HumVee, and matched the latter's speed. "Let's see if this works." He fingered a button on a lipstick-sized canister among the keys dangling from the ignition switch. "Patience."

Tipsy frowned. "Huh?"

"It's scanning frequencies."

Abruptly, every LCD screen in the HumVee went dark.

This cheered Tipsy immensely. "Wow. Am I a cheap date, or what?" She laughed girlishly and slapped the dash. "How'd you do that?"

Quentin flicked a forefinger at the little canister. "It's called The Quietus, and it's tuned for the frequencies specific to television remotes.

Fourteen ninety-five, double-A battery extra. It's great for restaurants with loud televisions, it works on modern jukeboxes, and for all I know it disarms IEDs, too."

The black BMW abruptly accelerated past them in the fast lane.

"No reason for tailgating now," Tipsy observed.

The HumVee driver looked up from his phone conversation and glared at the darkened display in his dashboard. He touched its screen, touched it again with greater authority, then slapped it. He leaned back in order to view the screen on the back of the headrest of the passenger seat, but couldn't see it. He leaned over the center console and, with some stretching, released the lock on the passenger seat with his phone hand, leaving the phone clenched between his shoulder and ear, talking the while, and driving too. The seat tilted forward and he could see that its video display, built into the headrest, had also gone dark.

The driver mouthed, "I'll call you back," closed his phone, and began pushing buttons on the dashboard. The three displays flickered alight, and the sexual activity resumed.

"He likes it on," breathed Tipsy, "I like it off."

"Don't stare or he'll know it's us," Quentin said, somewhat huffily. "If he's capable of buying a Hummer, he's capable of anything."

"What are you talking about? A guy with a pink Mohawk and a red and yellow pineapple shirt driving a burnt-orange HumVee with pornography on at least three video screens is going to get paranoid about people staring at him? Is that what you're saying?"

Quentin touched The Quietus. "You have a point." The screens in the HumVee winked out.

"Oh, look," Tipsy said, "he's pounding the dashboard with his phone."

"It can take it," said Quentin, with a glance at the passenger-side rearview mirror. "That car's built by and for Americans." A part flew off the phone. "On the other hand, his communications device appears to be an offshore production."

"Maybe it's still under warranty."

"It should be. People hit things with cellphones all the time. Each other, too."

Quentin let the Hummer pull ahead. It was followed by an F-250 Ford pickup, whose cab contained two rows of sleepy sheetrock tapers. A jumble of cardboard boxes, five-gallon buckets, and light trees heaped the bed, the whole ensemble bespattered with hardened joint compound. Quentin dropped into the lane behind the truck and took the Cesar Chavez off-ramp.

At the stoplight he said, "Well, what are we doing? Back to Townsend and Second during rush hour? How bad do you need that chart?"

"They close at 5:30," Tipsy said. "Feel like a beer?"

Quentin frowned.

"Yes," Tipsy said, anticipating his thought, "I am a bad sister."

"You sure?"

"Just one. Then, if you could . . ."

"Drop you at your DUI class?"

"You're sweet."

"In Diamond Heights."

"You've memorized the way!"

"You're buying. We'll get the chart tomorrow."

"Not tomorrow. Tomorrow I've got to get started on another essay for the DUI class. The one I'm turning in tonight took me two days to write. Writing, I must say, is not my fortay."

"Fort," Quentin corrected. "They really make you work that hard for a new license?"

"Are you kidding? They're serious up there. The assignment was to go to a party and not have a single drink the whole time I was there. Can you believe it?"

"How interesting," Quentin lied. "So you had plenty of time to write."

"First thing I noticed? Getting high and coming down take way more time than writing an essay."

"Not to mention concentration."

"That's what parties are for—no?"

"I've always wondered why anybody would waste a good high on a party."

"Well, to get laid, for one thing."

"Really?"

"And to dance. What's that quote you always quote?"

"'Dancing is the lowest form of social intercourse'?"

"That's the one."

"G.K. Chesterton."

"What a jerk."

"Takes one to know one."

"Takes one to memorize one."

"We were speaking of your essay."

"So I went to a party and didn't drink and had a great time. Danced, got laid, didn't spend any money, and there was no hangover."

"So what's the point? You can live a full life without drinking?"

"It seems like a stretch, doesn't it."

"Is that a question?"

"No."

"So?"

"So what?"

"So was it fun anyway?"

"No, it wasn't fun anyway. Do you have any idea how hard it is to find somebody you want to fuck when you're not drunk?"

"Well, no. I have the opposite problem."

Tipsy stared straight ahead.

"That dick," she said, after two blocks, "was really big."

THREE

ONE OF THE REASONS YOU WENT TO SEA, THE BOSUN REMINDED CHARLEY, is *shoddenfreude*, the pleasure to be derived from the fact that other people have to go about their business wearing shoes, while you don't.

Charley nodded. No wonder I'm slipping.

Ha ha . . .

Ah ha ha . . .

Ah HA HAAA . . .

As Charley rose to his knees, the boat lurched. Instinctively, his hips remained beneath his center of gravity. But the genoa flogged, the correcting bungees allowed the tiller to bang his left arm, and pain shot through his shoulder. A knot was rising on the back of his head. He was getting dehydrated. Funny, he thought, as he rubbed the knot with the heel of his right hand, I used to fancy myself a pretty good sailorman.

Ah, reiterated the bosun, shoeless and incompetent.

Only the sea laughed. Only the sea, as it slipped past the hull, pausing here and there to lap at the combing, to toss a cupful over the gunwale to test, always to test, for weakness. *Vellela Vellela* bucked and wallowed and took a little more water over her bow. The genoa flapped and the jury rig creaked. A little wall of brine an inch or so high trickled along the deck between the genoa track and the cabin trunk, spilled past the back of the house, ran out the after scuppers, and dropped but a foot, back into the sea.

Warm Caribbean brine.

Charley squinted east, toward the sun. He made the time for nine o'clock on what had already been a long day. The energy expended left a need, a vacuum, a void, an ache. Two aches. Three. Tea would be nice. Or hot oatmeal laced with salt, golden raisins, brown sugar and Haitian rum. Charley looked at the companionway, now entirely filled with the bright orange distensions of some miracle fabric, striped here and there by silver reflective tape. Beyond it lay trapped all the victuals, every one of them, including fresh water.

He pulled himself erect and worked his way backwards toward the bow, along the starboard side, using his right hand on the grab rail atop that side of the house. Each porthole he passed—there were three—

showed orange. At the foredeck he assessed the bow. It was riding pretty low. Sickeningly, it did not properly resist his weight. He looked aloft at the big sail. With a fresh breeze the genoa might actually drive her under. Was it worth cutting the sail to ribbons? Or setting it on fire? With what? The load was working the standing rigging by the minute. The three intact starboard shrouds were taut; they would hum if he plucked them. The single port shroud slacked as the bow lowered, tightened as it rose, and there labored a weakness that couldn't last.

He knelt at the skylight. It was secured from below but he might be able to breach it if need be. Might not, though, as it was half an inch thick. Tropical ultraviolet and years of sand-bearing saline spray had rendered the thick plexiglass nearly opaque. Charley leaned so that his right eye beetled six inches above it, then one inch. He thought he could see nothing, or perhaps he was seeing the heap of chain, a gleam in the gray gloom, and then the bow dipped. The thickness of the plexiglass seemed to ripple to its perimeter, then slowly contract to a point, which then slid off to the low side of the boat, to port, and disappeared.

Seawater.

Seawater had lifted up to the underside of the skylight.

Well then . . .

Charley sat back on his heels.

Well then.

A fin surfaced to port and, proceeding bow to stern, the shark's fuselage abraded the hull, making a sound as it passed fit to scrape paint off hulls and myelin off nerves. Charley watched the gliding fin as if enthralled. It must have been two feet high, and *Vellela Vellela* no longer had even a foot of freeboard on her port side. Then he snatched the boning knife from its sheath at the small of his back and slashed at the fin twice, nicking it the first time. The fin disappeared with surprising alacrity, leaving behind a little boat afloat an empty sea. More or less afloat; less and less afloat. And a sea not so damned empty.

Charley looked at his ten-dollar knife and recalled a line from Melville describing Ahab's *intense bigotry of purpose*. He turned the blade so that it glinted.

Best get bigoted, big boy.

He took a look over the side just to confirm the obvious. And there he could see the parallel lines of sprung planks that numbered below the boat's migrating waterline, a foot or so of them visible through the clear water as they laddered down the tumblehome and out of sight to the single strake, stove between frames. He lay back on his elbows and stretched his legs aft but the injured shoulder wouldn't let him relax into the pose.

He turned onto his right forearm and gazed between the stanchions upon the liquid expanse, thinking that the scene must much favor "Waterspout," the Winslow Homer painting. He knew the tables—and in fact had expended an idle hour on understanding the calculation—which told that, if one's head were five feet above calm waters, one would be able to see no more than about two and a half miles in any given direction, for a total scope of five miles. This gives a visual command of pi times the square of 2.5 miles equals nearly a twenty square mile circle of open sea. A mere patch under *visual command*. Interesting term. It smacks of the theoretical.

He was probably in non-visual non-command of several thousand square miles of deserted ocean. If he set off the EPRB he had a chance of getting rescued within a day or two, if the boat lasted. But if he were rescued there would be uncomfortable questions, and, no matter how vague or evasive he managed to be, there would inevitably be uncomfortable answers. Answers would lead to more questions, he'd have to stop being vague or evasive or cooperative at all, there would be a gathering of evidence, a public defender, a trial, and prison—hard time and no way around it. Back to school way up the river, a very tough school indeed, a silted-up river at that, and no paddles. If he were lucky it would be a federal joint, probably in Florida, where one of the chief rigors to be endured would be a perpetual onslaught of American television. If not—his mind cast a glance to the southeast—you're talking scorpions and lice. Cuban fauna. Ever felt a spider walking over your face in the dark? Well it's sinusoidal cascades of hirsute tootsies, mon vieux, in parallel syncopation and, leaving out what it does to your imagination, that's all there is to it. Nice, commented the bosun, who added, rhetorically—and how does that stack up against deliberately cultivating cataracts and deafness in order to shield oneself from the ablating rays of American television?

He noticed he'd been digging the point of the knife into the foredeck. His own or anybody's foredeck, this was a big breach of etiquette. A real no-no. Not Bristol. Besides which, it dulls the knife.

He refrained from throwing the knife at the sea.

The bow dipped and the genoa flapped and more water came aboard, wetting his legs. Because sunburn was becoming an issue the moisture felt good, short term; long term, its salinity would exacerbate the problem. It boded ominous. The sheet slacked and the tiller creaked. The sail filled and the sheet tautened. The vessel wallowed on.

Inflated below deck with no means of freeing itself, that damned raft might stand in for a water-tight bulkhead and keep *Vellela Vellela* afloat indefinitely. A serendipitously ironic fuckup, one might say, were it not for the fact that, by keeping the vessel afloat indefinitely, it would also be indefinitely prolonging the agony, not to mention preserving the evidence and effectively marooning the perpetrator aboard his own perpetration. Drifting around out here with no more wherewithal than a cockroach on a tongue depressor. Not my tongue, the bosun gleefully pounced. How about a cricket on a popsicle stick? Charley almost smiled. Shucks. What's a bosun for, if not to cheer a man up? Okay, Charley conceded, let's call it an ironically fucked-up serendipity.

The facts were flying in Charley's head, and it was getting a little confusing, but not for nothing was he a single-handed sailor. While he liked the call of the wild well enough, he was of course and above all an inveterate misanthrope. He was used to puzzling out dilemmas on his own, he enjoyed the independence afforded by his near-exclusive reliance on his own blunders or cleverness, and so he took the time to suss things out, when he had the time to do so, or he made a snap decision when he didn't. So now Charley just lay on the foredeck, watched the world go by, and brooded.

And sure enough, about two hours later, *Vellela Vellela* seemed to have come to some sort of accommodation with her circumstances. The hull had settled evenly, with about six inches of freeboard. The water level in the cockpit had evened out with the sea surrounding it. With the boat holding so much water the genoa was pulling much more of a load than it was used to, the stasis couldn't last. But so long as the breeze held mild the standing rigging might continue to stand. Charley tidied some of the debris left behind by the accidental jibe, shortened and cut away and hanked various lines and sheets. He stood on the vang track, which had bent double to port, until it more or less lay down on top of itself. He rigged the collapsed mainsail into a sort of ragged awning over the house, to afford himself some shelter from the sun; for the SPF 30-plus UV-protection sun block, along with the food and water, charts, navigational instruments, bolt cutters and other gear, remained trapped below.

And this stasis defined the terms of the dilemma Charley staved off all through the forenoon, while he busied himself with topside tidiness. No food, no water, no sun block, not much of a boat, and he didn't want to be found, either. There was one person, particularly, by whom Charley would not be able to withstand discovery. He was called Red Means and he was Charley's employer of the moment; he was an old friend, and he was also a pirate. Old school, shiver me timbers, you fuck me up, mate, I fuck you up. Why not work for the best?

In fact, Charley's below-decks cargo, carefully secreted in a small compartment in *Vellela Vellela*'s keel, belonged to Red Means, and only to Red

Means, until such time as Charley managed to off-load it in a tiny lagoon on a two-acre uninhabited islet just northwest of the back side of Boca Chica Key.

And if Charley failed? Well, even the best reason wouldn't be good enough. Was a collision with a submerged shipping container a better than best reason? Probably not. Not to mention, besides, that Charley had been asleep at impact. And if he'd been awake would he have seen it in time? Didn't the previous 72 hours of incident-free discontinuous wakefulness count for something? Charley rolled his eyes skyward, tracing the curve of the inverted cobalt bowl interloped by the odd westbound pod of cumulus.

One look from Red's red eyes and Charley would give up the truth with the inevitability of a bog regurgitating a mummy. The fact was that Charley was too honest, insufficiently ruthless, and maybe not even smart in the way that "smart" applies to the ins and outs of dope smuggling. He'd noticed this on his very first run, many years before. He just didn't have the nerve for it. The truth was that he was plenty smart in other ways, and a good sailor, too. But guns? The Coast Guard? Years of stir? Alcohol- and drug-fueled orgies? The excuse to not work for a year based on three weeks of adrenalized insomnia? Whatever happened to Calvinism, for chrissakes, work for work's sake? And what about the ennobling virtue of abiding by the law? Not to mention the salvation of the elect by God's will alone, so why play it any way at all? Had he gone wrong by being Charley instead of Elect? Or had he gone wrong by being Charley instead of Red? We'd best discuss that later, in the bar, cautioned the bosun. It's not going to do us any good out here; besides which, it makes you sound like you're crazy. But seriously, Charley persisted, does a mere temperamental unsuitability for any normal vocation, coupled with a love for all things maritime, necessarily lead to the criminal life?

In your case, the bosun stated, obviously.

It was true. Eleven years before, about eighty nautical miles off St. Simon's Island, Georgia, the Coast Guard had nailed Charley with 250 kilograms of Colombian marijuana. It was the same modus operandi, too: single-handing a modest sailboat with all the accoutrements of the carefree cruiser—solar panels on a hard dodger, barbecue hanging off the after rail, surfboard and a kayak lashed amidships—loafing along with wind and current, enjoying the freedom of the ocean. Charley didn't care for the toys, but he liked the show-business aspect. There he'd been, of a chilly Gulf Stream morning, all bundled up, tiller lashed, cup of tea in one hand and a wedge of Christmas fruitcake in the other, when the 102-foot Coast Guard cutter *Ineluctable*—white hull, orange diagonal stripe amidships, .50 caliber machine guns bow and stern, three radar masts rotating at the top of its house, and a double row of jagged green cannabis leaves painted along the base of its stack, each pentafoil representing a significant maritime interdiction—materialized out of the mist about two hundred yards aft of *Xanadu Caprice*. Charley was having such a nice time, with his dreamy thoughts amid the magnificent environment, a mere twenty hours or so from offloading his cargo and onloading his very own suitcase full of cash, that he didn't even notice the authorities until they hailed via loudspeaker, which, at 125 decibels, nearly started him overboard. Certainly the tea scalded the fingers of his left hand. The Coasties politely requested permission to board, he politely granted it, and they found the marijuana right away. There was so much pot aboard he'd been using the bricks as furniture.

It was the old days. Each kilo came with a gram of cocaine embedded in it. The feds never even noticed. After carefully weighing and photographing the bricks as evidence, they just went ahead and burned the lot. If they'd noticed the blow, things undoubtedly would have gone much harder with Charley. What you might call a bitch-slap of fate, the bosun never tired of reminding him.

On the foredeck of *Vellela Vellela*, Charley exhibited the rueful smile of a man taking a moment out of a busy day to indulge a reverie.

That fiasco turned into two and a half years in FCI Marianna, however, and that stretch only happened after a year and a half in the court system, during which, under the onus of astronomical bail, he cooled his heels in the Coast Guard's Savannah brig. Charley was a first offender, Marianna is a so-called country club, but prison is still prison. He almost certainly would have been sentenced to time served if he'd coughed up some names and testified against them. The feds told him so, and the feds are trustworthy—yes? No? They offered to build him a new identity too; reconstitute his essence as, say, a diesel mechanic at a 24-hour truckstop in Buffalo, Wyoming.

Jeez, moaned the bosun, you're making it sound worse than it was.

No or yes, they got nothing from Charley. Charley just sat there in chains while they ran their case, won it, and a judge sentenced him to prison. Well, he never talked about it, and this helped him to not think about it too very often. When he got off the subsequent two years of parole and could leave Florida and the country, Red got him a job in a little boatyard on Guadeloupe. After all, it was on account of Charley's keeping his mouth shut that several people had been privileged to spend the intervening years continuing not to work. Charley had never been the only iron in their fire, but they remembered him. These friends staked him to some considerable cash when he got out, another reason to park him offshore, and another reason Charley was able to efficiently refit the hulk that became *Vellela Vellela*.

He'd splashed her three years ago.

And now?

Well, here he was again, it seemed, close aboard square one. Although, as a one-time loser, the arithmetic really added up to less than square one. Less than square zero, in fact. For a second offense under mandatory sentencing, any judge would have to slam him for ten to twenty. Or was it fifteen to life? He didn't really know. He hadn't been keeping up with the legislation. Maybe he should have researched it, oh, say, a couple of months ago?

Back in the shade of the jury-rigged dodger he alternately studied the sea and the orange thing stuffed into the companionway and puzzled it all out. Various elements of the scenario began to assume the intractability he'd foreseen, and after a while the looser pieces fell into place. First, the authorities were not an option. He never wanted to see the inside of a jail again. Period. And despite the elevated stakes, he still would rat out exactly nobody. After all—irony curled his lip—he had a reputation to protect. Besides which, fuck the authorities. Doesn't misanthropy start with authority? And then, no matter how things worked out, the load and his boat were lost. More irony, they were supposed to be lost. Just not yet. Just not like this.

Plus he was hungry, thirsty, fifty-three years old, sunfried, childless, which has been mentioned once already today, and—but for the minor exception of a sister seen but once in twenty-something years—so how important could she be?—he was unattached.

From the recumbent slouch of the single-handed sailor, mesmerized by the bubbles trailing his transom, Charley sprang into a crouch, let out a roar, and knifed the life raft like it was the belly of a grizzly bear that stood between him and the exit. The upturned edge of the blade unzipped the miracle fabric from the threshold of the companionway all the way up to the hatch, with a stroke sufficiently convincing to gouge a two-inch splinter of teak out of the slide.

The CO_2 took but a second to escape, a harsh exhale of stale gas that, but for his fascination, almost made Charley turn his head. But then, engorged by the seawater pent up behind it, the companionway puked the entire raft inside out, a limp cascade of space-age fabric, followed by worldly goods. The level of water inside the cabin equalized with that in the cockpit and submerged the sill of the companionway.

Along with the raft came a plastic food container and a bottle of water, a sneaker, a hank of 1/4" polypropylene line, a hollow-handled Torx screw-driver, a can of yams, a dive mask with snorkel, a sodden t-shirt, and a few volunteers from the ship's library—Sterling Hayden's *Wanderer*, Harry Pidgeon's *Around the World Single-Handed*, Bernard Moitessier's *The Long Way*, Felix Reisenberg's *Cape Horn*, H. G. Creel's *Chinese Thought*, Vito Dumas' *Alone Through The Roaring Forties*, an out-of-date Caribbean edition of Reed's *Nautical Almanac*, Richard Henderson's *Singlehanded Sailing*, Homer's *Odyssey*, Jack London's *Martin Eden*, and *The Virginian* by Owen Wister.

He had always carried too many books.

Along with the sodden smalltime chattel sluiced the biggest centipede Charley had ever seen. A good eight inches long and an inch in breadth, not including the reach of its forcipules and many feet, the creature writhed and twisted in the cockpit brine as if caught by an invisible hand.

FOUR

IN THE BOATYARD QUENTIN PARKED AMONG A FOREST OF JACKSTANDS AND dunnage in the corner of chain link fence closest to the street, and he wasn't half out of the car before two men approached. One wore shades and a Forty-niners jacket, the other wore shades and a flannel shirt, and both wore moustaches.

"Tell me," Tipsy dared them over the roof of the Mercedes, "that you're not cops."

"Ms. Powell?" asked the one in the Forty-niner jacket.

"Who's asking?"

"Keep your hands where I can see them, buddy," the other said to Quentin.

"Huh?" Quentin said. "I'm rolling up the window."

"Button it."

The first guy pulled his jacket aside and showed a blue patch of nylon with a badge pinned to it. "SFPD."

"I paid all my fines," Tipsy protested. "And I signed up for the class. We've met four times already."

"What class?" the cop said.

"The DUI class."

The cop in the team jacket looked at his partner, then back at Tipsy. "So you are Teresa Powell."

"Everybody calls me Tipsy."

"Even in the DUI class?"

She shook her head pseudo-lugubriously. "Some guy called Tipsy registered before I did."

"There goes your identity," the cop lamented. "Did you quit drinking?" he asked, with unexpected sympathy.

Tipsy lied to the officer's face. "Absolutely."

Quentin rolled his eyes.

The cop's mouth tightened. "Too bad," he said. "You get through with us, or *vice versa*?" He nodded. "You're going to need a drink."

In the headquarters of the San Francisco Police Department, on Bryant at Fifth Street, they had a room to themselves. Quentin and Tipsy sat across a steel table from the two cops, also seated. There was no other furniture in the room, but there were two security-type cameras affixed to the ceiling, each trained on opposite sides of the table. The distinctive odors of burnt coffee and gastro-intestinal distress vied with that of the mildew peculiar to old mops.

"Ever heard of the Cavalcade of Wonders?"

They looked at each other. They looked at Officer Protone, they looked at Officer Few. "It sounds like a church," Quentin ventured. "Or a traveling circus," Tipsy submitted.

"Negative," Officer Protone said aloud. He touched a few buttons on a cassette recorder and set it on the table between them.

"Wow," Tipsy said. "I haven't seen a cassette recorder in a long time."

"My whole career is on cassette," Few replied. "I'm trying to be technologically consistent."

Quentin reiterated his skepticism. "This can't be important enough to record."

"It's being recorded for accuracy and mutual protection," Few stated perfunctorily. "So you've never heard of the Cavalcade of Wonders, one of which wonders is genetic predetermination shaped by nurture." Blank looks.

"Genetic determination?" Tipsy made a face. "Shaped by nurture?"

"Genetics is a crap shoot," Quentin said. "The progeny could come up, oh, I don't know, queer, let's say."

Tipsy smiled and shook her head.

"I more or less agree," Few said, "but they don't think so, and, in any case, it seems to be a risk they're willing to take." He indicated his partner. "Protone can explain it better than I can."

This guy Few is one nervous cop, Tipsy observed to herself.

Protone cleared his throat. "The Cavalcade of Wonders is an organization dedicated to the manipulation of the course of world history via that of American democracy. The so-called direction of so-called progress," he added ominously, "based on the bedrock principle that democracy is too important to be left in the hands of the people, and that maybe a line of genetically-designed and strictly educated royalty, disguised as elected officials, might be a better way to go."

Gobsmacked, Tipsy and Quentin remained silent.

"Well," Few finally said.

"Where were they," Tipsy asked, "during the three Bush administrations?"

"That certainly might have been the germ of the idea," Protone said.

Tipsy whistled.

"In other words," Quentin frowned, "it's a fascist or a nationalist organization?"

"Right in two. If you're really interested in the subject, you might check out this book." He produced it from his briefcase and laid it on the table. "*Wackos, Flacks and Apparatchiks*" Quentin read aloud. "*Sundown on American Polity.* J. J. Wadsworth." The dust jacket illustration featured a shot-raddled American flag flying over a half-toned mob of people bearing illegible placards, screaming and shaking their fists at the reader.

Tipsy turned out an inside flap. "Everything you ever wanted to know about spittle-flecked invective."

"Wadsworth, Wadsworth," Quentin said. "Wasn't he in the state department?"

"He's had several jobs in and out of the government," Protone confirmed, "including spook."

"A career bureaucrat," Few summed.

"You mean *American Polity* is some kind of insidious euphemism? How about a concrete example?"

"Sure. The privatization of public capital is a game they like a lot." Protone thought a moment. "Here's another. The so-called Middle East has been a source of global turmoil for, let's say, two thousand years."

"Pick a starting point—any starting point," Tipsy laughed, though uncertainly. Then her smile faded. "Are you guys serious?"

Protone pursed his lips. "In consideration of said turmoil, one might go back so far as Troy—"

"*The Iliad* concerns events that occurred 3,200 years ago," Quentin put in. Everybody looked at him.

"But the city itself goes back to the Bronze Age—about two thousand years before that," he added helpfully.

"But let's don't," Tipsy hastened to suggest, "let's please don't go all the way back to Troy."

"We don't have the time to do it justice," Protone agreed with barely a pause. "But my colleague can offer some pertinent details."

Few blinked rapidly, like a mechanical device waiting for the quarter to drop, then plunged in. "Let's go back merely to the Balfour Agreement and British partition that created Iraq in 1921 or, slightly less remote, historically speaking, to what Palestinians celebrate—"

"Wrong verb," Protone interjected. "Try lament."

"—as *Naqba*," Few nodded, "the Catastrophe."

"Otherwise known as the creation of Israel by the United Nations in 1948," Quentin put in.

Few continued. "Though the state of Israel consists of a mere four million people, it seems reasonable to stipulate that turmoil has been her inheritance and legacy to the Middle East throughout her existence. She possesses nuclear arms, not to mention cluster bombs, will not ratify the nuclear non-proliferation treaty and, whether offensively or defensively, she has taken up conventional arms against all of her neighbors. Something like ten million so-called Palestinians are hostage to Israel's sense of well-being. 'God' has telepathic relations with both sides."

"Naturally," Quentin muttered.

". . . In all of this, the United States has backed Israel with treasure, arms, and policy, both public and clandestine."

Protone lifted one hand off the table top in front of him and turned it palm up. "Fair enough?"

"Not if you're a Palestinian," Quentin frowned.

Tipsy shook her head. "You can get a very loud argument about everything both of you just said, including the verb tenses and the punctuation."

Few nodded. "Amen."

Quentin regarded Few. His hair was slicked back, and he hadn't shaved in two or three days. Not a strand of gray showed in hair or stubble, yet he seemed aged. The tone of his skin ran from pale to grayish, his eyes were tired and pouched, the left eyelid displayed an erratic tic. By the odor about him, he smoked tobacco, which may partially have explained the bluish tint to his lips. Quentin smiled.

"What's so funny?" Protone asked.

"I was just thinking," Quentin replied affably, "how some people assume that cops aren't smart."

"Long as they think so," Protone said, "our job is that much easier."

"Or educated," Few added.

"Let alone, human," Tipsy had to chime in.

"We get that all the time. People think cops are what they see on television."

"Those aren't cops," Tipsy pointed out. "Mostly they're actors."

"Yeah," Protone said. "We get them down here all the time. Want to ride around in a black and white, observe interrogations, spend an hour locked in a cell."

"You can do that on Alcatraz," Quentin remarked.

"Costs money out there," Protone pointed out.

Few almost smiled. "They know all about guns, too. Way more than I know."

Protone looked at him. "Almost."

Few made no response.

Has this guy been shot, Quentin wondered, or shot someone else? Or both? After an awkward pause he said, "Let's get back to the Cavalcade of Wonders."

"Well, like some of these wannabe cops," Protone said, "these Knights of the Cavalcade, as they call themselves, think they have a line on a better way to run the world."

"Oh boy." Tipsy shook her head. "Don't they know they have to get in line with the rest of the people who have lines?"

"I don't know," Quentin said thoughtfully. "It seems to me that the job is up for grabs."

"Who in their right mind would want such a job?"

"Another excellent question from the little lady," Officer Protone replied.

"That's quite enough of the little lady stuff," Tipsy suggested tartly.

"Point taken," Protone replied immediately.

"But *right mind* is assumed," Few jumped in, with unexpected fervor, tapping the table with a forefinger to emphasize his point. "As in the right man is one who does not question his moral imperative, nor his presumed mandate to affect—better, to wreak—changes upon those around him, changes up to and including those of life and death, and as such is more or less in line with the point, which is, Who, in the big picture, is in a position to do something about the big picture?"

Quentin frowned. "Are you talking *global ambitions of the last remaining superpower* kind of talk?"

"Sure."

"As in, *The United Nations exists solely by our discretion and at our pleasure*"?

"That's the way they talk."

"You're stipulating that the people in a position to do something about problems like the Middle East are the people in charge of foreign policy in the government of the United States?" Quentin looked to each of the people seated around him.

"I'm not," Few pointed out. "But they are."

"In view of recent history that hardly seems credible."

"The right man is no less right," Few declared, "despite or because of recent history, that is to say, despite evidence pro or con. The Right Man takes the long view."

"This Cavalcade is a think-tank?"

"That and more."

"I hate it when tanks think," Tipsy quipped, adding, "I think I wandered into the wrong classroom. Can I be excused? I have this essay to prepare for my DUI class. It—"

Protone shot a cuff and looked at his watch. "We'll get you there, Miss Powell."

Tipsy's expression clouded. "You know where I—"

Protone slipped his sleeve back over the face of his watch. "We know. We've been keeping tabs on you." Protone produced a rare smile. "That DUI made it pretty easy. Since you can't drive, we got cops on bicycles following you around."

Quentin chuckled.

"But I—," Tipsy began. She indicated both herself and Quentin. "We—"

Officer Protone held up both hands, palms out. "We checked you out thoroughly. We know you're oblivious." His glance included Quentin. "Both of you."

"If oblivion were against the law," Quentin quickly stipulated, "seventy-eight percent of the country would be in jail."

"Eighty-eight." Few's eyelid twitched. "Possibly ninety."

Whatever this is about, Quentin observed to himself, this guy Few is taking it very seriously.

"The Cavalcade is a think-tank," Protone continued. "And they are serious about making a difference in the world. Deadly serious."

"Different like how?" Quentin asked.

"Sticking with the example of the Middle East, they're serious about changing things there one way or the other, if you get my meaning, for good and for all, as in, permanently for everybody."

Quentin and Tipsy exchanged glances. "No," Quentin said, "we do not get your meaning."

Protone persisted. "Given its druthers, the Knights would take all the pieces and throw them up in the air." He threw both hands upwards. "Some pieces higher than others, of course. They're control freaks, cheating is expected, money talks, oil screams, human rights are for pussies, they're a red herring anyway, and in any case they're a luxury afforded us by our privileged status in the world. A lot of their so-called guidance comes from the Bible, and if they weren't so well financed, connected, determined, entrenched, crazy, and so goddamned determined, we could forget about them. Unfortunately . . ."

Tipsy thought to ask where it mentioned oil in the Bible.

"And so forth," Protone said, apparently agreeing with her.

"Don't these guys realize that controlling your history is not like controlling your mayonnaise?" Tipsy asked.

"No," Protone shook his head, "they don't. Worse, there's probably an argument to be made for their perceiving history as some kind of sandwich. A finite, vendible, and even stealable commodity, and certain to go stale if somebody doesn't eat it. And the sooner it's eaten," he added with emphasis, "the more nutrition it provides."

"What happened to the football metaphors?"

"As goes foreign policy, all football metaphors were exhausted by recent administrations. But as Joseph Campbell said, if you want to change your history, change the metaphor. Or was it the narrative?"

"Joseph Campbell?" Quentin marveled aloud.

"At any rate, it's about time," Tipsy remarked.

"But they're not asking for our metaphor," Quentin supposed.

"That would be correct."

"All the pieces?" Quentin asked. "Israel? Egypt? Lebanon? Palestine? Iraq? Jordan? Iran? Syria? Saudi Arabia? How about the background players—Russia, China, India, OPEC?"

Few nodded and nodded and nodded, as repetitiously as the tic in his eyelid.

Quentin looked from one cop to the other. "Who am I leaving out?"

Neither spoke.

"Turkey?" Quentin said, with an obvious tone of disbelief.

Protone nodded thoughtfully.

"But that's . . ." Quentin whispered. "That's crazy. If there are four million people in all of Israel, there are fifteen million in Baghdad alone. Or used to be. In any case it's like saying Squire Sancho Panza can throw some windmills higher than others, so Don Quixote can pick them off sequentially and at will as they come back down."

"Tilt," Tipsy quipped.

Nobody had a rejoinder to this miserable yet completely appropriate pun. But, "Your similes," Protone told Quentin, "are excellent."

"But then," Tipsy said, as if to convince herself, "pinball is so last century."

Protone nodded thoughtfully.

"Of course," Quentin said, speaking even more softly, as if to the table top, "nobody in Baghdad has nukes."

Nobody spoke.

Quentin raised his eyes and searched the face of each cop, twice. "Do they?"

"If you're asking me," Protone shrugged, "it's bad enough that Israel has nukes."

"They've had nukes since the Johnson administration," Quentin flatly stated. "Who killed Karen Silkwood?" he stage-whispered.

Few picked right up on it. "Probably the same people who paid Michael Crichton to write a novel declaring global warming to be a fabulist plot intended to further an agenda of left-wing environmentalist socialism, starring the environment as a deity," he said. "If you're asking me."

Everybody looked at him.

"Stupid cop," Protone said affectionately, adding, "Not that he has any facts to back that up. Hell, I can't even remember the name of the book."

"*State of Fear*," Tipsy said. "It's his most boring book."

"Wow," Few whistled.

"I wish I were illiterate enough not to know how boring that is," she added wistfully.

"Patience, darling," Quentin said, "you're well on the way."

"Have you considered becoming too literate to know it?" Few suggested solicitously.

Quentin held up his hands. "You didn't hear it from me."

"One woman's airport bookstore," Tipsy scowled, "is another woman's beautifully paneled library."

"Gentlemen," Quentin interrupted, his tone as sober as the three hours Tipsy was about to spend on Diamond Heights, "are you telling us that one of the wonders in the Cavalcade would or could be a nuclear weapon in the hands of any one of the dozens of so-called fanatic but in any case undoubtedly focused opponents to the state of Israel?"

"That's the kind of stuff they lecture each other about," said Few.

"As an incitement?"

"Isn't that obvious?"

Protone glared at Few with obvious annoyance. "There are other techniques," he said brusquely.

"Techniques?" remonstrated Quentin, much surprised. "Are you calling nuclear warfare in the Middle East, or anywhere else for that matter, a technique?"

"The Knights do," Protone said. "Drop a tactical nuke on Teheran, or Fallujah, or Gaza—like that. They can be hotheaded. Personally, I'm not convinced."

"Are you nuts?" Quentin expostulated. "Do you remain to be convinced?"

"Once you make up your mind, you forfeit your status as an intellectual," Protone pointed out. "Besides, they have a point about the Middle East."

"What," Quentin snapped, "that it's intractable?"

"Sure." Protone looked at him frankly. "You think it's not?"

"Okay," said Quentin, "let's concede that it's intractable. That doesn't mean you allow the place to blow itself up—not, at least, if you can at all prevent it. And it sure as heck doesn't mean you help them blow themselves up." He looked from cop to cop. Few's mouth was grimly tense. Protone looked almost bemused. "Does it?" Quentin asked. "Well, does it?" he demanded.

"Oscar?" Protone said. "Answer the man."

"Like you said." Few looked nobody in the eye. "The situation's intractable."

Quentin looked at Tipsy. Tipsy looked confused and disconcerted.

"Okay, it . . . it gets blown up. So then what? You put guys there in moon suits to tap the vast reserves of oil beneath the subfloor of a nuclear winter?"

"Nuclear winter is one thing," Few said glumly, ostensibly addressing the tabletop. "Guys with miscellaneous agendas blowing up vital pipelines is something else."

Nobody said anything.

"What—what about that nuclear winter?" Tipsy asked.

"Easy," Quentin quipped. "You contain it with a country-sized geodesic dome, and all the pipelines run underneath it."

"We had you wrong." Few pointed a finger at Quentin. "You're not oblivious."

Quentin sat back in his chair, stunned. "My God."

"You see?" Protone said. "Cops have opinions, too."

Quentin sighed loudly. "Stupid cops."

"Opinions are like assholes," Tipsy began.

Protone pinched his brow between thumb and forefinger, scrubbed his forehead, looked at Few, then at Quentin. "Of course, as mere cops, we're not in the business of nukes and zero-sum endgames and such."

"I wish you were," said Quentin. "I think."

Protone permitted himself a little smile. "I'm sure that's meant to be reassuring."

"Especially in light of knights and cavalcades and such like, who don't have such low opinions of their low opinions," Quentin adduced.

"Opinions are like assholes," Tipsy began again.

"That would be correct," Few confirmed acidly. "It's an understatement, too."

"Some people have more than one asshole?" Tipsy asked naively.

"Okay. Okay." Quentin placed both his hands flat on the table top. "If we're not suspected of smuggling nukes to the betterment of mankind, what are we doing here?"

"We can't go around arresting people for what they think or what they say," Few stated pedantically.

"Not yet, anyway," Protone put in.

"If you could, you'd probably have to arrest yourselves," Quentin observed.

"That would be correct."

"But what we can do is arrest people for committing crimes that are already on the books."

"Such as?"

Protone raised a few fingers from his folded hands. "Dope smuggling. Dope possession. Dope peddling. Burglary. Forgery. Murder."

A silence protracted until Tipsy volunteered that she personally drew the line at Driving Under the Influence.

"In a nutshell, Ms. Powell is related to someone who is running errands for someone commissioned by someone who is high up in the religious wing of the Knights."

"Related . . . ?" Tipsy repeated incredulously. "But I have only one living blood relation in the whole worl—" She stopped. Slowly, she covered her mouth with the fingers of one hand.

"The religious wing?" Quentin repeated incredulously. "What the hell do they believe in?"

"Sir, you astonish me," Protone said.

"Well?"

"They believe in God, of course."

"Jesus Christ," Tipsy remarked bitterly.

"When convenient," Protone nodded.

"The most useful idea, for tyrants," Quentin recalled thoughtfully, "is the idea of God."

"Marx?" Few brightened. "Lenin?"

Quentin fixed an eye on Few. "Stendhal."

"Got that?" Protone said to the tape machine. "Follow up."

"It doesn't make any difference who said it," Quentin assured Few. "It smacks of the truth."

"Think avatar," Protone nodded. "They have their leaders, their ideas of leaders, and, once in a while, one comes along whom they deem sufficient to the hour. But it seems clear that it's boiling down to some kind of royalist conspiracy. The idea is, they want to train a leader from birth."

"Kinda like the Israelis train their fighter pilots," Few put in.

"How is that?"

"They identify them at birth and go from there."

"Really? How—"

"Enough with the Israelis. Have they a motto, these eugenicists?"

Protone pursed his lips. "I'd say it would be 'The greater good for the few.' They'd never admit to it outside of chambers, of course."

"But it would look good on the coinage. In Latin, of course."

Few almost smiled.

"How few is few?"

"I'm Few through and through," Few offered half-heartedly, with the twitch of an eyelid.

Tipsy smiled. Quentin ignored him. "Ten million, for one random example, seems like a lot." Quentin narrowed his eyes. "Four million?"

"Far fewer than four million," Protone assured him. "Far fewer and not, uh, state-specific."

"And class specific?"

"Now you're talking."

"So," Tipsy interjected impatiently, "what are we talking about here? Fascist horseshit flying in the face of fascist history?"

Protone nodded again, but reluctantly.

"Yeah," Few said glumly. "It's the only way."

Quentin shook his head as if he hadn't heard correctly. "What?"

"He's speaking on behalf of the Knights," Protone assured them. "Don't pay any attention. Oscar has spent so much time under cover he occasionally forgets who he's talking to."

Tipsy regarded Few as if by a new light. "Oscar Few."

"It's his nickname."

"I get it. You're under-appreciated."

Few made a gesture of modesty.

"Anybody ever call you 'Happy'?" asked Quentin.

Few frowned.

"No," Protone answered for him. "Why?"

"Just curious." Quentin shrugged. "So you've attended their meetings?"

Few nodded cautiously.

"Police business is one thing," Quentin said, with grave sympathy. "I'm sure it has its moments. But show business?" He shook his head. "Show business is something else."

"That's true," said Few, brightening slightly. "One might even say that show business is the whole story."

They all looked at him.

"I can't believe you characterize a royalist conspiracy as show business," Tipsy admonished them. "So," she repeated, turning a nervous eye on Officer Few, "you've attended their meetings?" But her mind was clamoring: what in the hell had her brother gotten himself into?

"Only low level stuff," said Protone, speaking for Few, who appeared too disturbed to reply. "The high level guys would bust him immediately. The high level guys are just too weird to infiltrate easily. They're all graduates of Ivy League colleges, for example." Protone nodded. "Oscar works security details for them. Perimeters around meeting places, airport runs, the large conventions, stuff like that. Still, it helps us keep tabs on them, when they're around." He blew a little air out of his nose. "They don't come to San Francisco too often."

"So none of them live here?"

"I didn't say that."

Quentin and Tipsy both blinked.

"Anyway, the religious wing of this outfit sees to the careful maintenance of certain rituals they've codified and established. It's not like worship, exactly. They don't have a swearing-in ceremony, or articles of faith,
or uniforms—nothing like that."

"Except that many of them shave their heads," Few put in.

"When are you going to shave yours?"

Few nodded glumly. "Pretty soon, probably."

"Yes, but as a rule they recognize each other by what they've published
or otherwise communicated, their family connections, and the causes
they're willing to back with real money. In fact, there's hardly anything untoward, one might say, or anything one might consider seditious. Scenarios of
global catastrophe are the business of any number of organizations, after all,
from the Pentagon to the United Nations to, well, to dozens of think-tanks,
not to mention organs ancillary to every first-world government."

"Not to mention reality itself," Tipsy interjected.

"The thing is," Few blurted, speaking rapidly, "the inner circle of Knights
has dedicated itself to certain goals, and they are bound by certain articles of
faith. From the outside, there can be little doubt that this group of individ-
uals is committed and serious, almost religiously dedicated to modifying various vectors in world events to accomplish perceived goals and ambitions.
There is no doubt, for example, that they are very serious about having a
hand on the tiller of not only US foreign policy, but that of the developed
world in general. Most of them think it would be nice to eliminate what they
perceive as moral turpitude, too—although, so far as that goes, there are just
enough adulterers, closet homosexuals, wholesale fanciers of internet
pornography, and purveyors of corrupt influence among their ranks to keep
a lid on their hypocrisy. Factions want the Holy Land for Jews and
Christians, but even within the Knights, these factionals are referred to as
The Crazies, while petroleum haves and have-nots comprise the *realpolitik*
dialectics whereby expansionist nationalism or *democratization* is perceived
as a sufficient cloaking device, or justification, for the advancement of
national interest. The Crazies listen and are listened to, policy is agreed
upon, and the next step is implementation. Once implemented there's no
going back, the end justifies the means, and that's it. This does not prevent
certain elements from pursuing alternate, backup, and even contrarian goals,
however, and in fact the organization perceives such subsidiary efforts as
generally accruing to their well-being and interest, a kind of healthy discord,
within limits, naturally."

"A leader conceived of selectively procreated genetic material,"
Protone added, "raised and educated from birth, represents to them the

culmination of an idea they refer to as the charisma of secular fetishism."
He smiled wanly. "You've probably never heard of it."

"Not once," Tipsy flatly declared, "and I've lived in San Francisco all
my adult life."

"Agreed," Quentin said, "and I've been living in San Francisco for
twice that long."

Protone exchanged a glance with Few. "Here's the long and short of
today's meeting," he said. "We've told you we're keeping tabs on you. We
have reason to believe that, in a short time, other people will be keeping
tabs on you. We, and they, expect your brother to show up."

Tipsy pointed to the floor. "Here?" she asked in astonishment. "In San
Francisco?"

Officer Protone looked at Officer Few. The latter shook his head.
Protone dealt a pair of calling cards to the table top. "When you notice
them, call us. I needn't note," he added, "that you'll be only too happy to
have someone to call at that point but . . ."

"But you just did," Tipsy said. "And my brother?"

"Him too. He almost certainly will fail to elude both the authorities and
these other . . . people of interest. But if he somehow manages to get to
you before we get to him, by all means, call us. Immediately."

"But he's . . . my brother."

Protone looked at his watch and stood up from his chair. "You don't
want to miss that DUI class. Let's get going."

Tipsy shook her head, as if trying to clear it. "I haven't seen my brother since . . . since . . ."

"Since Thailand," Few said, watching her. "Maybe fifteen years ago."

Tipsy stared at him. Quentin blinked. She looked at Protone. Protone
was standing up. She looked at Quentin. Quentin raised an eyebrow and
opened a hand.

Tipsy rounded on the cops. "That's it?"

"For now," Protone said.

"You can't quit now," she declared.

Few looked puzzled. "Sure we can." He depowered the cassette
recorder.

"If you miss just one of those DUI classes," Protone reminded her,
"you have to start all over." He pushed his chair up against the table.
"Those DUI statutes are tough."

FIVE

THE CENTIPEDE WAS LONGER THAN THE TUBE OF ALOE VERA APRÉS-SOLEIL bobbing close aboard it, and not much thinner. Its body was the color of the porphyry grips on a much-fired pistol, its legs a dirty ivory blushing to ochre, and their spiculate extremities sported the fawn-colored translucence of the anthers in a pear blossom. Though he'd heard such an arthropod would, given the chance, feed on a cockroach, a tarantula, or even a bat, and therefore perhaps had its utility, Charley speared the creature to the side of the port cockpit locker with an inch and a half of boning knife and no remorse.

It was nice to nail down if but one of the many distractions current aboard *Vellela Vellela*. Perched on the starboard gunwale, he soothed his roasted flesh with aloe vera. The improvised dodger flapped. The cockpit drains failed to drain. The genoa tautened and slacked. The tiller and its bungees creaked. The sun blazed. The centipede circumwrithed the implacable axis of the blade of its fate.

Charley retrieved a plastic liter of water from a cabinet just inside the companionway. The water had come from an island aquifer, fetched by himself. Though it tasted miraculous, he sipped it judiciously.

He'd known for a long time that when things go awry at sea, the cascade of events can be very difficult to predict or to stop. Sometimes all it takes is for one insignificant thing to go wrong—a broken shackle, a misidentified light, an accidental jibe, a corroded through-hull—and it's all over. Every effect proceeds from its cause with impeccable logic. One thing wrong, two more, four, eight . . .

Or is it sixteen? Do fuckups proceed arithmetically or do they exponentiate? Do they double, or do they square?

What is it called, when right and wrong have nothing to do with it? Contra-Manichaeism?

Reality?

Of course Manichaeus, insofar as one recalls, considered the material world as innately evil, whereas the spiritual one, as embodied by mankind, he perceived as innately good.

Well, opined the bosun, as far as I can tell from an altitude of three and a half feet, the sea don't care one way or the other. And speaking for myself, I don't feel so good. Not good at all.

As goes reality, Charley mused, insofar as one has learned in, lo, these many salty years, good and evil are just so many streamers on the maypole.

Is it not always mostly pitiful, the bosun remarked, when a man is thrown upon his own philosophical resources?

Charley, studying the water bottle, grunted.

Its label long gone, only about two inches of water remained in it, and Charley finished it off. As if absentmindedly, he dipped the bottle into the brine that now rose to his knees. When the bottle was about one third refilled, he replaced the screw cap and dropped the bottle into the cockpit brine. The container bobbed up, lay parallel to the surface, and floated. Hmmm, the bosun said. For in the face of an entirely practical problem, the bosun would forget anything else. Charley unscrewed the top, added more water, and tried again. A couple of tries later, the bottle surfaced and floated cap down, leaving about a quarter of its length to bob above the surface.

Feeling the bottle brush against it, the centipede, though lethargic, darted its forcipules at its surface.

Attentively rinsing the area thus touched, for he knew the toxin to be allergenic at the very least, Charley plucked the bottle from the brine and set it on top of the house. Then he retrieved the mask and snorkle from the odds and ends floating about the cockpit, spat onto the inside of the lens, distributed the spittle with the ends of his fingers, donned the apparatus, and disappeared below.

Vellela Vellela wallowed sideways down the face of a mild swell, and the cockpit brine immersed the centipede.

Charley reappeared, wet from the soles of his feet to his sunbleached tonsure, perfunctorily cleared the snorkle of salt water before removing it, and dropped it into the half-submerged cockpit. If he noticed this minor irony, he made no show of it. Rather, he unscrewed the cap of the water bottle, dropped a small electronic device into its mouth, and replaced the cap.

I ain't believin' you, said the bosun.

You got a better idea?

Yeah, groused the bosun. Let's rewind the tape.

I hear you, said Charley, giving the cap a little extra torque.

Speaking of tape, observed the bosun, about one week's worth is all the UV is going to let that plastic live.

I'll take it, said Charley, and he launched the bottle as far astern as his good arm could fling it.

*   *   *

Working unguent into his left shoulder, which burned inside and out, and watching the centipede die, with an occasional glance toward the sun, which was watching him die, and aft toward the drifting water bottle, now separated from *Vellela Vellela* by two swells, Charley recalled a beautiful yacht he'd once come across at a wooden boat show in Tiburon, California. Though her beauty was unquestionable and what he was really looking for was a berth to Hawaii, it was her name that attracted him. She was called *Martin Eden*, and this seemed to Charley a strange name indeed to be calling any yacht, never mind a beautiful one. He had read the Jack London novel, *Martin Eden*, and though he'd found a lot to like about it—indeed, of all London's novels it was Charley's favorite— he could not square its final theses—that ours is perhaps the most degraded of all possible worlds; that the only way out is death; that the only question is how to manage that death—with the majesty of this eponymous yacht. Every inch of her teak was oiled, every stay taut, every line hanked or coiled down, her brass buffed, her log in order and neatly penned, too.

It seemed an ominous thing to name a yacht *Martin Eden*. An invitation to fate, even. And sure enough, asking and receiving permission to come aboard he met not the skipper, who may have known better than to have told the tale, but a salty waterfront type who lived aboard only to keep an eye on her. This individual happily gave Charley a tour, as the vessel was up for sale, and it took but a slow amble aft, after a saunter below decks, to get the prime story of her. Standing by the wheel, Charley noticed right away that the main boom, which appeared to consist of one entire tree of Douglas fir, while extending aft a good ten feet beyond the transom, also lay parallel to the keel a mere five and a half feet above the after deck, which let it run not an inch above Charley's shoulder, right beside his ear.

Adrift on the Caribbean a mere 2,600 crow-winged miles from Tiburon, Charley thoughtfully rubbed unguent over the trapezius of that very shoulder. The water bottle now lay four swells distant. It had become difficult to discern against the Caribbean dazzle.

"It seems an odd thing," Charley told the live-aboard, as he ran his hand along the varnished spar, "to have named the vessel after London's novel."

The live-aboard perked up. "Aye. . . ." He was missing several teeth and sported the grizzled rubicundity of a weathered alcoholic, the sun's rays vying with gin blossoms for the colonization of his parboiled cheeks. "Ye've read it, then?"

Charley said he had.

And the live-aboard recited:

> From too much love of living,
>> From hope and fear set free,
> We thank with brief thanksgiving
>> Whatever gods may be,
> That no life lives for ever,
> That dead men rise up never,
> That even the weariest river
>> Winds somewhere safe to sea.

This startled Charley. "Algernon Swinburne."

"Martin Eden reads it aloud, right at the end of the book," the live-aboard confirmed. "His, too: his end."

Charley shook his head. "I haven't read that book since I was a kid."

"Most people will never read it. Do ye recall the name of Eden's yacht?"

"Sure. *Mariposa*. Butterfly."

"That's true."

"London's yacht was *Snark*."

"Aye. Always wondered what it meant."

"How about, you're a frog with an extensible adhesive tongue, able to reach out and nail a fly instantly." Charley clapped his hands, once. "Snark!"

"Are you crazy?" the live-aboard asked, with no more inflection than if he needed change for a parking meter.

"No," Charley replied simply. "Are you?"

"Only when I get around people."

"Onomatopoeic?" Charlie coaxed, reverting to the earlier subject. The live-aboard shook his head. "Okay," Charlie admitted, "then it has to be Lewis Carroll."

The live-aboard nodded. "The Hunting of the Snark."

"A boat name we can understand."

The live-aboard nodded.

"Not like," Charlie returned to the subject, "*Martin Eden*."

"Aye. . . ." The live-aboard shook his head. Then he frowned and set an index finger aside his purpling nose. With a glance toward the harbor-master's office at the top of the dock, he said, "The owner don't like this story put about, being as the vessel's for sale and all. But . . ." He appraised Charley with a frank look. "Ye've not got the pelf to replace a bronze screw in the burgee halyard's horn cleat."

Charley smiled. "True story."

The live-aboard lowered his voice. "The man what commissioned this beauty was a doctor. She was built right over yonder, in the Nunes Brothers' yard, in the late nineteen-twenties." He hooked a thumb over his shoulder. Although the diminutive and extremely wealthy isthmus of Belvedere stood south into Raccoon Straits between *Martin Eden* and the town, Sausalito lay just a mile to the west, across Richardson Bay. There the ghost of the fabled shipyard, as Charley knew, now slumbered beneath an Indian restaurant.

"The last refit took three years. It's still goin' on. Everythin' has to be just right. So far it's cost the owner a hunnert large and he's hardly ever sailed her. He spares no expense keeping her Bristol, though, all with the ideal in mind of her original glory, as you can see for yourself."

"Job well done," Charley replied. "I'll give him that." Although, he added to himself, if some PhD ever publishes the authoritative text on maritime anal retention, this barky would sail fair on the dust jacket.

"So," continued the live-aboard, "comes the launch—back in the twenties we are—and with it the hour for our doctor to take possession of her. His beautiful society wife busts a flagon of bubbly across her stem and down the ways she slips. Sure, there's all kinds of swells aboard her, relatives and politicians and whatnot, and a smart crew to man her. Up goes canvas. It's one or two of a summer's afternoon and—by the time they pass Yellow Bluff?—the westerly's blowin' the dog off his chain. The hired skipper shapes her up for a beam reach heading straight for the Golden Gate. Mind . . . ," the live-aboard wagged the finger, "this is before there's a bridge."

Charley raised an eyebrow. "I hadn't thought of that. It must have been beautiful."

"Sure it was beautiful," the live-aboard scowled, no less certain than if he'd been there himself. "And they're just clippin' along on the starboard tack, all set up, tunin' this and that. Lime Point is abeam, with all the Pacific beckonin' 'em on, when the hired skipper invites the owner to take the helm." The live-aboard stepped back and saluted. "The kid—I say kid, but he was all of 35—has been waiting two years for this moment. He takes the helm eagerly. After a minute or two watching, the hired skipper says, 'Pleased to report, sir, but ye'll want to be comin' about to starboard or jibin' to port, and that sooner than later, on account ye needn't sail up onto Baker Beach yer first time out.'"

"Or ever, for that matter," Charley confirmed.

"'Immediately,' replies the doctor with enthusiasm: 'Ready about!'

"'On the owner's command!' shouts the skipper.

"'Ready about, sir!'" bellers the bosun, and man and boy they jump to the sheets.

"'Helm's alee!,' screams the owner. 'Helm's alee!' goes the call. The owner spins the wheel and *Martin Eden* passes her bow through the eye of the wind." The live-aboard struck his palms together. "Smart as a knife through spotted dick."

"That be smart," said Charlie, amused.

"Her foresail aback it's 'Leggo sheets!' Mind, it's the first the owner's steered the vessel under sail, let alone spun the wheel. Hell, it's the first time anybody's spun the wheel. It's the first time she's tacked! She's going as good as she'll ever go, in thirty knots of wind with everything up, and she's a sight to behold. All of ten knots she's makin', with a bone in her teeth, and all eyes lay aloft to witness the canvas crack round. But the owner has spun the wheel *all the way* to starboard. So that, as the hands smartly sheet her flat, the westerly near laid *Martin Eden* on her beam ends." The live-abroad sighed and patted the cheek of the boom. "'Ease sheets!' roars the hired skipper. 'Let us be chased back into the bay!' But the owner, inexperienced and out of his depth and panicked too, doesn't know what this means, and, not knowing what to do, he does nothing. He just holds his new wheel all the way to starboard in this great blast, and the next thing anybody knows *Martin Eden* has continued round, the sheets are eased but she's doing a doughnut, as the racers say, from a starboard tack to a port tack downwind—that's about 180 degrees of it. But she continues round! 'Harden the main!' roars the hired skipper. 'For your lives,' screams the bosun, 'harden the main!' But now it's her stern that swings through the eye of the wind, and quick as the fo'c's'le downs a ration of rum, this barkey jibes somethin' horrible." The live-aboard flattened the palm of his hand against the polished cheek of the main boom with a smack. "This great damn spar sweeps the after deck entire, starboard to port, and keeps right on going to the ratlines, gear and canvas aflyin'. That she wasn't dismasted on the spot and rolled to splinters in front of Fort Point was certainly a matter of luck and stout craftsmanship. But there wasn't luck sufficient to go round, not on that day."

The live-aboard paused. A Western gull lifted off the other end of the dock with a cry of protest and fled across the harbour. "As the leech shivered but before the boom could come back with a crack of canvas fit to alarm a seaman, the hired skipper tackled the owner's wife, who happened to be the one standin' next to him, and brought himself and her sprawling in a heap on deck as this tree of a spar swept overhead. Like the scythe of doom, it properly was. A seaman knew to duck, of course. And the other society swells just happened to be amidships or below, out of harm's way. But the menace cold-cocked the owner right on his punkin, crushed it proper like, right where he stood at the helm, blowed a load a bloody snot out his hooter, and launched the poor sod's remains clean over the taffrail." The live-aboard skipped one palm off the other, beneath the boom and to port. Charley followed the gesture with his eyes. "The young owner was dead before his ballast was overboard. He hit the water and kept right on goin', too. Never to be seen again."

In the momentary silence a mild surge entered the harbor and passed among the boats tethered there. Amid the creak of docklines, *Martin Eden* rose and settled in sequence with the rest of the craft.

"By the time they got *Martin Eden* shaped up to have a look around, the young doctor's body was gone with the ebb. They ranged all the way out to the western corner of Four Fathom Bank, about five miles, lookin' for him, to no avail, and sure, it must have been a quiet sail back to Sausalito. To this day the lad's Gladstone bag is buried in that little triangle of sod hard by the First Unitarian Church, at Franklin and Geary. Next to the preacher who built the place. Forget his name." The live-aboard cleared his throat, took two steps aft, and spat over the stern. "About six months later," he continued, wiping his beard with his sleeve, "she married that skipper."

"Who did?"

"Why, the doctor's widow. She waited a decent term, then married the bloke what saved her life. Brought him a tidy dowry, too. That sawbones owned half of Russian Hill."

Charley looked toward the city. Five miles across the bay, the front window of a northbound cable car glinted as it dropped off the crest of Powell Street.

"She sold *Martin Eden* before the wedding, though," the live-aboard added, "to the first willing man who come along with a dollar. And stranger to tell, maybe? In eighty years her berth has never left the San Francisco Bay."

The live-aboard passed a hand along the burnished taffrail, and shook his head wistfully.

"She's a lot of vessel for one dollar. . . ."

What's the moral of this story? yawned the bosun.

I don't know, said Charley, startled out of his rumination. The tube of aloe vera lay across the palm of one hand. A dab of its cream lay on the palm of the other. He squinted aft. The water bottle had drifted out of sight.

How about, suggested the bosun, you don't have to be a rich fuck to get ruined by an accidental jibe?

That must be it, Charley nodded, kneading salve into his trapezium.

Either that, the bosun added, or you might draw the conclusion that, if you bide your time? If you keep a weather eye?

Yes?

There will always be a deal on a boat. The bosun clicked his tongue. It's a buyer's market.

Always. Charley smiled faintly. Absolutely.

SIX

SKIP FAULKNER HANDED A LETTER OVER THE BAR. "THE LATEST FROM THE tropics."

Quentin ordered a beer and a glass of soda water as Tipsy opened the letter. *Sis*, the first line read, *I'm not going to bullshit you*. She put the letter down. "Goddamn it." She stared at the glass of beer. "I prefer being bullshitted." She picked up the letter. *I've gone back to work*. She put it down again. "Goddamn it."

Quentin didn't bother to tear his eyes from the television, which nattered in Spanish from a shelf above the far end of the bar. On its screen, the Secretary of Homeland Security stood behind a podium emblazoned with the seal of his authority and moved his mouth. Behind him multiple repetitions of the words *Código de Naranja* covered an entire wall. Beneath him a crawl announced a delayed start time of 5:45 P.M., Pacific Standard Time, for the Forty-niners game, due to the President's speech, followed by the headlines *Muerte Misteriosa Del Activista Famoso*, and *Este Noche á las 23 horas: ¿Numero Uno? ¡No Es Vale La Pena!* "What?"

"Those cops are on to something."

"I wish we could say as much for Homeland Security. Hey, Faulkner."

"Yo."

"May I ask why it is that you guys are watching TV in Spanish?"

Faulkner didn't even look at the screen. "What difference does it make?"

But this is it. The last job.

Tipsy said, referring to her brother's letter, "I don't believe it."

"I don't either," Faulkner replied, referring to the television.

"I don't think anybody does," Quentin said, referring to Tipsy and Faulkner.

I'm sick of working on the rich man's boat. But it's the only way to make an honest living down here, if you can call it honest, and it's that simple. Sure I've met a few owners of sufficiently kindred spirit. Interesting people, self-made people, kind and generous too, some of them. But it comes to nothing more than cocktails and servitude, sailing around with or without the owner to places they want to be or think they want to be or don't even show up to be. There's a certain pride to keeping things shipshape and bright no matter whose rig it is or how much it cost, pride being separated from vanity by the lonesome comma haunting the four figures of your cruising kitty. But there's fear among these people now, Tipsy. They're particular about every port they sleep in, they make sure they're surrounded only by others of their ilk. Security—as in how not to get kidnapped—has become an undeniable issue. Megayachts are carrying thugs and automatic weapons under the rubric of "Private Security." You raft up with one of these things—120, 150, 175 feet on the waterline—all night long there's a guy on the after-deck helipad with a weapon and an earbud. And it's not the Top 40 he's listening to, he's in touch with a similar guy on the bow. The boat's lit up or not. There's a party aboard or there's only the owner and a playmate. Makes no difference.

And it's not misplaced, this fear. There're places now these boats don't go. There's a very narrow strait called Baab al Mandab, for example. It's the gateway to the Red Sea from the Gulf of Aden. To the north and east for some four hundred miles the entire coast is Yemen, one of the most lawless countries in the world. I once met a guy who worked for the company that built the first jetport in Yemen, in the seventies. He compared the experience to landing a time machine in the Stone Age.

But the consensus is, the Stone Age needs money too.

The western boundary of Baab al Mandab is Djibouti, which isn't the smallest country in Africa, but it's close. To the north is Eritrea, to the south Somalia, and directly west, not a hundred miles from the main port, also called Djibouti, lies some hundred and sixty thousand square miles of Ethiopia.

To brand this part of the world a lawless place is to underestimate it. It's a lawless planet. And, an epifocus of this world, Baab al Mandab is fraught with piracy.

The stories are legion. You might recall an oil tanker getting hijacked there, but no yacht attempts the straights alone anymore, never mind singlehanded. If one were to be so foolish, he'd soon find himself buzzed by a panga—a type of long, thin, flat-bottomed skiff with a pair of 200 horse outboards hanging off one end. This is the outrider, the scout. Two or three passes and he's off. Come twilight, however, the lone yachtsman will find himself with a two-panga escort, each manned by three or four men. Each man is armed to the teeth—a knife, a pistol, maybe an RPG, and some type of automatic weapon, most commonly a Kalashnikov. It's a good choice. I remember guys in the American War, guys who had been in-country long enough, who tossed the AR-15 in favor of the AK-47 . . .

"The American War," Tipsy said aloud.

"Which war?" Quentin asked.

"The American War," Tipsy repeated.

"Oh, sure," Quentin replied. "That's what the Vietnamese called it— still call it."

"Charley calls it that, too."

"You mean the one we should have won?" piped a voice beyond Quentin.

Tipsy leaned back for a look. Two stools down the bar stood a thin young man in a pink polo shirt with a little American flag pinned to the lapel.

"But we didn't win it," Quentin pointed out, without bothering to turn around.

The young man's expression tightened.

"That'll be five dollars even," Faulkner told him.

The man retrieved a wallet from a back pocket of his khaki trousers and selected a five dollar bill from it, which he handed to the bartender. "So why didn't they call it the French war?" he said, closing the wallet and taking up his pint of beer.

"I'm sure they did call it the French War," Quentin replied in his most reasonable voice, "while they were still fighting the French. The Vietnamese won that one, too."

"So," said the young man, sipping barm off the top of his draft. "Are you a Communist?"

"Worse," Quentin smiled thinly. "I am the son of a Communist."

"Your paradigm is exhausted," the man replied. It was almost as if he were sympathetic.

"Now there's a leap of faith. But," Quentin shook his head, "no such luck. My dad was with Harry Bridges from the beginning."

"Sadly misguided," the young man sadly suggested.

Tipsy blinked at this individual, turned to look straight at the televised imagery for a moment, and then, hardly breathing, turned to Quentin, who sat to her right.

Quentin gestured toward the beer in the young man's hand. "You forgot to tip the bartender."

"No, I didn't," the young man answered.

"Stay thrifty." Quentin pushed a dollar off the top of his own change toward the beer tap. "Maybe you'll save enough to pay off the current American war."

Tipsy laughed aloud. It was a generous, inclusive laugh, much as if she were inviting the young man to laugh along at her companion's surly remarks. But the young man wasn't laughing.

"Dude," he said. "Are you serious?"

"As serious as a black man can be in this society."

"Hey, man," said the young man, holding the beer to his chest. "I'm black, too."

"Really?" Quentin looked him in the eye. "I hadn't noticed."

"Well." Tipsy politely cleared her throat. "It's been a long time since I've witnessed a conversation in which every word counted."

Quentin took it right up. "Which conversation was that?"

The young man started to say something.

"Get the fuck away from me," Quentin said abruptly.

The young man blinked.

"And, yes, dude," Quentin added, "I'm serious."

After a moment's thought the young man took up his wallet and his pint of beer. "I think I'll check out the patio."

"See what you can find out about the American War while you're out there," Quentin said to the man's retreating back. "Christ. What's this town coming to?"

"Quentin," Tipsy pointed out, "didn't your dad and Harry Bridges get their heads cracked, and more than once, up and down this very waterfront?"

"Yes, they did," Quentin said.

"Not only that, but wasn't your father the only black man in the Longshoreman's union?"

"No." Quentin took a sip of soda water. "There were two of them."

"So what's so new or even offensive about brain-boy there thinking along the lines of communism as evil and the Vietnam War as winnable?"

"Nothing," Quentin shook his head. "Opinions are like assholes . . ."

"Everybody has one," she finished.

"It's just that I expect more from my fellow Franciscans."

"He probably does too."

Quentin sighed. "At least it didn't come to blows. I might have hurt the kid pounding some sense into him."

"Are you kidding? He's probably got a black belt in tort litigation. One smudge on his alligator and he'd sue you for everything you own."

"It's a crocodile."

"Then he'd breed and spawn in the very house he took away from you."

"That's disgusting. Stop it. I'm trying to drink sensibly." He took a sip of water. "So what else does Charlie have to say?"

"When I left off, he was using one form of piracy to justify another."

. . . they have grappling hooks, radios, ammunition, and no scruples whatsoever. Some of them even see their cause as just. You can heave to and take your chances, but your chances are two: get cleaned out and stay alive, or get cleaned out and killed. If you have a woman with you—or are one—you have

to run, because slavery is her alternative. But they can outrun any sailboat or even a freighter. Some of these pangas can do forty knots. Or you can go down with a fight—but down is going to be the end result.

Why am I telling you this? The yachts I've been working on don't even think about Baab al Mandab. They meander from pleasure port to pleasure port here in the Caribbean and in the Mediterranean, seeking others of their class. It's not unlike squid mating. Remote travel doesn't faze them at all, but if you're not being seen for the sake of being seen, and sized up for the sake of assessing the degree of your excess, and by your own kind, why spend seventy or eighty million dollars on a boat?

But it's more insidious than that. These people don't want to see their boats in Baab al Mandab. They know it's dangerous. But it's no longer safe for them in certain anchorages on the west coast of Guatemala, like it's been almost any place in Colombia for years, like it has become up and down the coast of Brazil, and Panama, and Costa Rica . . .

The circle is closing.

What am I supposed to do? Get killed defending one of them?

Anyway, after bumming around for almost a year without a pot to piss in, other than Vellela Vellela, I've decided to undertake one more big score. A score modest enough, by most people's standards, but one sufficient unto my needs. I'm sure you're all too aware that I know but one or two ways to do that. But just in case the slots don't come up all cherries, I want you to know about it.

"Damn it," Tipsy said. "Those cops were right." She slapped the pages of the letter. "I don't want to know!"

"He's talking about smuggling, isn't he?" Quentin asked.

Tipsy made a face.

"I guess that rehabilitation stuff isn't all it's cracked up to be. Perhaps that explains the gloomy philosophical tone communicated by this particular epistle?"

"Charlie has been writing me letters since he ran away from home." She indicated the letter. "Almost since his friend was building jetports in the Stone Age."

"Tell me something I don't know."

Tipsy blinked. "Could I be squandering my adulthood by constantly restating the obvious?"

"I never thought of you as a progressive essayist."

"I love his letters. Email and cellphones have completely blown away snail mail, but Charley has never stopped with postcards and letters. Look at this." She showed Quentin the envelope. "Hand addressed, hand written. A careful hand. Stationery off a ruled pad. Exotic stamps. Water stains." She sniffed the pages. "Rum and kerosene smoke."

Quentin noted the edge in her voice. Instead of asking her to tell him something he didn't know he said, "Sure, baby."

On the other side of the bar, Faulkner paused for a look at the stamp as he dried his hands on a towel. "I already have that one." He mopped his forehead on his sleeve, hung the towel under the bar, and turned back to his work.

"Rum Cay. Can you imagine? Wouldn't you like to travel there?"

"Why would I want to go there when I can stay in San Francisco arguing about Vietnam and workers' rights? You think it's any different there?"

"Charley says it's hard to find somebody in the islands who gives a shit about what the United States is up to."

"Oh yes?" Quentin bristled. "That will all change the minute we start bombing them."

"That'll get their attention."

"Don't they know we're the most important country in the world?"

"I guess not."

"That's what my ironically pink brother on the terrace there thinks."

Tipsy turned to have a look. "I thought he left."

"Nope. He's out there telling his friends there's bogus negritude to be baited at the bar."

"Maybe they'll buy you a drink before your mind turns to dust in the Museum of Old Ideas."

"What do you suppose is going build that museum?"

"Money?"

"The evergreen idea that contains all other ideas."

"We're stoking its inventory by the hour."

"Point taken," Quentin muttered tightly. It was clear that he was genuinely annoyed.

"Quentin, answer me straight: Are we going to have to shoot our way out of here?"

"Hey." Quentin stabbed the bar top with a forefinger. "I am the regular here. That buppie out there is a fucking provocateur."

"I though you could hold your water better than this."

Quentin stiffened. "Water? Good idea. Let's pamper yourself with a shot of tequila. You know how I like to watch."

Tipsy didn't object.

"Faulkner."

"Yo."

"One shot of Casaderos."

The place had a good crowd in it. But Faulkner tumbled a shot glass onto a coaster and had it generously brim full and flanked by a lime wedge and a saltshaker, with the quart back on the shelf, before Quentin and Tipsy could resume their conversation.

"Poetry in motion." Quentin covered the orphaned dollar bill with a ten. "That's yours."

Faulkner gathered up the cash and rapped a knuckle on the bar.

Ignoring salt and lime Tipsy lofted the shot glass. Quentin raised his pint of water. "May the scales fall from their telemesmerized eyes."

"What are you talking about?" Tipsy said, backing her glass out of the toast. "They're running the country. They're running the goddamn world. Toast something plausible, for chrissakes."

Without hesitation Quentin came back with, "May their telemesmerized eyes be poached in light sweet crude and served up to the delectation of voracious hapkeite miners between shifts in the cafeteria of our first lunar maquiladora, as mandated by the Extraterrestrial Lunches for Labor Act of 2052."

Tipsy smiled. They touched glasses.

You'll remember Red Means as the guy who once took care of you as a favor to me while I was on vacation, as the euphemism goes. Add to that the hulk of Vellela Vellela, the shipyard job in Guadeloupe, and a bunch more stuff. Long story short, three years ago, when I splashed Vellela Vellela, we went our separate ways.

Well, not much has changed, so far as Red is concerned. He could be living high on any one of the more expensive islands around here. He's got money buried in suitcases on half the beaches in the Caribbean. He's a legal, passport-bearing citizen of at least three sovereign countries, the United States among them, but he prefers to live modestly aboard his fish boat, wherever she may be docked or anchored. His employees make landfall there all the time, of course, here and there in the Keys, off the coasts of Florida and Georgia, up the St. John's River, the Barrier Islands, Cape Fear, and so forth.

This reminds me of the story of a certain barrier island community. This is in the early nineties. Red had the local sheriff in his pocket, you understand, so every couple of weeks or so this sheriff would have pressing business on the mainland. An hour or two after the eastern taillights on his westbound patrol car disappeared over the causeway, some slab—which is what they call a rotten-hulled shrimp boat up and down the Gulf Stream, the type that has to get towed in half the time it goes out—would come listing out of the mist and tie up at the town's only wharf. The only paved road on the island runs from the causeway through the outlying swamp and three blocks of ersatz urbanity to dead-end onto that very dock. And this slab is gunnels awash with dope. Five *or six guys and a box-bed truck materialize and twelve hundred pounds of marijuana transship, quick as a knife through spotted dick.*

"Through what?" Quentin asked.

"Some kind of seagoing comestible," Tipsy shrugged.

> *. . . Later it was cocaine. Still later, the Drug Enforcement Agency showed up and took everybody away, including the sheriff—who by the way managed to beat the rap and hang on to several hundred thousand francs he'd parked in a Swiss bank account.*
>
> *I ought to know.*

Quentin leveled the edge of his hand between his nose and upper lip. "Doesn't your brother know the general public is up to here with dope stories?"

"Who says this is a dope story?"

Quentin looked at her. "It appears that, not only does our man not hear his own music, neither does his sister."

Tipsy sighed. "Yes. . . ."

Quentin grunted. "Faulkner."

"Yo."

Quentin moved his chin at his empty glass.

"The same?"

Quentin nodded.

"Not for me," Tipsy said modestly. "I've had enough."

"The heck you say," Quentin pointed out, "it's your round."

"Oh, shoot. In that case . . ." She glanced at the page beneath the one she'd been reading. "We're almost to the end."

"Let's hear it."

> *. . . part about the rainy day bank account I somehow never learned, when you come right down to it. Although, in a slightly different context— Somebody's knocking on the hull . . .*

"Now I see the point," said Quentin. "It's not how you lose the game, but how you play it."

> *Okay, it's two hours later. I'm going to put a stamp on this and send it to town with the guy who just dove the hull. I'm set to weigh anchor at first light. Lots to do between now and then. Much love.*

"Way out there on the vast blue sea," Tipsy folded the letter, "my brother Charley's thinking of me." She batted her eyes.

"Better he were thinking of his lawyer," Quentin muttered.

"There you go again." Tipsy folded the letter into its envelope and set it aside. "Always the level-headed pessimist. Who says he's going to get caught?"

"Are you kidding? The cops are waiting for—"

She covered his mouth with the fingers of her free hand and with the other touched the shotglass to his fresh pint of water. "Let's keep it a secret until it's over?"

Quentin thoughtfully took up his glass. "So, Tipsy," he said as if casually, "What do you know about this Red guy?"

"Red is the guy Charley refused to drop the dime on."

"So Red owes Charley—no? Owes him big, it sounds like."

"Big." She raised an eyebrow. "Yes."

"So he couldn't—you know—just bail Charley out?"

"Instead of giving him a dangerous job, you mean?"

"Exactly."

"I don't know. I've never met the guy. I've just heard about him over the years. The first time was while Charley was still in prison. One day I received a money order for five thousand dollars." She tapped the bar with the bottom of the shot glass. "Right here. Out of the blue. I was still living aboard *Dhow Jones* at Mission Creek."

"That was one leaky scow, as I recall."

"It was one leaky scow. In fact, at that point she had flooded and settled onto the bottom—which was only about four feet below her keel at maximum flood—but it was time to find a new home or die from breathing mold spores. I was at my wit's end when all that money showed up."

"But you didn't know about spores and mold at that time."

"That's true. I thought I was asphyxiating on my lifestyle."

"Explain the difference to me again?"

"That money bailed me out for close to a year."

Quentin smiled and began to sing. "Once upon a time, life was cheap and easy, in the most beautiful town in the world . . ."

"Tell me about it. These days, I'd be lucky to stretch five grand for five months."

Quentin looked at her and smiled. How perfectly charming. Once upon a time in the most beautiful town in the world Quentin Asche had been known to make five thousand dollars in five minutes, and they both knew it. "Anyway, the money came from Red."

"It came from Red, and Charley had asked him to send it. Reimbursement wasn't expected. And I still haven't met him." She paused. "It was only much later that Charley happened to mention the source of the money."

"It was dope money?"

Tipsy shook her head. "If only."

"Whatever could you mean?"

Tipsy sighed and shook her head. "Red had a wife at the time. She was the mother of two of his kids."

"How many kids does he have?"

"No idea. She was strung out when she got pregnant, she was strung out when she gave birth, she was strung out the whole time she was nursing."

"Oh, please," Quentin said.

"Yeah. Well, anyway, when Charley got busted, it was a very near thing that Red wasn't caught, too. Red and the wife farmed out the kids and went underground for a year or so. They lived in a fishing shack jacked up on cypress posts in southwest Florida, somewhere in the swamps around Watson's Store. You needed an airboat to get near the place, and just about anybody you ran into out there would just as soon shoot a stranger and feed him to the gators and use his airboat for parts as talk to him about, I don't know, the Battle of Hue, let's say."

"How about," Quentin suggested, "the American War of 1959-1975."

"Quentin . . ."

Quentin stabbed the bar top with a forefinger. "First American officially killed in action in Vietnam? July 8, 1959. Very good. Last American officially KIA in Vietnam? April 29, 1975, right again. We qualify the qualification *officially*."

"You're making me sick."

"Here's a tougher one, so tough I won't phrase it as a question. The first American shipment of arms arrived in French colonial, pre-partition Vietnam on August 10, 1950. You heard me. It's reasonably safe, as it were, to assume that somebody died as a result, so that adds up to a 25-year engagement. And by the way, young lady . . ."

"Yes?"

"It's not me who's making you sick, it's the mold known as your government."

Tipsy shrugged. "Roll the blank dice."

"What is that, fatalism? The dice are government-issued," Quentin muttered darkly.

"That would appear to be correct, as Officer Few might say." She brightened. "I like that expression."

Quentin shook off the malaise of his statistical foray with remarkable aplomb. "Do you like Officer Few, too?"

"He is kind of cute. . . ."

"One story at a time."

"But Quentin, darling, it's all one big story."

He waved this off.

"Anyway, Red had kept this woman loaded the whole time he was a high-flying dope dealer. Now they were up against it, with damn little money of their own, and no way to access the various suitcases buried on half the beaches in the Caribbean, as my brother would have it. Red figured he'd kill three birds with one stone. Make good this solid he owed to Charley by helping Charley's sister; help his wife; help himself. Marriage sure is complicated."

"I wouldn't know," said Quentin archly.

Tipsy gave him a look, but Quentin rebuffed it with one of his own. "So," she continued, "long story short, one night by the dark of the moon they slipped into some illegal clinic in Miami where, longer story shorter, Red sold one of his wife's kidneys."

Quentin's face went slack. "That's too short."

"It turned out she was dying of cancer anyway. . . ."

"That's supposed to increase my understanding?"

". . . which is why she was a junkie the whole time. The habit helped her deal with the pain, which is why Red let her stay strung out, and it's at least one of the reasons why Red stayed with her."

Quentin blinked.

"It's what happened." Tipsy shrugged. "According to Charley, anyway. He wrote me a long letter about it. He likes to tell stories in his letters."

"As perhaps I've noticed."

"Her name was Carmen. Charley liked her."

"I can scarcely believe it."

"So," she said, "scarcely believe it."

"So he didn't send all the, er, kidney money to you?"

"He sent half the money to me. The rest he used to keep her supplied with narcotics until the time came for her overdose."

"Because—what? How . . . ?"

"Because the wife owed one to him, and he owed one to Charley, and I am Charley's sister, and Red loved her, and they knew she was near the end." She spread both hands over the bar. "Simplicity itself."

"It's not euthanasia that's complicated, it's marriage."

"That would be correct."

"Wait." Quentin reanimated his face sufficiently to frown. "I'm trying to get a grip on . . . I mean, how do you fit into that equation? I mean . . ." He touched two fingers to the bartop, between himself and Tipsy, and struggled for an appropriate expression. "I mean, what is this? Karma?"

Tipsy drew away from him. "They're going to have to give you a couple of rooms to yourself,, in that Museum of Old Ideas," she pronounced solemnly.

"In other words," Quentin surmised, "you certainly hope not."

SEVEN

CHARLEY HAD HEARD OF CURIOUS THINGS RISING FROM THE BILGES ONCE a vessel is certain of going down, especially a vessel that has passed years in the tropics. Vermin of course, insects and little mammals of every description, but also reptiles, originally attracted, perhaps, by the other denizens of the below-decks ecosystem. A Nicaraguan skipper once told him of clambering all over his foundering schooner in the midst of a hurricane with all manner of creatures slithering and scurrying about the deck under his bare feet. Though the odd blast of lightning gave him a glimpse of what he might expect to be stepping on at any given moment, at the time it was, as he pointed out, the least of his worries. The hurricane lasted three days.

Charley wondered what port the centipede hailed from. Could it have been aboard the entire time he'd owned the boat? Watching him as he slept? But the speculation was half-hearted, a holding action to fend his imagination off brooding over what else might go wrong, and it soon petered out.

No need to brood, counseled the bosun. Just stick around.

As if in response to this fatalism, despite its remaining unexpressed aloud—though that's ridiculous, Charley autoremonstrated, for, once an idea has been consciously articulated, even if in silence, it's donned clothing, become real—something bumped the starboard bow. The sound reminded him of a rug, perhaps burdened by the weight of a corpse rolled up in it, being dragged along an unfinished concrete floor. Not that he'd ever been in such a circumstance, but hey, let the imagination run full and by, since nothing else is, then check in on the reality—another shark scraping along the hull, testing, testing. . . . And this sharp reminder of his true circumstance led Charley to wonder, insofar as it may or may not be within his power to affect it, what manner of death might the skipper prefer to the one of being eaten by a shark?

And so it's now we find the time to be askin' the big questions, growled the bosun.

Charley ignored him. Not a protracted fade while languishing in prison. We decided that. Nor being keel-hauled by Red Means. We know that, too. Dehydration? Too slow. He considered the centipede.

Knife to the heart? Does a centipede have a heart? Now there, he reflected, languishes a subject for a book I'll never read or write. Although it certainly seemed preferable to death by shark, he had to wonder if he had the nerve to knife himself. So perhaps that's the threshold between passive and active? But Charley had a memory of attempting to inject himself with a tiny dose of heroin, one fine summer's afternoon, in a rundown bunkhouse behind an Orlando truck stop. Tied off, syringe loaded, vein thumped up proud, his best fair-weather buddy watching—fair-weather because Charley had purchased enough dope for two—he couldn't bring himself to do it. And it wasn't fear of the poppy that stayed his hand; it was fear of the needle. They must have a term for it, though "smart" might do. In the end his fair-weather buddy did it for him. His fair-weather buddy was good at it, too. So good that he kept right on until he killed himself doing it just a year later. For his own part, Charley didn't like it in the first instance and never injected anything again. And the high? Well, there's high and there's high, Charley thought wryly. All he could really remember, some thirty years down the road, was the puking. Right now, though, the bosun reminded him, you're high on suicide and estate planning. Charley surveyed the empty ocean beyond the transom. What euphoria could possibly eclipse the contemplation of a saline eternity?

He carefully worked the point of the boning knife out of the teak, keeping the centipede skewered, and flipped the corpse through a steep arc, over the side. The creature landed with a barely discernible plash about ten yards abeam of *Vellela Vellela*, only to be, much to Charley's astonishment, immediately disappeared from below by a first rate shark's maw. A really big one. The deed could not have been accomplished more greedily or efficiently, that is to say, it was a perfection of ergonomic gluttony. The profusion of teeth was followed to the surface by a single eye that unmistakably took in the scene afloat, glowering as if resenting the paucity of the immediate sacrifice, yet without restraint in its Precambrian delectation of the menu to come. This assay was followed by a sinuous presentation of a dorsal fin, a starboard fluke, a tapering anterior, and a deltoid tail, until all revolved again into the bottomless repository of briny prodigy that is the unlimited sea.

The genoa slacked and cracked taut. The tiller creaked. I'm slated to be unnerved in the end regardless, Charley reflected. He tried the point of the knife against his naked chest, below the left nipple, just where he imagined his heart to . . . lurk? Wrong word. Cower, more like it. Come on, lad, Charley urged himself, take your medicine. . . .

It was a thin, sharp blade which would no doubt do its job efficiently.

He flattened the point against his breast. And as he did so his eyes unfocused from the dimple indented by the knife point, just below the *Pectorallis major* . . . and refocused on a translucent amber bottle, bobbing in the twenty inches of seawater now in the cockpit. For, congruent to Charley's circumstance, *Vellela Vellela* was no longer holding her own. Slowly but surely she was going down. No more than three feet of airspace remained between the surface of the water in the cabin and the cabin's top. Even as he tabulated this progress, a bleach bottle bobbed to the surface within the submerged galley, and its blue cap dinged the brass bowl of the chart table lamp.

Perhaps Cedric Osada hadn't raided the oxycodone after all.

Charley sheathed the knife at the small of his back and plucked the canister from the brine. After some to-do, not all of it unattributable to his nerves, he managed the canister's childproof cap. Its interior had remained dry. Among fat pastilles of Vitamin C, stress doses of Vitamin B, still-redolent echanasia, golden seal, pseudoephedrine (to open the sinuses for scuba diving), Dexamil (for alert passage-making), aspirin, ibuprofen, penicillin, and streptomycin—four bright blue 80 milligram doses of oxycodone asserted themselves amongst their more salubrious ilk like interbred queens in a termite's nest. He coaxed them onto the palm of his hand and threw the bottle over the side.

Oxycodone is synthetic morphine. A quarter of merely one of those blue pills would sled a normal person straight to oblivion. Taken all at once and chewed to obviate their time-release function, Charley figured, certainly four of them should comprise a thorough overdose.

As he computed these matters, *Vellela Vellela* lurched. Charley pitched backwards but managed to turn, too. His left shoulder impacted the back of the house, on the starboard side of the companionway. He contrived to roll his momentum through the cockpit water, making a fist around the pills as he rotated. He wound up on his back, head underwater, pills held aloft. The pain was sufficient to take his breath away, but not so much that he couldn't roar as he surfaced. He rose to his knees in two feet of brine and looked forward. The bow and the foot of the genoa were awash. Still the breeze was sufficient to fill the sail, yet insufficient to drive her under, or lay her on her side, not yet anyway, and Charley momentarily entertained the strange idea that *Vellela Vellela* might sail on despite her hull and the entire rig being submerged.

The logic wasn't something he wanted to hang around to witness. Dream logic.

Now the useless left arm depended from his shoulder like a long sock full of saturated sand. He opened his right hand. The pills were wet. Bits of them clung to his palm. One, two. Three? Okay. Four. He clapped his palm to his mouth.

Five.

The pills lay on his tongue, bitter and insidious.

Six.

He began to chew.

Seven, eight, nine . . .

He crushed the acrid pills between his molars, licked the palm, then washed it all down with two hastily cupped handfuls of sea water. The whole tasted like a vile cocktail of kelp and battery acid, but the deed was done. He resisted gagging. He blinked. Yes it was done. As he tried to think what he thought, the following swell attempted to accelerate *Vellela Vellela's* waterlogged stern past her awash bow. The genoa flapped and the tiller creaked and one of its bungees snapped but the swell carried on and the jury-rig returned her to a broad reach, more or less. But a little puff, a capful of wind, a mere teenaged sprite might lay her over, and that, no doubt, would be the end.

Sitting on the cockpit sole, chest deep in water, Charley ran his tongue over his gums, probing the several gaps among his few good teeth for orts of medicine. The tip of a dorsal fin, gliding close aboard, had an inch or two more altitude, above the surface of the sea, than his own head.

It won't be long now. I might yet experience those teeth. What to do? And in the calm afforded by the first glimmerings of the narcotic haze, sure to eventually overwhelm him, if only he could mine the time in order for his metabolism to do its work, he recollected a length of chain and two padlocks he kept with the dock lines in the port cockpit locker. Quickly, or so he thought, he undid the fastening and lifted the lid. On his knees, up to his ribs in seawater, a rummage among fenders and lines and life vests turned up twenty feet of 5/8" case-hardened BBB chain. He smiled a strange smile. He dragged the chain out of the locker with no regard to the damage its links inflicted on the wood. With the chain came not one but two padlocks, each of the pair of keys threaded onto the locked hasp of the opposite lock. Many's the time Charley had used this rig to securely iron *Vellela Vellela* to a dock or buoy ball in a strange or dicey harbor. Now he would use it to iron himself.

He crawled out from under the makeshift awning, forward to the mast, dragging the chain after him. There, he figured, the extant rigging might afford him some little protection from the predation of the ocean, a sort of shark cage within which he might stall for time. He sat against the foot of the mast, facing aft. He passed the chain around both his waist and the mast below the gooseneck. He keyed open a padlock, cinched the loop of chain tight, passed the loop of the hasp through two links, and snapped it shut. He wriggled to test the rig and decided, if he were sufficiently desperate or panicked, he might actually make himself thin enough to escape. He reopened the padlock.

As he did so the second tiller bungee snapped, the bow sloughed around, the genoa backed across the bow to starboard, and the chainplate retaining the single remaining shroud came away with a moist crunch. The wire tore out of the grip of the mangled boom as the mast snapped a few feet above Charley's head, and with a sigh of canvas and a clatter of turnbuckles and blocks, the entire rig lay down to starboard.

Without the pull of the sail, and with the new drag of the rigging, the little vessel slowly set about presenting its starboard side to the following sea.

Charley retrieved the knife and parked it between his teeth.

Though gear settled all over the deck, not a line touched him. The makeshift bimini had parted like a tissue. He didn't even turn around to assess the damage. Quickly Charley improvised a five-point safety harness, of the sort commonly found in a race car, a loop behind the mast and under the gooseneck, the ends down between the thighs, up and X-ing behind the mast again, over the gooseneck, over the shoulders, X-ing over the chest, down and criss-crossing behind the mast again, to meet over his sternum where, the oxycodone allowing increasingly painless gymnastics, he snapped closed a padlock hasp just as *Vellela Vellela* began to side-slip under the surface in an apparent attempt to follow her rig. A swell washed over the boat, carried away the rest of the awning, and wetted Charley to his chin.

Charley's legs and lower left arm surfaced just as a pair of jaws closed around the wire and turnbuckles snarled around the starboard chain plates, two feet away from him. The metal rent the monster's mouth bloody as its impact staggered the entire vessel. The beast's exhalation reeked of a presidential pardon. Momentarily awed, Charley snatched the blade from his teeth without noticing the nick he inflicted on the corner of his mouth and slashed at the beast. But it slid away untouched. So the cage of rigging worked, Charley noted, with no great satisfaction, as he replaced the knife between his teeth. At perhaps twice its usual rate his nerve-wracked heart broadcast narcotized erythrocytes through his vascular civilization like so many monsoon-driven propaganda leaflets among a credulous population. Nor was he unaware of how preposterous this assessment might have sounded to an impartial bystander. On the contrary. Let him apostrophize unambiguously: Woo-eeeee, he extolled, this drug be skankin' *strong*! And he pitched the padlock keys over his debilitated shoulder as if they were salt for luck.

And then, as if the impulse were continuous, Charley wrest the waterproof satchel from under his belt at the small of his back, using his bad arm at that. He opened it, removed the manuscript of his incomplete novel, and launched thicknesses of unbound pages over his shoulder with no more deliberation than he'd given to the impalement of the centipede hours earlier. The pages bloomed on the wind into a pixelated plume, a white and very modest white cumulus tumbling like a reflection over the translucent green of the swell far beneath the cerulean sky. And then it was as if the sea, by some sleight of hand not visible to even an attentive onlooker, reached up and captured each and every rectangle of it, by ones and threes and tens until, altogether, the whole thing was as drowned as so much erratic linoleum uselessly tiling the unpavable. Just like the keys, just like a pinch of salt, just like the possibility of luck, yet another streamer on the maypole of reality, 276 pages settled to leeward like rain-driven leaves, like rectilinear puffs of an ephemeral smoke, the paltry sum of a whimsical concession to fortune.

Not that Charley saw it. How strange, he thought, still facing aft with a knife between his teeth, how strange that I feel liberated. Holding it above the surface he zipped the waterproof satchel and replaced it between his belt and the small of his back, now at least eighteen inches underwater. To protect the ship's papers, her log, a chart, a few empty envelopes pre-addressed to his sister, which he'd stashed there just to keep them dry, his passport and wallet—this was mere habit. With his bad arm, now but for a dim metabolic peep nearly freed from pain, afloat like a stalled log line, he thought to himself, that was the most satisfying thing I've done in a long time. What else can I get rid of? Except for writing letters. Even with only the one correspondent, I like the writing of them. But to get rid of those pages! ¡Adiós! He watched the swell for a full minute without really seeing it, thinking of little else than how very queer that deliquescing satisfaction had tasted. Perhaps in death, Charley fancied with a marvelous, mad detachment, I shall crack the nut that was— is—the novel.

Now the hull of *Vellela Vellela*, the boat that Charley had worked two years to refit and refloat, and had lived aboard for one of those years and three more of cruising, ebbed to starboard, flooded to port, she settled deeper with each iteration, a foundering, dismasted wreck. Her genoa billowed in the water, surrounded by detritus, like the saturated bodice of Ophelia's frock.

The shark didn't reappear. But as Charley slipped beneath the surface entirely, a shadow wicked through his peripheral vision. I've almost made it, he thought. But I must brace myself for multiple incisions. He plucked the knife from his teeth. But what if I were to approach the novel as if I were writing a letter to a friend? Better to inhale, stupid, inhale, or get shredded to chum. Where's the bosun? But his spirit wouldn't voluntarily surrender its lease on his body. On the contrary, his larynx battened its little apartment against the landlord. Plus, he had this idea about The Novel. Which was? Write it like a letter. Why hadn't this idea occurred to him before? Maybe writing has something to do with dopamine? The chain prevented him clawing back to the surface in order to write a novel. He moved the point of the knife through the water in front of him as if fencing with it. To live? To write? To research the effects of alkaloids on the central nervous system? So, but London had been right. The organism will strive for tone. Don't laugh or you'll drown. You meant life. Strive for life. What difference does it make? That's its job. I'm telling you. London told you. It ain't about you. It's about getting your genetic material into the next generation. That's the last piece of advice I'm givin' ya, declared the bosun, because, believe it or not, bein' underwater and all, I'm evaporatin'. Huh? Charley laughed until his eyes began to bulge. Well, we blew that mission! Hello? Hello—. Multiple incisions. Hyah, thrust, hyah! But as the shadow descended in the water before him, his eyes discerned vestiges of non-shark technology. Black fins with . . . chartreuse highlights? A sheath knife strapped to a hirsute shin. Brown fabric billowing. Unbuttoned pocket flap, pocket inside out. Gray weights on a yellow belt. The black bib of a farmer john. A fat watch. Hoses and bubbles. Around the yellow rostrum of a face mask, auburn locks swirled. A living wreath of cinnamon sea snakes, was what it occurred to Charley to compare it to. Charming simile. But you can't fool me, boy-o, this is the Caribbean, Charley remonstrated, feeling immensely canny, sea snakes are a scourge specific to the Pacific. It's the sharky-warkies you got to worry about in these wa-wa-waters. . . .

In his left hand the scuba diver held what looked for all the world like a pneumatic impact wrench. A yellow hose spiraled from a bib on its pistol grip, up and out of sight, toward the surface. Memory of surface. A hammerhead shark appeared at the diver's elbow, half again the diver's length. Look out, Charley yelled, expelling air. The diver turned and without hesitation touched the chuck of the wrench to the center of the creature's head and pulled the trigger. A plume of bubbles rose from the tool's pneumatic vents. The shark vanished.

That sounded exactly, Charley marveled, like somebody changing a tire underwater.

With his free hand the scuba diver drew his knife. One entire edge of the stainless blade's considerable length was serrated like a limb saw.

Sheeit, man, said Charley, laughing the ultimate paucity of his oxygen into the brine, *don't you know you can't cut no five-eighths chain with no dive knife?*

Ah hahahahahaha . . .

11
The Weevil of Habitude

EIGHT

CEDRIC OSAWA ENTERED MIAMI INTERNATIONAL AIRPORT WITH A SEA BAG labeled 150% Genoa, a brand-new copy of *The Rivers Ran East* by Leonard Clark, and a knackered windbreaker. He checked the bag and was on line, happily digesting an excellent Cuban lunch, when Miami Homeland Security confiscated his marlinspike knife, given him on his fifteenth birthday by the first skipper he'd sailed under, and which, unlike everything else in his life, he'd managed to hang on to for thirty-five years.

There was some discussion about arresting him for attempting to board a commercial aircraft with a weapon, but when the security supervisor became convinced that not only had Cedric not been on a stateside airplane for fifteen years, but also that he intended to stick to the claim that he'd only ever heard of the Chilean version of September 11, itself heretofore unknown to the interrogating supervisor, he told Cedric to put on his shoes and get back in line with the rest of the weary travelers. Instead, Cedric put out his hand and asked for his knife back.

"You don't want to go there—" one of the two security guards hastened to suggest.

His supervisor cut him off with a gesture. "We're talking Homeland Security, here, Mr. Osawa. Which of those two words don't you understand?"

Cedric pointed to the knife, marooned on a tray on a stainless steel counter flanked by the two lesser functionaries. "That's a tool of my trade," he said simply, "and I've owned it all my adult life."

Thusly Cedric won himself a trip through a nearby unmarked windowless door.

"Mere sentiment withers before the necessity of a secure homeland, Mr. Osawa." The supervisor showed him a book, fat and tattered, with the limber morocco covers of a Bible, except they were red, white and blue. "The Patriot Act says as much."

"I need my knife," Cedric insisted quietly.

The supervisor cast a frustrated glance at the disputed object. "How much could it cost to replace?" he asked reasonably.

"How much you got?" Cedric replied.

The supervisor declined to consider this.

"Point being," Cedric elucidated, "it's not enough."

The supervisor gestured toward the door, beyond which rumbled a cavern of passengers layered like pastry, with belts, shoes and tickets in hand, their individuality demarcated by a maze of nylon straps and chrome stanchions. Two bumper stickers were affixed to the inside of the windowless door.

I ♥ GITMO

I ♥ WIRETAPS

"Don't you want to catch your plane?" the supervisor asked.

"It wouldn't do me any good without my knife," Cedric stated simply. "I'm going west to work."

"And what is your trade, Mr. . . . ." The supervisor glanced at Cedric's 100-ton Coast Guard license.

"Osawa," Cedric said. "I do anything on a boat that needs doing."

"So you're going to San Francisco for a boat job?"

"Yes, sir."

"What sort of boat job?"

"Why, sailing, sir," replied Cedric patiently, though he was beginning to wonder what order of stupidity he was dealing with, "by way of delivering a boat from San Francisco to Zihuatanejo."

"Is that why you have those tattoos?"

"I beg your pardon?"

"To help you deliver boats?"

One of the two subordinates snickered.

"Aids to navigation?" the supervisor continued, glancing behind him at the snickering subordinate in order to conceal a smile of his own.

"Actually, skipper," Cedric said evenly, "I got this one here," he touched his right forearm, "when I was in the service."

The supervisor raised an eyebrow, then turned his head to read what was inked on Cedric Osawa's right forearm. He did this cautiously, as if he were afraid that the subject was laying for a chance to kick him in the privates. The supervisor had learned this precaution the hard way.

"Semper—?" he read aloud. The supervisor's eyes snapped up. "Semper fidelis?" he recited rather than read. "You're a United States Marine?"

"Marine?" Cedric cocked his head as if puzzled. "Why would I join a pussified outfit like the Marines?"

Now both subordinates snickered. With startling alacrity the supervisor whirled and barked. "Stand down!" The subordinates wiped their smiles, assumed parade rest, and stared straight ahead. The supervisor turned back to Cedric. "Well?"

"Merchant seaman. Four years." The supervisor took the forearm by its wrist and read aloud, with difficulty, "*Semper Voco Imp* . . ." He flung the arm away in disgust, annoyed at obviously faking, if even momentarily, a pretension to fluency in non-leatherneck Latin. "What's that mean?" he gruffly demanded. "What outfit's that?"

"*Semper Voco Imperium Dubium.*" Cedric generously supplied a translation, "Always Question Authority." Then he added, not flinching from the supervisor's glare, "Outfit's kinda loose."

The supervisor was incredulous. "What the hell's that got to do with the goddamn service?"

"Everything. Do I have to spell it out for you? Some people don't like to be told what to do."

The supervisor was visibly fuming. "That's not how it works, sailor. Semper Fidelis is how it works."

"With Semper, I agree."

"That's enough." The supervisor stood aside. "Escort this man to his gate and see that he doesn't miss his flight."

"The knife . . ." Cedric began.

". . . Will be melted down," the supervisor finished the sentence for him, "prior to being cast along with many others into one-liter beer steins embossed with patriotic tableaux vivants of battles fought and won throughout US history, given away free in PXs all over the world with the purchase of two cases of 3.2 American-brewed beer or the rental of any ten made-in-America DVDs or a down payment on a combat life-insurance policy. It's not much but it shows support for our troops and every little bit helps. You do support our troops?" the supervisor thought to query.

Cedric looked from the supervisor to his knife to each of the two subordinates and back to the supervisor again. "I can see," he said with quiet assurance, "that you add up to little more than a middling bureaucrat with a substandard dick." He sighted through a thumb and middle finger, held a half-inch apart, and Cedric's eye did not quail before the bulging orbs of the supervisor's.

Later, in the break room, one of the two subordinates would recall for some colleagues how the back of the supe's neck turned redder than Stalin's nuts.

For Cedric's more or less generic insult turned out to be all too deliciously near the meta-mark. The very same two subordinates had also been on the scene when the supe had yanked a French socialite out of line because her jewelry kept setting off the metal detector, plus she was a MILF. When this lady, already late for her international flight, objected in a reasonable if slightly haughty tone, the supe had demurred in a vulgarly

smug one, and things rapidly deteriorated until she called him, as it happened, *un vrai fonctionnaire avec de bonheur de posséder un pipe
diminutif* in front of the two or three hundred other native speakers waiting to board a jet to Paris. When the shrieks of amazed laughter had died
down, amid cluckings and exclamations of *Oh la la la*, and on the outside
chance this foreigner was talking code, the supe insisted on calling for an
official translator, refusing to accept the proffered offices of any number
of bilingual travelers. That took a while. But the moment he'd been
informed as to what the woman had actually said, the supe radioed for the
dykes and ordered a strip search, and the woman missed her plane.

About a year after that, the supe discovered that the socialite's husband
owned a big piece of the bank that held the mortgage on the supe's house,
and he found out the hard way.

Ever since, the supe had applied the strictures of Homeland Security
with a fine discernment for those without recourse. Cedric Osawa, it had
seemed to him, fit the bill perfectly.

In the meantime, behind the supe's back of course, his subordinates
and all their brethren at the airport had taken to calling him Needledick
the Gnatfucker.

Now the supe's eyes assumed a steely glint, and, at least to his subordinates, the very paint on the walls of the interrogation room seemed to
sweat. When the supe's mouth opened it looked much like the wound a
chef might twist into a bratwurst with the corner of a spatula in order to
ascertain the degree to which it has cooked.

"I care about Homeland Security," the supervisor said in a barely audible voice, "like everybody else cares about football. It's my top priority.
It's my career. It's my life. Nothing could be more important. I lose sleep
over it."

"You care for Homeland Security," Cedric Osawa countersuggested,
"like pigeons care for Grant's tomb."

"But tonight," the supe persevered with leavened certainty, "I'm going
to sleep very soundly. Merkin."

"Yessir."

"Mr. . . ."

Merkin looked at his clipboard, which he'd been holding behind him
while at parade rest, and hastily turned it right side up. "Osawa. Sir."

"Enter Mr. Osawa's name on the No-Fly watch list. Under Remarks
make the entry, *Hates America*. Under *Last known address* enter," and
here the Supervisor could not refrain from a condescending sneer, *"The
Everglades."*

To give him credit, the subordinate glanced at his coworker and blinked. His coworker continued to stare straight ahead.

"Well, Merkin?"

Merkin stammered in the affirmative and reached for a ballpoint pen clipped into his breast pocket. Its activating click was loud. Everybody waited for him to finish copying the number of Cedric Osawa's passport onto the form on the clipboard. It seemed to take a long time.

"Finished?" the supervisor finally asked.

Though he was still writing, Merkin nodded nervously.

"I can't hear you," said the supervisor.

The supervisor had Merkin sufficiently buffaloed that he stammered. "All f-finished, s-sir."

"That's fine. Now be so kind as to escort Mr. Nigawa, here—"

"Osawa," Merkin corrected. "Sir."

The supervisor stopped speaking long enough to favor Merkin with a slow look, then continued, "—to the taxi stand outside the baggage terminal. Bosworth."

"Sir."

"Find Mr. Osawa's baggage. You do have baggage?"

"More than when I came in here," Cedric stated mildly.

The two subordinates exchanged a glance, then looked to their supervisor. A puzzled expression passed over the supervisor's face. It looked, as Merkin later remarked, as if interviewer and interviewee were going to follow the logic of this contretemps to a violent conclusion.

Almost imperceptibly, the supervisor smiled. "Find Mr. Osawa's baggage, return it to him at the taxi stand on the Arrivals deck, watch him get into a taxi, and watch the taxi until it has disappeared over the horizon."

Pulling a radio from his belt with one hand and retrieving a magnetic key from his breast pocket with the other, Bosworth activated the door lock and exited. The supervisor said to Cedric, "If you're otherwise clean, Osawa, you can apply to be removed from the No-Fly list within six months to a year. Visit our website for the appropriate forms and procedures. And if you're not clean? Don't apply. Because if you're not clean, we'll know. And applying when you're not clean, by the way, is a felony. Get me? Until then," he turned one hand palm up, as if the situation were soon to be beyond the scope of his power, which no doubt it would be, "you're going to have to take the train. Or the bus. The train and the bus are a little looser about security than we are. For the time being, anyway."

At the curb Bosworth handed Cedric his sea bag. Merkin walked up the sidewalk against traffic with one arm raised, signaling for a cab.

"Your boss is a piece of work," Cedric observed matter-of-factly.

"You should see him at the end of the shift," Bosworth said morosely.

"This is the beginning?"

Bosworth nodded.

"Let me think. A forklift loads him and his heartburn into a half-track drawn by Clydesdales?"

Bosworth gave him a look. "Funny you should put it that way. I was going to mention the supe's heartburn. Also, he's got the acid reflux."

"I could give a shit about that guy's metabolism."

"What's funny is, you're almost completely right. At the end of every shift the supe squeezes himself into a perfectly restored 1957 Alfa Romeo Giulietta Spider Veloce convertible. It's the apple of his eye and the pride of his existence and, on account of his blood pressure, his complexion perfectly rhymes with the poppy-red paint job. He even wears a special black shirt with red stripes when he drives the machine to gymkhanas, along with a black cap with a little red pompon on top, all of it rhyming with the red piping on the black leather upholstery."

"Your boss lives alone. Weekends, he details the car. He refuses to drive it in the rain. At night he sits beside it in his garage on a shooting stick and sips single-malt whiskey while listening to *Madame Butterfly*."

"What!" marveled Bosworth. "You know this guy all your life?"

Cedric modestly shrugged.

"It's just like you said. Supe restored the car entirely by himself. Took him years. Did the body work, the paint, blueprinted the engine, tracked down and paid double for original parts, waited eighteen months for the custom upholstery, rewired the entire electrical harness by himself. The job got him through his divorce and the loss of his house so he didn't kill himself or his ex-wife or any lawyers or nobody from the bank or me or Merkin either. But anyway, no, that's not what I'm talking about. What I meant was, this is just the beginning of the shift. By the end of the shift, he's much worse."

"What time's the shift end?"

Bosworth shrugged. "Twelve-thirty in the a.m."

"He could easily blow a gasket by then," Cedric hypothesized optimistically. He considered Bosworth. "Miles to go before you sleep."

Bosworth sighed wearily. "Tell me about it."

A cab pulled to the curb. Merkin exited the front passenger seat and opened the back door for Cedric.

Cedric said, "You guys graduate from college for this?"

"For this," Merkin shook his head, "I should go to college?"

"I graduated," Bosworth affirmed. He blinked. "That was fourteen years ago."

"*Quod erat demonstrandum*," Merkin pointed out.

Cedric nodded. "Maybe see you guys in a year or so."

"Maybe," said Bosworth.

"I buy two Lotto tickets every Friday night," said Merkin.

"Sucker," said Bosworth.

Merkin eyed him coolly. "That what you learned in college?"

Cedric threw his sea bag through the open door and followed it into the back seat. Merkin closed the door and saluted. The taxi pulled away from the curb. As instructed, the two functionaries watched it go.

Cedric asked the driver for the time.

The cabbie glanced at the back of the cellphone clenched between the palm of his hand and the rim of the steering wheel. "Four thirty-five."

The cab merged onto a freeway. Cedric asked the driver if he knew of a chandlery.

The cabbie frowned into the rear view mirror. "A what?"

Cedric told him.

"I got a buddy just bought a boat," the cabbie said to the mirror. "Says he's going to cruise the Bahamas." The cabbie touched a preset on his phone and instigated a consultation in Sranantongo. Presently he hung up the phone and spoke English to the mirror. "He leases something called a side-tie about a half hour from here. There's a boatyard, a marine supply store, and a bar. He needs all three." He shook his head. "It's going to take a whole lot of work to get that boat cruising anywhere."

"You know what boat stands for?" Cedric asked him.

The cabbie shook his head.

"Break Out Another Thousand."

The cabbie grinned at the mirror. "I'm gonna call him right back."

He wasn't on the phone a minute.

"Well?"

"He heard that one already."

Back at the airport by eleven, wearing baggy brown thrift-store shorts and a matching short-sleeved button-down shirt with KEN embossed on its breast pocket in white letters, Cedric boarded the employee shuttle-bus. With a pair of sunglasses worn backwards on his head and a beaded chain around his neck looped through the corner of a credit-card-sized piece of laminated plastic cut out of a bar menu and tucked into his breast pocket, Cedric looked every inch the baggage handler. The few employees on the shuttle were beat and said not a word, except for two stewardesses and a steward who carried on an animated conversation about a movie star who had gotten drunk in first class and exposed himself in coach coming back from London.

Miami International is a large airport, and the employee parking lot contains many vehicles. But the lot is well lit and, soon enough, among row upon row of conveyances, a gleaming red two-seat convertible made itself perfectly obvious. Eight or ten rows later, Cedric stepped down from the back door of the shuttle.

He was a little drunker than he should have been while undertaking a serious piece of work, but his contempt for the job made up for it.

The new knife had been among the cheaper models offered by Tropicana Boat and Marine, and it was a no-nonsense example of its type. Its curved marlinspike easily penetrated the sidewall of each of the Alfa's steel-belted radial tyres. Its bluff-bowed blade made short work of the black canvas top, and easily plowed a deep fissure through any number of hand-rubbed coats of red lacquer, well into the sheet metal, from head-light to taillight on the passenger side of the roadster.

As he mirrored the first incision on the driver's side of the car, taillight to headlight, it occurred to Cedric that the odd size of the tires might make them a special-order item.

He hoped so.

NINE

I WORKED THE BOAT INTO PORT NELSON ON RUM CAY JUST BEFORE NOON, having hove to outside to wait for the sun to get out of my eyes. The entrance is tricky, although others might call it a challenge.

Well, start them bastards with a properly crowned rope. There's ledges and coral heads and wrecks and old pilings and all the rest. Fishermen love it here and that just adds to the obstacles. There was a dinghy with five or six sets out, right in the middle of the channel. And having said that, I feel better. It's their island, after all.

I set stern and bow anchors in 2 meters of water so that whatever the tide is up to around here it might proceed more or less parallel to Vellela Vellela's *keel and leave us more or less out of it, and maybe I could get a night's sleep into the bargain. I noticed we were well out of sight of the little ice and bait shack at the top of Government Pier. That's for appearance's sake, I'm sure. No way that guy's not a friend of Red's. In fact, Red emphasized this as the ideal place to park.*

I made a call on Channel 21 as prearranged, going to 42, the doubled frequency, after the acknowledgment. Sat in the cockpit with a bottle of rum until the noseeums got to be too much. The mosquito fly was stowed forward of the Danforth and the ditch kit too, like I'd maybe never spent a twilight in the Caribbean. But it's more like I have no idea of the plan. I mean, I'm just a mule. Why should I have any idea of the plan?

"Hey, Tipsy."

Tipsy looked up from the letter.

Faulkner pointed. "That's one I don't have."

Tipsy lifted her glass off the envelope. Faulkner took it up and narrowed his eyes at the prize. "Crooked Island. That's new. Almost four months ago."

"I noticed that," Tipsy said.

"What's he up to?"

"Same old epistolary novel," she said evasively. She took a sip of beer. "The book he's always been meaning to write but never has written. While this opus, here," she lifted the pages, "has been writing itself."

"Does he get laid in it?"

"Why do you ask, Faulkner?"

"Epistolary novels are always about getting laid. Think of *Les Liasons Dangereuse*."

It was hard for Tipsy to think of a book she'd never read. "Don't you have glasses to wash?"

"If it's intended to justify his existence," Quentin persisted, "it's either going to be infinitely long or infinitely short."

"I'm not even sure it's real." Tipsy favored Quentin with a glance of annoyance. "What's with you today?" Quentin raised an eyebrow and indicated the pile of pills heaped on their own coaster next to his pint of soda water. "Nobody to fight with," she guessed.

Faulkner held a corner of the envelope under the bib of the espresso machine and cracked the valve. A serrated corner of the triangular stamp lifted into the steam.

The next day the funkiest little boat you ever saw turned up, first thing in the morning. I was below when she arrived, making myself some breakfast and thinking about going ashore for groceries and a look around the ville. After all, I'd never called at Rum Cay before. I stuck my head out the companionway, and what should I descry but an old Monterey, Jambo by name, which is Swahili for Hello, or Greetings, as I'm sure you know. The stack was rusted through in so many places it looked like a vine trellis.

How in the hell that little guy got here all the way from California, to which the design is native, its skipper couldn't tell me. He's only owned her for a couple of years. Arnauld's Dive Service was lettered along either side of the hull. Fore and after decks and even the roof of the house were festooned with gear—an old compressor for tank and hooka diving, wire brushes, stiff-bristled nylon brooms with long and short handles, all kinds of scrapers and tools, coils of line, heaps of chain, oxy-acetylene tanks, a gasoline-powered welder/generator, a milk-crate each of new and used zincs, a crate full of solvents and epoxy products, and so forth.

He pronounced his name the way the French pronounce it—Ar-KNOW. Raised in a boatyard in Guadeloupe by an American father and a French mother, he learned to sail before he could walk, and to race before he could properly read. And if there was anything besides hotel servitude to be had on an island, he had called there—damn near every island in the Bahamas, Windwards, Leewards, Antilles, assorted Gulf ports up the east coast of Central America, Texas, Louisiana, Alabama, and the Florida panhandle down to the Keys, too.

That bit about Guadeloupe was a nice coincidence. I know the boatyard—it's where I rebuilt Vellela Vellela—*and I know his mother. She still*

*runs the place. Dad long gone. Good name for a song. Probably the name
of 200 songs. Alcohol got him. So that more or less puts to sleep wondering
about what the connection with Red is.*

*Arnauld was friendly enough, but after those few preliminary remarks
he was all business. So much for a lube and tune-up, so much for going
aloft, so much for roving halyards, seizing lines, such-and-such markup on
parts, and a minimum fee for scrubbing a bottom, compounded by the
number of feet below the waterline, compounded by an hourly rate if the
job goes long. We haggled, but Arnauld wouldn't budge. Within the context
of a charade, you'd think it wouldn't matter. But Arnauld seemed to enjoy
the play-acting. It was a pretty exorbitant price by Florida standards. But,
as Arnauld needlessly pointed out, we weren't in Florida, and it wasn't my
money. In the end I agreed to his price for keel, rudder, and through-hull
inspections, as well a thorough scrape of the bottom and zinc replacement,
paid in advance. I gave him cash and Arnauld wrote me out a receipt. He
prepared to dive* Vellela Vellela *and I went back to my breakfast.*

*But sitting below and listening to somebody thump around your hull is
an uncomfortable feeling. So I finished the dishes, borrowed Arnauld's
dinghy, and rowed to town.*

*Ah, sister Tipsy. Shall I go into the languorous delights of out-of-the-way
tropical ports? The little towns associated with them can be somewhat the
same, and they're not all good, but I never tire of them. There's every sort
of strange vegetation, of course. And racially, too, the whole Caribbean is
mixed up. There's Spanish and French and the whole east coast of Africa,
and American English and English English and all kinds of derivative pat-
ois and Creole. Great people, in any case, right down the line. And have I
mentioned the food? You tasted a good conch fritter lately? Of course not.
Are you still living off beer and chips? And I bought some stamps at the little postal window in what they call the Administration Building.*

"French fries, he means," Tipsy said helpfully. "That's what they call
French fries in the islands. Like they call them in England."

"Freedom fries," Faulkner goaded, handing her back the stampless
envelope.

"*Frites de liberté!*" Quentin declared. His chin rested on his crossed
forearms, which in turn rested on the bar. Inches from his eyes, little bubbles rose through the clear body of the pint of soda water, beyond the
diminishing selection of medicaments. "*Frites de liberté, d'egalité, de fra-
ternité, et de mort.*" Quentin smiled contentedly. "Fries of death."

"You're already paying me to help you die," Faulkner pointed out.
"Ready for more? Tipsy?"

"I'll have another."

"Quentin?"

"What is it, anyway? What's so attractive about drifting aimlessly on the face of the sea, year in and year out?" Quentin muttered at his glass of water.

"You should try it sometime," Faulkner suggested, as he landed Tipsy's next beer in a fresh, frosted glass.

Quentin rolled his eyes toward Tipsy's new beer, then up at Faulkner, then away. For twenty years Faulkner had worked every spring and summer in this bar, saving every dime he earned. Come October, Faulkner flew south with his bankroll, two or three bags of gear, and his guitar. Every October his 34-foot Columbia lay waiting for him in Zihuatanejo or in a cove in the San Blas Islands or in a little port in Honduras, Guatemala, Belize, or maybe even way down the coast of Chile. He'd had wives and girlfriends, though none currently. Faulkner was another one of these guys who sailed out the Golden Gate on the tide one fine morning thirty years ago, took a left, and never really came back.

"Sounds too much like unpaid work to me," Quentin said.

Faulkner didn't give a damn what Quentin thought. But at the moment he was washing glasses in the sink under the bar and his mind was unoccupied. "Aren't you listening to Charley's letter, Quentin? Does it sound like work?"

Quentin made a face. "I'm sorry, Skip, but my opinion is that, in general, there is no free lunch."

With a soapy hand, Faulkner indicated the menu chalked onto a slate above the back of the bar. "Where's it say anything about a free lunch?"

"All over the place, but perhaps most especially in the gringo's view of the tropics. And it's never real."

"Okay. Speak for yourself."

"I was speaking for myself."

"You think that all cruisers do is bob around and talk to each other on the radio while drinking rum and harmonizing sea chanties over fresh fish for breakfast?"

"Yes." Quentin sat up. "I do."

Faulkner set the last glass to dry on the mat and toweled his hands. "It's hard to explain the mysteries and pleasures of the sea to somebody whose idea of a rough ride is a restaurant table with one short leg."

"Hooo—no!" whooped Tipsy, looking up from her letter. "That got a rise out him."

Indeed it did get a rise out of Quentin.

"Last month some yahoo on this side of the bar calls me a communist as if the adjective were an ultimate pejorative—worse than *executive talent pool*, say, or *exophthalmic spirochete.* . . ."

Tipsy's eyes rounded with anticipation. "Go get 'em, Quentin."

". . . And today," Quentin continued, "from the other side of the bar, a potentially simpatico soul, a working stiff like myself, is accusing me of—what?—Black Urban Professionalism? I'm not sure when it was that I got to be It around here, but hey, Faulkner, take your choice. What's it going to be? Little fucking twits with crocodiles on their shirts, or me—" Quentin jerked a thumb at his own chest—"who at least knows which end of the fucking glass to drink his water out of?"

"I changed my mind," Tipsy said. "Take it easy."

Faulkner folded the dishtowel lengthwise in the gutter on his side of the bar. "Aside from the fact that buppies, as you call them, spend real money on real drinks at this bar, as opposed to free glasses of soda water on account they know the bartender, I don't really give a shit."

"That's right," Quentin retorted, with not a moment's hesitation. "You don't give a shit because in one month or two at the most, you're going to be some thirty degrees of latitude south of here, sitting on your ass in a deck chair as the sun comes up trying to figure out the three chords to 'Margaritaville' when all you really want to do is open that first beer and forget the whole thing."

"Five," Faulkner said.

Quentin started. "Five what?"

"'Margaritaville' has five chords."

"*And you call that a life?*" Quentin suddenly shouted.

Faulkner stabbed a soapy finger at the compartmentalized box of pills on the bartop and hissed, "And you call this a life?"

"Low blow!" Tipsy scolded Faulkner.

"No!" Quentin, smiling viciously, stood up on the lower rung of his barstool and spread his arms to encompass the entire bar. "I don't!"

In the silence that followed this exchange, somebody somewhere in the bar emitted a long whistle that started out on a middling pitch, rose to another, then elided smoothly down through ever-lowering pitches until it petered out.

Quentin cocked an ear in the direction of the whistle. "You know what I think this is all about?"

Neither Tipsy nor Faulkner made an answer.

Quentin nodded. "It's about the great cloud of ineffable guilt hanging over this entire country. Here we sit, boozing it up, money in our pockets, psyches intact—at least we think our psyches are intact—while in various locations on the other side of the world, our armies—yes, the Armed

Forces of the United States of America—are blowing the shit out of anybody who gets in their, which is our, way. Men, women, children—all life
forms, dogs and infrastructure and entire cultures included, are inciner-
ated daily on behalf of the most beknighted, misguided, and crypto-impe-
rialistic foreign policy this country has ever espoused, and that includes
the Vietnam Experience and the Monroe Doctrine and the so-called
Spanish American War. And, however, as with various doomed, dreadful,
mendacious conflicts, ostensibly carried out on behalf of the good citizens
of this country, and for the good of the good citizens of this or that occupied country, and not under any circumstances for the good of the bad
people of this country, any more than it's on behalf of the bad people of
that country, they're terrorists if they're against us, they're patriots if
they're with us, whose job it is of our armed forces to hunt down and kill
wherever they may be found, if they can be found, which they can't,
because they don't per se exist, because their name is *legion*—this
endeavor, as I say, foisted on ourselves at least as egregiously as it is on
our supposed enemy, has *twisted the national psyche*. Are we not all in
this together? Is it not as James Baldwin said, that all men are brothers?
That's the bottom line? If we can't take it from there, we can't take it
at all?"

"Amen, brother," Tipsy encouraged him.

"Must you lecture us?" somebody shouted.

"Let him speak!" insisted another.

"Shut up!" shouted a third, although it was not clear whom they
addressed.

"Guilt," Quentin persisted, "and guilt alone, brings us low. For we, as a
polity, have transgressed our global brothers and sisters. Every one of us
knows that at this very moment men, women, and children are being dec-
imated by a wide selection of the most vicious weapons ever assembled by
any technology in history. Forget nukes. Who needs them? We got
radioactive bullets, we got Thermit mortars and phosphor grenades, we
got five-hundred-pound laser-guided bombs, we got helicopter-mounted
Gatling guns that spit 2,500 exploding .50 caliber rounds per minute, we
got unmanned drones armed with air-to-ground missiles. No! Ladies and
gentlemen," Quentin slapped the bar with the flat of his hand, and his
pills jumped. "The real question is how anybody with a brain in this country can sleep at night. Every endeavor is no more or less than a distraction
from the horrible truth, that, even as we sit here and argue about it, inhu-
man acts are being performed upon our fellow humans in our name,
whether you spend your life meaningfully or not. And I ask you . . ."
Quentin placed the palm of one hand over his heart and scanned the bar,

"has not a concerted regime of cruelty and excessive brutality replaced that of due process, habeas corpus, and impartial justice? And for what? For one thing, and one thing only."

"One thing?"

"Shaddup!"

"Did he say one thing?"

"Who cares!"

"*And free the pandas while you're at it!*"

"What thing is that?"

Quentin raised a single index finger. The bar fell silent. "So that many people, mostly Iraqis, but also young American men and women, just like you and me—except that most of them grew up poor and, wanting to make something out of themselves, volunteered for the armed services, whereas we did not—can die face down in the sand in a foreign land. And why? I'll tell you why. So that China will be guaranteed the oil reserves she needs to take over the world."

Silence overwhelmed the bar. Tipsy, beside him, and Faulkner, across the bar, stared.

"Hear hear!" somebody erupted. "Yes yes!" shouted another. "It's China's war," acclaimed a third. "Who knew?" queried a fourth. "Buy the dude a drink," clamored a fifth. "Left-wing cunt!" "Right-wing shill!" "Centrist pawn!" "Gung hay fat choy!"

Quentin collapsed onto his stool and stared rigidly over his glass of water. His upper lip quivered. "There," he declared unequivocally. "I've said it."

"Said what?" Tipsy and Faulkner replied in unison.

TEN

CEDRIC OSAWA AWAITED THE WESTBOUND HOUND, SCHEDULED TO DEPART Miami at midnight.

The No-Fly list was going to be a pesky impediment to a comfortable retirement, if he ever found the means by which to retire, just like the lack of health insurance was going to be a pesky impediment to a healthy one. Retirement? Health insurance? Hah. Plot no flies on me. Samurai laugh, Doppler down the centuries, Ah ha, ah ha ha, ahhh hahhahhahhahahah. . . .

The Hound grumbled out of the haze of humidity and into the dimly lit station like a ghost of transportation past. Cedric hadn't been on a Greyhound bus since his long-squandered youth. At the time, as he recalled, the encapsulation of despond available for inspection in every seat had been sufficient to kindle a nascent ambition to make something out of himself.

A sailor, maybe, who finds the pungencies of bilgewater preferable to that of undifferentiated upholstery vapors.

Things appeared not to have changed much. The placard over the windshield said El Paso. El Paso is a long way from Miami. The placard might just as well have posited Alpha Centauri. Although, Cedric reflected, as he watched eight or ten passengers disembark, the latter is less than five light years from Miami. But El Paso? Miami to El Paso is a rat fur piece. The Pelt of No Amigo. Warrior delectation, chortle down unnumbered eons . . .

> *The Felt hat of El Paso*
> *Is the skint Pelt of No Amigo*
> *Epidermis of nary friend of mine.*
>
> *Take it sleeeeezy*
> *Don't be queeeeasy*
> *Ye olde diastole lifts entropic*
> *Slurry from the Blue Hole of Time . . .*

Sometimes those old songs just get stuck in your head, and you just got to embarrass them until they go away. Benevolent robins of mortification beak Mind Worms out loamy furrows of corpus coliseum. Ahaha. . . .

Names for nameless things. Fears and trepidations and places never plotted by the theodolite of man, whatnot. One of mankind's specialties, naming things. Another is messing them up. Crocheted Encomium No. 1: Those with no imagination are destined to commit the unimaginable.

On the back it reads: Put another way, those who do have imagination are destined to have the unimaginable committed upon them—a textbook example of a contrapositive clusterfuck.

Thank you. It's kind of you to say so. May I go now? Sure. Take the bus.

I'm in a pleonastic mood tonight. Either that, or my dura mater is on fire. Doppler burnin' fu down the smokin' centuries, cha cha, chachacha, cough cough, coughcoughcough. . . .

Merdre alert, Cedric reflected, I haven't had jingle-revenge fantasies like these since I left the States for Alfa Centauri, how many egg cycles ago? Let alone acted one out. Jingle revenge? Egg cycle. Oviposit the offender. The mature three-foot worm breaks through the skin from the inside, broadcasting eggs like soap bubbles on Telegraph Avenue circa 1970. Hold him down. Ah ha, ah ha ha, ahhhhahahaha. . . .

The driver was a black gentleman in shirtsleeves, visored cap set back on a perspiring forehead surmounted by thinning gray locks, insomniac pouches under roadmap eyes. Cedric nodded hello as he boarded and received in response a request to show his ticket. Cedric showed it: all the way to El Paso, two days, three transfers, thirty-six stops: $134. The driver looked like a perfectly natural extension of the driver's seat. If there's random drug testing for drivers, Cedric thought, "random," or having no specific pattern, purpose or objective, must indeed be the kind of drug testing the company was carrying out, for something had this individual Wide Awake. Existential Awareness, perhaps?

"Nice evening," Cedric allowed, as the driver returned him his ticket.

The driver ducked his head for a look through the windshield at a large clockface set into the wall above the exit door of the terminal and checked his watch against it. "Eleven minutes."

Cedric always found himself reluctant to get off his boat. He liked his fun. He enjoyed a hospitable port. But *Tunacity* was his home. Its environment consisted entirely of things he understood. He was comfortable there. Every night, the thing rocked him to sleep. Ashore was another story. Once docked, it always took him a long time to actually step ashore, find a bar, take a taxi into town, find another bar. And the present perfunctory social interaction only served to emphasize Cedric's isolation in the teeming greater world.

Between the green dash and the illuminated Occupied sign over the toilet in back, the entire fuselage was an impenetrable darkness with the odor of a vehicle that had been making round trips between the Miami chapter of Alcoholics Anonymous and the El Paso cognate since Gulf War

I, with the occasional side job of hauling raw kelp to a psoralen process-ing plant with the windows closed in order to trap nutritious edible insects as they bred. Fruit flies (*Drosophila melanogaster*), for one example.

On the other hand, nobody else had waited with Cedric in the termi-nal for this bus. Nor had anybody asked him for identification, nor scanned his shoes with a metal-detecting wand, or swabbed his sea bag for traces of explosives. Nobody had asked him for anything other than the price of the ticket. Sure it's a hole in Homeland Security, Cedric reflect-ed, but it's a nice hole. Nostalgic, almost bucolic. Conducive to relaxation. He tripped over ankles and baggage straps in the darkened aisle and received not so much as a muttered remonstrance in return for the cour-tesy of apology. Two-thirds back he found two adjacent empty seats on the port side, right in front of the entire row of empty seats situated above the wheel wells, which had no leg room at all, and so stood a good chance to remain unoccupied for the entire trip. He punched a divot into one end of his sea bag, laid it transverse against the back of the window seat for lumbar support, and laid claim to both seats. The window was functional and he opened it, letting in the hiss of airbrakes, incomprehensible rumi-nations on the public address system, fumes of combusted diesel, and a damp amnion of tropical humidity, toward the latter of which his nostrils discerned greedily. A halo of four or five people watched someone shuf-fle luggage in and out of the cargo hold, just forward of the wheel well on Cedric's side of the bus, directly beneath his window. Without exception these people looked worn out. They watched the baggage process as if it were yet another waiting-room television, as if, with absolutely no place better to be, they had surrendered to its presumed technological superi-ority, manifested as deft maneuverability of purpose, in this case, pneu-matic hinges.

> Paranoia infuses the mountain
> Gnosis planktons the sea
> If nourishment sprang from fountains
> hinges would bear squeak free
>   the weight of karma
>   the weight of dogma
>   but never the frolic of allegory!

The first person to see her luggage placed on the concrete took it up and embraced it gingerly, her eyes darting shyly, her mouth partly open, her expression one of timid vulnerability. Clearly, this girl-woman had no place to go. She may not even have known she was in Miami. The features of the tall black man next to her had spent themselves almost entirely in a battle between rage and exhaustion. When his big plastic suitcase appeared, with half the cuff of a flannel shirt dangling from its hinge seam like a bookmark in a thick lucubration whose subject was despair, he manifested uncertainty, as if torn between punching out the baggage handler and getting hauled off to jail or crawling into the baggage hold—angling, in either case, for a good night's sleep. Lastly stood a Cuban couple with a baby asleep in a blanket slung from his mother's shoulder. Glacial resignation showed in both the parents' faces. She was pregnant again. Work was seasonal. Here came one, two, three pieces of luggage, each more threadbare than the last. The man managed to wrangle all three, one in each hand and the third under his arm, and they walked away. *Bien providencia.*

By the bluish-gray of the terminal lights coming through the window Cedric resumed the chapter entitled "Brother of the Snake" in *The Rivers Ran East.*

"There is something here I don't like!" he said.

The Indian was nowhere in sight; the clicks stopped. We hurried along, and after half an hour, I experienced an unaccountable chill when Jorge suddenly halted in his tracks and I bumped up against him:

"Be prepared to go back," he said after some hesitation, in a very quiet voice. "There is a snake here."

For some reason I breathed in relief. "Go around it," I suggested. "We don't want to lose that Campa."

"No! Stand very still. I can't see. But I know it is close—I just heard it hiss."

Not knowing whether the snake's head was suspended in the darkness somewhere around our faces, or wriggling toward us over the ground, we must have stood there a full five minutes, not daring to move a toe or bat an eye. The mosquitoes were awful. I began sweating, while my lower leg muscles crawled and my face twitched every time a bug touched it. Suddenly, a yard away on our right—of all things—came the faint quack of a duck. It sounded pathetic and distressful, as if it were lost.

Jorge sprang instantly ahead, crying "Hurry!". . .

Very tired after an hour of rough going, we rested on a fallen log, and the guide back-tracked, standing like a shadow twenty feet away. All about now was a thunderous ear-splitting orchestration of frogs, insects, animals, and night-birds. From the roaring the *cochas* on all sides must have been crawling with crocodiles. I remarked to Jorge that he usually didn't sweat so much even on a burning hot night. His leather shirt was wringing wet.

"That snake back there—" he answered, "was a *shushupe.*"

When I failed to register, the Peruvian explained that this was a maroon-colored twelve-foot reptile of intense cunning, who lured unwary victims to him. It would attack man, and in five to eight minutes, the paralyzing venom would cause death by shock. "We lose three or four *caucheros* every year out of La Merced."

"I guess the snake was after that duck," I suggested, adding, "lucky of us."

"No, it makes the sound itself—a decoy. To strike effectively, the *shushupe* calls his victim up close to him. Then strikes."

"There couldn't possibly be anything more diabolical out here than that," I ventured. Jorge made no answer.

Cedric's eyelids accrued density. The book fell against the sill. A muted conversation had begun several seats forward. Diagonally across the aisle, metallurgical insect noises leaked from an invisible pair of earbuds. His lashes fluttered, his lids lowered. He couldn't decide what language the conversation was in. He couldn't make out what kind of music was being listened to. That was fine. His eyes closed. Aft, below the toilet, the big diesel started. An initial burst of black fumes swirled past the open window. He let his temple lie against the window's metal frame. Vibrations from it, conducted via the bone of his skull to his brain, felt oddly comforting. It was as if the quarter inserted into the slot of the coinbox wired to the VibraBed in an ancient motel room, with arrow-pierced hearts and pairs of initials carved into underside of the shelf above the headboard, actually worked. Eyes closed, Cedric heard the hinges creak on the awning door of the baggage compartment below his window. It's all good, he thought, and he smacked his lips softly. If but only a momentary goodness. Maybe I can sleep through the seventeen waypoints to the first baloney sandwich. Although the morbid fascination of steamy ghost-lit tropical whistlestops is hard to resist. . . .

Someone walking across the tile floor of the echoing terminal wore heel taps. It had been a long time since Cedric had come across anybody who nailed crescents of metal to the heels and sometimes the toes of their shoes, ostensibly to protect them. A lot of people, in the tropics, and sailors in particular, didn't wear shoes at all; for that matter, despite "progress," much of the tropics remains unpaved. Heel taps don't amount to much on roadbeds of crushed seashells or pure sand. But here in Miami each footfall sounded of ceramic and steel. Clack-a-clack cla-clack. Cedric idly wondered if there were sparks. He supposed he might have cared. The baggage door slammed. Unexpectedly loud, its boom reverberated throughout the hall. Cedric opened his eyes.

The baggage handler was walking diagonally across the terminal, away from the rear of the bus. Beyond him a rail-thin man in black chinos, cut

fairly tight, with a long-sleeved flowered shirt, a sallow complexion, a pen-
cil-thin mustache, and a black straw stingy-brim with a yellow band atop
a full head of oiled black hair slouched through the terminal toward the
bus. Better to say that he modulated over the tiles like a tall saw-toothed
wave with a short period. A new filter cigarette lay pinched between the
flat of his head and his right ear, filter forward. For that taste of Macassar,
Cedric thought sleepily, although the thought belied the alacrity of his
wakefulness. Each footfall clicked, some of them twice, and with them the
figure's Information slotted into Cedric's main board.

Well well well, Cedric blinked, if it ain't Felix Timbalón.

The man in the flowered shirt carried a small brown and black tool
tote, with pockets all around its exterior, of the type a cable TV installer
might carry, who would require little more than a pair of pliers, a crimp-
ing tool, and a pad of invoices. Multiple pockets and sleeves for tools were
stitched around the exterior of this bag, none of which contained anything
at all, let alone a tool, let alone a comb or toothbrush. A copy of *Nuevo
Herald*, the *Miami Herald*'s Spanish language daily, protruded from the
bag's mouth.

The man with the toolbag disappeared around the front fender of the
bus just as the driver closed the door. Cedric had nearly closed his eyes
again when he heard the door open and shod hooves mount the diamond
plate entry steps. There was a brief, muffled exchange. The door hissed
closed again. The pinion in the transmission under the bathroom at the
rear of the bus chattered and slowed until it meshed the first ratio cog
with a clunk. The driver revved the diesel, eased the clutch, and the
Hound undertook to lumber.

Cedric could practically feel the lights of the terminal as they slipped
along the side of the bus and over his face. He could make out the various
respirations of his fellow travelers within the sparsely tenanted vehicle,
altogether not unlike a redolent den of hibernating bruins.

The carpet, though abraded to a meager molecularity by decades of
woeful brogans, would yet be damping the heel taps. The footfalls tentatively made their way aft down the darkened aisle, pausing here and
there as if to suss a seat's potential for maximum comfort with minimum
company.

At last the footsteps arrived at Cedric's row, where they paused again.
And though the bus now pitched and rocked its way diagonally over the
gutter that separated the bus station exit from the street, Cedric affected
sleep.

The figure loomed over Cedric's row, took two steps toward the rear of
the bus, and stopped again.

Long enough, thought Cedric, whose pupils strained to discern through their closed lids and in the dark the figure in the aisle not three feet away, plenty long enough to notice the carpeted sheet metal cowl over the wheel well.

The man slid into the seat anyway. He slid all the way across the aisle seat and into the seat next to the window, directly behind Cedric.

What, thought Cedric, a coincidence, and on this of all the clapped-out buses in South Florida. Not to mention how one marvels at the masochism sufficient to ride a nearly empty bus fifteen if not fifteen hundred miles while seated with one's knees flanking one's earlobes like moons to the minor and questionably inhabited planetoid of one's head bone, his coccyx on fire and blood clots in his ankles—and for why? Because his daddy used to beat him for wetting the bed?

What are the chances?

I ask you.

No, no, ask me. Thank you. Slim to none, is the answer. Very slim to totally none.

Among hitchhikers, Florida's Alligator Alley, more recently known as the Everglades Expressway, is legendary. It stretches some 110 miles across the southern tip of Florida, from Miami to East Naples, right through Big Cypress Swamp and the Everglades. There's a fence on either side of it now, and it's four lanes in many places. But not so long ago Alligator Alley was two lanes of macadam atop a dirt berm with not two feet of altitude bisecting ten thousand square miles of otherwise undifferentiated swamp with no fence in sight. And to this day there's exactly one paved exit off Alligator Alley, about halfway across the peninsula, which, having provided access to a gas station and store, turns immediately to mud and disappears north, into the Seminole Indian reservation.

For fifty miles in either direction there are no services, no lights, and no respite from the wildlife that inhabits the swamp. This includes alligators, of course, for the highway was not facetiously named, as well as cottonmouth water moccasins and mosquitoes, of which the latter's profusion can envelope an exposed human with the claustrophobic efficiency of the thread count of a minus-fifty mummy bag. But even since the erection of the fence this is no highway on which to find oneself stranded after dark. Before the erection of the fence, certain locals would amuse themselves by picking up a naive, westbound hitchhiker in Coral Gables, say, at dusk, and transporting him about twenty-five miles down Alligator Alley before affecting to remember that they had left the stove on in the trailer. They'd drop the unsuspecting and often grateful hitchhiker in the middle of the swamp, giggle through a slow U-turn, and make it back to the east coast, guffawing over their poptops all the way.

The only way to deal with the fauna was to walk all night. But in the face of invisible rapacious wildlife heeding nature's imperative to get across to one or another side of the road, the most ginger ambulation failed. Plus, giant palmetto bugs, whose diminutive brethren are cockroaches, make themselves constantly available to be crushed blindly underfoot. It sounds exactly as if one is stepping on sodden boxes of kitchen matches, and is fundamentally unnerving. Excepting such muciferous evidences of passage, many's the hitchhiker who headed out Alligator Alley only to vanish without so much as a habeas corpus. The stranded motorist disappears, too, leaving the sun to come up on the empty red one-gallon gas can, bobbing forlorn in black ditchwater, a mile or two from the abandoned vehicle.

Those palmetto bugs can fly, too.

And the literature says they're only about an inch long?

Hah. Double it for antennae, and square that for legs.

It's a romantic place.

Cedric didn't know why or how Felix Timbalón had come to be on this particular bus, but he knew what Felix was good for, and, as regards what Felix was good for, proximity counts.

As the lights of civilization thinned away from the westbound bus vector, Cedric calculated Timbalón's move. After he made it, as soon as possible, Felix could want to be stepping down; whether to meet a car, or catch the next bus eastbound, or whatever, Felix would want to be off this bus.

Ochopee would be the only stop between Miami on the east coast and Naples on the west coast. Cedric had visited Ochopee once before and remembered it as a pretty rough place. A concatenation of unpainted board cabins for truck drivers, each one with an air conditioner roaring, a pair of canopied picnic tables on a plywood deck next to a pair of outhouses, the whole spread sharing a single bug light on an eight-foot post, a pair each of diesel and gas pumps, and, behind the store, a much-rutted dirt lot full of idling 18-wheelers. The store sold chips, beer, candy, country-western CDs, and truck paraphernalia such as chromium girl-silhouette mudflaps and pine-scented air-fresheners alongside ersatz Seminole artifacts—rubber-headed tomahawks, chicken-feather clutches labeled Eagle Medicine, and denim shirts with a yawning, well-fanged snake and "Moccasin Power" embroidered on the breast pocket. To the man seated behind Cedric, there could be only one genuine attraction to the place: a ride back to Miami.

Would a car wait for him there?

Cedric considered this. After a while he dismissed it. No car, he decided, for this would be a one-man operation. It would be more secure that way, and less expensive, for Felix would want to conserve money for his rapacious heroin habit. Not for nothing did Felix Timbalón wear long-sleeved shirts in the tropics.

As the density of electric lights on either side of the highway thinned to none, Cedric spared little thought to how much he was worth and why he was worth it. He could wonder about that later.

It would be a delicate thing, but he could predict how it could be handled. There were variables and considerations, but Felix was a specialist. It would be best not to make a big fuss on the bus, not to be noticed. No shooting, for an obvious example. Or the thrashing and gagging involved in garroting, for another. Cedric knew, as he quietly opened both ends of his new knife, that not to make a big deal out of the job might be imperative, and to this end Felix had a stock in trade.

Through the open window came the compound reek, sullen and unmistakable, of reptiles and mud. If it were daytime one might see any number of alligators ranked along the swamp side of the chainlink fence, black alligators, ten and twelve and even fourteen feet long, laid up like logs in a boom, deposited along the fence as if by a high tide or the Department of Tourism. Motorists in Disney World t-shirts, Bermuda shorts, and flip-flops would be tenderfooting through the saw grass on the highway side of the fence taking pictures. Every now and again one of the reptiles would yawn and cough, a hideous sound the direction from which true denizens of the swamp are cautious not to overlook. And Cedric fell into a reverie concerning the first time he'd encountered Alligator Alley, long before there was a fence, at a time when there was no night traffic at all along its 110 miles, at a time when even the sole exit at Ochopee offered no services, not even so much as a yard light sufficient for your inner Gregorians to chant by.

> The Lord is my shepherd, I shall perhaps bleat
> The Lord harvests those who form a line on the left
> The Lord addeth, the Lord subtracteth
> For Life exhibiteth the associative property
> For God so hard-wired the World
> Forgotten googol of centuries ago . . .

He'd seen a cotton mouth water moccasin in a shoal alongside this road as thick as a barge hawser. . . . The passenger in the seat behind him unzipped a zipper.

Cedric affected restless sleep until, forty-two minutes into the trip, he felt just before he heard a subtle pressure against the back of his seat, level with the top of his spine. Then came a slight pop, so quiet as to be almost inaudible, no louder than a raindrop on a calla lily.

Ah so. The method and its path stand revealed.

"Oh baby . . ." Cedric whispered, and he shifted and resettled sufficiently to slip *The Rivers Ran East* between the nape of his neck and the seat back, smacked his lips twice, thrice, and sighed contentedly.

The warm and humid slipstream of the bus, traveling at seventy miles per hour, blustered fitfully at the open window.

The steady pressure resumed. Cedric's forehead chilled. A bead of sweat trickled from his throat over his Adam's apple to the hollow beneath and hovered there, like a bubble in a compass. A hand clamped over his nose and mouth. It smelt of cigarettes and piss and ropa vieja.

The Rivers Ran East is one and one-eighth inches thick. The ice pick penetrated to one and one-sixteenth inches.

Cedric spat ten cubic centimeters of saliva into the hand and shivered like a bride.

The ice pick withdrew and came back with a vengeance, making a new bore into the book to a depth of an inch and a quarter. Next to a mole that always itched unpredictably, in the dimple just to the right of the top of Cedric's spine, the steel tip drew blood.

Cedric released through his frame a single, spasmodic shiver.

With a jerk, the ice pick withdrew through the thicknesses of both book and seatback. The palm remained cupped over Cedric's mouth, and now its thumb and forefinger pinched his nostrils shut. Cedric didn't breathe, but his eyes were open, and his marlinspike was poised to gimlet the wrist to the ceiling. The hand relaxed but lingered. Still Cedric did not breathe.

The hand released his face.

Cedric slowly sagged against the window frame with a bubbly sigh. *The Rivers Ran East* tumbled to the sea bag, thence to the empty seat, thence to the carpeted floor.

The passenger behind Cedric stepped into the aisle, cleared his throat, and hawked a twinkling bolus of mustard-colored phlegm at the hollow below Cedric's right ear. The passenger watched it glisten as he straightened his shirt. He removed his little hat and absently shaped its creases, all the while studying the motionless figure slumped in the darkness below the window beyond the sea bag.

The passenger smoothed his hair with one hand and resettled the hat onto his head with the other. Then he took up his little tool tote, zipped it shut, and began to make his way toward the front of the bus, swaying with its motion as he went.

Not a minute later the Hound with the El Paso destination placard slowed and arced off the highway, circled through the service apron in front of the Ochopee pump island, and hissed to a stop facing west again. Its diesel settled into an irregular idle. Its door opened with a clunk. One passenger got off. Nobody came out of the store to greet the bus.

The disembarked traveler didn't enter the brightly illuminated store, its every exterior source of light orbited by insects and bats. Behind the building, rain caps rattled atop the stacks of idling diesels beneath a haze of carbon monoxide and humidity. In the dark swamp beyond throbbed the entire phylogenesis of *Amphibia*.

Walking purposely, cla-clack, unhurried, clackaclack, the thin traveler dropped a folded newspaper into a trash can as he passed between the two gas pumps, before he faded into the shadows beyond the far corner of the store. A moment later he reappeared on the brown cement path that meandered past two unlit outdoor privies, whose doors tilted open, admitting their fetor to the night, and he finally disappeared among the gaily colored running lights of tractors and trailers.

The door closed and the airbrakes coughed. The bus wallowed through the compliment of a wide right strophoid, regained the pavement of Alligator Alley, and accelerated though six ratios into the night.

ELEVEN

ACCORDING TO ARNAULD, THERE WASN'T A TORX WRENCH ON THE ENTIRE *island. Torx technology hadn't arrived there yet. But it was time. Arnauld made one by square-cutting the tip off a screwdriver and grinding six flutes parallel to the shaft. Then he locked a pair of vice-grips perpendicular to the handle, and voilà—a torque-able Torx wrench. It worked great. Arnauld dove the hull a couple more times, we had a tin cup each of sun tea with a little rum in it. He casually asked whether I'd visited Boca Chica lately, that's all I needed to hear, and soon enough he was on his way. That little stinkpot of his sounds like a seagoing mambo lesson.*

Cargo secure, the next anchorage is Albert Town on Long Cay, blue water all the way. So after I spent a couple of hours laying our course, I passed the rest of the afternoon in a hammock strung from the mast to the forestay—never underestimate the holding power of the icicle hitch!—sipping tea and reading Konstantin Paustovsky's The Story of a Life. *Ever read it? If you haven't, do so. It's a beautiful book, a memoir of Russia at the turn of the last century, a stunning banquet of melancholy, adventure, horror . . . all of it depicting a world long gone. I'm very taken with it. Let me copy out a passage for you. (Copying favorite passages, by the way, or reading them aloud, is how I taught myself to write, insofar as I know how to write at all, as if you didn't know.)*

Volodya Rumyantsev was the brother of Uncle Kolya's closest friend at the Bryansk arsenal, Captain Rumyantsev. Volodya was hard of hearing. There was always hay in his red beard, because he slept in the hay barn. He despised every kind of human comfort. He would put his folded student's overcoat under his head instead of a pillow. He dragged his feet when he walked, and he talked indistinctly. Under his overcoat he wore a faded blue Russian blouse, and he belted it with a black silk cord with tassels.

. . . He was filled with love for provincial Russia. He knew it intimately—the fairs, the monasteries, the historical estates, the customs. He had traveled to Tarkhana, to Lermontov's birthplace, to Fet's estate near Kursk, to the horse fair at Lebedyan, to the island of Valaam, and to the Kulikovsky battlefield.

Old ladies everywhere were friends of his, former teachers and officials. He used to stay with them. They fed him cabbage soup and little cakes filled with fish, and in gratitude Volodya taught the old ladies' canaries to whistle a polka, or he gave his hostesses superphosphate. They could spread a little in a geranium pot and produce the most enormous blossoms to amaze their neighbors.

He took no part in the arguments about the fate of Russia but he would move in when the conversation got around to Tambov hams, or the frozen apples in Ryazan, or Volga sturgeon. No one could compete with Volodya in knowledge of these things. Uncle Kolya used to say jokingly that Volodya Rumyantsev was the only man alive who knew how much sandals cost in Kineshma and the price of a pound of chicken feathers in Kalyazin.

One day Volodya Rumyantsev went to Oryold and brought sad news back to us. We were playing croquet beside the cottage. The game appealed to all of us. Games dragged out sometimes after it had grown dark, and lamps were carried out on to the croquet ground. We quarreled at croquet more than anywhere else, especially with my older brother Borya. He was a good player, and quickly became a "rover." Then he would knock our balls so far that sometimes we couldn't even find them. This made us very angry and, when he was aiming, we would chant, "The devil under your hand, a toad in your mouth!" This tactic sometimes helped and Borya would miss.

We also quarreled with Gleb. When Gleb played against Sasha he always missed and lost on purpose, just to please her. But playing with Sasha against us, he performed miracles of skill and daring, and always won. All the inhabitants of the cottages usually gathered for our croquet games. Even Uncle Kolya's two dogs, Mordan and Chetvertak, ran up to watch the game, although they then lay down cautiously under the pine trees so as not to get hit by a ball.

On this morning it was just as noisy as always on the croquet ground. Then we heard the sound of wheels; Uncle Kolya's springless carriage was driving up to the cottage. Someone cried out: "Volodya Rumyantsev has come!" No one paid any attention to this: we were all used to Volodya's private departures and arrivals.

A minute later he appeared. He walked up to us in loose overalls and boots. His face was all creased up, as if he were going to cry. He was holding a newspaper in his hand.

"What's the matter?" Uncle Kolya asked him, frightened.

"Chekhov has died."

Volodya turned and walked back to the cottage. We ran after him. Uncle Kolya took the paper from Volodya, read it, threw it on the floor, and stalked off to his own room. Aunt Marusya went anxiously after him. Pavila took off his pince-nez and cleaned them for a long time with his handkerchief.

"Kostik," Mama said to me, "go down to the river and call your father. Let him interrupt his fishing for once."

She said this as if my father should already have known about Chekhov's death but with his usual flippancy had attached no significance to the news and had not grieved over it. I took offense for my father, but I went down to the river. Gleb Afanasiev walked with me. He became suddenly very serious.

"Yes, Kostik!" he said to me on the way, and he sighed deeply.

I told my father that Chekhov had died. My father suddenly grew pinched in the face and all hunched over.

"Well, well," he said, in confusion, "how can it be? I never thought that I would outlive Chekhov . . ."

We walked back past the croquet ground. The mallets and balls lay scattered on the ground. The birds were making a racket in the linden trees, the sun shone through the leaves and made green spots on the grass.

I had already read Chekhov and I liked him very much. I walked away, and thought that such people as Chekhov should never die.

Two days later Volodya Rumyantsev went to Moscow to Chekhov's funeral. We accompanied him to the station at Sinezerki. He took a basket full of flowers to put on Chekhov's grave. They were common wild flowers which we picked in the marshes and in the woods. Mama packed them on a layer of wet moss and covered them with wet linen. We tried to pick as many country flowers as we could because we were sure that Chekhov loved these. We had a lot of Solomon's seal, pinks, and camomile. Aunt Marusya added some jasmine which she cut in the park.

The train left in the evening. We returned on foot from Sinezerki to Ryovna, and we got home only at dawn. A young moon was hanging low over the woods, and its tender light shone in the pools of rain. It had rained not long before. The grass had a wet smell. A late cuckoo called in the park. Then the moon disappeared and the stars came out, but an early morning fog soon blanketed them. The fog rustled for a long time, trickling down the bushes, until a calm sun came out and warmed the earth.

Volodya's peregrinations aside, as well as my own, you may think the Ukraine on July 2, 1904, a long way from the Bahamas a century later— and you'd be right. But so what? As Louis Armstrong said, if you can't hear the music, I can't explain it to you.

But Sis, I'm sure you can hear the music.

You'll discover that it's a hard book to find as it's been out of print, in English at least, for something like thirty years. I paid four dollars for my used copy in Key West. Could it be any more expensive on the West Coast? I'd never heard of it before. One day, as I was hovering over a bin of tattered spines, the book just jumped into my hand. The Story of a Life has a deservedly famous first chapter. A few lines and I was hooked.

Famous. Listen to me. Since I discovered it for myself, I've never met anybody who has even heard of this book, let alone read it.

But you're in San Francisco, for chrissakes. Surely you can find a copy in San Francisco?

Thirty years! Did I point that out already? I'm pointing it out again. Injustices too numerous to number happen every day, and perhaps each and every one of them is a greater crime than the misdemeanor of this memoir's neglect. But, so, let them be greater. How is the mind supposed to compass a so-called civilization that daily squanders such gems or, put another way, engenders such philistinisms. Engenders? Hah! Manufactures wholesale, is more like it, and vended at a great markup, down the throat, with a funnel. If paté likewise lacked flavor and nutrition, the force-feeding of geese wouldn't even be an issue.

There's a long list of these cultural atrocities. I needn't retail them. It would spoil the intense pleasure I took in copying out the passage, despite my penmanship.

I'm reminded of another book. A History of Pi by Petr Beckmann. It's full of interesting things, if you happen to be interested in a certain transcendental number; among them, Beckmann estimates the success of a given civilization in terms of its advancement of mankind's knowledge of pi. By this measure the Roman Empire, despite its might, power, scope, and longevity, achieved very little; not only did it advance mankind's knowledge of pi not a whit, but in the course of its conquest of Carthage it slew Archimedes, who was arguably, among many other accomplishments, one of pi's greatest exegetes. Exponents? Ah! A lousy pun at last.

Perceived by this light, American civilization has sporadically achieved a great deal. But does not its attempt to preserve the cultural legacy of one of its great immigrant populations, namely, the translation of The Story of a Life, add immeasurably to this achievement? And will not future historians rank the subsequent neglect of that book among our culture's most intimate diminutions?

Ah, I'm just gassing on. Maybe if there's some bread left over after this score I'll bring Paustovsky's book back into print myself. How do you like that idea, Sis? After all the miles I've sailed, the navigation I've sussed, the uninhabited cays I've camped on, the fish I've caught, the reefs I've dived, the books I've read, the money I've pissed away, the drugs I've consumed, the women I never married, and the rehabilitation I've undergone at the hands of the state—perhaps I'll wind up being remembered for the republication of a single, obscure work of literature, and nothing else.

But that's a pipe dream, yet another among Charley's pipe dreams. The only reason I know the name of the translator or the publisher of The Story of a Life *is because I took the trouble to glance at the title page. The name of the editor who caused the book to be translated and published isn't mentioned.*

Not to mention there's never enough money. Goddamn money.

The boat floats, the boatwright is forgotten, and maybe that's as it should be. Paustovsky's book, in my mind at least, remains. And when I die, and the book remains out of print, what will become of this impression? Perhaps above my grave a leaf will tremble. Perhaps, one warm day, in the little grove adjacent the cemetery, a visitor, seeking shade, will find a lost croquet ball. Hah. Faded and checked, dotted with the little perforations peculiar to powder post beetles, half-buried in pine straw.

A forgotten hemisphere. A microcosmic Ozymandius.

On the other hand, maybe if this last score comes through, and it really is big, and there are no legal fees or repercussions, maybe I can find a snug harbor for me and this damn boat, and read and read and read.

Much as I do now, plus or minus a certain exhausted restlessness.

When I first went to sea, I had this idea that there'd never be a dull moment. There would be danger, whiskey, storms, women, big square-riggers, strange cultures, pirates. Well, there have been all that and more. I had certain charts for so long they fell to pieces. I lost half my left pinky to a back-wound jib sheet—and I've probably never mentioned that to you before, have I. I saw a crew member on an ocean racer fall overboard and get nailed by a shark while he was still tethered to the boat. I saw a pregnant woman get knifed in a bar. I can splice double-braid or crown a rope end or throw a tugboat bowline with the best of them. Tune rigging, even tame a diesel engine. I've been hauled up an 85-foot mast in a bosun's chair in heavy seas. I watched a hurricane slam that same boat against a jetty and reduce her to splinters—a million-dollar loss, technically; a one-of-a-kind loss in reality. The first night on my first ship I punched out the second mate, who was drunk and coming on to me. I snorted pure pink Peruvian flake off a 19-year old girl's ass cheek and chased it with rum the same age. The first and third of these were gifts from a provincial governor's personal stash. Later, he got his throat cut. The girl married a Swiss surgeon. I pulled a stretch in prison. I never got a tattoo. At least I'm not a vegetarian. I lived aboard with Sandy for almost three years in Key West, put up with her Scientology, took a berth on a rich man's boat to make ends meet, came home three months later to find the woman gone. The boat was still there, locked up, it's true, but with her interior mildewed beyond redemption. The note Sandy left on the berth had been reduced to illegibility by mold, and I never discovered the text. My complexion's as wrinkled as an old sail but I didn't get melanoma—not yet, anyway. I helped one of the best boatwrights in the Caribbean shape a hull from scratch. I never killed anybody. I moved a lot of dope for some very tough people. I got caught. I started over again. I squandered money, energy, health, decades. I had a blast or, better to say, I had what passes for a blast. Often I had no fun at all. I contributed to the ephemeral. I spent a lot of time at sea. That's how one gets healthy again. And recovers time. And space. Spatiotemporal salubrity—you read it here first. I engaged a vast deal of spatiotemporality alone. I'm not sure what that means.

Of one thing I am certain. The price of freedom was—is—a lot higher than I thought it would be.

TWELVE

"THAT CHARLEY," TIPSY SIGHED. "DO YOU THINK CHURCH BELLS WILL RING across America when, say, Philip Roth dies?"

Quentin frowned. "No. But perhaps, in homage, some New Jersey masturbator will prolong his ecstasy by one or two strokes."

"Whoa, Nellie!"

"Consider such remarks," Quentin said modestly, "the prerogative of an old man."

Tipsy shook her head. "Some days, next to you, I just don't feel like a fully developed character. Still," she folded the letter, "it's sweet that Charley thinks I'm even capable of reading some Russian memoir."

Quentin made no response to this.

"Let alone, Philip Roth."

Quentin made a delicate sound in his throat.

"Know what I mean?"

Quentin turned a page in his newspaper.

"Take Sarsaparilla Candy, for instance, which she spells Sasparilla. Plodding along in the porn industry, she was getting by on her looks and a certain natural talent. She thinks, 'Where's the future in this? I'm going to turn fifty on my hands and knees?'"

"That's right about the age when you begin to suspect that if you don't take the action as you find it, you may never find it again." Quentin observed, not looking up from his paper.

"So," Tipsy continued, "having long recognized a need for makeups that won't smear in the clench, Sasprilla goes out and starts her own cosmetics company. She calls it Gentilia. Sole proprietorship. She does a little research, finds a Korean company that has the knowhow, establishes a brand, gives it away free to her friends and fellow practitioners in the porn industry, works day and night, builds it up, takes it public—and voilà: five years later she's a millionaire. Five years!"

"A million bucks," remarked Quentin, "the be-all and end-all of life."

Quentin knew the Sasparilla Candy story. Tipsy had worked for Gentilia, on and off, almost since its inception.

"For the sixth time since 1995," Quentin read aloud, "the House of Representatives has passed a bill recommending a constitutional amendment banning the desecration of the American flag."

"Where does that leave freedom of speech?" Tipsy queried.

Quentin scanned ahead. "It doesn't mention freedom of speech."

"After all, how could they?"

"The bill reads, in its entirety, 'The Congress shall have power to pro-hibit the physical desecration of the flag of the Untied States.'"

"That's entirely consistent with throwing people in prison and torturing them because, quote, 'They hate our freedoms.'"

"Actually, I'll go you one better than that." Quentin folded his paper. "It goes right along with arresting people for using photographs of George Bush II for target practice."

"Whose picture should they use?"

"Osama bin Laden's—of course."

"Why not Thurgood Marshall's?"

"Now you're thinking. But watch out that your brain doesn't generate too strong a field. They have ways of detecting your thoughts."

"Then what?"

"First, they will de-habeas your corpus. Next, they will allow an indef-inite period of time to elapse before your process comes due. And while you're hopping up and down on the griddle trying to keep your feet from getting burned, they will gut a half-century of environmental regulatory reforms and plant an oil rig every four miles between San Diego and Crescent City, right up the entire coast of California."

"But," Tipsy raised a finger, "while 'they' are depriving the world of its natural heritage, China—the nation, not the boyfriend—having pur-chased Unocal and established it as an off-shore, non-taxpaying entity, will make its move on Chevron, having already put its moves on Shell, British Petroleum, Nigeria, and Venezuela."

"Hey," Quentin observed, "capitalism needs elbow room."

"That's probably one free market fluctuation certain prominent freemarketeers are willing to interdict. Or at least retard. But wasn't it Marx who predicted that, once capitalism goes global, it will destroy itself? Everybody in Congress knows their Marx—right?"

"In your mind, my friend," replied Quentin, "a little knowledge makes for a dangerous opinion."

"No, really. I couldn't give a hoot about Karl Marx."

"How could it be otherwise?" Quentin observed coolly. "You barely know who he was."

"But it's an interesting idéa," she parried.

Quentin unfolded his paper. "Do you really want to discuss Marx just to prove you're a fully developed character?"

"Yes," she said emphatically.

"But you're preaching to the converted. I know we're in a world of shit. Go convince somebody who thinks everything is fine."

Tipsy fidgeted. "Just contemplating that conversation makes my skin break out."

"Don't call me. Call Gentilia."

"Not *that* skin. . . ."

Later, walking on Potrero Hill, Quentin realized that, bad as they were, the national and international scenes had little or nothing to do with Tipsy's skin rash. He wasn't even so sure that her nervous condition had anything to do with her brother's return to harness, as it were. It should do, though. While dope smuggling once had its romantic side for people like Charley, when what was being smuggled was marijuana and not yet cocaine, or hashish and not yet heroin, when it was the hipsters versus the squares and not narcoterrorists versus the Drug Enforcement Agency, when the whole thing wasn't orchestrated and driven by some cocka-mamie CIA scheme involving purchasing dope from Jacobins in order to buy weapons for Ultras—and other inappropriate scenarios for an impen-etrably mendacious foreign policy etc. etc.—, the salad days are long gone. They're two generations gone. Maybe three. The picture of Charley Powell making one last run at fifty-four years old in anticipation of early retirement hardly made for appealing statistical analysis.

Why, Quentin wondered, stooping to retrieve a roofing nail in a crosswalk, don't people like Charley do desperate things for love instead of money? He tossed the nail into a tree box, wondering if a little rust wouldn't do a bottle brush tree some good, nutritionally speaking. Because Charley's too shy or damaged to come to terms with his emotional reality? On second thought, that nail was galvanized, coated in zinc to prevent it from rusting. Well, he thought, looking over his shoulder toward the tree from the far end of the block, people take zinc for their health, don't they? To boost their immune system. And to damage their prostate. Between the devil and the deep blue sea. What do people and trees have in common? The Republican Party? Of course! It exists to snuff out both!

He turned back. But if one were to grind up, say, Republican environ-mental strategy and sprinkle the result in tree boxes all over town, surely the trees would flourish?

Am I under arrest? Are such thoughts metaphorically consistent with using an American ex-president's face for target practice?

One strives for consistency . . .

Quentin, he chided, you'd think that a dying man would have better things about which to remonstrate.

Well, he reflected, quite the contrary. One treasures the details, the *fiddly bits* of life.

The roofing nail bounced out of the tree box and came to rest between two russet Krugerrands of neatly minted dog feces. Quentin hesitated. That nail will probably remain right there, intact, and this tree will get struck by lightning, in a town where lightning is rare, before somebody's dog steps on it. The latter thought pained him, but he had to be careful about this. His compromised immune system left him wide open to opportunistic infections, every kind of cold and virus and even plant diseases.

Quentin retrieved his fountain pen from an inner pocket. He paused to regard it fondly. Many's the mortgage agreement . . . He tried to flip the roofing nail into the tree box. But the nail hit the trunk of the acacia and ricocheted off the curb and thence into the street where, immediately, the right front tire of a passing Ford Excursion (sage green, 6280 lbs., 14 mpg city, 17 mpg highway) gleaned the nail as if on cue. Vehicle past, nail gone. When the big SUV slowed before running the stop sign at the end of the block, Quentin could see that it bore a BUSH/CHENEY '04 bumper-sticker. A navy blue latex sack, ostensibly containing a pair of oversize testicles, dangled from its trailer hitch.

"But," Quentin maintained aloud, "I still don't believe in karma."

He consoled himself with the thought that this particular bumper-sentiment presented an uncommon sight in San Francisco; not precisely rare, however, he perceived it as an accurate reflection of the "evolving" state of the municipality.

One admires American democracy, Quentin paraphrased Stendhal, but the trouble with it is, one has to discuss it with one's local Republican.

Much more common in San Francisco, during the '04 campaign, had been the sight of 14 mpg SUVs with a John Kerry for President sentiment on the left bumper and NO WAR FOR OIL bleat on the right. How to suss that one? How about: In this country, there is no Left. Yes, Quentin didn't say aloud, that's why I'm walking by myself, and talking to myself. . . . You'd think a mortally ill man would have better things to think about. You'd be disappointed. The Mercedes is in the shop again, and that is altogether too stupid for a sick man to think about. That car is almost as much of a turkey as a Ford Excursion. Always has been.

What is it a sick man is supposed to consider, anyway? Should he reread *The Death of Ivan Ilych*? No. *The Magic Mountain*? Please. *Diary of a Mad Old Man*? Maybe.

Arrived at his house on De Haro Street, Quentin noted, as he engaged the bannister and the first of the 69 redwood steps that rose up the hill to his aerie, that his other dead car, a 1968 Datsun 510, on the concrete pad half-way up the hill, where it had reposed for some six months now, had accrued quite a volume of trash and eucalyptus leaves in its shadow. Originally black, now blistered gray by salt and sun, the car had over 400,000 miles on it, dating as it did from an era when Japan made cars cheap and hardy enough to take over the world—and, at 26 city miles to the gallon, decades ahead of its time. Now the 510 needed a clutch—its fourth—and China, to whom Quentin had given the car, didn't want to pay for it. Or couldn't. So, as an example of how *his* mind works, China claimed to be embarrassed to be seen driving such an old car. Quentin thought it was more about the manual transmission, which China could-n't handle either. In any event, the hills of San Francisco eat clutches and brakes; it's a law of nature. Quentin had paid $400 for the car in 1977, and clutches and brakes were the only things he'd ever replaced on it. Okay, okay, in the nineties he'd replaced the rubber belt by which the crankshaft drives the camshaft, back when there were still homosexual mechanics in this town, whose shops maintained immaculate waiting rooms with comfortable chairs and fresh flowers and *All My Children* on the television, with names like Gay Motors, Sweet Motivation, and Let Us Turn Your Crank.

Maybe it was the eighties. The very early eighties.

After three stops to catch his breath he gained the top of the stairs, where, after a fourth pause to allow the perspiration to at least partially evaporate, he let himself into the cottage, failing the while to dodge a line of mental patter he'd pursued a hundred times before. No doubt about it, in a town rich in quaint abodes, this had to be one of the quaintest. It couldn't have been fifteen hundred square feet—in fact, as he happened to know, it was 1347—including the bathroom, which was on the ground floor, under the kitchen. However, since Quentin and China—the boyfriend, not the nation—had stopped sleeping together, the size of the place had become all too apparent.

Before the railroad yards in the flats of Mission Bay were developed into a biotech complex, complete with a street called Stem Cell Way, the Bay Bridge had been visible from the kitchen window. Half of this marvelous wood-mullioned unit, seven feet wide and four feet high, two sashes of some sixteen 8 x 12" lites each, slid behind the other half, mak-ing for an always-astonishing blast of birdsong surfing a cold, eucalyptus-tinctured fog, as one did the dishes.

Quentin had owned the place for forty years, since long before China made the scene, maybe even since before China was born, if of woman the little Caliban had been born. Yet another stub in the real-ity checkbook.

China never gave anywhere near the damn about the view that he gave about being coy on the subject of his age. When and if he was home he smoked dope and watched his 36" flat screen television which, after protracted vituperation, China had insisted on hanging right on top of the view of De Haro Street to be had from the big window in the east wall on the first floor, adjacent the front door, from which one could see the gantries and spectral illumination of the dry-docks at the foot of 18th Street, for just one example, two miles away. Not to mention the sunrises. And moonrises! Quentin had managed to draw the curtains before China mounted the thing. Otherwise, all you'd see from the street would be wires, cooling vents, and a chassis of a color Quentin liked to call Storm Trooper Gray. The damask curtains between it and the window glass were much more pleasing to the eye, but, still, the setup rendered the spectacular windows useless. China didn't care about quite a bit of other stuff, either. What did ring his gong were the ostensive results he was getting from a new trainer at his gym, complimentary gallon jars of nutritional supplements, and a turnip-shaped quartzite crystal he parked between the cheeks of his ass when the latter wasn't otherwise employed, in order to re-harmonize his wracked prostate.

In exchange for discounts on membership fees, the vitamins, and crystal tuneup, China was boffing the trainer. Not that Quentin cared. "Hey," he could hear China shrugging it off, were Quentin foolish enough to bring it up, "every starlet does it."

Tedious, tedious, tedious.

Quentin had always suppressed his bisexual streak, and it's none of your business, thank you very much, but it was times like these that women like Tipsy started to look good to him, and he knew he was in trouble. Tipsy was his closest friend, she was intelligent, and she was good-looking, too, but she was a lush and, at this stage, that's just about all that remained to that story. Personal matters like love and sex came a distant fourth or fifth with Tipsy. Even politics outranked them. Not only that, but Tipsy had a longstanding monthly champagne brunch and hotel-room nooner with a married doctor. Once, Quentin had made the mistake of asking her about the guy. "Well," she confided at once. "After tipping and dismissing room service, right before we pop the cork on the champagne, he sets his pager to 'Vibrate.'"

"That's enough!" Quentin had declared, showing her the upraised palms of both hands. And the subject was closed.

What with one thing and another, Quentin had been sleeping the last six months on the upstairs couch, crammed against the west wall of the dining room, with stacks of books and the window wide open and the wonderful view of the sub-iconographic rooftops of biotechnology, enduring the soundtracks of old movies, the canned laughter of "situation" comedies, and the exhortations of shopping channels rising from the floor below, if and when China was home. But at home China wasn't much of, lately, and when he was at home he was either loaded and belligerent or hungover and sullen, with passed out cold the only stop in between. China clung to a job wheeling cartloads of interoffice mail between the multiple floors of a big downtown law firm, a form of employment he'd maintained for something like four years with absolutely no intention of improving or advancing himself. His idle chatter consisted almost entirely of office gossip, of which he possessed a detailed surfeit, of which Quentin, by mere apposition, and despite a matured facility for tuning out his bunky's prattle, himself possessed way too detailed a map.

The punk couldn't even cook.

So what's this about? Quentin asked himself one more time, as he surveyed the dishes in the sink. Downstairs, China's unmade bed, heaps of clothes, his open gym bag, his poster of Governor Arnold Schwarzenegger—"Married men love what I can do for them," China would wistfully invoke the image, every night or day as he retired, "and it's guaranteed to improve the nuptial contract. Arnie," he'd blow a kiss, "call me." The flat screen, the matchbooks with hastily scrawled phone numbers, half-consumed half-pints of brandy, the odd black beauty or triazapam caught between the sofa cushions—these comprised a world for which Quentin never had been able to muster a care. Yes, he had always been kidding himself about China. And it wasn't that he hadn't been aware of China's miscellaneous but rather complete if equally concise list of shortcomings; it was perhaps that all of these banalities had finally added up to the man in his entirety, which, if sad, scarcely amounted to anything of substance, which left Quentin acedic and bored. And sex? Well, come on, darling. Quentin almost blushed. But his expression went wry even as his cheeks tinctured with shame. He knew any number of seventy-year-old queens who chased the young boys, went to their clubs and did poppers with them, even snorted methamphetamine to keep up with the demands of a strenuous sex life. In fact, you only had to know one of them. Gay or straight, it was an unusual man who could pull it off. The rest of them, the balance of them, just looked silly.

He recalled four lines by Thom Gunn. How could he not recall them?

> Then dawn developed in the room, but old.
> . . . I thought (unmitigated restlessness
> Clawing its itch): "I gave up sleep for this?"
> Dead leaves replaced the secret life of gold.

What's the difference between a seventy-year old rake and one of fifty?
Twenty years of dead leaves.
He chuckled.
And maybe a couple of teeth.
His smile faded.
Night sweats.
The Man With Night Sweats—a Thom Gunn title.
Toothless Rake With Night Sweats—a Quentin Asche title.
Life can be so . . . circular.
The right-hand pan of the balance has crashed to the desk.
It's time to go.

Quentin surveyed the second floor. It was all one room. Even with the window open the musk of unwashed dishes in the sink would always linger above the far end of the couch. There were several boxes of books, which he would sell, if only to pre-empt China's selling them. The modest assortment of clothing he'd been buying to accommodate his thinning frame would fit in a svelte suite of three valises, two of which he could lock in the trunk of the Datsun for the time being. He toyed with the idea of leaving the dishes, so that maybe China would appreciate his absence.

"What's that about?" Quentin asked the room indignantly. "I, yes I, am the one who's going to appreciate my absence." He glanced at the clock over the sink. He had a minimum of four hours before the first possibility of China's appearance. He could be gone by then.

After he'd packed up the necessaries he did the dishes anyway. Then he delivered the luggage down the steps to the Datsun. Somebody had scrawled NATURE BATS LAST with a finger in the grime on the back window. After four more round trips, all the way to the bottom of the steps and back, each trip with two boxes of books, four and more rest stops, and weight loss through perspiration, he washed down a fistful of pills with an entire liter of water, and called a cab. With a final box of books on one shoulder, and a valise in the balancing hand, he walked out.

Click of lock, end of chapter. Forty years passed through him like a breeze down a canyon, the last two of these years a mere dust devil at the far end of it. From a wire across the street, a mockingbird loudly proclaimed its freedom. It sounded a lot like a car alarm.

The staircase ended at the sidewalk on the west side of De Haro Street. He sat on the third step, waiting for the taxi. Far beyond the roof of the old Pioneer Soap Factory, two blocks away, now converted to live/work lofts—all meanings of those three nouns long since up for grabs, and are we hysterical yet?—tendrils of fog flirted with the south end of Yerba Buena Island. The lower deck of the Bay Bridge thronged with the evening's traffic, a slow-motion existential bullet that he had managed to dodge all his working life. Engrave it on the toothless old rake's drawer in the columbarium: NEVER COMMUTED. There's an accomplishment.

As for the present view, encroaching development would soon demolish it. Quentin permitted himself a rueful smile. He had enjoyed his use of that view, the memory and the reality of which might well die with the rest of him. Somewhere along the waterfront, probably at Pier 35, a cruise ship gave a long blast of its horn, a warning to its passengers that but half an hour of shopping remained before departure. Three chuckling ravens barreled over the hill above the cottage.

The driver sized him up at once. He insisted on loading the trunk and back seat of the cab while Quentin waited in the front passenger seat. When the cabbie had joined him, Quentin gave their destination as Green Apple Books.

"Sixth and Clement," the cabbie said.

The books were quality titles in poetry, fiction, history. Much of the contemporary work was signed by the author. The Thom Gunn titles, for example. *Jack Straw's Castle. Boss Cupid.* Long gone Thom Gunn. The signed books might be worth something. The poetry was. It developed that the cabbie read history. Quentin made him a gift of Shelby Foote's Civil War trilogy, boxed.

Signed or not, the remaining books were all in good shape, they would find good homes. The transaction would precede a delicious supper in an excellent Burmese restaurant on California Street, not far from the bookstore, followed by a good night's sleep in a room rentable by the night, by the week, by the month. And maybe, Quentin thought with a twinkle in his eye, some paid companionship. Gourmet room service or bathroom up the hall, what difference did it make?

The succeeding units of time he would take as, and if, they were served.

THIRTEEN

TIPSY LEFT THE BAR, ABOUT AN HOUR AFTER QUENTIN, IN HER CLAPPED-
out Beamer. Green exterior, black interior, no back seat, a bag of golf
clubs in the trunk forgotten since the last time she'd had a flat tire, it started and got her home. DUI be damned. She was legally drunk, too. DUI
be double damned.

She had offered to give the clubs to the cute guy from AAA who came
to fix that flat maybe five years ago. Six? Seven? He declined to accept
them. You don't play golf? Tipsy had asked him, not even half seriously.
By way of a serious answer, however, the lad had recited a few verses from
Robert Fitzgerald's translation of *The Odyssey*.

> Sing in me, Muse, and through me tell the story
> of that man skilled in all ways of contending . . .

Goddamn it, Tipsy had thought at the time, doesn't anybody in this
town read trash anymore?

As the air wrench spun five nuts off the Beamer's left rear wheel, the
strophes kept flowing.

> . . . the wanderer, harried for years on end,
> after he plundered the stronghold
> on the proud height of Troy . . .

He set the flat to one side, saying, "There're twenty-four books in
Homer's *Odyssey*. I've got ten of them puppies memorized." He rolled
the spare in front of the wheel well and lined up the holes in the rim with
the lugs on the hub. "I don't have time to play golf." He lifted the wheel
and seated it. "Book Eleven is called *A Gathering of Shades*." As he hand-
started each of the five nuts, he recited.

> And Heraklês, down the vistas of the dead,
> faded from sight; but I stood fast, awaiting
> other great souls who perished in times past.
> I should have met, then, god-begotten Theseus
> and Peirithoös, whom both I longed to see,
> but first came—came . . .

he forestalled an interruption by raising one hand. Darren, as was stitched on his shirt, getting cuter by the minute, rested his forehead against the sidewall of the newly mounted tire, and closed his eyes. With a curious sense of anticipation, Tipsy watched as his lips moved in silence. At length the kid nodded.

> . . . but first came shades in thousands, rustling
> in a pandemonium of whispers, blown together,
> and the horror took me that Perséphonê
> had brought from darker hell some saurian death's head.
> I whirled then, made for the ship, shouted to crewmen
> to get aboard and cast off the stern hawsers,
> an order soon obeyed. They took their thwarts,
> and the ship went leaping toward the stream of Ocean
> first under oars, then with a following wind.

He cross-torqued the lug nuts with an airwrench. "That's the last stanza of Book Eleven," he said between nuts one and four. "Thirteen books to go." He looked up at her and smiled. His smile dazzling, his skin unmarked by care or time, he squinted against the sun and told her, "I don't have no fuckin' time for no fuckin' golf," and they both laughed.

He spared a little time for Tipsy, though. Darren's wrecker spent a weekend or three parked in front of her house, a spavined copy of the old Doubleday Anchor edition of Fitzgerald's translation of *The Odyssey*, a rubberband holding it together, on the dashboard. It turned out it was one of several knackered copies, from one or another of which Darren was seldom to be separated. One thing led to another, accompanied by deepening mutual awareness and, after a few weeks, Darren didn't come around any more.

She liked to tell herself she had inspired him.

It was also possible that he went away because she drank too much and had lousy taste in literature.

Of course the thought occurred to her that she'd taken Darren home—the other end of the driveway—at least in part because his love for a good book reminded her of her brother. The thought occurred to Quentin, too.

"Yeah, well," she said to Quentin, "that's nice and neat and psychofuckingtheoretical."

She hadn't had a flat tire since, but she had momentarily tuned up her taste in reading. She took a hiatus from cozies, thrillers, crime novels, mysteries, political memoirs, and White House tell-alls to embark upon Robert Fitzgerald's translation of *The Odyssey*. Even though tonier literature interfered with her drinking, on account of its demand on her attention span, she continued to drink. And eventually the quantum in literary quality succumbed.

Darren's business card surfaced occasionally in the glove compartment, whence, most recently, she'd had to produce the registration and proof of insurance prior to being handcuffed and hauled off to the four hours of jail time mandated by current drunk-driving statutes. That's why she was thinking of Darren, at the moment . . .

Sure, baby. That's right.

The driveway and her home were in that block of Quintara that fronts a big playground, way out in the Sunset District, between 40th and 41st Avenues, not a mile from Ocean Beach. A ground-floor beauty parlor had been converted to a modest studio apartment, whose signal virtue was a south-facing pair of warped and paint-peeled French doors that opened onto a neglected garden behind the building. This luxury possessed a single fig tree whose fruit Tipsy had never tasted, despite living hard by it for the twelve years since *Dhow Jones* settled to the bottom for good. A weathered and unpainted Adirondack chair, pushed into the corner between the house and the fence in the northwestern quadrant of the yard, faced the tree. In front of the chair stood a milk crate with a sofa cushion on top of it, her anti-macassar, as Tipsy had called the footstool until she looked it up.

> A protective covering for the backs of chairs and
> sofas. [Etymology: anti- + Macassar, a brand of
> hair oil.]

After that, she called it a footstool.

She often read in the chair, wrapped in a blanket, with a hot toddy to ward off the chill of a summer's fog. She kept her 2,000-page Webster's New World Dictionary out there, too, where it lived underneath the chair in a four-bottle wine crate with a hinged lid. She'd paid two dollars for the dictionary at a yard sale. Every time she purchased a bag of potato chips she saved its desiccant pouch for the dictionary crate. Thus the tome mildewed but slowly, and remained equally capable of coughing up etymologies for words like anti-macassar, as well as hibernating patiently in its wooden box while its mistress breezed through hundreds of pages of undemanding prose.

By the way, here is Tipsy's toddy recipe.

INTO an 8 oz. mug
POUR 5 oz. boiling water
STIR IN 1 teaspoon wild mountain honey
ADD the juice of 1/4 lemon
(DISCARD the rind—or SAVE for ZEST)
FINISH with 1-1/2 oz. rum, brandy, or bourbon

Guaranteed to keep you warm on the inside while you pursue low-calorie reading in the lee of an unpainted board fence creaking in 25 knots of a fifty-five-degree westerly.

Which was what was happening by the time the Beamer got Tipsy home. The fig tree was positively hustling in the wind, the ground beneath it littered with fresh and rotting fruit. Since neither Tipsy nor the landlady—who, living in her other house in Napa, was rarely seen, but she kept the upstairs apartment and the parking garage for herself—harvested the fruit, their decay had nurtured a green and orange froth of furiously blooming nasturtiums that had pretty much taken over the garden and most of the fence with the exception of a seldom-trod path of redwood cross-sections that meandered from the active left-hand door of the French casement to the foot of the fig tree, with a well-trod bifurcation to the chair.

She had a chair at the foot of her bed, too, for the numerous days when it was too wet or cold to read out back. Flush with both arms stood a stack of paperbacks, whose spines retailed the zeitgeist of Tipsy's reading list. The thrillers of Ross MacDonald, Agatha Christie, Sherlock Holmes, Dashiell Hammett, Raymond Chandler, many, many Simenons, even the detective novels of Faulkner and Gore Vidal, along with Eric Ambler, Wilkie Collins, Ruth Rendell, Dick Francis, Robert Parker . . . and the entire early to middle career of Françoise Sagan, *Bonjour Tristesse* through *The Unmade Bed*, and, once Tipsy discovered that Sagan had taken her pen name from a character in Proust, the C. Scott Moncrief translation, arrived in the form of a gift from Quentin, soon comprised a footstool of its own. Quentin, who had read *Remembrance of Things Past* twice, nevertheless predicted that Tipsy would never read it. In fact, stacks of books encased the little overstuffed chair not like concrete surrounds a gun emplacement on a Liberty ship. Books spilled into the bathroom, the kitchenette (*The Nero Wolfe Cookbook*), and the entryway (Dorothy Sayers, Amanda Cross, Judge Dee, Josephine Tey), and she had improvised a unique method of storing these works, which was simply to stand them side by side and let them march along a wall, through doors, into and out of whatever room came next. Good thing she had two rooms—three counting the bath. Periodically, she and Quentin would journey to Green Apple with several boxes of each other's books and sell them. Buyers at the store always harvested Derek Raymond, Jean-Patrick Manchette, Iris Murdoch, or Wilkie Collins from her boxes, but Quentin always got more money for fewer books.

The only domestic event which even came close to embarrassing Tipsy was the weekly Dumping of the Bottles. No matter when or how she did it, it made for a lot of noise. And one bottle at a time, carefully placed atop its predecessor in the recycling bin, seemed to take forever.

"An alcoholic just can't catch a break," Tipsy mused to herself, as she carried out the week's empties and dumped them. And who cares what the neighbors think anyway? And, really, what could they think? That I'm a faded beauty who lives on booze and trash literature? Score one for neighborly percipience. "You would think," she said to herself, mimicking Quentin, "that after weeping to Edith Piaf while dancing naked in front of the full length mirror on the back of the bathroom door at two o'clock in the morning, you'd be forgiven for making a little noise with the recycling."

Ouch, and nevermind. A girl has her secrets. She thinks.

When the job at Gentilia dried up, as it were, Tipsy had tried to care. But she'd been there for over four years, long past the time to move on. Back in her mind—sometimes not so far—lurked the specter of suicide or, perhaps more precisely, the lure of suicide. In any case, it was an act she considered inevitable rather than rash. By way of a sort of security deposit, she had purchased a .32 caliber automatic pistol in a Reno pawnshop ("That's a nice example of a purse gun you've bought yourself there, little lady."), along with a couple of boxes of rounds, and passed an afternoon in the desert on the east side of Mono Lake teaching herself how to shoot it. Pistol and the remaining cartridges now patiently awaited the Big Day in the bedside drawer. Health insurance, she called them. She had no other.

Not that she was ready to consummate that particular inevitability, not just yet. Not even close. Beginning with its simplicity and its solitude, there was much about her routine of drinking and reading that she genuinely enjoyed. An afternoon passed comfortably sipping a drink with Quentin sufficed as a social life. She was under no delusions about what it meant. She knew he sat with her only to humor her. If he canceled a date, it wasn't because he didn't enjoy her company, but because he couldn't gin up, as it were, the stamina sufficient to while away yet another afternoon watching her drink. "The quality of life," he would apprise into the phone, "is diminishing."

Tipsy, on the other hand, had no interest in doing anything else. She'd found that she could read one dynamite thriller after another with no ill effects. Drinking herself to sleep every night had proved equally reliable.

The real problem was money.

Once she'd been laid off she qualified for six months of unemployment benefits, with the potential of extending the coverage for another nine months. Sasparilla had helped her con a small disability check from the state due to carpal tunnel syndrome brought on by typing invoices for nipple clamps and the like. You'd think they'd cut her a separate check against her wonder over guys from Iowa who would order penis bracelets big enough to wear on her wrist—but no.

That had been fourteen months ago.

Two months left.

Though the job was waiting for her, Tipsy had put off thinking about the inevitability of going back to Gentilia. She was a woman of a certain age, after all. She'd worked a lot already and had damn little to show for it. Why keep trying? She'd learned any number of little economies. She didn't have a pet so she didn't have to buy pet food. She'd learned to live without heat. Her landlady deducted $250 a month from the rent for sweeping the sidewalk in front of the building, for putting the recycling and trash bins out on garbage day and taking them in again, for washing the windows in both apartments. For another $100 a month she allowed two elderly parties who didn't care to qualify for medical marijuana to come by and pick up the monthly package left for them by that same landlady, who did qualify and resold the benefit. These chores didn't add up to two full days out of the month. Three hundred fifty bucks left a mere one hundred owing on the rent. The unemployment and disability checks covered that and left her $950 monthly for whatever. Booze. Vitamin C. Used thrillers. A slim margin, but not bad. And when Quentin was around, he never let her pay for anything. She'd often wondered what people saw in the novels of Stendhal, or of Elizabeth Taylor, or Dostoyevsky, or Marguerite Duras, or Tolstoy, or Mary Renault, or Faulkner or, god forbid, Doris Lessing. *The Golden Notebook*, in Tipsy's opinion, was a fine example of a modern novel that put people off reading for keeps and drove them wholesale into the insatiable gorge of television. Nothing Quentin could say had convinced her to reattempt it.

By Tipsy's lights, the unexpected twists and surprise turns, the ghastly crime and the fitting comeuppance, the Moral Imperative, that old here-we-go-again feeling, explained things in ways literature did not. Not any literature she'd ever taken the trouble to read, anyway. I mean, a memoir written in 1917? In Russian? Charley, please. Be serious.

Charley. There sails a guy who took life by the horns, went ten rounds with it, got flattened, picked himself up off the deck and threw himself back into the storm.

They were born and raised on a dairy farm in Wisconsin. Charley attempted to run away two or three times before he actually made it, and still he was only sixteen years old when he got out for real. A year later his first two postcards appeared in the mailbox, one week apart. They came from Egypt and the second one, which appeared first, depicted burning sand, a camel, a squinting man in a djellaba holding the camel's bridle, a wind-blasted pyramid in the background, it bore a triangular stamp with serrated edges, and it was addressed to Tipsy care of their parents. Likewise the first one, which arrived second, which depicted a nineteenth century drawing of the entrance to a tomb in the Valley of the Kings. Put together they read,

> *Hiya, Sis. Took ship in Philadelphia. The very first night at sea I got in a fight with the second mate, who wanted to "turn me out proper." He was drunk and I was scared so I hit him. Down he went. One punch! We made friends later because, he said, I stood up for myself. The crew loved me because, they said, he had it coming. Jumped ship in Marseilles. Hitchhiked around. Picked grapes in the Sevennes. Learned enough French to fall in love . . . II . . . Then she went away! So did I! Took a job crewing a yacht in Cap d'Antibes. Speak pretty good French now, which will serve in much of North Africa. Got to Alexandria, now Cairo. Spanish will have to wait till I get to Argentina. Later this year? Then, overland to Chile. Patagonia! Every day, I'm glad I'm not where you are. All I can say is, I hope you get out of there one day too. I'm sorry I had to leave you behind. I'm running out of room. The name of the guy with the camel on the reverse of the other card is Akmed. All love, Charley*

Twenty-six years later, she still had the cards. Charley still had his guilt, too. For, in fact, he had left her behind. Twenty-six years later she remained convinced that, if she were to wake up in Hell one fine morning, the Devil would immediately put her to milking an infinite row of cows, every single one of them with the scours, and the infinite pile of manure at the far end of the infinite barn would be frozen solid enough to walk on.

Tipsy got out too, but it had taken awhile. Unlike her brother, Tipsy liked to know what lay at the bottom of the cliff before she jumped. And how far down it was. And what the weather was like. And who was going to catch her.

So she left Wisconsin with a guy. He drove her all the way to San Francisco and only wanted sex in return, which were the two things she wanted too, at the age of seventeen. Having arrived, her driver quickly got a job on a crew remodeling a Victorian. Within months, he asked her to marry him and have his babies. Two months after that, Tipsy took up with a coke dealer she met in a bar. Not long afterwards she let herself into the carpenter's little apartment during framing hours, gathered up her few belongings and departed for good, never to see the guy again. The city is easy like that: A slight variation in your normal path, and everything changes, including the people.

Actually, "never" wasn't quite true. Years later, passing through the San Francisco airport on the way back from Hawaii, she spotted the carpenter waiting outside the International gate. A young boy and a younger girl, both blond, waited with him. He'd lost most of his hair and gained some weight.

It had been annoying, fifteen years ago, to see him in the airport, and it was annoying to think of it now. In the event she could flippantly dismiss their incompatibility as a mere astrological distinction. Later she had come around to thinking that the guy merely knew exactly what he wanted, and she had freed him up to go about getting it.

As a girl who had never figured out what she wanted beyond a certain degree of comfort with a lesser degree of responsibility, Tipsy never understood how other people brought ambition to bear upon such decisions. And standing there in the airport, fresh from a month of responsibility-free tropical sybaritism, tanned and just the least bit malnourished, she found herself marveling at the fact that she had never conceived so much as a mote of curiosity about what impulsions might drive a man such as her carpenter. But he'd long since ceased to be hers. A woman such as Tipsy had once been—quite attractive, but as restless of spirit as she was terrified of domesticity, so that the one tendency reinforced the other—would always think of a former beau as at least partially hers. Then, at the airport, she realized that if she stood there long enough she might glean some insight into the woman her carpenter had chosen as her replacement. This thought naturally flew in the face of the fact that it was Tipsy who had left him, not the other way around, and it flatly denied any agonies of heart or conscience the poor carpenter might have endured in, say, the first year of her disappearance.

In the end Tipsy realized she cared not a whit for the woman upon whom the carpenter's stationary affection had devolved, and certainly not for her carriage or looks or the telltale marks of endearment she might lavish upon children and father. Tipsy passed through the exit door, caught a taxi to the apartment she shared with the latest man in the string she'd known since arriving in California, and never gave the carpenter and his wife another thought.

Until this afternoon, for some reason; in the short inventory of her curtailed emotional existence, she found herself fetched up against this last memory of her carpenter.

The coke dealer had been found welded into a fifty-five gallon drum in a slough far up the San Joaquin River about a year after he had inexplicably disappeared, leaving her to move out of the apartment she couldn't afford.

The guy with whom she'd been living for over eight or ten months at the point in time in which she noticed her carpenter at the airport never did come back from Hawaii. In the course of selling his furniture she found $10,000 in cash hidden in the back of a leather couch. And that's how she got the two grand to purchase the scow *Dhow Jones*, and live aboard for a year without working.

She'd not had a credible attachment since.

Unless you counted Charley.

She placed the letter from Rum Cay into the little chest, hand-carved in Thailand, which contained twenty-six years of postcards and letters.

She counted Charley.

III
Phantom Caravan

FOURTEEN

HE DIDN'T HAVE MUCH TROUBLE SLEEPING FOR THE REST OF THE TRIP—IF
you call sleep what happens to a man folded into a bus seat for 144 hours.
Loss of consciousness might better describe it, but that would be wrong,
too; better to term it a kind of option. You become exhausted, you become
passed out, you become awakened by an unusually percussive gust of
methane from the seat in front of you. Aside from discomfort, Cedric had
a couple of other things keeping him awake. The first was the residual
motion of the sea, as transmitted to a man's inner ear by the deck of a
boat. Cedric could do anything that needed to be done on the deck of a
boat, and one of the results was that he could hardly walk a straight line
on solid land anymore. It customarily took him a week or so to lose the
sense of a world seesawing—let's spell it seasawing—as he read a newspaper or stood at a bar. His gyroscope continued to compensate for a sea-
kindly motion that wasn't there any more, the only solution to which was
standing or walking with knees bent, as if the substrate could at any
moment heave up in an attempt to fling him off its back.

In and out of this fitful sleep, the memory of a certain sexual antic favored
by a girlfriend from his deep past brought with it the unmistakable sound of
a concrete saw kerfing its way along a white line painted in the street; of "Just
Walk Away Renee," a popular song released seven years after he was born but
never removed from the jukebox in a certain bar in Key West and often to be
heard there; of the scrumptious shrimp and oyster Po' Boy sandwiches made
in that same bar by an enormous black man from St. Thomas, Tracy by name,
who was "god-muscled," as a regular worshiper, a retired specialist in the
Homeric hymns, repetitively opined from the corner barstool; Tracy's fore-
fingers were the size of the dill pickles he sliced every morning in advance of
the arrival of his Po' Boy fans, of whom there were many; Tracy had nothing
to do with the ownership of the bar; all he took, and all he wanted, were the
proceeds from the sandwich concession; Tracy lived comfortably on a house-
boat; his avocation comprised of an ongoing attempt to collect of all the
known recordings of the tenor Beniamino Gigli; his favorite among these
many sides was the Gigli and Giuseppe DeLuca duet on "Del tempio al lim-
itar" from Bizet's *Les pêcheurs des perles*, and it was on the jukebox;
"Nietzsche," Tracy would say, as he bladed mayonnaise over the open face of

a sourdough roll, "thought Bizet superior even to Wagner"; Tracy always had a toothpick in his mouth, never perspired, always dressed sharp, yet his clothes never evoked their milieu of shredded lettuce and vinegar; a real sawdust joint with peanut hulls and oyster shells on its floor of dished planks and a tiled gutter that ran a stream of water underneath the foot rail, for cigarette ends and spit, although you could get thrown out for pissing in it; a gallon jar each of dill pickles, hardboiled eggs, and pig feet; many signs and bumper stickers papered the foetid walls, prominent among them "Intelligence Is The Best Aphrodisiac," "Adlai Stevenson / Harold Stassen / Nobody for President," "Who Licked The Astral Envelope?," "Eat More Possum", "Square Dance Tonite," "GAY UFO," "VOTE," and "You Want To Get Laid? Crawl Up A Chicken's Ass And Wait"; the men's urinal was a porcelain trough irrigated by streams of water leaking from 1/8" holes drilled at irregular intervals along a six-foot length of half-inch galvanized pipe; surmounted by a verdigrising bronze plaque that read, "Please flush twice, it's a long way to the White House"; no self-respecting woman would use the lady's facilities, which didn't mean they didn't get used; no air conditioning; the very bricks perspired; oddly enough, the woman Cedric met in that bar was named Traci, spelled with an i instead of a y; so maybe it was true, as one of the regulars opined that, as Freud zoomed away from the remains of his lunchtime Po' Boy on his 750cc Norton, with sidecar and spare tire, he missed a gear; Traci operated a concrete saw for the city; something about her caused men to fight one another, but another trick she practiced was serial monogamy; one guy for Traci, Traci for one guy; Traci was new to the bar since Cedric had last been in town; her pheromones indicated that she was between stints of serial monogamy; one thing led to another led to a guy named Jedediah, who didn't like the attention Traci was showing Cedric; Jedediah called him out; Tracy, the beautiful black man, did not pause the assembly of Po' Boys; Cedric and Jed took it outside; only Cedric returned; that was the end of the beginning; Traci took Cedric home in her flatbed truck with the city insignia on the driver's door, the monster saw in back restrained by chain binders among a spare three-foot blade, 500 feet of hose, various pressure reducers, gun muffs, orange traffic cones; so "Just Walk Away Renee," the sound of a concrete saw, the reek of vinegar, Bessie Smith calling for a pigfoot (or Bizet, presumably, though it had yet to happen); the composting miasma of rotting yeast, cockroaches stupefied by the *largesse*, enough time to run out of other things to think about, such as a cross country trip on a Greyhound bus, each and all sufficient to evoke in Cedric's mind feckless replays of various of the hours he'd spent orbiting Traci; on that particular shore leave; in that particular epoch of Key West, the Conch Republic.

The other thing to always overcome ashore was a reluctance to leave the home that a good boat with a good crew always became, or one with just himself and no crew at all. He liked it. Time ashore interrupted his routine. So he was reluctant to get off the boat, made various excuses about how he could buy shaving cream next port, there was plenty to drink aboard, he never drank half so much at sea as he did ashore, and so forth. Standard seadog.

But now, 144 hours after leaving Miami, Cedric had had it with muscle cramps and nostalgia. He was tired of thinking about Traci, tired of the mind worms of popular music, tired of sifting a past that meant nothing— just plain tired, and hungry, too. After the initial prepackaged baloney sandwich, five days ago, he'd quit eating.

So he stepped down in Las Vegas.

At the door he asked the driver a question. "If I get off your bus and get back on the next one, or two or three after that, is the ticket still good?"

The driver yawned. "That's what they all say." He squinted. "You a Chinaman?"

"Could be, I guess."

"That what they do in China?"

Now it was Cedric's turn to yawn. "How's that?"

"Let a man get off a bus and back on whenever he's a mind to."

"As a matter of fact," Cedric answered, "it seems like a good idea."

"Well, that's not how we do it here."

"How do we do it here?"

"You get off the bus and get back on, you got to have a special ticket. A Ticket To Ride, they call it."

"How do you know that's not what kind of ticket I bought?"

"'Cause you're a Chinaman. How would a Chinaman know to buy a special ticket?"

"I'm a Chinaman that's been here before?"

The driver shook his head. "Then you'd know better than to ask me."

Cedric looked through the windshield. A lot of people were taking buses into Las Vegas, and a lot of people were leaving on them. The ones arriving looked a lot more hopeful than the ones departing. He sighed aloud. He hadn't had a square meal in six days, ditto a bath, a shave, or an hour's uninterrupted sleep. He wanted to sit on a barstool, stretch to his full height, maybe get a masseuse to walk barefoot on his back, maybe look up concrete sawing in the yellow pages. "Man," he said, turning to descend the stairs. "Riding this bus is like having insomnia for a livelihood."

"You should try driving one for a livelihood," the driver said. "If you don't keep your lid cracked," he touched the side of his head, "you'll blow your top."

The Las Vegas air was hot and dry. Every room he stepped into had air conditioning, televisions, and slot machines. The lobby of the tiny motel he found on a back street was no different. A pair of electronic slot machines stood next to the desk. They looked like identical robots and they made slot machine noises whether anybody played them or not. "Pay the winner!" one said, and emitted the digitized rattle of a cascade of silver dollars. "We pay more than any Indian casino in Nevaaaadadadada," boasted the other machine, and it emulated the digital algorithms of gunshots and the whoops of celluloid Indians.

The woman behind the desk wore very long appliqué red, white, and blue fingernails, and she made him wait while she manipulated her computer keyboard. All Cedric wanted was a room so he could sleep in a horizontal position, but he couldn't keep his mouth shut. "I can see that you're a patriot to your fingertips," Cedric quipped aloud. The clerk manifested a technique of touch-typing that reminded him of a gamelan orchestra, and if he didn't soon get a hot bath and some rest everything was going to remind him of everything else, with the sole caveat that he'd forgotten whatever it was in the first place. But at least she didn't remind him of Traci.

Jesus Christ, he thought to himself. Ten years, maybe more, and there's absolutely no reason to think of that woman, except to remember that she manifested a generosity of spirit that touched me then and lingers as one of the signal interactions in a life singularly lacking in signal interactions. That perpetual source of simile; that gamelan orchestra, for instance. Debussy and gamelan music. That, and the concrete saw. I've got to get some sleep.

"Pay the winner," a slot machine declared. "Ding ding, ding ding ding." The other machine made like a police siren. "Pow pow, pow pow pow."

"You listen to these things all day long?" he asked idly.

The woman finished typing before she looked up. "What things?"

Cedric indicated the two slot machines.

"Just eight hours," she said, extending a claw toward Cedric's receipt inching out of a printer slot.

"That printer slot," Cedric pointed out, "doesn't go ding ding ding."

She frowned. "Is that a pun?"

"I guess they're a mercy," Cedric observed.

"Puns?"

"Those sixteen hours off."

"Shoot." She caged a mouse within the nails of her spare hand and moved it atop a clutter of papers. "You can't get away from that stuff in this town. Doesn't matter where you go."

Cedric affected mild alarm. "You mean to tell me I can expect to find a couple of those things in my room?"

She shook her head. "Can't do that."

"Why?"

"You might rob them."

"Rob them? I might murder them."

"Easy there fella. This is Vegas, and that's treason you're talking. They could put you away for just thinking such things. Hell. All I'd have to do is report you and—" she drummed a patriotic tattoo atop the mouse with a talon—"Gitmo."

"Winner! Ding ding, ding ding ding."

"Damn," Cedric said.

"To hell and forever," she said. "Parboiled al Dante."

"Like the poet?"

She frowned. "Like the spaghetti."

"Say," Cedric brightened, "anybody got a good spaghetti around here? Good salad? Good red wine?"

"Sure," she said. "Majesto's. Here." She produced a pamphlet map of Las Vegas, took up a pen and, gripping the latter as if it were the handle of a butter churn, carved a circle on the street grid. "Only three blocks from here. Tell the mayterdee the Silver Peso sent you. You'll get a free stack of chips."

"Winner." The slot machine made a sound like a police siren. "Ding ding ding ding."

"What do I do with free chips?"

"Gamble 'em away. Just like everybody else."

"Where?"

"Anywhere. Right at your table if you want. While you eat."

"So Majesto's is a casino?"

She looked at him. "You from China or something?"

"Why?"

She tapped the map with the pen. "This is Las Vegas. Gambling built this town. The construction is still going on. I doubt it's ever going to stop. Gambling is what we do here. Gambling pays for everything. This town is so on the boil, the phone company has to reprint the yellow pages four times a year. You come in from the airport?"

Cedric shook his head.

"Well if you leave by the airport, you'll see a big pyramid out there."

"A pyramid? Like in Egypt?"

She frowned. "It's on the dollar bill, man, and nobody in this town believes in anything else. Except America, of course. Everybody here believes in America." She narrowed her eyes. "They got dollar bills in Egypt?"

Cedric said he didn't know, but he'd ask his friend Charley. Charley had been in Egypt. "Except," he remembered aloud, "I can't ask Charley."

"How come?" the lady asked.

"Charley's dead," Cedric said.

"I'm sorry to hear it." She handed him the printed receipt. "Take a right out of the elevator on the second floor."

In a bar. He wasn't sure when, where, or how he got there.

Another guy, already in there, was already drunk.

Cedric was loaded, too. This bar lacked a television, it was fairly dark, the sound seemed to be turned off on all the poker games, though their lights flashed, and Frank and Nancy Sinatra were singing "Something Stupid" together.

The nap had worked out okay, but he woke to the reverberations of televisions in every room around him—one above, one below, one each on two sides. So he checked out.

The spaghetti had been soggy, the meatballs tasteless, the Caesar salad frozen, and the wine a vinegar—an al Dante meal, indeed. The free poker chips never materialized, perhaps because, having tasted each of the servings, he put down his fork and waited for the next installment, only to find himself repeating the performance. The thing that protracted the meal beyond a half hour was the whiskey-rocks he enjoyed between each disappointing performance from the kitchen.

He had an hour to kill before the next bus.

The jukebox fell silent. Cedric dropped his sea bag next to a stool and ordered Irish whiskey from the well and on the rocks. The bartender wore a flannel shirt, black jeans, athletic socks, bedroom slippers. Her hair was carelessly piled atop her head and affixed there by two black enameled chopsticks with ideograms stenciled along their length that wished everybody, no doubt, a happy new year.

"That looks like a double," Cedric observed.

"Let me guess," the woman said. "You can't control yourself so you want me to dole it out slowly."

Cedric smiled and raised the glass. "Cheers."

"What are you looking forward to?" said the man at the corner of the bar.

"Who?" Cedric looked around. "Me?"

"You," the man said. "I'm buying you that drink and I want to know what you're looking forward to."

Cedric shrugged. "San Francisco."

The man blinked. "That's it?"

"You don't like the answer, don't buy the drink." Cedric counseled him.

The man shook his head. "You look to me like one a them immigrants that stretches carpet in high-roller suites. Either that, or you're going to San Francisco because you're queer." He squinted. "Which is it?"

On the coaster in front of Cedric, "Winner!" was printed in a red arc of wanted-poster type surmounting a two-inch disk of mylar in which, if the angle were correct and the light sufficient, the drinker would see a reflection of his own face.

Cedric took a second look at the character across the bar. This individual had a very closely shaved pink face beneath a drying-at-low-tide peninsula of thin hair. Although he probably weighed two hundred pounds he looked as though he might be in some kind of shape, despite the gin blossoms that festooned his upper cheeks and the fractaling veins that empurpled his nose. Bags subtended his eyes, which distension served to sadden his malignity. His labored breathing reinforced the banality of the drivers X-ed over the words Desert Golf on the breast of his polo shirt, open at the neck and displaying a lot of hair among which nestled a chain of miniscule links from which depended a droplet of gold resembling a molten spermatozoon.

Cedric always noticed the hands and in this case the man wore on the third knuckle of the middle finger of the right hand a ring set with a large hemisphere of garnet. A proper delivery of this stone could pop the orbit of a man's eye like a ball-peen hammer shattering a light bulb.

Cedric leaned one elbow on the bar, pinched his nose and upper lip between thumb and fingers, and said tiredly, "I don't know a goddamn thing about carpet or high rollers or homosexuality—although," he added thoughtfully, "I am a sailor." He turned his head and scratched one ear, then looked back at the man and added, "But even if I did, I fail to understand why I should even entertain the idea of discussing it with a peckerwood such as yourself."

Six days of boredom is enough already.

"What did you call me?" the man replied after a stunned silence.

The bartender had retired to the far end of the bar to page through a copy of *People* magazine, but now she looked up.

Boredom aside, Cedric couldn't have said exactly why he responded thus to a perfect stranger. Maybe the stranger didn't strike him as perfect? The bar was sea-sawing? Maybe whiskey actually worked? "Look," he said reasonably. "Is this nineteenth century behavior in the twenty-first century, or what?"

"No," the man replied smugly, saliva evident in his sibilants. "This is

Nevada." The menace in his voice was sufficiently histrionic as to be only slightly less implausible than it was unmistakable.

Cedric turned to the bartender. "Is this any way to let your customers talk?"

"What way is that?" the woman asked him, wide-eyed.

Cedric jerked a thumb toward the man in the catbird seat. "His way."

"Mister," she said. "Talcott there is a regular, and I don't know you from Charley Chan."

"Charley Chan." Talcott guffawed caustically. "Fucking queer."

Cedric blinked, sighed, set down his glass. "How much for the drink?"

"I done told you, immigrant," Talcott said, before the bartender could reply, "I am buying your goddamn drink."

Cedric looked at Talcott. "I don't accept drinks from racist pecker-woods."

The bartender gasped.

Talcott manifested a grin of intense satisfaction. "What'd you call me?"

"How much for the drink?" Cedric repeated to the bartender.

"I'm talking to you," Talcott said.

"Racist is nothing you haven't been called before." Cedric looked from the bartender to Talcott. "Unless this entire town is chickenshit."

Talcott's mouth deployed a leer and he straightened up on his stool.

My my my, Cedric observed to himself, the corpse sits up in the sun. And it's tall, too.

"Never have I ever been so disrespected." Talcott's expression subsided into one of aggrieved sincerity. "I'm not sure I appreciate it."

"One of the things about getting infantilized by alcohol," Cedric advised him, "is that you have to get used to deriving less and less nutrition from eating more and more shit. The upside is, from early on, it all tastes the same."

Though he frowned at this, Talcott pushed back his stool.

Make that two-thirty, two thirty-five, Cedric thought, and maybe six foot three.

"Double down!" one of the bartop poker machines suddenly erupted. "Pow pow, pow pow pow!"

Cedric stood and dropped a ten dollar bill on the bar. "I sincerely hope there's enough in there for a tip," he said to the woman without looking at her, "I've got a bus to catch. By the way, I'd like to thank you for pouring an honest drink." He rattled the ice in the empty glass and fed a couple of cubes into his mouth. "I am a little concerned, however," he allowed, as he set the empty tumbler on the bar, "about your taste in customers."

Talcott stepped around the corner of the bar, buffing the ring on his right hand with the palm of the left, and waxing with pre-coital anticipation.

Cedric chewed ice and pointed at the street door, which was now directly behind Talcott. "It would be a very easy thing to abstract yourself from between me and the exit. Smart, too."

Talcott shook his head. "I am the red carpet to your future, you immigrant pissant."

"Well," Cedric said, manifesting resignation as Talcott approached, "I guess we're about to determine who is the bigger sociopath in this joint." He stuffed his folding money into a back pocket of his jeans. "Or the dumber," he added.

A diminutive wisp of a premonition wafted from the left side of Talcott's brain to the right side, as mirror-imaged in the man's eyes, but it radiated little more comprehension than the ghost of a man who has spent forty-two years as the host of a television game show, only to drop dead in the studio parking lot of a massive coronary.

"Peckerwood," Cedric said wearily, "you're in my goddamn way."

Talcott, each hand balled into a fist, advanced a step. He might have had something going for him, other than the punch he could throw with the ring, but Cedric, who liked his eye sockets just the way they were, didn't wait to find out. Before Talcott could uncork the ring, Cedric sortied a left at his nose. Talcott brushed it clumsily up between his two crossed forearms, completely exposing his torso, and all went irrelevant. Cedric's right jabbed twice the base of Talcott's sternum. The blow would have been damaging in any case, let alone that blow repeated, but Cedric had taken the precaution of striking with a fist clenched around the heft of his new rigging knife. The knife was not open, to be sure, but it added considerable linear momentum to the two blows. Talcott exhaled so thoroughly that his lips flapped, covering the backs of his own wrists with saliva. Cedric administered a third blow to the abdomen, right above Talcott's dick, if he had one. Then the insides of his knees touched, he evacuated, and his entire anatomy transmogrified into primordial pith.

Little else mattered. Cedric stepped back. Talcott reeled, sagged, clasped both hands to the afflicted part, and collapsed into so abject a genuflection it might have shattered both patellae. Adroitly set up for the kill, had Cedric skewed homicidal, Talcott looked up at his new master, whose head appeared to him to be rising toward the ceiling. A singular pallor suffused the bepuzzlement that transfixed Talcott's visage and, though he waited, the blow did not come. It didn't have to. Talcott fell forward like a timbered redwood and kissed the floor a dreadful smack, snapping off both of his upper incisors. Talcott made no move to break the fall. The impact sounded as if someone had swatted the parquet with a sock full of nickels. Talcott was spared awareness of this ignominy, however, for on the way down his right temple glanced the two-inch brass knob on a footrail stanchion, and by the time the bar flooded to bursting with paramedics, firemen, and police officers, Talcott's enjoy-by date had expired.

The owner appeared, too, an older individual with a tousled cowlick who had obviously been napping in some back room. "Thank you, stranger," the man said, pumping Cedric's hand. "That Talcott prick was the bane of our establishment. Until you came to town, nobody would go up against him. Good riddance to bad Irish rubbish." He indicated the bartender, who modestly touched her hair. "As a fit reward, I want you to marry my daughter. Someday," the owner spread his spare arm, "all this will be yours."

The woman behind the bar smiled. Cedric hadn't noticed the gap between her teeth. Nor the freckles in her flanneled decolletage. The package looked rather attractive.

"I'm deeply gratified," Cedric said, "but I think we should have sex first."

This startled the owner. "Say," he narrowed his eyes, "are you from San Francisco?"

"Not you and me," Cedric hastened to clarify. "Me and your daughter."

"Oh, well," the man beamed, reassured. "That's different."

The daughter beamed too, and she set aside her copy of *People* magazine.

Cedric woke up.

The bus roared out of a narrow gap rockdrilled through the shoulder of an arid butte, and the highway descended into a long, sun-blasted valley. A sign, faded from the green of pool table felt to a sage without chroma, loomed large in the windshield

> Right Lane   Route 68
> KINGMAN   1-3/4
> BULLHEAD CITY   40

and disappeared into the rearward bluster of the Hound's blowby.

When Cedric attempted to rub the glare out of his eyes, he discovered that his right fist was balled up around the marlinspike knife. Jesus Christ, Cedric thought, looking at the knife, whose blade was closed, if I don't ease up on that brown liquor, these blackouts are going to make a monkey out of me.

The Greyhound took the exit without slowing.

FIFTEEN

WHAT WITH ONE THING AND ANOTHER, I'VE GOT THE MOOD AND THE TIME FOR *this last rumination. There's some guys fishing small boats around here today. For a few bucks I'm sure I can get one of them to take a letter into Landrail Point, whence eventually it will make its way over to the post office at Colonel Hill. Latter is slam on the other side of Crooked Island from here, a matter of some fifteen miles as the fish flies, way more than that as the ambulation rambles. Not to mention, the supply boat only stops by there once a week. So it's probably going to be a good long time before this gets to you, Sis. And that'll be it for a good long time after that. A real long time.*

Early in his career Red stole two kilos of cocaine right out from under the mule smuggling it. On the car ferry from Port Angeles to Victoria—that is to say from the US to Canada—the mule met a pretty French Canadienne and spent the trip in the lounge chatting her up. The language barrier didn't seem all that much of a problem, for she laughed at everything he said. She was working for Red, of course. Red had been waiting for his chance and this ferry ride was ideal.

Ironically, if the authorities were slaying the guy, Red might have been doing him a favor. If they were going to pounce so as not to lead the mule's organization to suspect it had been penetrated, a customs bust at an international border would be an innocuous way to do it. We say nothing, here, of what the mule's organization might do to him for blowing the run, regardless of the reason for his failure.

But Red couldn't give a damn about that angle. As far as he was concerned, if the guy had been paying attention to his job, Red would never had gotten his chance, so the responsibility was on him. Or, as Red himself put it, "While his jaw was flappin', my claws was scrappin'."

Once aboard the ferry, the mule waited for everybody to go upstairs to the snack bar. Then he moved the load, two one-kilo parcels, each including a powerful magnet, from his own vehicle to the inside of the back bumper of a tricked-out Winnebago with Arizona license plates, which was parked on the car deck a couple of vehicles in front of him. You know the kind. A motorscooter on a rack out front, awnings and bay-window extensions on either side, a Jeep on a towbar out back, the whole rig is forty feet long, it takes three or four people to jockey it onto the ferry. This was in springtime, when the snowbirds head north to British Columbia. The retired couple driving the Winnebago wouldn't know a thing, and Canadian customs would wave them right through. Altogether an excellent choice.

Then the mule went to the bar, and Red's move was simplicity itself: he swapped Winnebagos.

Once off the ferry, the mule trailed after the first Winnebago, and Red followed the second one. All either of them had to do was track some ignorant tourists around Victoria for the day. Every tourist eats, has a few drinks, goes to the bathroom, visits a museum. Somewhere along the line, Red would seize his chance.

Meanwhile, up the coast of B.C. in the next day or two, enacting a similar pattern, the mule would make an unnerving discovery.

In Vancouver—ideal on account of a big population base in which to get lost, not to mention a large demand for product—Red would be looking at something like $1,700 Canadian per ounce times 16 ounces per pound times 4.4 pounds equals $119,680 Canadian, depending upon how he moved it, minus the price of the girl. (As it happened she was Red's partner at the time, name of Darla. So there was a fifty-fifty split. What a babe. And smart? She was faking the Quebeçois accent.) And what, two ferry tickets? Gas? A hotel room? Two tickets back to Florida? Pure profit with very little risk. All you needed was the nerve to do it.

All this by way of reassuring you that, while there are other people out there doing what Red Means does for a living, I work for Red because he's the best.

Vellela Vellela and I had an uneventful passage to Albert Town from Port Nelson. Sixty-seven miles on a rhumb line, straight out the Crooked Island Passage, never less than a thousand fathoms of blue water under the keel. Excellent and beautiful open ocean sailing under ideal conditions; a broad reach in ten to fifteen knots of trade wind, clear blue skies excepting voluminous cotton balls of cumulus blowing southeast to northwest topped by the odd thunderhead. Barometer steady. One mild squall mid-afternoon, fifteen minutes of solid rain, faired off not long after.

We spoke not a single vessel. Only the stack of a cruise ship rose over the horizon, easterly, at about eleven hundred hours. It looked to be heading on nearly a reciprocal course, and until it disappeared I amused myself calculating how far away it much have been. Estimating the middle of the stack, cut as it was by the curve of the earth, to be maybe 100 feet above the surface; and my eye, with me seated in the cockpit, maybe six feet above the surface (almost exact: I measured it), the vessel figured to have been some 24 miles distant.

That, Sis, is what I call elbow room.

It may well turn out to have been the nicest day of the whole voyage. Only *trouble was no trouble at all. The main halyard was frayed, but I gleaned a nice trick long ago from one of Bernard Moitessier's books, which is, when you reeve a new halyard you cut it long, five feet or more. Every halyard will fray where it passes over the sheave in the masthead block. Before the line breaks you cut off a foot toward the standing part, re-reeve the thimble into the new working end, and presto—an unfrayed halyard.*

Moitessier wrote that, as he was sailing around the world or making an extensive passage, he re-rove each of his halyards every week. I don't need to do that, of course. Moitessier's running rigging almost certainly was hemp. But I've been more or less continuously at sea for three years. So fatigued and frayed lines are an issue.

So are sails, for that matter. Mine are sagging like a cheap suit. Sorry. But if I get to San Francisco I expect to be able to order a new suit of sails.

And yes, that means I'll be staying a while.

Tipsy. How long has it been since we met in Thailand, and I gave you that cedar box. You still have it? I can't remember what year that was. I can't imagine you've changed as much as I have. I'm bald, for instance. You're not bald, are you? I guess I never told you that before. Pelón is the Spanish, which also means skint, as in broke. So I'm Pelonito Doble, twice-skint, the little bald broke guy, and have been for years. And skinny. Skinnier than ever. I'm missing a couple of teeth and half a pinky finger, too. Lost the latter to a backwound sheet winch on a great damn spinnaker in a big boat race from Antigua to St. John's. Took it off clean and I only ever thenceforward saw the bitter end. I see it now. Its absence aids the pen to trace more smoothly the paper. A grinder bound up the stub in strips of cloth torn from his own t-shirt, and we kept on racing. We figured the faster we ran that boat the faster my finger would get to a doctor. And you know what? We were third to finish and corrected out second. A doctor on the race committee sewed me up at a dockside sink usually employed for the cleaning of fish. I was at the bar with the wounded pinky in a glass of ice water and a beaker of rum in the other paw by the time our skipper had ordered the second round. The stump looks pretty good, considering. Excepting this clumsy attempt to dampen your shock at the sight of it, after all these years, I rarely think of it.

Okay. I've been at sea for a day and on the hook for two, and I've been trying to figure out how to broach this subject and I can't see any way around it, so here goes.

In letting you know that I'm going to be showing up in San Francisco in a few months, I have probably fucked up. But, maybe not. It all depends. What I need from you is total discretion. Please and thank you, tell no one—no one—about my destination. In the first place, many sea miles lie between thought and deed. In the second place, well, I probably don't need to spell it out to you, and we can talk about how stupid it all was if and when I ever get there. I'm not going to let you know I'm in town until the job's over. Somewhere in there I'll have a bath and a shave, then we can meet for dinner. On me. And talk all night, I imagine.

Until then, mum's the word. Can I rely on you in this?

Except for the fact that we haven't seen each other for so long, I might have waited until I got there to contact you. But, to tell you the truth, except for the fact that this job will afford me the voyage to San Francisco, I might not have taken it. Always the money. But I found myself so filled with anticipation over the idea of meeting you again after all these years that I couldn't wait to tell you, and again, I might not get there at all. . . .

Faulkner passed by the catbird seat, where Tipsy sat reading. "You want another?"

She nodded.

"How's the only sibling?"

Tipsy folded the water-stained letter. "All at sea, as usual."

Faulkner ploughed the mouth of a frosted glass through a sink full of ice. "When's he getting here?"

Tipsy looked up. "Huh? Oh. Well, now it seems . . . he's not coming."

"Is he okay?"

"He sounds fine."

"Are you okay?"

She feigned confusion. It didn't take much.

Faulkner considered the news. "I thought this was a big reunion happening here."

"It's like I told you," she said testily. "First it was happening, now it's not happening."

"Just so," Faulkner transited smoothly. "What's another year after twenty-five?" He patted her hand. "Don't let this family meshugaas get under your skin."

Annoyed, she moved her hand. "Does family meshugass ever get anywhere else?"

Faulkner pursed his lips.

Tipsy rolled an unlit cigarette between thumb and forefinger. A lot of smokers were in that DUI class, and she'd taken it up out of boredom. "May I have some matches?"

At the opposite end of the bar a door led outside to a narrow deck above the water. Once there, Tipsy snapped a pair of matches into both hands, cupped against the afternoon westerly. Even with the bar between her and the east side of Potrero Hill, the flame blustered quite desperately. Cigarette ignited, she cued a preset on her phone.

After one ring a computer answered and told her that the number she had dialed, which the machine then recited with rote courtesy, had been disconnected, helpfully suggested that she check the directory listing, and hung up. Tipsy snapped the phone shut and placed it on top of the book of matches, which quivered in the breeze as if it meant to take flight from the weathered and unpainted 2x8 which capped the pier railing. The breeze smoked her cigarette faster than she could. She didn't like the taste anyway. She adjusted the location of one of three dilapidated barstools and perched on it.

She hadn't seen Quentin in five weeks. His phone had been disconnected for three. It was a land line. Once quit of his high-flying real estate business, about two years ago, Quentin had dropped his cellular service. She'd gone by the cottage he shared with China—China Jones, on stage in his own mind, as she never failed to think—but there'd been no sign of either of them. The Datsun was parked on the little concrete pad, halfway up the stairs amid windrows of leaves, but that didn't mean anything. It had been parked there for close to a year, awaiting repairs China would never afford it. No sign of the Mercedes.

She found it hard to believe that Quentin Asche, who had all the money a man could reasonably need, was now reduced to letting his phone be disconnected. It seemed more like a symptom of self-administered ostracism, rather than a slide into penury. Penury it wasn't. That much she knew. But didn't he realize that in one week life could pass a girl by entirely, let alone five?

Yes, she ruminated. Of course he did.

The thought occurred to her that Quentin might have died. She brusquely dismissed it.

Tipsy had always enjoyed Quentin as a drinking companion, even after his health forced him to quit drinking, but now she really needed to talk to him. The warning in her brother's letter was clear. Tell no one. It was like a dare. How can you possibly ask a gossip as consummate as herself, not to mention Quentin Asche, to tell no one about anything, let alone the prospect of a second meeting in a generation with your only surviving kin? Let alone the apparent prospect, only hinted at in this most recent letter, that he might chicken out altogether?

Oh my god, she suddenly admitted, I have to talk to somebody about this.

The wind had smoked her cigarette down to the filter. She flipped the butt into the bay and was considering sharing another with the elements when Faulkner called her name.

She turned for a look. Behind the bar, Faulkner held up the receiver of the in-house telephone.

She looked at her own phone. Then her heart skipped a beat. With a shaking hand she retrieved Charley's letter from beneath the phone and squinted at the Bahamian postmark: nearly three months before. She gathered her things and hurried inside.

"Hello?"

"Tipsy . . ."

She caught her breath. "Quentin! Are you okay?"

"I'm okay."

"Oh. I—. Oh."

"Try not to sound disappointed."

After a moment she found her voice. "Where the hell have you been?" she demanded sternly. "Your phone's disconnected, I've been by your place, you haven't come around for drink or . . . or companionship—what gives? Did the meds quit working?"

"So he couldn't even keep the phone going," Quentin said thoughtfully.

"Who couldn't? You mean China?"

"I left China," Quentin stated unequivocally. "Left him for good. If the phone's not working, it's because he didn't pay the bill. And maybe he's gone, too."

Tipsy welcomed this development; as a sensitive friend, however, she needed to react appropriately without lying.

"At fucking last," she said frankly.

Quentin ignored the remark. "A month ago. The day we last saw each other."

"That's five weeks ago."

"Okay, five weeks. I went home and took stock. Not much to take. I sorted my worldly goods and walked away." After a pause he added, "I sold all my books, and the house is for sale, too."

Tipsy exhaled loudly. This, all of this, was a big deal for Quentin. He'd been letting that kid torture him from day one, starting some 750 days ago. One of the many ways China had been tormenting him was by selling off Quentin's books by the half-dozen behind his back. So, in a couple of deft blows, Quentin had deprived China of his supplemental income and his free place to live. Cold. Nice and cold.

"It's about time."

"Oh, Tipsy," Quentin said bitterly, "you always know what to say."

"What do you expect me to say? I've never seen you so happy? How about, Oh, Quentin, what could possibly have gone wrong? Was it the sex? You were never happy, everything was wrong, and what sex?"

"Yeah," a guy standing next to her turned to say, "What sex?"

"Hang on a second." She pointed one end of the receiver at the guy and said, "Mind your own business or I'll jam this thing so far up your ass you'll be able to hear both ends of the conversation."

The guy's eyes got big, then started to narrow.

A man behind him put his hand on the guy's shoulder. "Don't."

Faulkner appeared, patting the fat end of a long-necked beer bottle against the palm his free hand. "Another round, gentlemen?"

"Sure," the second man said. He jerked a thumb toward Tipsy. "And one for the lady."

"Very civilized," Faulkner said, dropping the empty into a bin.

"Tequila," Tipsy said to the first man.

"Top shelf," his friend quickly escalated. Letting a moment expire, he elbowed his friend.

"Yeah," the friend agreed sullenly. "Top shelf."

"Sorry," Tipsy said into the phone.

"Has China—by any chance—has China called you? Looking for me, I mean?"

"That avaricious little fuck knows better than to call me. He knows how I feel. He knows how all your friends feel. This protracted infatuation has cost you damn near every one of them."

Quentin ignored this. "To—you know—hasn't China been looking for me? Isn't he worried?"

Tipsy rolled her eyes. "I wouldn't give that little cocksucker the time of day," she said coldly, "let alone tell him where you are. I wouldn't even take the call." She paused. "While we're on the subject, where are you? Because I, yes I, have been looking for you."

"Oh, come on, Tipsy. He's not such a bad kid. He—"

"Listen to me, Quentin Thomas Asche. China Jones, if that is indeed his real name, isn't fit to wring the rainwater out of your shoelaces."

"Tipsy."

"Yes?"

"I wear loafers."

She laughed. "Of course." Quentin was a connoisseur of colloquial expressions for queerness, and "Light in the loafers" was one of his favorites. "Yes, of course." But, "He's been nothing, and, I mean, nothing but poison to you," Tipsy persisted. "I know from poison, and I know precisely what he's done for you, it adds up to way less than zero. Nothing but grief. Not only that, but you've let him take a nice casual year, or more, to perform all this marvelous subtraction. You don't even have a perspective on it. You used to laugh. You used to be witty. You never obsessed on politics. I've heard of slow torture, but this China guy—"

"Oh," Quentin protested weakly, "you just never took the trouble to get to know him. None of my friends did."

"Will you pull yourself together? What's to know?" Tipsy exclaimed, so

loudly that Faulkner and the two patrons renewed their attention to her.
"Listen," she said, lowering her voice. "Why aren't you calling me on my
cell phone?"

"I . . ." Quentin hesitated, then resigned himself to a little bit of the
truth. "I was hoping to leave you a message, to let you know I'm okay." He
paused, then added, "You're in the bar early."

Tipsy glanced at the Olympia waterfall behind the bar. It twinkled gold
and blue and told the time, too, a throwback to another era of beer consumption; two o'clock of an afternoon in whatever era she and it currently cohabited. "I got here about an hour early, it's true. Faulkner called to
tell me there was a letter here from Charley. I came right over."

"Oh." Quentin spoke with little conviction. "Good."

"Plus I've been taking the bus to my DUI class. It's a long haul."

"Oh. I . . . forgot about the DUI class."

"Tonight's the last one."

"That's . . . marvelous."

A short silence ensued.

"That's okay, Quentin," Tipsy began, "you've got a lot on—"

"Tipsy," Quentin abruptly interrupted. "I've been so very lonely."

"Listen," Tipsy said after a moment. "Call back on my cell." No reply.

"Quentin. Are you there?"

"I'm here."

"Look. I'm . . . standing here in the bar with rather a large audience
overhearing my end of the conversation. I can take my cellphone out on
the deck. It's colder than Dick Cheney's titanium stent out there, but I'll
have the place all to myself. Plus, I'm wearing a sweater. Call me back and
we'll talk as long as you want. It'll be more private. I'll have a smoke while
you tell me your troubles."

"Smoke?" Quentin repeated, alarmed. "Do you have any idea what
second-hand smoke smells like on a sweater?"

She paused. "Then, maybe, I'll tell you mine."

"Oh," Quentin said after a moment, in his flattest voice. "Trading cigarettes for peccadilloes. That sounds divine."

"I didn't say it would be divine," Tipsy retorted. "But it might be
therapeutic."

"You think?" Quentin replied, not quite hopefully.

"Hang up and call me back, Quentin. Now. Promise?"

Silence.

"Where are you, Quentin?"

After a moment Quentin said, "In a . . . hotel."

Tipsy narrowed her eyes. "Where is this hotel?"

"Eddie at Taylor."

She cast her mind's GPS across town until she saw a playground with a chainlink fence around it on the northwest corner, a parking lot ditto on the southeast corner, and the live porn theater on the northeast corner. Was it the Pussycat Lounge?

"Are you upstairs over St. Anthony's soup kitchen or the sex arcade?"

"The sex arcade. Even four stories up, you can smell the disinfectant. The stench of that roach-and-flea-bomb stuff is equally inescapable."

Tipsy puffed up her cheeks and exhaled in exasperation. "Bathroom down the hall?"

"Yes. But I won't be here long enough to use it. Besides which, there's way too much hair in the drain."

"The telephone, too? Down the hall, I mean?"

"Yes."

"A pay telephone, then."

"Exactly."

"Can I call you on it?"

"This telephone no longer accepts incoming calls," Quentin read aloud. "It's a hand-lettered sign."

"They're trying to cut drug dealing back to less than forty percent of the Gross National Product."

"Oh? Since when did they get it that low?"

"Nice hotel. Well, do you have another fifty cents?"

"I do, as it happens."

"Call me back on my cell. At once."

"Okay."

"Promise?"

"I promise."

He rang off. She handed the receiver to Faulkner. She took up her fresh Casaderos, saluted the two bravos, who returned the greeting, and headed for the smoking porch.

"Is he okay?" Faulkner called after her.

"He's okay," she answered as she backed through the door.

She managed to share another lousy-tasting cigarette with the wind and finish half her tequila, pondering the whole time, before her phone rang. Its display spelled HOTEL VERLAINE.

"Sorry. A guy had to make a call."

"Can you talk?"

"Not for long. He went for change and there's another guy waiting."

"Okay. Look. Before we get into you and China, I need to explain something."

"Sure," Quentin said, sounding less than patient.

"I mentioned a letter from Charley."

"When's he coming?"

"That's it. That's exactly it. Yes. But I mean, no, he isn't coming. I mean, he doesn't want anybody to know about it. I shouldn't have told you. Have you told anybody?"

Quentin made no response.

"He made it sound like we know what he's doing and maybe we shouldn't know what he's doing. At least, you shouldn't know what he's doing. Have you told anybody what he's doing? Have you told anybody Charley's coming? To San Francisco, I mean?"

Quentin, somewhat confused said, "Who would I tell that your brother's coming to San Francisco?"

"That's a good question," Tipsy said, somewhat prosecutorially. "Who?"

"I mean," Quentin continued, as if annoyed, "I don't know your brother. I don't know anybody that knows your brother—except you. And by now, after twenty-five years, you probably don't know him either. You probably don't even remember what he looks like."

"By now he looks like our maternal grandfather, probably. Little potbelly, a tonsure, gray and thinning, warts in the folds around his eyes, potato nose, bald for sure—the works."

"I was so happy for you. You are—were—going to see your only living kinfolk at long last. Every last member of my family went to their grave not speaking to me. All it took was for them to find out I was—am . . ."

"Light in the loafers."

"That's it."

"I know."

"I was happy for you, Tipsy. But who else would I tell?"

"I don't know, Quentin," Tipsy bore in. "And I don't know why you would, either. But that's not the point. The point is whether or not you've told anybody that Charley is coming to San Francisco. Have you?"

Silence.

Tipsy swallowed half the remaining half of the tequila.

Quentin said, "You don't give an orphaned thong sandal about me and my problems, Tipsy."

"It's all about you, isn't it."

Tipsy paused the glass halfway back to the 2x8 and smiled.

Tipsy stopped smiling

"Some friend you turned out to be," Quentin added.

Tipsy could hear tears in his voice. She put down the glass. "Quentin. . . ."

Quentin hung up.

SIXTEEN

China Jones sashayed along Geary Street in buff-colored ass-cheek-hugging felt bell-bottoms with a skinny concho belt threaded through its loops. The belt's ten inches of extra tongue terminated in a chrome ferrule that dangled over his basket like the head of a serpent whose hollow tooth might excrete a syrup of venomous glitter, were it to be teased. Above the belt a form-fitting t-shirt with horizontal blue and white stripes with a pack of smokes rolled into one of its sleeves exposed his midriff. Its hem was high enough and the belt was low enough to permit all the world to see that he had a prominent inny that looked like a tree ear with a chrome stud in it, and that he waxed regularly. He wore a women's cologne named *Fumarole*, and mousse in his hair sufficient for Tipsy Powell to have once referred to his head as Manitoba, and to the person beneath the hairdo as the veritable Dauphinette of the Manitoban Bratocracy, Population One. Emphasis on the diminutive feminine ending. He'd never spoken to the lush again.

The pants were snug enough that even a mere half a gram of meth bulged a rear pocket like the head of a nail under a coat of paint. China affected a disco purse, too—chrome sequins sewn to black satin suspended waist high by a thin silver chain—that held a couple of poppers, another half of methamphetamine, a driver's license that said he was 28 years old (he was 38), three twenty-dollar bills, the key to the DeHaro Street cottage, and a card identifying him as a member of Balls to the Wall, a Folsom Street gymnasium with fifty or sixty weight-lifting trophies displayed in a glass case that enclosed three sides of the dutch door at which members queued for towels, vitamin supplements, steroids, growth hormones, glass pipes, and prophylactics.

He'd not been home since the kitchen sink backed up. He wasn't sure how many days it had been, but he knew, for he'd counted, that it happened one month to the day after Quentin bailed. Quentin had absconded with all his books and clothes, too, and hadn't so much as texted who what when where why, leaving China to conclude he'd been dropped like a dirty communion wafer.

But then, China had always known Quentin for the emotional coward that he was. From the beginning, he'd seen right through him.

Funny, mulled that diminutive module of his mind least concerned with his appearance and the buzz he'd been minting for some 36 hours, how empty a bookless room can look. Maybe that's the idea? He hadn't really given much thought to how handy books were but, as goes décor, they were almost as good as magazines. Quentin's floor, even with China's TV and cellphone charger and some clothes, which China had moved upstairs as soon as he'd figured out Quentin had gone for good, looked strangely denuded, almost Arctic, without the books. That the fog had decided to come back and sit on San Francisco for three weeks in a row only served to reinforce the impression of gloomy desuetude. That, and the eviction notice. That, and the For Sale sign.

For a while China had tried to liven up the room. He uprooted a sunflower from somebody's front yard on the way home from work one evening and put it in a sake bottle with some water and a crushed aspirin. The bottle was transparent, however, so right away the display looked a little grungy, and, soon enough, the flower drooped. He'd thought aspirin was supposed to cure a hangover. Hahaha. And the only place it seemed to really fit was on the small dining table under the window. But it got in the way of the flat screen there so China really found himself at a loss as to where to place the display. Finally he put it on the back of the toilet where it soon died and where it yet languished, moribund, half its water evaporated and the other half a flocculated louche of ditch water.

Quentin had mentioned once that sunflower seeds are arranged in some kind of special spiral but China had paid no more attention to that than he usually paid to the rest of the overeducated poofster's observations. Quentin was a study. He could go on and on about San Francisco real estate, economic trends, poetry, history, American foreign policy— "so-called," as he used to say, "foreign policy"—let alone the spiral in the arrangement of seeds in the head of a sunflower, but Quentin knew next to nothing about contemporary music, television, cosmetics, sado-masochism, the Hollywood closet, or pharmaceutical stimulants, for a few of the more incredible examples. Quentin didn't even care about the Giants, for chrissakes, and remained absolutely clueless about the Forty-niners. It was little wonder he could hardly hold up his end of an intimate dinner conversation. But in that, at least, Quentin wasn't alone.

Having topped a block of Taylor at Bush, China, slightly winded, paused to raise the ever-so-lightly-tinted-ochre lenses of his charcoal-spotted butterscotch horn-rimmed glasses (shoplifted) for a squint at the tiny woman's watch (ditto) whose jeweled dial barely covered the racing pulse on the inside of his left wrist. One fifteen. He'd only been up for twelve hours. He still had forty-five minutes of the lunch hour. He never

ate lunch and didn't go to work anymore but he always took the hour, usually whiling away the allotment with a toddy or two backed by a rail of
crank in one of the many so-called pocket bars to be found around the
purlieus of the Financial District. These bars were of a type—small, dark,
not too loud, stiff drinks reasonably priced—tenanted by regulars who
would leave you alone if that was the vibe you put out, while yucking it up
with anybody willing to talk with them. The customers were rarely strati-
fied into gay or hetero, young or old, transvestite or transgender, like they
could be in other parts of town, usually holding no more in common than
that they were thirsty and lonely whether employed or not, or, the Big
Casino, lonely and independently wealthy. There were a lot of hotels in
the neighborhood, too, which, vis-à-vis lonely big casinos, could come in
handy.

As if the very street had read this thought, it presented China with an
invitingly open door he'd never noticed before. A modest living room of a
joint, it was called Patsy's.

Inside Patsy's was cozy, dark, and cool with but a single customer.
Giants and Foroty-niners memorabilia festooned the walls, along with the
usual booze advertisements, salted among photographs from both earth-
quakes, '06 and '89. The jukebox was a semi-modern affair, a small console full of compact discs hanging off the wall next to the bathrooms, of
the sort that Quentin's Quietus thingie could snuff. Although, as far as
China was concerned, all Quentin's Quietus thingie was really good for
was embarrassing China. But from this machine, Frank Sinatra declaimed
"You Make Me Feel So Young," with Nelson Riddle, and not too loudly.

> You make me feel so young.
> You make me feel spring has sprung.
> Every time I see you grin
> I'm such a happy in-di-vi-du-al . . .

China had ever heard of Nelson Riddle but, cheered by the illusion of
youth regardless, he took a stool midway along the bar and ordered a
brandy with a soda back. The bartender, who may have been Patsy herself, filled a rocks glass with ice, cleared a selector spigot with a spritz into
the undercounter sink and covered the ice with soda. "Lemon?" she
queried. China nodded. She cleft a wedge on the rim of the glass. "Any
particular brandy?" She placed two cocktail napkins on the bar in front of
China, and set the glass of soda water on one of them.

"What's in the well?"

Patsy leaned back to survey the counter under the bar. "Crocker's
Golden Spyke."

China frowned. "Never heard of it."

"You might want to keep it that way," said a new voice.

China turned to face the customer wearing impenetrably dark shades sitting on the stool at the corner of the bar with his back to the front door.

"That's not an attitude I find particularly fruitful," China said with a certain coyness. Turning back to the bartender, he added, "At least, not when it comes to the fruitful experiences often to be risked by venturing into the unknown."

"Fruitful experiences? Venturing? Unknown? Risk?" The customer groaned. "Ye minor fucking deities and extended clown triggerfish."

The woman behind the bar leaned on her two outstretched arms, each hand of which gripped a few inches of the gutter on her side of the plank, and waited.

"Fruitful experiences," the man repeated incredulously.

"Let's try the well," China said quietly. "Neat."

"Was there some kind of high tide last night?" the customer inquired of the room in general. "There seems to be a deal of flotsam ringing the hills this morning."

China checked the inside of his wrist. "It's one forty-five, sir."

"Try not to dry out," the customer growled. "You'll raise a stink."

This guy thinks I'm some kind of pansy, China sniffed to himself. He doesn't know rough trade when he sees it. Or, he reflected slyly, maybe that's exactly what he knows?

This kind of thinking was informed by one of the generalities China thought he'd discovered about life, which is, every straight man is at least a little bit queer, and a lot of them are way more than that.

The bartender set a rocks glass on the other napkin and poured the tumbler half full of an amber fluid. China took up the glass and saluted his gruff colleague. "Precisely." He took a healthy swallow and choked a little. "Say," he managed to fib, "not bad."

"Three bucks a shot," the bartender pointed out. "Although you should know that this is the kinda joint where management might throw a kid a freebie every third drink or so."

"A vanishing paradigm," the drunk pointed out contentedly.

China finished the drink. Is there a feeling in the whole wide world comparable to that of one and a half ounces of ethyl alcohol drowning one hundred billion neurons in a heart that has been up all night?

"On the other hand," the other customer added, "there's no accounting for taste."

The bartendress dried her right hand on a towel and extended it. "You're a brave man. My name's Patsy."

"Thank you," China croaked weakly, taking the hand in his own. He set down the empty glass. The bartender refilled it.

Suddenly, China experienced a vision. I could start all over, he thought to himself. I could become a virgin again. I could pass the high school equivalency test. I could work in this bar part time. Patsy could play my mother. I could drink in moderation, or not at all. I could sleep only with people my own age or younger, and not for money or in-kind services. Maybe do the whole beard—wife, kids, career, and confine my flings to politicians and evangelists and this drunk over here. Although he's kind of seedy. What's the difference, anyway? Maybe I'd dress a little more conservatively. Though that doesn't sound like much fun. I used to get health care at the law firm. Better I should re-up that job and help out at Patsy's after work. Stop by the Cala Foods at Hyde and California for limes, lemons, and olives on the way in. Nice routine. A simple life. Quitting steroids and gak alone would certainly tilt me toward moderation, once abstinence had permitted my personality a certain refractory period. . . . He looked slowly around the bar, his hand still firmly in Patsy's. Patsy had seen her share of bad men and crashed alcoholics, not to mention flamed-out dot-commers and their descendants, economists and bond brokers, not to mention—he assessed the woman across the bar in shrewd slow motion—the hippies, punks, and military personnel of bygone eras. Men, mostly. Patsy had the look about her of a grandmother who kept a sap under the bar. That's it, China thought dreamily to himself, I could reduce my thirty-eight years of lies, deceit, and irresponsible cocksucking to one half of a simple moral dichotomy: give me your money, and I'll give you a drink.

"Excuse me," said a voice next to him. "Is this seat taken?"

"Why . . ." China abruptly emerged from his reverie. "No. It isn't."

"May I?"

"Absolutely," China graciously responded. "The more the merrier."

Patsy's hand released his and, with a reassuring pat to his forearm, she replaced the bottle of Crocker's Golden Spyke in the well, rapped the bar twice with a knuckle, and turned her attention to her new customer.

China took stock of him, too, and was immediately impressed. Well-barbered straight blond hair with traces of gray at the temples. Tanned and fit. Mid-fiftiesh. Sharp suit of a blue so dark it seemed black, with a tastefully muted and micronometric lavender pinstripe. Blue hosiery in the same value as the avocado shirt, lavender tie to match the pinstripe. Chocolate-colored shoes, possibly handmade. A modest but inescapable hint, in the cologne, of leather and money. China recognized the marque as *Justine*.

In the vast but quantum bitch-slap between the gakked-up diastole and ethanol-soothed systole, all of China's well-intentioned resolutions regarding the future disposition of his character evaporated.

"I'll be right back." China stood off his bar stool and placed a coaster over the mouth of his brandy glass.

In the men's room he tapped a little mound of crystal into the fold of skin between the clenched thumb and forefinger of his left hand, snorted one such bump with each nostril, then fell into an intimate inspection of the face in the mirror over the sink. It was miraculously unlined, this face. Moreover, his torso stood in excellent shape, and its costume projected a decisive chasm of caste between himself and, say, buff guys who drive delivery trucks for a living. China's true portrait, in short, yet tarried in the attic of his soul. The speed burned his maxillary sinuses like he'd inserted a length of red-hot wire into each of them. Someone tapped at the locked door.

"Five minutes," he said over his shoulder, hooking the toilet seat with the toe of his shoe so that it fell with a clatter.

"So sorry," said a man's voice, and, after a pause, the door of the adjacent women's room opened and closed.

Best to bump the bump, China decided, and he snorted half again as much as previously. Tears started to his eyes. Putting things away and holding his head back to ensure there were no telltale granules clinging to the well-scoured bore of either carefully depilated nostril, dabbing the tears with bath tissue, he flushed the toilet, turned to the door, threw a mouthed "Wish me luck" with a wink and the tissue over his shoulder toward the chancred mirror, and, smoothing and resmoothing the fabric of his trousers over the cheeks of his ass with the flattened palms of both hands, he debouched.

Back at the bar, he found himself alone.

"Where's my fan club?" he asked Patsy.

"Lon the homophobe, there," Patsy indicated the catbird seat, "drinks the morning shift. Don't make no difference what kinda argument he's started, he goes home every day at two. Like clockwork. This other guy," she indicated the stool in front of which a drink waited, "will be right back."

Sure enough, the handsome gentleman in the expensive suit duly reappeared, leaned casually against the bar, and looked very frankly at China.

"Cheers," China smiled. The speed had ignited his speed-dependent tinnitus. No problem. What's to hear? The news? More than once, China had done an amount sufficient to incite a sloughing of audio frequencies of the sort to be heard when tuning a short wave radio. He knew his limits and—he cranked a rictus smile for no reason apparent to anybody else—he wasn't there yet. He knew this because, at the moment, the tinnitus was a discreet frequency of 5,000 hertz, and the only thing twenty decibels of 5,000 hertz gets in the way of is a whistling tea kettle.

The handsome stranger returned the smile and took up his glass. "You should have let me in," he said quietly. "I had something for you."

China could have idly strung out this banter for an hour or so, via protestations along the lines of, I'm just off the bus from Boise and I'm sure I don't know what you mean, or, there are some things a girl just doesn't share with strangers and the bathroom is one of them; but he sized up his man and cut to the chase.

"You might have passed a note under the door."

The man smiled. "I didn't have a pen."

China extended his hand, knuckles up, fingertips down. "China."

The other responded reciprocally, knuckles down, fingertips up. "Holden. But you can call me Miou Miou."

"We could go back later," China suggested, "Or any time for that matter." He made a little face. "It's just a bathroom, after all. Unless . . . ?"

"Tea," the man shook his head modestly, "is not my scene."

"Nor mine," China hastened to assure him. "It's just that, when in Rome. . . ."

"Understood," the man agreed, "and enough with the sotto voce already. Would you like another drink?"

"Absolutely," China replied.

Holden pointed. "That's brandy?"

"It was," China said, downing it. Thanks to the crank, China could barely taste the cheap brandy. He showed Holden the empty glass and redeployed the rictus smile. His teeth looked like the tiles on a much-used re-entry vehicle.

"Bartender," Holden said.

"Her name is Patsy." China was not the one to pass up an opportunity to come on like a regular.

"Yo." Patsy looked up from a copy of *The New York Times* double-trucked flat on the far end of bar, between herself and the now vacant cat-bird seat, where the light from the open street door favored reading.

"What's your best brandy?"

Removing and folding a pair of half-lens reading glasses, Patsy walked down the bar as she surveyed the top shelf. "Looks like this *Amygdales d'or* shit." She pronounced it *Amig dah-lee's door*. Holden smiled. "It sounds Irish."

China shrugged.

"I don't think so," Patsy said doubtfully.

"Let's have a look," Holden told her.

Patsy produced a milk crate and stood on it to reach the bottle, and displayed the courtesy of blowing off the dust before she placed the flask on the bar.

Holden produced his own, very elegant, pair of folding reading glasses with thin gold temple bars and a golden chain with tiny links, and studied the bottle through them. "My goodness," he said at length. "It's a calvados." He looked up. "It's never been touched."

"At fifty bucks a pop," Patsy said, still atop the crate, "I'm surprised it ever got purchased, let alone touched."

For once, China volunteered the truth. "I've never heard of it," he said, referring to the genus.

"Nor have I," Holden declared frankly, referring to the species. "My curiosity is piqued. Patsy?"

"Yes?"

Holden tapped the bottle with a corner of his glasses. "How utterly charming."

Patsy shrugged. "It was here when I bought the place in 1991."

Peering through the lenses of his folded spectacles, Holden's eyes ranged over the label in question. "So it's at least eighteen years old," he marveled. "Right here in San Francisco."

China touched his chest and blushed convincingly. "What a coincidence. It's the same age I am!"

Holden looked at China. "You don't say."

"I'm half deceased," China glumly posited.

"Shut the fuck up," Patsy admonished him. "You're half alive."

"You . . . You're . . ." China gulped histrionically.

"Yes," Patsy lied, "I'm almost forty."

"You don't look a day over thirty," Holden countered suavely.

"Yeah," Patsy laughed, "and the Iraq War was a boon to the economy."

"That clenches it." Holden replaced the bottle on the bar and tucked his spectacles back into the inside breast pocket of his jacket—where, as China had already noted, also resided a wallet of tanned ostrich, iguana, or alligator skin. Holden hailed from neither Texas nor Australia, by his accent, so China's money was on the alligator.

Holden's hand lingered at the pocket. Patsy stepped off the milk crate. China's breath quickened—might it be rhino? Elephant? Holden inclined his impeccable hair toward the bottle. "We'll have a glass apiece."

Patsy tapped the bar three times with a middle finger.

Patsy, China thought to himself, how disappointingly boorish. Such a lack of faith. Can't you see what we have here?

"Ah," said Holden, getting the drift. He retrieved the wallet, and from it, at arm's length, he far-sightedly fetched a C-note, laid it on the bar, and crossed it with a twenty. "For you," he sweetly declared to Patsy, replacing the wallet. Still and all, China thought begrudgingly, business is business.

"Excellent," said Patsy, not touching the notes. "Now my grandson can finish college."

Holden bethought himself and half-retrieved the billfold. "Unless you would care to join us?"

Patsy shook her head. "Too early for me," she declined. "But that's very kind of you."

"Another time, then." The wallet settled back into its burrow.

Without turning to look at it, Patsy gave the milk crate a kick that sent it back under the sink. "Do you mind if I take the trouble to serve it correctly?" She took away China's brandy glass, swabbed the bar in front of her two customers, and dealt a clean napkin to each of them. "I get so little practice."

Holden raised an eyebrow. "Patsy," he declared, "that's a congeniality most unexpected." He turned to China. "Don't you just love it, when somebody fetishizes the secular?" China rewarded this query with a completely blank look. Holden said to Patsy, "I'll wager the warmth will coax this liquor into divulging the most divine secrets." He turned aside again. "China?"

At this, China barely hesitated. On the one hand, while he always wanted to appear more sophisticated than the people around him, on the other hand he'd learned that it was rarely true. This was especially the case with older men, more experienced than himself, and especially with the kind of men in whom China tended to be most interested, older men in funds, the majority of whom, moreover, took singular pleasure in schooling younger men in various of the pleasures of life. "I'm sure I don't know what that means," he admitted simply.

Holden placed a reassuring hand on China's forearm. China readily colored, a trick he had learned in acting class. This guy's faster than I am, he observed to himself, he's making it easy.

"We'll certainly follow your advice," Holden said to Patsy. He let the hand linger.

Upon each of the two fresh napkins before her two customers Patsy had soon erected a modest brandy globe half-full of water heated to piping hot by the steam spigot on the espresso machine, each surmounted by a second glass, its globe gimbaled by the mouth of the first, and tilted so that its charge of calvados did not quite spill.

China, for one, was especially appreciative of this novel etiquette, for, in the meantime, his epiglottis had been encapsulated by a bolus of meth-raddled mucus of prodigious dimension, so that he feared he must soon loudly clear his throat and hawk the result out the street door or choke. But, and just in the nick of time, Holden adroitly plucked erect his snifter, its warmed elixir the brindle of a million-dollar foal, with a bouquet quite the equal to that of old money, and toasted Patsy, then China. Making haste to follow suit, China downed his entire drink.

It felt like someone had opened an emergency exit on an intercontinental flight at the polar zenith—in first class, of course! The bolus disappeared without a trace.

Patsy was staring at him, but if China's gaucherie had nonplussed Holden, it also amused him, and only the latter showed. "To a fruitful evening," he smiled, before he allowed a mere dram of calvados to flow over his lower lip. For a long moment afterward, the beam of a connoisseur suffused his features. Then he closed his eyes. "Un . . ." he opened his eyes, "believable." He touched the base of his glass to the rim of China's empty one. "Patsy?" he said, but he was looking at China. "Another, if you please."

Patsy didn't wait for him to produce the fifty bucks.

"To the delights of the unknown," Holden toasted, "and to unknown delights." He paused to study the light that appeared to slowly pierce the nostrum of his raised glass. "This is most auspicious," he pronounced, with the confidence peculiar to a man who can back up his most recently dispensed hundred dollar bill with another. Again, he took a very small sip. And this time even China siphoned off but a quarter of his calvados, as if to savor it, demonstrating, in fact, remarkable restraint.

Holden smiled broadly. "Most auspicious indeed."

China could not have agreed more. "Thank you, Holden."

"Miou Miou," Holden sweetly smiled. "Call me Miou Miou."

SEVENTEEN

QUENTIN REPLACED THE RECEIVER ON THE HOOK. AT THE FAR END OF THE hallway a man and a woman haggled in stage whispers. "I'm tellin' you nigga—" said the woman. "Fuck you, bitch," the man retorted. "Who you calling bitch, nigga?"

"Is this what I get for reading two newspapers a day, year in and year out?" Quentin asked himself.

The two people at the end of the hall exchanged money and drugs. "That's my last two dollars," said the one.

"Then I'm outta here," replied the other. "I don' wanna be hangin' 'round no broke people."

Quentin continued his train of thought as he returned to his room. "I suppose the first year or two of fascination with the human trainwreck comprises the fault of the seducer; but surely, do not the next fifty-odd years imply the complicity of the seduced?" Opening the door to his little room he caught sight of the hot plate on which smoldered the remains of two cups of instant coffee. A cockroach stood on the counter beside it, its feelers raised inquisitively toward the steam. "Such are the chambers allotted to what folk as remain in the world with the leisure to consider life's weightier propositions. A blanket as coarse as possible, a window covered with aluminum foil, a constant welter by which the most basic of human functions as well as every television channel are conducted to the sphere of contemplation by virtue of three thin walls and one each of floor and ceiling, all of it ameliorated by the odor of cigarettes combusted decades ago, mildewed carpet, dead mice, and the reek of disinfectant borne upon the updraft in the light well, if the one window isn't nailed shut. And what about the brown corona of tobacco residue on the ceiling above the bed? Even cockroaches have a peculiar odor, if there are enough of them, and not to exclude the tenacity of the odor of the rough trade lately paid off and sent away. . . ."

Anyhow, he sighed, as of today, at long last, sex is over.

And other than that resolution, or realization, or resignation, enough with the asceticism already.

Beyond the front door of Hotel Verlaine the air was rank, but this distinction was not specific to Eddy Street. No rain had fallen in northern

California for three months. With luck, only another three months would elapse before the rains returned. Six months between downpours and even the cleanest block in Pacific Heights would accumulate a stench. But the reprieve in the Tenderloin didn't last two weeks.

But Quentin's new-found freedom from the passive-aggressive oppression of the China regime gave him all the sweet tastes he could have wanted. Sure he was lonely. The liaison with China had cost him most of his friends, who could not abide the boy. Only Tipsy had hung in with him. But clearly, she now had more important salmon to poach.

Or could it be that he had leaned on her once too often? Quentin racked his brain to discover some equation of emotional interdependence between himself and his remaining friend. He put up with her drinking, for one example. Discussing books with her, for another example, was even less interesting. And yet, sit through it he did. Was this not friendship?

A perfunctory cafe on the corner of Jones and Bush served him a cappuccino and a "chocolate croissant" for $6.50. The price point, Quentin thought, as the clerk laid three dollars and fifty cents in change on the counter, allows me to tip this young fellow a magnanimous buck, thinking the while that I, too, was once a *barista*, though in those days the term was "backbar talent." One of my regulars, who drank white wine on ice morning noon and night, was smitten with me. He was also a professor of Middle Italian. He would sit in the corner, where the glass rack met the bullfight poster, and watch me work. When I'd come near he'd stage whisper,

Ogne pense vole . . .

and bat his eyelashes.

Had Quentin been rude to that old man? He hoped not. Such indiscretions can come back to haunt one's geriatric reverie.

"You know," Quentin observed, as the young man placed the pastry next to a bowl of coffee and steamed milk, "that's actually a *pain au chocolat* and not a *chocolate croissant*, as you call it. *Croissant* is French for *crescent*. Like that almond *croissant* in the display case. See? It's crescent-shaped. There's nothing crescent-shaped about this *pain au chocolat*. It looks like a wallet. Better you should call it a *portefeuille au chocolat*."

The clerk slid his eyes from the *pain au chocolat* to the almond *croissant* and back. Neither crescent- nor wallet-shaped, his eyes were slits. They looked like they'd been up all night, smoking kif and playing the nose flute. They regarded Quentin, then languidly blinked.

"For me," the clerk said, "French pastry is a potent symbol of the yoke of colonialism." He looked past Quentin. "Next in line, please."

At the door a rack displayed the *Chronicle* and *The New York Times*. PRESIDENT DEFENDS FOREIGN POLICY headlined one, PRESIDENT COUNTERS CRITICISM headlined the other.

Not today, Quentin said to himself, resolutely stepping past the rack; today, I take off.

On the sidewalk a pair of tables flanked the door into the cafe. One of them had a large planter upwind of it. Now who's the Philistine, he grumbled, as he dropped his valise beside a spindly wire chair, whose back he turned against the planter and the fog wind making a good ten knots down Bush Street. Chocolate crescent, indeed. He retrieved his morning pills from the valise. This goddamn so-called culture takes what it wants from the rest of the world, renames it by way of laying claim to it, and jettisons the rest. If I weren't getting on in years and had the money, I'd start another planet. What am I supposed to do, he fumed, just sit here eating this crap without reading a newspaper? I'll go mad. And just as he thought this thought, a folded copy of *The Wall Street Journal* dropped on the table in front of him. "May I join you, Mr. Asche?"

The man familiarly yet politely addressing him wore a costume to go along with his Russian accent. From the sidewalk up, Quentin considered well-polished black shoes, sharply creased black trousers, a lint-free Chesterfield coat over a jacket that matched the pants, and a silk shirt, all of them black. A white silk *cravat*, a homburg hat, and a furled black brolly completed the ensemble.

"The Russian consulate," Quentin said, squinting against the diffuse sunlight that backlit the man's face, "is on the corner of Scott and Pacific, about forty blocks that way." He pointed into the wind. "It features twin surveillance cameras over every door and a two-story, cruciform radio antenna on the roof. You can't miss it."

"That's true," the man smiled pleasantly. "Although I haven't been there since the celebration of the Pepsi-for-Stolichnaya deal."

Quentin frowned. "That was in the seventies of the last century."

"I was young but, insofar as I remember it," the man pushed back the brim of his hat with a single forefinger, "that was one hell of a party." He smiled thinly. "Not to mention, it was the very eyetooth of *perestroika*."

Quentin shook his head. "If you'd told me then that one day I'd miss Richard Nixon. . . ." He sighed. "How do you know my name? Have we met?"

"Good question, the first, and no to the second. But, if you don't mind, your cappuccino and *pain au chocolat* look very appetizing." He hooked the umbrella on the back of the empty chair. "Why don't you have a look at the paper while I retrieve a modest repast for myself?

Then we'll talk." He tipped his hat and slightly inclined his head. "But only if you care to talk."

Quentin gestured at the newspaper. SECRETARY OF DEFENSE BACKS TROOP BUILDUP, the headline read. NO HONOR WITHOUT SACRIFICE, ran the subhead. "I'm not one to judge a person by his reading material but— really—*The Wall Street Journal*?"

The Russian shook his head. "But of course you judge people by what they read, Mr. Asche. As for me?" The man smiled and shrugged. "I'm just trying to keep up with the Joneses."

"Maybe you should move into my hotel," Quentin suggested, as a somewhat sour reaction to his own presumption that the man was referring to the Dow Jones Company, which used to own the paper. Quentin added, "I swore I'd take today off from this nonsense," even as his eyes had begun to scan the various texts legible above the fold.

"Quite so," said the stranger. "Better you should get the news from poetry."

"See here," Quentin unreasonably expostulated, "that really is a most tedious admonition."

The man smiled as he passed through the front door of the cafe. "You're easy this morning."

Recollecting why he was ostensibly sitting there in the first place, Quentin took a bite of his chocolate crescent and chased down his pills with subdainty sips of cappuccino, which had already cooled by half. Flakes of pastry fell to the newspaper. He was quite hungry, and he had choked down his morning pills with what remained of the pastry and coffee before the stranger returned.

The Russian was followed by the opinionated clerk, who took away Quentin's empty cup and saucer and replaced them with full ones.

"*Menu redux*," the stranger pointed out. "My treat. You look a little lean." He removed his hat and set it on the table, alongside a coffee and chocolate wallet of his own.

"It's my gay aesthetic," Quentin said suspiciously. "But thank you." He fell upon the second pastry. "Indeed I am hungry," he allowed, catching a crumb fallen from his mouth and replacing it. "Although I'm not certain of the nutrition to be gained by consuming multiple chocolate wallets."

"Yes," the man said, taking a seat. "Maybe if you consumed real ones." He tore two sugar packets in half and let their contents cascade into his black coffee. Taking up a spoon he stirred the coffee and watched Quentin eat. The man's eyes were intelligent, measured, steely.

"So," Quentin said, when nearly finished with his second breakfast. "You were going to tell me how you know my name."

"No, I wasn't." The man replied pleasantly enough. "But I will if you'd like."

"I'd like."

"Charley Powell," the man said.

Quentin frowned. "What about him?"

The man shrugged. "Charley said you'd provide the answer to that."

Tipsy's admonition to mumness, phoned in not two hours ago, and which had seemed merely superstitious then, now appeared prescient. "That's interesting," Quentin said offhandedly, "if only because I've never actually met Charley Powell."

"But his sister is a close friend of yours," the man reminded him.

Quentin deflected this. "You know what, pal? If you told me you were Charley Powell himself, I wouldn't have much reason to believe you one way or the other. That's how much I know about Charley Powell."

"Oh," the man said mildly, "you know a bit more than that, Mr. Asche."

"Asche," Quentin said. "That's right." He extended his hand. "And whom do I have the pleasure of addressing?"

The man looked at the proffered hand. "Vassily," he said easily. He took the hand, not with palm across palm, as in a handshake, but thumb interlaced with thumb, and he smiled thinly. "Novgorodovich."

"Like the city," Quentin said.

"Yes."

"Son of the city of Novgorod."

"Yes," Vassily said, looking curiously at Quentin. "Do you speak Russian?"

"Only to the extent of pronouncing the names in big Russian novels like, say, *The Story of a Life*?"

The son of Novgorod's expression did not change. And he retained his grip on Quentin's thumb. This in turn prevented Quentin from retrieving from his valise his copy of the book, against which he had redeemed a trade slip at the used bookstore.

"Konstantin Paustovsky?" Quentin clarified.

"Never heard of him," Vassily replied.

Vassily might not know Charley Powell after all, Quentin concluded. So what use would there be in actually showing him the book?

"He sounds like a Jew," the Russian speculated.

Quentin had never thought about it. He had no idea. But—"So?"

"They shouldn't let Jews write novels," Vassily said.

Quentin laughed in his face.

The Russian laughed too.

Each of them laughed as if he knew something the other didn't.

"Pleased to meet you. Thanks for the coffee." Quentin waited a moment. "Now what? We thumb wrestle?"

"Sure." Vassily curled a lip. "Why not?"

Quentin made as if to shake loose the grip. The other man held firm. "I'm not your buffed gym rat," Quentin winced. "That's why not."

Vassily released the grip. "Quite so." His smile hardened. "I know."

Quentin opened and closed his hand a few times. "You seem to know a great deal. Would you like to explain this knowledge? Otherwise, since I don't wrestle, maybe we should call it a day."

"Oh," Vassily said, "it's too soon for that." He sipped his coffee and set the cup back on its saucer. "Far too soon."

"Look." A gust of wind blew the flakes of pastry off the *Wall Street Journal*. It almost took the paper, too, but Quentin slapped it back to the tabletop. LET THE DOMES BEGIN, another headline read; LIBERAL FILIBUSTER FAILS, read its subhead. "Since you know so much, you probably are aware that I'm sick, homeless, and alone. Which of them is it, exactly, that you find so attractive?"

"Charley Powell," Vassily repeated.

Quentin rolled his eyes and fixed them on Vassily. "I wouldn't know Charley Powell if he fell out of the awning," he pointed upward, "onto this table," he pointed downward. "Do you not understand?"

"His sister," said Vassily.

"His sister," Quentin stated flatly, "is a lush who doesn't make very much sense most of the time."

Vassily nodded, as if in agreement.

"Especially after dark," Quentin added gloomily.

"But he loves her," Vassily replied. "Or thinks he does. At any rate, she's all he has. And she loves him." Vassily opened a hand and studied its palm. "Or thinks she does."

Quentin took up his coffee spoon, idly parted the foam atop what was left of his cappuccino, and set it down again. "Why are you bothering to know these details about two people who don't know you?"

"Which two people?"

"Which two people? Why—Charley and Tipsy—Teresa—Powell."

"It's true that I don't know Teresa," Vassily said. "But Charley, I do know."

Quentin eyed Vassily. "You know Charley?"

Vassily showed Quentin the back of his left hand. "Pinky finger: gone." With a curious dexterity, he curled that finger out of sight. With the other hand he removed his Homburg, revealing a bald head, and passed the theoretically maimed hand over it. "Bald—like me." He replaced the hat and pointed at his left forearm. "No tattoos." Vassily smiled without humor. "Unlike me."

"Well," Quentin said slowly, "you certainly know more about him than I do. It sounds like you know more about him than his sister does, too."

Vassily replaced his hat and leaned over the table. "Charley's coming to San Francisco," he said matter-of-factly.

Quentin said nothing, but he felt certain that Vassily could read this truth in his eyes. He didn't bother to deny it. "I've heard that his visit has been postponed or canceled. But, either way, what of it?"

Vassily sat back in his chair. "Charley is my friend. He did a big favor for me once. In Florida."

"Yes? What was that?"

"It's not important."

"It's not? You came all the way from Florida for something unimportant?"

Vassily shrugged. "Everybody wants an excuse to visit San Francisco."

"Do I assume that you were in prison with him?"

Vassily said nothing.

"So what are you telling me? That you've come to California to return the favor?"

"Exactly," Vassily said. "To return the favor."

"So what's that to do with me?"

Vassily tilted his head to one side, considered Quentin, and then tilted it to the other side and considered him some more. At length he said, "Very little, one hopes."

This made Quentin uneasy.

The Russian stood up. "Sincerely." He fished a black leather passport wallet from the inner breast pocket of his Chesterfield and, making no attempt to conceal the fact that it contained many banknotes, he selected a twenty and a business card and dropped them on the table. "I was a waiter for a while," he said, setting his saucer atop the twenty, "in Brighton Beach, when I first came to this country. If you would see that the young man receives this before you leave? I've enjoyed our little breakfast, Mr. Asche. If you hear from Charley, please pass him my card. Or, if you like, give me a ring yourself. In fact, if you would take the trouble to call me without letting Charley know anything about it, I could surprise him. That would be fun for us both."

I wonder, Quentin thought to himself, what Novgorodovich considers fun.

"I'd be only too happy to make it worth your while."

It was only then, as the Russian was replacing the wallet into his jacket, that Quentin noticed the tattoo. It was a teardrop, in black ink, and it had been needled into the fold of skin between thumb and forefinger of the Russian's right hand.

So, Quentin thought to himself. If I were possessed of a similar tattoo, our teardrops would have kissed, so to speak, as a result of that curious handshake.

The Russian retrieved his umbrella. Quentin took up the business card.

Vassily Novgorodovich
PetroPozhirat, LLC
Moscow, London, Havana
Beverly Hills, Guandong, Caracas
33-01-46-09-88-88

That's almost certainly a Paris phone number, Quentin thought to himself, yet the city isn't named. "What," he said aloud to the card, "no email?"

Vassily smiled. "Too insecure."

Quentin bowed the card between thumb and forefinger. "How grateful?" he asked abruptly.

Vassily blinked.

"Did you hear me?"

"I heard you."

"Well? Charley shows up. I call you. What's it worth?"

Without another word, Vassily hooked the handle of the umbrella over his left arm and retrieved the wallet. His thumb pulled the corners of bills over the tips of its adjacent fingers with practiced celerity and when finished the Russian slipped the wallet back into the depths of the Chesterfield with the one hand while the other slipped one edge of a thickness of bills into the little chrome coil that held the cafe's laminated menu and wine list, on the table, hard by Quentin's elbow. The uncaptured edges of the banknotes fluttered in the breeze.

"A retainer, Mr. Asche." Vassily unhooked the umbrella from his left elbow.

"And after the call?"

"I'll double it."

"What if he doesn't show? After all, it's been years since he and his sister last met. What if he remembers that they both must like it that way?"

"This may be his last chance to see her," Vassily said.

"How is that, exactly?"

"Prison was hard on him." Vassily sucked a sympathetic tooth. "His whole life has been hard on him. His health has suffered. His liver is compromised."

Quentin said nothing.

"The shock of seeing his old friend Novgorodovich will do him good. And when Charley sees what is coming to him because of me, because of what he once did for me, well . . ." Vassily spread his hands and smiled. "Maybe it will do him two worlds of good. Maybe he doesn't have to work so much anymore. Maybe he can stay in San Francisco and take care of his sister." Vassily smiled.

"Change his life, you mean?"

"Both their lives. For good." Vassily nodded at the business card. "That telephone number rings anywhere in the world. Except Patagonia."

"Patagonia . . ." Quentin repeated thoughtfully.

"An excellent provider." Vassily raised the umbrella. "Unfortunately, it's not publicly traded." As if by magic, a taxi pulled to the curb. The Russian tipped his hat. "I look forward to hearing from you, Mr. Asche."

The Russian opened the curbside door. Crisply displayed in bright red LEDs, the fare on the meter was one hundred and twelve dollars.

That's a busy cab, Quentin thought.

The door closed. The taxi motored up the hill and took a right on Taylor.

Quentin counted hundred dollar bills. They were crisp, and there were twenty of them.

He'd just sold Tipsy's brother to a total stranger for two thousand dollars.

He didn't even need the money.

He folded the bills in the middle and began to turn their thickness end for end, between his thumb and forefinger and the tabletop.

At length, when his eyes refocused from a distant third-story architrave, he saw that the Russian had forgotten his newspaper.

No, he said to himself, as he dropped the money and the Russian's business card into the side pocket of his jacket, today I am not reading a goddamn newspaper.

EIGHTEEN

WHEN CHINA JONES RETURNED TO THE DE HARO STREET COTTAGE AT 3:30 in the morning, Pacific Standard Time, he walked right past the For Sale sign posted on a stake at the foot of the sixty-nine wooden steps.

True, it was still dark.

Having achieved the top of the steps, however, he could hardly have missed the Notice to Vacate Premises by Order of the Sheriff of the City and County of San Francisco. But he might as well have. He punched his key right through the lower right hand corner of it, and penetrated the lock.

It takes quite a few glasses of calvados to get on top of three grams of blow especially, good blow. Fortunately, that well-groomed poofster in the cashmere Chesterfield had been willing to stand China all the calvados he wanted, at fifty bucks a pour, so long as China went home with him afterwards and wasn't too metabolically awry to stay awake while the guy did his thing, and asking all kinds of irrelevant questions the while, chattering quite like a proper blow monkey himself, and China, plied with more than his share of the eight-ball of veterinary grade cocaine, could hardly get a word in edgewise—China snapped his fingers—he, China, was right on top of just about everything, and the client did his part to ensure this by buying the rest of the bottle. At five hundred dollars, Patsy had cut him quite the deal. China noticed that the snap of his fingers conveyed little actual snap—in fact, it had been inaudible. He hadn't felt it, either. But, as with almost everything else in his life, he didn't wonder about it. He had his priorities. And a nice home it had been, too, high atop Nob hill with a wall of windows overlooking the roof of Grace Cathedral, not to mention a sound-proof room full of toys nobody under twenty-one should ever be allowed to know about, let alone to look at. Make it eighteen. Well, China reconsidered, speaking as a former prodigy, make it sixteen. Not the front door of the cathedral, mind you, but the roof. Gargoyles and spires and tiles the color of post-vampirized complexions in bad light, which is to say, ashen by design, cinereous by proclivity. He snapped his fingers again. How come no audio? Was he that fucked up? Don't push it. Don't ask, don't tell, don mask, do swell. Take responsibility for your excesses. He'd often been loaded sufficiently to delay the auditory coordination between a given sound and his conscious perception of it, but he'd never been sufficiently loaded to block audio reception altogether. Well, there's always hope. Or had he? He frowned. Does coke-induced tinnitus block all audio input up to a certain volume? Or just some of it? He couldn't remember. Maybe he never knew. He could hear the tinnitus, 5000 hertz and maybe 40 decibels—pretty loud. Plus several other frequencies, none of them harmonic. Loud to the exclusion of nocturnal fog susurration among eucalyptus leaves, a key turning in a lock, the snap of thumb and forefinger. He cocked his wrist and poised one finger atop the thumb. Had he? Did it? More to the point, was he? Temporarily deaf that is? That is, that is, is? He studied the setup. The cuticles were discolored. Did he really want to know? He opened the hand. Better not. He uncocked the wrist. The keys fell to the floor. Home anyway. He lowered the hand and looked at the keys. Soundless impact. Footfall on the moon. Spooky keys. Spookeys. He skirted the keys gingerly. Home, anyway. He glanced over his shoulder. Pick up those gleaming-in-the-gloom suckers later. On the way out. On the Way Out.

Something special there is about a trick who isn't worried about the money, even if there are other issues, like total absence of post-fellatio remorse for example; like here's an extra hunnie for barebacking; like here's five hunnies for letting me tie you up; like don't worry about the whip, it's a small one; Miou Miou the Inquisitor, China the quizzed; like I must have passed out, because the next thing I know, it's like, don't let the door spank those tight little buns on their way out, Honey. Different kind of honey. What's the Spanish for honey? *Miel*; and the Spanish for adios is *adiós*.

"Oh, Daddy," China remembered himself as suggesting, "don't you want me to stay over?" He pointed at the window. "We could attend early Mass." What he was really thinking was he'd never get a cab at that hour. But what he said was, "Don't you just love it when Monsignor lays that cool wafer on your hot tongue?"

Miou Miou, who had exchanged his beautifully tailored ensemble for a kimono and an ascot beneath which he sported fuchsia polyvinyl chloride lederhosen with appropriate zippers, blue nylon suspenders embroidered with little white anchors curlicued with rope, a chrome dog collar, and a cattle prod in a belt holster—started laughing and couldn't stop. His face turned red, he started to cough but, still, he couldn't stop laughing. Finally he had exhaled a plume of Turkish tobacco smoke, extra-fragrant because cut with tarball, toward the ceiling, wiped the smile off his face, asked China what part of *Adiós* he didn't understand. It means *goodbye, you are out of here, go with God, pick your deity, think of it, glamourpuss*, more laughter, *as a school night*, contemptuous laughter, *a rough trade-school night*.

China considered his mental hologram of the apartment. Deep-cushioned chairs and two divans upholstered in striped silk, a well-stocked bar, Dalidá's smokiest on the sound system, ruby velour drapes framing two floor-to-ceiling window walls, it was a corner unit, carpet to die for or face down in, hand-blown glassware on display in beveled glass cabinets, a fourth wall of books, among them two leather-bound meters of a lasciviously illustrated *Oeuvres* of the Marquis de Sade. China had none but the vaguest notion of the author, but lascivious he understood. The edition was impressive. He would have bet all those old bindings smelled good, too, but by then his sense of smell was totally AWOL. Despite forty-five minutes of methodical sex, not a hair of the client's expensive coiffure looked out of place. It wasn't a rug, either, as China had ascertained by palpation. What brand of mousse could it be?

I could choke this guy in the midst of hot sex, China had mused to himself, and live here for a month before anybody became the wiser. But, he sighed, that would be murder. And for what? Mere luxury beyond a mere mortal's mere imagination?

Plus, if the client's mother were still alive, she would be calling every day.

The client had ushered China towards the front door with his cigarette hand, palm up. The gesture appeared quite gracious and, suddenly, China found himself in the hall with the apartment door closed behind him. The building was so quiet, its paneling so opulent, its carpeting so thick, China barely heard his own footsteps as he failed to walk a straight line down the corridor to the elevator. Even the tinnitus seemed muffled. The buttons were old, a black ceramic pair vertically stacked in a brass escutcheon. Why not me? he rhetorically asked, pushing the Down button. As the car soughed and clacked its way up the shaft to meet him China noticed a security nacelle, a black hemisphere about four inches across. It glowered down at him from atop the gilt frame enclosing the brightly buffed brass arrow, which tracked the elevator's progress through a semicircular arc—L, G1, G2, 2, 3, 4, 5, 6, 7, 8, PH: that's us. The car's doors split open, silent as a bivalve. China dispensed a little salutatory wave toward the security camera, entered the car, and it wasn't until after the doors closed that he realized that he was so high both his ears were ringing, not just the one, in multiple frequencies, too, and he had cottonmouth sufficient to desiccate a rain forest. He touched the seam of his back pocket, then cannily stole a glance from beneath the ledge of his sagittal crest at one and another corner of the elevator, where its walls met its ceiling. He saw no camera, but that didn't mean there wasn't one, nor did it mean Security wouldn't be waiting for him downstairs anyway. He pressed his ass against the wall. He could feel it. The bindle of meth was extant. He'd managed to get through a date without sharing his personal stash with the client.

They'd exhausted the client's own bindle, guy wanted some more, fuck him, he had the money, he could buy it himself. But if China were going to sleep before noon he would need some booze or downers.

Halfway down the nine stories China impulsively depressed the button marked PH. Could a satisfied client refuse him the dregs of a lousy bottle of calvados? The machine did not respond. Instead it deposited him on floor one, where its door opened onto the narrow and oppressively bright art deco entrance lobby. China looked at his own reflection in a floor-to-ceiling mirror directly across the hall from the elevator. Not particularly flattering. He punched the PH again. Again, nothing happened. He tried the button that closed the doors. Nothing. He tried the button for the garage. No response. This elevator, he realized, would yield not to a passenger's whimsy, but to a code or a key. How discerning. How discrete. How secure. How exclusive. How excluding. How lonely the loneliness of the nocturnal blow monkey.

The entrance lobby was deserted. The two other doors that opened onto it, from a bar/restaurant and a janitor's closet, were locked. The elevator doors remained open. Only the street door yielded to his touch. He passed through it. A brass mechanism closed it on his heels with efficient, silent dignity, and locked the rough trade into the night.

He stood in the entry of the cottage, unable to recall how he got there. He liked to think of it as his home, though he was rarely there anymore, and though it was less and less habitable, and, as it were, he watched himself watch himself, as he denied that some part of him was denying the import of the Sheriff's notice permission to sink in.

Quentin had been gone for well over a month with no contact. Maybe it had been two months. Truth be told, China had made no attempt to contact him. The phone had been disconnected. Portentous notices had arrived concerning it and water, garbage, gas, electricity, their unopened envelopes neatly swept against the baseboard by the lower rail of the front door. The angle of repose possesses a certain inevitability. China ignored them in much the same way as he had ignored gas gauge, water temperature, oil light, registration renewal, insurance premiums, parking tickets, and unusual noises before the Datsun broke down completely. And then it turned out that Quentin had long since transferred the title to him, to China! Now he'd have to get a whole bunch of stuff square with the DMV before he could legally own another car. Either that, or manufacture a new identity. And so what? China had seen all these speedbumps before. He liked that term. Speedbumps at the other end of the straw of life.

All he did anyway when he was home was bathe and watch television. No doubt the water and electricity departments would have their say in that. Whatever. His hair wanted 100 strokes before he went to sleep. He flossed meticulously. There were manicures and pedicures to be self-administered, because he no longer had the wherewithal to purchase professional attention. There was a machine hooked up to the TV which enabled him to stay current with a couple of soaps and a so-called reality show he couldn't bear to miss, about a gay hustler trying to cope with the aftermath of Hurricane Katrina, as well as the latest movies here and there on the schedule. But then, after several unopened notices, the cable service had been disconnected, too.

Had he told Quentin he'd been fired? That he'd spent what little money he had from his severance check on cocaine? Until, when he was down to tens and twenties, he blew them on speed on account of it's better value for the dollar?

No matter. Unemployment had finally kicked in, he had thirteen months to go, and, because nobody could afford to pay rent in San Francisco while holding these kinds of jobs, inter-office gofer gigs were a dime a dozen. China smiled his best post-trick smile. Paying rent in San Francisco was not his problem. His brow furrowed. Or was it?

He used to spend a lot of time studying his face in the bathroom mirror, shaving carefully, mugging, tweezing eyebrows and nostrils, tracking a wrinkle or two, particularly the so-called crow's feet that opened from the back corner of each eye like two miniature coral fans. After a while all of Quentin's and even his own cosmetics and beauty products had been exhausted. The bathroom trash can was overflowing with empty tubes and vials and unguent bottles. But since the trash can and recycling bin at the foot of the sixty-nine steps were overflowing because the scavenger no longer picked them up, what use would it have been to take them out anyway? He had long since switched out the smaller bathroom trash can with the larger one under the kitchen sink.

Then he'd run out of toilet paper. Quentin had taken all the books. Which left the magazines. Which would eventually clog the waste line. Ask me if I care. Not enough traction either.

The laugh track of whatever sitcom crackled around the rooms, day or night, when China was around. Too loud, always too loud, it wasn't the same as when Quentin was upstairs to be annoyed by it, but, in point of simple fact, China was too stoned to turn it down. No, that wasn't it. The real reason was that China was too depressed to turn it down—that's right—too depressed. The laugh tracks kept him company. If he ever got a cat he would call it Laugh Track. If it was stupid he'd call it Half Track. Ah haha. Now he was too depressed to turn one on, even if he could. He loved his routines, he needed his routines, and his routines were coming apart. And what difference did it make? There was nobody there for it to bother but him, and he could care less one way or the other. It was all the same to him. He could turn a laugh track on or off in his head anyway, anytime, just like that. Just as if he had some kind of mental remote up there, click and the sound was muted, or greatly diminished, and he could think for hours, undisturbed, with car commercials and talk shows and football games and braying celebrity pundits—it made no difference to him. His concentration was that great. So focused was his mind on—nothing. The Void. Embrace the totally carved city block. Visualize the empty parking space. Harmonize your tinnitus. Follow the ball that never bounces.

Wide awake, he spent fifteen minutes searching both floors of the house for an unidentified hum that ultimately eluded him.

He had already reread all of the glamour, movie, gossip, and celebrity magazines in the cottage, preparatory to stacking them on the floor next to the toilet, in anticipation of the final frontier. Except for the ones that had really interesting articles, which he would clip when he could concentrate long enough to find the scissors, and eventually went upstairs to raid Quentin's bookshelves—only to find them completely empty. But wait: he already knew that. Just checking. In the time he'd been downstairs, looking for the hum, he'd forgotten the books were gone. Quentin's clothes were gone, too, which China had once freely borrowed. Quentin's newer clothes fit China rather well. In fact—he touched it without looking at it—this might once have been Quentin's belt. No way, it's too chic. But too bad, he thought idly, standing at the bathroom door, those magazines are all pretty much alike. Some of the articles, though, especially the deeply researched ones about any royal family, Princess Grace, for one outstanding example—the rest of those poor Grimaldis, for another—are really good. My god, the life they live or lived. The glamour, the tragedy. . . . And not a faggot among them, by all accounts. Satellite faggots, though. Oh yes, your quality people have your satellite faggots. . . .

Suddenly and copiously, his nose began to bleed. He'd thought it was snot, but blood is thinner than snot. As a rule, China thought, as he watched the water—he blinked: hadn't they turned off the water? Evidently not. But it was cold. That's right. They turned off the gas but not the water—as it diluted the red to pink.

That bitch Quentin was always on my ass to improve my mind, always recommending this or that book to read, and now that I have the time to read he's cleaned out all the books. What a hypocrite. He probably sold them to support a drug habit I didn't even know about, some shit he took to keep him from pissing his pants. These old queens will have their secrets. He abruptly experienced a pellucid recollection of the man in the lederhosen. Laughing at something, wielding that truncheon. What was his name. . . . Can't remember. Got away. Probably remember it at three o'clock . . . this afternoon. China suddenly felt confused, or stupid, even. And cold. What's that about? And what's so funny? What . . . Aloud China test-drove a laugh, and he was startled, about halfway through to suddenly hear it. So he stopped laughing. Always too loud, China's laugh was never appropriate or appreciated or contagious and, always, betrayed a hysteria perilously close to the surface of his shoal personality, no less dreadful than the screech of tires behind you in a crosswalk, this laugh was perhaps his biggest social weakness—if you didn't count his intelligence and level of education and drug habits and vanity and so forth. China's jaw tightened. Occasionally he let slip a risible shriek in a bar where they didn't know him too well. It happened in that one on 18th Street, Bareback Mountain, it's called, where many faggots gather to watch Monday Night Football. Capital letters, that's right. Bit of a clubby group, if you're asking China. Quite the shrill fan base however, if you're asking people in marketing. Quasi-religious, really, like elevating the host only televisual and loud, all the way though football season which, these days, runs from July to February. Or . . . Isn't it through March, now? Some people say I'm stupid, but I say some people don't have a life. A lot of older men cruise the scene for jocks—I got real estate, you got a big dick, let's get together and transactionally analyze that. In fact there's usually a lot more old Nellies in there than jocks, so it's easy pickings for somebody of China's build and looks. . . . Used to be, anyway. Why doesn't this bleeding stop. . . . Did I take aspirin recently? But one Monday night China was in there and he'd snorted a little gak and downed a couple brandies and got himself caught up in the game unawares. There was a mark sitting one stool over, obviously a little uncomfortable and surreptitiously eyeing the talent around the place—such talent as there was to be discerned amongst the other customers who were mostly carbon copies of the mark—and carbon copies is a most appropriate image, given their average age, digital copies being an appropriately modernized figure of speech to describe the five or six hustlers up and down the bar more or less interchangeable with China himself. He'd long since discerned that the mark's excitement favored the team wearing the red and blue uniforms, and as he thought this thought about the carbon and, skipping xerox, digi- techno- generation on-beyond-zed gap, a red and blue jersey intercepted a pass meant for a chartreuse and gold jersey and—well, out it slipped, that shrill bray that sounded like a car accident, and the mark, who heretofore had looked just about prime to pick up the tab on the next drink China had already ordered over his shoulder, blanched, shook his head, excused himself to the toilet (two toilets back there, both labeled MEN), never came back, and China had to pay for his own drink. Ten minutes later he noticed his mark working another corner of the room, speaking and gesticulating animatedly. China hadn't even turned around to check out the source of the general hilarity that erupted into the momentary silence that had engulfed him. He knew it was aimed at him, and his cheeks burned. . . .

So he comes home to an eviction notice. Pesky pesky memory node, somehow cycled around it again. Something else to ignore, for sure, but China was no longer loaded enough to ignore this additional little fact of life as it got under his skin and ran riot. Otherwise he'd suppress the real impetus of whatever feelings generated, his highly-evolved excuse machine would kick in and hatch various scenarios, like him standing before a judge saying "Not tonight, honey, I have a headache 'cause I ran out of Percocets," or, "Because the deputy here impounded my stash" and so forth. Lame lame lame. Which would then piss him off of course, but, properly set up, the next moment he'd totally forget what pissed him off in the first place. It's good policy to be pissed off, but every now and again somebody will ask you why you're pissed off. You can tell them it's none of their business, but what if they're into real estate? But there's little real estate sufficient to compensate for this vague sense of foreboding hovering in some disused part of the back of his head, which was most of the back of his head, and therefore capacious, and certainly adequate to contain entire caravans of phantom forebodings, free-floating neuroses, polyvalent anxieties, with plenty of uninhibited blackness left over, and all of it with a bottomless appetite for drugs, as insatiable as a developing country's appetite for petroleum.

As for the front of his head, the bleeding had stopped. Christ, that took long enough. He rinsed his hands and turned off the ever-cold water. It's a wonder I have any blood left at all. Wasn't there something I was supposed to be doing? Scissors? Asswipe? Princess Diana? Sourceless hum? He looked up. Gone. He blinked. Job, maybe? Oh yes, the job, maybe. And come to think of it, there was that job to be showing up for, at nine o'clock. Although he had the place so wired he could get there at ten and by eleven and he'd have everything done that needed to be done by lunchtime. . . . The problem was to get there by lunchtime. But wait, wait—he'd been fired! A not-so-tiny *frisson* of panic darted from the back of his head all the way to the front. All fucked up and no place to go—again! Can I somehow blame this on 9/11? Maybe that's what the hum is about. A little reminder. Something along the lines of, get all of those damned rubber dinosaurs out of your locker in the mail center and hand over your security badge. He frowned at the kitchen window. Something about the portrait reflected there caused him to dismiss what he was trying to remember as unimportant in the greater scheme of things. He could understand that he could see the lights of the city as if through the image of his face: but, still, did this image have to look so ghastly? Is it the hair? He cautiously turned his head to one side.

But he didn't want to tough it out. Not just now. Not this minute. So he didn't.

His friend Nikki the tranny who styled wigs for oh, you wouldn't believe the socialites and celebrities and entertainers who send Nikki their wigs—Nikki never got going until ten or eleven. Of course Nikki runs her own business and always has time to watch daytime television, just beyond the wig. A girl has to keep up with this stuff. *Exactly*. Daytime television is all about wigs. *How true*. It's hard to believe it's about anything else. *Darling, wigs rule. . . .*

So maybe after a few drinks China would snort two reeealely long lines and, say, maybe, say, maybe trash Quentin's house. That's it. Pure rage. He only takes this stuff out on the inanimate, on other people's stuff you understand. Never on his own stuff, and never other people *per se*. Well, okay, there's verbal abuse—come on, you old queen, get it up! I'm waiting! Flex it! But the sun's coming up! Your surgery looks terrible no matter what time of day it is. How do you feature that? But not physical abuse. Never. China is gentle like that. And there's a way of looking at his relationship with Quentin—and they did have a relationship, make no mistake about that; Quentin was the only person China had met in a long time willing to take him seriously—as a person, China said to the face in the window, which seemed to be watching him. You could consider that China deliberately torpedoed Quentin's every intention as a sure-fire way to hurt, not Quentin, but China himself. Self-defeating. Counter-productive. Passive aggressive, one might say, toward oneself. A sad case. Appalling really. It's because I never had the money to see a shrink. No, darling, wait a minute. There you go again. It's because you never took your own money and spent it on a shrink. Did not Quentin himself, not two years ago, back when he was still a high-flying real estate broker, put you on an allowance with the proposition that you spend a hundred of it a week or whatever it cost for an hour with a good shrink of your own choosing, an elective selection he left up to you, one he trusted you to make by way of encouraging you to take on a little responsibility for yourself?

Well, yes, it was back when he was a high-flying real estate broker, but it was also back when he thought I was worth the trouble.

I know where I can get two, two and a half grams for a hundred bucks, China said to the window, without moving his lips. I need a barstool in here, he thought, so I can sit and watch the mirror I mean window and lean over and snort dope and pour myself a drink without standing up all the time. He tried to remember the last time he'd been home. Probably Thursday night. He'd made it into work Friday morning, got fired, and

now it was Monday of next month. Or was it the following Friday. Still no
leads on a new pad, somebody who needs a roommate, a fuck buddy, a
concubine, a tweezer of nose-hair. Hey, sure, put a roof over my head, of
course I'll tweeze your nose hair. Happily. No problem. Try me. Nikki
acted like she hadn't even heard the question. He knew better than to try
to get a job delivering dope. Or thought he did. Tricky without a car.
Anyway, the only dope delivery system he really understood was a soda
straw, or the bottom half of a ball point pen, or a snapped-off car antenna,
or a rolled up hundred dollar bill, although it had been a queen's true age
since he'd held on to one of those latter delivery systems long enough to
use it for delivery. A single is more like it. A hundred dollar bill, he thought
wistfully. . . . Do queens really live to be so old as that? Wait a minute.

Wait a minute. What the fuck am I thinking? He dipped two fingers
into the watch pocket of the designer jeans he'd scored in a thrift shop on
Market Street and—voilà! A C-note! And a bit o' bindle right behind it!
God is great! The client had tipped him before showing him the door!
How could he have forgotten this? Well, hell, they always tipped, for one
thing. If it's one thing China-boy knows how to do, it's get tipped. Never
fails. There's a special place on every circumcision! But not that often is it
a hundred dollar bill. He smiled with toothsome satisfaction as he rolled
the bill perpendicular to its length into a tight little tube of uncounterfeit-
ed parchment. What a life. If somebody managed to figure out a way to
make casual sex between consenting adults disappear, little faggots like
me and that Nob Hill client would re-invent it before you could say
three-day weekend. China hoovered two immense lines, unrolled the bill
and licked it clean. Centilingus, Quentin had disdainfully called it. China
had made him spell it out for him. People laughed when he repeated it.
Later Quentin came up with centillatio, then shortened it to C-llatio.
China made him write it down. People laughed when he repeated it. You
should write for television, he told Quentin. So that I, Quentin had archly asked, might find fulfillment in life? Over-the-hill bitch. He'd heard
somewhere that sixty percent of the hundred dollar bills in circulation in
the United States bear detectable traces of cocaine. The fucking feds
probably can't tell the difference between cocaine and methamphetamine. Or maybe that accounts for the other forty percent, and they're
being coy with the statistic. You can sure tell the difference when you
snort it, though. Maybe the feds will give him a job. Federal Shit
Detector. Makes one think that, if the feds somehow figured out a way to
make cocaine disappear overnight, people like China Jones would re-
invent it faster than you can say In God We Trust. Sister, China thought,
as his laryngealpharynx vibrated like a reed in a bass saxophone, that

would be something. A real accomplishment. A contributor to the history
of mankind like Lindbergh, say, or Pasteur, or George W. Bush. A succulent raisin in the unleavened bread of life. A plot device, in—face it—the
unexamined plotlessness of my own post-modern narrative. A clothesline
strung between tenements, teeming with plot devices hung out to dry.
Blow Reduxer, it could say on my tombstone. Or just plain *Blowmo erec-
tus*. *Ass to ash*. *Centilinguist*. Incised on a marble cenotaph, tomb of the
missing hundred dollar bill, white as pure veterinary blow, carved to
resemble so many bricks of cocaine stacked in a federal evidence locker.
Talk about your fulfillment late in life!

Late? He glanced over his shoulder at a battery-powered clock radio
beside the sofa bed. Late? Crimson numerals fresh as nose blood, carry
the two . . . No time whatsoever had passed.

Soon, however, it will be six o'clock, China said to the clock radio, but
addressing without speaking aloud or at least without hearing himself
address the diaphanating portrait in the dark window, which he now
turned to face in the mirror, window, he meant window. The face's lower
jaw had gone missing, making it appear, though China did not know the
word, like a calvarium, a skull without a jaw, the kind you keep hard by
your lucubration as a candle stand. He touched two fingertips to the puffiness visible below his left eye and felt nothing. Is the picture coming
down from the attic? He glanced down at the fingers. The hundred dollar bill was gone. He looked at his other hand. It was empty, too. Funny,
he giggled, he hadn't noticed a string. He looked at the window. Blood
streaked the reflected face. He looked at his hands. Why had he not
noticed the string attached to the c-note? A string that led all the way back
to the penthouse? And the bindle, too? Monofilament, maybe? He flicked
his tongue at the blood at the corner of his mouth. Whoa. The tongue in
the reflection was forked. It can't—. Wait. Don't try that again.

Half an hour. Half an hour to six, when the liquor stores will open, even
if it's Sunday. Thank god for California.

But ghosts don't need liquor. Ghosts don't need money, either.
Genuflect at the readyteller, that this may be so. There is a rumor, however, going all the way back to *The Odyssey*, that ghosts do need blood.

Okay, stay calm, so now China needs blood. But so, see, he has blood.
Blood running down his reflection. Blood on demand. Though the pressure is diminishing, pulse has become flow has become seepage.

The bindle was still there though. He had already checked. Don't jinx
things by checking again. He'd take it to hell with him. Gak in hell: redundant? If things got too real, he'd trade it for blood.

NINETEEN

THE ENERGY IN THE HALL WAS AS PALPABLE AS IT WAS AUDIBLE.

Officer Few's nerves were already plenty wracked. He'd unexpectedly blundered into a new security gate at the employee's entrance. Normally he'd have been informed. Normally, he might well have been manning the metal detector, or a wand, himself, rather than roaming the lecture hall in a rent-a-cop uniform with Mace, a pair of handcuffs, his media watch, and Tipsy Powell, his newly uniformed guest.

They'd never put him on a strip search team. Not yet, anyway. He suppressed the imaginative clusterfuck of himself and Tipsy assigned to separate strip-search teams.

The whole thing had been Protone's idea, the bastard. What skin was it off his nose? While Few and Tipsy were playing with fire in a drought-blighted briar patch, Protone was sitting on the couch in his rented garage with a beer in one hand and his dick in the other.

As backup, few had an eight-gigabyte media pen mixed in with the various writing implements in the breast pocket of his uniform. But if they caught him with either one of these toys, bad results would ensue, and the boys upstairs would know from nothing.

Visual deterrent, they call it. Just a guy in a uniform standing around would keep people in line, particularly these people, unless they were drinking. Entitled people, when they were drinking, were worse than fraternity boys, and way worse than bikers.

The gavel struck the podium.

"Oscar," Tipsy stage-whispered. "Who is that weird fuck up there?"

"Anybody looks you in the eye," Few hissed, "just let your eyes slide right off him, like you're perfectly confident he don't have the balls to pick a fight."

"Fight?" Tipsy hissed back. "These people don't—"

"Has anybody ever remarked how good you look in a uniform?"

"Really? You think—"

"Hey, Frank," Few abruptly addressed a guy in a cheap suit, who appeared out of the crowd. "Everything cool?"

Frank pointed. "What happened, you get the bud implanted?"

"Uh, no," Few replied. He fumbled in his breast pocket, a thing he

hated to do. If and when he or anybody else reviewed the recording, the
audio would be predictably sandblasted. "I'm running a little late, here.
That new checkpoint—"

"Hey," Frank agreed, "I told them to text you guys."

"Yo," Few said, "that might be it. I'm switching providers."

As Few hastily screwed the little bud into his left ear, Frank adroitly
changed the subject. "Who's the babe?"

As Tipsy's complexion flared, Few jumped in. "Officer Powell, a
high-school buddy from Park Station. Her kid's got a problem, she
needs the OT."

"Sorry about the kid," Frank lied unctuously. If a fly were to land on
this guy's face, Tipsy thought to herself, it would slide right off it.

"Yeah," Few agreed.

"Your old man can't cover the three of you?" Frank asked, as if to
impugn a husband's virility by way of hitting on his wife.

"Ahm," Tipsy replied, usurping her temper with a glance at Oscar, "he's
doing two shifts for the Petaluma PD as it is, and he was lucky to get the
duty. They've got the budget problems too. . . ."

"Mm," Frank assented.

Oscar beamed.

". . . There's two other kids, the insurance is balking at covering the sick
one. . . ."

"No way you got three kids," Frank said.

"The one is Dan's by his first marriage. So we took out a second on the
house. . . ."

Oscar raised an alarmed eyebrow.

"MS," Tipsy elaborated, unfazed. "They claim we must have known
when we expanded the coverage."

The gavel struck closer to the microphone.

"That's tough," Frank lied.

"Yeah," Oscar agreed.

"So," Tipsy said, "Oscar, here, is doing me a solid."

"Oscar's a good man," Frank chucked Oscar on the shoulder. It was as
much as to say Keep it up, Oscar, you'll get laid yet. Bad for the audio,
Oscar was thinking. I should jam this chucklehead's earbud up his urethra
for him, Tipsy was thinking.

"Order in the hall. Order . . ."

Oscar had started the pen and the watch before he entered the hall,
before he'd cleared security, so nobody would see him messing with buttons. But he shot his cuff anyway. One minute after eight. "They do like
to go off on time," he said.

"Speaking of which . . ." Frank said, and he abruptly took his leave.

"That's . . ." Tipsy said.

"Our boss," Oscar said.

The lights dimmed.

"Great," Tipsy said.

"Yup," Oscar agreed. "Especially if he doesn't check with Payroll."

"Tonight's topic: The Cycle of Desacralization."

Unbelievable, thought Few.

The what? thought Tipsy.

The speaker was a woman in a big hat with a dahlia on it. "Nature," she began, "it was first held sacred by Paleolithic man. Witness the exquisite paintings on the walls of Lascaux."

Several slides, stored and presented by computer.

"Nature imposed and supplied all things—food, wonder, fear, thunder, water, fire, thrills and terror, life and light, death and darkness. By mankind, nature was worshiped and defied, carnalized and spiritualized."

Several slides. A lava flow, a full moon, waves of sand dunes, the jaws of a spider.

Being the Rudy Gelder of sub rosa audio, Few leaned back against a wall with his hands folded in front of him, at parade rest, immobile, the better not to rustle the dry goods.

"At first, religion sacralized nature, too."

That's true, Tipsy thought to herself, as Frank walked by, going the other way, with a wink.

Slides of a reindeer headdress, eagle feathers, a golden calf, a mastodon hunt.

"After eons," continued the speaker, "this gave way to the desacralization of nature by the self-aggrandizement of its main sacralizer, religion. The sacralizer usurped the sacred to itself, and itself became sacred."

Irish dolmens, Stonehenge, St. Peter's basilica.

"Interestingly, Stonehenge, a site of worship thought to be at least five thousand years old, also is of great astronomical interest. Outside of tools used for hunt and harvest, we see here an interesting first example of a new sacralization, that of technology."

Several slides of Stonehenge in apposition to solstice sunrises, equinoctial sunsets, and phases of the moon.

"The pyramids likewise, whose builders made use of a vast number of employees, as we might term them, along with an equally vast technology, now mostly lost to us."

Slides of Cheops and the Valley of Kings.

Oh, wow, Tipsy realized. That's exactly the same view of a tomb entrance that Charley sent me on a postcard a hundred fucking years ago. . . .

Sarcophagi, hieroglyphs. "Engineers became legendary, mythical, godlike. Why? Because they implement and augment technology." The step pyramid at Saqqara. "Here's a fine example. We find Imhotep—who designed this structure for King Neterikeht, around the turn of the twenty-sixth century B.C., and who is widely regarded as the first architect—and, for those of you who think Frank Lloyd Wright was the first architect to be deified, wrong, it was Imhotep."

Laughter.

". . . To this day his cult is significant. And why?" The arrow of a scarlet laser triangulated the pyramid. "The artifact. His artifact remains, and the spirit of the man is sacralized by his powerful relic."

I never thought of it that way, Tipsy thought.

"Hey," a voice hissed. Tipsy turned to find Frank's face immediately next to hers in the darkness. "What's happening?"

Over Frank's shoulder, Tipsy could see Oscar Few's shape in the darkness, his eyes on them.

"This is really interesting," Tipsy ventured.

". . . Relics have their place throughout history, as we have seen. The eagle feather headdress and the bear or lion claw necklace, the tusk of the narwhale, the wrist bone of a martyr . . ."

"That's not what I'm talking about," Frank replied huskily. His breath was redolent of Tampa Jewels and salami.

". . . The pyramid constitutes a change in that it was spawned of man, not of nature. . . ."

"What are you talking about?" Tipsy asked loudly. Two or three people in front of them glanced over their shoulders.

"Keep your voice down," Frank said, equally loudly.

". . . And here we trace the roots of the sacralization, first, of the technologist, the scientist, the engineer. . . ."

Frank put a hand on Tipsy's shoulder.

". . . And at first, of course, all the works of these technologists are dedicated to the sacralization of nature, then of the religion of nature, then of the exponents of such religions. Royalty, in other words, who were deified, often after their deaths, but increasingly in their lifetimes and finally by the mere fact of their birth within the context of a properly curried—or sacralized—bloodline."

Tipsy wasn't all that worried about this Frank guy. After all, as she reassured herself, she had a truncheon on her belt, and she knew where his nuts lived. But a scene was precisely what nobody—neither Frank, nor Tipsy, nor Oscar Few—wanted.

"This bred men with great sway over their fellows, and this power accrued to their factotums as well. The warrior caste, generals and tacticians make for obvious power figures, direct and fearful. But these usually toiled in the name of some greater good, and this good was guided by a king, if this figure were strong, or by a king's advisers who, until very recently in our history, were usually religious figures."

"Well?" Frank said, squeezing her shoulder.

The slides became portraits.

Tipsy winced under his grip. "Okay," she whispered, "this has gone far enough. My old man walked after he shot the last guy who laid a hand on me, and now he's got a taste for it."

". . . Cardinal Richelieu, 1585-1642, makes for an excellent example. Prince of the Church and a statesman virtually without peer in or out of the spheres of religion and monarchy, he ran France, nominally for his King, Louis XIII, for forty years. . . ."

She put her lips right next to Frank's ear, whispered, "Me, too," and elbowed him right at the bottom of his ribcage, just under the offending arm. The hand promptly went away.

Oscar stepped between them. "What's up?"

"I need bitches for strip search," Frank rasped.

"That's a volunteer gig, Frank."

"Frank didn't tell me that," Tipsy said, regarding Frank through slitted eyes.

Oscar looked at her. "Frank?" he said, looking back at his boss.

"Yeah," Frank said. "I forgot."

Tipsy nodded. "I decline."

"That's it, then," Oscar said.

"Yeah," Frank said. "That's it." There was an edge in his voice.

"You'll find somebody," Few assured him.

Frank melted into the crowd without a word.

"Great," Few said.

". . . Richelieu, too, retains his cult. But as politician and prelate he left precious little behind to be cherished by any means other than scholarship. And while this scholarship is sincere enough, and richly rewarding, Richelieu left no pyramid, no relic. And so, as a personage fit to be sacralized, his record will have to do. Down through the decades his name fades in human memory and his idolization becomes more difficult to maintain, and thereby less and less . . . useful, shall we say?"

"You okay?"

"I'm fine," Tipsy nodded. "Who put that creep in charge?"

"He's not in charge of us. He coordinates services for the organizers. Security is just one of them. But he'll probably look into your credentials."

"Which he won't be able to find."

"That would be correct."

"Great. Do I have time to listen to this?"

Few shrugged. "That's why we're here."

". . . Richelieu's amorality is a tactic to be remarked—by this assembly, at least. For it is in the evolution of Richelieu's thought that we can clearly see the needs of the state rise above those of religion, in which we perceive the change that put religion at the service of a state that ultimately —it took three hundred more years—became one of the major western democracies in which religion played a smaller and smaller part."

More slides. "These are from Rapa Nui. They're called moai." So as to linger, the speaker slowed the projection rate. "I like them. The big heads of Easter Island all have a three-to-five head to body ratio. Very handsome."

Rows of moai. She sped up the rate again.

"But what is the state if it is not the most efficient use of its constituent entities? Religion, labor, industry, technology, military . . . ? Here we might discuss the twentieth century's three or four really impressive fascist states: Japan, Italy, Germany. But don't forget Franco's Spain, Pinochet's Chile, Mugabe's Zimbabwe . . ."

Tipsy glanced over her shoulder. Oscar had merged into the crowd to take a few infrared pictures. Am I hearing this correctly? she wondered, looking back at the screen.

". . . And don't forget their mistakes. In Japan, the emperor was still considered a deity. In the European states, however, this notion barely survived the eighteenth century. Certainly this is true of France, despite the very real presence of royalists there even today, not to mention the half-hearted deification of Napoleon."

I have to get a grip here, Tipsy thought to herself. I'm in danger of becoming gobsmacked.

"But a true fascist, you see, deifies the state, because he—or she— embodies it. By this light, the pace of the sacralization and desacralization of one or another so-called reality constructs has increased. And we note that, while religions come and go, nature has outlasted everything. Nature Bats Last, says the bumper sticker. But this slogan, as with so many others, may turn out to be nothing more than a religious homily."

Gobsmacked and stupid . . .

"Technology, in a word, is what we face. And, in the face of overweening technology, what do the people seek?"

"A Messiah," replied about eighty voices.

The speaker chuckled. "Or a man, at the very least. A man to stand up to the onslaught. As Jacques Ellul spent his life annotating, by the middle

of the twentieth century, technology had effaced all previous environ-
ments—nature, religion, even the state. Insofar as the efficiencies of either
collude with the progress of technology, so much the better for them.
Insofar as they hinder or interfere with the efficiencies of the new sacral
reality, so much the worse for them."

Either you are on the same page with the momentum of history or
you're not, Tipsy concluded for herself.

". . . It's that simple. There are two rules. (1) Never deviate from the
message, the rationale of which, meanwhile, is ever mutable. And (2),
never cease to vilify, disdain, calumniate, discredit, and slander anybody
who speaks or acts against the message."

And all messages boil down to a single message, Tipsy thought, which
is, since technology represents hope rather than monstrosity, get with the
program or perish.

". . . Or perish," the speaker concluded.

Murmur murmur murmur, responded the audience.

A slide of a bank exterior, marble pillars, leaded glass windows, big
double doors atop a few granite steps up from the sidewalk.

"Democracy, as Marx pointed out, paves the road to socialism."

"Fuck him!" someone in the crowd shouted.

"Yes, yes," the speaker turned her palms toward the crowd, "I know.
You'd think we could cite somebody else who has pointed it out."

Oh, man, Tipsy thought, where is Quentin when I need him? Did Marx
really say that?

". . . Nevertheless, the younger here among us will almost certainly live
to witness the complete privatization of public capital, and the national-
ization of all responsibility for private debt in excess of as little as one million euros."

"Dollars!" someone shouted. "Yeah," responded another, "Why not
dollars!"

"Whatever," the speaker shook her head. "Mark my words, the children
of our children will live to see the no-bid privatization of all public functions and systems."

"We've gained control of our schools. By flooding the student mind
with unassimilated information geared strictly toward their contributing
to technological efficiency and not having the time for anything else, we
simultaneously weed out rebellion simply by setting rebels up for impov-
erishment. Train a technician and you breed innovation. This individual—
one deploys the term *individual* strictly in the sense of a biological entity
—will find him or herself attracted by the sense of accomplishment he
can be taught to anticipate, and lulled away from any notion that what he

might be doing conspires to achieve nothing less than the culling of any instinct that might deviate from one hundred percent efficient participation in the subservience of the scattered needs of humanity to the specific requirements of technology."

I'm back to gobsmacked, thought Tipsy.

"But, surely," someone shouted, "do we not remain, at bottom, human?"

Laughter.

"Do we not recognize the hunger of the human spirit in each human breast?"

More laughter.

"Are we not all, still, despite various artificial anomalies, human beneath our rip-stop exteriors?"

General hilarity.

More of the same. Then . . . "Yes," the speaker beamed, "that's exactly the sentiment. And that's why we need to put a human face on reality. It is for this reason we pursue our short-term goal of creating and introducing a relic to which only the chosen will be rewarded with access, as if to a beacon suited to the navigation of the soul."

Wild applause.

"Remember, *relic* derives from the Latin for *remains*, which in turn comes down to us from *relinquere*, to leave behind. This relic will have been as it were, not the subjunctive, condition contrary to fact . . ."

Knowing, if uncertain, laughter.

". . . left behind, to guide us, to reassure us, to remind us to behold our future as promised by our past and guaranteed by our present. . . ."

I'm getting dizzy, Tipsy realized.

". . . For the true believer, there will be veneration. For the skeptic, there will be DNA evidence. Dare we imagine a deity right in our midst? Brother Imhotep . . ."

A spotlight found a man in the audience. After a pause, delighted laughter. Tipsy could see nothing. She looked over her shoulder. In the darkness behind her Oscar Few had lowered his head and was shaking it slowly. As she turned to look around, the projection screen flickered and a real-time image filled it. The man in the apex of the spotlight appeared to be dressed as a full-on, 3,500-year-old Egyptian dude, all cornflower blues, liquid tan complexion, Masonic dividers in one hand, a carpenter's square in the other, silhouetted hieroglyphs gliding over his entire carapace. A smattering of applause. The actor took a bow. The reaction is tepid. People are talking about other things.

". . . There will be pews comfortable enough to encourage meditation but not sleep . . ."

Amused laughter.

". . . Votive candles for purchase, a dedicated library, a portrait gallery, an audio tour, pedagogical holograms, graduated levels of membership strictly related to generosity, and so forth."

Groans, laughter, teasing remarks. "Why not shut up and get everyone here to sell one of their Hummers!" "Yeah! Hum up or shut up!" "Put your Hummer where your mouth is!"

Privatization of public capital, Tipsy thought. And, as if the crowd had read her mind, a communicable chant arose from it. "Hey, ho, whaddya say, how much we gonna privatize today? Hey, ho . . ."

"Loath as I am to quote him," the speaker insisted, "it was Goebbels who said, 'We do not talk to say something, but to obtain a certain effect.' Put another way, it doesn't matter what we say, but how we say it. Our reliquary will do just that. Written materials will be made available, if only because some few riders of the Silver Tsunami cling to the printed word. Also videos, of course, inspirational music, and devotional talks. Be assured that the experience, in and of itself, will be nothing short of inspirational. . . ."

Murmurs of knowing assent.

"Ladies and gentlemen," the speaker bowed from the waist, "I thank you for your time and attention." She checked her watch. "See you at the no-host bar."

The lights come up amid desultory applause.

An hour before the show, Tipsy had picked up Few in front of the cop shop on Bryant Street.

"Ahm, look," she began, after he'd climbed into the Beamer. "Since this is our first date, you being a cop and all, full disclosure, I still don't have a driver's license."

"Not my department," Few announced. He showed her the uniform she'd be wearing that evening. "Like it?"

A few hours later, eight or ten blocks after they'd departed the lecture hall, Tipsy stopped the Beamer at a red light, and Few observed confidently, "Pretty crazy scene, huh."

Tipsy watched the cross traffic. "Crazy?" she said after a moment. "You mean, as in wild?"

"No," Few said. "I mean, crazy. Insane. Loco. Nuts."

The light turned green and they were across the intersection before she told him, "I was *fascinated*."

Few's lips parted, he turned his head slightly in her direction, then he

turned back toward the windshield. My Daddy always told me, he
reminded himself, that if you're going to spend your life as a cop, you're
going to spend it with crazy people.

Exhaustion seeping into his voice, he said aloud, "Just drop me on
Bryant Street."

Normally, Few might have filed his report on a thumb drive, including
cellphone photos of rapt faces and license plates, along with random communications intercepts, if any, the audio of the proceedings dubbed off his
pen or his watch or both, along with any notes he might think germane.
The normal surveillance stuff.

Of course he went through the motions; he turned in his data and filled
out a report. But normal, it seemed to him, had petered out a while back.
So, two weeks later, on his monthly hike in the Marin Headlands, Oscar
Few deposited first generation cassette dubs of all his raw data in the
Shock & Awe commemorative lunch box he'd concealed in a gopher den
at the foot of a century plant left behind by long gone squatters twenty
feet above the high tide mark in an out-of-the-way place called Pirates
Cove. Few no longer trusted any other form of media or repository. You
seen a five-inch floppy drive lately? How about a zipdisk?

He had little fear of official repercussions, no more than he had hope
for making headway on this case. He was already being asked to justify his
overtime expenses. Like, fourteen dollars for a thumb drive?

Still, he figured, some day, when this park would be in the midst of
being turned into a vast housing project, the raw materials of his secret
history might provide a clue as to how it all was allowed to happen.

IV
DEAD MEN'S POCKETS

TWENTY

BEFORE SHE WAS PROPERLY SEATED ON THE STOOL NEAREST THE SMOKING deck, Faulkner plunked down a coaster, a draft of Anchor Steam Beer, and a sealed envelope.

The envelope had been addressed by Charley. Inside, however, she found a note from someone else.

I have news of your brother.

Tipsy turned the note face down on the bar, covered it with her hand and looked around as if she were a tourist from Kansas to whom, concerning this dive, some bribed concierge had conveyed misleading information. Nobody paid attention.

She took a sip of beer and turned the page face up.

Of necessity, I'm on the move. Discretion advised. But if you're interested in Charley's news, I'll telephone the bar at nine o'clock on Sunday night.

The note was unsigned.

Three men, one on a stool and two standing, dressed according to a variation on a theme: torn hickory shirt, paint-streaked bib overalls, a striped engineer's shirt flecked with little holes burnt by slag. Two of them wore moustaches, the third a full beard. The three were in there doing the same thing she was doing, which was taking the edge off a hangover and starting in on a new one. One of them had a shot of bourbon lined up behind his beer glass: the avant-garde.

None of these guys paid any attention to Tipsy, either. Unlike herself, all they had to do was get drunk, get some sleep, get up, go back to work, and persist with the notion that, beyond the gallon of paint, beyond towing some hulk to Oakland, beyond that coffee can full of valve springs, the future didn't exist.

"Faulkner."

"Yo."

She held up the envelope.

"It was stuck in the door when Walter opened up this morning."

"At six?"

"Five-thirty."

She let the envelope fall to the bar.

"I thought I'd find you here."

She looked up.

His face fell. "Didn't you miss me?"

"Miss you . . . ? Oh! Yes—yes of course I've missed you." She stood and tendered a distracted hug.

"Gee," Quentin said, as she pulled away. "That's what I call a perfunctory salutation."

She waved this off. "Sit down and have a drink. You'll feel better about it."

Quentin didn't sit down and he didn't order a drink. "Am I interrupting something?"

"No more than usual."

"Okay," he snapped.

She shook her head. "This is coming out all wrong."

"There are other bars," Quentin pointed out, "and other lonely female drunks in this town, and if I can't do any better than stand here and take this . . . this *chill abuse*—"

Tipsy shook her head. "Will you please lighten up and sit down?" She jerked an empty barstool a foot closer to her own. "Where the hell you been?"

"Sensitivity training."

She didn't give it a thought. She tapped the envelope with a fingernail. "I need to ask you something."

"Sure." Quentin sat on the stool. "We can discuss my problems later."

Tipsy frowned. "Where'd you get that jacket?"

"Downtown."

She fingered its sleeve. "There's still a thrift shop downtown?"

Quentin archly drew away from her. "I beg your pardon?"

"Then it's as new as it looks?"

"You like it?"

"It's beautiful."

"Thank you, darling. I'd tell you that I bought it exclusively because I dress for you, but that wouldn't be true, if only because I never see you anymore."

"You never see me any more? The truth of the matter is, I, we"—she indicated the rest of the bar—"nobody sees you any more."

"That's all in the past," Quentin said. "Faulkner."

"Mr. Quentin Asche," Faulkner said, coming down the bar. "Long time no see." They shook hands.

"What time is it? Wait. I forgot." Quentin shot his cuff and had a look. "It's seven-thirty."

"Nice watch," Tipsy said, as if perplexed.

Faulkner spun a napkin onto the bar. "What'll it be?"

"Whiskey sour. Hold the whiskey."

"No fruity drinks."

"An Old Fashioned, then. Hold the bourbon."

"I'm outta cherries."

"Soda water, rocks, maybe a lime?"

"I can do that."

"Thank god. I'm exhausted."

Faulkner went away.

Quentin watched Tipsy watching the watch. "You like it?"

Tipsy frowned. "What the hell is going on?"

"I put the house on the market, served China with eviction papers, China made himself scarce, I took the house off the market, cleaned it up within an inch of its life, took out a second, had a guy draw up some plans and get a building permit, hired a contractor for the remodel, and moved my skinny portfolio into the nicest hotel money can buy."

"Wow," Tipsy said, after a long pause. "And here I was thinking maybe you had committed suicide."

"Well," Quentin admitted, "the thought crossed my mind. But then I realized I have no heirs—see?"

Tipsy shook her head. "Negative."

"If I were so foolish as to blow myself away, without the proper paperwork, whatever assets I left behind would go to improve some bridge in Yolo County."

"You mean, probated to the State of California."

"Exactly. It was China's *Pumping Iron* poster that reminded me of it."

"He didn't take it with him?"

"He didn't take it with him."

"Huh. He must have been pretty upset."

"I sincerely hope that was the case."

"You don't know where he went?"

"No idea."

"Not at the house, at any rate."

"The house least of all. We hauled two twelve-yard debris boxes out of there, stripped out the fixtures, the lath and plaster, the insulation, even the plumbing and electrical—the place is down to the studs and uninhabitable." He touched her arm. "Even the Datsun has been hauled away. And I sold the Mercedes to my mechanic for what I owed him.

Now it's his nightmare, and I'm taking cabs everywhere I go."

Tipsy put her hand on his forearm. "You didn't throw out that kitchen window?"

Quentin smiled and patted her hand. "Not on your life."

Tipsy relaxed. "Twelve yards of debris. . . ."

"Twenty-four."

"It sounds like a lot."

"It was. But it's what it took to get the place back to zero. By the look of it, China ran the facilities into the ground before he took off. I mean, darling," Quentin made a face, "the toilet was clogged with magazine pages."

Tipsy made a face. "Nice."

"It cost me close to ten grand just to clean the place up enough to gut it."

"How much for the whole remodel?"

"Depending on fixtures, eighty to a hundred."

"Just out of curiosity, what'd you list it for?"

Quentin smiled. "A conservative one point one million."

Tipsy, who had raised her drink halfway to her lips, set it down on the bar again. "I'm gobsmacked a lot lately."

"Be very gobsmacked. It would have gone for more. And," Quentin raised a forefinger, "it's a tear-down."

"But it's your home!"

"Maybe that's why I took it off the market." Quentin shook his head. "On the other hand, I am so over the past-tense aspects of that place. Let's look at it from the point of view of an inveterate real estate developer."

"How's that?"

"Would you spend eighty to a hundred grand to make three to four hundred grand?"

"Does unilateral foreign policy make me sneeze?"

"Right you are. Meanwhile, darling, it's first-class hotels and organic luncheons."

"You'll do design and décor yourself."

"Correct. When the project is finished, oh, eight or ten months from now, I'll figure out what to do with it."

On the television over the far end of the bar a couple of steroidally overdosed women in sequined patriotically-colored bikinis and crash helmets bashed each other with electronic pugil sticks that lit up whenever they scored a solid hit. A crawl across the bottom of the scoreboard read, *Sabotaged pipeline scorches 10,000 acres, 5 villages.*

"I finished the DUI class."

"Congratulations."

Tipsy studied her beer. "Thanks."

After a short silence Quentin said, "You should see this hotel. Fabulous restaurant. We'll go there later. Their cocktails start at nineteen dollars." He spilled a little carton of pills on a napkin and began to sort them. "A very nice bar," he added significantly, talking to Tipsy but addressing the pills, "where they don't resent fabricating a whiskey sour. Entertainment, too. Real entertainment, I mean. Musicians who can play music."

"You know perfectly well, Quentin, that you're the only customer in here who can get a mixed drink." Tipsy touched the base of her glass to the rim of Quentin's.

"The Margaritas and Bloody Marys in here," Quentin reminded her, "are pre-mixed. The margin on top-shelf Margaritas is something like three hundred percent."

"Just like your house," Tipsy observed.

"Oh really, darling." Quentin closed his eyes and segued directly to realtor mode. "I bought DeHaro Street in June of 1977 for $45,000. The down payment was sixty-seven hundred and fifty dollars. It's been paid off for twenty years, and now it costs about two thousand a year, in insurance and taxes, to own. Let's generously suppose that I put $35,000 in it over the years—a new roof, two paint jobs, two dishwashers, new cabinets, like that—plus the ten thou I had to throw in on account of that parasite that was living there." He set his glass on a coaster and lowered his voice. "I priced it low." He threw two pills to the back of his throat and chased them with water. "With multiple bids, I probably could have cleared the asking price. One-time deal on my primary residence after the age of fifty-five—I'd get out from under tax free."

Tipsy drew back. "Get the fuck out of here."

"The line of credit on it," Quentin lowered his voice, "is a cool two hundred grand."

"Get further the fuck out of here."

"They didn't even want to see my tax returns. There would have been a bidding war." Quentin looked at her. "What part of Kansas are you from?"

"Mars."

"Let me get that drink." Quentin put a hundred dollar bill on the bar.

"You really refinanced your gutted house?"

"A new owner would have knocked it down, built a new place for another million, and wound up paying some $37,500 a year in property taxes alone. Plus insurance, debt service, and blah blah blah." Quentin drew himself up to his full height. "I felt it incumbent upon myself, as a citizen of this community, to prevent this calamity from overwhelming some hapless buppie."

Tipsy shook her head. "That's mighty civic-minded of you."

"It's a new era, darling," Quentin assured her. "I'm telling you. If I die the day before I spend the last dime," he touched the bar with the tip of his index finger, "I'll be getting out in the nick of time."

"Let's hope you live that long."

Quentin looked at her. "Thanks."

"I didn't mean it that way."

"Just exactly in what way did you mean it?" Quentin ignored his own question. "I really put my house up for sale." He sounded a little hysterical. "I'm going to live the rest of my short life in interesting hotels. When I mentioned to the bank I needed a little money to tide me over until the house sells, they fired up that $200,000 line of credit faster than you can say Roy Cohen. Times have changed." Quentin moved in close, nudged her elbow with his own, and tilted his head. "It's a different world than the one I plundered."

Tipsy looked down, only to see a roll of cash halfway out of his trouser pocket. It was the thickness of the business end of a baseball bat.

"Criminey," Tipsy whispered. "That looks like enough money to jump-start the Cuban economy. Don't be flashing it like that. Christ, I've never felt so weird about money in my entire life. What's the deal? You're paranoid without it, you're paranoid with it?"

"Who's paranoid?" Quentin giggled loudly.

Faulkner looked their way from the other end of the bar. Quentin waved the fingers of his empty hand at him. Tipsy rolled her eyes. Faulkner looked the other way.

Quentin took up his water. "Need any cash?" he whispered over the rim of the glass.

Tipsy nodded her head, yes, then began to shake it. "No. I don't want to foul up our relationship. It's fouled up enough as it is."

"What relationship?"

"But, oh," she hooked her arm through his, "I've missed you so."

Quentin sipped. "Just so you know it's there."

Tipsy's eye fell on the envelope. She pursed her lips. "There is one thing I have to ask you."

"Shoot."

"Who did you tell about Charley?"

Quentin narrowed his eyes. "You're causing me pain."

"I asked you once before and you didn't answer me."

Quentin gingerly set down his drink. After a pause he said, "Okay." He tented his fingertips below the tip of his nose and looked straight ahead. "One night, three, maybe four months ago, when you first started getting the letters about Charley's recent . . . his projected . . . his . . . that he was contemplating . . . a trip—China was waiting for me when I got home."

"China . . . ," Tipsy breathed. "I knew it."

"Hear me out?"

"Sure," Tipsy nodded. "What do I have to lose?"

"I don't know."

She caught her lower lip between her teeth.

"He was reasonably sober for a change. It was a warm night. China had the big window open, and he was cooking the one recipe he's really good at."

"Chipotle and green olive chicken with wild rice and okra."

"Very good. You could smell it from De Haro Street. Plus—and I don't know where he got them—he had chilled a bottle of Pinot Grigio and opened another of Crozes-Hermitage. Just on the off chance, you understand, that I'd like to taste them. Which I did. One sip each. Delicious."

"Which of your books did he sell to pay for them?"

Quentin closed his eyes.

Tipsy sipped her drink. "Anyway, China doesn't know anything about wines. He must have looked them up on the internet."

"Just . . ." Quentin's eyes moistened. "It was unbelievable. The aromas of Côtes du Rhône and roasting chicken were competing for my saliva. Do you know how long it's been since I could really taste anything?"

"He wanted something," Tipsy began. "He—"

Quentin held up a forestalling hand. "Oh, thought I to myself, the child can't help himself. He wants something." He shook his head. Tipsy nodded hers. "I braced myself for a fine meal and maybe even some sparkling conversation, followed by the kind of sex that suckered me, if you'll pardon the expression, into that domestic morass in the first place. Enjoy yourself, I told myself; but drink very little, and don't get too relaxed, because, after everything else—"

"Comes the bite," Tipsy concluded.

"That's right. But I was wrong and so are you. He didn't want anything—at least," Quentin hastened to add, "not right then he didn't want anything."

Tipsy waited.

"It was just like the old days," Quentin posited with a smile. "Before he got involved with all the wrong people, too much alcohol, the drugs . . ."

"The personal trainer . . ."

"Yes, yes . . ."

Tipsy had her doubts about the rosiness of Quentin's recall, but she said, "Delicious food?"

Quentin nodded. "Great conversation . . ."

"Come on, Quentin," Tipsy insisted, annoyed. "Passable conversation."

"No . . ." Quentin began.

"At least you weren't fighting," Tipsy suggested.

"We weren't fighting," he conceded.

"And finally, great sex."

"No," Quentin hastened to correct her, "it was . . . meaningful sex."

"Oh," Tipsy said, slightly clearing her throat. "Meaningful sex."

"He was just as loving as the China I remembered. Firm without being too demanding, not too strict, took his time . . ."

"Oh, please," Tipsy said. "I'm going to puke."

"Nobody puked . . ." Quentin continued dreamily.

"Okay okay," Tipsy hurried him. "Afterwards you lay in each other's arms and talked. Just . . ."

". . . talked," they said together.

Tipsy swirled the last inch of beer in the bottom of her glass. "About anything in particular?"

"At some point," Quentin sighed, "he asked about you."

"Oh," Tipsy said. "This is about me?" She pointed a finger to her breast. "China Jones asked about me?"

"And I told him your great news," Quentin said simply. "We were talking about the things that we both cared about," he added defensively. "After all . . ."

"After all?"

"I care about you, Tipsy."

"And I you." She patted his arm. "What exactly did you tell him?"

"Just that Charley had gotten in touch after months of silence."

"Did you tell China that Charley had work?"

"Well, that was good news, too, wasn't it?"

"Did you tell China what kind of work?"

Quentin held up his hands and inverted them, palms up. "Do I even know what kind of work?"

"Did you tell China about Charley coming to San Francisco?"

Quentin frowned ingenuously. "Charley is coming to San Francisco?"

"Charley was coming to San Francisco." She made a fist and stabbed the bartop with her middle finger. "I sat right here and read it aloud. You were here."

"So you must have done. I'd forgotten."

"I thought you were all bent out of shape about my good news?"

"Totally," Quentin insisted, "absolutely one hundred percent infatuated with your good news. It had been a long time since you'd had any, and I was happy for you." He faced her, as if frankly, and placed one hand on her forearm, as if in sincerity. "Put yourself in my place. China was making nice and he really really wanted to know what else was going on in my life. I couldn't wait to tell him. I was so happy for you!"

Tipsy removed her arm from his touch. "Blabbermouth."

"Blabbermouth?" Quentin sat upright and touched the fingertips of both hands to his chest. "How dare you. I've been keeping your counsel for just about as long as I can remember, and I know it's been going on for as long as you can remember."

Tipsy paused the rim of her glass before her mouth and raised an eyebrow. "You have a point there."

"I," Quentin said forcefully, "think so."

"Don't get worked up."

"Now she tells me."

"China's it, right?"

"What do mean, China's it? Aren't you the one who's always telling me he's not unique?"

"Far from it. What I meant to say was, is China the only one you told about Charley?"

"Who else would I tell, for God's sake?"

Tipsy handed note and envelope to Quentin. Quentin read it. She showed him the envelope. Quentin didn't have to be told to compare the handwriting. He noticed the uncanceled stamp. He read the note again. He handed envelope and note back to her. "Have you heard from Charley lately?"

Tipsy shook her head.

Quentin indicated the note with his chin. "Are you going to meet this guy?"

"You bet I am." Tipsy nodded gravely. "Are you coming with me?"

TWENTY-ONE

RED MEANS STARTED OUT IN LIFE THINKING HE WANTED TO GET BY DOING as little work as possible.

That didn't fly.

So he got energetic. He'd found that so long as you didn't mind working up a sweat and getting your hands dirty, you could always get a job. And what's the dirtiest job you can do without getting too dirty?

Dope smuggling. That's right. Not dope dealing, but dope smuggling. There's a difference.

It's the immigrant way, it's the path of upward mobility, it's the booby-trapped shortcut out of the wilderness of impecuniosity and into the freshly manicured lawns of financial stability, where the water in the swimming pool is always blue and the beer is always cold and it's against the law to fire up a leaf blower before nine in the morning.

And that's only the rosy side of the picture.

Do something illegal, and do it well, you get paid a hundred, a thousand, ten thousand times the guaranteed minimum wage. Play your cards right and the sky's the limit. Play your cards wrong and, if you live, time is all you will get. Either way, as went the universal perception of every dope smuggler he ever met, it beats a day job.

Dumb. In all his years in the game, Red Means had played his cards so as not to get caught. Money was the second priority.

In his day Red had made many hundreds of thousands of dollars, perhaps even a million or two. He'd started out with a partner. She turned out to be smarter than he was, which was okay so long as they were in business together. But later, when drug smuggling became much more heavily penalized than it had once been, except in Texas, and commiseratively more dangerous, too, even in Texas, she bent her superior mind toward getting out of the business altogether, with a reasonable amount of money to boot, but her primary objective was to get out in one piece. No jail time, no scars, but not wholly destitute, either. She made it, and with enough money to buy a house. In due time she married a building contractor, produced a couple of kids, the husband added a room onto the house, and her homemade jam won a prize at the county fair.

Now that Red was sixty years old, the thrill of living on the edge had lost most of its luster. He never liked to admit that his partner had seen a light twenty years ago that he himself still preferred to pretend didn't exist; but, in the event, after his first twenty years of being a full time criminal, he thought himself tired. Plus, his partner's departure was disorienting. So he'd turned his talents to various cons.

He started a sailing school. At first he was its only instructor. Soon enough however, various other reprobates, themselves tired of the game, thought to turn their more dubious hands toward something more or less honest, and turned up at his doorstep asking for work. Relieved of his teaching duties, Red turned his considerable talents toward cooking the books. Right away it became obvious that his various old cronies weren't any more interested in teaching than he was. Rather, they preferred to countervail the boredom induced by honest endeavor—knot tying, man-overboard drills, setting and resetting the anchor—by getting loaded; although one fellow, in particular, hove to with a lovely solo student and let the vessel drift aground while assaulting her. It turned out that the student was a lawyer who was learning how to sail so she could spend more quality time with her lawyer boyfriend on his very large yacht. Before the lawsuit could really get going, Red had to disappear his old crony, who could not bring himself to consider the situation in any but retrograde terms, *viz.*, "If she don't want to get laid, what's she doing on a boat with the likes of me?"

Red fit him for the shingle chemise and declared bankruptcy.

Next he started a money management fund. And who were his clients? Successfully retired and ambitious-to-be-retired dope dealers, of course. A bottomless client pool. Red began receiving threats offering to fit *him* for the thousand-fathom turtleneck from idiots who expected better than a 10% return on a legitimate investment. He didn't take them seriously. After somebody blew up his car, however, that business, too, went south.

Finally Red turned to real estate. Florida real estate, in particular, presented many of the elements lacking from his other businesses, and many in common with dope smuggling. Piracy, back-stabbing, and throat-slitting, to name three. Coke whores were replaced by real estate whores. It wasn't difficult to distinguish between the two. The former rubbed whichever of your knees was closer to the mirror, the latter rubbed the knee closer to the stack of comparables. But here, too, he met with less than spectacular results. Realtors of both sexes with frosted hair and sensible shoes and Jaguar convertibles with A-frame OPEN HOUSE signs piled in the back seat drove circles around him. No commission was too small to be undercut, no state-wide real estate license examination was so stringent that it couldn't be made more difficult by industry-lobbied legislators, no oddball request by neurotic snowbirds from New Jersey was too demeaning to be fulfilled.

Red just couldn't hack it. He was not a people person. You can't fit a jerk for the sandy loam hoody just because they don't like the charcoal flecks in the alabaster granite some overextended speculator had spirited off some other job to spruce up the half-bath in a condo he desperately needed to flip.

Finally, at a greyhound track outside of Miami, Red found himself sitting at the bar with about two hundred dollars to his name, an empty glass in front of him, and the slip fee overdue on the mildewed 32-foot nonnavigable Chris-Craft he called home at the time. Miami had changed around him, the Keys were too hot for him, he had no friends, most of his former associates were dead, in prison, or permanently retired to South America, and, as a musician acquaintance had observed about a trumpet player, if there had been any design changes in women over the last year or two, Red would be the next-to-last person to ask about them: the last one being the trumpet player.

Not that Red was bereft of experience with women. He had at least three grown kids scattered around the trailer parks of south Florida and another married to a socialite up in Newport, R.I., so the procreative aspect of living with a woman no longer interested him at all—which had in fact been true the whole time. What he did miss about having a woman in his life was the fighting. A good fight, in Red's experience, meant that he was alive. After the fight, of course, they should lick each other all over. It is so stipulated in *The Dope Dealer's Handbook to Domestic Bliss*, right after the illustrated sidebar that shows how to sharpen a hypodermic needle on a brick.

Smuggling carried a similar appeal. The adrenaline of the chase, the furtive, mosquito-infested nights, the extreme risk and proportionate rewards—these were clues, in Red's experience, that he was fully alive. The seventeen months he'd spent living in the Everglades with the mother of two of his kids? The nadir of his life. Boredom incarnate. If it hadn't been for convincing her to donate that kidney, which was illegal, he might have killed her and himself too. Little else in those days eclipsed the satisfaction of pulling off that deal—well, except maybe the day he'd forced a recalcitrant debtor to feed his favorite pit bull to an alligator the guy kept in his swimming pool. Payday is payday.

He didn't particularly care about snorting the fruits of his labors. He preferred staying clean, the better to savor every detail of existence, not to mention the competitive advantage it gave him. He'd learned that from Darla. Everybody in the business knew better than to short him or vend him inferior product. Besides, the way all of his wives and girlfriends had looked at it, it meant more dope for them. Every woman in his entire life, without exception, elevated that priority over every other. It was a feedback loop of self-defeat if ever there was one, from which he didn't at all mind taking a year or two off.

In a weak moment he'd tracked down his erstwhile partner and called her. A little girl answered the phone, then turned it over to her mother.

"Darla?"

"Yes?"

"Red."

Silence.

"Darla?"

"Red."

"How's it hanging, babe?"

Silence.

"Hello?"

"Red."

"Darla?'

"We no longer have anything to discuss."

"Well, hell, babe, I know that."

"Then why are you calling me?"

"Well I—I miss you. Kind of."

In her phone's background, a doorbell rang and a dog barked.

"Darla?"

"I'm here, Red."

"We had our fun, didn't we?"

"Did we?"

"Sure."

"I don't remember it that way."

"You don't remember it that way? How do you remember it?"

"It's simple: I don't remember it."

This stumped Red. After a pause he said, "Is that your little girl?"

"That's my little girl."

"How old is she?"

"Nine going on seventeen."

"That's nice. That's real nice."

"Red, look."

"Yes, Darla?"

"I've got to sign for a UPS package and rustle up some supper."

"Oh." Pause. "You cook now?"

"Not only do I cook, I run a catering business."

"And you cook at home, too?"

"Frankly, Red, I can't get enough of it."

"How's it doing?"

"We're barely making it. Every time we sit down to do our taxes we—"

"Taxes?" Red laughed.

"Yes," she said simply.

I forgot about taxes, Red thought to himself.

"We wonder," Darla continued, "where it all goes."

"Never enough," Red concluded.

"Seems that way."

"Well, say . . ." he began.

"Don't even start," she advised him.

"You don't need a little help?"

"No, thanks. We'll make it."

"You don't need a dose of . . . supplemental income?"

"I've got to go, Red. Please don't call me again."

The simplicity of this plea, which so lacked in urgency as to be matter of fact, left him, for the moment, at a loss for words. Finally he said, "Sure. Sure, Darla."

"Promise."

He nodded without saying anything.

"Red?"

"You got it," he assured her, lending a vocal energy to the response he in no way felt. "This is goodbye."

"Thanks." She hung up.

It might have been the only emotionally straightforward decision, untinctured by profit motive, he'd made in his adult life.

Now, years later, this still remained true, and he still wasn't sure why he'd made it. Was it because Darla had made something of herself? Even if it was something he couldn't respect? Or had her honesty embarrassed him into acquiescence? Imagine that. If, where he'd spent the last forty years, honesty was a species of respect among thieves, it was despised in all its many other forms. What power could a housewife hold over Red Means?

Maybe one day, as he occasionally thought, he'd drop by and ask her.

Her phone number hadn't been too hard to find. Her address wouldn't be all that much trouble either. It's all on the goddamn internet.

Yet, as the years went by, Red somehow never found the time to make good on—what? Was it a threat? Not a threat, precisely. Well, then, was he afraid of Darla? That wasn't it, couldn't be it. But he did understand that crossing the wire of his own life with the wire that was hers could only bring grief to both of them. The truth of this seemed plain. What was he supposed to do, show up just to ruin her life? Just because she'd asked him to butt out?

This rumination was quite aside from the fact that, if he messed up her life, Darla would hunt him to the farthest ends of the earth and fit him for the Smile Mon shroud, do not doubt it.

He'd always liked that about her.

The way around that would be to wipe her out along with her entire family. . . .

How nowhere, Red smiled, is *that*?

Still, he thought, as he familiarized himself with the console, the memory of Darla arose to nag him occasionally. She had been one of the most capable people he'd ever dealt with. One of the smartest, too. Should he admit that maybe he'd been a little bit in love with her? That it had been lonely without Darla's steady hand in even the smallest decision?

Easy now, big boy. Or the old Gotcha Devil-djinn of Squirm is going to be laughing up at you from the dregs at the bottom of the Beaker of Beers Past. . . .

He glanced at the analog clock, whose second hand ticked through the bearings of a compass. . . . I'm left with the obvious, which is that this woman whom I deem so smart took a powder fifteen years ago.

Check that, check that: make it twenty.

—Okay, she quit the business twenty years ago. So what. And why did she quit the business? Because she's smart, that's why. Look at what happened to Alice, for example.

Oh, please. Alice was a drug addict. What did you expect? It was Alice's habit that did her in. Not me.

Drug addict? Before she took up with you, Alice was good-looking, smart, and an accomplished musician with a working band and boyfriends coast to coast.

Sure, Red agreed. But it's not like I forced her to throw it all away for dope.

Nevertheless, in the end she died friendless and alone in a Tampa motel with a needle in her arm.

And in between, pal, she did what, three and a half years? Hard time, at any rate, from which she emerged a changed woman.

She went in at about the same time as Charley, as Red recollected. A completely different bust. Just driving a car load of weed up to New York. Christ, she didn't even get out of Florida. . . .

All because she wouldn't give you up to the cops.

Him, too. Neither of them would dime me to the cops.

You know, Red said to himself, as he reached for the cellphone, Charley used to tell me how he got this character going in his head while he was in the joint. He called him the Bosun.

The Gotcha Devil-djinn of Squirm knows the Bosun. They attend the same lectures together. Topics like Stellar Navigation, Oppositional Defiant Disorder, and The Blue Hole in Lucayan Culture. Serious stuff.

Red selected a number from his phone's memory. Is talking to yourself a sign of maturation?

Hell, Red admonished himself, as he listened to the phone ring, it's a sign of being alive. The Gotcha Devil-djinn of Squirm . . .

"Red Spot, Junior."

. . . Author of all Chaos . . .

"I'm calling for Tipsy Powell."

"Hang on."

Bar noise.

"This is Tipsy."

"This is Red Means."

Bar noise.

"You got my note?"

Bar noise.

"Hello?"

"I have it right here. I just didn't know it was you."

"Well?"

"Is this really Red Means?"

"Look out the window."

Bar noise.

"I'm looking."

"See the big yacht behind the sloop?"

"I see it."

"I'm aboard."

Bar noise.

"I want to bring a friend."

He might have known, but Red said, "Sure," without the least hesitation. "I would, too."

Bar noise.

"We're on the way."

She hung up.

Red hung up.

"You got that right," he said to the windshield.

TWENTY-TWO

THE DOCK WAS A BADLY MAINTAINED AFFAIR THAT CREAKED WITH EVERY passing ripple and wavelet, never mind a real swell and the stumbling footfalls of a pair of landlubbers. Quentin had known practically from birth that he had not the adaptable quality sailors call sea legs, but he also knew that a boat would have to be having a rough time of it, indeed, before its decks heaved and yawed with the likes of this ramshackle dock.

Kreutzer's Revenge was a big motor yacht whose twin V8s, even at idle, burbled puissance. No tuna tower, stabilizers or harness chair gave the least hint that it might be a fishing vessel. The boat was a sleek VIP lounge dedicated to a version of comfort and coddling not often witnessed by mere mortals. Amenities included multiple staterooms with private baths, satellite television, central heating, hot tub, sauna, dining for eight, a tender that cost more than a Hummer, a saloon that converted into a movie theater at the touch of a button, a wine cellar, etc etc. Not a book in sight, if you didn't count the chart room, but if you did include the latter, every chart was electronic, no paper data aboard, stupid but why not, for if her power should fail, no chart minted could prevent this boat from instant transubstantiation into a very expensive piece of driftwood.

Red greeted them amidships, at a set of gleaming teak stairs suspended over the side. "Tipsy."

"Red."

He offered a hand. "We meet at last."

Quentin watched for Tipsy's visible reaction, but none was forthcoming. The man greeting them was a burly devolution of what surely had been a hale and vigorous youth. Framed by the tendrils of a sun-blazed tonsure once golden red and now cinnamon, the face bore the permanently scalded look of a complexion peculiar to a northern gene pool not bred to the sun, but deliberately and relentlessly exposed to it for years on end, its intelligent eyes surmounted by devil's horn eyebrows. The man had the labored breathing of someone who had perhaps used tobacco for years or been exposed to mustard gas or an electrical fire or too many pipes of crack.

Tipsy accepted the hand and stepped aboard. "We meet at last," she repeated.

Red beamed. "Charley never told me his sister was a babe."

"You got birds roosting in those eyebrows?" Tipsy sniped.

"Mere squabs," Red replied easily. "They show up every year, right around mating season."

Tipsy laughed.

Red laughed.

Tipsy laughed a little louder. A gay laugh.

Red shook his head. "I'll be damned."

They both laughed.

I'll be doubly damned, Quentin surmised. If these two were gay and this were a cruise ship, nobody would see hide nor hair of either one of them until it docked in Hawaii.

"This is Quentin Asche," Tipsy said, abruptly remembering him.

Means proffered the hand. "Welcome aboard."

Quentin affected a frosty hauteur. What's the matter with you, Quentin, he admonished himself. It's not like *you* sleep with her.

"Watch your step." Red solicitously took Quentin's elbow. "You don't want to fall into the wrong drink. Make yourselves comfortable in the saloon. Is it always this cold in San Francisco?"

"Always," Tipsy assured him.

"We'll organize a toddy as soon as we're under way." He dropped a rail of hinged teak across the gap and touched a button. An electric motor flattened the stairs against the side of the boat.

"I've got a great toddy recipe," Tipsy chirped.

"Under way?" Quentin said uncertainly. He looked from Means to Tipsy and back.

"Quentin gets seasick," Tipsy advised the skipper.

"Who said anything about going to sea?" Red opened the after door into the saloon. "Watch the threshold."

"You did."

"Nah." Red shook his head. "We're just going for a little cruise on the bay. Aboard a barky of this tonnage, you won't even know you left the dock. Well," he corrected, "you might know you left this dock." As if to answer this slur, the dock buckled with a loud thump. "Besides," Red added, "there's nothing like a little nocturnal cruise with a drink in your hand to ease the flow of talk."

The saloon was lots of teak, discrete lighting, and polished brass.

"*Kreutzer's Revenge*," Quentin observed. "Interesting name for a boat."

"How's that?" Red paused at the door.

"You don't know?"

"It's a charter," Red explained.

"'The Kreutzer Sonata' is a Tolstoy story. As she is dying Kreutzer's wife tells him, and I quote, 'You have your way now; you have killed me.' She just had to get in that parting shot. But, if the story were a little more modern, perhaps the day after he buried his wife our widower might have gone straight to the yacht broker, paid cash for this baby, and christened her *Kreutzer's Revenge*."

"Well," Red asked. "Did he kill her?"

"Yes. He stabbed her."

"Quentin," Tipsy said, "that's a marvelous story. Our new friend, here, will now need to be dissuaded from the opinion that you're morose."

"Hey," Quentin pointed out, "I didn't name the damn boat."

Privately, of course, Quentin was thinking that there appeared to be quite a deal of Russian this that and the other about the town lately.

"Quite the contrary," Red told them. "Thank you, Quentin. I had no idea. And, as you can already see, cruising the peerless San Francisco Bay with interesting people is eminently conducive to conversation. Not to mention carousing. I don't think, Quentin, that you'll be seasick. We'll be motoring strictly upon the gentle breast of the Bay."

Tipsy told Quentin it was entirely up to him.

"God forbid I should be so seduced by present company as to impair my judgment, Tipsy, darling, but we don't even know this man."

"Quentin's not impugning your hospitality," Tipsy hastily intervened. "But he has a point."

"Then let me put it this way," Red said simply, with an unctuous smile. "If you want to have a conversation about your brother, it's going to be out of earshot from the rest of the world. The way to ensure that privacy is to conduct the conversation aboard this yacht in the middle of the bay. So what's it going to be?"

Tipsy didn't hesitate. "I'm game."

"Well . . ." Quentin looked from Tipsy to Red. "Do you have a passable soda water aboard? Is that the term? Aboard? And a lime?"

"A man after my own heart!" Red slapped Quentin on the back, which precipitated a brief fit of coughing. "Step up to the wheelhouse while I cast off."

Only the colored lights of a hundred thousand dollars worth of electronics illuminated the wheelhouse. Beyond a pair of awning windows and one story below them, Red coiled a line, hanked it over the pulpit railing, and scampered aft to deal with the line astern. Fifty or sixty yards forward of the bow, framed by the window in the door beyond the little porch, Faulkner leaned on the counter, talking with a customer. Three or four miles west, beyond the roof of the bar, a dense fog followed the contours of darkened inland vales and ridges of the coast range, snuffing lights as it advanced, breaking and tumbling like an immense, slow-motion wave, plunging the east-facing foothills into such obscurity that not so much as a single gleam penetrated to the outer world.

Tipsy shivered.

"Maybe this tub's got a locker full of sweaters," Quentin quipped, "with *Kreutzer's Revenge* stenciled mammilla to mammilla." As he spoke, a pair of vents in the bulkhead below the console began to puff warm air at them. "I'll be damned," Quentin said. "Central heating."

Lost in thought, Tipsy made no response. After a moment of silence, Quentin asked her why she trusted their host.

She shrugged. "Charley trusts him."

"No," Quentin corrected her, "Charley works for him."

"So what?" she replied stubbornly. "If he has news of Charley, I want to hear it."

The back door of the saloon opened and closed. "Someday," Quentin said, changing the subject as Red mounted the companionway ladder, "we're going to kick back in the old folks home and re-examine every line of dialogue we ever uttered."

"The ones we can remember, at least," Tipsy agreed.

"No problem. Your grandchildren will remember them for you. Especially the embarrassing ones."

"Grandchildren?"

"Dialogues."

Red put one hand on the helm, another on the throttles, and eyed the recalcitrant dock. "Good thing this beast has a bow thruster."

"In any case," Quentin continued, "I'll bet that not a damned line of such dialogue as can be recalled will turn out to mean what we thought it meant. Irony will have expired at last."

"You really think anybody will be able to remember anything at that juncture?" Tipsy wondered. "Or, perhaps more to the point, that anything will be worth remembering?"

"I've got a good memory," Red assured them, as he reversed both engines. "Ask me anything."

"All right," Quentin nodded, "who was Konstantin Paustovsky?"

Tipsy shot Quentin a look. Quentin watched Red.

"One of Charley's favorite writers," Red replied, without a scintilla of hesitation.

Quentin's eyes widened. He looked at Tipsy.

"You see?" she nodded. "The important stuff never goes away."

"How ironic," Quentin added, with a little frown.

"Was it him who wrote about this guy Kreutzer?" Red asked, giving the engines a little more throttle.

"That was Tolstoy," Quentin said.

"This thing," Tipsy said after a pause, "sounds like six trucks."

"That's about what's back there," Red confirmed.

Kreutzer's Revenge rocked back through her own prop wash until her bow cleared the end of the heaving dock, at which point Red spun the wheel to starboard and gave her a little port thrust. The bow swung to starboard. He re-centered the helm, shifted both throttles to forward, and eased her away from the various dinghies arrayed along the ends of the rickety piers flanking the empty slip.

Red soon had the vessel heading for the Bay Bridge at a modest and comfortable four knots. Nothing showy, nothing excessive, no strain on the passengers or demands upon the lusty V8s.

Lights along the eastern waterfront streamed lazily past—the vast biotechnology complex, the Lefty O'Doul drawbridge, the three-story high skeleton of a soda bottle fronting the baseball stadium, the myriad masts of the South Beach marina. To starboard, across the bay, a haze above the water diffused the powerful illumination rising from the cranes of the Oakland container terminal. Beyond the bow, black water sinuously reflected the southern string of illuminated bulbs that traced the western catenary of the Bay Bridge.

A silent VHF scanner abruptly caught the tanker *Hercules Perforce* announcing its approach, under pilot, to the Golden Gate Bridge. The skipper of a tugboat awaiting the tanker responded by suggesting they switch their communications to Channel 37, and Channel 16 squawked silent.

The three of them succumbed to the spell of these waters in darkness. The city to their left drifted past, a towering spectrality. High above them, on the lower deck of the Bay Bridge, traffic streamed east, demarcated by orange and red lights along the upper edges of truck trailers scattered among five lanes solid with vehicles. As *Kreutzer's Revenge* passed beneath the bridge, despite the grumbling of its twin seven-liter diesels, the friction of tens of thousands of tires rolling over asphalt and the clatter of expansion joints two hundred feet above the surface of the water, were clearly audible.

Then they sailed out from under the span, the rumble of traffic receded, and the bay opened before them, the lights of the Ferry Building to port, those of Coit Tower on Telegraph Hill a little further north, and those of Treasure Island to starboard.

"All these years I've lived in San Francisco," Quentin marveled at the windows, "and I've never been on the bay at night. It's beautiful."

"Yeah," Red replied absently. "You gotta admit."

Tipsy agreed. "Why not just do all your sailing right here?"

"Aside from the fact that it's always cold as hell? Everywhere you go you'll find that most yachtsman spend their lives doing exactly that," Red agreed. "They sail strictly local, and not very often. And why should it be otherwise? Most of them slave away seventy percent of their lives at some job so they can barely afford their water toys."

"Well," Quentin cleared his throat. "And what do you call this thing?"

Red nodded. "A real big toy. But it's some rich guy's toy. Somebody who can afford it. Not to be confused with your average blue-collar chump's hole in the water."

Quentin studied the man at the wheel, who appeared to be wearing not a stitch of clothing with less than five years of wear on it. "And who is this rich man?" he asked mildly.

"Beats me," Red replied easily. "Like I said, it's chartered." He fiddled with some switches. "And like all charters, something's broken on it." He rapped a knuckle against the glass of a dark screen mounted above the console. "In this case, it's the radar."

"Is that bad?" Quentin asked.

A voice broke in on channel 16. "—Inbound—" and broke up. Red fiddled with the squelch knob. "Nah," Red said. "We'll get by."

"So where are we going?" Tipsy asked.

Red pointed forward. "I thought we'd drop the hook and have a couple of drinks behind Angel Island. I'm told it's a quiet anchorage." Red was watching their route but, for a moment, his eyes focused narrowly in front of him. "And Charley is a lot to talk about."

"Where is Charley?" Tipsy frankly inquired.

Red said nothing.

"Come on, Red." Tipsy repeated. "If anybody knows Charley's where-abouts, it's you. Where is he?"

Red looked at her. "Good question."

"What's wrong?" Tipsy said.

Red shook his head and returned his attention to his piloting.

Tipsy and Quentin exchanged a glance.

"When's the last time you saw Charley?" Red asked the windshield.

"A question answered with a question," Quentin observed.

"Fifteen years and about eight months ago," Tipsy answered without hesitation, ignoring Quentin. "We spent two days in Phuket."

"I remember that trip," Red said. "But he made no mention of a sister."

"Maybe he was being protective."

"That's a long time ago," Red smiled, stating the obvious. "You were probably under age."

Quentin rolled his eyes.

"When's the last time you heard from him?" Red asked.

"I got a letter—when?" She looked at Quentin.

Quentin thought about it. "The last one I saw came at least three months ago."

She turned to Red. "There was one after that. But it's been a while."

Red thought about it. "What'd it say?"

"The usual, mostly about books and sailing."

Red watched the windshield. After a while he said, "When Charlie was in prison, I sent him a box of books, via my wife, every month. Charley would send me back long letters, via her, all about them. I enjoyed those letters. After he got out, he quit writing to me." He looked at Tipsy. "That was maybe six years ago."

"Now he's working for you again."

"Did he tell you that?"

"He wrote me that. Yes."

Red pursed his lips. "That was supposed to be on the q.t."

"Not to worry," Tipsy said, with a glance at Quentin. "Who's to tell?"

Red nodded. "Good question."

"So he's still working for you," she persisted. "Right?"

"Not any more," Red said. "Charley quit me."

This took Tipsy aback. She looked from Red to Quentin and back to Red again. "Well if he's not working for you, who is he working for?"

"Funny." Red glanced at her, then went back to watching the windshield. "That's what I was going to ask you."

"Me?" Tipsy frowned. "When's the last time you heard from him?"

Red didn't hesitate. "Assuming that letter took its time getting here, about two months before you last heard from him."

"Is that the so-called news you've got for me? That you haven't heard from my brother since five months before I last heard from him?"

Red lifted two empty hands. "And how was I supposed to know that?"

"He has a point," Quentin observed.

"Thank you," Red said over his shoulder.

"Yeah." Tipsy expelled an exasperated sigh. "Thanks."

As they cleared the northeastern tip of the city, just east of Pier 39, the ochre lights of the Golden Gate Bridge hove into view, three miles to port.

Red pointed out a mass of bright lights, floating in a fog bank below the bridge. "Freighter."

"Don't change the subject," Tipsy insisted, ignoring the view.

"I thought we'd try to put two and two together," Red said simply. "See what we could figure out."

Tipsy stared at Red. "Every time that son of a bitch gets my hopes up," Tipsy abruptly declared, through clenched teeth and to nobody in particular, "he dashes them."

"That's what family is for," Quentin suggested, "if you're asking me."

"This conversation isn't one," Tipsy announced. "What's a girl gotta do to get a drink around here?"

"Step into the saloon and help yourself," Red said. "There's ice in the countertop reefer." He readjusted the squelch on the VHF. "She looks like a freighter," he added, "which means she's probably headed for Oakland." He moved his chin over his shoulder. "You guys got a big container terminal over there."

"Oh," said Quentin.

Red touched a GPS display in front of him. "So she'll probably nip between Alcatraz Island, here, and the city front." Quentin pretended to be interested. "In the meantime, we'll dodge behind Alcatraz, across this stretch of open water, here, to the back side of Angel Island." He touched up the throttles.

Tipsy paused at the companionway. "Anybody else?"

"I'll wait," Red replied.

"I'll have a soda water," Quentin said. "With lime."

Tipsy disappeared aft.

"What'll she be drinking?" Red asked Quentin after a moment. "Will she be able to think straight an hour from now?"

"It depends. Usually she just drinks beer."

"Beer, we have."

"Occasionally, she likes to back it up with a tequila."

"Tequila, we have."

"In the pinch, she'll go for whatever's around."

"Is she a lush?"

Quentin shrugged. "She's one of those smart people who drink too much. If she had a purpose in life, she'd put it down and blow away the competition."

"She doesn't have a purpose in life?"

"Not since she escaped her family."

"When the hell was that?"

"About twenty-five years ago."

"Christ."

"A long time," Quentin agreed.

The sound of a glass rattling against a bottle reached them from the galley.

"I'd best get us to where we're going while everybody's still thinking straight." Red trimmed the wheel and gave her a little more throttle. "You can't believe how fast these big ships go," he said after a moment. "Sixteen, eighteen, twenty knots, more. They can't stop, they can't turn, and these channels are barely big enough to contain them. Us little guys need to steer clear."

"You call this thing a little guy?"

"Hey," Tipsy called from the galley, in between the opening and closing of drawers. "Do we have a knife?"

"Sure," Red said absently. "Look around." Alcatraz Island now lay directly between *Kreutzer's Revenge* and the bridge, obscuring the latter. The old prison, now strictly for tourists, was closed for the night, but remained sufficiently illuminated to render legible the largest of the historical graffiti.

"INDIAN COUNTRY," Red read aloud. "Imagine that."

"You don't remember when the Indians took over Alcatraz?"

"No. And if it's got to do with prisons, I don't want to know about it."

They exchanged a glance.

"I guess you had to have been here," Quentin said. "It was pretty exciting."

Red returned his attention forward. "There should be a green light flashing every five seconds over there somewhere." He pointed. "It's called Point Blunt."

"I spent an entire day on Angel Island once. It's a park." Quentin blinked. "I think it was in 1978." He couldn't make out the flashing green light. As he searched for it, what sounded like glassware crashed to the saloon deck. "Oops," Quentin said.

A scream pierced the air.

"What—" Quentin started.

Red closed a meaty fist around Quentin's thin arm without a word. "Let's let her deal with it," he suggested mildly.

"Tipsy is screaming," Quentin said. "Deal with what?"

"Is she saying anything?"

"No," Quentin answered, struggling. "She's screaming no, over and over."

"That's not going to do her any good," Red said.

"Tipsy!" Quentin shouted. "Tipsy—!" He lurched toward the companionway, but Red held the arm. "See here, Mr. Means!" He squirmed and twisted, but he was frail and Red's grip was irresistible. "What—? Unhand me! What's going on?" Quentin looked at Red's fist, which entirely encapsulated Quentin's reedy biceps. He looked at Red. Red steered *Kreutzer's*

Revenge and ignored him. Just beyond the spume-lofting rocks at the northern tip of Alcatraz, the advancing bulb of *Hercules Perforce* appeared and steamed across the bow of *Kreutzer's Revenge*, not a hundred yards away. "What's happening?" Quentin screeched, as the monster's bow wave lifted the bow of *Kreutzer's Revenge*.

"That sonofabitch is a tanker, and she's bound for Richmond," Red said calmly. "No wonder we can't see Point Blunt." He backed the throttle. The enormous, rust-streaked hull of the eastbound *Hercules Perforce*, now a mere seventy-five yards away, filled the forward windows. As the bow of *Kreutzer's Revenge* dropped into the trough, Run spun the wheel. Glassware crashed in galley, and Tipsy's moans were no longer heard. "To hell with these damned boats," Quentin screeched. "What's happened to Tipsy?"

Red's hips swung to the motion of the deck as if they were gimbaled. "I can make an informed guess," he told the windshield, wheel in one hand and Quentin's arm in the other.

Quentin, staggering on the same deck, looked at Red as if he were mad. And now he gripped Red's shoulder with his free hand and shook it. "You can? Well? Let's have it, man!"

Unmoved, Red nodded. "She found her brother's head."

TWENTY-THREE

SHE CAME UP THE COMPANIONWAY WITH A CARVING KNIFE. IN THE OTHER hand she wielded an unopened bottle of beer by its neck as if it were a chisel mallet.

Throwing the wheel over, Red Means neatly rolled Quentin Asche over his hip and launched him at Tipsy, who turned her back in order to avoid impaling the featherweight. Before she could repurpose, Red boxed her ears and kicked her down the companionway. She landed face down on the saloon deck, knife and bottle clattering down the teak steps in her wake, her head ringing like a steeple the day Pushkin died.

In the countertop of the cabinet at her shoulder yawned the teak lid of a top-loading refrigerator, which contained the severed head of her brother. Tipsy had recoiled without closing the lid. She didn't want to stand up because she didn't want to look at it again, and she knew that if she did stand up she wouldn't be able to not look at it again. In any case she was so stunned she probably couldn't stand up anyway. But if she didn't stand up she might never see her brother again. Or what was left of him. Suddenly she understood the idea behind the open casket funeral. In this case the casket could be a hatbox. If she'd had a gun she could shoot Red. Or herself. She started to cry.

Quentin's head, having struck the finial of the upper end of the companionway handrail, now lay, still attached to the rest of him, on the wheelhouse deck, bleeding and unconscious. Not three steps away, Red held the wheel as *Kreutzer's Revenge* churned through a second three hundred and sixty degree turn. Fifty yards away, a magnificent view of the lights of Sausalito was occluded entirely by the stern quarter of *Hercules Perforce*, itself three hundred yards long and a hundred feet high, steaming at twelve knots against an ebb tide, bound for Southampton Channel, there to dock and spend the night mainlining petroleum into the long arm of Chevron.

Fifty yards between a vessel a mere twenty feet high and one at least ten times that looks like a near miss, and five panicked blasts from the *Hercules Perforce* air horn—meaning Ahoy, pissant vessel, change your course immediately or die—confirmed this impression. The sight of its bow wave alone, flashing over the tanker's keel bulb, had filled the windscreen of the smaller boat and rocked her beam end to beam end. The loose beer bottle careened back and forth over the saloon deck, as did the senseless Quentin Asche on the command deck. Even in her grief, Tipsy clung to the pedestal of the chart table. Red had the wheel to hold onto, and his sea legs to keep him vertical.

The wave passed. Red got *Kreutzer's Revenge* straightened out and heading north, passing aft of the stern lights of a tractor tug which steered the tanker by means of a taut wire hawser that stretched from a winch on the bow of the former to an after bitt on the stern of the latter.

At a steady six knots Red brought the cruiser across from Alcatraz, well astern of the tug, until the Point Blunt light, flashing green every five seconds, bore directly to port, about half a mile away. This placed *Kreutzer's Revenge* midstream of the dredged shipping channel, which suited Means just fine. Outside of the paper chart on the chart table, which he had purchased himself and taken an hour to study, and a splendid full-color GPS display on a stalk screwed to the overhead, which refreshed itself every few seconds, he had little idea of local conditions.

Such local knowledge as Red did have he'd picked up over the last few days in a tour of waterfront bars along Fisherman's Wharf, where he'd found knowledge of the San Francisco Bay a paucity indeed. He'd been more likely to receive uninvited a discourse on hotel conditions in Anaheim, should he care to visit Disneyland during his tour of the West Coast. He did find a chandlery, and therein his chart and a tide table. All else was tourism—Alcatraz sweatshirts, cotton candy, hamburger and crab restaurants, mimes and street musicians; there was even a western-wear store, the only one left in San Francisco. But fishermen? So far as Red could tell, Fisherman's Wharf was all wharf and no fishermen.

The boats were there, all right. But, in chatting up the skipper of one, who was handing out flyers advertising his gaily painted trawler as a handy vehicle for a sight-seeing trip to the Golden Gate Bridge and back, at $25 per pair of touristic eyeballs, Red discovered that the man hadn't pursued a fish in some years; on the contrary, he'd converted his boat to tourism at the behest of, and with some financial aid from, the City and County of San Francisco. "Local color," the skipper told him, as Red handed back the folded brochure. "There's no more fish to catch. They're all gone."

The fisherman-turned-tour-guide told Red that, since Red seemed interested in bare-boating overnight with his wife and kids on San Francisco Bay, the backside of Angel Island between Quarry Point, to the south, and Point Simpton, to the north, formed a lovely protected anchorage. There he would find shelter from our famously freezing thirty-knot westerlies and our Hawaiian and Alaskan rainstorms as well, both of which almost invariably blow out of the southwest. There's good holding ground, too, if one steers clear of cables and a wreck, both charted, that will surely foul an anchor. Best to buoy an anchor with a trip line anyway, just to be sure. If you lose the anchor the charter company will charge you twice what it's worth. Anyway, point being, if a man sails out there Monday through Friday it's a near certainty he will have the little cove to himself.

Red stood aside so that each member of a passing family, fresh from Disneyland, judging by the branding on their five identical sweatshirts, could take a copy of the ex-fisherman's brochure.

"They just want something with San Francisco printed on it," the ex-fisherman lamented, as they watched the five tourists jaywalk across Jefferson Street. "And they want it for free."

Behind the dark mass of Angel Island—a national park with no public lighting—all would be snugly private. If there were any screams to be heard, there would be nobody to hear them.

Red had anticipated Tipsy's keening Eureka; indeed, he'd been unable to devise a way around it. In the end, he came around to thinking it not such a bad idea. Get things started with a bang, what the hell.

So far, so good.

Now they could get down to business.

Anchor set and buoyed with one of the boat's big green fenders, Red killed the engine and all lights in the wheelhouse except those on various instruments and the VHS radio. Almost straight north, beyond the bow roller of *Kreutzer's Revenge*, the entire oil terminal at Richmond Long Wharf abruptly illuminated, as the maneuvers necessary to dock and pet-rosuction *Hercules Perforce* got underway. This was precisely the kind of operation Charley could have watched all night by way of amusing himself, Red reflected.

Maybe I'll park his head up on the dashboard, here, let him enjoy an uninterrupted view.

Red's smile revealed a missing tooth.

He stepped over the unconscious Quentin and reversed himself in order to back down the companionway, despite the fact that the vessel was not underway and no unpredictable sea tossed her. Gaining the saloon he nearly stepped on Tipsy, who lay whimpering on the carpeted sole.

He left her to it. He retrieved the carving knife, the beer bottle, and a lime from the deck and put them in the sink. Next to the sink stood Tipsy's empty glass. Next to the drink yawned the open mouth of the top-loading refrigerator. Up out of the refrigerator beamed Charley's severed head.

"You scared her good, Charley. Almost got me cut." He lifted the head by its tonsure and raked a fistful of ice out from under it. "Sometimes I think you lack subtlety."

He shared the handful of ice between two glasses, then paused as if to regard Charley by various angles of light. Wraiths of condensation trailed the head as he turned it. Only the ragged flesh of the severed neck showed signs of freezer burn. So far, so preserved. He considered the logo on the inside of the refrigerator door. He'd never heard of the brand, but it seemed to do the job. He replaced the head on the bag of ice and dropped the door, which latched itself. If I get my ass out of this fix, Red mused, one of these units might serve well in the tropics, where you can trade ice for anything. Anything at all.

"Okay, little sister." He gripped Tipsy under her shoulders. "Sit up. Let's get a little grog in us."

Overcome by apathy, Tipsy made no effort to resist.

Red eased her onto the bench, the upholstered back of which was the refrigerator cabinet.

Red drew the cork from a bottle rum and sniffed it. "I know you're not going to believe this." He half filled each of the two glasses. "Not at first, anyway." He nodded at her over one of the glasses. "But I had no choice in the matter." He threw back the contents of the glass at one go, squeezed shut his eyes, and smacked his lips. "Damn," he said, "that's some trophy shit." He poured three more fingers of rum in his own glass and offered her the second one. "Fact is, I liked your brother."

After a long pause, Tipsy accepted the drink. She took a sip, paused, took a second sip. After a third pause she took a longer draught, and then the glass was empty. Gingerly, as if it were made of the thinnest crystal, she set the glass onto the table.

Red recharged it. He showed her a bottle of soda water. Tipsy shook her head. Red put his hand on the latch of the refrigerator. "More ice?"

Tipsy looked up from the glass, at which she had been staring, and refocused her eyes on some middle distance. The refrigerator compressor switched on. Tipsy winced.

"I guess not," Red surmised.

Tipsy opened her mouth.

Red held up a hand. "Before you start casting about for someone to blame, I need to point out that I didn't kill your brother, you have no idea what's going on, and we need to talk. Because," he smiled without mirth, "things are even weirder than you think they are."

Tipsy put the glass to her lips, glanced down at its rim, then set it on the table. As the boat gently rocked, the liquor remained level in the glass, upon which was embossed a crossed pair of yacht club burgees, one blue, one red.

"Charley's dead," Tipsy finally said, her voice dull. Then: "What could possibly remain to discuss with a piece of shit such as yourself?"

"Since you bring it up," Red raised an eyebrow, "wouldn't you like to know how he died? On TV, they call it closure."

A shadow passed over Tipsy's face. "My brother . . ." she repeated softly.

". . . Was a friend of mine," Red said.

Tipsy exhaled. Her disgust, if unqualified and profane, had never been long-suffering. "He was your gofer. That's all. Your errand boy."

"I prefer the term contract employee. But after what—sixteen years?" Red shook his head. "We were friends."

Tipsy made an ineffectual gesture toward the refrigerator. "Where's the rest of him?"

"The sharks got the rest of him," Red replied truthfully. "It wasn't pretty."

Tipsy looked up. "You were there?"

Red nodded.

"He's aged," Tipsy said after a pause.

"Decapitation will do that to a man." Red shot up a hand. "So will twenty years," he added, by way of a kindly correction.

"Twenty-five," she corrected him. "Fifteen since I've seen him." Tipsy continued, as if talking to herself. "He never told me about the earring."

"He got the ear pierced in Brazil," Red supplied helpfully. "A long time ago."

"Brazil," Tipsy repeated with little inflection.

"These days, it's a fad for men to wear earrings," Red told her. "A hundred years ago, a sailor got his ear pierced for a reason."

"Do tell," Tipsy said.

"You rounded the horn under sail? Cape Horn? Down there at the bottom of South America?"

Tipsy made no response.

"You got your ear pierced. West around? The right ear. East around? The left ear." Red pinched his left earlobe with the fingers of his left hand. "I never made that passage. But your brother did."

"Really?" Tipsy showed a little curiosity. "Charley rounded Cape Horn? Under sail?"

"East around. That he did. That's why the earring is on his left ear."

"Wow . . ."

"Aboard a thirty-four-foot gaff-rigged ketch." Red sipped his drink. "Wow, indeed."

Tipsy showed more interest. "By himself?"

Red shook his head. "Just one other guy, but he was a very experienced skipper. Charley was his crew."

After a long pause, she sighed again. "What's . . . what's with . . ." She moved her thumb over her shoulder.

Red opened the palm of his left hand, lifted it, and let it fall onto his thigh. "I need to prove it."

"Prove what?"

"That he's dead."

"To me?"

Red shrugged. "For starters."

"Consider it proved."

"Yeah." Red nodded.

"What's wrong with a simple death certificate?" Tipsy asked.

Red shook his head. "Too easy to forge."

"And you didn't do it?"

Red shook his head.

"Promise?" Her voice sounded very small.

Red nodded.

"Okay." Tipsy collected herself and sat up straight. After a moment she sighed deeply. "So where did this . . . evidence . . . get collected?"

"In the Straits of Florida. About halfway between Havana and Key West. He was damn near home free. At least," Red added darkly, "it looked that way."

Tipsy sat up a little straighter. "What stopped him?"

"His boat hit something. Could have been a balk of timber torn off a dock by a storm, could have been a palm tree or a shipping container, it could even have been another wreck. It was bad luck, pure and simple."

"Charley had bad luck? Surely not."

"Yeah, well . . ." Red managed a smile. "He was on an uptick. A couple of years worth of uptick, I'd say."

"And then he signs on to work for you again. Brilliant."

Red considered her. "What do you know about it?"

Tipsy blinked. "You sent your note in one of his envelopes."

"How do you think I found you?"

Tipsy answered the question with another. "Aside from his head and some envelopes, what else did you take off his boat?"

"Not nearly enough."

"Couldn't you have left him alone?"

"Going back to work was Charley's idea."

"Couldn't you have told him no? Why Charley, of all people? Hadn't he suffered enough? Don't you have any number of idiots hanging around, looking to make a quick buck?"

"I wasn't picking on—. Besides, Charley was good. He—" Red held up both hands. "I don't want to get into a pissing match with you, Tipsy. You've had a bad shock. Besides which, you took a shot to the head."

"Two."

"I'm surprised you can remember that."

"I'd be more surprised if I forgot it."

"It was an automatic reaction," Red said defensively. "Like taking—" He failed to arrest a gesture toward the refrigerator. "Come to think about it, you may have a concussion. You shouldn't be drinking."

Tipsy wasn't missing much. "Cutting off my brother's head was an automatic reaction?"

"I had to do it," Red insisted. "I need to demonstrate that things have gone . . . awry."

"Awry?" Tipsy shook her head as if trying to wake up. "Awry, you say?" She spoke through clenched teeth. "What things went . . . awry?"

"It's going to be all I can do to get my ass out of this sling."

"What—? You mean your proof didn't . . . work?"

"I haven't tried it." Red chewed his lip. "Not yet."

"Why not?"

"Things have indeed gone awry, and that's a fact. But they may not have gone permanently south. Not yet anyway."

"Unless your name is Charley Powell."

"But not if your name is Tipsy." Red blew air through pursed lips. "Can we get on with this? I would like," and here he smiled, "not to be shouldering the blame for wiping out the entire family. You hear what I'm saying?"

"Oh? And how do I fit into this mess?"

Red brightened the smile. "Reluctantly?"

"You can say that again."

"You're already in it," Red told her, "up to your neck."

"And how do you figure that? I don't even know what mess you're talking about. Are we dealing in dope or shrunken heads? Even if Charley got himself decapitated over a lousy boatload of dope, what the hell, and I repeat"—she pointed a finger at Red—"other than the fact that I no longer have a brother, what in the hell does it have to do with me?" She frowned. "Does somebody think that I somehow have this boatload of dope? Is that the deal?" She glared at him warily. "Do you think I have it?"

Red put down his drink opened the door of the top-loading refrigerator. When he plucked Charley's head up out of it by the hair, Tipsy yipped. Holding the head to one side, Red used his free hand to remove the bag of ice, which he dropped unceremoniously onto the countertop. The free hand then produced a package wrapped in black plastic and sealed with gray duct tape, which he pitched onto the saloon table.

"Would that it were that simple." He gestured toward the counter. "More ice?"

"No!"

Red dropped the bag of ice into the mouth of the refrigerator, punched it twice with the fist of his free hand, lowered the severed head onto the divot, and let the door fall with a bang.

Then, with silent courtesy, he poured Tipsy another drink.

About a minute passed.

"Is that what I think it is?"

"I don't know." Red raked a few shards of ice off the counter and dropped them into his drink. "Do you think it's one kilogram of pink Peruvian flake?"

"It really does look like a brick," Tipsy marveled ingenuously. Then she lied. "I've never seen one before."

Red just shrugged. "Some people don't get around like other people do."

"So now what's the hassle?" Tipsy asked. "Shouldn't you be celebrating while I make funeral arrangements?"

Red solemnly shook his head. "We got nothing to celebrate, and the funeral's going to have to wait."

Tipsy toyed with her drink. Finally, just to make conversation, she inquired after the value of the brick.

Red responded as if he were bored. "Wholesale, forty-four thousand bucks. Retail by the ounce, maybe seventy thousand. Gram-wise on the street it could go to ninety thousand." He closed his eyes and massaged the wrinkles in his forehead. "Ordinary cops would exaggerate the price, but the feds would double it to the media, to 170 thousand, say. If you asked them again they'd round up to two hundred thousand." He smiled wanly. "The feds got a lot of overhead."

Tipsy's face hardened. "You killed Charley for—"

"I did not kill Charley, Tipsy," Red reiterated patiently. "For reasons I don't entirely understand, Charley got himself into a pickle, and for reasons I more or less have come to terms with, he took the permanent way out."

"What's that supposed to mean? My brother cut off his own head?"

"It's effectively true," Red affirmed grimly. "Your brother might just as well have gone ahead, as it were, and committed suicide."

"After all he'd been through," Tipsy responded incredulously, "Charley committed suicide?"

"I saw it with my own eyes."

"I don't believe it."

Red made no response.

"How?" she asked softly.

"He chained himself to the mast of his sinking ship in shark-infested waters."

Tipsy opened her mouth. Nothing came out. She closed her mouth. After another moment she said, "That's redundant."

"That it was."

"I don't understand. Was he sick?"

"No."

"Was he about to get caught?"

Red hesitated, then shook his head. "Not till his boat got stove."

"Well why, then?"

"At the time, I had no idea."

"About what?"

Red nodded severely. "It took me a long time to believe it. Weeks, in fact."

"Believe what? That he would he kill himself?"

Red balled his left hand into a fist. He stood still but he shivered, the very picture of inarticulateness. The ice in his drink rattled. He set it down. The he leaned across the table. His shadow fell over her. His face, reddening as if from its own power source, hovered inches from hers. She could see every detail of his sun-blasted complexion, the purpling veins in the flesh of his nose, flecks of dead skin on his chapped lips, the gap where his lateral incisor had been, and the pink fractals in the whites around his startling blue eyes. His breath enveloped her, an intimacy sweetened by rum. His hair and clothing reeked of fish and diesel and exhaustion. The welt of a scar on the cheek beneath his left eye whitened visibly. His unkempt hair virtually writhed with energy. Tipsy shrank away from this visage until her shoulders came firmly against the upholstered side of the refrigerator behind her.

"Your goddamned beloved brother double-crossed me." Red spoke almost tenderly, but his rage was barely contained.

His anger charged the air around him, but Tipsy could see that Red was confused, too. He was also amazed, confounded, frustrated, even hurt, and he was having trouble admitting to himself the truth of his own assertion. Perhaps this was the first time he'd said as much aloud. His eyes bore into hers, questing, searching, unrequited. Tipsy, inexplicably and to her surprise, realized that she felt some kind of sympathy for the man.

"What are you saying?" she asked softly, so softly that she might have been asking the question of herself.

Red blinked the blonde lashes that sparsely tenanted his translucent eyelids. "Sixteen years," he growled in wonder, "and Charley decides to go it alone. Why?" He straightened up and downed his drink. "He was the best at what he did. And suddenly he decides to become the best at what I do? What possessed him? It's like he took leave of his senses." Red regarded the black package. "And of all the deals to screw me on, he has to screw me on this deal? Well," he nodded, "that part I understand. That part is pure, shit-bird Charley. Perfect bone-head timing. The exact wrong deal at the exact wrong time. But that he did it at all?" Red shook his head. "I've thought about it for almost three months. It makes no sense. An entire lifetime." He blew air between his lips. "Forfeited. I just don't get it."

"What about the first time?" Tipsy asked quietly.

Red frowned. "You mean the prison thing?" He shook his head. "That wasn't a mistake. That was the luck of the draw. Could have happened to anybody. Charley knew that. And Charley did the right thing. He didn't squeal. Took his medicine. He knew he'd be taken care of when he got out. And he was. Sure it cost him. But he knew the risks. We all know the risks. Everybody does his part. Everybody takes his lumps."

Tipsy cleared her throat. "So what was different about this time?"

Red's eyes refocused on a picture only he could see. "This time, it was a mistake. This time it was just the one deal. One lousy deal, but it was a big one. The biggest. That's why I let Charley do it! Hell." He looked at her. "I was glad he turned up. I'd been sitting dockside and thinking I'd take a pass on the job because I didn't have the right guy for it." Red shook his head. "Charley should not have tried to think for himself. Out of all the deals, it was the wrong one. He wouldn't have gotten away with it. And it's the one deal that could get us both killed. Not incarcerated, mind you, but killed. That's the alternative to success. Charley must have known. So—why?" Red's eyes showed no remorse or guilt or evil or beatitude—on the contrary, his eyes were as neutral as a pair of marbles in the blank visage of a limestone faun. "You too, Tipsy, you could die because of Charley. Even you." Red looked at the refrigerator, at the drinks, at the melting fragments of ice on the countertop, at the black package wrapped in duct tape. "You gotta understand this part. You and—" He pointed at the companionway. "—and that guy," Red said. "Your friend could die, too."

Tipsy started. "Quentin!" She stood up. "I forgot about Quentin!"

TWENTY-FOUR

TIPSY STOOD OFF THE BENCH AND ALMOST FELL OVER. "WHAT DID YOU DO to me?" she wailed, holding her head with one hand—and the edge of the chart table with the other.

"Pure reflex," Red said, steadying her. "Plus, don't forget, you're on a boat."

"How could I forget this nightmare?" She tore herself away from him. "Quentin!"

He lay on his back, right where Red had left him, with his head on the sword mat at the top of the companionway, its bleached sisal soaked in blood. Just as they reached him, Quentin began to spasm and vomit.

"Quentin!" Tipsy grabbed his shoulders. "What are you—" She shook him violently. "You choke on own your puke and I'll kill you!"

"Son of a bitch," Red groused, as he tried to push her out of the way. "Every time I turn my back on this job, it goes straight to shit."

"Stop puking!"

"You know CPR?" Red demanded. "If not, move!"

"Are you kidding?" she replied, pushing back. "I can't even swim!"

Red brushed her aside. "Call his name." He rolled Quentin onto his stomach, with his head slightly beyond the top step of the saloon companionway. With an adroit, simultaneous push on either side of Quentin's spine, he caused a bolus of mucus and vomit to be ejected from Quentin's nose and mouth.

"Call his name!"

"Quentin! Goddamn you, answer me!"

Red rolled the half-conscious Quentin onto his back and swept the mouth with his forefinger, bringing up more mucus. He placed one hand atop Quentin's sternum, his other hand atop that, and pushed down and released fourteen times, counting aloud. Then he pinched Quentin's cheeks so that his mouth opened, leaned over, and his mouth was an inch from Quentin's when Tipsy yelled, "Stop! Wait! Stop, stop!" and yanked Red by his hair.

"What the fuck are you doing?" Red angrily stiff-armed her. "I'm trying to save this guy's life!"

Staggered by the blow, Tipsy began to hyperventilate. "He—He—"

"Out with it!"

She slid to the deck. "He has AIDS, you fucking idiot!"

Red blinked. "This guy has AIDS and I'm the idiot?" Tipsy's eyes enlarged. Then she kicked him. Red ignored it. After a mere second's consideration, he applied his thumbs to either side of Quentin's jaw and thrust them upward. More mucus appeared at the corners of Quentin's mouth, but not in such quantity as before.

"Soak a rag in cold water and bring it here. Maybe there's a pair of gloves under the sink. If not, look in the engine room."

It wasn't the napkin with the yacht's name embroidered into it that took her so long to find, it was the pair of rubber scullery gloves, neatly folded behind the trash can under the sink. By the time she returned to the bridge Red had air flowing through Quentin's throat, and his chest and stomach were moving, though somewhat spasmodically. "Fold it up and press it against the head wound. Steady pressure, not too firm. Call his name."

"Quentin . . . Quentin!"

Quentin groaned.

"Excellent! Call him!"

"Quentin." Her voice broke. "Quentin, please!"

"T-Tipsy," Quentin whispered.

"That's it, old man." Red belayed the chest compressions. "What's your name?"

"Asche," Quentin stammered feebly. "As in p-pain in the Asche. . . ."

Red raised an eyebrow. "I believe he's going to make it."

"He'd even make jokes at your funeral." Tipsy took Quentin's hand.

Red frowned as if puzzled. "What better place to make them?"

Quentin now breathed, if laboriously. His eyes remained closed. "I'm exhausted," he whispered. "And I've got a splitting headache. What have you been drinking?"

Tipsy smiled through her tears. Back when he was a hypochondriac, before he had real medical problems, Quentin was a student of contact hangovers, to which he often referred as *near-field wickedness*.

"Let's put him to bed," Red suggested. "When he feels up to drinking some water, we'll try to get some aspirin into him."

"Are you sure it's okay to let him sleep?"

"Why not? If he can't sleep, we'll have to deal him in on the rest of the pain that's available around here."

"You're right. If he goes to sleep we can—" She stopped and frowned. We can what—take turns holding Charley's head? And abruptly she realized that it had been some fifteen minutes since she'd last remembered to be upset about her brother's head. Damn, came the very next thought. If that doesn't prove you can get used to anything. . . .

One arm under the shoulders, the other under the knees, Red cradled and lifted Quentin as if he weighed no more than a bolt of velvet. They bundled Quentin into a bunk in the captain's stateroom, which opened off the pilot house. Donning the blue gloves, Tipsy rinsed the blood out of the cloth napkin and reapplied it to the head wound. The gash, though two inches long, did not appear to include a skull fracture. Even so, the sight of it rattled Tipsy.

"Head wounds always bleed disproportionately to their severity," Red reassured her, as well as Quentin.

"And proportionately to how much blood thinner you're taking," Tipsy pointed out.

"Warfarin, probably," Red speculated. "Same shit they use to kill rats."

Tipsy scowled. "You're just a walking physician's desk reference, aren't you?"

"Maintain the pressure," Red said. "It'll just take longer for the platelets to rally to the cause."

Two rinsed napkins later, the blood had slowed to a trickle.

"This boat is bigger than your apartment," Quentin whispered, as Tipsy tucked the edge of a Tartan blanket under his chin. He lowered his eyes. "What's with the tacky plaid?" And he fell asleep.

"He's going to be fine," Red said, as Tipsy closed the stateroom door.

"Thanks to you."

Red regarded her. "Why didn't you keep your mouth shut?"

"About the AIDS?" She shook her head. "Don't be ridiculous." The gloves were streaked with saliva, mucus, and blood. Red found a box of latex gloves in the engine room, and without a word they set about cleaning up the boat. They took up the sword mat, which was Velcroed to the deck, and put it into the washing machine, along with Quentin's bloodied shirt, various cloth napkins, detergent, and bleach. They found a mop and a bucket and detergent and swabbed the deck and companionway steps. When they'd finished they returned to the saloon and washed up.

As he added a capful of bleach to the last basin of water, Red asked how long Quentin had been living with AIDS.

"It's been about five years since the diagnosis," came the answer.

Red rinsed his hands. "Is that why he's so thin?"

"He's always been slim, but, yes, he's slimmer now."

"Does he do the various medications?"

"A three-way cocktail. Plus the blood thinner, vitamins, and I don't know what-all else."

"What's the prognosis?"

She shook her head.

"Nature will take its course," Red adduced. "Some people survive for a long time. It helps to take care of yourself."

"Hanging out with me probably doesn't do him all that much good. He'll get vituperative with anybody he disagrees with, which, while it stimulates him, makes demands on his energy. But he no longer drinks. That was a big step. The worst thing—" She lowered her voice. "The worst thing is—was—his fast lane with no-brain boyfriend, who'll down any drug that comes along and still likes a popper as he's coming."

Red raised an eyebrow. "That's bad for you?"

"It's bad for Quentin. Not anymore, though, maybe?" She crossed each middle finger over its index finger. "Quentin seems to have broken it off with him."

"Does he have anybody else?"

She shook her head. "Just me. His family quit talking to him decades ago. Now, ironically enough, he's outlived every one of them."

"Why'd they quit talking to him?"

"He's gay, and they hated him for it."

"Stupid," Red said. "But at least he knew why they hated him."

Tipsy considered this. "You know," she said, "I'll have to point that out to him. Anyway," she added, "you saved his life."

"I'd have done the same for you."

She looked at him. "Mouth to mouth?"

He looked at her. "You know, when we were fighting back there?" He snapped his fingers. "I just about got wood."

So much for coquetry. Tipsy's jaw dropped, but she didn't manage to suppress a smile, and she blushed.

Red preceded her to the chart table and poured two glasses of rum. As she was drying her hands, he said to his drink, "I'd have done the same for your brother, too, if I'd gotten there in time." She added the hand towel to the washing machine, a compact Italian front-loader which would make an astonishing variety of audible machinations as it both washed and dried. After a prolonged study of its control panel, she managed to start it.

As she closed the teak bifold doors that concealed the laundry closet, Tipsy was nearly overwhelmed by feelings such as she had not experienced in a long time, if ever—tender regard, gratitude, the fatigue that succeeds a surge of adrenaline, the incongruous opulence of the amenities which presently surrounded them, anger, shock, a severed head in the refrigerator. When you drink yourself to sleep most nights, she thought to herself, it's hard to articulate any feeling at all. Aloud she said, "Are you ready to tell me what happened to Charley?"

"Are you ready to hear it?"

She nodded. "Yes."

Red wasted no time. He stepped to the wheelhouse, returned with a briefcase, cleared the saloon table, and unfolded a bedraggled chart. NOAA 11013, Tipsy read at a corner of its margin, *Straits of Florida and Approaches.* Also from the briefcase Red produced dividers, a pencil, parallel rulers, a navigation triangle, a knackered copy of Reed's *Nautical Almanac for the Caribbean*, and lastly a school copy book, its cover a mottled black and white to which was glued the type of label one might expect to find on a jar of home-made jam, white with a red border and chamfered corners. On it was written, in Charley's careful script,

Log of Vessel
Vellela Vellela
Vol. XI

"Volume Eleven," Tipsy read aloud. "He was only aboard that boat for three years."

"Charley tended to bloviation in his logbooks."

"And the other ten?"

"Gone down with the ship." Red tapped the copy book with a finger. "He made the last entry in this one the day before she foundered."

Tipsy stared at it.

"Wrap yourself around a drink," Red suggested.

She looked at her glass. "I've had enough for the moment."

Red took a sip from his own drink and set it aside. "Where was Charley the last time you heard from him?"

Tipsy indicated the bottle. "A place called Rum Cay. Wait. It was the next stop. He sent me a rambling couple of pages from his next stop. I can't remember the name, but it was a day's sail from Rum Cay."

"Long Cay." Red took up the dividers. "They're quite close together, and either one is a good place to begin the tale of *Vellela Vellela*'s last adventure."

"Charley's last adventure," Tipsy qualified glumly.

"And your next one."

She shook her head. "I don't do adventure."

Red produced a pair of reading glasses from the briefcase. "You do now." Displaying the habitude of a man unused to wearing them, starting with one ear and working toward the other, he wrapped the temple bars around his face by hooking one onto his left ear, then turning his head inside the spectacles until he'd hooked his right ear. He cocked his head back, so as to read through the half-lenses, and touched the dividers to the chart. "Rum Cay."

Tipsy leaned over the chart. "It looks tiny."

"It is that." Pricking one leg of the dividers into a pre-existing hole at Rum Cay, Red stretched the other leg of the dividers almost due south, until its pin touched another island. "Long Cay. See this symbol?" He touched a finger to the chart. "That's a wreck. Probably more than one." He moved the dividers over to the latitude scale, on the right-hand edge of the chart, and read off the distance. ". . . About sixty-seven nautical miles. Rum Cay is big enough for a bar, diesel and groceries, a one-man dive outfit, not much else. Albert Town, on the other hand, on the south end of Long Cay, is deserted."

"You've been there."

Red shook his head. "Never had a reason to visit Albert Town. I own a piece of a little business on Rum Cay, however, that silk-screens t-shirts, which I then import into the States. They're designed by my former wife and screened by her current boyfriend. They've lived on Rum Cay ever since she got out of rehab."

"I thought your wife died of cancer."

"Different wife."

"How many wives have you had?"

"I can remember two. Your brother was talented, you know."

"Sure. I . . . Well, actually . . . You know, Red, I haven't. . . ." She arrested a glance at the refrigerator behind her. "I'm surprised I recognized him." She managed a small half-laugh before her voice trailed to nothing.

"Are you okay?"

"No. Should I be?"

Red nodded. "Charley was an accomplished sailor, among other things. Good sextant navigator. Handy with the marlinspike. A fine boatwright. And he could cook, too." Red leaned over the chart, waggled the folded dividers between fore and index fingers, and peered at the speck at the far southeastern edge of the Bahamas, pale green amid soundings of thousands of fathoms. "Let's pretend we're calling in at Rum Cay." He took up Reed's, consulted its index, and found his place. "Port Nelson, Rum Cay," he read aloud. "You may be able to tie up at the government dock temporarily. Depths are reported to be less than 6 feet." He looked up from the book. "Six feet is one fathom." He touched the chart. "Just here, on the northwest corner of the island, soundings exceed 2,000 fathoms. If you could see a topographical representation of this tiny island, rising from a bottom two miles deep, you'd probably find it frightening." He glanced at her over the half-lenses. "*Vellela Vellela* had a draft of a little less than five feet."

"Sounds like a near thing."

Red shrugged. "It's mean lower low. *Anchor west of town,*" he continued to read, "as depths permit. The charted approach takes you through a deep passage between several coral reefs. A bearing of 013°T—the T stands for True—on Cotton Field Point brings you safely across the reef. When the dock at Port Nelson bears 081°T steer for the dock. . . ." He turned a page and flattened the book on the table so she could see it. "Here's the local chart." He moved the stainless steel points of the dividers over it. "Heads up, the soundings on this chart are in meters. I've marked the bearings. Here's Cotton Field Point. Here's the approach. Thirteen degrees bears like this. These are reefs. Prevailing wind and current both come out of the southeast until you get inside, where the wind drops and the current tends to come round this way. . . . There's the tide to take into consideration, of course. Here's the Port Nelson bearing. Come to starboard. . . ."

"Jeez," Tipsy said. "Is the point that it's complicated?"

"Yes, and more so because your brother did this stuff under sail, without an engine."

"Really? Why?"

"Well, for one thing, his boat didn't have a goddamn engine. But, for another, that's the way he wanted it."

"Is that as difficult as it sounds?"

"Very few modern sailors have what it takes to do it. Skill, patience, nerve—and two anchors immediately to hand."

"Or stupidity. Or foolhardiness."

"As you like." Red took up the logbook. "Let me be straight with you, Tipsy—"

"Oh, do," she retorted.

Red's eyes met hers. "Settle down," he suggested. "I'm hoping that somewhere in here . . ." He burnished the cover of the logbook with his palm. Tipsy noted, not for the first time, that his hands had been calloused and thickened by work. ". . . lies a hint or a clue as to what Charley did to himself and, in turn, what he's even now doing to us."

"From beyond a watery grave," she qualified bitterly.

"As I said before," Red's eyes were steady on her, "we're stuck with each other. We don't have the time to get pissed off about how we got into this. We need to get pissed off about how we're going to get out of it."

"Maybe you could start by telling me what 'this' is." She assessed Red with a frank look.

Red assessed her back. "There will be no wriggling on the hook," he told her. "We're going to be partners on this problem until it's solved. You hear what I'm saying?" He shook his head. "We have no choice. You have to trust me; I have to trust you. For the time being, please take my word for that and," he handed her the logbook, "give this your undivided attention."

She looked at it but she didn't take it. "But what—?"

"Before we get off this boat," he interrupted, "you will have the whole story, I promise, even if it takes all night to explain it. I'm hoping for a little enlightenment myself. Okay? And don't worry." He placed the logbook on the chart in front of her. "It's all going to become too depressingly clear what we're up against."

The logbook's pages, once soaked in water and now dried, looked as if they were stacked in waves. "I dried it with a thermocouple heat gun," Red noted. "I keep it on the boat for shrink." She looked up, puzzled. "It's like a hair dryer," Red waved a fist back and forth. "Heat-shrink? For sealing electrical connections? It's a kind of tubing. . . ." She shook her head. He shook his head. "Skip it." He opened the logbook to a page marked by a paperclip. "Read aloud. We'll follow the voyage on the chart."

TWENTY-FIVE

DATE	TIME	LOG	COURSE	WEATHER	POSITION
3/16	0430	0	165°C	NE 10-15	23°39'2" N. Lat.
				1005 mb	74°51'6" W. Long.
				Fair	(Cotton Field Point Light)

Remarks

Note: Mag Var. 8°44'W

Stood out of Port Nelson before dawn. Set a course of 157° True, which I expect to hold for some 68 miles, with corrections for set and drift, until we close with the Albert Town Light on Long Cay. At five knots that's about 13-1/2 hours, which should get us there in plenty of daylight. Current hereabouts, according to Reed's, looks to be about 0.6 knots SE, going our way.

DATE	TIME	LOG	COURSE	WEATHER	POSITION
3/16	1830	72	At Anchor	Clear	22°35" N. Lat.
			Long Cay	1008 mb	74°22'5" W. Long.
					(Windsor Point)

Remarks

Actually, we're maybe one mile NNE of Windsor Point, but I'm beat and feel a fit of introspection coming on. I'll do the exact position in the morning.

Anchored in a shoal west-facing inlet within spitting distance SSW of a pretty wreck. She's been stripped, of course, no doubt within days of her stranding, but what a fair-weather example of a saloon deck whorehouse she once must have been. Only her steel hull has allowed her to resist the depredations of the natives and the sea for as long as she has. One good hurricane bearing NW will be the end of her, and the beginning of yet another uncharted maritime hazard teeming with edible sea life—good fishing, of which there is already plenty around here.

Cedric and I once fouled an anchor on a reef not too far north of here, and dove it only to find two more anchors, both of them better gear than the one we were trying to save. Wound up spending a week within a three or four mile radius diving shoals and inlets for fouled anchors. We found a dozen. Some of them were too big, of course. We used fenders and gallon jugs to buoy the ones we thought we could handle, then came back about two weeks later with tools aboard For Tuna, *Cedric's boat at the time. (His current one's called* Tunacity. *Get the drift?) Oh for an acetylene torch!—in spite of the lack of which we wound up with nine dandy examples of modern and ancient anchor theory, and so much barnacle-encrusted rode we had to leave most of it behind. Ever optimistic, we sank a lot of chain way up a tidal creek, just as far as we could push the dinghy under the load, gunnels awash even with us over the side, on the theory that some day we'd come back for it. There are excellent directions to the trove in one of my old log books—don't forget to allow for something like ten years' migration of magnetic variation. Tonight, from this anchorage, I can see the mouth of the creek. Oddly enough,* Vellela *is anchored on the exact back bearing of the vector from the creek to the middle of the entrance to Man of War Channel—277° True. Anyway, whether it's been silted over or not, anybody close aboard the trove will know it, for the iron there will box his compass. I can just see the expressions on the treasure hunters' faces when they realize they're excavating something like 1,352 pounds of 5/8" BBB chain!*

Intervening hurricanes, economic circumstances superior and otherwise, a bad back, these and more have precluded recovery—by me, anyway. As for Cedric, I haven't the slightest idea where he is these days. I had to put a few cables between me and his substance abuse, and now we've drifted apart. I mean to ask after him in Key West.

We weighed our nine anchors and made straight for Man-O-War Cay, about ninety miles and almost due west of here, just north of the channel, the gateway to the Great Bahama Banks, where the fishin' is bitchin'. Sold every hook to D-Ray's Vintage Marine for two thousand bucks Bahamian. Cedric took two hundred off the top for gas and we split the rest—voilà, a $900 jolt to the kitty. Kitty likes being jolted!

I know it's considered déclassé that is to say unsalty to commit personal ramblings to a ship's log. On the other hand, who's watching? Besides, I've been alone for so long I need someone to talk to, I can't afford a shrink, I'm too mean and old and ugly for a girlfriend, the bosun is a figment of my imagination (you've never met the bosun but don't worry, nobody else has met him either) and—well. Did you know that Albert Town has been officially declared a ghost town? "American Loyalists" first settled this islet in 1783, bringing with them slaves and cotton seed. The enterprise ultimately failed. Man-O-War Cay has similar Tory antecedents. I'll bet that when the wind blows just so, Albert Town has quite a tale to tell. Ours are not the only chains buried around here. . . .

DATE	TIME	LOG	COURSE	WEATHER	POSITION
3/19	0620	72	285°C	Cloudy	22°33' 55" N. Lat.
				1001 mb	74°25' 20" W. Long.
					(Albert Town Light
					bearing 191°M.
					Long Kay Light
					bearing 98°M.)

Remarks

Mag. Var. 8°44'W

Okay. Note Position correction, derived above.

A couple nights of sleep. Excellent. Proper dawn breakfast of fresh snapper, beer-bread, black tea. Replaced bowl with chart, fork with pencil, knife with dividers. Kept teacup, plotted course. Weighed anchor, departed in good order. Set a course of 277° True, straight for Man of War Channel, some 85 miles distant, though I have no intention of going there.

DATE	TIME	LOG	COURSE	WEATHER	POSITION
3/19	0735	76.5	231°C	Scattered small cumulus 1003 mb	22° 35' 40" N. Lat. 74°26' 20" W. Long. (Albert Cay Light bearing 105°M; Long Cay Light bearing 97°M —which is the reciprocal of the Man of War Channel bearing, 285°M less 8° var = 277°T!] (Note: Logging course notes because on-board chart almost obliterated by previous plots, erasures, prickings, and rum rings.)

Remarks

223° True is an 87-1/2 mile rhumb line that gets us across Crooked Passage, Mira por Vos Passage—how I love that name!—and West Channel, not quite at right angles but in daylight and short order.

(Note: At approx. 22°7' N. Lat 74°W. Long we cross mag var curve after which mag var will be an even 8°W.)

Beaucoup shipping, fishing, and cruising, which is good on the one hand, as it provides a cloak of anonymity, and bad on the athwartship paw, as maintaining vigilant watch means the skipper and crew of Vellela Vellela *are going to see damn little rest between now and Boca Chica Key, maybe a week's time hence, weather permitting, touch the wood.*

Haven't been voyaging down this way in a long time and I'll tell you what, it's beautiful. If I weren't working I'd take a month to get to Florida. Maybe six months. Maybe never get there.

When the light on Santo Domingo Cay bears 312° Magnetic we'll come up to 287-1/2° True, which should put us on a dead run up Old Bahama Channel. The most visible Cuban light charted is at Cabo Lucrecia, visible for 25 miles, 29 miles off which we'll make the turn. If the night is as clear as it is now, we should be able to navigate by its loom and the Santo Domingo vector. But there's the usual ominous Notice to Mariners on my chart. "CAUTION: Many lights on the Cuban coast have been reported to be irregular or extinguished." Your embargo at work, my gringo compatriots, and doesn't that make you feel all warm and fuzzy? Too bad the Cubans can't sell a little sugar, some rum, and a few cigars on the American market. It might give them the extra bucks to be maintaining their aids to navigation, not to mention medicine for their children, felts for their pianos, not to mention a taste for capitalism.

Sticking one's nose into Reed's Nautical Almanac *and looking up the lovely Bahía de Banes, whose entrance is about fifteen miles east around a half a circle south of Cabo Lucrecia, one reads the following.*

This pocket bay is currently being developed as a tourist center. If arriving from the Bahamas, this is an excellent place to clear in. Entrance is straightforward, deep, and all-weather. Line up the conspicuous white building until it bears 115°, and steer straight for it until you reach the new marina. Much of the bay has been designed as a national park. . . . A new aquarium is accessible with a good dinghy; nearby is a new deluxe hotel that is open to visiting sailors for excellent meals.

An excellent place to clear in, that is, if your haling port is almost anywhere in the world except the United States.

DATE	TIME	LOG	COURSE	WEATHER	POSITION
3/19	1630	165	281-1/2°C	Lucid	21°33' N. Lat.
					75°30' W. Long.
					Santo Domingo Cay
					Light bearing 312°M
					Loom of Cabo Lucretia
					light bearings 196°-207°;
					Average=201.5°
					Depth 8730 ft., 1430
					fathoms charted.

Remarks

Made good the WNW turn around S. Domingo Cay at 0700 hrs. Not too shabby for dead reckoning. Plenty of shipping. Hauled down the radar reflector, polished it, sent it back aloft. Looking forward to little or no sleep all the way to Key West, which is about 450 miles from here. As goes single-handed passage-making, that's not a lot of time to go short on sleep. As go 54-year-old sailors, well . . . If there weren't all this political bullshit going on with Cuba, there would be a dozen snug little ports to put into along its north coast and get some sleep, along with beer and empanadas. Then, too, I don't want this vessel searched no matter who's searching it, do I.

DATE	TIME	LOG	COURSE	WEATHER	POSITION
3/19	1930	182	281-1/2°C	Still Lucid	21°36' N. Lat.
					75°47' W. Long.
					Santo Domingo Cay
					Light bearing 20°M;
					Loom of Cabo Lucrecia
					light bearings 164°M
					to 177°M. Average =
					170-1/2°M. Depth
					Sounding 8782 ft.,
					1470 fathoms plotted.

Remarks

If there's salt water in your veins, this is fun. This time tomorrow we won't be eight miles from Cuba, which should be showing the light on Cayo Paredon Grande, halfway up the Old Bahama Channel. I think that means Big Wall Cay. *My Spanish dictionary only has* pared—*wall*—*which seems pretty close.*

Eight miles is well within the twelve mile limit of course, where the Cubans will have every right to board Vellela Vellela.

Man, would it be fun to visit Cuba. What a place. I haven't been there since the late eighties. It's big, you know, like about 700 miles long. There are hundreds if not thousands of islands, bays, inlets, and harbors. The chart shows railway lines that start and stop, bays large and small, barrier islands, cays, reefs, rocks—an entire world, in short, which, so far as I can tell, has barely made it into the twentieth century, let alone the twenty-first. Navigation around the island is probably of the ancient mariner ilk—hand-held compass, lead line, water color, dead reckoning, local knowledge, and luck. GPS cartridges or cards for Cuba exist, but all the gringo ones claim to be about someplace else. Maybe the French have a good one? Maybe nobody does—in other words, just Vellela Vellela's cup of tea-laced-with-rum, a perfect place for an anachronism like me, who sails a boat with no engine.

Anyway, I can't be thinking about Cuba now. It's the hour to adhere to Red's First Postulate, which is, never break more than one law at a time. It's engraved on a brass plaque over the door to his engine room. Yes . . . would that things were so simple. . . .

Anyway, it's you, dear logbook, to whom I confide the plan. We should make landfall in Boca Chica within a week. On board we have a significant stash of Bahamian t-shirts. Each and every one them sports a caricature of Old Helios, with sunglasses and dreadlocks, surmounting the invocation that you Don't Forget To Inhale, Mon! S, M, L, XL, XXL. They could have been made anywhere, of course, but in fact they come from a little silkscreen outfit on Rum Cay. It's one of Red's laundry operations. Get it? Ah ha, as Cedric would say, ah hahahahaha . . . We've got a license to unload these things into the hands of a wholesaler of shirts to tourist shops and kiosks headquartered on Boca Chica Key, yet another of Red's laundry operations.

Looked up late this afternoon to see a very large shark fin not twenty-five yards abeam. Close aboard! These waters are famous for their sharks, as well as their fishing. But it always amazes me that the creature can find a little vessel like Vellela Vellela atop 1,300 fathoms. I mean, don't they hunt in three dimensions, or what? That's a lot of room.

It's also why it's hard to find a life jacket on a boat in these waters. People would rather drown than be eaten alive.

Hey. I got nothing else to do, so let's see here. Say Vellela Vellela is 28 feet. (Note: She started out 37 feet and nine inches, bumpkin to bowsprit. But you'll recall she was a wreck when I took receipt; and what, you might well ask, would be the first things to go in a wreck?) Way out here, you would probably think 28 feet to be cutting things a mite fine by way of modesty. To wit, charted depth hereabouts is 1,300 fathoms; times six feet per fathom makes 7,800 feet. Call Vellela Vellela's overall length the diameter of a cylinder, with the charted depth the cylinder's height, you get—it's a simple formula—area of the cross-section (which is a circle) times the height. . . . That's it: Pi times the radius squared times the height equals (the calculator battery died awhile back so I'm doing this longhand, in the margin, at the helm, and not without consulting my *trusty* Mechanical Engineer's Handbook), *4,802,867 cubic feet of water. Which means that a shark has*

$$\frac{\Pi^*r^2_xh\ ft^3}{0.13368\ ft^3/gal} = \frac{4{,}802{,}867\ ft^3}{0.13368\ ft^3/gal} = 35{,}928{,}088\ gallons$$

of brine merely straight under the keel in which to look for food. That's if he happens to intersect the "keel cylinder" at all.

Wow. That's what you might call sharkly acumen.

But not to worry, dear logbook. Vellela Vellela *is as seaworthy as hard work can make her—to which labor your earlier installments can attest.*

Still, one ponders, as one sees the occasional fin streaking through the water, how in the world do they find anything?

Earlier today, I saw a yellow fin tuna chase a flying fish straight up out of the water. The latter lived to fly another day.

DATE	TIME	LOG	COURSE	WEATHER	POSITION
3/20	0045	213	292°T	Clear	21°42-1/2' N. Lat.
				1003 mb	76°21'6" W. Long.
				NE 10-15	

Remarks

(Note: position coincident with charted mag var curve; magnetic variation now 7°W.)

Mild dogleg around shoal vaguely charted at 21°48' 20" N. Lat 76°18'5" W. Long last reported in 1978. Can't be too careful.

Spectacular shooting star. I'm writing by headlamp. I can't help myself. It's just too beautiful. Not my writing, but the night. Pronoun reference. Sailing at night is just too beautiful. What's that line from Baudelaire, about a heart seeded with stars?

Course bearing on Cayo Confites Light, 76 n.m. distant, which is the SE corner of the entrance to Old Bahama Channel, with Labaderas Reef on the NE corner and not 10 navigable nautical miles between, plus all the two-way traffic. Sailing directions predict one knot of current setting NW. Going our way.

According to the charts there's a navigable parallel channel by which Vellela *could skirt this bottleneck, some 20 n.m. NE. All the shallow-draft smugglers, fishermen, and a very few cruisers use it. But the navigation is intense, what with uncharted shoals, rocks, etc. abundant. And at night? Forget it. Cedric used to call freighters and container ships and the like "inverted reefs" with the added caveat that not only are they uncharted, but they move. But at least you can see them, even at night—most of the time, anyway. On the other hand, they can't see us at all, most of the time, which is probably why they universally refer to small shipping as "speed bumps."*

Hm. Paging back, I see I've been inconsistent in recording course bearings.

Magnetic, Compass, and True all mixed up. Tsk. Have to go back and set my house in order. . . .

DATE	TIME	LOG	COURSE	WEATHER	POSITION
3/20	2300	287	318°C	NE 15	22°6' N. Lat.
				1005 mb	77°24' W. Long.
				Vivid	

Remarks

Light on Cay Lobos bearing 33° Magnetic off the starboard bow, and light Cayo Confites bearing 297° Magnetic almost dead ahead. Changed course to 320° True. There's only twelve miles across the Old Bahamas Channel here, between a dark and shoal stretch of islands and reefs and cays, off the north coast of Cuba, and more of the same along the southern edge of the Great Bahama Bank. It's the middle of the night and I'm wearing a t-shirt. It's balmy, mon! In most choke points around the world lately you could expect pirates. I guess Cuba doesn't have any. I've never heard of them here, anyway. Lots of shipping going the other way for some reason. Where to? Haiti? For what? Arms smuggling? Rum? Lots of small fishing boats.

DATE	TIME	LOG	COURSE	WEATHER	POSITION
3/21	0915	325	297°M	NE 10-15	22°35'30"N.Lat.
				1003 mb	77°59' W. Long.
				Hallucinatory	

Remarks

Maintained this course for 37-1/2 NM. Log read 33 NM, but the Shadow knows! Raised Cayo Paredon Grande light to port about 2/3rds of the way, at 0320 hours. Tired. Washed down a Dexamil with a cup of hot green tea. Stomach agrowl, naturally. Steady on, with Cay Lobos light rising and dipping off the stern quarter just to make me nervous, until latter bore 120°C astern and Cayo Paredon Grande bore 268°M, almost dead west.

DATE	TIME	LOG	COURSE	WEATHER	POSITION
3/21	1120	340	297°M	NE 10-12	22°35'N. Lat.
				1005 mb	78°8' W. Long.
				Vivid	

Remarks

Magnetic Variation now 6°West.

Fell off to 297°M at 1120 hrs. Lots of shipping. Chop making a pain in the ass of taking accurate bearings or sights. But this is the last general course change for something like 146 miles. That will make better than a full day, something like 29 hours. Flying the genoa, poled out.

DATE	TIME	LOG	COURSE	WEATHER	POSITION
3/22	0530	381	277°M	NE 15	22°56-1/2' N. Lat.
				1006 mb	79°8' W. Long.
				Light haze	

Remarks

I happened to be on the bow, taking a bearing, when a marlin breached, not fifty yards forward, and arced right over the compass I held at arm's length. I could hardly believe my eyes. Magnificent. Why would somebody want to kill such a creature, only to mount it above a fireplace?

DATE	TIME	LOG	COURSE	WEATHER	POSITION
3/22	2035	452	273°M	NE 18	23°23' N. Lat.
				1001 mb	80°19' W. Long.
				Hazy	Cayo Bahía de Cadiz
					Light bearing 228°M

Remarks

It just does not get any damn better than this. What a way to go out. I'm going to miss this boat. Have I made the right decision? Too late now, buddy! What a legacy . . .

Three days at the helm and I'm remembering the Sevennes and Marie and that Apollinaire poem she taught me by way of advancing my French. A long time ago. Probably it's the other way around—Le Voyageur, then Marie, then the Sevennes, and don't forget grapes picked, wine drunk, fromage consumed on bread with butter . . . Marie! What if what if what if. Oh, the wondering mind of man, not to mention the wandering vessel that contains it. And while it's been filling up with Life ever since, the mind I mean, most of the Apollinaire has been superseded. But, cut to the chase, what really made me think of the snatch of verse was its reference to Euripos, or Euripus, another place I've never been! Euripus became generic for a dangerous channel because it's notoriously rough, swift and unpredictable. It's in the Aegean somewhere. They say its currents can run to twelve knots—yikes—and not only that, they reverse direction seven times a day! Jaysus! Does Apollinaire know whence to fetch his similes, or what?

Ouvrez-moi cette porte où je frappe en pleurent

La vie est variable aussi bien l'Euripe
Tu regardais le paquebot orphelin vers les fièvres futures
Et de tous ces regrets de tous ces repentirs
    Te souviens-tu . . .

Hey, logbook, don't worry, I'm about to translate it. The title should maybe be "The Traveler," but of course us salty chickens aboard Vellela Vellela *prefer "The Voyager."*

Open up this door on which I pound, weeping

Life is at least as unpredictable as Euripos

You watch the orphaned packet breaching a feverish future
And remember every regret, every repentance . . .

Sorry Guillaume, that's all I can remember. That's all I've been able to remember for years.

Twelve knots! Jaysus . . . !

DATE	TIME	LOG	COURSE	WEATHER	POSITION
3/22	1900	559	020°T	NE 15	23°27' N. Lat.
				1001 mb	80°19' W. Long.
				Hazy	"MON DOME" charted
					light bearing 208°M.

Remarks
Havana! Mira por vos!

TWENTY-SIX

THE SUBSEQUENT PAGES, ABOUT A THIRD OF THE BOOK, WERE BLANK.

"That's it?"

"He died the next day."

Tipsy determinedly kept her eyes on the logbook. "A few pages seem to have gone missing."

"The last ten," Red agreed. "I counted the stubs."

She looked up. "Who tore them out?"

He shook his head. "That's the way I found it."

"Maybe it means something?"

Red shrugged. "He was pinched for blank paper."

Tipsy closed the book. "Volume eleven," she said thoughtfully. She shook her head. "It seems funny that a guy so conscientious about his logbooks would tear a bunch of pages out of one, just for scratch paper."

"Charley was particular about his logbooks," Red acknowledged.

"So it's not like you tore them out because there was more nasty stuff in there about what a criminal you are?"

"Worrying about stuff like that would be a full-time job," Red pointed out. "They were gone when I fished the book out of the drink."

"Say," Tipsy said after a while, "that reminds me."

"You want a drink?"

"No. What's a Torx?"

"What?"

"No, really. I've never heard of it."

Red straightened one leg, dug two fingers into the watch pocket of his jeans, and produced a hex drive Torx tip. "This is a No. 2, or a T2. Hold out your hand." He dropped the tip onto her palm. It wasn't three-quarters of an inch long.

"I've never seen one of these before. They make screws that fit this thing?"

"The six-point star configuration gives you a lot more torque than a Phillips tip, forget a slotted one. They've pretty much taken over the machine tool industry. You buy a screw gun or a power saw these days and they're entirely assembled with Torx screws. I always carry a tip for the common ones, and there's a full set on my boat."

"This didn't set off the metal detector at the airport?"

Red smiled bemusedly. "Not like Charley's head did."

Tipsy's expression soured.

"I chose to see a bit of America via the windscreen of a drive-away Mercedes," Red explained. "I bought two bags of ice every eight hours all the way across the country."

"That's real funny. Of course you didn't fly." She handed back the Torx tip. "You're reminding me . . ."

"Yes?"

"That diver guy from Rum Cay."

"Arnauld?"

She pointed. "He had to make one."

"How do you know that?"

"Charley wrote to me."

Red grimaced. "That stupid conch told me he had a full set."

"Does it make a difference?

"Maybe no." Red frowned. "Maybe yes."

"Okay. That's lucid. So why did he need one?"

Red dug into his briefcase, produced a copy of *Twenty Sailboats to Take You Anywhere*, by John Vigor, and opened it to a page with a turned-down corner. "This is a schematic of a Bristol Channel Cutter." He flattened the book on the table. "Your brother's boat—minus the bumpkin, the bowsprit, and about a hundred thousand dollars." He touched the drawing. "He shortened the boom to clear a narrower backstay triangle, extended the mast by a couple of feet, so on and so forth. He had to get all new sails and rig, spars and the stick anyway, so . . . He did a cool job. The boat sailed great."

"This is really *Vellela Vellela*?"

"That's more or less her."

"Charley's boat. . . ." Tipsy's eyes devoured every detail of the sail plan and hull. When she looked up: "While we're about it, just what the hell does the name of Charley's sailboat mean? It sounds painful, like veil of tears or something."

"You're reading a bit much into that one," Red laughed, "but, well, funny you should ask that question, because Charley seems to have anticipated it. Were you guys twins?"

"Charley is—was—two and a half years older."

"So there's no chance of telepathy?"

"You mean," she tartly retorted, "am I getting messages from my brother's frozen head?"

"Right." Red retrieved a clutch of papers from the briefcase. "These were in the waterproof envelope with the logbook. You live in California. Ever heard of a book called *Between Pacific Tides* by Ed Ricketts and Jack Calvin?"

"No," said Tipsy.

"Me neither. So I did a little research. The book concerns itself exclusively with the intertidal denizens of the Pacific Coast."

"Sure," said Tipsy.

"It was perhaps the first book to do so."

"Fascinating."

"It's a classic. After fifty or sixty years, it's still taught in the California school system."

"Let's get a move on."

Red brandished two printed pages, annoyed. "These were torn from a copy."

"So maybe it means something?"

"Try to show a little enthusiasm, woman. Charley liked books. If mutilating a logbook was distasteful to him, why would he trash a real book? Maybe it means something, maybe not, but there's an interesting literary angle. This guy Ricketts was the guy upon whom John Steinbeck based the character of Doc in his *Cannery Row* stories. Cool, huh?"

"Cool," Tipsy acknowledged coolly.

Red frowned. "You ever read any of the *Cannery Row* stories?"

Tipsy made no reply.

"Any Steinbeck at all?"

Tipsy sighed an acediac sigh.

"Huh. Well, Steinbeck and the man he called Doc—who was this guy Ricketts—made the trip together that Steinbeck turned into *Voyage to the Sea of Cortez*. Later, Ricketts was run over by a train and killed."

Tipsy sneezed. "My tongue is going numb." She sneezed again. "Where the hell has this stuff been?"

Red moved the various materials to his side of the chart table. "Some of it's a little moldy."

Tipsy sneezed again, hard, and a fourth time. A large black bandana blossomed from Red's hip pocket. "Jesus," she said, blowing her nose into it. "Don't let any pregnant women get around that stuff."

"Oh," Red said, affecting startled deference. "Are you—?"

"Not on your life."

"So, I dodge another lawsuit. Well." Red sorted through the moldy papers. "Since you can't get near them, let me read something from them."

"I'm out of rum."

He pushed the bottle across the table. "Pages 226-228. I'll keep it short."

> Some years in early spring vast swarms of by-the-wind sailors, *Vellela vellela*, often mistakenly called "Portuguese man-of-war," are blown toward our coast, and great numbers of the little cellophane-like floats, with their erect triangular sails, may be cast ashore in windrows (Fig. 173). Often the fresh specimen is intact enough to place in an aquarium jar of water to observe its details. The animal, beneath its transparent float, is bluish to purple; contrary to older zoological opinion, it is not a colony of specialized individuals, like the Portuguese man-of-war, but a highly modified individual hydroid polyp that has taken up life on the high seas (Fig. 174). This can be visualized as the upside-down hydranth of a hydroid like *Polymorpha*, which has been developed from a larva that did not descend to the bottom to settle and grow a stalk but has since settled at the surface and grown a float, so to speak. *Vellela* and two or three lesser-known relatives are properly called chondrophores. . . . *Vellela* is one of the few examples of high seas life that a beachcomber may expect to find.

"I've seen those things," Tipsy said, peering at the illustration, her voice entirely nasal. "Out at Ocean Beach, not far from my apartment. I never knew what they were called, but I can see how somebody might think it a perfect name for a sailboat."

"Maybe especially Charley's sailboat," Red added absently, his eyes scanning the text.

"Is there more?"

Red turned up the second page. "Here's a diagram depicting Vellela's characteristics, the sail's angle relative to the body, whatnot. *Vellela vellela's* pretty much a downwind sailor. See?" She saw, with no idea what she was seeing. "Ricketts goes on to suggest that specimens from the eastern and western sides of the Pacific are mirror images of each other, so far as their sails are concerned. Since they tack at about a 45-degree angle from a following wind, he speculates that the two species commingle mid-ocean by design. When big spring winds blow, however, the design fails and they're herded ashore instead of out to sea. That's if a natural design can be said to fail. Because, you know," he thumped the stack of books and papers, "God sees the sparrow fall."

"What," Tipsy asked incredulously, "did you say?"

"Just kidding."

"Good." She sneezed. "I always start sneezing around Big Questions." She sneezed again. "Not to mention large assumptions."

"Then let's don't go there." Red set the spoor-lofting materials on the bench on his side of the table. "We have enough questions as it is, and no assumptions to base on them."

Tipsy perused the text accompanying the drawing of her brother's boat. "A Bristol Channel Cutter is expensive?"

"That's only until you run her up on a reef, strip her of all her gear, and salvage her as a total loss."

Tipsy sneezed. "Will you stop already with the epistemology?" She sneezed again. "Or is it ontology?"

"You're cute when you sneeze."

Pausing the handkerchief on its way back to her nose, she gave him a look.

"But not completely," Red hastened to add. "We've strayed from the point. Right here," he touched the dividers to the silhouette of the hull, under the stern, "below the waterline, there was a compartment. For what it's worth, it was right where the through-hull for a saltwater intake used to be, and there was a zinc screwed to the center of its cover plate, so it didn't look out of place at all. The cover plate was held in place by Torx screws."

"What's a zinc?"

"A sacrificial anode."

Tipsy evinced annoyance. "I'm not even going to ask about the salt-water intake."

Red smiled thinly. "Eight Torx screws." He indicated the black package on the countertop. "That compartment fit this payload like a Triple-X condom fits—" He didn't finish the simile.

Tipsy ignored it. "Torx screws. Now I get it. Not to mention I forgot all about this package. Huh." She shook her head. "Amazing."

"What's amazing is," Red agreed, "some people would have killed us already over this deal, and a lot sooner in the conversation."

"Is that what happened to Charley?"

"I told you already," Red firmly reiterated, "if I had arrived in time, Charley's sorry ass would have been snatched from the jaws of death. I might have roughed him up for fucking up the deal, but hey, what's a long-suffering employer to do?"

"You were almost there to catch the falling sparrow," Tipsy suggested.

Red scratched his under chin with the dull end of the dividers. "But then," he said without a smile, "I might never have met you."

"So he drowned," Tipsy, sticking to the subject, said. "But wait a minute." She gave Red a hard look. "You almost got there in time, you say. But what were you doing there at all?" She narrowed her eyes. "You mentioned that Charley had double-crossed you. Had you figured it out?"

Red shook his head. "I didn't figure it out until I got back aboard *Tunacide* with this package."

Tipsy frowned. "What's wrong with it?"

"It's not all there."

"Some cocaine is missing?"

"What's missing is the real reason for this ill-advised adventure."

"Well?"

Red lay the dividers over the mouth of his glass and fiddled with them, as if intent on perfectly bifurcating the circumference. "You're not going to believe me."

"Try me."

Red watched the dividers.

"Come on, Red. Out with it. How weird could it be?"

Red raised an eyebrow and nodded at the dividers. "Pretty weird."

"Really?" Tipsy said. "Come on . . ."

"Okay." Red looked at her, lifted his head, scratched his chin. "I was hired," he said to the overhead, "to smuggle a DNA sample into the United States." He lowered his eyes.

Tipsy blinked. "A DNA sample." She halved a laugh. "A DNA sample?" she repeated incredulously.

"I know you don't believe it."

"You're right." Tipsy nodded. "I don't believe it."

Red shrugged. "The cocaine is—was—a beard, a cover."

"But why? Aren't DNA samples, like, saliva on a cotton swab at the end of a little stick? What's the big deal? You could smuggle a saliva sample in a perfume bottle, or a cigarette filter, or a . . . a snow globe."

"No." Red shook his head. "It's much more complicated than that."

Tipsy was shaking her head.

"Much more complicated," Red assured her, "and I don't even know the whole story."

"What do you know?"

Red pursed his lips. "You're not gonna believe me."

"I already don't believe you."

"See? Why should I tell you anything?"

"Well, gee," Tipsy said. "How about we go back to I'm in this deal whether I like it or not?"

"True story."

"So why in the hell would somebody hire you to do a job any kid could do?"

Red chewed his lip. "I got hired because I'm a professional, not a kid. I designed the job in such a way as to maximize the chances for success, and part of that, it seemed to me, meant that I had to have a really twisted cover story for maximum credibility, which was that we were smuggling drugs, real drugs but not too much drugs, so that most people wouldn't bother to look any further into our business. Because most people would have bigger fish to fry."

"But I still—"

Red held up a hand. "Unlike your basic dope deal, different parties are interested in this particular DNA sample for different reasons. I was— am—working for only one of them. So staying undetected was a prime directive. Second, one of the parties I'm not working for is the feds, and even that's complicated. There are feds and there are feds, or so I'm told, feds who work for Dynamo A and feds who work for Dynamo B, separate government fiefdoms, each with its agenda. There might even be Dynamos C and D. Third, actual law enforcement appears to have little or nothing to do with any of this. There are other forces at play, about which I know next to nothing, so it was important that I appear to be doing business as usual,f and steer clear of anything else. Fourth . . ."

Red stopped.

"Fourth?" Tipsy prompted him.

Red grinned. "This is gonna gobsmack you."

"Try me. I spent five years working for a sexual cosmetics company. I'm pretty hard to gobsmack."

"This DNA," Red said, "isn't just anybody's DNA."

"Oh," Tipsy concluded, "it comes from somebody special? Who? Einstein? Edgar Allan Poe? Liberace?"

Red watched her. "It's from a former president of the United States."

"What?"

"You heard me."

There came a pause.

"Well don't just sit there like a wart on a genital," Tipsy suddenly shouted. "Which goddamn former president of the United States?"

"That's another wrinkle," Red said. "You put your finger exactly on it."

"Come on, Red! Which president?"

"As far as I can tell," Red said, grinning from ear to ear, "nobody knows which president."

Tipsy blinked. "So now what's the goddamn point?"

Red raised an eyebrow. "Feeling gobsmacked?"

TWENTY-SEVEN

"SON OF A BITCH, GIVE ME SOME RUM."

"Sure." Red smiled. "Want some ice?"

"Yes—I mean no! I mean—just don't make me watch."

Red retrieved ice for two.

"You'd think a boat like this would have an icemaker," said Tipsy, through clenched teeth.

"There's an icemaker aboard," Red replied mildly, "and it's broken." He swirled the ice in his drink and smiled. "Break out another thousand."

Tipsy spent the next few minutes muttering "Son of a bitch" between sips of drink. It sounded quite mechanical, but there was no pattern to the cycle of it, and in fact her mind was thoroughly on the boil.

"It seems to me," she finally said, "that we have a clear choice between doing our patriotic duty and not doing it."

"How's that?" Red asked, frankly curious.

"Well," Tipsy said. "Don't you see? What if somebody's going to use this presidential DNA to build a clone?" She frowned. "Is that even possible?"

"I have no idea."

"Well, still, let's say it is possible."

"Sure."

"Let's further guess that since somebody is taking the trouble to smuggle this presidential timber it must be stolen, and if it's stolen, this somebody intends to build a clone from it."

"Okay," Red said, "but that's two guesses."

"Yes, yes, I understand that part. But what I'm getting at is," Tipsy leaned over the chart, "what if it's the wrong president?"

"The wrong president?" asked Red ingenuously.

"You know," Tipsy insisted impatiently. "One of the bad ones."

"Hmm," Red mused. "Should I be naming names?"

Tipsy narrowed her eyes. "Do we need to name names?"

Red nodded sagely. "I can see, with a girl like you, this could be some kind of deal breaker."

"You got that right, pardner."

"Let's see. Without getting into who we voted for in the last election . . ."

"And why wouldn't we want to do that?" Tipsy inquired icily. "Is there some uncertainty?"

"Are you suggesting that if it's the wrong president's DNA, and if we somehow manage to get our hands on it again, at that point our patriotic duty would be to somehow lose it again?"

Tipsy nodded. "I should say so."

"And if it's the right president's DNA," Red held the palm of his hand up and gently slashed it down and forward, "we should let it go on through?"

Tipsy nodded gravely.

"I see." Red cleared his throat. "Let me help you out here with something, Tipsy."

Tipsy waited expectantly.

Red lowered his voice. "If we don't find this DNA and deliver it to the next pair of hands down the line in a timely fashion, no matter whose DNA it is?" Red nodded. "You and I are going to be playing three-dimensional chess with your brother in Davy Jones' locker." Red jerked a thumb over his shoulder. "And you can probably throw your old friend over the side while you're at it."

Tipsy blinked.

"Do I make myself clear?"

Tipsy's expression hardened.

Red sat back in his seat. "I, for one, intend to earn my forty thousand dollars and live long enough to spend it. And you, for another, need to confine your political aspirations to the voting booth." He patted the chart. "Understood?"

"Yes but—"

"No," Red shook his head. "Say 'Yes, sir.'"

Tipsy wrinkled her lips. "But—"

"No buts."

"Yes," she finally said. "Sir," she added. But she was thinking, but. . . .

"In conclusion," Red concluded, "I propose a sweetener. Charley got out of my office with $12,000, or sixty percent of the twenty thousand he was to earn by merely sailing from one end of the Bahamas to the other. I of course allotted forty large to myself, for management and P&O."

"P&O?"

"Profit and Overhead."

Tipsy made a face.

"Hey," Red touched his breast, "I'm a businessman. You want to do this for free?" He extended the hand. "Next time around, help yourself. This time around," he nodded, "we're doing it my way. I thought your brother had no idea about the DNA, by the way. Unfortunately, that turned out not to be the case."

"What! How do you know that?"

"I thought Charley thought he was running a load of blow and it was simple as that. Wrong. Somewhere along the line he figured out what was going on and pulled a switcheroo on his old pal Red, the little bald-headed bastard. And no, I'm not over it. But I took the trouble to visit Arnauld on Rum Cay before I came to California, and I'm fairly convinced that both dope and DNA got aboard *Vellela Vellela* like they were supposed to. So that leaves Charley as our number one rascal. But what I wanted to say is, Charley only had $2,500 Bahamian aboard when the boat went down, which I took off with the logbook and paperwork." Red dipped into the briefcase and pulled out a much-abused wad of legal tender. "As of now, that twenty-five hundred is yours." He handed her the cash. "When, not if, but when we find the rest of the package, I'll deal you in on Charley's balance, which is eight thousand dollars. Not only that, I'll pay you in American,0'cause that's the kind of guy I am. What say?"

Tipsy didn't know what to say.

"I understand that you're speechless with gratitude." Red smiled thinly, drumming his fingers on the chart. "But since you can't say no, say yes."

Tipsy looked at the money.

"You can leave out the 'sir,'" Red added.

"Yes," Tipsy finally said. She set the money aside. "Let's go."

"We're off," Red said. "Damn. Okay. Please begin with the first Rum Cay entry and read through to the end, one more time. Any thought that occurs to you—anything at all?—please share it. I've pored over it so many times I've got it memorized. I can take my drink up to the captain's chair and watch the bay for a while. Or, if you like, you can read aloud while I retrace his course. Whichever makes you comfortable. Whatever helps."

"Are you kidding? Retrace the course."

It was Charley's handwriting, no doubt about that. Letters small and carefully formed and highly legible, the lines lay straight across the page despite most of them having been written at sea. The writing carried his voice, too, a voice whose audio signature Tipsy barely remembered, but whose tone she recognized from the many documents that had found their way from him to her over continents and seas and years, full of digressions and naive dreaminess which almost always belied the seriousness of whatever Charley was really up to.

Tipsy had no idea what the navigational notes meant. But Red patiently measured off longitude and latitude, and pricked the chart accordingly, double-checking the plot of Charley's course as the log recorded it. She quickly learned which data were important to the plotting, read them out as Red needed them, and skipped the rest. Occasionally he would frown and ask if the notation were "true" or "magnetic" or "compass," or consult the logbook for himself. In less than an hour they'd double-checked the penciled lines from Rum Cay to Albert Town, around the southeasterly tip of the Great Bahama Bank, west by northwest along the coast of Cuba, through Old Bahama and Nicholas Channels, and into the Straits of Florida. By the time the log book entries ended, 21 nautical miles north of Havana, Charley's script showed signs of haste. The charted course ended, too. But the log included *Vellela Vellela's* last change of course, 20° True, and Red himself had recorded the wreck's location, 24°56'30" north latitude, 82°2' west longitude, 32 miles north of the last change of course, which he now plotted as well.

"She went down fifty-three miles north of Havana and forty miles south of Key West."

"I had no idea Havana and Key West are so close to each other."

"Aye," Red growled. "And in that ninety miles lies many a tale!"

She cast her eyes over the chart, fascinated by names she'd read in Charley's letters but had never bothered to envision, let alone research. She blushed to admit she'd never taken the trouble to pull out an atlas or purchase a chart in order to study her brother's career—or his geography at least. The shape of Cuba—an island, after all—charmed her. Names exotic, foreign, colonial, and just plain piratical flowed along either side of his course. Double Headed Shot Cays, Lavanderas, Hurricane Flats, Cayo Coco, Bahía, La Gloria, Larks Nest, Guantánamo . . . Way points, lights, rocks, cays, islands, shoals, soundings, reefs—these salients teemed in variety and such detail as to practically demand curiosity. As she expressed interest in one or another location, Red went from the big chart to Reed's and looked it up, there to find virtually microscopic detail, right down to important punctilios such as whether or not one might find a bar on even the merest rock to have lifted its snout out of the sea.

"It sounds," she said finally, "as if bar-hopping would be a great way to waste two or three years in the Caribbean."

"Hey." Red affected a blank look. "You think so?"

"Don't make fun of me. Is that what Charley was doing? Drinking his way from port to port?"

"No. Your brother drinks, of course, drank that is. But he'd rather sail over the horizon than eat, let alone spend money in bars. Let alone socialize at all. Charley kept to himself. The one and only thing he preferred over sailing was reading. And that narrowly. Your brother taught me everything I know about books." Red tilted his head. "Did you know he was a writer?"

"Well, sure. He wrote me letters all the time."

"That's not what I meant."

"You mean, a writer-writer? As in journalism?"

"Novels."

Tipsy's eyes enlarged. Yet another fundamental of his life Charley had never bothered to mention? "A published writer?"

"Never published, so far as I know. Quite the opposite. Once when I was drinking with him I watched him feed a manuscript into a wood stove. He said it was a novel. It certainly looked thick enough to be one. Like this." Red held thumb and forefinger about an inch and a half apart.

"I had no idea. He never said a word to me about it."

"He never sent you anything? A story, a sample chapter, an outline, a character study?"

"Nothing."

"I'll be damned. Not that I ever read any of what he wrote either, but, all the years I knew him, Charley always owned a typewriter." Red held a forefinger aloft. "A manual typewriter."

"Of all the letters he sent, not one was typed." Tipsy smiled, but she felt distressed. How could Charley have kept this ambition from her?

"He always kept a notebook, too. Even at sea, even in the tropics, with lots of rain and few if any clothes on, there were always pen and paper within reach. He'd find a solitary lagoon somewhere and anchor out for weeks, reading, typing, writing. He told me he'd tried at one time or another to write everything but screenplays because, he claimed, screenplays aren't really writing."

"That would be Charley. Why aim for real money when there is so much non-money lying around all over the place?"

"Charley always maintained that whatever amount of money you make, no matter how you make it, sooner or later you're going to earn it."

"What are you saying? That Charley is now his own best paradigm?"

"True story. His prior example, however, was a Miami guy who sold his very first screenplay for something like sixty grand."

"That sounds like real money."

"Really?" Red shrugged. "Anyway, next this guy spends two years rewriting the thing, after which there was nothing left but the title. By then the coked-up producer who called him at all hours of the day and night for 24 months could no longer be found, the sixty grand was long gone, he sold his new car for half what he paid for it and blew all the money at the dog track, and finally he got evicted by his own mother. Charley never heard about him again. Point being . . ."

"There's no free lunch."

"Not even close."

"Quentin has a similar philosophy." She cocked an ear aft.

"Quentin's okay," Red assured her. "But, truly," he resumed, "Charley never sent you any fiction?"

"None. He's sent me a hundred and fifty, maybe two hundred letters and postcards. But no novels."

"You counted them?"

"No, but I still have every one of them."

"How'd you manage that?"

She smiled. "I keep them in a box that floats, as it turns out."

"You dropped it overboard?"

"I lived on a boat. It sank."

"At sea?"

"Dockside."

"Oh, well," Red said, losing interest. "When was that?"

"Oh, about the time a certain party sent me five thousand dollars."

"Yeah?" he brightened. "How timely."

"By the way," she straightened up a little. "Thanks." She offered her hand.

"Don't mention it," Red said. They shook hands. The clasp lingered through an awkward pause. "You know," Red finally said, "I took care of Charley like he was my own brother."

She took her hand away. "What's that supposed to mean?"

"I don't know. Nothing? What do you think it's supposed to mean?"

"Did you ever write back to him?" she responded defensively.

"No," Red said simply. "Did you?"

"I—I never knew where to write to him. Then," she added truthfully, "there was the question of motivation. I'd get a letter off to him every year . . . or three. It might have been three years," she finished lamely.

"I see," Red said, displaying little sympathy. "Anyway, for me to write to him would have been stupid. But every month, my wife sent him a box of books. She picked them out, I paid for them, and the postage, too." Red shrugged. "She and Charley shared an interest in novels. And history." He nodded. "Everybody in the joint read every one of them." Red gave her a frankly appraising look. "You don't know anything about me."

"True. Well? Now who's ungrateful?"

Pause.

"What was the name of the book he burned?"

"*Windward Passage*."

Tipsy brightened. "That's a perfect title for a movie."

Red laughed.

"Did he tell you what it was about?"

"A prison novel. A sailing novel. Or maybe it was about a novel about the sea written in prison, or a novel about prison written at sea." Red shrugged. "He was always going at it from a different angle. After he burned it, in fact, he just started over. Or maybe he just kept on typing."

Tipsy's lips formed a quizzical smile. "How thick?"

Red raised the thumb and forefinger. "Maybe three hundred pages, typed, double-spaced, and single-sided."

"He fed all that into a stove?"

"We were drunk. I happened to mention it was chilly. Next thing I knew . . ." Red opened a hand. "He said it wasn't good enough, it wasn't going anywhere, he was sick of thinking about it, he felt trapped by it. Maybe it was that simple." He closed the hand. "It kept us warm for about half an hour."

Tipsy said nothing.

"Charley was working on a new version when he died."

"How do you know?"

"I saw it."

"Where?"

"All over the Gulf Stream. Pages and pages of it. If we'd been some place with deciduous trees, it could have been fall. Leaves everywhere."

Tipsy frowned. "That's quite an if."

"Anyway, Charley submitted his novel to the House of Neptune, and Neptune accepted it. I was busy trying to save everything else." He indicated the taped-up brick, the water-stained logbook, and the refrigerator. Then he turned to the briefcase and retrieved three or four business envelopes. "These are addressed to you care of Red Spot, Jr. It's how I found you. There were seven of them." He fanned them.

"They look just like the last four or five I received from him. Only the stamps varied."

"There you go."

"He kept them pre-addressed?"

"By the dozen, I guess. However many come in a box from the stationery store. In the tropics," he added, "you have to buy these envelopes with the pull-off tape covering the adhesive. Otherwise, the humidity will seal them. Same problem with stamps. Either that, or you have to keep them in a refrigerator." He added the clutch of envelopes to the pile of effects. "Charley had no reefer on *Vellela Vellela*. . . ."

Tipsy glanced behind her, thought better of it. She lifted her glass and thought better of that, too. Instead of taking a sip of rum, she set the glass on the chart, north of a compass rose in the Gulf of Mexico.

Red watched her.

"Okay," she said quietly. She raised her eyes and looked at him. "Tell me the story."

TWENTY-EIGHT

"It should have been a straight-ahead job. You never know, of course. Charley had been out of action for a long time. I thought he liked it that way. But when he learned he could make twenty grand in two or three weeks from this deal, he wanted it."

"Did you ask him why?"

"He told me he wanted enough money to go visit his sister in California."

Tipsy chewed her lip.

"Red, I naturally asked myself, why now? Well, I answered myself, it's not your business. Maybe Charley is feeling mortal? Maybe he's had a portent or a sign, maybe he's pissing blood, say, or something has shaken him sufficient to make him go up against his fear of a bad result versus the imminence of mortality? Maybe an albatross flew over his bow from port to starboard."

Tipsy blinked. "Is that bad?"

Red laughed. "You're easy."

"Well, what about it?" Tipsy glowerd. "Maybe a doctor gave him some bad news."

"The only bad news Charley ever let a doctor give him was that a race had been canceled. You submit to a doctor about anything other than sailing, Charley used to say, he'll find something wrong with you. That's his job. I couldn't agree more."

"You never see a doctor either?"

"Just to get sewn up. But hell, a veterinarian can sew you up. So can a competent sailmaker."

"Sewn up from what?"

"Fishhooks. Gaffs. Marlinespikes. A machete." He indicated a series of scars on his right forearm. "Teeth."

The scars looked like a pink oath in cuneiform. "Shark?" Tipsy asked.

"I don't count sharks," Red said. "Sharks don't know any better. Anyway, I was worried about Charley. I didn't think he was in shape for the job. Ever since he came out of prison . . . I don't know. Yes I do. Prison changed Charley. He was cavalier about it, but anybody who knew the before-prison Charley and the after-prison Charley could see it. He'd had enough of the wrong side of the law. If that meant poverty or a whole new set of friends or dying instead, so be it." Red held up a forestalling hand. Tipsy had already noticed that it, too, displayed a scar, a diagonal slash across the palm, but this one was recent.

"I know all this," she said with a trace of impatience.

"Even so, if Charley met a blind fed under the clock in Grand Central Station," Red continued, with a trace of satisfaction, "Charley wouldn't tell him what time it was."

"I think that's what you might call obstreperous."

"The hell you say. Anyway, he got hard time for that particular trait, and his un-snitched-upon colleagues gratefully took care of him when he got out. That's how he got the job in the boatyard, that's how he got his boat, that's how he could afford to refit her. That's how come, three years later and six months ago, I rolled over and promised him a milk run. In between, he didn't ask me for anything. Not once."

"Smuggling a kilo of cocaine into Florida in the hull of your engineless sailboat is a milk run?"

"The current security climate makes it a little trickier than it used to be, but, you know, really, aside from the fact that the feds don't know their ass from a hole in the ground, there's so much dope being smuggled into the United States at any given hour of the day or night the authorities cannot possibly keep up with it. In light of which a mere kilogram is insignificant. Virtually nonexistent. And that's a true story."

"Can I ask you a question?"

"Sure."

"Why didn't you just give him the twenty thousand?"

"What am I," Red touched his chest and looked over the rims of his half-glasses, "made of money?" He lofted the injured paw. "Just kidding."

Tipsy conspicuously looked around. "Nice boat."

"Suffice that you be reminded," Red repeated, "that it's not my nice boat."

Tipsy narrowed her eyes. "We're down to who you work for."

Red ignored her. "I knew if I offered him the money outright, he'd turn me down. So I offered to loan him the money at zero percent interest, or whatever terms he wanted. He turned me down. He insisted on earning it, and he pointed out the obvious, that I was the only person who could help him earn that much on short notice. Make that any notice. In retrospect, I should have jammed the cash up his ass in small denominations. In a moment of sentimental weakness, however, I capitulated."

"Seems like a lot of rigamarole for an insignificant kilo of cocaine."

"Well, sure, now that everything's fucked up, of course it looks that way. Meanwhile, complete idiots get whatever shit they want into the country by the metric ton on a weekly basis. Some of these guys are pretty mean, too. A man gets on in years, he doesn't care to deal with such guys. Besides," he gestured at their surroundings, "you couldn't load a ton even on this tub. To move a ton, you need a real boat. A ship. And you need real connections. Somebody almost has to be on the inside of the feds' deal at the harbor, or in the airport, or on both sides of a given border. Such operations are big and expensive and there's leaks, weapons, treachery, and a lot to lose. Sooner than later people get killed, and it's almost always the little people. I don't know why; maybe it's because there's more of them. Anyway, in the space between the giant steps, the likes of me discover plenty of opportunity for modest markets."

"How little was my brother?"

"Tiny. But your brother killed himself."

"Oh," Tipsy choked out the obvious retort, "autodecapitation."

"No," Red replied, as if patiently, "that part I did. But I did it only after he had already drowned himself. Why are you rubbing this in? You think I enjoyed it or something?"

"Did I say that?"

"Then lay off it!"

A passing swell gently lifted the big cabin cruiser and let it down again. The brass oil lamp, a pricey and highly polished anachronism, creaked as it swayed over the chart table.

"You cut . . ." Tipsy began, but she felt stupid repeating it, so she didn't. "I saw it. I could see it again. So it must be real."

"He was already dead," Red took the trouble to remind her. "In the moment, I felt that I had no choice." His fingers turned his glass on the chart.

"You had no choice?" Tipsy said tightly. "Thousands of people die every day. Maybe it's millions. How many of them get their heads cut off? Before the invasion of Iraq, I mean. But in Iraq it happens before they die. But after? What's the use? Wigs? Cornea transplants? Or have they perfected brain transplants? And besides," she started to cry, "who the fuck would want my brother's stupid brain anyway? What sort of people are we talking about, here? Morons who need implants in order to pretend they have beautiful memories of sailing the Caribbean?" The tears flowed at last. She drummed the chart table with her fists. "If that's the problem, why don't they just buy themselves bigger Travel Channels!"

Red stood and attempted to comfort her by putting his arm around her shoulders. She hit him in the gut as hard as she could. He took it. She hit him again. "Go on, tell me," she said through her tears. "I can take it. I've been taking it all my life." She angrily wiped her eyes. "See how tough I am?"

"I was there because I was tracking him," Red said, almost as if he were speaking to himself. "And self-pity is going to get us exactly nowhere."

"You son of a—" About to strike him again, she stopped. "What did you say?"

"I was worried about him. So, instead of fretting for two weeks, I decided to do something about it. What the hell, I figured, I hadn't been fishing for a couple of months. So I gassed up *Tunacide*, laid in a bunch of supplies, and took off."

"Who?"

"That's my fishing boat. Man, you oughta see her. She—"

"Skip it," she said fiercely. "I wouldn't know a fishing boat from Proust." She took up the black bandana, touched it to her eyes, then slammed it down on the chart. "I want my brother!"

"I can't help you there, Tipsy," Red said quietly.

She squeezed shut her eyes and shook her head. "I know I need to get a grip. I will get a grip." She shook off his arm. "Tell the goddamn story."

"She's got a fishfinder fit to spy on a guppy's private life at a thousand fathoms. Radar, sonar, global positioning, satellite television, Vessel Identification, so forth." He touched Tipsy's shoulder reassuringly, then began to pace. "The whole time Charley was out there, I was just over the horizon, keeping an eye on him. Unbeknownst to Charley, along with the blow and the DNA, I got Arnauld to put a transponder aboard *Vellela Vellela*. Only I knew its frequency, which mutated daily according to the first eleven terms of the Fibonacci series."

Tipsy blew her nose. "The what?"

"You know, 0,1,1,2,3,5,8,13 . . ."

Tipsy pounded the chart table with the bandana-wrapped fist. "You're taxing me!" Her drink, his drink, the dividers, and the brick of cocaine, all jumped. Abruptly, Tipsy's eyes unfocused and slowly refocused. "A transponder?"

"So," Red resumed, "I was keeping an eye out for Charley, not really all that worried about him, you understand, and getting in some fishing, too. In fact, right here," he touched the chart with a forefinger, "about a mile east of Bird Rock, I nailed a magnificent yellow fin tuna, the prettiest one I ever caught. Incredible fish." He moved his finger an inch. "The day after Charley anchored off Albert Town."

"So you shadowed him from Rum Cay onward?"

"The whole way. And it was spectacular. I hadn't spent so much time on the water in years. Some places in the Caribbean have changed a lot. Other places, it's like Columbus never learned to sail.

"The reefer was damn near full of fish by the time that ten days was up, and it's a big reefer. Much bigger than this one. Not as cold, though," he reflected. "Anyway, mornings I'd while away fishing. Just let her drift. Afternoons I'd spend catching up with Charley. Evenings I'd crack a beer and put her on automatic pilot, or even anchor out if the surroundings were interesting or the next morning's fishing looked promising. *Tunacide's* good for sixteen knots. With Charley traveling at four, five knots at the most, it was a bigger problem not to overrun him than it was to lose him. I just had to be sure I kept him hull down and traveling away from me.

"How far away was that?"

"Twenty-five, thirty miles. The tower on *Tunacide* is pretty high and pretty distinctive. If Charley had ever seen it, I'd be busted toot sweet."

"It sounds like a setup."

"Stop." Red held up the hand. "I'm the one got set up."

The tears had ceased but Tipsy remained fragile. She had a headache. Her eyes were swollen. She blotted them with the kerchief. "I'm all right," she finally sniffed.

"The unexpected is what happened. *Vellela Vellela* holed herself for keeps. I don't know how. It could have happened to anybody. To me, even. Nighttime, broad daylight, awake or asleep—it was an accident. Anyway," Red opened the logbook. "Except when he's hallucinating French poetry, the last few entries are cursory, as opposed to the chattier ones." He leafed back a few pages. "He last slept . . . here. Two full nights." He touched the chart. "Albert Town, four days before. After that," he drew a finger along the plotted course, "four days with no sleep, the last two on uppers. He was bushed. After he turned north he almost certainly set up the boat to steer a course unattended, and passed out in his berth."

"But you were right there. Couldn't you have gotten to him before the boat went down?"

Red grimaced. "You ever fought a tarpon?"

"A what?"

"It's a fish."

"No. What about it?"

"It's a game fish."

"So?"

"They don't call it 'game' for nothing. That very morning a tarpon hit my troll rig so hard he almost turned the boat around." He showed her the palm of his left hand. "See this?"

"I noticed it, yeah."

"The bastard snatched my best rod right out of the gimbal. Sure, I had a sennit on it. But before I could get the rod back aboard and set the brake and so forth the sonofabitch had peeled maybe five hundred yards of No. 18 wire off the reel. It sounded like one of those wind-up penguins on speed. About half of that wire went through the meat of my hand. Cut it right down to the bone like one of those things you slice cheese with."

Tipsy winced. "Why didn't you just let the poor fish go?"

Red gave her a look. "Not bloody likely." He jerked a thumb at his chest. "Am I not a man?"

"My brother was just over the horizon," she shouted, "dying!"

Red held up both hands. "Last time I checked Charley's position he was just fine. Loping along at a good four and a half knots, according to my reckoning, keeping a perfectly straight course, hitting his waypoints dead on, sailing by vane and log and the sextant and dead reckoning as if he had the finest automatic pilot money can buy. Like," he jerked his thumb toward his chest again, "I did. He was a fine sailor. I wasn't worried about him. I was worried about that damned fish. And my rig, of course, by the by, which is worth something north of a thousand bucks if you had to buy it new."

"Which you didn't," Tipsy guessed.

"No, of course not. What's that got to do with anything?" Red shouted. "First," he resumed, moderating his tone, "I let the fish run against the drag while I knotted a t-shirt around this hand with my teeth and strapped myself into the chair besides. So right away, I don't mind telling you, there was blood all over everything. Slippery as hell, too. It looked like I'd already killed a bunch of fish and cut my throat into the bargain.

"Anyway, having gotten my act together, I had but one thing and one thing only on my mind. I went to fighting that fish."

"Well, come on," Tipsy asked impatiently. "How long could it take for a macho man to land a goddamn fish?"

"In this case, six and a half hours."

"Six and a half hours? I don't believe it."

"At the end of which he got away."

"Oh, no," Tipsy sympathized unconvincingly.

"It happens." Red drew himself up to his full height. "Do I detect irony in your voice?"

"Sure. As well as pity for the fish."

"I thought as much. Anyway, when you play a fish like that fish there's a lot of work, as I think you'd call it. You've got to let it run, reel when it gets tired, let it run, reel, run. Meanwhile, don't let it pull the line under the boat, don't let the line foul the prop, don't give the fish enough slack to spit out the hook, don't let yourself get dehydrated, do not get sunstroke. Pace yourself with the fish, ration your strength, and so forth. It's a lot of trouble, especially when you're by yourself, and it's a lot of fun, too, and don't give me any of your shit, 'cause you don't know what you're talking about. Cut to the chase. By the time it was all over we'd had a good fight and the fish was gone. I'd drunk one beer and opened another before I remembered what I was really doing out there. I checked the screen and right away I could see that Charley's boat had only moved a few miles while that fish dragged me and *Tunacide* all over the place, and while, by then, forty-odd miles separated my boat from Charley's, it should have been something like sixty.

"Now, there are a lot of reasons for a boat not to be moving, especially if it's a single-handed sailboat without an engine. The wind might have died, for instance. Or some part of the rig might have failed. More likely the single-hander is hove to for a little shut eye under the premise that if he's not moving in broad daylight he's got a diminished chance of getting run down. But maybe he broke something, too, or maybe the wind piped up and he had to shorten sail and fouled a halyard, or hey, maybe he hooked a real nice fish and he fought it and won and now he was sitting down to his own grilled tuna, with two or three bottles of beer followed by a nap into the bargain. There's a lot of variables. Did you ever think of any of this?"

"No," she said decisively. "None of it."

"Well I did. There was plenty of reason for Charley to be dawdling out there, and every reason for me not to expose myself. So I cleaned up the boat and doctored my hand, both of which were pretty near ruined, drank two liters of water and two more beers, turned up the audio warning on the radar, as well as the volume on the VHF scanner, and passed out in the shade of the master's berth with an electric fan on my face. You ever sleep with a fan? It's—"

"You may be much man, but you're human, too," Tipsy concluded.

"Thank you. That's right. When I woke up I made myself a big breakfast, and—remember that yellow fin tuna?"

Tipsy nodded.

"While the tuna steak was poaching in butter and white wine with a couple of bay leaves and some fennel," Red smacked his lips, "I got around to checking on Charley's position. Not to mention my own position."

"And?"

"We were both drifting with the current. In the better part of nine or ten hours, he hadn't made six miles over the ground. Like me. But he'd been at it about twice as long as I had. So maybe something was up."

"You made a beeline for him?"

"Not a bit of it. I'll finish my breakfast, I said to myself, and then, if Charley still appears to be adrift, I'll figure out a way to sneak up on him. After dark, maybe."

"Jesus," Tipsy said through clenched teeth.

"I know what you're thinking," Red said. "But for a tarpon, there went a live sailor."

"Not to mention a live brother."

"Not to mention," Red nodded grimly, "a double-crossing son of a bitch."

TWENTY-NINE

"THE TUNA WAS DELICIOUS, BUT I DIDN'T ENJOY IT. STARTED WITH BEER and finished with coffee, watching the screen the whole time, and finally I couldn't stand it any more. I fired up the engines and headed for Charley. Slowly. I helmed from the flying bridge, which put my eyeballs maybe twenty-five feet above the water. Higher than this thing." He indicated the overhead. "All things being equal, I might have managed a glimpse of him sternwise, and, what with rising and dipping and the sun behind me, he might not notice me at all.

"But the closer I got to his signal the more fucked up I knew things were. At a range of about thirteen miles I should have been able to see the top of his mast—that's nautical miles, about fifteen statute or land miles. It's a long way to see the tip of a mast but it should have been easy. There would have been sails attached to it. Big white sails. I knew what direction to look, and I had stabilized binoculars. It was a typical Caribbean day, clear as a bell with passing pods of low cumulus. There's tables that tell you what's visible at such and such distances and heights above the water and so forth. All I had to do was look it up and I did. Like the mast of *Vellela Vellela* was, says right here in this book, forty-one feet six inches above the waterline, to which Charlie had added a couple of feet, and my eyeball was maybe twenty-one feet above the water, so the tables allowed for a sighting of Charley's main trucks at 17.73 nautical miles. Round up to eighteen. I remember it clearly. It's like I'm looking at the figures as I speak.

"A pretty fair swell was running, maybe seven feet, so there was the added plus and minus of a glimpse of her from atop a swell, then losing her in the trough. That would be cool. If I could get a gander and all looked well, I could just fall off and lie over the horizon with Charley none the wiser. But I had to be careful. Charley was good, like I say. If he was on deck, he would be sweeping the horizon, albeit likely with the naked eye unless he spotted something particular he wanted to study, like for instance the glint of a stainless tuna tower with a hank of red hair under a straw hat contrasting nicely against the blue sky. But more likely he'd be on the lookout for an official-looking vessel, or a freighter or a tanker.

"I didn't go straight in on the eighteen-mile vector. I worked a tangent. But not a mast tip, VHF antenna, windex, not the wink of a stainless tang or halyard shackle, not a rag of sail were to be seen. Not at seventeen point seventy-five, anyway. Nor at seventeen, sixteen and a half, sixteen, fifteen and a half . . .

"I kept looking at my instruments like I was going crazy. But they had to be telling the truth. The instruments said Charley was right over the horizon and getting closer, just a few points off the port bow, but the horizon showed no sign of him.

"I eased off the tangent until I was headed straight in. Cautiously, but straight in.

"Then I had a dark thought. What if Charley had figured out what I was doing? What if he had found the transponder? But that was almost impossible, for it was inside this brick of cocaine which was under that zinc which was below *Vellela Vellela*'s waterline, and the cover plate was secured with Torx screws. Of course, he may have dived the hull. He didn't have a good reason to do so, but suppose he had done it? Suppose Charley dove on the hull, got the hatch open with a Torx driver he'd professed not to have, retrieved the payload, and discovered the DNA and the transponder as well? That's two surprises. What would he have done?

"The same thing I would have done. Dropped the transponder into a mayonnaise jar with an airtight lid so it would float, dropped the jar into the drink, and changed course toward any of the 359 points on the compass rose that had little or nothing to do with the one vector parallel to the Gulf Stream that the jar would follow, which current, in that vicinity, sets nearly two knots per hour to the northeast. And then I would keep on sailing until I got caught or changed oceans, whichever came first. If, indeed, that's what Charley had been paranoid enough to do, which is what I might have done too, with a fair wind he could be a good seventy, eighty, ninety miles away, and right next to impossible to find.

"But I was fantasizing about the unthinkable. What good reason could Charley give himself for suspicioning me? Me, of all people. Me who had given him his start and staked him again after he got out of the joint, and had handed him this recent job as well? Why would he think I didn't have his best interest at heart? It didn't make sense that way. Maybe Charley had concluded that some third party was interested in him. So something was wrong with what was wrong—you hear what I'm saying?

"Still I crept up on him, because I just couldn't bring myself to admit that this operation even had a chance of going sour. I was in denial. I continued to cautiously motor, closing up with the position of the transponder the while, continued to glass the horizon, and continued to see nothing. Eleven miles, ten, nine . . .

"An hour and a half later, I motored directly over the transponder signal, and there was not a sign of a boat. Nothing but empty ocean.

"What the fuck.

"So now the unthinkable was fully engaged, and it was one shitty feeling, I can tell you.

"There was no debris. I glassed circle after circle. Wherever that transponder signal was coming from, I couldn't see it. I had no idea of the accuracy of my gear, a detail I should have known, but hell, I was looking for a thirty-foot boat, not a two-inch electronic gadget. Even if you're ten miles away from the damn boat, you should be able to see it.

"Had the boat gone down and the transponder was still working? The guy I bought it from told me it might transmit through maybe half an atmosphere, or about sixteen feet of water, maximum—in which subject I was very interested, of course, because it would be stashed below the water line. But he also told me that, deeper than about a quarter of an atmosphere, its range would be severely curtailed. This led me to suppose that *Vellela Vellela* may have swamped and now lingered, just under the surface.

"If the transponder was still aboard, that is.

"At that point I got so annoyed by the screen that told me I was right on top of the transponder signal, I turned the damned thing off.

"Now my overworked brain was really ginning up the scenarios. I probably hadn't expended that many neurons since I sat for my 100-ton license, forty-something years ago. I turned the engines off and listened. I randomly stabbed the binoculars at empty stretches of ocean. I looked high for flares. I looked low for debris. I tuned and studied the radar. Nothing. I fiddled with range and sensitivity, setting both at their maximum. Nothing. I went back upstairs with the binoculars, if only because all that fresh air and sunshine on the fly bridge made me feel better. Nothing. And I had no patience for any of it.

"At some point I finally admitted that I was bobbing around in an empty seascape and I had to do something, even if it was wrong.

"So I consulted the chart. I'd been plotting Charley's course as well as my own. I've never been able to break the habit of a paper chart, and now it came in handy. I knew where Charley had turned north. I knew where the transponder signal had started moving at the same speed as the current in the Gulf Stream. And, in fact, I wasn't all that far away from that point.

"I plotted the route from Charley's course change to Boca Chica Key. I did a careful job, too. I knew how much time had elapsed since the course change, since the transponder signal had slowed. I knew that Charley would steer a westward course to allow for being set eastward by the Gulf Stream. And so forth.

"It seemed to take forever. But I worked it through, picked a course, and headed out.

"A mere half an hour later, the longest half-hour I've ever spent, the radar acquired a very small target. Strangely enough, it was a fifteen miles away, well within the limit of *Tunacide*'s radar range, which is twenty-five miles. The image came and went, it was well north and east of the course I'd set, but it was the only target I'd seen all day, so I steered for it.

"Another hour, and the unthinkable happened again. *Tunacide* topped a swell, and the eyepiece of the binoculars filled with the one sight I didn't want to see: a naked stump of mast, its upper end a jagged flare of an aluminum splinter not five feet above the deck. And then it was gone.

"We were in the trough and all I could see was water. I took a bearing and passed it to the autopilot. The swell was too big for full speed ahead, but I fed her some throttle anyway. Not too much, though, because if you jam into heavy seas, the autopilot gets confused, and I needed the autopilot. While she labored for the derelict I sprang to the deck and broke out everything I could think of. A messenger line, a grappling iron, a couple of life vests, a boat hook. Flippers, mask, snorkel, tank, weight belt, buoyancy conserver. A coil of fat towing line. I put fenders over. There's a compressor aboard *Tunacide* for topping off scuba tanks or running a hookah or sandblasting or painting, whatever, and I jumped on deck and fired it up.

"Then I clambered back up the ladder and glassed the bow from port to starboard and back. As we crested a swell I caught another glimpse and, I don't mind telling you, I almost lost heart. At first I thought she was hull down, of course. The mast was stripped of rigging, except for a thickness of sail clutched in the track, below the fracture. Everything else was a tangle on deck and spilling off the starboard side. Charlie sat back of the stub facing aft, right in the thick of a snarl of rigging and canvas, and he was throwing fistfuls of paper into the air.

"What in the hell, I said aloud under the binoculars, is going on?

"A trough swallowed the freeboard of *Tunacide*, and *Vellela Vellela* was lost from sight. I went to manual helm, but when I gave her some more throttle the seas wouldn't allow it. She was just digging a hole, as the sailors say. I throttled back. Four miles. Atop the next sea I brought the glass to bear again. These are high-tech binoculars I'm using, with a built-in gyroscope to steady the image. One thousand bucks. You know what "boat" stands for, don't you? "Break Out Another Thousand." Sure it's not funny. It's a context thing. I almost puked. *Vellela Vellela* wasn't hull down over the horizon at all. She was decks awash. What I was seeing—the stub of mast, Charley's head and a bit of his shoulders—was all of *Vellela Vellela* that remained above water.

"I gunned it. Equipment on deck, hatches and companionways open, to hell with it. *Tunacide* rose to the challenge and did better for herself than I expected. Old sailors always bear a prejudice against the stinkpot. We never think a stinkpot can handle a sea like a well-founded sailboat. She took green water over the foredeck but *Tunacide* did well until she took a tanker load down the companionway, too, and I had to back her off, bilge pumps whining. I mean, *Tunacide* isn't one of those speedboats that can go from wave top to wave top, at a speed limited only by how tight you can hold on. Nothing was lost overboard except a deck chair, which I didn't even miss until I wanted to sit down much, much later.

"Sometimes, at sea, things happen so quickly you can't grasp the sequence of events. Other times a single event will take an eternity to happen, and this was one of them. We closed the gap at eight knots. Three miles, two, one, a half, a quarter . . . It took at least twenty minutes, maybe a few more, but it seemed like forever. By the time we got there only the shredded tip of the mast was above water. Charley's head was lifting up out of the swell and dropping back under.

"A hundred yards away I forced myself to put the engine in neutral. There was a lot of stuff floating around the wreck—bottles and cans, clothing, a boat hook, books, all that paper, a blue plastic jerry can, a long spiral of yellow polypropylene line, to which was attached the deflated remains of an orange liferaft—all of that, plus mast and rigging. Not to mention that the simplest and least paranoid scenario was that *Vellela Vellela* had been holed by a submerged object, and, if so, where was it? The current was with us, and there was way on *Tunacide*. Best to drift down on *Vellela Vellela*. Best not to let the prop get involved with what surely was a tangle of lines and gear and canvas, not to mention a live skipper. Who knows, maybe he had a tank on, or a snorkle, or something. I couldn't tell, but as we closed that last hundred yards at the rate of one year per yard, I could see the hair on the top of Charley's head, right against the mast, rising and dipping, rising and dipping. Occasionally his whole head submerged, then he'd come up spouting. So he hadn't drowned yet. His back was to me, but I couldn't figure out why he hadn't paid me any attention, let alone, how he'd managed to trash his own liferaft. But a lot of smart money will tell you that abandoning a vessel at sea is strictly a last ditch effort, because many's the abandoned vessel found still afloat weeks, months or years after anyone has last heard from her crew. Of course, if you've holed your raft too, that's all kinda irrelevant. And need I mention a nice big fin circling the wreck? It disappeared as *Tunacide* bore down, but still . . .

"For Charley even to be in this pickle, something had gone mighty wrong.

"Well, and maybe I was his guardian angel, although, if so, it was going to be a close thing and, anyway, I didn't have time to be digesting details.

I sprang to the after deck and hefted the single scuba tank. Put it down, donned the BC. Resumed with the tank. And then I thought, sonofabitch, what am I doing, there's work to be done. I sprang below and dumped a whole drawer of tools onto the sole of engine room until I found the air wrench, a No. 2 Torx bit, and a goddamn half-inch to three-eighths drive adapter, and it had to be a half-inch female to three-eighths inch male adapter at that. If you haven't gone pawing through boxes of greasy tools looking for three things without one or another of which you will fail from square one, with no time to lose, well, you haven't really been nervous.

"A hose, too. Two hoses, I should say, for I had two fifty-foot lengths of 3/8" pneumatic hose aboard, for a total of one hundred feet, and why not? The entire damn boat is only fifty-three feet, and the compressor sits amidships, belayed to the back of the house, its thirty-gallon tank red as a new nun. Fifty feet of hose would reach anywhere on the boat, double up for backup or two tools, and break out another thousand.

"But you see what that meant. I had maybe eighty, eighty-five feet of hose and who knew how little time to dive the hull of *Vellela Vellela* and back out eight Torx screws on the—what was it, the port side? Hell, I didn't even know. Port or starboard, toss the coin, but aft for sure. But there was Charley, too. I had to see to Charley as well as the payload.

"I plugged the male end of the hose into the air tank. With a hundred and ten pounds of air on it the hose went stiff as a rusted cable. I plugged the male fitting on the air-wrench into the female end of the hose and pulled the trigger twice, vroom vroom. A second time, vroom vroom, and the compressor bore down under the governor until the pop-off valve popped off. So far so good, but would it work under water? Who the fuck knew. Good question though. I sprang below and pawed through tools again until I found a No. 2 Torx driver, manual version. It looks just like a screwdriver. Sure to god I'd be down three or four atmospheres, 90 or 120 feet, with my back to the sharkosphere, before I got eight screws backed out by hand. I grabbed a roll of duct tape, too.

"Gaining the after deck once more I opened the valve on the single tank and fumbled into its harness. Nervous as a cat. Then I remembered the swim ladder. I scrambled aft and put over the swim ladder so I could climb back aboard my own goddamn boat. Don't laugh, the swim ladder has been forgotten by better sailors than me on boats with less freeboard than *Tunacide*, and they did not live to tell the tale. I buckled on the weight belt, sat on the fighting chair to put on the fins, and, bethinking of it at the last minute, I strapped on the sheath of a dive knife a guy named Cedric Osawa gave me years ago. That's right, Charley knew him too. Biggest dive knife you ever saw, a blade sharp as a serpent's tooth and a serrated spine fit to limb oaks with. Cedric's a fucking idiot. I laughed at it when he gave it to me but was reassured to hold it at that particular moment, on the bounding main. I left the spear gun. I had enough stuff. And there, on deck, was the duct tape. I stared at it. What the hell was the duct tape for? I ran through every move I could foresee having to make on the dive until I remembered. I tore a couple of inches off the roll and wrapped it two or three times around the Torx tip, the female-to-male adapter and the chuck, too. Those rigs fall apart all the time in thin air, you know, let alone under water.

"By then *Tunacide* had drifted down on the wreck, as if this were a perfect man-overboard drill. *Vellela Vellela* lay downwind and down current, so *Tunacide* covered her. A fin reappeared in the old peripheral vision. There was a rifle aboard, a shotgun too, but it's counterproductive to have blood in the water if you're going for a swim. Peaceful coexistence is the key. I spit in the mask, centered it on my face, cleared the regulator and fell overboard backwards, the mask clasped to my face by the ruined hand, impact wrench in the other.

"I fell right down past a maze of rigging and torn canvas, a fucking miracle I missed it. I didn't even think about it. If I'd hit the middle of that stuff, that would have been the end of the job. Best case scenario, I might have gotten myself untangled before it took me to the bottom.

"The hull lay close aboard, just above me, and right off I spotted the zinc. A stroke of luck. Now for Charley. I flippered through a loop and exhausted the BC a little. The belt dropped me amidships, and there he was, chained to the goddamned mast.

"Charley had chained himself to the goddamned mast.

"Or had somebody else done it?

"I couldn't believe my eyes, I didn't know what to think, but there it was, some kind of harness of chains. Right out of an S&M catalog with a padlock, yet.

"I floated there, incredulous. My eyes must have bugged sufficient to fill the mask. Charley was still alive and he noticed. Plus I was holding an air wrench, for chrissakes. An air wrench! I must have looked just like I was fixing to rotate his tires. It's like that test they give you to see whether you're dumb enough to join the army. What's wrong with this picture? My mind was nearly blanked by the image of a big pair of red-handled bolt cutters I happen to own, red handles with black rubber grips and black jaws to hold the blades, and they were aboard *Tunacide*, too. I had just seen them in a cubby below the tool bench in the engine room, right next to the drawers I'd rifled for the other gear.

"Why the hell hadn't I brought those bolt cutters! Fucking lot of good an air wrench was going to do Charley.

"But the bolt cutters wouldn't have made any difference either. The links looked to be at least 5/8", and case-hardened, end of story—too much for my bolt cutters, too much for most bolt cutters. Too much for one man to handle. . . .

"Charley pointed. Did he think the joke was on me? I glanced away, as if to work up a good curse, only to look straight into the starboard eyeball of the biggest hammerhead shark I ever saw.

"It was the shark Charley was pointing at, and if I hadn't looked I might have been the creature's lunch. Do hammerheads attack people? I don't know what possessed me. The wrench was more or less floating there, right between us. All I had to do was pull the trigger and ratchet the cartilaginous motherfucker right between the eyes. Actually, I'm not even sure the wrench came in contact with the shark at all. With the sound, with the eruption of bubbles, it simply vanished.

"I turned back to Charley. What could I do? The thought occurred to me that the mast was aluminum. Maybe I could prize off enough fittings to slide Charley up the mast? I drew the knife . . .

"That's when Charley laughed. Charley saves my life, I'm trying to save his, and he thinks it's funny.

"I yelled 'fuck you' so sincerely I spat out the mouthpiece.

"Charley got the last laugh, all right, but then he drowned. Right in front of me. I think it must be a horrible death. At first you realize you better not breathe. Then you realize you won't be able to breathe. Then you realize you have to breathe but you better not breathe, then you realize you're going to try to breathe anyway and it's not going to work but you have to inhale, it's too painful not to breathe, and anyway, that's it, you're not a fish, you're drowned.

"It's the realizing ahead of time that makes it painful. The more realizing you do, the more painful you think it's going to be. That's the horror. The more imagination you have, the worse the anticipation. In the event it's not so bad. That's the way it looked to me anyway. Charley's eyes got big. He looked scared. He also looked amused. Then the bubbles stopped. He gaped like a fish out of water, which kind of makes sense, then he relaxed, and then his eyes stopped moving. He was gone.

"I attacked the chain and lock and mast and gooseneck. I clambered at the first fitting I could get the point of the knife to do something to, which was a deadeye that captured the becket on the downhaul block. Stupid. I cut the lines between the two blocks. Next came the gooseneck, a serious obstacle, and I worked at it, too. Eventually the head popped off a screw, but not before I broke the point off the knife. This was not progress. I watched the triangle of stainless steel and the head of the screw bounce

off the deck in slow motion, through little somersaults like they were pursuing one another, and slowly accelerate into a plunge as if with every
intention of spiraling straight through the 821 charted fathoms yet to go
before they beat *Vellela Vellela* to the bottom. Four thousand seven hundred and twenty-six feet. A hundred and forty-three atmospheres. If you
sent a styrofoam coffee cup to that depth, the pressure would compress it
to the size of a thimble.

"How much time passed, I don't know. Finally, working behind him, I
realized that Charley's bald head was slowly bobbing from one shoulder
to the other, the strands of his tonsure wallowing willy-nilly. Then the tank
gauge floated up in front of my mask. I seized it and had a look. After all
of this exertion, my air was better than two-thirds gone. That was it.

"I gut-stabbed the mast hard, so hard that the pointless blade penetrated it up to half its length. And it got hung up in there, naturally. Think of
a lobster trap. I used up a lot of air trying to get it back before I gave up.

"And then I bethought of the hundred feet. I looked up. There wasn't
so much light as there once had been, and this is the Caribbean, where
the water is clear and light penetrates deep.

"The half inch or so of water in my face mask had turned pink. Pressure
was forcing blood through my sinuses and out my nose.

"One atmosphere is thirty-three feet. The hose was one hundred feet,
at least fifteen or twenty of which were involved with the compressor, the
freeboard of *Tunacide*, and the nice overhand knot I'd taken the precaution of tying around the handrail.

"I breaststroked my way over the deck and down along the hull of *Vellela
Vellela*. No zinc. Where's the zinc? I had become disoriented. It was on the
other side. I had to swim back up the hull, over the foredeck and back down
the side of the hull, tugging the hose free of various trailing lengths of line
and rigging. There it was. Screw number one. Whoops. Put the tool in
reverse, stupid, and be glad you didn't cam out the head. Screw number one.
Okay. Screws number two, three and four . . . And just as I spun the next-to-
last Torx screw loose, holding onto the rudder with the fucked up hand and
the wrench with the other, the descending *Vellela Vellela* tore the air wrench
out of my grip. End of hose. Beginning of third atmosphere.

"I retrieved the manual Torx driver from the knife sheath and backed
out the last screw by hand. This is a lot harder than it sounds, in weightless conditions, but by and by, screw and cover plate soon followed the
others to the bottom, and the brick was mine. No sign of the transponder,
of course or the DNA. This didn't surprise me at that point, but there was-
n't time to be brooding about it, either.

"I keep a small game bag, a kind of net purse, on the weight belt, for spear fishing. I shoved the vacuum-packed brick into it.

"I cleared the blood from the mask and blew some air into the BC. The hull descended past me, bearing with it Charley's corpse. The sharks would be tending to it soon enough—maybe sooner, if their brains could comprehend the fact that I no longer had the ability to change their tires for them. I looked up. The impact wrench dangled about thirty feet above my head.

"I usually take a decongestant before I dive. Years of blow-induced nasal congestion make this necessary. Now I felt like I was about to lose an eardrum. I raised the mask, pinched my nostrils closed, and blew against them. This ear cleared. This one ruptured. And yes, it was painful.

"Another fuckup. I turned in the brine and watched a thin tendril of my own blood lift away from the side of my head. Maybe some shark would soon be interested in helping me feel sorry for myself.

"I added air to the BC and augmented my rise past the hull with the flippers.

"There Charley hung, slightly buoyant, belayed by his own hand to his own rigging. I could have saved the fuck. He knew I was out there. And then I thought I got it: Charley hadn't wanted to get saved.

"Proof, I realized. Who or whatever caused this, I'm going to need proof that it happened, and a mere kilo of cocaine isn't going to speak loud enough.

"It was about then that I noticed that the wreck wasn't sinking anymore. Not rapidly, anyway. I blow out an eardrum and now I get time to think? We hung there, boat and I, in almost neutral buoyancy. I might have gotten a good daydream going, if for some reason I hadn't looked up, and realized that the pneumatic wrench and maybe ten feet of hose had gotten tangled in the welter of rigging, and now this rubber thread was attempting to arrest the descent of this seven-ton boat. If I didn't do something, there would be consequences. There are always consequences. When things go wrong at sea, things do not fuck around.

"And now I realize that not only is that fucking hundred-foot hose not going to part, it is not going to pull the fucking compressor over the side after it, either. And why not? Because two hoops of eighth-inch iron strap belay the compressor's thirty-gallon tank to the back of the wheel house, that's why. Not to mention, the hose is looped over the handrail. Therefore this setup has a damned excellent chance of capsizing *Tunacide*. Or, how about this: since her engines are still idling, maybe the load will list her sufficient to heave the intercooler intake above the surface, there to suck air instead of salt water. Either way, the weight of the sinking *Vellela Vellela* is well on the way to turning my fish boat into a turkey farm. All it would take after a certain point is a broach on a good swell or some green water aboard and the whole works would be underwater—two boats, Charley and me, with Charley suddenly the one better off.

"I won't bore you with what it took to get that knife back. Suffice to say, it came away in my hands like that aluminum mast was a length of suet.

"I clawed frogwise straight up, ruptured eardrum and the bends be damned, till I was above the wreckage and all its tendrils, and slaughtered that air hose. Just get me back to Florida, I was thinking, and I'll buy all the goddamn air hoses and pneumatic wrenches and synthetic eardrums money can buy. Break out another thousand.

"The severed hose belched air with a robustness sufficient as to be quite audible. The bubbles expanded in size, too, violently undulating until they disintegrated into smaller bubbles, as the mouth of the severed hose released them, which in turn drove the hose around in the water like it was a demented snake. The compressor would already have kicked in, trying to keep up with the demand, and unless somebody got aboard *Tunacide* to turn it off, the little three pony engine would burn itself up. And the air wrench? I caught a glimpse of it far below, going down, down, down, trailing twelve or fourteen feet of yellow rubber hose like it was a strand of bull kelp.

"Break out another thousand.

"But down the Y-axis is the negative direction. I looked up. Up is the positive direction. *Tunacide* was safe. Slowly but surely, the hull of *Vellela Vellela* was getting serious about resuming its descent, bow and Charley first, as if backlit by darkness. I looked down upon that sight with these very eyes, and I will not soon forget it.

"I sheathed the broken knife, exhausted the BC, and crawled straight down after her. It felt like somebody was trying to back a Torx screw out of my ear. You get on this side of me, now, you're going to have to talk loud. But at the time I was thinking, I knew, that the testimony of a lousy water-stained kilo of cocaine was going to fall on nothing but deaf ears. No way it would speak loudly enough. Ever.

"Now I'm thinking, what about a head? Mute, loud, rude—I liked the idea. It didn't even shock me. Why not give it a try? What is there to lose? A head might provide, how to say, incontrovertible evidence that the stakes had elevated. What the fuck. What the fuck, and why not?

"Just like that last Torx screw, the head wasn't all that easy. Weightless conditions.

"What the fuck, I kept telling myself, as I sawed away, descending into darkness and running out of air, with my legs wrapped around the mast and a corpse, blood not pumping but leaking out of the jugular, a surprisingly thin thread of blood. What the fuck, I told myself, it's not like Charley needs a head anymore. . . ."

V
THE DROIDS OF SÍ

THIRTY

EVEN WITH A FAMILY, SUICIDE IS AN OPTION; BUT IN ORDER TO MAINTAIN A family, you have to want to live.

Complex.

Without a family, suicide is simple.

These and other oddly coherent thoughts teased awkwardly his mind, even as an emergency room orderly shaved his head. A cop studiously recorded his description of the two people who had mugged him.

Everybody who came near him wore gloves. The cop had none and didn't come near him.

His feet not touching the floor, one hand covering the other in his lap, the very picture of composure, Quentin carefully described two dead ringers for Tipsy and Red as his thin hair fell to the sheet covering the gurney upon which he perched.

"Caucasian female," the officer read from a 3x5-inch spiral notebook. "Medium-length reddish hair, probably henna. Freckles. Pasty complexion. No makeup. Gin blossom on left cheek. Puffy facial features. Alcoholic? Early to middle forties—"

"Middle to late forties," Quentin corrected. "Don't sustain her illusion. On the other hand," he reflected coldly, "drink may have prematurely aged her."

The officer dutifully appended the correction. His pencil was a yellow three-inch stub from the Presidio bowling alley.

"Such pencils," Quentin observed, apropos of nothing, "are designed to inhibit cheating."

The officer looked at the pencil, then waggled it between his fingers. "First thought, best thought," he suggested gravely.

Quentin closed his eyes and concentrated. "Stanford sweatshirt," he continued. "Newish blue jeans, clean pink sneakers—make that low-cut dirty pink sneakers."

The cop looked up. "You think they might have been designer sneakers?"

"No more than I think she graduated from college," Quentin sniffed. "Let alone Stanford."

The policeman, the black letters engraved onto whose brass name plate identified him as VENTANA, frowned. "How can you be certain of that?"

"Because I," Quentin assured Officer Ventana with all due gravity, "graduated from Stanford."

"Okay, okay," Officer Ventana compliantly repeated aloud as he wrote, "probably . . . not . . . much . . . education."

"Magna cum laude," Quentin added, talking to himself. "Ouch."

"Sorry, darling," said the orderly. "Some of this cheveaux is pretty crusty."

"Have you no aspirin in this facility?"

"Sorry again, darling. Only the doctor, and I'm not one—"

"You're a movie star," Quentin interjected.

"Screenwriter, actually."

"Is that not just another word for autoinfantilization?" In posing the question, Quentin did not miss a beat.

"Well gobsmack the populace." The orderly took a step back from his task and folded the wrist holding the razor against his hip. "And aren't we in the mood for love."

"Well?" Quentin said, leveling his gaze at him.

"Honey," the orderly said, turning his head to one side, "what in the world would a girl like me do with an over-the-hill queen like yourself?"

"I came here to get better?" Quentin suggested.

"Now, girls," Officer Ventana began.

"You keep out of this?" the orderly suggested back, subtending, with a coy smile, "Cupcake."

Officer Ventana frowned. "The Castro was my beat for three years. I got called every name in the book. 'Cupcake' was not one of them."

The orderly wagged his scissors. "You must have kept your hat on."

Maybe Ventana had been trained for this. In any case, he blushed.

"Why," the orderly lamented to Quentin, "are straight men always so serious?"

"It's not that," Ventana volunteered. "It's that I just completed six months of anger management. So when it comes to the little outrages of life I'm kind of . . . neutral. That's it. Then there's my serotonin uptake inhibitors. Plus I'm still on probation for clocking a dyke on the jaw because she gave me the finger after I wrote her a citation for a lesser misdemeanor than the one she had committed on account I thought she was such a spectacular piece of ass. Next thing I know, her mouth turned the air blue around my head with a string of obscenities such as you never heard on the waterfront—when this town had a waterfront. Fucking blue collar's been gone from San Francisco going on three generations now. If my grandmother hadn't left me her house in the Excelsior?" He jerked the thumb of his pencil hand over his shoulder. "I'd be outta here. Point being,

she called me every name in the book, but she never called me 'Cupcake.'"
Almost angrily, he elucidated, "The dyke, not my grandmother."

Quentin and the orderly were observing Officer Ventana. "Point taken," the orderly ventured cautiously.

"I left the syllabus in the car," Ventana added, his voice beginning to crack. "For anger management, I mean. First title in it is *Notes from Underground*. But even if I had it with me I wouldn't begin to know how to look up such a slur. Besides—I get worked up like this? I can't read so good. The words go double and the lines undulate. Needless to say, the sentences don't make any sense. It's like watching the constant stream of crazy people at Mission and 16th. They're all unique but they're all different—you know what I mean? People are all the same on the inside, I mean they're all made up of oxygen and hydrogen, mostly, and I guess carbon too. On the outside, they all got different rap sheets. But on the inside for sure it can't ever be more than the ninety-six naturally occurring elements. Can it? Maybe someday somebody in some lab will clone a lifeform from some synthetic element. Lawrencium, say. After all, Lawrencium was made from Californium." Ventana exhibited the rapid eye movement of a dreamer. "Some people are more radioactive than others. It's just natural. Take our former president, for example."

"No," everybody in the room responded, "you take him."

"But in the end it doesn't make any difference. They're all the same to me, they're all just plain crazy." He looked from the orderly to Quentin and back again. "Not me." His jaw twitched. "I'm not crazy. I'm not crazy at all." He smiled crookedly. "See?"

"Crazy, man." The orderly's tone conveyed empathy.

"Wild," Quentin agreed.

"Like that word you used," Officer Ventana continued. "That big one."

"Word?" Quentin blinked

"Autoinfantilization," the orderly recalled.

"Very handy," Quentin looked at him, "with the recitation."

"Mary," the orderly said, not without theatrical inflection, "you are so testy."

Ventana pointed his pencil. "Spell it. So I can look it up."

The orderly spelled it.

"Pretty good," Quentin said to the orderly. "But you can't look it up," he told the cop.

Officer Ventana looked up from his notebook. "Why not?"

"Because he invented it," said the orderly.

"Voilà," said Quentin.

Officer Ventana flushed with anger. The flare was so abrupt that the orderly and Quentin were taken aback. "What the fuck you mean he made it up?" Ventana demanded.

"Take it easy," the orderly said.

"It's a, uh, I, it's merely a combining form, a neologism. Like, for example, when Shakespeare made up incarnadine."

"Incarnadine? Neologism?" Officer Ventana sputtered at, rather than to, Quentin, as if a preliminary to striking him. "What the fuck's it mean? Huh, faggot? You ain't seen—" He stopped.

"Hey, hey," the orderly interrupted. "Talk about autoinfantilization."

Despite a concussion, a scalp wound, and seventy-three years, Quentin drew himself up. "Did I ever suggest that I was the victim of a hate crime, Officer?"

"Huh? Well, no, you didn't," Ventana admitted. "But why else would somebody clock a faggot on the cantaloupe? Did they take your wallet? Your cash? Your ATM card?"

"They took my dignity," Quentin stipulated.

Officer Ventana pointed his pencil. "You're queer—right?"

"How—how can you tell?" Quentin said uncertainly.

"Jesus, Joseph, and Mary," the orderly said, raising his eyes to the ceiling. "My god," he said abruptly. "There's blood on the ceiling."

Quentin and Officer Ventana, though wary of each other, looked up.

"I guess that's why they call it the Emergency Room," Ventana said.

Quentin nodded. "Put that in your screenplay."

"The day autoinfantilization gets used in a movie," the orderly assured the ceiling, "is the day my dick stops getting hard."

"Hollywood would excise incarnadine from Macbeth," Quentin said.

"They already did," the orderly sighed. He returned his eyes to Quentin's wound. "Speaking of which."

"Be sure to wear your little gloves," Quentin reminded him. "I'm positive."

"Don't worry about me," the orderly assured him, snapping the cuff of the latex glove on his razor hand. "If I get the HIV, I'm going to get it the right way."

"That's not even funny," said Quentin.

"I know," said the orderly. "It's my way of keeping you awake."

"I think I'm going to throw up," Officer Ventana announced.

The orderly was examining the top of Quentin's head. "Does that mean you're through being pissed off?"

"Negative." Officer Ventana shook his head. "I'm permapissed."

Quentin, whose head was tilted forward, beamed without moving. The orderly directed a wide grin at Quentin's wound. "Excellent!"

Officer Ventana affected bashfulness. "You think?"

"You are too cute," the orderly affirmed. "And you have no idea what I could do for your marriage. Hold still."

Quentin frowned. "That's . . . uncomfortable."

"I'll be finished eventually. How'd you let all this blood get so dry?"

"I spent a weekend in Cabo before I came to see you?"

"Why didn't you call me? I could have met you there."

"So, listen," Officer Ventana interrupted. "What did the guy look like?"

"He was a redhead, too."

"What did we do to piss off the redheads?" the orderly asked.

"I haven't the slightest."

"Redheads are all permapissed," Officer Ventana offered. "Little guys need to steer clear."

"There he goes again," the orderly remarked. "In all of Macbeth—in all of Shakespeare—incarnadine occurs but once—you hear what I'm saying?" He dabbed a sponge soaked in warm water over the coagulated blood caked in and around Quentin's scalp wound. "That's aside from making outrageous generalizations about minorities."

"Is that all you remember about him?"

"He looked like an over-the-hill pirate. Far beyond anything I ever saw in the nineties real estate market. Lots of scars, balding on top, heavy set, another alcoholic, probably. Or a fellow who likes to eat. He used a lot—" Quentin stopped himself quite suddenly.

Ventana waited.

What the hell am I doing, Quentin said to himself. I must be more debilitated than I realized. The theory was that if I told this cop exactly what Tipsy and Red look like, he'd never find them. It seemed like a reasonable approach at the time, and easier than making it up, which I'd then have to remember, and which almost certainly might get innocent people arrested. But if I go so far as to tell this cop that for example Red Means talks a salty lingo and most assuredly knows his way around boats and drug smuggling, why, Officer Ventana might guess Red's identity without any more assistance than that! On those few clues alone! Admirable deduction. Besides, it was just a perverse joke I was playing, mainly on myself. What was it Genet said about betrayal? It aroused him? Something like that. That, and the act is ecstatic. Plus, the result is freedom. Or liberty. It's like Jesus at the moment of realization—or of presumption—that he'd been betrayed, not by Judas, but by God. Is not the agony of our Lord fueled by the knowledge that, once God has betrayed His own son, God is rid of mankind forever, thereby freed and, therefore, Himself ecstatic? Liberated from wrath? What am I? Quentin wondered, Martin Buber on mescaline? Officer Ventana's walking, talking syllabus? Is this a trauma-induced epiphany, or is it chopped liver?

"Hold still," entreated the orderly, sounding very far away.

It's Tipsy and Red who got me into this mess. Not God, not Jesus, not Jean real-estate-free Genet. Except for myself, of course. I, myself, didn't have to leave the dock with them. Or *cast off*, as they say.

I wonder what they talked about during that hour, while I lay bleeding on the floor. The deck, I mean.

Damn them anyhow.

Maybe I should describe the severed head for the nice, neurotic officer? They thought I didn't see the severed head. Silly conspirators. The Shadow knows!

Oh dear. I'm deliberating the consequences of betraying my dearest friend, along with her newest friend, as well as her brother's severed head. Can you betray a severed head? If this were a detective novel, the head would give me nightmares. One doesn't often encounter severed heads in mainstream novels. But there's one in Stendhal, bless him. It's hard to have nightmares when you have insomnia. Inconsolable insomnia, that ol' alligator of alliteration. This way, he vaguely pointed, madness lies. That way, he vaguely pointed, madness tells the truth. Which way is which? Weren't we just talking about alligators? Anyway, it's a crocodile. No. That's not the problem.

"Mr. Asche?" The orderly snapped his fingers in front of Quentin's nose. "Hello?"

"Yes? Yes, what?" Quentin drew away from the snapping fingers. "What is it?"

"Are you okay?"

"Sure I'm all . . . What's the matter?"

"Don't get your panties in a bunch," said the orderly. "I was thinking the concussion had kicked in. No big deal."

"Why would I wear your panties on my head?"

The orderly looked at him and blinked.

"I thank you for doing your job," Quentin persevered. "But that's a bit rich. Don't you think?"

"Man," groused the orderly. "You're plenty mean enough to survive a conk on the head. What's this?" He stood on tiptoe as if to peer at the top of Quentin's head. "I can see your brain."

"You can see my what?" Quentin screeched.

"It's pulsing red."

"Pulsing?"

"When it's not pink," said the orderly, giggling.

Officer Ventana sniggered before he could cover his mouth with his notepad.

"How professional," Quentin sniffed, with as much hauteur as any man with a half-shaved head and wearing a backwards nightie can muster. He flicked an imaginary speck of lint off his exposed kneecap. "It goes right along with the television. Imagine."

Both Ventana and the orderly glanced toward the platform above the hallway door on which a television squatted. On its screen, a sports journalist soundlessly proclamated. Beneath his image crawled the message, *. . . Gasoline at the pump: UP 27 Cents. . . .*

The orderly reverted his attention to the wound in Quentin's scalp. "I forgot that infernal machine about seven thousand shifts ago."

"A television," Quentin replied, "complete with fluorescent lights, blood on the ceiling, mustard walls, a battered linoleum floor, and crude jokes about homosexuals with head injuries. It's all of a piece. I'm surprised you don't have a shopping cart in here for body parts. It's a cul de sac of the civilized world."

"I'm not arguing with that one, Mary," the orderly muttered decisively.

Officer Ventana gestured with his notebook and pencil. "Red hair and a pirate," he prompted.

"Hold still."

"Insomnia's not the word I'm looking for," Quentin said. "It's not about not being able to sleep after a head injury, it's about not being able to remember things. Like in the detective novel."

"Amnesia?" both Ventana and the orderly said.

"That's it." Quentin blinked. "That's it," he said again, though with less certainty. He laughed. "Gentlemen," he addressed the room, "since when can't I remember amnesia?"

Officer Ventana's expression of expectation, surfing weakly on boredom and exhaustion, didn't change. Quentin angled his eyes toward the orderly.

"Since when can't I remember amnesia?" Quentin repeated thoughtfully. He didn't want to supply an answer. Or couldn't. However, his fascination being on the order of one unable to look away from the enfeebling agonies of a crushed spider, arachnid allegory for one's own mind, eight legs sapped, sixteen knees unstrung, fit her for the cobblestone web, Quentin took a guess. "Since I got hit on the head?"

The orderly pursed his lips. "Makes sense."

Quentin looked at Officer Ventana.

"Red hair and—?"

Quentin sighed. "That's all I can remember."

"That, and autoinfantilisation," the orderly reminded them both.

"On the contrary," said Quentin. "I made that up on the spot. Think of it as spontaneous bop neologia. It has nothing to do with amnesia."

"Hup you," said the orderly, "finger-poppin' daddy."

"Bullshit," said Officer Ventana.

"More words you never heard before?" the orderly asked.

"No, but . . ."

"Speak up. It's busy in here."

"In general I hear only a very limited subset of any given human language, English or otherwise," Ventana explained. "Including click languages."

The orderly hesitated, briefly resumed, then stopped what he was doing. "All right," he said, "I'll bite. What does 'Fuck you' sound like in a click language?"

"Which one?"

"Bad-géd asshole," the orderly announced. "This guy's a—."

But when Officer Ventana spoke, it sounded like August grasshoppers in a sheetmetal duct.

"How dare you speak like that to me?" the orderly demanded.

"That's what I tell them," said Officer Ventana. "Right after I chill them with my sap."

Quentin and the orderly repeated in unison, "Chill them with your sap?"

"You never hit nobody with a nightstick," said Officer Ventana, "you ain't no friend of mine." Officer Ventana blushed. "I accidentally killed a guy with one," he blurted. "My first unpaid leave."

"And how long was the administrative leave?" the orderly demanded.

Quentin found himself transfixed by the expression in Officer Ventana's eyes—nostalgia? dismay? regret? The door beneath the television swung open. The orderly heard it, threw a glance over his shoulder, and looked to his work, speaking rapidly. "This is San Francisco. Guys kill to get a residency here. Kill, I tell you. We take our pick from every medical school in the hemisphere. Of all the bright, motivated people, we get first choice. And whom does the system cough up?" He made a noise a like a dog dislodging a hairball. "The Heterosexual Sawbones from Hell."

Unable to move his head, Quentin rolled his eyes. "The what?"

The orderly distributed emphasis equally among the meticulously enunciated syllables of his hushed reply.

"What part of Heterosexual Sawbones from Hell don't you understand?"

THIRTY-ONE

"Listen, Oscar, there has to be a way."

Officer Few stared into his coffee.

"I mean, where do these people come from?"

Oscar sighed. It happens every time, he thought to himself. Every time I meet a woman I think I can get something going with, it turns out there's an ulterior motive. A ray of sunlight fell across the table, and in it his coffee cup gleamed like diction in a symbol, as the poet Darrell Gray once noted. Few pursed his lips. Shadows cast by a ceiling fan fluttered on the surface of his coffee. A motive ulterior to my ulterior motive, that is.

"Well . . ." He touched his spoon to the rim of the cup. "There's this thing they do on Tuesday nights."

Tipsy narrowed her eyes. "That's tonight."

"They call it the Newbie Scooter. It's an open mic kind of deal. You sign up, you do your thing, they measure the result the old-fashioned way."

"How's that? By the amount of money people throw at you?"

Few made with a rare smile. "You wish. It's called an applause meter, but it's nothing more than a VU meter with a tell-tale. They don't even use a separate mic. More's the pity, because the speaker's mic is a cardioid. They should really should be using a—"

"What time?"

Oscar Few could always warm to the subject of audio gear, but one thing he'd never met with was a woman whose enthusiasm for it equaled his own. "They go up at seven-thirty. If you don't want be hanging around listening to a bushel of half-baked bromides, we should get there by seven."

"We?"

"Until they extend you an invitation, or you meet somebody else, you'll still need me to get you in there."

"I'll meet you on the steps in front of Bryant Street at six-thirty."

"I advise you to sign up second or third so you can get a feel for how it works." Few sighed at his coffee. "Six-thirty it is."

"Thanks, Oscar." Tipsy stood and retrieved a twenty from her hip pocket. "Let me get this." She paid and tipped at the counter, dispensed a little wave in his direction, and left.

Few remained sitting at the table for a long time, lost in thought. His cellphone irregularly vibrated in its hip holster, like a cicada nested on the bark of his being, but he ignored it. By the time he took a sip of coffee, it had become too cold to drink. He got up and left the cafe.

After the volunteer techie got more or less on top of some pesky feedback, the third speaker got down to it.

"Iraq, as we all must know and admit by now, is intractable."

The room was packed, and seventeen of the attendees had signed up to speak.

Rooba rooba, the crowd responded.

"Iraq has cost the developed 'hood blood and treasure beyond measure, blood and treasure, beyond measure."

Rooba . . .

Not a bad start, Oscar thought. Despite a thick sheaf of notes, she addresses the crowd directly. They usually just sit there. To get any reaction out of them at all on her first go was somewhat marvelous.

"Yet the developed 'hood needs, must have, calls out for the petroleum reserves of Iraq."

Rooooooba . . .

"For what we've squandered on this war, we might have bought oil from Saddam Hussein for the better part of the century!"

Rooooooooba . . .

"What is to be done?" Tipsy held up the sheaf of papers. "This afternoon, riding BART home from work, knowing I'd stand here before you tonight, I came up with a plan."

"Where do you work?"

"City Hall."

"Where do you live?"

"Sixteenth and Mission."

"That's one stop!"

"Hey," Tipsy said, "I'm good."

Rooooba rooooba rooba . . .

Goddamn, thought Few, with a covert glance at his own VU meter. She lives in the Avenues, she mentioned in passing that she never rides BART, I know perfectly well she doesn't have a job, and, something like five hours ago, she didn't have any plan at all.

The chick's a natural.

A voice cried out from the back of the room. "That's ten minutes longer than the Bush Administration spent on the entire Iraq invasion strategy!"

Rooooooba . . .

"I couldn't agree more," the speaker acknowledged. . . .

Oscar had audited five or six Newbie Scooters, and, excepting Tipsy, it was pretty much the same people. But since he had taken the trouble to show up he insisted that he document the entire event. So they stayed till the end.

Seventeen people had signed up; in the end, fifteen of them spoke. Aside from Iraq, topics included the Super Bowl, Afghanistan, Columbia, the depredation of Antarctica, trees in Berkeley, 9/11, the rudderless Republican party, the rudderless Democratic Congress, the hideous *Chronicle* redesign of 2009, Woody Guthrie, the economic meltdown of 2008, the alarming rise of ocean acidity, "How Neocons Hibernate In The Mud, Like Locusts," How Jews Can't Catch A Break, followed by How Palestinians Can't Catch A Break, Corporate Media, and the globalization of shade-grown coffee.

None of this had anything to do with why Few attended events thrown by the umbrella organization, the Cavalcade of Wonders, and he would have been bored out of his mind regardless.

Not so Tipsy Powell. Tipsy was fascinated. So far as she was concerned, if there'd been a bar to go along with the open microphone, the setup would have been perfect.

To make up for this default, they repaired to a Mexican restaurant on Folsom Street, where Tipsy proceeded to hammer three Margaritas before Few got a second pour out of his bottle of Bohemia.

"I got a million ideas," she told him, and proceeded to continue with the body of a rant only hinted at by her open-mic ramble, which had been limited to five minutes.

Few watched the bubbles in his beer.

In between her first and second margarita, Tipsy asked him why he wasn't recording what she was saying.

Few lifted his eyes from his glass long enough to stare at her, then shook his head.

"I only got twenty-three terabytes of storage," he said, his voice flatter than roadkill. "It's a budget thing. And, as usual," he took a sip of his beer, "the budget's threatened."

Dismissing Few's zinger as more mere bureau-techie talk, Tipsy proceeded to elaborate on the possibilities brought to light by the Newbie Scooter forum.

Few let her rabbit on.

I've been wrong about women before, he understated to himself.

Maybe her brother will show up sooner than later and I can file this chrono-sink under Daytime Television.

Half an hour later, at approximately eleven-thirty, at home on Quintara Street, Tipsy poured herself a shot of tequila with a beer back, wrapped herself in a Oaxaca blanket for consistency, snuggled up in the backyard chair, and, despite being more excited about the Newbie Scooter forum than anything she'd visited in years, she passed out.

Her dreams were, for the most part, fantastic. But a thread ran through them that had remained coherent, for lack of a better term, for many years.

Tipsy had often experienced the sensation of reading, or reciting, or conversing in dreamscapes, but it was the rare session in which the text made sense, for lack of a better term; it was an even rarer occurrence if, when the sugar resulting from the metabolism of alcohol consumption shocked her awake four hours after it knocked her out, she remembered such texts.

This night, loaded on beer and tequila, wrapped up in the Adirondack chair under a howling westerly and a starless sky, her dream was startling in its, for lack of a better term, clarity. Among other unrealistic characteristics of its tenor—for this was a dream, after all—was the unlimited amount of time she had to articulate her thoughts. And the size of the venue in which she performed. And the size of the crowd, attending her every word. And the fantastic lighting . . .

When the metabolism of alcohol into sugar and acetylene kicked her awake four hours later, she was cold and had a crick in her neck.

The clatter of fig leaves sounded like applause.

". . . As some of you may remember, the great Buckminster Fuller rediscovered ancient truths as regards solid geometry and pioneered their contemporary and future utility. Though much of his work in this regard occurred mid-twentieth century, he himself realized that, his engineering skills aside, it would be a generation or more before the properties of materials caught up with and were able to realize the innovation inherent in his calculations."

The screen behind and above the speaker's head illuminated. Its corona did great things for her hair.

"Here we see a simple geodesic. In this case, a 20-frequency icosahedron. For you, of course, mere policy makers," and here the speaker permitted herself the toothy grin, much-practiced before the arms-length camera lens of her Committee Digital Assistant, by which cognoscenti recognized her world-round, "the mathematics are irrelevant."

Laughter.

"Why?" the speaker asked.

"Engineers are a dime a dozen!" screamed a voice from the floor of the assembly.

"Winner!" boomed an asexual tweeter, accompanied by sirens and the fluting tones of a ballpark pipe organ. Confetti rained parallel to the directrix of a narrow cylinder from the stratospheric ceiling of the hall onto the mown dome of a single audience member, already triangulated by a pair of roving spotlights, and not so incidentally encompassing a radius of three people in any direction around her. "A vacation for two innnn—" timpani crescendoed and stopped: "—Langley, Virginia!" Cymbal crash. "The Safest Place to Vacation in All of Cryptopolis!"

The hall erupted. A tall and blonde young man in tennis shorts, the sleeves of a cabled V-neck letter-sweater draped over his shoulders, and designer reading glasses with an italic CW in the blind spot appeared bearing an envelope. "You and the sexy wonk of your choice," boomed the announcer, "will tour the CIA Gatehouse, the outer ring of the Pentagon, the unlabeled parking lot of one of the many unmarked buildings in the area, and, as a special donation from a concerned network, you and he or she will receive free lifetime transfusions of State TV."

"And you know this is a big deal, folks," the speaker addedd, lowering her corona to speak softly into the microphone, "if only because you also know how the State prefers the delicious irony of making people pay for it. It's no different than paying 250 shells to a manufacturer to walk around in a pair of sneakers with the manufacturer's logo on them. Not different at all."

Fists pumped. "It is The True!" Polite applause persisted desultorily, which served to make the ruckus of the claquers a tad obvious.

Before the applause could die out completely the tennis player, in a single continuous move, handed the startled winner the envelope, draped an arm over her shoulder, pointed at a camera, pinched her ass, mugged for an exploding strobe light as she squealed, stepped aside, thrust both arms in her direction, and backed into the darkness defined by the perimeter of the spotlight. "Winner!" redundated a computerized voice amid a renewed clamor of sirens, cowbells, and the nasal, fluted tones of a ballpark pipe organ. "Because," roared the announcer, "there is no place in all of Cryptopolis in which to so safely vacation as Langley, Virginiaaaaaaa!" The crowd responded with a full-throated roar.

The speaker prolonged her smile as screens shuffled. "That's one lucky policy-maker down there," she said warmly. She looked directly into teeming darkness. "Enjoy your trip. You can catch up on your work the following weekend."

"Ah ha. Ah hah hah hah hah," agreed the claquers. "Did you hear what she said?" yelled one member to another. "Fucking great!" said the woman next to him, barely audible through the hilarity and applause. They high-fived.

The computer materialized a map of the Middle East on the screen, and the crowd settled down. The speaker adjusted the dahlia on her hat.

"Kurds to the north of the country, roughly from the Iranian border beyond Al Sulaymaniyah, north to Turkey and northeast to Syria," the speaker recited. Little narghile icons appeared on the map as she ticked off the locales. "As many of you have cause to regret because you came to the knowledge so late, Iran is home to the largest Shia population in the world. This influence extends west, throughout eastern Iraq, from Al Sulaymaniyah all the way south to Basra." Quarter-moons appeared, coping varying distances east of the Iraq border, their concavity facing Iran. The map scrolled as she spoke. "The extent of this border is about five hundred miles as the crow flies, but its reality is more complex, and in truth it's perhaps half again as long. Here is Kuwait, secularized as most of you know, firmly under the sway of western influence and, thus, endangered. Now." The speaker caused a laser pointer to highlight the three-way border at the corner of Kuwait, Iraq, and Saudi Arabia. "Who among you knows which of the countries bordering Iraq shares its longest border? Which country shares the shortest border? Which country has accepted the most refugees fleeing the civil war?" If the speaker had been a superannuated professor in a flowered hat teaching political geography in a small two-year college on the banks of the Pecos, she couldn't have presented a more benign aspect as she surveyed the audience. "Anybody?" She darted her laser pointer about the audience at random. "Speak up."

"Saudi Arabia!" someone said.

The speaker raised an eyebrow. "Saudi Arabia, you say?" The map scrolled west. The crimson dot of the laser circled a line on it. "Here is their border. What do they offer? Sanction for refugees?"

"No!" chorused two or three voices.

"Shia sympathy?"

Two or three people laughed.

"The longest border!" yelled the first voice, overcompensating for the boredom inherent in it.

Abruptly the map zoomed out. "That's not quite correct," said the speaker. "Saudi Arabia shares the second longest border with Iraq. Iran comes first. See." The map zoomed out. Figures crawled up and over it. Saudi/Iraq: 900 km; Iran/Iraq: 1,200 km . . . "And the refugee statistics?"

"Jordan," came a woman's voice out of the darkness, "has taken upwards of 750,000 refugees. Syria has accepted one million."

"And Saudi Arabia?" asked the speaker.

A voice piped up. "Saudi Arabia doesn't make a statistical showing, refugee-wise."

"How about the United States?" asked a voice.

Laughter.

"Ahem," the speaker resumed, "so it's Jordan, the country sharing the shortest border with Iraq except for Turkey; and Syria, whose common border ranks third in length after Iran's and Saudi Arabia's. Between them, Jordan and Syria account for nearly two million of Iraq's refugees, which is some 85% of the total. Correct?"

"But they're all Arabs!" somebody pointed out.

"That's true," the speaker confirmed. "The Iranians are Persian and Shia. Jordanians and Syrians are Sunni and Arab."

"So," spoke someone very near the foot of the stage, "they are looking after their brothers."

"How very good of them," confirmed someone else.

"But what of Saudi Arabia?"

"They have their own agenda."

"Which includes Wahabism."

"Which includes American Air Force bases."

"Used to include American Air Force bases."

"Wait." The speaker held up a hand. Far above, her laser pointer described little ruby bundles of quantum string on the ceiling. "Let's not confuse issues. Setting aside the military question, how may we best characterize the refugee crisis?"

"It's a humanitarian issue!" someone shouted.

"Yes! It's a humanitarian issue!" several voices responded.

"And so?" queried the speaker.

Many voices roared as one voice: "And so it's a dispensable issue! Negligible! Antithetical to good policy!"

The speaker did not repress a smile. To Demagogue Is To Rule, proclaimed the flybutton discreetly nestled under her lapel. She looked up at the screen. One by one the east-facing crescents, the west-facing crescents, and the narghiles winked out.

In the ensuing bath of applause, a pair of dotted lines began to propagate northwards from a common vertex at the base of the Shat al Arab.

"This is the waterway in the northwestern corner of the Persian Gulf which drains through both the oil port of Basra, in Iraq, and the oil port of Abadan, in Iran. Watch me now," cautioned the speaker.

Dreamwise, it might rank with flying. The lines snaked like meridians, parallel but diverging, north through Iraq. The line on the east more or less followed the Iraq-Iran border. The second line sidled west as it progressed north, flanking An Nasiriyah, An Najaf, Karbala, and Ar Ramadi. The two lines met again in the Jabal Hamrin, south of Kirkuk and southwest of Al Sulaymaniyah.

"So," said the speaker contentedly, as she caused the ruby dot of her laser to circumnavigate the pair of lines, "from Basra to Tuz Khurmatu, in the Jabal Hamrin, to Basra again."

"The oil fields of Iraq," various of the awed spectators realized.

"It looks like a purse," said one.

"The Purse of Oil," agreed another.

"What's the Arab for purse?" asked the speaker.

"Hafiza!" shouted someone. "Zayt! Zayt is oil! It's the Hafiza min Zayt!"

"Winner! Ding ding ding . . ."

"Damn," said another, "does this dream have Vision, or what?"

"Winner! Ding ding, ding ding ding . . ."

"By all that is right," objected another, "much of that territory is Persian!"

"Fuck 'em," someone said.

"Fuck them!" shouted another, and many took up the cry. "Fuck them! Fuck them! Fuck them! . . ."

"Now, now," beamed the speaker, "that's not very diplomatic."

Led by the claquers, the hall was subsumed by sycophantic laughter.

"What of the rest of the country?" someone asked when the hilarity died down sufficiently for a single voice to be heard.

The pointer circled. "This swath of eastern desert—which is called, by the way, the Syrian Desert"—a smattering of cheers—"may be easily divided by lofting a perpendicular bisector from the Jordanian border"—a line appeared—"and extending it to the western border of the Hafiza min Zayt, thus." A line traced a path through the desert along the highway connecting the border town of Trebil to a severely depopulated area about seventy-five miles southwest of Al Ramadi, where it intersected the western border of "the newly christened, as it were . . ." the speaker noted, to derisive snickers, ". . . Hafiza min Zayt. So that everybody doesn't feel completely shafted, this highway"—the laser pointer traced the road back to Trebil—"becomes international territory." The perpendicular bisector split into two parallel lines and proceeded to cope to the highway, forming as it were a corridor for it.

"Although," the speaker apostrophized, "it will probably remain unsafe to travel until at least the end of the Epoch of Capitalism." He turned to the audience. "And about how long will that be?"

"One thousand years!" came the ready reply of many voices speaking as one.

The speaker cupped a hand to her ear. "How long?"

"One thousand years!" came the response.

"I can't hear you!" roared the speaker.

"ONE THOUSAND YEARS," came the redoubled roar.

"Thank you." The speaker smoothed the front of her flybutton display.

"That's longer than the heckafucking oil is going to last!" someone pointed out.

"Winner!" Everybody laughed. "Ding ding ding . . ."

The speaker returned her attention to the screen. "Saudi Arabia gets this half"—the laser pointer scribbled in the desert south and west of Karbala, An Najaf, and An Nasiriyah—"and Syria gets this half." The crimson dot spiraled in the deserts surrounding Baghdad, Kirkuk, and Al Mawsil.

"Those aren't halves," someone pointed out.

"More or less half of something beats the heckadarn out of more or less half of nothing," another voice pointed out.

"Just ask Kuwait and Jordan," another chimed in.

"Or Iran, for that matter," a woman interjected.

"Who is making these decisions?" someone asked loudly.

"Who's asking?" the speaker asked, turning toward the crowd.

"You're answering a question with another question," the first questioner boldly responded—so boldly indeed, that there could be little doubt that he was a claquer and his statement scripted.

"On the contrary," the speaker stated forthrightly, as if patiently. "What we are doing here is exploring a White Paper by way of brainstorming an intractable problem. *We're not necessarily determining policy.*"

"Po tee weet!" someone shouted.

"You'd think they'd come up with a packet-burst for these disclaimers and be done with it," muttered someone in the Very Important Apparatchik Suite. The speaker picked it up in her earbud. "Make a note."

"Fair enough," the audience member responded, to much good humor. "But how do you propagate your solution? How do you enforce it?"

"Yes," responded several voices. "How, for God's sake?"

"God does not come into it!" the speaker roared, and the dream gelatin quivered. "Let there be no invoking of deities within this assembly. Is that clear?"

"Clear! Ma'am!" The entire assembly responded with a single voice.

"I can't hear you."

"Clear!! Ma'am!!"

"I can't hear you, you pussies."

"CLEAR! MA'AM!" echoed the ineluctable response.

"That's more like it." A little dehydrated, with a headache coming on, the speaker cleared her throat. "As you were." She darted the laser about the twinkling audience. "And we were . . . ?"

"Dividing up the Middle East, as the world has otherwise known the vicinity in the post-colonial era as demarcated by the Balfour document." The response, though coming from the proceeding's official stenographer, was appropriately timorous. "Ma'am," it added.

The stenographer, formerly a journalist, was no longer he nor she. The change was necessary.

"Right. And the question concerned?"

"Imposition, sir."

"As in . . . ?"

Someone in the audience found the courage to speak. "As in how do we propose to impose the demarcation of the new Purse of Oil?"

"Ah," said the speaker. "That is where Mr. Buckminster Fuller comes in—whether he likes it or not." Laughter. The crimson dot traced the borders, the in-country rotations of troops, the Hafiza min Zayt. "We build a heckadome over the entire thing."

"A heckadome!"

"A synergy of domes, plural, yields one . . . singular . . . heckadome!"

"It's totality exceeds the sum of its parts!" someone declared, to cheers of agreement.

"But is it possible?"

"Absolutely!"

On-screen, an animated time-lapse sequence of struts, girders, beams, columns, and hubs assembled itself and arced as if overhead.

"A heckadome!"

"A mere ten stories high. Segmented to allow for salients of geography, control vertices, points of egress, and, of course, the heights of derricks."

"Carbon fiber . . . ?"

"Did Fuller know carbon fiber . . . ?"

"He must not have. . . ."

"Pyrolysis of synthetic fiber would be a fruitful area of res—"

"Para-who?"

"Don't worry about it."

"Technology is your friend—"

"—Or Else!"

"Ding ding, ding ding ding. . . ."

"Plus, of course, Avogadro ratios favorable to inert gas dispersion." The speaker tugged at her lip, which elongated disconcertingly. "Argon, maybe."

"It almost has to be carbon fiber. . . ."

"The substance is classified. But, be assured, it exists. The technology is approximately the same as that pioneered by NASA in anticipation of the hapkeite mining colonies soon to be constructed on the moon."

"Pure genius!"

"Pow pow, pow!"

"A triumph of tax-funded engineering!"

"But again—I say, ladies and gentlemen! Be reasonable! Be rational! Be realistic . . . ! How do we enforce it?"

"Yeah. What about the people?"

Laughter.

"No, really. They'll get in the way."

"Winner! Ding'ding ding . . ."

"Not to panic," soothed the speaker. "Once the dome is constructed, we'll leave a few doors open and flood the place with fire ants."

"Fire ants? Fire ants, did she say? Fire ants . . . !"

The speaker folded her arms across her chest and appeared very smug. "An Avogadro number of fire ants."

"That's brilliant!" enthused a statistician. "The great storms in east Texas coincident congruent to the Era of Non-Compliant Weather Models has us knee deep in surplus fire ants."

"Brilliant!" yelled the claquers.

"Perfect!" agreed others.

"Everybody will leave," hundreds roared. "Can't stand no," cued Condor Silversteed's seventh consecutive No. 1 hit, "fire factions, pow pow, pow pow pow, f-f-f-factions . . ."

"What an artist!" whispered an awed denizen of the Very Important Apparatchik. "The very apotheosis of prolepsis!" soughed another.

The hubbub rose to a cacophony of argumentation, pontification, vituperation, the whole tempered withal by enthusiasm and doubt. The speaker wielded her twenty-eight-ounce Japanese framing gavel, so beautiful in design and fabrication, it looked as if she were about to smite the podium with a stainless steel orchid. The headache quantized accordingly. "There is a solution," the speaker winced. "Ladies and gentlemen, there is a solution . . . !"

The map of the Purse of Oil reappeared on the screen, a grid of triangles and hexagons superimposed upon it.

"Construction time: ten years. Cost: seven trillion Euroshells . . ."

"Euroshells!" came the shocked response.

"Why Euroshells?" someone shouted.

The Speaker shrugged. "More hell for the shell."

Some speculators laughed, some speculators cried. "It is The Fiduciary

Territory Imposed By Progress," intoned the announcer in his best *basso profundo.*

The Speaker nodded slowly. "And what of the additional two or three million who will have fled?" she reminded them. "Will they not be of sufficiently resilient and coherent stock to re-seed their cultures?" She folded her arms. "Where's the goddamn problem?"

Several audience members made sounds like a buzzer on a door lock. "That's a humanitarian issue!" Others took up the cry. "Out of the bounds of the debate!"

"Oh, of course," the speaker responded. "I'd forgotten."

"Oh, of course!" They all laughed at the quaint joke. The speaker had forgotten! That's what a good night's sleep in the Xolotel™, otherwise known as the backyard, will get you. Proof positive!

"Visionary!" stipulated a telegate.

"The speaker makes sense in her sleep!" enthused a hologate.

"All in all, it will be no different than working on the moon. Heckafucking employment opportunities . . ."

Nothing happened.

The speaker leaned into the microphone. "Jobs?" she prompted. "Jobs, you knuckleheads!"

The place went nuts before eventually dissolving into contented laughter. "No singing." The speaker glanced at an imaginary watch on her wrist. "Not until Condor Silversteed holos in at eleven hundred hours!"

"Winner! Ding ding ding . . ."

Everybody cheered. But before the crowd could erupt despite the conspicuous silence of the claquers, the speaker held up both hands. "Please reserve your passionate subjectivity until then."

The crimson dot of the laser pointer spiraled.

"The Shrine," the speaker concluded, "will be erected in the very heart of the Hafiza min Zayt."

The dot held steady at the confluence of the Tigris and the Euphrates Rivers. "Every hundred kilometers or so, transverse tunnels through the ripstop—heavy security of course—will periodically be opened to accommodate Bedu migration, as well as limited commerce, because, after all, we can't eliminate people altogether. Not yet, anyway!" Sustained laughter . . .

. . . Quentin, said a voiceover in the dream, where are you? I'm having my first authentic political nightmare while actually asleep . . .

Oscar Few spent the night in Pirates Cove.

It happened to be a night of extraordinary clarity. After he'd parked a month's worth of tapes under the century plant, he lay in his sleeping bag on the driftwood platform built over a crevice well above the tide line and counted stars and constellations. Some he could name, some he made up names for. Arcturus which is a constituent star in Boötes, Pygmalion, Virgo, Sagittarius, Cygnus, and Bellerophon, as well as Alice, the Rabbit, and the Mad Hatter.

Truth of the matter was, although he could spot a mad zealot in a radio-neutral suit from forty yards, the only constellations he was really sure of were the Big Dipper, Orion, and the Pleiades. He liked the story that the latter were named for the seven daughters of Atlas who were metamor-phosed into stars, despite the fact that only six of the stars are visible to the naked eye. This stuff is hard to keep up with, but not so hard as keep-ing up with the Cavalcade of Wonders, he reminded himself with a shud-der. Not to mention the net they somehow manage to cast. When was he going to meet a woman he could talk to? And there were Mars and Venus, too, but they aren't constellations. Which reminded him of a t-shirt which proclaimed, Pluto: Always Remember. As to the rest—the Crab, the Bear, the Archer—or was the Archer also called Orion?—he knew their names but not those of their constituent stars.

He also knew that, in China, these same constellations were called Rat, Dog, Boar, Snake, Dragon, Horse, Sheep, Monkey, Ox—like that; because, like the Greeks long after them, the ancient Chinese, too, had, you know, imagination and stars to foist it on.

Nice and simple. That's the way he liked his explanations.

Either way, the night sky was a wonder seldom paid attention to, these days, by man or beast—and there goes a satellite. Someday there'll be orbiting prison platforms—and he would be possessed of an Extra-terrestrial Vehicle Identification Scanner by which to log them. Gitmo_6 would no doubt be the name of one of them, although ex-cons in the know would refer to it as Tweeker's_Roost. But, except for the cassette tapes, he never carried any tech along on these solo hikes. He spent enough time dealing with tech. Besides, even cellphones didn't work out here, let alone non-existent ETVIS units. Although, he sighed, that too, might one day change.

He lay on his back, gazing up at the night sky, nary a cloud above him, only the nimbus of San Francisco to the south, the city itself hidden by the loft of Coyote Ridge, with the big Pacific rollers booming and seething against the rock outcrop that rose out of the surf on the south side of little cove like a big stump. Stump Rock, in fact, was its name. Maybe thirty feet high and not more than ten feet across at the top, it wasn't a difficult climb, at low tide, and in his long-gone youth he'd spent many an hour up there sunning himself. Occasionally he still took the trouble to wade out and climb it. The last time, at least a year ago, he'd noticed that some long gone pothead had left a pipe with a baggie up there, in a cleft between rocks under a stunted coyote bush. He'd ignored them for a long time until, noting that the marijuana had turned solid black with mildew, he'd taken a look. Nothing special. A little pipe made of plumbing parts, the weed was mostly shake and no bud with lots of seeds; a cop knows about these things. Two of the seeds had sprouted within the residual humidity of the bag and subsequently shriveled. All of it turned to dust at his touch. And this led him to the conclusion that, despite its proximity to a metropolitan area whose population exceeded six million people, it had been a long time since anybody had taken the trouble to scramble up to the top of Stump Rock.

Stretched out on the platform above the surf he could hear the intermittent buoy off Duxbury Reef, six or seven miles due west. He rolled over. After a minute or two he picked it out, flashing green. He counted the flashes. One came every six seconds. It was a so-called whistle buoy, but the whistle sounded more like a forlorn moan, its audio driven by and therefore subject to the whims of the swells, and he'd loved it since he was a boy. He fancied that it must be the most melancholy sound he'd ever heard.

This thought caused him to remember a guy last seen pushing his surfboard off Abalone Flats, at the northern end of Duxbury Reef, a mile or so north of the buoy and the reason for its placement. A curious bystander asked him where the fuck he thought he was going, because there was no surf to be had west of there for some 3,000 miles.

"I'm looking for a good dentist," the guy told him.

Officer Few had read about it in the *Chronicle*. So it must be true.

Take me with you, man, Few said to himself, not even half facetiously.

THIRTY-TWO

CEDRIC OSAWA SMELLED THE BRICK ON THE CHART TABLE THROUGH TWO layers of seven-mil visquine before he sniffed out the light switch. In fact, having detected the former, he skipped the latter.

Anybody else would have smelled Cedric Osawa first. He'd been on the road for two weeks without a bath. A number of the conveyances he'd been aboard were abluted far less frequently than that, and many of the odors to be encountered were adhesive and communicable. He'd left Vegas without showering, haunted by indigestion and dreams full of nostalgia, strange portents, and the apparently permanent mind-worm of a snake that quacks like a duck.

Cedric himself, though inured, could discern the redodences of popcorn, of fluid attributable to the human condition, of flea and roach powder, compressed air, skunk, disposable diapers, combusted tobacco, molten upholstery, antifreeze, roofing tar, pine sap, newsprint, burnt coffee, unbleached wool, clove bidis, chlorine bleach, mildewed books, vulture neck feathers, the Four Corners power plant, gun powder, burning tires, rubbing alcohol, acetone, xylene, toluene, carbon tetrachloride, carpet mold, gorgonzola cheese, No. 2 diesel, sweet basil, decomposing chitin, sintered brake linings, and . . .

Justine.

Cedric didn't know one couture cologne from another, let alone *Justine*. But if *Justine* is anything it's unique, and Cedric recognized it as a significant deviation from the stink of the everyday, of the hoi polloi, and of most navigable vessels. Plus it was new. Its freight aboard the olfactory after deck gave him pause.

Still, the light switch could wait.

Cedric tuned the short-range night vision that had enabled him to avoid a collision with many an unilluminated breakwater, and scanned the cabin. Lights from adjacent vessels penetrated the yacht's lites here and there. The yellow loom of a municipal dock light slanted down the bridge companionway.

Justine. He reached for another name. Male or female? Immediately upon the assumption, pheromones pressed the air. It was involuntary. A certain levity returned the metabolic semaphore. Deadly levity. Levity implied perversion. Propaganda. A deliberate mistake.

Despite his concentration, he recalled the snake.

Shushupe, native to the high Amazon Basin, is nocturnal, long, and extremely venomous. It is also wiley. *Shushupe* finds a game trail, coils itself into a pile, and quacks like a duck. In the dark, it sounds just like a duck. Might it smell, as well, like *Justine*?

In broad daylight, it would probably sound just like a snake.

Having sounded just like a duck, *shushupe* waits with unhinged fangs. The methodology must work, for the species thrives.

Why not name an odor for a snake?

One trip up the Amazon was all Cedric Osawa had required. Of the twenty-six venomous reptiles cataloged in one of the appendices of Clark's book, he remembered only *shushupe*. But *shushupe* was enough. A surfeit, really. If you ordered a Greyhound bus full of poisonous snakes, and only one *shushupe* turned up, you could sign the bill of lading. After that trip, and once this one was over, Cedric would re-up for the snakeless isles of the Caribbean Basin, and turn his back on the reptile catalog of *The Rivers Ran East*.

The lesson, however? Easy. If it quacks like a duck, it may not be a duck.

. . . So maybe it isn't a cologne for women. Maybe it's a men's cologne. Maybe it's a woman's cologne on a man. The mores of the mainland can be so deceptive.

Meanwhile, if that isn't a brick of blow on the chart table, Cedric Osawa is a duck's uncle, for whom the snake of fate can wait.

The snake of fate does wait. It's one of the things it does best.

His footfalls on the carpet of the saloon were soundless. A dock line creaked. Along the pier a halyard plaintively flagellated its aluminum mast and fell silent.

A shadow arced over the row of windows to port. Cedric tensed. The shadow landed on the dock in full view.

Night heron.

A west coast bird with whose east coast cousin Cedric was familiar. But just a bird, after all.

His shoulders remained as tense as newly tuned rigging. Accustomed as he was to medicating various ailments accumulated over a lifetime of physical endeavor, some part of Cedric texted with that part of his cortex concerned with such things. Yo, U B hurtN. U B holdN? U B Kray-Z. Yo fool! U need tht brik 2 hit U upside U hed befo U geddown wid it?

Years and years ago, Cedric had taken a shotgun to a television. To consolidate the mess, he'd removed the television from his boat to a nearby dumpster arena. Gave the TV both barrels. Most satisfactory. Now he'd like to give both barrels to his mental server. U, yo. Kind of tricky, though. Might take out the host, too. As went the television, it might have been nice to take out the host too, but it doesn't work like that. It works like, take out all the entities you want, the host lives on.

Fukkin insidious, yo.

Tired as he was, Cedric recollected himself. He wasn't sure what he'd do when Red showed up. Kill him outright? Probably best. Cedric wasn't one for the lingering adiós of torture. Plus Red was dangerous. But no rush. Tonight or tomorrow or the next day, Cedric would settle a score.

Man O man I B tired, Cedric thot. My brain, Cedric thought, seems to be making a cameo appearance in the texted movie of its own existence. When's the last time I saw a movie? Decades. Why should I sit through a movie when—this is serious, man. Wake the fuck up. Before you hit the mainland, you never even heard of texting.

Cedric wanted to wake the fuck up, as his brain would have it, but he was, in fact, bone weary. Wasting a night on that asshole's car in Miami took some energy, sure. But taking a bus all the way across the goddamn United States took way more. He should have stayed in that hotel in Vegas and slept for a week. Better it should have been in Palm Springs. Bakersfield? It would appear that the business with the knife was going to cost him a lot of time and a lot of sleep. Fucking asshole bureaucrat. Two weeks on the bus and a missing knife had helped Cedric catch up on current events. "Fucking asshole country gets its architectural penis cut off by fucking fanatics and what does it do?" a guy who got on in Albuquerque and got off in Flagstaff told him. "Declares war on two countries. Flails around like a thousand-pound semi-aquatic, egg-laying mammal with a ripped toenail. You heard me. That's what it does, and it flattens any number of hapless cultures and jack-lit people while it's doing so."

"And dings me for a knife I've had for thirty years."

"Yeah." *Yeah.*

It's a wonder they didn't blow up the Bahamas while they were at it. I guess I should consider them and me fortunate in that regard. And if Charley hadn't gotten his ticket punched I'd be on the hook in some quiet cove with me precious Lacayan forkéd nose pipe and a wahine and a quart of rum and a half-decent guitar. . . . Altogether, an alternate reality.

Cedric gave up. Fuck it, fuck them, and fuck you, whoever it them and you are. I can take out Red Means no matter what shape I'm in.

He crossed the cabin. He'd hefted a few bricks in his time—bales, bundles, bushels, and suitcases, too. He made this brick for good weight. A righteous one thousand grams. Two point two pounds.

The night heron emitted a *quock* and recrossed the port- and dock-side lites. Cedric froze. Birds and snakes are related—no? Scales became feathers—no? Other way around? California has exactly one poisonous snake, he consoled himself, and it doesn't quack.

The night heron rose and settled on the next boat over with a thump.

Cedric forced himself to swallow.

The next boat over was a Cal 20. The entire boat, rigging, house, decks, tiller, cockpit, even its dock lines, was flocked in black mold. What showed white was seagull guano or, as witnessed, the droppings of a night heron. Bluish white, by the yellow mercury light. The color of . . .

Cedric's new knife made quick work of the gray duct tape, the black polyethylene, and the clear vacuum-sealed plastic within. He didn't need to turn on a light to get a better look. Cocaine, too, has a certain odor. Cocaine smelled to Cedric like ice smells to an Eskimo, like home, like the great outdoors, like yo natural habitat. It smells like one kind of ice as opposed to all the other kinds of ice. It smells like the blade of a harpoon left overnight on the sled under an exuberant aurora borealis.

Cedric put the new knife to work. He chipped a quantity off the brick onto the door of the countertop reefer, hacked at it for a while, aligned the resulting smithereens into four rails like he was building a switchyard for the Sierra Pacific, and then rolled a hundred dollar bill into a tube with a quarter-inch diameter, helped himself, and, soon enough, Cedric found himself thinking he was thinking straight.

Charley Powell, now, what a study.

Many's the adventure Cedric and Charley had shared. Boats in all weathers, for example. Although they'd never, Cedric thought, glancing at the Cal 20, gone out in a boat that fucked up.

Fucked up in a boat, however, Cedric thought, as he happily doubled down, that much we've done. "Winner!" oddly occurred to him. "Pow pow, pow." Goddamn that Las Vegas. *Justine*. Cedric hesitated over the rolled bill. *Quock*. Cedric glanced out the window.

The night heron had moved. Now it stared into the black water between the boat and the dock.

The boat tested its dock lines.

Just above Cedric's head, the bail of a brass lamp creaked.

Cedric sniffed. Not kerosene. Odorless lamp oil.

And a singed wick.

And what's that?

Rum.

Ah, Cedric thought. Excellent idea.

The bottle stood on the counter. Haitian, it was, too. Not often seen. Mighty genial. Cedric drew the stopper and sniffed. Damn.

For the first time in two weeks, Cedric smiled.

If Cedric knew anything at all, he knew this: there is nothing—nothing—so mutually copacetic as clean cocaine and a fine Haitian rum.

He drank it straight from the bottle. The rum cut through the bolus of cocainized mucus encapsulating his epiglottis like a herd of alligator shrimp eating through dead bottom paint—or, for you landlubbers, like baby formula cut with melamine will eat through infant actuarial tables. Take your pick. Centuries away, the Samurai knows. Ah ha ha hahaha . . .

Double D damn. Text that. Cedric stood up and rummaged around until he found a glass, half-filled it with rum, and took another sip from the bottle before he stoppered it.

Ice? What am I? A fucking Eskimo? Fuck ice.

After years in the tropics, Cedric had learned to do without ice—not rum, just ice.

He paced back and forth along the edge of the chart table. This is perfect, he thought. Fucked up on rum and blow and surveying forty feet of mercury-lit dock and a rotting Cal 20, who the hell cares if it's in San Francisco as opposed to somewhere within a hundred miles north or south of latitude 25? He saluted the row of windows. That will come, that will come. I will discharge my pact with Charley and make my way home, bus or train or walk if I have to, though I may never again have the money for a bottle of this rum. Let alone and forget a kilo of blow. Maybe there's some way I can get both across the country? This is aside from the fact that at my age I need either stimulant like I need a snake that quacks like a duck. On the other hand, at my age, what difference does it make? I've already seen hurricanes, Latin spitfires, megayachts in flames, a shark-sundered water-skier, the wrong end of an automatic weapon—and still I have not been forced to grow up. What's to get older about? But now—he held up a forefinger—I must sin.

Cedric looked around. Yes. Of course there's one. He carefully lifted the door of the reefer so as not to cause the diced cocaine to slide off its face. It's a sin to put ice in a rum like this. He ran a hand under the lid. But . . .

"So you found your friend at last."

Along with the voice wafted *Justine*.

The lid fell open. Two protracted rails of cocaine disappeared over the side of the cabinet and into the whorls of a damp sword mat on the cabin sole below. Charley's head by the hair in one hand, glass of rum in the other, Cedric turned slowly.

"Now at least you can say that your commission is based on more than a mere supposition."

Though half-cloaked in shadow, the man addressing him was dressed head to foot in black, including his shoes. His sleek blonde hair and a beautifully tanned complexion stood away from the gloom of the cabin like the recently cleaned visage of a saint in an otherwise begrimed peristyle.

Outside of the many and perpetual discussions he carried on with and within his own mind, Cedric was not a man of many words. But in this case he was moved to communicate. He held up the head. "You know who this is?"

The blond-haired man nodded. "Yes."

"Do you know how he came to be . . . like this?"

The blond man nodded again.

"Did you have anything to do with it?"

The blond man turned his head slightly. "Not really," he told Cedric. "Not directly."

"Not directly," Cedric repeated.

"No."

Cedric set Charley on the counter.

"How, then?"

"I'll have to think about that," the blond man said. "It's an interesting question."

"You do that." Cedric raked a little ice up out of the refrigerator and added it to his rum.

"In the end, however," the blond man said, with no outward sign of cogitation, "it all comes to the same thing."

Cedric took up his knife and stirred his drink with the blade. "What's your name, why are you here, and what comes to the same thing?" He wiped each side of the blade on his tongue.

"They call me Miou Miou."

Cedric's face wrinkled into a mask of revulsion botoxed with incredulity.

"Not that it matters," continued Miou Miou, "in the eye of Allah. It's you—"

"Allah?" Cedric said quickly. "What's Allah got to do with it?"

"Nothing." Miou Miou smiled. "It's just an expression. You know, like, Allah sees the sparrow fall?"

"I been hearing about fucking ragheads running round the world these days, blowing shit up," Cedric said, thinking he might piss this guy off enough to get him to make a mistake. He took a sip of his drink. "But," he admitted, taking another sip, "you don't look like no raghead."

"Rags mean an entirely different thing to me," Miou Miou affably agreed.

"Is that affirmative? You're not a raghead?"

"More like a raghorse."

"Me," said Cedric, rattling the ice in his drink, "I don't care about a man's affiliation. So long as he lets me alone, he can affiliate all he wants."

Miou Miou appeared to consider this. Then, "Sometimes," he said, "affiliations are hard to avoid."

"How's that?" Cedric took a sip of rum.

"Take your friend Charley," Miou Miou said.

Cedric didn't look at Charley. "What about him?"

"Late in life, he acquired a certain . . . affiliation."

"So?"

"So look where it got him."

"Where did it get him?"

Miou Miou smiled. "It got him to where he fits very neatly into a top-loading countertop refrigerator, like a six-pack. Like a gallon of wine. Like a frozen chicken."

Now Cedric realized that, along with his sense of humor, he had better put down his drink. Not the knife. Just the drink.

"I'm sorry about your friend," Miou Miou said unexpectedly.

"That," Cedric answered, "is kind of you." Not taking his eyes off Miou Miou, Cedric pointed his blade at the severed head. "Did you do this?"

The blond man shook his head.

"Do you know who did?"

The blond man nodded.

"Who?"

"Red Means."

"I'm very disappointed," Cedric nodded back.

"Yes," said Miou Miou.

"Yes what? What do you know about it?"

"Charley left you a note, I believe."

Cedric frowned.

"A note," Miou Miou added, "and some chump change."

Cedric is not liking this, Cedric thought.

"It said, in effect, in case anything happens to me, Red Means is the party responsible."

Cedric blinked.

"Correct?" Miou Miou asked.

"What business is this of yours?"

Miou Miou dismissed this. "It's true?"

Cedric made no response.

Miou Miou answered his own question. "So you've come to avenge your friend."

Cedric said nothing.

"How loyal. How quaint. How stupid."

"What would you know about it?"

Miou Miou spoke in the dark. "If you promise not to mistakenly avenge the death of your friend and go straight back to where you came from, I'll let you go."

"*You* will let *me* go?"

Miou Miou nodded in the dark.

For the first time in two weeks, Cedric laughed.

In the dark, Miou Miou did not laugh.

Cedric abruptly turned serious. "Not bloody likely. Aside from the fact that it's none of your business, what do you have to do with this?" Cedric moved his head toward Charley's. "How do you fit in?"

"You're the one," Miou Miou replied, "who doesn't fit in."

"Felix Timbalón," Cedric realized aloud.

"An unreliable hophead," Miou Miou said with contempt. "Obviously."

"At least he was working for a living," Cedric observed.

"And what would it be, precisely," replied Miou Miou, "that you think I am doing?"

Despite the rather intense atmosphere presently reigning over the main cabin, Cedric thought that what he'd really like to do before they continued with the conversation was help himself to another blast. At a minimum, it would delay the hard work of trying to figure out what was going on, let alone doing something about it.

"Normally I'd be considered the perfectly amoral man," Miou Miou said to Cedric. "A job's a job and, so long as I get my money, it's all the same to me. Naturally, I get my kicks. But from where I stand, it's not difficult to surmise that not a soul in the world is going to miss you, high or not."

Surprisingly adroit, considering the addled metabolism that made it, Cedric locked open the spike in the handle of his knife as he lunged. Spike and blade formed a T, with Cedric's fist balled around their handle, and they appeared to comprise a formidable weapon.

But Miou Miou was a little too far across the deck for Cedric to cover the distance in less than a measurable amount of time. Plus, truth to tell, Cedric misjudged it. Cedric was loaded. Miou Miou was a professional, and he didn't show up for work loaded. Cedric was just a dope smuggler, retired, with compromised reflexes. Before Cedric really realized it, but as a result of a move Cedric found sickeningly familiar, and slow even, he watched himself find himself face down in the carpet with his arm twisted high up between his shoulder blades, its shoulder dislocated, and the knife tumbling uselessly off the small of his back to the deck.

The end will converge quickly, he thought to himself.

"Have you ever heard of a snake that quacks like a duck?" Cedric feebly inquired of the floor.

Miou Miou broke Cedric's neck and stood up. "No." He shot a cuff. "Can't say as I have."

The business end of a boat hook speared Miou Miou through his right ear drum, inducing a shrieking tinnitus that Dopplered through his brain like an oncoming rape whistle. So that's what a mistake sounds like, Miou

Miou thought, as the impact shattered his skull. I wonder if mistakes are communicable.

"Nobody's going to miss you, either," Red said, as Miou Miou collapsed on top of Cedric, "motherfucker."

I figured that out, Miou Miou thought, as he died, a long time ago.

Red opened and closed the torn palm in the dark. At this rate, the son of a bitch is never going to heal.

He leaned the boat hook in a corner. "Sorry I'm late, Cedric." He stepped to the sink and inverted Cedric's drink over the wounded paw. "I'm late a lot lately."

Red raked some ice out of the reefer with one hand, replaced Charley with the other, and dropped the lid. He recharged Cedric's glass with ice and rum, keeping a few shards for the palm of his hand, and sipped judiciously. When the ice in his palm had melted, he set down the glass, knelt on the floor, and methodically turned out both sets of pockets.

Miou Miou, being a professional, had nothing but cash on him, maybe five grand in dollars and euros.

Cedric had his 100-ton Coast Guard license and a familiar-looking envelope. Inside it, Red found $504 Bahamian, $112 American, and a note, which he read by the glare of the dock light.

> Cedric,
> Long time no see. I've been owing you this grand, plus vigorish, for a while. Try not to put it all in one arm.
> Unfortunately or otherwise, if you don't see me face to face before the beginning of hurricane season, then I'm toast and Red's the reason.
> See you around the blue hole,
> Charley

Red scrutinized the envelope. The postmark was faint and the light was bad, but eventually he made it out as Colonel Hill, Crooked Island, Bahamas. "I'll be a son of a bitch," Red told the ghostly darkness. He read the note a second time. He read the postmark a second time. Nothing had changed. He brought his fist down on the lid of the countertop reefer hard enough to dent it, which started the palm bleeding again.

Then he stood in the gloom of the cabin for a long time. After a while, the night heron flew between the dockside illumination and the cabin windows.

Red thoughtfully folded envelope, note, Coast Guard license, and money into his hip pocket.

Then he took up the glass, finished the rum in it, and chewed up the ice.

"Miou Miou," he said finally, "I owe you one." He shook his head and set the glass in the sink. "Fucking Charley."

THIRTY-THREE

SCREAMS FOLLOWED THE DOCTOR THROUGH THE OPEN DOOR. AN ELBOWED lever closed it behind him, silent as a bivalve.

"Medical ethics prohibit my calling a patient, especially one with so dire a need, a fucking cunt," declaimed the doctor, calmly stripping off a pair of bloodied latex gloves. The lid of a stainless steel trash can yawned to the touch of his foot, and he fed the gloves into its mouth. "But I've just about had it with ethics."

"About time, if you ask me," commented the orderly.

"Nobody asked you," said the doctor, rolling on fresh gloves. "People who'd siphon a fix from a fentanyl drip in the orthopedic ward should not be allowed to hold opinions concerning ethics."

"That was Johnston," the orderly corrected him gravely.

"Let alone express them."

"Now he works at St. Petrale."

"Oh, so," said the doctor, "we're in touch with the base scum? Are we texting him?" He sequentially slotted each finger of one hand at right angles to the fingers of the other to seat the latex. "Is it a union thing?"

"Everybody knows he's at St. Petrale," the orderly responded calmly without answering the question. "I was present at the staff meeting at which you yourself suggested the efficacy of our highly recommending him to there by way of speedily jettisoning him from here. You—"

"I'm sure I don't know what you're talking about," the doctor cut him short. His eye fell on Quentin. "What have we here?" He did not deny himself a little sneer.

Quentin drew himself up. "And whom do I have the honor of addressing?"

"We, in the trauma center, find ourselves shorn entirely of manners," the doctor said.

Quentin's eye involuntarily fell to the man's breast, which bore a name-plate not unlike the orderly's. "Doctor Felton-Foote," he read. "Didn't I know you in Guadalajara?"

Felton-Foote favored Quentin with the regard of a colonial entomologist. "I daresay you knew everybody worth knowing in Guadalajara."

"Except you, it would seem."

"I've never been there," Felton-Foote sniffed.

Officer Ventana was looking puzzled. "What's going on in Guadalajara?"

"Medical school," the orderly informed him, in a stage whisper sufficient to be heard in the back row of the balcony. "It's a good one, too."

Felton-Foote favored the orderly with an icy regard. "And what exactly
would you know about the disparate, not to mention relative, merits of a
given institute of medicine?"

"I judge them by what they send me," the orderly answered, in all simplicity.

"All I know," Felton-Foote grimly regarded Quentin, "is what the
streets of San Francisco send me. So." He pulled Quentin's head abruptly
forward and peered at his shaved scalp. "Gay bashing?"

Quentin cracked aside the forearm of the doctor with his own and leveled eyes with him. "Not yet," he snarled. "Not just yet."

Dr. Felton-Foote's cellphone rang a vaguely familiar tune. He retrieved
the device from a holster beneath his scrubs, frowned at its readout, and
took the call. "What is it?"

"The theme from *Doctor Zhivago*," the orderly stage-whispered helpfully. Quentin and Ventana looked at him. "He holds an undergraduate
degree in Comparative Literature. His thesis posited that Boris Pasternak
admired Petrarch sufficiently to have named Zhivago's Laura after the
poet's Laura, and there's a long appendix with genealogical charts showing how the real Laura, on which Petrarch's idealization was based, married into the family that produced the Marquis de Sade."

"There's always a Russian connection of late," Quentin marveled, "but
I didn't know that about the Marquis de Sade. Is it true?"

The orderly shrugged. "He writes cementitious poetry, too."

Felton-Foote did not bother to leave the room or even walk away. "Call
me when you've debrised the wound." He tried to hang up, but the caller
forestalled him. "So start an IV," Felton-Foote barked. "What are you,
helpless?" He listened briefly. "No, no, no." He stabbed a latexed forefinger into the air in front of him as if it were a lofty prostate. "It's a simple
gunshot wound. Of course she's going into shock. Start the IV, give her a
local, debris the wound, call me when she's ready. What part of Service
and Humility don't you understand—?" He listened some more. "Ms.
Thomas," he said, as if patiently, "gunshot mothers are delivering babies all
over the planet at any given moment within the context of less than two
percent of the resources available to this hospital. As a theoretical part of
these vast resources, have you never heard of an epidural?" He listened
briefly. "Look look look," he said, obviously interrupting. "Don't get hysterical. Do as I've told you, and I'll be along. Is that clear? Christ, look at it
from the point of view of your residency. To wit, do you want to assist on a

caesarean on a gunshot victim, or—" he contemplated Quentin, "—or do
you want to suture a quotidian skull laceration?" He waited. "Okay." He
holstered the phone. "Residents," he apostrophized in disgust.

"I got into this business," the orderly observed, "to alleviate the suffering of mankind. But," he indicated Quentin, "this gentleman has been sitting on this gurney for two hours already."

Ventana indicated the television, at which he'd been staring as if fascinated. "That's about how long that guy's been dissecting a Superbowl that
hasn't happened yet."

The orderly didn't even look.

Quentin glanced up at the digital readout in the lower right-hand corner of the television screen. "One hour and forty minutes."

"Mm," replied the doctor absently. After a pause, he smiled. "I've just
bought a Porsche."

"Not again." The orderly closed his eyes and shook his head.

"Wow," said Officer Ventana, wrenching his attention away from the
television. "What model?"

"Carerra Turbo S," the doctor answered him. "Priapic Red."

"Whale tail," said Ventana, "cookie-cutter wheels, sunroof, fog-lights,
seven-speaker stereo, and a black Naugahyde brassier?"

"The works," the doctor assured him. "Her speedometer reads to 165."

Ventana whistled appreciatively.

"And you believe it?" the orderly surmised.

If Felton-Foote noticed the fumes of acid rising from the orderly's
tone, he made no sign. Quite the contrary. "You take a nurse up through
the gears and back down inside of a mile?" The doctor snapped his latexed
fingers. "She's ready to deal."

"I'd give it up too," the orderly hinted broadly.

"The problem is," the doctor continued, evincing earnest petulance, "I
can't come up with a proper license plate."

"A license plate?" Officer Ventana asked.

"He means a vanity plate," the orderly informed him.

"Oh, no," Ventana adjoined sympathetically.

"Every tag I think up is already taken," Felton-Foote explained sadly.

"FELTFOOT is already taken?" the orderly asked.

"Gone," the doctor nodded, aggrieved. He looked up with anticipation.
"How did you know?"

"We had this conversation a shift or ten ago," the orderly pointed out.

Dr. Felton-Foote vaguely frowned. It was clear from his expression
that if it weren't the conversation he couldn't remember, it may well have
been the orderly himself.

Quentin bore witness to this exchange with mounting incredulity. "Say, have you a couple of aspirin around—?"

"And what about FOOTFELT?" Ventana suggested.

"Yeah," put in the orderly, not bothering to conceal his acedia, "have you thought of FOOTFELT?"

"Taken." Felton-Foote retrieved a roll of paper from the side pocket of his white smock and handed it to Quentin, of all people.

Quentin accepted it. Or rather, his incredulity accepted it, or maybe it was his concussion. Something, at any rate, had rendered him passive.

The orderly nudged him and winked. "Let's see." Officer Ventana came round behind the gurney to look over Quentin's shoulder as he unrolled the piece of paper, revealing a list in which each entry had been scored through by pen or pencil.

FELTFOOT
FOOTFELT
FLTFT
FTFLT
FLEETFT
FLTDOC
DCTRFLT

"I got it," Quentin said.

"Good." The orderly patted him on the shoulder. "That's the first step to canceling autoinfantilization."

The doctor hushed him.

"TOOTELFF," Quentin said, "is an anagram of FELTFOOT. Only the Shadow will know."

"And those with secret decoder rings," the orderly added with admiration.

Ventana look mystified.

Felton-Foote counted on his fingers. "Too many letters."

"Perfect," Quentin declared, "then make it TOOTELF. Or—will they give you a space between syllables? As in, TOOT ELF?"

"Oh no." Felton-Foote made as if to hold back the wave of sentiment with the latexed palms of both hands. "That's too close to BLO MNKY, with or without the space."

"No anyway," Ventana volunteered. "I've cited that one for blocking a crosswalk. Jaguar XKE." He backhanded his notepad. "$375."

"Time was of course . . ." As if to exchange the reverie of excesses past for the exigencies of matters present, if a tad reluctantly, Felton-Foote arrested the reflection. "But, no. Inspired by the example of a recent president, I sacrificed the enjoyment of that product in order to reify my personal integrity."

"To reify," Quentin said thoughtfully, "is to regard or treat an abstraction as if it had concrete or material existence."

"Alas," stressed the orderly.

"After my residency," the doctor added, somewhat petulantly.

"Say," said the orderly, "wasn't that about the same time that Johnston got nailed for siphoning fentanyl?"

"What are you," snapped Felton-Foote, "Thucydides?"

The theme from Dr. Zhivago sounded again. "All those other ones are taken, too. Hello."

Quentin shared the list with the orderly and Ventana.

CADUCEUS (too many letters)
CADUCUS
CADUCS
CDUCS
CDCS
CDS
SAWBONES (too many letters)
SWBNS
SAWBNS
SAWBONZ
CADUZEUS (too many letters)
CADZEUS
CADZOOKS (too many letters) (doesn't make sense)

"Sure it does," said the orderly.

SURGEON
SRGEON
SRGEN
SRGN
SRGN1
SRGN2
SRGN3 &c &c

"That's so depressing," the orderly said, not without a certain satisfaction.

"I'll say," Quentin agreed, gamely swallowing a wave of nausea.

"It's hard," Officer Ventana reified.

"Is ER on there?"

"Um . . . Here."

"How about ASSHOLE?"

"Um . . . Yep."

"What? Where?"

"Just kidding." Quentin offered him the list. "Anybody want to add to it?"

"Yes," the orderly said, "but no thanks."

"Boy or girl?" Felton-Foote said into his cellphone, turning his head to study the readout on a beeper vibrating on his belt.

Quentin let the list collapse into a tube. "Aren't you supposed to suture a wound before it heals?" He touched the wound in his scalp. "Despite my daily dose of warfarin, even, it's quit bleeding."

"You know that stuff started out in life as rat poison?" The orderly gently inclined Quentin's head for a look. "So it has."

Quentin blinked. "Warfarin?"

Officer Ventana came back around the gurney. "We're still lacking a complete description."

Quentin blinked twice. The officer seemed a bit . . . fuzzy. His glasses must be in his jacket. "Description? Description. . . ."

Ventana read from the notebook. "Red haired pirate. Burly, brusque, sunburned . . ."

Quentin frowned. "I can't remember a thing," he said after a moment.

"Get an Ob/Gyn down there," Felton-Foote said into the phone. "I don't know a thing about preemies." He hung up. "Well?"

All three looked at him. "Well what?"

"Did you think of a plate for the Porsche?"

Quentin held out the roll of paper. "You already thought of them all, it would seem."

"Pretty resourceful," the orderly agreed. "We're stumped."

"Stumped," Officer Ventana agreed.

"It's a difficult problem," Felton-Foote said, retrieving the list. "I'm not surprised you couldn't cope with it."

"Especially since I'm injured," Quentin remarked.

"A head injury," the orderly hinted.

"Yes . . ." the doctor murmured thoughtfully, tapping the tips of the latexed fingers of one hand with the rolled list.

"How about HEADCASE?" the orderly suggested.

The doctor looked up and appeared to think about it. "I'm not a psychiatrist," he said at last.

"Probably taken anyway," consoled the orderly.

"Besides," said Officer Ventana, counting on his fingers, "it's too many letters."

"I'm not feeling so well," Quentin said truthfully. "Woozy, like. *Mal de mer*." He flattened a hand over his stomach. "Or maybe the sushi's still alive." He looked puzzled. "Except I don't eat sushi."

"Must be tough," Officer Ventana said.

"Not-eating sushi?" Quentin asked uncertainly.

"Owning a Porsche."

The doctor availed himself of a fretful sigh. "It's a matter of discipline."

Quentin fainted.

"Now," said a man seated behind a microphone on a desk within the tele-vision above the door, "maybe the lovely Doris can get this picture up where we can see it." The camera cut to a slim brunette in a black cocktail dress who also wore a blinding smile. A tiny gold cross dangled from a thin gold neck-lace over the hollow of her throat, and she held against her abdomen below her décolletage a photograph which reflected glossily in the studio light. She watched for direction as the camera slowly closed on the photograph, until the photograph filled the screen, except for Doris' manicured nails, and the cam-era pulled focus sufficiently to sharpen the image, which was of a young girl squinting and smiling uncertainly while her picture was being taken. "Now look at that," said the man who had been speaking before. "Have you ever seen such an ugly little girl? Look at that hair. Look at those teeth. A disgrace to the race. I don't mean Caucasian people in particular, ladies and gentlemen, because, as you all know, I'm not a racist. I mean hominids in general. Look at that squint. I bet she's already near-sighted. Her daddy may have went to Hollywood, and her other daddy might have been a Rhodes Scholar, and both mommies might have went to both Hollywood and Yale, but it's ugly progeny like this that make you wonder what in the hell is going on at our elite univer-sities today. Ever think about that? Huh? What, in the hell, is going on, at our—yours and my—elite universities today. Thank you, Doris." The camera pulled back to a long shot of a still-smiling Doris, and then cut to the man behind the desk. He smiled, too. "You'll never have a kid looks like that, honey," he reassured Doris, out of the shot, stage left. The shot awkwardly cut to her laughing, without sound, and cut back. "Ever think about having kids? Huh?" He leered. "We'll talk about it later." Again the camera cut to the girl, who feigned shock, and the shot cut back. "Thanks again, Doris, honey." He turned to face the camera again. "Never mind what's going on in the halls of Congress. By all that's decent about this country of ours, it's people like the parents of this hapless, ugly, deformed child who are determined to ruin it. Educated, wealthy, liberal—that's a deadly combination. That ugly little girl's parent's unregistered interest group has undertaken a tireless campaign against the Redfern Efficacies Act. Can you believe that, ladies and gentle-men? The Redfern Efficacies Act! Who in this great wide country of ours can possibly be against Efficacy Number One?" He held up a forefinger. "The criminalization of flag burning. The criminalization of flag burning! Who could possibly be against it? Give me that." The photograph entered the frame

of the shot and he leaned out toward the camera to take it. He sat down again and steadied the photograph in the glare of the studio lights, watching a monitor out of the shot as he did so. "This little girl's parents have but one purpose, one single aim, and that is no less," the photograph steadied, he looked directly into the camera. "No less," he repeated calmly, "than the implosion of this great democracy of ours." He shook his head. "This little girl's parents' unregistered interest group and their cronies will not cease until their efforts have brought this great country of ours to its knees. . . ."

What in the hell is going on? Quentin wondered. Who is this guy? But the people bustling around him took no notice of his queries, if indeed they could hear him; if indeed, he suddenly realized, he were uttering them aloud or, if aloud, coherently. Officer Ventana? he pinged. Doctor Felton-Foote? Is television the only thing I can hear or understand? Is this my fate? But I don't understand it. . . . He was no longer sitting on the gurney, he lay on the floor next to it. He was on his back, looking at the ceiling. In a circle around him he could clearly make out the features of the kindly orderly, of Officer Ventana, and of Felton-Foote, who, turned away from the gurney and on the phone, seemed to be lip-synching the words, "Get a traumatologist down here, stat!" As he screamed soundlessly at the phone he was also squinting at the tiny screen on his beeper.

The man grimaced and let the photograph of the little girl fall face forward onto his desk. "I urge you," he said, addressing the camera, "to call your senator, your congressman. Call the White House, because, you know, because the White House wants to hear from you." He pointed directly at the camera. "If you feel that your representative in the House or Senate somehow got there despite your honest vote, we have an 800 number that you can call." He lowered his eyes as if looking over the forward edge of his desk. "Don't we," he said, letting his eyes slide to one side. "Don't we have an 800 number the folks at home or in their workplace can call?" A hint of menace colored his intonation. The digits of a telephone number began to crawl across the bottom of the screen. Whatever device the studio was using to create this effect conjoined a slight buzz to the audio signal, while a translucent sawtoothed wave undulated a couple of scan lines along the bottom of the video signal. "Here we go. What you're seeing on your screen at home or in your office is the toll-free number of the National Redfern Efficacies Act Emergency Response Political Action Committee. Operators are standing by to take your comments, your suggestions, and, if you possibly can help, your donations. Yes, ladies and gentlemen," he sighed, "it's a sad fact of life that money talks. Heck," he touched his breast modestly, "you can listen to me all day," he smiled and inclined his

head, "and I hope you do, too. But," he resumed his severity, "money is what
makes this thing we call democracy go round. You know it, I know it, they
know it. By they I mean them up there in Washington, and by them I mean
folks with an agenda, like the cronies and the unregistered interest group
fronted by this little girl, here." He turned down the corners of his mouth, as
if lowering them toward the photograph, now face up on his desk. "With your
help, ladies and gentlemen, we can pass the Redfern Efficacies Act. Call us
now." He recited the 800 number. "Put your hard-earned dollars where your
mouths and your hearts and your minds are. We'll do the rest. Now." He sat
back from the desk and drummed the fingers of both hands along its edge.
"When we come back, we'll take a closer look at the Twelve Efficacies, as well
as some of the activist judges who call themselves Americans but don't think
the Efficacies worthy of the sanction of law."

Sandy, Quentin said to the orderly, for the orderly wore a nameplate
too, make them turn it off. Who the hell is that beastly man? Why is the
administration of this hospital torturing us with this rubbish? Is State TV
the only channel you can get down here in this sub-basement of an emergency room?

His own eyes informed Quentin's unpleasant realization that, whatever
his impression of what he, himself, Quentin, was saying, it wasn't what
other people were hearing. The orderly's professional mask had slipped
sufficiently to let show his true feelings, and what Sandy the orderly was
feeling was sorry for Quentin. It was evident that Sandy and everybody
else in the room were hearing gibberish.

And then Sandy's voice burst through the envelope of silence that
cloaked Quentin's conscious faculties like an unexpected radio transmission on a heretofore silent frequency.

"—Baby," Sandy the orderly said, tears welling over the lower lids of his
eyes. "He sounds like a baby."

And then the door to the hallway opened and closed again, silent as a
bivalve, and there-through passed that Russian guy. Quentin recognized
him, but couldn't place him or his name. The doctor said something
Quentin couldn't understand. The Russian answered and the doctor
asked something and then Quentin tried to speak. The orderly had to
restrain him and Officer Ventana pitched in and, unfortunately, it
appeared Quentin had wet himself. Officer Ventana made a face and
stood away but the orderly hung in there. Doctor Felton-Foote watched
the scene over the mouthpiece of his cellphone, whatever he was saying
he was saying into the cellphone and, anyway, it made no sense to
Quentin. With doctors as with poetry, sense derives from sound like a

steady rain on an ocean swell as it dissolves among the rocks at Land's End on a big winter's day. Those swells come all the way from Japan. Where did this guy come from, Quentin managed to shout, and the orderly looked at him as if he were really worried about what was happening to Quentin and suddenly his audio was interbenightedly lucid.

". . . calling card in your pocket . . . cellphone number . . . He's the only friend/colleague/acquaintance or family member, check one, here, that's it—we could find. Short notice, dire circumstances, nobody here's got time to do it anyway . . . We need him to sign off on drilling a hole in your skull to relieve the pressure. Don't worry, just a little pinch . . . But surely you recognize him? He's here to help you. We're bending the rules, here. We all want to help you."

Benighted again. The sounds of big surf, of bad shortwave reception, of deciduous leaves. Sferics from purgatory, from the past. Tour Hue during Tet with the Marquis de Sade by Pedicab at No Risk . . . ! I fade your offer, said the television, Tour Basra with British Commandos, Special Effects Guaranteed Realistic, No Live Shrapnel—Bonus: Home For The Niners Game! Complimentary non-alcoholic drinks and snacks included. No host bar. Offer good only in select markets. Paint balls extra.

Stroke, said Officer Ventana's mouth. Officer Ventana's audio was turned off, too. Heart attack, mouthed the orderly.

"Well, my dessicated friend, what's happened to you?" said Vassily, his solicitude abruptly surfing the surf with equanimity. "Perhaps," Vassily urged him, "perhaps you might put me in touch with our friend Charley so as we might coordinate your out-patient arrangements . . . ?"

Just like a poor baby, the orderly mouthed, his eyes brimming with silent tears. Only the noun surfaced in the susurrant spume. Although, Quentin feared, if one of them fell over the edge it might hit the floor with a tremendous crash. Edge of the abyss. Hear its hiss.

Wicked! Quentin squirmed away from Vassily and writhed ineffectually, *most wicked and to be avoided*, even if his nightie were a leaden foil to go with his leaden feet and the leaden credit card that guaranteed enough bonus miles to medevac him the fuck out of here.

Stroke, repeated the cop's mouth. Massive coronary, repeated the orderly's labial choreography. Why not both, Officer Ventana asked in his most reasonable mime.

Wicked, Quentin chalked up to experience one more time, chalked onto the slate held by the clown who waited at the cable car turnaround, a guy he used to tip twice a week after he finished rowing at the Bay Club, when he could still row, two decades ago. Row, row your decades ago. . . .

"Baby," bi-valved the orderly, his eyes brimming with silent tears.

A baby? Quentin drew himself up, as it were, though he remained supine. *An infant?* What happened to the prefix and suffix? His strength evaporated like a blister of water in a heated wok. He hadn't realized he'd been trying to sit up. Okay then, let's sit up. Follow through. Slippery when wet. Slight alarm: when's the last time I took my medicine? Yesterday? Day before? Panic. An expired meter. Stuff got me this far. Yesterday. That far. Needle goes to red. I got quarters. Gentle hands restrained him, increasing their strength as he increased his. He gave up the struggle and fell back to the floor, fetal. Full-body pronation. Someone rolled the gurney out of the way. If we're clearing the decks, he thought, let's turn off this disgusting television, too. He reached in his pocket for his key-chain Quietus. *Won't they think I'm clever, conspiring to achieve peace and quiet in an emergency bistro in which they think it's totally beyond my ability to order. Doesn't bistro mean* quick? Except he wasn't wearing a pocket, no more than he was wearing trousers, and he pinched between thumb and forefinger and middle finger an old man's cold and fearful penis, wrinkled and diminuendoed, not standing up to all and sundry circumstances as of yore, we're talking regression, cradle to realtor-of-the-year to cradle again, perigee apogee perigee, el señor character arc, mostly a fold of skin and tinier than ever because he was wearing a disposable puce paper smock with off-white centime-sized quadrifoliate pansies printed on it and a great slit all the way up the back so it was cold on the emergency room floor, cold in more ways than one. And pockets on these things are not covered by your insurance? Maybe your deductible? Don't get hysterical. They get you coming and going. Russian for quick. *Oh*, Quentin thought, as he lay back on the publicly traded frigid linoleum, this stuff will never last, can you short stock in managed care linoleum? Better yet, how about a breath of fresh air? Ye merchant could charge at least as much as ye merchant charges for water. Whatever the traffic will bear. *Oh it's wickedness, a wicked world infested by State TV and latex gloves, which means I still have a sense of smell and a long-dead family propagating wicked aggrandizement. I could learn the Russian for almost anything, starting with get me out of here, I could readily exchange rubles for Euros, forget the dollar, the dollar is toast, and why must I think about money just now? Now, when a man might mistake wicked for a wicket, wicket through which a forgotten mallet might sleekly facilitate a wooden ball's exit, a graceful soughing amble through whispering long grass . . .*

THIRTY-FOUR

THE RUSSIAN HELD OUT A BURLY PALM, FACE UP. RED DROPPED THE KEY onto it.

The Russian closely inspected the key, as if it were an earring or broach with a valuable stone. He dangled its flotation fob as if to hypnotize himself. He looked past it at Red. Red looked past it at him. The Russian let the key drop out of his hand onto the table.

A waiter appeared. "Would either of you gentlemen like a cocktail before dinner?" He leaned over the table to light a pair of candles in a sconce on the wall.

The Russian didn't wait for Red. "I'll have a double shot of the cheapest vodka in the house, ice-cold, neat."

"Shall we make that a vodka martini, sir?" the waiter suggested. "That's cold and neat."

The Russian smiled. "Only if it's in—how do you say—a nervous glass?"

"Very good," the waiter said.

"You've mastered the vernacular," Red observed.

"Vernacular focuses the mind," the Russian declared.

"No vermouth, no olive, no ice?" the waiter asked.

"No fruit," Vassily said. But he was looking at Red.

The waiter turned to Red. "Sir?"

"I'll wait for the wine."

"Very well. And may I run down tonight's specials for you?"

"First the vodka," said the Russian. "And a wine list."

"Very well, sir. You'll find the wine list under your menu."

"So it is," said the Russian, not looking at it. "What do you have from the valley of the Rhône?"

"Red or white?"

"Red."

The waiter opened the wine list to its seventh or eighth page and ran a finger down it. "These are all from the Rhône, sir. Do you have a specific preference?"

"Vaqueras, St. Emillion, Châteauneuf du Pape, St. Joseph—but only if it's really, how you say . . . top shelf? And, by the way." The Russian shifted his eyes from Red to the waiter. "None of this fifteen percent alcohol bullshit—capiche? When I say I want to drink French wine," the Russian touched a fingertip to the tablecloth, "I expect to drink French wine."

The waiter's eyes slid toward Red, then back onto the Russian. "Very good, sir."

Red smiled thinly. Red knew the Russian knew that Red knew that the Russian spoke better English than Red did. So how long did they need to stay cute on the subject of *vernacular*?

The waiter smiled and touched a marque. "An excellent Hermitage. . . ."

"Done," said the Russian. "We'll order entrées when you return." He did not look at the price.

"Very good, sir." The waiter went away.

"They say this place has the best steaks in San Francisco," the Russian said.

"I don't give a shit," said Red.

"You are welcome," the Russian said. "But, of course, I don't care that you don't, as you put it, give a shit. We came here because I like a good steak. Have a salad, if you like. Or drink an entire bottle of expensive wine for yourself. Tonight, you are my guest."

"I couldn't be more thrilled if I was an astronaut and this was Venus."

"Cosmonaut." The Russian folded his hands on the place setting in front if him. Diamond chips in the form of the letter P, embossed on a gold ring on the pinky of his left hand, glinted in the candlelight. "Does she have it?"

"No," Red said. "She doesn't have it."

"Gee." The Russian sat against the back of the booth. "That makes two of you."

"Three, if you count Charley. Four, if you count the poor mother-fucker who installed it in the bottom of Charley's boat."

The Russian opened one hand. "He was really, really difficult, that guy."

"His name was Arnauld."

The Russian covered one hand with the other. "All he had to do was tell us the truth."

"Like you'd know from the truth."

"I'll know it when I hear it," the Russian assured him.

"He put it in the keel—right?"

"Yes. He convinced us of that much."

"With his last breath, no doubt."

"There's no better certificate of authenticity. Although, as regards cer-tificates?" Vassily smiled. "The head was a stroke of genius."

Red made no reply. A fat lot of good this sparring was going to do Arnauld, who had only been doing his job. Had done his job. Or Charley either, for that matter. Red sighed. Twenty years ago, smuggling had been

easy. It had even been fun. Or had he thought that nostalgic, useless bit
of rote already today?

The drinks appeared. By the time the waiter had shown the Russian
the label on the bottle, cut its foil, and drawn its cork, the Russian had
tossed off half his vodka. When the waiter offered to pour a taste for the
Russian, he waved it off. He poured the taste for Red. I know from wine
like I know from cosmonauts, Red brooded. He swirled the wine in its
globe. "Nice color," he said without enthusiasm. He drank it off, letting it
stay in his mouth for a moment before he swallowed. "Damn."

The waiter beamed.

"Next time," the Russian said, as the waiter half-filled his glass, "we'll
call ahead. Get them to open the bottle a half-hour early."

Next time, Red thought, I'm going to be a lot harder to find.

"Excellent idea, sir," the waiter agreed. He half-filled Red's glass and
declined to advance the caveat of credit card and authorization, when
ordering by phone.

"To that end, as I'm sure this bottle won't last long enough to realize its
full potential," said the Russian, his eyes still on Red, "perhaps we should
proceed without delay to a second one. So it will be awakened by the time
our steaks arrive."

"Suit yourself, Vassily," said Red.

The Russian nodded at the waiter.

"Another?" said the waiter, in a neutral tone. A second two-hundred-
dollar bottle of wine came with the potential of thirty or forty dollars
added to the tip, which would make it a hundred-dollar table, and a horse
the waiter liked was running at Golden Gate Fields tomorrow. Otherwise,
neither the floridity nor the extravagance of the order impressed him.

"So that, having properly breathed, the wine will realize its potential,"
said the Russian. By the tone of his voice, he might have been counting
pigeons at a bus stop.

"I'll see to it at once. And since you like this wine so much, sir, with
your permission I'll send over a salver of three or four starters, gratis. Beef
tartar, onion rings, green beans in olive—"

Red sighed abruptly. Vassily waved a hand. "Skip the starters."

"Very good, sir," the waiter segued smoothly. "Have you selected your
main course?"

"The biggest steak you have, and still walking," replied the Russian,
again not waiting for his guest.

"That will be the Vaquero Porterhouse. Thirty-four ounces. Very rare.
Sir?"

"The smallest steak you have," Red said, "medium rare."

"That's our pepper steak, sir, grilled with sweet onions and a cognac and peppercorn sauce."

"Perfect."

"Any legumes?" asked the Russian, throwing back the last of his vodka.

"Two vegetables come with it, sir. You have a choice . . ."

Goddamn this is excruciating, Red thought. Why force me to sit through this meal when we both know it's going to come to an unpleasant end? I might have to kill this guy to get him to let me alone. Unfortunately, as Donald Rumsfeld is on record as having mentioned in reference to himself, no man is irreplaceable. Like me and like Rummy, Vassily is working for somebody else. If something happens to Vassily, they'll just get another boy. And, as with the Rummy, they started out with a proper motherfucker. So I've got to try and satisfy him somehow.

The waiter departed. The Russian drank off half his wine, stuffed his mouth with a large tuft of bread pulled off the loaf, and chased it with the second half of his wine. "So." He refilled his glass from the bottle. "Where is it, Mr. Means? Where is our prize?"

"If you're talking about the brick, it's on the chart table on your boat."

Chewing more bread, the Russian looked at him sadly. "I told you that you could have that for yourself, Mr. Means. Your brick holds no interest for me."

"I'm not interested in it either, Vassily. Take it as a token of my good faith."

"Mr. Means." Vassily leaned over the table. With a glance toward the aisle, he stipulated in an undertone, "We are quite beyond good faith." The burgundy Naugahyde complained as he resettled his weight against the cushions of the banquette. "It's results or nothing."

"Nothing is a big word."

"As far as you—or I, for that matter," Vassily touched the breast of his shirt, "are concerned, nothing is everything except the desired result. There is no other path. You know it, I know it. And I, for one, am tired of talking about it."

"Well I'm here to tell you, Vassily, nothing is all I come up with. What else can I do? Arnauld convinced you he didn't pull a fast one, and you should have left it at that, by the way. It's been a long time since anybody got himself murdered on Rum Cay."

Vassily held up his glass. "Drowned," he said. "Servicing a bottom. Got tangled up in his hookah. Tsk."

"I don't think so. Nobody thinks so. He lived there fifteen years and never so much as ran out of air. And besides, Charley makes two."

"Charley?" Vassily frowned. "Charley . . ." He brought his wine glass to his nose and savored the wine's bouquet. "And what have I to do with Charley?" He moved his glass so that its contents spiraled up and down its interior. "Charley worked for you."

"Yeah, well," Red sighed. "I never lost an employee. And the reason I never lost one is that I never exposed them to risks they—or I—couldn't handle."

"Well, now you've lost two. It's probably got something to do with averages." Vassily smiled. "Welcome to the big time."

"Yeah," Red said without enthusiasm. "The big time."

"I wish I could have seen the sister's face when you showed her the head." Vassily chuckled.

"She's kind of plucky." Red smiled. "She came at me with a knife and a beer bottle. Better you weren't there."

"That's true," Vassily agreed simply. "I might have killed her."

Red nodded. "Like I said."

"Where is the head, anyway?"

Red shrugged. "Right where you last saw it."

Vassily's smiled waned. "Still on the boat?"

Red touched his butter knife. "Still on the boat."

"My . . . With the brick of cocaine?"

"On the chart table. Is it really yours?" Red smiled thinly. "The boat, I mean?"

Vassily set his glass to one side.

"I presume the reefer isn't all that far from the registration papers?"

Vassily said nothing.

"You're supposed to keep them on board at all times," Red reminded him, "in case the Coast Guard boards you."

Vassily retrieved a cellphone from the breast pocket of his Chesterfield, which was draped next to him on the settee, and keyed a preset. "And where, exactly, is my boat, Mr. Means?"

"Oh," Red said, "it's around."

Vassily made a face. "Is it legally parked, at least?"

Red affected surprise. "You know, I didn't even think of that."

"Miou Miou." Vassily lifted his eyes to the ceiling. "Call me." He closed the phone and set it on the table, next to his wineglass. "I see."

"Good," Red said. "That's good that you see."

Salads arrived. The waiter showed them a pepper mill the size of a bowling pin. "Gentlemen?"

Red smiled at him. "Please."

After dusting Red's salad, the waiter asked Vassily if he wanted some pepper.

"Yeah." Vassily's listless surliness implied to Red that Vassily may well have been capable of wringing the waiter's neck just to make himself feel better. He'd seen this level of frustration before. It was one of the wild-cards of the business.

The waiter went away intact.

"So," Red said, stuffing roughage into his mouth, "*Kreutzer's Revenge* is registered in your name."

Vassily's eye fell on the key. *Delta Bait and Tackle* was embossed in white on the unsinkable blue fob. "Twenty years I wanted a boat," he said simply. "I bought her brand new."

"Well," said Red, "you keep her Bristol, all right."

"Guy works on her two days a week," said Vassily dully. He looked at his salad. "So how's it going to be?"

"How it's going to be is how it already is, Vassily."

"Which is?"

"The sister has no idea—none—of who we are, what we're talking about, or what we're after. Let alone what her brother was up to. Which is as it should be, because he didn't know what he was up to either. No more than Arnauld knew what anybody was up to," Red added pointedly.

"So you say."

"The thing I regret is, I need to prove it to you."

"And how do you propose to do that?"

Red's salad was nearly finished. "I want to tell the sister what's going on."

Vassily blinked.

"Look at it this way. If she already knows what it is, all you have to do is keep an eye on her and sooner or later she'll lead you to it. I mean, it's not like it has a . . . how should I put it . . . a limited shelf life?"

"That's for the employer to decide, not the employee."

Red turned his head to one side.

Vassily realigned the pair of forks next to his plate. "Not to mention, they would think nothing of appealing to your innate . . . patriotism."

Red smiled. "Patriotism may be a lot of things, Vassily, but innate isn't one of them."

"You mistake my meaning. In the circles I normally inhabit, patriotism is synonymous with greed."

"Ah," Red nodded. "Greed, I might consider innate. Yes . . . you may have something there."

"May I, as you say, sweeten the pot?"

"You can try."

"Find it," Vassily said quietly, "and live."

"Oh come on, Vassily," Red replied. "I know what's at stake. I'm seeing dead people—"

"You have no idea," Vassily cut him short.

Red considered this. "Okay, " he said at last. "I have no idea."

"Surely," Vassily frowned as if in disbelief, "you don't conceive of yourself as in a position to demand more money?"

"On the contrary." Red shook his head. "If returning your deposit would square things, I'd happily give it back. With interest."

"Deposits are nonrefundable," Vassily pointed out. "Your very words. Not only that, you lost the consignment. So there's the matter of . . . insurance."

Red sighed.

"So," Vassily said. "What do you propose?"

"I want to cut her in. If she knows what's up or can figure it out, and she's in on the action, her mind will clear, if she's got any sense, and it won't get any messier than it already has. I could hang around, drink with her, ask her all about her brother and sneak a peak at the letters he's been sending her for twenty years, talk about her boyfriends, and maybe even become one of them myself; but it's not going to help us find what we're looking for if she doesn't know what it is. If she has no idea what we're talking about she's not about to find it, or even to look for it, and meanwhile she's merely mourning her brother. An opportunity, combined with the threat of death, might sharpen her mind." Red took up his steak knife. "But I'm willing to bet you on something."

Now Vassily sighed. "How melodramatic." Clearly he was disconsolate. "But," he said, "what's that?"

Red touched the point of the knife to a crust of bread. "Charley left Rum Cay with your package in his keel. Arnauld told you that much, and it's true."

Vassily's lower lip spilled up and over his upper one, which had the effect of adding a layer to the cascade of his chins. "He told us that much," Vassily agreed. "Considering the . . . position . . . he was in, we believed him."

Red's own jaw hardened. "You killed a man for nothing," he said quietly.

Vassily touched his breast. "I wasn't even there." After a moment: "We generally try to kill them for a reason," he added with a vague smile. "It's true."

"You talk like a kid who's delivered a newspaper to the wrong house."

"Quaint simile." Vassily passed a hand over his face. "It's quaint to think that one or two lives mean anything at all. Is this a conch thing," he asked, as if exasperated, "or are you just stupid?"

"The latter," Red assured him. "I thought I was in this for the money. Then I thought I could help a friend. Kill two birds with one stone. Well, the birds got killed all right. It wasn't about the money. It was about the friend. The kind of friend you don't know anything about. Or, come to consider it," he reflected bitterly, "maybe you do. All the same, it's my mistake."

"Who? This Arnauld? A bum who scrapes boat hulls only to eat?"

"Well, yes, there was Arnauld. But I was talking about Charley."

Vassily waved his napkin. "Another bum. What the hell did your Charley ever do besides wander around on his boat? But I'll tell you something." Vassily dropped the napkin onto the table. "If this deal went the way you think it did, this guy Charley is not your friend."

"He was, though," Red said stubbornly. "Charley was my friend."

"I thought you were smarter than this, Mr. Means."

"I thought you were smarter than this, too, Vassily."

"I hire the likes of you to do a job, and you think I'm smart?"

"You got a point."

"I have another point. Turn that sister of Charley's or we're all going to learn a lesson about how cheap life is." He refilled his glass and toasted Red. "Even in America." He sipped a loud sip. "Maybe then, that stone will stop with just the two birds." He took another, smaller sip. "Instead of five."

"Me, the sister," Red counted, "and you?"

The steaks arrived. The two customers watched glumly as two waiters arranged glasses, plates, silver. When his two colleagues had departed, the original waiter arrived to top off both wine glasses. Setting the nearly empty bottle aside, he flanked the existing wine glasses with two fresh ones and presented a new bottle for Vassily's inspection. The Russian glanced at it and grunted. The waiter proceeded to draw the cork. Vassily declined to taste. So did Red. The waiter placed the bottle on the table so that both diners could see the label. "Anything else, gentlemen?"

Vassily sighed loudly. Red said it was all fine. "Enjoy your dinner," the waiter said. He set the two-hundred-dollar cork on a little saucer and went away.

Vassily contemplated his meal. The thirty-four ounce steak draped over its plate like an overcoat over a footstool. "What is this?" Vassily said after a moment.

"Carrots," Red told him.

"No. This."

"Okra."

Vassily blinked.

"Americans are crazy," he finally said. "I'll give you a month."

THIRTY-FIVE

OFFICERS PROTONE AND FEW, A STUDY IN CONTRAST. BUT THEIR PINCER was mighty, they had produced a high rate of evidentiary proceedings. If the District Attorney's office ever got its act together, they might even generate a high rate of conviction, too.

Take Laval, for instance. When Protone was a beat cop, Laval was one of his pet projects. Laval's end-all desire was junk, of course, but anything else would do: Seconal, Toluene, cough syrup; Vicodin, Oxycontin, Oxycodone; Percocet, Darvocet, Demoral; Morphine, Laudanum, Paregoric; Mandrax and so forth, ad nauseum.

Alcohol, Laval never touched.

Laval's specialty was the quickie car break-in, the smash-and-grab. He walked a grid in Hayes Valley, west of the Symphony, the Opera, the Ballet. In the vicinity were many tony restaurants and bars. City Hall was just across Van Ness from the various edifices of culture, too, but those people went home about the time the culture vultures were showing up—although there was some overlap; so, once in a while, Laval would nick a city employee for a laptop or a briefcase. But usually it was people from out of town looking to cop a parking spot for cheap or for free prior to spending an hour and a half in a $250 seat at the opera or symphony. For cheap, that is, until they had to buy a new window along with a new computer, or a designer purse, or an in-dash stereo, or twenty CDs, or whatever else it is that people are naive enough to leave in their cars in Laval's territory.

Metastasize naive to stupid, and voilà, you have Laval's way of looking at it: people leave stuff in their car, they're stupid, they deserve to get ripped off. Cops look at it the same way, Laval would argue, and he should know, he talks to them all the time. He was no punk who busted a window on some stiff's car just because the stiff hadn't left him a little something on the back seat or in the glove compartment. Laval would never take a chance on breaking into a car without having a pretty good idea there was something to grab and run with. When the whole operation took thirty seconds, that was a good job. Conversely, when the whole job was too juicy not to take three or god forbid four minutes, well, there was an element of resentment there, as in like, man, how can you do this to me? You think I can just pick and choose from among all this shit, and in the dark? The fuck you think I am? Superman and shit? See in the dark and shit? So, once in a while, he'd take a shit in the back seat, or set the dashboard on fire, just to even the score.

But sometimes . . . Once, he spotted the job from the other end of the block. White hybrid, out of town license plate holder—Merced or Modesto or Fresno or Chico or some such fucking place, UCSB decal in the back window with JUST MARRIED soaped over it. He stalked nearer. He bore down. Sure enough, the entire back seat was heaped with wedding presents.

Still in their wrappers, pink, white, baby blue, some tie-dye, with cards on them. And, courtesy of Laval's beard du jour, a homeless guy collecting bottles, he was pushing a shopping cart that night. Freight forward? No problem! And what a haul. Blender, iPod, copper cookware, microwave oven, four-slot toaster, X-box, matched set of cutlery, briefcase full of sex toys . . .

It might be three days before he would have to go back to work.

Laval made no bones about his approach. He stalked the 'hood like a zombie on a mission, which he was. Every four hours, rain or shine, holiday or hump day, full moon, sixty knot wind, gay pride parade, whatever, Laval was on duty. No matter that he'd jonesed on the floor of a jail cell times beyond ordinality, a most unpleasant experience, guaranteed to cure all but the hardcore, the equation was simple: fifteen, twenty years max, and he'd be unclaimed on a slab, done. Retired, after a manner of speaking. Laval stalked the 'hood like a soldier on a twenty-mile hike with Sarge right at his ear calling him a roundheeled pussy, a limp-dick failure, a stretch-elastic pantywaist—not that Laval had served. One look at the abscesses inside either of his elbows, between any pair of toes, on the back of either hand, all up and down his calves, the odd, desperate puncture about the carotid artery in his neck, exempted Laval immediately as already a lifer in a different kind of army.

Tonight he carried a bicycle lock and wore a little purple backpack. He walked against traffic on a given side of the street, on the principle that any do-gooding driver seeing him bust out a window couldn't pursue him without doing a drastic U-turn and making a scene to the extent that Laval would be long gone before the citizen got his or her wheels straightened out, sure, but the real principle was that walking against the parking vector maximized his view of front and back seats.

Being a masochist of the primordial fluid, Laval entertained certain fantasies, and in this he had certain archetypes in common with his victims. For example: who hasn't dreamed of embedding a hand grenade inside their car radio, its pin rigged to a loop of wire captured to some part of the underdash infrastructure, such that yanking the radio without taking a certain precaution pulled the pin on the grenade which, preset to explode after four-and-a-half minutes, would blow Laval's backpack right through his thorax?

But only when he was sufficiently high could Laval entertain any fantasy at all. Which on a good day amounted to about four fifteen-minute time periods, in between which he was all business, work work work, add it up it's a life. Balance of his time, Laval was of one mind, one course through life, restive as a shark. So focused was he that he seemed to possess a sixth sense as to whether or not some wily suburbanite had stashed the removable face of his fancy CD player under the passenger seat, so as to outfox the Lavals of the city's night.

Merchandise to hand, Laval made it on over to an apartment in the projects, one of the few with a door direct to the street, wherein the mummy of the original lessee lay shrunken and desiccated in a wheelchair reeking of terminal decomposition, while her grand nephew dealt in stolen pawnables.

Additional foetidities, lit only by a television, included mildew, scorched ham hocks, dry rot, burnt spoons, stale vomit, instant-coffee urine, cat piss on polyester carpet and drapes, decayed breakfast cereal, burnt cheese, rotted masonry, and pillow mites, among other things.

Never more than ten bucks per item. Two items, twenty bucks, unless the Flake—that was the guy's handle—could smell Laval's need as especially pressing. Then, "Fifteen, baby," the Flake would say, and without touching the merchandise he would add something along the lines of, "You ripped them wires pretty bad."

"Come on, man," would whine Laval, "it's my birthday."

And the Flake's great aunt, in the wheelchair with one leg lost to diabetes and the establishment waiting for her to come back so they could get the other one, interested only in cigarettes, Spam, and cola, would squawk like a parrot. Or, every once in a while, just to throw Laval off his feed, she would screech like a macaw.

"Don't upset Nana," the Flake, inscrutable behind tinted lenses and oblivious to the brazenness of this filial presumption, would warn Laval. "And, say, Laval?"

Laval, disgruntled: "What?"

"Quit scratchin'."

When he had been a beat cop, Protone having made a special project out of Laval, busted him fourteen times. Fourteen. Count them. Laval never did more than ninety days, and most times they'd turn him loose because the jail was too crowded, because Laval would get a public defender who would plead and win no contest, because Laval would promise to go to rehab or Narcotics Anonymous or maybe even career redirection, get some computer skills, start fresh, commute to a tall building downtown—whatever he had to say to get himself back on the street before the monkey incisors started working him over for real.

Protone had been in court for every one of Laval's appearances. He'd testified every time, too, at first. But eventually the public defender would see him coming and advise Laval to plead nolo contendere. Finally a judge who'd gotten tired of seeing Laval in her court gave him a ninety day stretch—the first in Laval's then nine-year career.

Laval's personal best? One Christmas Eve Protone had busted him, booked him, and thrown him in the clink by nine o'clock. By midnight, however, Laval had been sprung on his own recognizance by the necessity for additional jail space precipitated by the mass arrest of rioting Santas outside a karaoke bar in the Castro. While this manipulation spared Laval the spectacle of several adjacent cells full of inebriated Santa Clauses chorusing on "Christmas in Jail," it did not spare a brand new Range Rover from the ministrations of Laval. Forsaking the D-shaped bike lock, confiscated by Protone as evidence, Laval fell back on an old stand-by, the ninja kick. The porcine Range Rover's passenger window is pretty high off the ground, however, and Laval's various kicks twice indented the passenger door panel before he managed to land one on the window, dead center at that, and fall right back on his ass, narrowly missing the occupational hazard of shredding his left leg and perhaps the femoral artery, a death sentence even for one so bloodless as Laval. But a titanium iBook was the result, along with a cellphone and its charger, and Laval beat feet down Linden Alley pursued by the useless klaxon of the Range Rover.

"Damn, pretty good," Flake told him. "Twenty-five bucks."

"Awk," screeched Nana, who was still alive at that point.

So that Laval was fucked up enough to have wandered into traffic on Van Ness, get busted for public intoxication and obstructing traffic, and land back in the can by 2:30 in the a.m. of Christmas morning. Making for a solid two and one half hours of liberty between incarcerations. A record, maybe. Maybe not. There's a lot of competition for these kinds of achievements.

Protone, as he lay on a piece of cardboard next to a shopping cart on Ivy Street, an alley whose eastern end terminates across Franklin from the back of Louise Davies Symphony Hall, had figured it out. The calculation was a simple one. All one had to do was take Laval's age when his rap

sheet started, 14, and subtract it from his age when last he'd been col-
lared. Laval looks 57 but don't be fooled, 37 is the correct answer.
Multiply that figure by the number of nights per year Laval reasonably
could be expected to be servicing his habit, 365—cut him some slack for
Leap Years, and you come up with 8,395. Let's cut society some slack and
back out the average amount of time Laval spends scoreless or in one
lockup or another, say thirty days per year—that ninety-day ticket was a
serious anomaly, and Laval really browbeat his public defender about it.
So that's 335 working days per year times 37 - 14 = 23 years equals 7,705
working days. And, go ahead, back out the ninety-day ticket: 7,615 working days. Fog rattled the leaves overhead. Protone shifted his cold ass
over the layer of cardboard flattened under it and raised the collar on the
quilted hickory shirt.

The cheapest removable-face stereo you can buy, legitimately, runs
about $175 plus tax and installation. Let's say $225. The cheapest you can
replace one of those wing windows in a gracefully aging pickup truck, if
you can find it in a junkyard, is about $150, plus maybe $50 for installa-
tion if the frame isn't damaged. That's $200. Window plus stereo, you're
talking $425. We'll leave out the laptop computers, musical instruments,
baby pictures, sterling silver dinner service for eight, stacks of CDs, rhine-
stone dog collars, walking sticks, boxes and boxes of tools (not so much
any more, however, as Protone had noted, on account there are no blue
collar residents left in San Francisco), binoculars, cameras, bracelets, rolls
of quarters and on and on and on. Stick to the basic statistical unit of window plus stereo, round down to four hundred dollars so some liberal soci-
ologist can't say you're exaggerating, and get a career take of three million
and forty-six thousand dollars. Round it down to three million. Why not?

One fucking junky.

But hey. You want to get really pissed? After taxes Protone takes home
$35,272.57 a year if he pulls no overtime which will never happen but
that's beside the point. Divide that into Laval's lifetime take, and how long
before Protone achieves parity? Eighty-six years and a little over four
months. Round down: Eighty-six years of this shit.

But now a shadow entered the western end of the 400 block. There was
a tree up there with two vehicles parked beneath it. Ivy is a narrow one-
way street, heading west, with parking on just the north side. The shadow
moved east, with little pretense of doing nothing other than hesitating
over each window on the sidewalk side of each parked vehicle. Then came
a protracted section of driveways and end-out parking—culs de sac not
worth the risk. The shadow stalked on.

And here the motherfucker is, Protone said to himself.

Protone had a flat little unregistered snub-nose .32 automatic in an ankle holster tucked into the thick athletic sock that billowed up out of his left sneaker. He had a snub-nosed .38 Police Positive, one of his service weapons, nosed into the small of his back under his belt. While Laval would never offer resistance sufficient to quell with a bullet, one could always hope. And one could always kill the bastard anyway. A homicide detective busted back to beat cop is a pretty frustrated guy. It is however a mark of a professional to face temptation, even go armed against it, and not succumb. If only Laval knew how close he had come, over the years. But Laval knew little. He had a belief system, a structure of denial, a way of getting by that brooked no compromise, no systemic augmentation other than confinement or death.

Since his divorce, rather than go home, Protone had renewed Laval as his special project. He hadn't told anybody—not even Laval. He'd quietly gotten a colleague at Parkside Station to assign him the extra duty. He told him he needed the overtime for alimony, and how much of a lie could that be? It wasn't a lie at all. Meanwhile the Hayes Valley Neighborhood Association had besieged its supervisor, the cops, the city, the mayor, and anybody else they could think of, with letters and petitions and phone calls and emails and en masse appearances. For, indeed, Laval wasn't the only smash-and-grab guy working Hayes Valley. In this neighborhood the light of every dawn twinkled among shards of safety glass. People were pissed. So the old friend gave Protone the assignment happily. Staking out a single dark block, disguised as a homeless person, night after night, was an assignment few cared to undertake. It was cold and unsanitary, it was generally fruitless, and it could be dangerous.

But here he was, prone on the sidewalk, and there Laval was, casing his way down the block, coming directly at him. It was almost too good to be true. It was almost too tempting, too. Maybe I should just shoot the motherfucker, Protone thought. But then he rethought. If he took out Laval, Protone would be faced with going home every night instead of coming here. Home to the crummy sunset garage apartment the divorce settlement had left him enough money to rent. Home to Chinese take-out, to 275 channels of belligerently inane television, much of it cop shows, home to the two or three pillow cases bulging with soiled dry goods that doomed him sooner than later to two horrible, feckless hours in a brightly lit laundromat.

He heard the crunch before he'd even realized that Laval was making a move. Protone rolled into a crouch behind the shopping cart. You got to admit, Protone admitted, Laval has gotten good over the years. He pulled a pair of cuffs and a sap from his hip pocket.

And tonight, as Protone could see as he stole along the sidewalk, Laval had his act together. He had on batting or cycling gloves, so as not to cut his hands. He was dressed mostly in black clothing, culled no doubt from the free box at St. Vincent de Paul. Even his day pack was a dark color, and a dark hood blended his head with the night.

By the time Protone made it across Octavia and the fifty yards up the sidewalk to the scene of the crime, Laval had the passenger door open and only his left leg was visible on the sidewalk, in the full extension peculiar to the short-burglar. The victim was a late model Ford Excursion. No alarm sounded. The distinctive sounds of road maps, of insurance and registration papers, of an operator's manual reached Protone, as they hit the floor mat after being swept from the glove compartment. Then came the clatter of jewel cases as with both hands Laval swept CDs from the center console into his day pack, unzipped on the passenger seat.

The odor, from three feet away, stopped Protone in his tracks.

Laval-odor, distinct and immutable and rank enough, this was not. Laval released the passenger seatback, the seat sprang forward, and he set to rummaging. The edge of his hand found a wristwatch, which he transferred into the backpack. Under the back seat he found a small telescoping umbrella, which he dropped into the gutter.

Protone stood at the rear bumper, astounded. All the years he'd spent on the force, all the nights he'd stalked Laval, all the crime scenes, the aberrant behavior, the perversions, the charnel basements of sex slave massage parlors. . . .

"Fuck me," he growled aloud. Laval didn't react. "Fuck you," Protone shouted. Laval showed his head. "Don't you know a cadaver when you smell one?" Protone screamed at him. He waved his cuffs and sap. "Look at the flies!"

"Flies," Laval said, backing out of the crevice behind the passenger seat, "are a fact of life."

"Something's dead in there!" Protone yelled.

"Leave me alone!" Laval screamed at the top of his voice. "You're hurting me!" He slapped the top of the Excursion with the bike lock sufficient to dent it. "I got *enough* problems!"

"You can't smell that?" Protone lifted his instep toward Laval's balls and missed. "Drop the weapon!" He kicked and missed again. "You can't smell that dead body, you useless piece of shit?" And, despite his mouth filling with flies: "Lemme see your hands!"

Laval took a swing with the lock. Protone smiled and whacked the wrist with the sap. The lock clanged to the sidewalk. Then he clipped Laval behind the ear. Laval went down. As Protone resisted the urge to hammer

Laval into the substrate, Laval sank his teeth into Protone's ankle. "You're under arrest!" Protone declared, spitting flies, and he brought the sap down on the side of Laval's head. "Off!" Laval turned loose long enough to scream, "Help!" before he bit down on the toe of Protone's sneaker.

Plainly, Laval was hopped up beyond pain. This called for tact. "Give me that swag, you cocksucker." Protone clutched one of the backpack's straps and yanked. CDs spilled onto the sidewalk.

"Get away from my stuff!" Laval yelled. He gave a vicious twist to Protone's ankle. "Don't touch my stuff, man!" Beneath the struggle, an inch or two of crushed safety glass rasped like gravel. Laval grabbed the other strap.

He doesn't recognize me, he attacks a cop, he's far gone tonight, Protone thought, as he fell on his back, parallel to the Ford. Adding his other leg to the captured one, he levered Laval almost straight overhead and rolled back onto his shoulders. His legs and Laval kept right on going, like the hands of a clock going backwards, until Laval's head completed a full half circle truncated by the sidewalk, pursued by all of his pitiful but not discountable inertia, down the axis of his junk-whittled frame, collapsing vertebrae like they were saucers in an industrial plate stacker.

With a pause, then a sigh, Laval sagged against the right rear tire of the Excursion like a sack of autumn leaves.

Protone had lost the cuffs. He rolled over and did a two-handed pushup, only to discover that each palm was attempting and failing to flatten dozens of shards of safety glass. He collapsed, turning his head so as to lacerate one ear instead of his face. He rolled through the glass onto his back and lay still, panting. Sweat rolled from his hairline. The watch cap was gone. Advanced putrefaction, cooped up in the vehicle for only a coroner would be able to tell how long, assailed his nostrils. Thousands of flies darkened the air between the Ford and a lit storefront at the Octavia intersection. Protone knew the smell. He didn't like it. Nobody liked it. Masticated croissant and two cups of coffee assailed the valve at the base of his esophagus. How the hell could Laval stand to shake down such a vehicle, despite the sweetly pungent reek savory only to maggots and turkey vultures?

"Laval . . ." No answer. "Hey." Protone rolled over and shook Laval. "You okay?" Laval lay still. "Laval! Lie to me. Tell me you're sorry . . ."

A shudder extenuated Laval's 125 pounds. His lips slowly parted and stayed that way. A black rivulet, not an eighth of an inch across, ribboned over the downside corner of Laval's mouth, darker even than his complexion.

So much for job security.

Before the coroner got there the rivulet would follow an expansion joint to the curbstone, still granite in this part of town, and build there until it spilled over it, to disappear into the gutter in the shadow of the Explorer.

The coroner would count three bodies, once he'd sorted them out, including Laval. BTW, the email would read, there was an extra head. So there were actually four dead people. Laval was the obvious stiff. The coroner's assistants referred to the other two bodies as "hairball stew," which remained unidentified. Murdered, though. That much they could tell.

The head showed signs of having been frozen and thawed. No cause of death. Unless you count decapitation. Ah. Ah ha. Ah ha ha . . . ha. The coroner, Jimmy Nix, was a card. There were three parking tickets on the Excursion, which had been stolen in Berkeley.

In truth these facts told little more about Laval than they did the three unidentified victims. Dental records got nowhere. Even a tattoo, decipherable only as *Semp . . . Imp . . . Dub . . .*, yielded no tip. A scan of the only distinguishing mark on the other full set of remains, a high resolution bar code lasered onto the perineum, yielded a meaningless fourteen-digit alphanumeric string. There was nobody to call, no record of any next of kin, no corresponding missing person report. No loved one came to blink back a tear as Jimmy Nix drew open the respective drawers in the big freezer. Not even Laval's social worker showed up to gaze with regret and opine, "What a waste."

The paramedics gave Protone a tetanus shot right there at the scene, the skipper took a statement, gave him a bye on the paperwork, and damn if he didn't grant administrative leave on the spot. The skipper thought he was doing Protone a favor.

A black-and-white gave Protone a ride home. Despite a long hot shower and two ice-cold bottles of beer, there lingered a stench about his fingertips and the taste of flies on his tongue, and anyway it had turned into yet another of those nights he so dreaded. A night endured at home staring through the not-so-fun house lens that is the vitrified teton, seeing only the two weeks of administrative leave, his mouth locked up by a kind of vocal tenesmus, something to say, nobody to say it to, and no words to say it with anyway, no way to express anything at all.

THIRTY-SIX

THE THIRD GIN MARTINI, HOT-RODDED WITH A SHOT OF ABSINTHE, PUT HER right over the top.

LECTURE 4

La Bwana waited for the crowd to get over the umpteenth iteration of the chorus to the Condor Silversteed megahit, "Asian Dollars ('Scape My Grasp)."

> The markets are tumblin'
> The polls are aghast
> For the keys they are fumblin'
> And the locks are all trashed
>
> Succor's for sale
> But we know nothing lasts
> Umbrage ain't happenin'
> Cause everbody
> Ev'ry bod eee
> Ev'ry bod eee
> Can reeeeeeeeeead
> Your mail . . .

After enjoying the Quietusation of a few antigroupies the crowd settled sufficiently to be gaveled to order.

The gavel, by the way, is a *Yubiwaza*, a Japanese framing hammer with a twenty-eight ounce kryptonite head able to bang a 16 d. greased sinker (3-1/2") flush at a single blow, and yank them likewise thanks to its 18" handle sculpted from pure Rain Forest Crunch™ in the shape of the lithesome stalk of an otherwise extinct orchid.

"I don't have enough computer up here to show the videos . . ."

Knowing laughter from the darkened hall, as it was a long-establish fact of cunning, industry, and espionage that the Committee controlled the most powerful computers in all of Cryptopolis.

". . . but you should note the etymology of zeitgeist, a German word— zeit equals time, geist equals spirit. Thus its definition, the spirit of an era." As La Bwana recited, the big screen above and behind her, as well as those at eye-level over every wall-hung urinal in the building. etc., spelled them out. "The intellectual mores and cultural climate of a specific epoch or age. . . ." The salients of La Bwana's smile beamed benevolently over the hall, the expensive teeth, the sculpted lips, the diamond Skoda-Benz logo lasered into the right front incisor. ". . . which I generally interpret as the here and now, along with its logical extension, here today, gone tomorrow. Think bell-bottom trousers, Herbert Marcuse, Don't Ask Don't Tell"— gales of laughter—". . . responsible environmentalism," chortles and snorts, ". . . not to mention plenipotentiary democracy—i.e., the stratum of forgotten detritus left behind by every so-called culture, society, civilization, and empire—nationalized banking and privatized mass transit, for two—of which subsequent states remain more or less completely unaware, not to say, institutionally amnesiac."

"Young, dumb, and full of come!" someone shouted from the floor.

La Bwana leaned into the microphone, took a beat as the laughter swelled and evanesced, then said huskily into the microphone, "That's disgusting."

Knowing laughter.

"There's no way," La Bwana resumed, "to predict what this may consist of. For example, we still have the Mayan calendar—a so-called continuum I pick deliberately if only because so many of you still refer to it." Here La Bwana held a wallet-sized Mayan calendar aloft for all to see, which gesture was duly iterated 100X in the screen above and behind her, at eye-level on the inside of restroom doors, etc. "Let's see those Mayan calendars!" Dozens, then hundreds, and finally a total of 758 left hands shot aloft, each bearing a wallet-sized duplicate of the Mayan calendar, all of them compliments of BiggieBank, part of the convention grab-bag. In the screens appeared long panning shots of shadowy wallet-sized cards held aloft by phantom limbs.

"But we have no idea what happened to the Mayan culture, do we?"

Vague muttering.

"So think about it."

Rhinogenerics suffused the hall with the smell of burning electronics. The crowd began to chant. "Think, baby, think. Think, baby, think . . ."

"If you were Mayan," La Bwana resumed, as the chant wilted beneath her stentorian bellow, "with your half-paid-for condominium in Cryptopolis, and that BiggieBank promotion in the works, and your world suddenly came to an abrupt and complete end, what would look more important to you as 'they' (an invading, slave-taking army, possessed of and driven by an idolatry the exact contrapositive of your own to wit videlicet: They is not us therefore Not they is us) or "it" (an earthquake, an asteroid, a plague), carry off you and your family, or kill the women and rape the men—what, I say, would look more important to you in the moment: the calendar on the wall, the rivets in the slave-taker's armor, or the symptoms peculiar to the iBola virus? That's the one where your phone hemorrhages," she added helpfully.

Complete silence descended upon the hall. Even the pink noise of various spheroidicentric events, oxidizing from a wide spectrum of generation-old skull chips, faded to a barely discernible hiss.

"Zeitgeist, adiós. And then, just as abruptly, you are brought back to consciousness a mere five hundred years later, or, better, a thousand, only to discover that all anybody knows about you and your era (and the few who do know are specialists, and much of what they know is wrong) is the partial remains of your calendar some contractor found in a stratum of ash a mere three inches deep, some five feet beneath the compaction of subsequent shopping-middens, not unlike the one in which you yourself, teased along by your grandfather, discovered a blue glass patent medicine bottle in Darwin, California, in 1985, except, as it was about two inches below the surface, maybe it had been there a mere one hundred years. And even the calendar is mostly the pinup part of it, a nice Mayan boy in a negligee twirling a solid rubber basketball on the tip of his index finger, chiseled into stone with a few box scores below him, mostly Arabic numerals, base ten, and of course the Mayan boy thing means nothing because sex means nothing now, in our era . . ." Tittering among the young, sighs among the old. ". . . so nobody knows what it's about, but that doesn't stop them from speculating, quite the contrary, the dearth of fact fuels speculation, that like for instance a full moon on July 13, 1987, in apposition with Venus and transiting Sagittarius later that evening, portended the demise of your civilization twenty-five days, weeks, months, years, decades later, with huge—and I'm talking enormous—implications for the fate of our own egregiousness a thousand years afterwards—which is now! And everything else—the text messages from the party of your choice which continued to assure you that everything was okay, the buboes on your face in the mirror, the dust raised by the invading army as it rumbled over the Bay Bridge (an engineering marvel dating from 2013 which the last man in charge of saving the city couldn't bring himself to destroy, but the invaders will take great pleasure in so doing, after they're done with it)—all these and almost everything else have disappeared without a trace; of which we, now, a thousand years later, have not even a rumor upon which to base a fantasy concerning your. . . ."

"Zeitgeist!" a hundred voices supplied.

"Zeitgeist," La Bwana repeated, as if introspectively. "A German word, a combining form meaning time and spirit, thus, the spirit of the times and, by implication, no more or less ephemeral than fashion, than technology, than motorized transportation, than the printed word, the printed circuit, the cathode ray tube, the four-inch diameter basketball of solid caoutchouc—gesundheit—" Laughter. "—and of course the silly custom of sacrificing the losing team: than almost any cultural artifact you could name. How did you feel the night your phone died of the plague, or on the day it first showed the deadly symptoms? Except for the fact that a human might empathize with your loss, and perhaps even join you in mourning, though a thousand years separate your loss from their empathy, it's equally possible and much more likely that someone postdating you and your culture by a thousand years won't even have an inkling that your culture, your epoch, your zeitgeist so much as exited, let alone existed. Let alone that you were there, too." La Bwana pointed into the lights left right and center. "And you and you . . . Ah hahahaha . . ."

"Ah hahahaha," the audience repeated.

"Zeitgeist," La Bwana intoned as if introspectively, "might well be interpreted as the tendency of an era to overestimate its relevance to history—or to anything else. Boil it down to this!"

The Moscone Holodome fell absolutely silent. You might have heard a screw creak in a veteran's ankle.

"What have you done for pi today?"

"Huh?" three hundred voices asked. "Huh?" the other 458 asked.

"I said," La Bwana restated, "What have you done for pi today!"

Silence.

"See? The collective unconscious is not dead!"

The silence peculiar to a mob that has just experienced a moment of sympathy with a true thing, that fleeting elision between one state of ignorance and the next, like a flash of daylight from the air vent in the roof of the tunnel vision through which the room is traveling at a high rate of speed, other than which there is no evidence that any motion is happening whatsoever, the moment at which, despite all efforts of the subcommittee that dispenses the Wonders of History, a particle of truth trickles down the angled berm of the Comfort Zone like a pubic hair down a trouser leg.

The audience gasped and went nuts, and while the telepathic simile caused Tipsy to frown and stir in the Adirondack chair, she did not wake up. Buffeted by a clamoring fog wind, the martini glass fell soundlessly into the embrace of the nasturtium bed.

"Zeitgeist," La Bwana reiterated, as if suffused by introspection, "hales from the same German era that bequeathed us heroin and propaganda. Zeitgeist, heroin, propaganda—what a legacy!" La Bwana declared, *"And yet, these, too, shall pass . . . !"*

Animatronic simulacra of *hypsignathus monstrosus*, the female of which has an ovipositor the size of a cutlass hilt, Möbiused the microsphere, ovipositing flybuttons throughout the holotorium, each of which displayed one or another of the sanctioned logos appropriate to the current Info. ("The State Is Best Served In Silence," "Immediately Following The Game," read one, "The Losing Team Shall Be Sacrificed," read its companion, along with the old standby, "Resist Little, Obey Much," as well as the classic, "Ahhhh hahahaha . . .") The flybuttons disseminated themselves Poissonately beneath the pyrolyzed acreage of the Holodome, among delegates, telegates, and hologates. Beams of enlightenment swiveled amongst the crowd. The smurfs kept their Planck distance. Shadow9s slept in dark louvered lockers, in rows, like bats, like hypsignathus monstrous, like in shifts. It's a budget thing.

Fade to black amid the strains of the old Condor Silversteed standard,

> You came to me
> Like a bill from nowhere . . .

Tipsy frowned and shifted in her chair. Had she mailed a check to PG&E? But she did not wake up.

. . . The spotlight reignited as Condor Silversteed himself made a surprise appearance, not to perform but to wave at you, ready on the left, at you, ready on the right, and at you, ready down the middle. . . .

A girl standing right next to the moonlighting Officer Few screamed "He looked at me! He looked at me!" and fainted of happiness.

It is The True.

VI
WINDWARD PASSAGE

A day spent sailing is not attributed
to the sumtotal of those allotted
to a man's life

On the wall at the Cat 'n' Fiddle
Sausalito, California

THIRTY-SEVEN

THE CARIBBEAN LOOKED GOOD. ITS BLUES WERE CERULEAN. PORPOISES swarmed under the bow, laced air to water beyond the pulpit, and squealed. Gulls trailed after the stern and snagged bits of smoked ham launched off the tips of her fingers. Fish claimed what little the gulls missed. A million dollar yacht motored in this direction and a two million dollar yacht sailed in that direction, and everybody looked good. Having been gone for a while, Red engaged a lovely suite in a beachfront motor court while the bottom was waxed and the stainless polished. He loosed a curious mixture of bleach and white vinegar in a glass chafing dish below decks, left closed the port holes and sealed the companionway for twenty-four hours, aired it out for an additional day and, voilà, no mildew, no mold, not a single living creature survived the resulting chlorine gas.

"That ordnance sounds dangerous," she observed.

"Only if you inhale," Red pointed out.

"Do insects inhale?"

"No. They bite."

Red even went with her to the supermarket, the first man in her life since the carpenter to do that, and picked up the tab for $450 worth of booze and groceries. Then they went to a big chandlery and spent a comparable amount on gear—foulies, sun block, shorts, hats, flares, batteries, charts. Red insisted that Tipsy wait until he had departed the building before she paid cash for the charts. Then they went to a bookstore where she stocked up on mysteries plus titles concerned with women living aboard, women at sea, *The Idiot's Guide to Radar*, and a book specifically about catching and preparing edible Caribbean fish. If it was inedible, there was an appendix on taxidermy.

"Man," she said, "look at the tools you need."

Red had a look. "It's the same stuff you need to bleed a diesel."

"Then we're covered?"

"We're covered."

"Good. You can mount the trophies." She added the book to the pile. Red just laughed and paid the bill.

Tipsy had never seen anything like it. After a week or so, the realization dawned that San Francisco had fogged her brain as well as her weather, and that, until this trip to Florida, a very fundamental thing about her brother had escaped her notice: the Caribbean is a beautiful place. So what if it's hot? Some people consider that a plus.

"If you stay on the water," Red pointed out, "it doesn't matter how hot it gets." When they first walked down the dock, pushing a cart full of books and supplies, Red had stopped them alongside a huge boat. "Welcome aboard."

Tipsy couldn't believe her eyes. "This is *Tunacide*?"

"According to the transom."

"Red—it's beautiful!"

"So are you," Red said. "You really like it?"

"Like it? It's the nicest boat I've ever been this close to."

"But it's way smaller than *Kreutzer's Revenge*."

Tipsy frowned. "Never heard of it."

"Well," Red said, unabashedly enthusiastic, "get closer."

On the trip across the country, they had become inseparable. They consulted each other over the smallest decisions. Peanut butter, for example. Smooth or crunchy? Whatever you want, darling. No no, dear, you decide. . . . How about this motel? Sure, why not . . .

The captain's berth was as expansive and comfortable a place as anyone with reasonable appetites for such things might have hoped for, in which to wait out the tail end of hurricane season. They went to bed early and got up late. They anchored out in various secret spots scattered about the Keys, they snorkled, they prepared excellent meals and consumed them at their leisure, they drank all day but rarely to excess—spoken like a true alcoholic! Truth to tell, however, it was too hot for heavy drinking. Tipsy took to sunbathing on a thick towel on the foredeck with sun block, hat, and a Simenon wedged between the anchor rode and the deck so it wouldn't blow away before she may or may not get around to finishing it. She developed a nice tan and a thorough one too; nude swimming and sunbathing were entirely acceptable at every one of Red's solitary anchorages, as were eating and drinking in moderation so as to look good doing it. Tipsy quickly narrowed it down to iced white wine spritzers and a drink called a Stormy Weather—a pint glass brimful of cracked ice, a jigger of a cheap, excellent black Haitian *rhum* called *Dithyrambe du Gonave* of which *Tunacide* carried two cases, a squeeze with its wedge of fresh lime as an antiscorbutic, topped off with an English brand of ginger beer of tart piquancy such as she'd never tasted, of which there were at least four cases in the hold. Fit to slake the thirst, sting the tongue, and mellow the hemoglobin—delicious.

It turned out Red could prepare any kind of fish any way she wanted, let alone ways in which she didn't know she wanted but learned to crave, so there went that cookbook, but he also had in his head a quiver of odd recipes for, as an example or two, a killer Caesar salad, another salad, perhaps Thai in origin, based on jicama and serrano peppers, as well as a Moroccan dish made with apricots and lamb served over couscous. Tipsy eventually let Red do at least half the cooking because, although she wasn't incompetent in the kitchen, most of their meals consisted of seafood complemented by a grain and a fresh vegetable.

"Ice," Red told her, "is a pain in the ass to keep on board a boat, even a big power boat like this one. The systems necessary to maintain refrigeration and manufacture ice probably cause more problems for recreational boaters than any five or six of the common hazards to navigation—excepting, of course, diving under the influence."

"So," Tipsy said, rattling the ice in her empty glass, "why maintain them?"

"Anywhere in the tropics," Red said, "ice is a number one trade item. You can get anything in return for ice." His eyebrows waggled like a pair of time-motion studies of pupa gestation. "Poontang, for instance."

"Really?"

"Check it out." He cleared his throat. "Hey, babe." He rattled the melting remnants in his empty glass. "Want some ice?"

"*Yeah.*"

While Tipsy sunbathed the days away on the foredeck, Red whiled them away astern, sipping beer and keeping an eye on a pair of fishing poles. His fair skin prevented Red from going entirely naked, so he costumed himself with a long-billed fishing hat with flip-down shades and a neck curtain, a pineapple shirt marketed as *The Octopus and His Friends*, cargo pants with their belt threaded through the holster of a multitool, and a pair of flip-flops as, around midday, the deck became too hot for bare feet.

So, around midday, Tipsy and Red convened for lunch and a nap.

In the shade cast by the visor on his cap, Red's eyes twinkled as he marveled at his luck. Well into his sixties, it had been a long time since he'd had a fling purely for the fling of it. He'd look up and realize that a half-hour or forty-five minutes had gone by without leaving a discernible trace in his mind. Or that the bait had been stolen off both lines and he hadn't even noticed. He discovered that his hands, the one with its scarred palm, the two of them calloused and hardened by years of boat and fishing gear, had developed a new sensitivity. His center of gravity had lowered and his physical presence, never mild, became more assured than ever.

Late in his fifties, having concluded that the casual and convulsive sexuality that had characterized his youth had, while he was thinking of other things, become a thing of the past, he'd tried hookers and call girls and old girlfriends and even a new name or two. No soap. It just wasn't there. So instead, he concentrated on seeing how much money he could make with the least amount of effort, and how many fish he could catch while he was sitting around thinking about money.

And now, here he was, bobbing around the many coves and inlets and shoals and reefs of the Keys, basking in the unalloyed attentions of a babe almost fifteen years his junior, and it seemed like the most natural thing in the world. Just when you've lost interest in the subject . . .

Things weren't entirely carefree, of course. The problem needed to be dealt with.

And so, one night after a fine meal of fresh tuna poached in white wine and tarragon, with wild rice, golden raisins, walnuts, and fresh asparagus, and as Tipsy was taking her turn at the dishes, Red topped off both glasses and broached the subject.

"We need to take care of business. Otherwise this idyll," he moved his glass through a small circle, "will come to an abrupt end."

Tipsy wore an apron and nothing else. The tapes of the apron trailed from a bow tied at the small of her back. She made room for a saucepan in the back corner of the lower rack in the dishwasher, and stood up. "Is that all there is to it?"

"That's all there is to it."

She closed the dishwasher door, started the machine, and turned to face Red. "Well," she said, "we have the boat."

Red frowned. "What boat?"

She was drying her hands on the skirt of the apron. "This boat."

"We need a boat?"

"We need a boat."

"Why?"

"Because," she said. "I figured it out."

Red raised an eyebrow. "Thanks for telling me."

She shrugged. "At least, I think I figured it out. Besides," she looked at him frankly. "I'm enjoying myself."

"I'll not dignify that with an answer."

She shed the apron, handed it to him, and headed for their bunk. "Bring out the stuff you took off *Vellela Vellela*."

Red stepped into the engine room. When he returned with the briefcase, Tipsy was dressed and waiting for him. "Two heads are better than three," he said, apropos of nothing.

"That's not funny."

"Honey," Red said, "I—"

"Don't call me honey."

"Oh, now. Is this our first fight?"

"Who's fighting?" she said through compressed lips.

"Good." Red tapped the waterproof envelope with a forefinger. "The sooner we figure this out and do something about it, the sooner we can get back to doing nothing."

"Not to mention you'll get paid," Tipsy discerned. "Don't give me that bullshit."

Red drummed a mild tattoo with a fist on the chart table. "Damn straight I'm going to get paid," he said quietly. "*We*—" he pointed at her "—are going to get paid. And why not? Are we supposed to go through all this horseshit for free?"

"Are you referring to my brother's death as *horseshit*?" Tipsy shouted back.

Red took a breath. Then: "You know exactly what horseshit I'm referring to. You—we—are icing on the cake. Completely unexpected. That you and I . . . that we . . . it's . . ."

Tipsy brushed past him into the forward stateroom. Red sat at the chart table and fumed. What is it about this deal, he muttered to himself, that impels me to be behave irrationally? He studied his glass. Am I becoming sentimental?

Tipsy reappeared. "Here." She set a carved cedar box on the chart table. "All the mail I've ever received from Charley." She pushed the box to one side. "But this," she took up *Vellela Vellela*'s logbook, "is all we're going to need."

Red brightened. "Now you're talking." He pushed her drink across the table. "Have a seat."

THIRTY-EIGHT

"I'm convinced it's in the log."

"I'd have guessed the letters."

"He never said anything in the letters."

"He never said anything in the log, either."

"I beg to differ. Given that the log is genuine—"

"Is there some reason to think it's not genuine?"

"What I mean is, we don't have any reason to think the log is misleading."

"True story."

"Okay. So what if it's really not misleading."

Puzzled, Red shook his head.

Tipsy pressed on. "He made exactly one stop after he left Rum Cay."

"Albert Town."

"Find it."

Red opened the warped boards and had a look. "He arrived the night of March 16."

"What's the date of the next entry?"

Red turned three closely written pages. "March 19." He paged back. "There's a lot of blather in between."

"But he hasn't set sail."

"No."

"What's the next dated entry?"

Red turned the three pages. "March 19."

"What's he doing?"

"Weighing anchor. I see where you're going with this. No matter what he was up to, Charley wouldn't skip a navigational entry."

"Therefore, he spent three nights and two days at Albert Town."

"True story."

"For what? There's nothing there—right? A ghost town, you said."

"Charley said. I've never been there."

"What were you doing in the meantime?"

"Fishing."

"You didn't mind the delay?"

"Nope. Charley was facing a long passage, so I figured he was banking some sleep; or, since he was sailing, maybe he was waiting on the weather; or, for that matter, maybe he was fishing, too. Charley liked to fish as well as the next man. And to tell you the truth, he could have stayed at Albert Town a week for all I cared. It was beautiful out there."

"Not a bad story. In fact it's such a good story, I'm betting he made his move behind it. And there's something else. Read on."

"Albert Town light bearing so and so, Long Key light ditto. . . . Anchored in a shoal west-facing inlet within spitting distance SSW of a pretty wreck. . . . Is that it?"

"A fit of introspection, he called it."

"Good memory."

"You think you could plot his position from what's in there?"

Red scanned ahead. "The rest of this is just a bunch of bullshit about salvaging anchors and rode."

"With Cedric Osawa," Tipsy noted.

"That's true," Red pursed his lips. "With Cedric Osawa."

"He gave you that dive knife."

"Sure. I knew Cedric."

"Knew?"

"Long time, no see." Red shrugged. "Good seaman, good mechanic, excellent fisherman. For a long time, Cedric was a particular friend of Charley's. Due to Cedric's persistent dedication to blow and alcohol, however, Charley had distanced himself. Cedric's habits made him less interesting to run around with than he once was."

"He's a lush?"

"So it would seem."

"Well that's no reason to—" Tipsy stopped, thought about what she was saying, and abruptly reverted to the subject at hand. "Even so, I think we could use him about now."

Red looked at her, then shook his head. "We need somebody else in on this deal like we need a . . ." He stopped.

"A hole in the head?" Tipsy finished for him.

Red grimaced. "Let's just say that I hope Cedric isn't the answer. Last I heard, he'd become completely unreliable."

She nodded. "I think Cedric's superfluous. Although, if things had gone another way, he might have come in handy."

Red frowned. "Like how?"

She pointed. "Like if you hadn't found that logbook."

Red was thinking about something else.

"Read on."

Red cleared his throat and continued. "Wound up spending a week within a three or four mile radius, diving shoals and inlets for fouled anchors. We found about a dozen. . . . This?"

"Keep reading."

". . . too big for us to deal with . . . nine dandy examples of modern and ancient anchor theory, and so much barnacle-encrusted rode we had to leave most of it behind. . . ."

"We're getting warm."

"I don't expect anybody to believe this," Red continued, adding, "I don't either. [B]ut we buried all that extra rode way up a tidal flat, as far as we could float the dinghy under it, with us outboard and pushing . . ."

Tipsy clapped her hands once. "That's it."

"That's it?"

"Keep reading."

". . . on the theory that someday we'd come back for it. There are excellent directions to the trove in one of my old log books, and don't forget to allow for something like ten years' migration of magnetic variation."

"Stop," Tipsy said.

Red blinked. After a pause, he counted the fingers of one hand against the chart table. Then, more slowly, he counted them again. "Ten years ago, Charley was in prison."

"Getting warm," Tipsy said.

"You might have something here," Red muttered. Then he quickly read, "Tonight, from this anchorage, I can see the mouth of the creek. Oddly enough, *Vellela* is anchored on the exact back bearing of the vector from the creek to the middle of the entrance to Man of War Channel—" Red looked up. "It's a map."

"To a bunch of anchor chain," Tipsy cautioned.

". . . [O]nce you're close you'll know it, whether you can still see it or not, for there's enough iron there to box a compass. I can just see the expression on the treasure hunter's face when he realizes he's excavating 1,352 pounds of 5/8" BBB chain . . ." Red stopped reading. "One thousand three hundred and fifty-two pounds of chain," he repeated thoughtfully. "Five-eighths triple-B." He tapped a forefinger on the page. "That's a damned specific accounting."

"What's with the triple-B?" Tipsy asked.

"It's a low-carbon chain with short links that are standardized for most windlasses," Red said, obviously thinking about something else. "It's a weight of chain he might have been able to establish," he allowed. "But why would he take the trouble? Plus," he frowned, "it's one size up from what's readily seen on your average yachts on the hook."

"How much trouble?"

Red nodded as if to himself. "A lot of trouble."

Tipsy nodded. "I was pretty sure of that."

"I'll be a son of a bitch," Red said simply.

They looked at each other.

"How far is it from here?" Tipsy asked.

Red unfolded Charley's copy of *Straits of Florida and Approaches* and opened the dividers to straddle a degree of latitude on its right-hand border. "Sixty minutes comprise one degree of latitude. One minute is one nautical mile." He held the dividers aloft. "This is sixty nautical miles." He walked the legs of the compass from Albert Town to Key West. ". . . five, six, seven and then some—let's say maybe it's 450 miles as the crow flies. An actual voyage would be more like 550."

"How long would it take?"

"Well. . . ." Red studied the chart. "If *Tunacide* were a crow, and if we traded off watches 24/7 at ten knots—a mere forty-two hours. Two days. We can't travel that fast or that straight, however, as it would be rough on us and the boat, nobody would get any sleep, and the fuel would be expensive. Alternatively, we could travel by day, anchor out at night, and take our time. At that rate the trip might take, let's say, ten days to two weeks. Do a little fishing, eat proper meals, take naps, get eight hours of sleep every night. . . . And make sure we're alone out there."

"Does this thing have the range?"

"Hell, yes," said Red.

"What about groceries?"

Red shrugged. "Another trip to the store."

"What are we waiting for?"

Red knew the date, but he glanced at his watch anyway. It was the first of November. "The end of the hurricane season," he told her.

"Which is . . . ?"

Red smiled. "Right after the last hurricane."

After only two days, any trace of seasickness dissipated. She'd never experienced anything like it. Sultry days. Sultry nights. Always a breeze. Stars overhead she'd never seen. Red pointed out five or six of them every night.

"Okay, sister. There's the Big Dipper."

"I know the goddamn Big Dipper."

"Oh? So, starting with the handle, name its constituent stars."

Silence.

"Come on. You rarely get so clear a shot at it from the continent, not unless you're in the Rockies at 12,000 feet, anyway. Freezing your ass off, I might add."

Stubborn silence.

"Starting with the handle it's Alkaid, the middle one is Mizar, which is a double star, by the way, Alioth, Megrez, down to Phecda, over to Merak, up to Dubhe, extend that line and you get to Polaris. The pole star."

"The North Star."

"You're not so ignorant after all."

"Call me that again and you're gong to be naming stars a lot closer to your face."

At first Red stayed with her in the house on her watch. But Tipsy quickly picked up the rudiments of reading the GPS, correcting for set and drift, and pricking their position on the paper chart every hour, a practice upon which Red insisted. When she asked him why, he opened a drawer. "See that?"

"What about it?"

"That's a sextant."

"I've heard of them."

"You should learn how to use it."

"Are you kidding?"

Red swept an arm at the dials and knobs surrounding the helm. "This stuff goes south, this thing will bail you out."

"But is this stuff going south?"

Red shrugged. "It never has. And I take good care of *Tunacide*. But, electronic navigation or not, I like knowing where I am."

"Is there math involved?"

"You bet there's math involved."

"I like knowing where I am, too," Tipsy assured him. "But math? Forget it. Show me how this modern stuff works. At least I'll be as good as the lowest battery."

She cut way back on the sauce, with no drinking at all while standing watch, which was more than Red could say about himself. He shared her watches until they both gained confidence in her ability, and Tipsy proved a quick study.

Seas were mild. Except for high cumulus there wasn't a cloud in the sky. There wasn't even much shipping to worry about.

They did get approached by a Coast Guard cutter, maybe 150 feet long, deck-mounted weapons fore, aft, port, and starboard. The vessel cruised them slowly. Red happened to be minding the wheel at that point. He watched the cutter glide by, its skipper mindful of his wake and the current. Tipsy lay face down on a towel on the bow with the copy of Charley's logbook and *The Corpse on the Dike* by Janwillem van de Wetering. The strings of her halter top lay on the deck on either side of her. The pages of the novel flapped in the breeze, but she smiled and waved the logbook at three pairs of binoculars on the cutter's bridge.

That girl, thought Red, is supporting our troops. Though he had no contraband aboard, the idea that Tipsy knew how to behave in proximity to authority soothed him. *Tunacide* adjusted her course. Waypoint, he realized, glancing at a display above the helm. Ignoring the cutter to port he scanned the horizon to starboard until he spotted a flash . . . two, three, four . . . At the count of ten the light flashed again. That would be the light at Puerto Sagua de Grande. He plucked a yellow hand-compass from a drawer, stepped out to the afterdeck, and brought the instrument to bear on the horizon. When the light flashed again he corrected the bearing and read it: 172°, more or less. The little compass wouldn't do for two or three degree increments. He checked the chart and noticed an anomaly. The pilot described the light as visible at fourteen miles, but the chart said ten. He fiddled with the touch-screen buttons along the lower margin of the GPS display until it coughed up a bearing of its own. But of course that bearing was the one he himself had laid in yesterday, based on the chart. He took up the parallel ruler, old enough to have been wrought from brass, and given him in Haiti years before by an old man who'd admired Red and Charley as they had taken an entire day to scull one of Charley's engineless scows from one end of a becalmed Baie de Fort Liberté to the other. Talk about your blisters and your sunburn. . . . He walked the bearing vector from a compass rose south of Cuba to the charted position of Puerto Sagua de Grande light. He did it again for the light at Cabo Sotavento, six miles east. He noted a minor issue of compass variation, a difference between that on the rose and that obtaining in the zone of their position, but it easily fell within the margin of error due to the hand-bearing compass. He penciled the traces until they intersected their corrected course and came up with a position-to-light distance of twelve miles, half way between the two plotted values. Not bad for broad daylight.

At half a knot the current was hardly an issue, though they were stemming it, but the wind came aft and built some chop. By now, however, Tipsy had her sea legs. Her appetite was fine. Through his every watch the pilot could smell something cooking. An hour after sunrise the third morning out she had presented him with a plateful of eggs perfectly scrambled with garlic and asiago cheese, with sides of thick bacon, buttered grits, two biscuits, juice fresh-squeezed from ruby grapefruit, and an entire pot of coffee. Red ate every bite. . . .

"Ahoy the bridge," he said an hour later, "now it's the Cuban Coasties." And so it was.

Tipsy waved. The Cuban swabbies waved back.

"That's a Pauk II," Red said. "A Soviet vessel. I only ever heard they had but one of them. This must be our lucky day."

"I've never seen the Cuban flag before," Tipsy said.

"I've got one below," Red said. "I fly it on January 1, which is guaranteed to piss off a certain fraction of the Miami population."

"Which is why you do it." Tipsy concluded.

Red beamed. "Say, doll," he burped somewhat indiscreetly. "What say we pull this crate to the curb and grab us a little siesta?" Red waggled his eye brows.

"What's the matter with the automatic pilot?"

"It doesn't know from nothing about navigational hazards." Red took up his dividers. "Look here. Don't worry." He glanced aft. "The Cubans are going about their business and there's no traffic at the moment. Let's see—" He touched the dividers to the chart. "When Cay Lobos bears . . . 94° True, wait, the variation here is only 6 degrees west, west is best, that's 100° degrees Magnetic. Now take a bearing here to the Cayo Confites light, chart says twelve miles visible, pilot says eighteen miles. You gotta watch these discrepancies. They happen all the time. Let's reverse-cock the hat onto our course here, transfer the dividers to latitude, thirteen miles." He slapped the chart. "Good enough for a fishing boat." He marked the chart. "We program a waypoint just here. We pull the distances off the marked location to the closest abscissa of latitude and ordinate of longitude, read them against their respective scales here . . . okay . . . and here . . . good. Then we write the result directly onto the chart, close aboard the anticipated change of course, and the reckoned location." He didn't even look up. "Now," he enthused. "We bust out on this course here, see." He dragged a pencil line along a knackered edge of the ancient ruler. "And the course is. . . ." He walked the ruler over to the nearest compass rose, just north of the eastern tip of Cuba. "Can you read that? I don't have my glasses."

His glasses were heaped with pencil shavings and a lime-green architectural 30/60 triangle with a half-inch strip of tape along each of its three edges. The triangle was unusually small. Its hypotenuse couldn't have measured five inches.

She had a close look at the compass rose. "The outer ring of mensurations," Red said. "Each one is one degree. Small, aren't they?"

She began to count. "One, two, three . . ."

He wrapped the spectacles around his face. "Start with sixty. See the sixty?" He pointed.

"I see it."

"The next long mark is seventy." He handed her the pencil, and she counted the smaller marks ruled around the circumference of the rose.

"Seventy-nine." Red recorded the figure on a pad of scratch paper. Across the top of it, a cartoon face chewed a cigar.

> *Scowley's Marine Diesel*
> *Boca Chica Key*
> *Florida*
> *1-305-GET-BLED*
> *One look from Scowley?*
> *She'll be runnin' scared!*

"And what's the variation?"

"Huh?"

"Move the ruler. In the middle of the rose—there. VAR something something, annual increase something something. It's always on the increase, this far east."

"Eight degrees."

"That's good. But that's not the variation way over here. See?" He pointed at a purple line that angled across the chart, not far from their projected course change. "Put your finger on it." She did. "Now run north along it until you find a purple logo along side it." She did. "What's it say?"

"VAR 7° W. (2002)."

"Chart's getting old. What was that annual increase?"

She returned to the fine print at the center of the compass rose. "Seven. . . ."

"That's minutes. We needn't take them into consideration. But, okay, the course true was," he consulted his pad, "seventy-nine degrees."

"West is best," she said brightly, "and east is least."

Red slapped the chart. "You're getting salty, girl."

Tipsy smiled modestly. "This is just good clean fun, isn't it."

"Yes," Red replied happily. "So that's—"

"Eighty-six degrees," Tipsy declared.

"Our new course." Red leaned over the chart. "Eighty-six degrees magnetic." He pulled the pencil alongside the ruler. "To just about . . ." He pulled pencil and ruler off the chart and studied it. "Hmmm."

"Hey, Red?"

"What," he said, not looking up.

"What's that masking tape for, along the perimeter of that plastic triangle?"

Red didn't even look at it. "That's so ink won't run up under the edge of the triangle and smear the line."

"Ink?"

Red blinked, looked up at her, then looked back at the chart. "Once upon a time, humans actually inked architectural and engineering drawings. Back in the old days. Before computers."

Tipsy smiled at the triangle. "Like when Trafalgar was just a gleam in Admiral Nelson's eye?"

"Aye," Red heartily agreed. "And, now, lemme ask ye, here, darlin', don't ye think there's naught but a poor substitute for a paper chart? Be honest, now."

She surveyed the chart. It covered perhaps some ten or eleven square feet. It had been wetted and dried more than once, about it lay scattered pencils and their shavings, a hand sharpener, dividers, two different rulers, the little triangle and a bigger one, a gum eraser, a coastal pilot, a copy of Reed's Caribbean almanac and a glass with a finger of rum in it. Her brother's last course lay plotted across it, increasingly laced with the ongoing course of *Tunacide*.

"Yes," she said. "It's very handsome." She ruffled his hair. "Unlike you." Red surprised her. "I feel like a puppy with his first chew toy."

"I guess that's better than being a puppy with his first bee sting." Tipsy's laugh had a girlish lilt to it, but it reverberated with the first news to come from a certain part of her being in a long time. Red laughed too.

"There's thirty or forty feet of water behind Cay Lobos." Red dragged the points of the dividers along the surface of the chart. "It's the Great Bahama Bank back there. No shipping whatsoever and fishing to die for. Look here." He took up Reed's and thumbed through the pilot index. "Marlin, blue and white. Sailfish and swordfish. Dolphin, wahoo, kingfish, mackerel, tuna all kinds, bonito, bonefish, amberjack, tarpon, barracuda, and sharks sharks sharks. . . ." Tipsy stood beside him, her arm on his shoulder. "Fishes and anchorages fit to exhaust any number of lifetimes."

"Fine by me," Tipsy said. "But what about our greater purpose?" Red nodded. "Once we get five or ten miles behind the light we'll duck in here." He touched the chart. "Labanderas Reef lies between us and the channel, there's shoals here and here. We'll show an anchor light, and it's an excellent place to spend the night, but we could easily have it all to ourselves. Tomorrow, we'll rejoin our course . . . here. It's fifty nautical miles to the next waypoint." He pulled off a couple of dimensions. "Twenty-two degrees forty minutes north . . . Seventy-six degrees, eighteen minutes west. We'll make a day of it. Troll for lunch, stop to prepare and eat it, take a nap. . . ." He touched the small of her back. "Then we'll haul around for a short leg to . . . here. From there we'll follow soundings to the mouth of Man of War Channel. From there," he dragged the dividers east across a bight of open water, "a straight, blue-water shot to Albert Town."

"And our manifest destiny, I suppose," Tipsy said, with a thoughtful nod.

"Whatever that means," Red said, not lifting his eyes from the chart.

THIRTY-NINE

JUST BEFORE NIGHTFALL THEY ANCHORED BEHIND LABANDERAS REEF. THERE they had the sea to themselves, and the sea was the world. On deck after drinks and supper, scattered lights in the darkness marked fishing vessels, and a bigger light marked Cayo Lobos. "The Milky Way certainly puts the rest of this fooling around down here into perspective," Tipsy murmured as she nestled against Red's hirsute chest. They were seated on a pile of cushions on the afterdeck, leaning against the back of the house. *Tunacide* lay easily to her anchor. A wave occasionally washed over a drying rock a quarter of a mile or so to the north of them, phosphorescence flashing like teeth. Red had a set out, but he paid no attention to it.

"Yeah," Red said. "I'm sure you know that it's the edge of the galaxy?"

"So I've been told. But you know, it's a rare night that a San Franciscan can see the edge of the galaxy. Conceptualizing it," she chuckled, "that's something else."

"True story. Ours is a spiral galaxy, and what you're looking at, when you're looking at the Milky Way, is one edge of it. If the galaxy is a doughnut, you and your head and San Francisco, too, are all in the hole."

"God, doughnuts," Tipsy said. "Do they even have doughnuts in the Bahamas?"

"I've never seen one."

"In San Francisco, we have organic doughnuts."

"I don't doubt it. But why would Bahamians have them? Do doughnuts go with fish?"

"Not like cornbread does."

"I've got an excellent recipe for cornbread. The secret is honey and buttermilk."

"That's two secrets."

"Nah. Everybody uses buttermilk."

"They do?"

"Carmen used to get her honey from a guy who kept hives in an orange grove way down on Cape Sable, just south of Whitewater Bay."

"Who was Carmen?"

"That would be the Carmen whose kidney generated your five-thousand-dollar bailout."

After a pause Tipsy asked, "Didn't she have a couple of your children, too?"

"That she did." Red cleared his throat.

"There must have been something going on there."

"There was," Red allowed. "At one time we couldn't get enough of one another." After a pause he added, "It seems like a very long time ago."

"She died, I'm sorry to recall."

"She died."

"And the kids?"

Red shifted. "Your bony forehead is cutting off circulation to my arm."

Tipsy didn't move. "What are their names?"

"Pink, was the girl's name."

Tipsy smiled in the darkness. "Pink? Really?"

"What's so funny?"

"Nothing. Well . . ."

"It was Carmen's idea."

"Was she a chip off her mother's block?"

"She was—is—that. I guess she is, anyway. I haven't laid eyes on her in a long time."

"Why not?"

Red shrugged. "She took her mother's death hard. Blamed it on me, even though she knew better. I guess she knew better. She was fourteen at the time. A tough age for a girl to lose her mother."

"You don't even know where she is?"

"Atlanta, last I heard. She went there after she got out of prison."

"What?"

"Like I said."

"How old is she?"

Red thought about it. "She must be in her late thirties by now."

"She could be a mother."

"That," Red affirmed, "she well could be."

"Which would make you a grandfather."

"True story." Red looked up and scratched the underside of his chin. "What about you?" he asked, lowering his hand. "You ever have kids?"

"We're not through with your kids yet. What about the other one?"

"The boy. Ernesto. Che without calling him Che."

Tipsy stirred and resettled. "I wouldn't have figured you for that."

"For what?"

"For naming your only son after a revolutionary icon."

Red sucked a tooth. "Taking your points in order, it was Carmen who named him, since when is he my only son, and there's at least two sides to that icon business."

From somewhere across the water, far enough away for its source to be invisible, came the faint sound of a generator.

"Meteor."

"Where?"

He pointed. "Right through the swan."

She sighted along his arm. "There?" She pointed.

"That's a satellite."

"Really? You can see satellites?"

"They're hard to get away from these days."

"Then I missed the shooting star."

He let his arm hand fall to her knee. "There will be another."

Across the water, close to the horizon, a tiny flame erupted. "What's that?"

Red squinted and chuckled. "That would be someone lighting their charcoal."

She laughed. "A verifiable cosmic event."

They watched the orange flare diminish until it disappeared.

"And where is Ernesto?"

Red said nothing.

"You don't know?"

"I . . . lost track."

"Do you even know if he's alive, for chrissakes?"

"Last I heard, he was living in a dumpster in Orlando. Dope got him. It's been . . . I guess it's been ten years." Red turned up his injured palm in the shadows and turned it down again. "Last time I saw him, I had to punch him out."

"You punched out your own son?"

Red sighed. "I hadn't seen or heard of him in at least a year. He showed up on the dock at something like eleven-thirty one night, out of his mind on crank, announced that he needed a thousand bucks, and that I was going to give it to him. We exchanged words about money and amphetamine-fueled filial piety and the next thing I knew, Ernesto pulled a knife on me. My own son. But a knife is a knife. I clocked him." Red flexed the fingers covering her knee. "He was always after me to treat him like I'd treat any other man."

"Sounds like that part worked out."

"Yeah."

They fell silent.

Hard by the boat, a fish jumped. Red glanced at the set. The rod couldn't have been straighter if it were in the rack.

"What about you?"

"What about me?"

"Kids?"

"I skipped that phase."

Red glanced her way in the darkness, then returned his gaze to the sky. "Nobody skips that phase."

Tipsy looked out over the reef. "It was a funny combination of exclusionary circumstances. Early on it looked like a trap. Later the right guy was not in evidence. After that it looked like a lot of work, and for what? Just to take part in the big crap shoot. Look what you—" She didn't finish the thought.

Red grunted.

"Plus, it's another mouth to feed. And besides, I always maintained the illusion that I came to this planet to do something else besides breed."

"Really? What else is there?"

"I don't know. How about politics?"

Red didn't think that was funny.

"Okay, fishing. How about fishing?"

"Now you're talking. . . ."

After a leisurely breakfast they weighed anchor and trolled a rhumb line to a waypoint some twenty miles southwest of Man of War Channel. Tipsy watched the world go by. Soundings were never more than twenty-five or thirty feet, often much more shoal than that, with the bottom perfectly visible, along with schools of fish, forests of coral, sea fans, vast banks of white sand, and the occasional shark. Schools of little fish seemed to prefer the shade beneath *Tunacide*, and sometimes it was as if they were all traveling together. There were wrecks, too, and every now and again an eddy would swirl past choked with weed, bits of driftwood, a plastic sandal or water bottle or styrofoam cup, a cooler lid, a dead gull, a snarl of monofilament.

Red caught a bonito on a strip of uncooked bacon. They anchored, and he cleaned and cooked the fish; they ate it for lunch. He surprised her by presenting a beet salad alongside the grilled strips of fish and the ubiquitous bottle of ice cold Kaliq beer. She'd never tasted anything like it.

They never motored at more than four knots, often much more slowly, and after a while it became apparent to Tipsy that Red was in no hurry to get where they were going.

At the waypoint Red took the wheel from the automatic pilot and steered southeasterly until they found the next waypoint, some twelve or thirteen miles southwest of the eastern mouth of the channel. From there he watched the depth sounder and zigzagged a visual course among sand ridges and coral heads until they raised a couple of markers.

"We'll gas up at Man of War Cay," Red told her. "There's one grocery and one restaurant. We'll take a night off from our cooking, restock the dairy products, get a night's sleep dockside, and start the crossing to Albert Town bright and early. Weather permitting."

"How far is it?"

Red moved his chin at the chart. "You tell me."

Two minutes later, and not without a touch of pride, she told him it was eighty-five nautical miles.

"A straight shot," Red said. "But there's shipping and a little smuggling, too. It's best done by daylight. We can take it at eight knots, depending on sea conditions. It's a blue water passage, so a good night's sleep is in order. By the time you're ten miles east of Man of War?" He moved his chin in that direction. "The bottom has dropped well over a mile."

"Wow," was all Tipsy could say.

"If you're going to get seasick, that's where it'll happen."

"I'm not going to get seasick."

Red glanced at her. "You should try some of that aloe vera cream. From the green tube. You're showing a little color."

Tipsy frowned.

"Did you put on more sun block?" Red inquired tenderly.

Tipsy almost scowled, but she turned her back on him before she could do so. It had been a very long time since she could describe herself as smitten.

"I haven't seen old Perry Joseph in a long time," Red said. "It's years since I've been out here. I wonder if he's still alive?"

After his third query on channel sixteen, identifying only the vessel, Red got response. "Switch to 21."

Red switched to 42. "Talk to me."

"This is not an unexpected pleasure," a voice stated flatly.

Red's demeanor went serious, but his reply was neutral. "It is to me."

"What's your LOA?"

"Fifty-five feet."

"Take a side-tie behind the paint shed," came the reply. "Past the crane dock."

Red nodded but said nothing. The other correspondent clicked his mic off and on and back off again. Transmission over.

Red thoughtfully clipped his microphone to the side of the radio.

"What's that about?" Tipsy said.

"Not sure," Red said. "You mind waiting aboard while I find out?"

"Do I have a choice?"

"No."

"Then I'll wait aboard while you find out."

"Thank you."

There were all kinds of boats moored in and around Man of War Cay, in all kinds of condition. Some of them looked like they'd not sailed in years and might never sail again. Others looked as if they'd been delivered straight from a boat show. Still others looked like they'd seen every port in the world, with more to come.

When Red came back he looked less than carefree.

"Well?" she asked after he'd gotten aboard.

"Somebody asking after Charley," Red said. "About two weeks ago."

"Are they still around?"

Red lifted a shoulder.

"Who were they?"

"All Perry Joe knows is what they weren't."

"Which is?"

"Cops, feds, Interpol."

"Just plain folks." Tipsy studied him. "Does that make sense?"

Red chewed his lip. "Yes, unfortunately."

"It's a big ocean," she said after a while.

"True story. Stupid," he added abruptly, and he turned off the Send switch on *Tunacide*'s VIS unit. Since the engine wasn't running the unit wasn't sending, but still. He tapped the side of its chassis with a fingertip. "So why here," he said, after a little consideration. "Of all places."

"Why not?"

Red nodded thoughtfully. "If they started from Rum Cay, this would be a place to look." He waved a hand without looking. "They've got more facilities here than most places."

Tipsy raised an eyebrow. From where she stood, the place didn't look like much. "Looking," she said, "for Charley?"

Now Red studied her. "Who else?"

"For us, that's who else."

Red nodded.

Tipsy narrowed her eyes. "The logbook," she said, "has been in your possession."

Red nodded. "It still is. And, to answer your question, nobody else has seen it."

"More to the point, who else knows about Albert Town?"

Red shook his head. "Nobody."

Across the channel lay a schooner, though Tipsy wouldn't know to call it that. She, the schooner, was eighty feet long and one hundred years old. Her decks were unfinished teak and her brightwork was oiled teak and the rest of her was painted black or forest green. Her spars were finished natural and her sails were neatly flaked into well-stitched canvas covers, also green. Her standing rig was taut and her running rigging was all modern synthetic rope and winches had been added. Between her main and fore masts rose an amply proportioned house, with windows and lace curtains and flared bronze dorad vents. Everything about her was perfect except for her name.

"*Laburnam Villa*. What kind of name is that?"

"There's all kinds of vessels," Red said, "and all kinds of people naming them." His eye fell on the chart. "Let's have a drink."

Tipsy continued to study the schooner. "How much does a boat like that cost?"

"How much do you have?" Red said, not looking up from the chart. "And then some."

A spout of water erupted from *Laburnam Villa* amidships, about a foot above the waterline.

"What's that?"

"Bilge pump," Red said.

"It leaks?"

"Wooden boats leak." Red smiled and added, "Darling."

"And *Tunacide*," she asked after a pause. "Does *Tunacide* leak?"

Red nodded. "Not yet."

They fueled *Tunacide*, bought some groceries, and ate conch fritters ashore in a deserted cafe. Red introduced Tipsy to nobody. At first light next morning, *Tunacide* cast off.

Within an hour, as Red had promised, they were motoring over a mile of blue water.

FORTY

AT LEAST SHE DOESN'T THINK I'M THE KIND OF GUY LAYING BACK IN CON-
versation, over the evening meal or deep into the cocktails, just waiting for
her to say something stupid so he can pounce, humiliate, deprecate.

Just last night she told me, "Quentin always said, you want to have a hot
time with a guy? Go for the older ones. You'll never look back. You know
what?" She snuggles up to me. "He was right."

When I was in my twenties I figured, a girl in her twenties? Forget it.
Take this dime, call me in ten years. Girl needs experience, seasoning, a
trip around the block. Three trips.

Damn. A waterspout. Innocuous black cloud. Low and long and southeast. Steady on. I haven't seen a waterspout in . . .

Abruptly, the temperature began to drop. "Hey," he yelled down the
companionway, "Batten the forward skylight and all the portholes." A
glance at the barometer showed a falling needle. "Never mind the stuff on
deck. I'll get the stuff on deck."

He touched up the autopilot and hustled astern. Bait bucket, ice chest, net,
gaff—into the locker, hasp pegged shut. The wind picked up and brought
with it an ominous whistling, which, in turn, rose in pitch. He unclipped the
more expensive of the two rods, a Casa Vigía model, and backed into the
house to sit facing aft in the pilot's upholstered swivel chair while he reeled in
several hundred feet of wire just as quickly as he could turn the crank. He was
wondering whether this was a best use of his time when the jig jumped the
transom, bounced off the flybridge ladder, and the wind hit.

He'd put *Tunacide* to steaming southerly of the spout's apparent
course. But the wind knocked the bow north and laid her on her port
beam. Everything on the foredeck, suntan lotion, a chair, a towel, a pair
of sunglasses, a cocktail glass, a cop novel, disappeared. Red dropped the
rod to the deck between the pedestal of the command chair and the console, and overrode the steering. "Hang on!" he shouted over his shoulder,
perhaps unnecessarily. "Forget everything else and hang on!" He could
hardly hear himself above the screech. A wave reared up. *Tunacide* took
it head on. The boat breasted the face at a steep angle. A protracted concatenation of crashes arose from the galley. Behind him Tipsy did a good
thing, grasping the railings at either side of the companionway and pick-

ing her feet up, so that she was gimbaled, as it were, but even so she
became weightless and airborne as the bow dropped into the trough.
When the stern rose to follow, *Tunacide*'s screws rattled in thin air, and the
engines raced. The eighty-pound Danforth anchor snapped its gasket as if
it were a length of string and became airborne, hovering above the bow
as if weightless. When she buried her nose in the bottom of the trough
and came to a near standstill, the anchor came back and smote a fine hole
right through the deck just aft of the windlass. Now a wall of wind-borne
water plus a sea engulfed the bow and perhaps a foot of brine washed over
the deck, fore to aft. Water poured into the hole in the forward compartment, and as the thickness scoured amidships and rebounded off the
taffrail, put about six inches of itself over the raised threshold of the cabin
door, and down the companionway steps, wetting Tipsy to her knees,
while flooding up to the footrest of the captain's chair.

And just like that it was over. The shadow that had darkened the boat
fled into the northeast, leaving *Tunacide* bathed in pure sunlight. The
whistling diminished until it was indistinguishable from the sounds of
three bilge pump diaphragms, the two Caterpillar V8s, and water pouring
from every scupper.

Red turned to watch the weather go, and saw that the second rod and
reel had gone with it. A pawnshop purchase, its loss didn't command much
regret. Easy come, thoroughly dramatic go. It was his own fault, too. He'd
been caught out. A mere week, cruising the Great Bahama Bank, drinking
and eating, fishing and V-berthing, navel- and stargazing, these must have
reduced his vigilance to mush. This here now is the open sea, stupid, and
all that your non-vigilance has cost you to date is the number two rig, a hole
in your bow, and a deal of moisture below decks. Considering the broad
scope of the possibilities, so far, so cheap. Ready to tighten up?

The wind dropped to a steady ten knots and the sea re-cohered into a
long swell, both out of the southeast. Red was mindful of the conditions,
but what stood out was Tipsy's reaction at being caught clinging to the
companionway handrails, with the water rising up to her knees and
throwing capfuls higher than that.

She had grinned. A mad, maniacal grin, fit to suit any adventurer.

She's enjoying this, Red realized.

All the years he'd been in the Caribbean, nothing like that waterspout had
happened to him, and no woman he might have been with would have handled it with such equanimity. She doesn't know enough to be frightened,
Red told himself. But all she said was, "What about that hole, forward?"

She was still grinning. Red had seen this grin before. It was the expression of the thrill felt by the natural sailor. She could have been a kid, who,

taking the tiller for the first time, abruptly realized herself completely in charge of her manifest destiny, and conning like she'd been doing it all her life.

Not one of his kids, Red adduced sourly, no tiller for them. No rudder, either. Rudderless children. Red had no faith at all in psychiatry, but at one point Carmen convinced him to take their daughter to a shrink. After just a couple of sessions the chick had taken Red aside and asked him if he'd ever heard of the reality principle. You mean like, he'd responded, do your job or die? Well, she'd frowned, the textbook definition refers to a person's awareness of and adjustment to the world around her so as to assure herself of the ultimate satisfaction of her instinctual needs. It sounds like you're talking about happiness, Red had said. Yes, the shrink had agreed, your daughter is unhappy. I paid two hundred bucks so you could tell me that my unhappy daughter is unhappy? Red exploded. Things went downhill from there. Point being, this woman, Tipsy, is her brother's sister—she likes being at sea.

"Now you've seen a waterspout," he told her.

"Is that what that was?"

"I've not seen one in a while, myself. And I've never seen one that close up."

"Is it possible to get closer?"

"You go ahead," Red said, affecting a frank invitation, "I'll wait here."

They laughed.

"Let me patch that hole before we try it again. Sit here and let Otto steer. You see another one of those things? Take the wheel, cut Otto loose, and point her southeast of the disturbance." He glanced at the GPS display. "Otherwise, steady on at eight knots and ten degrees."

Tipsy restored the course and reset the pilot. "Tell you what, Skipper. Do your thing topside. I'll take charge below."

"Where have you been all my life?" Red responded, smiling despite the hole in his boat.

"San Francisco," replied his wringing-wet crew.

After retrieving and properly belaying the anchor, he used a pair of duckbill pliers to break off a few fiberglass splinters around the perimeter of the hole in the foredeck, pitching them overboard as they came away. When the wound was reasonably debrised he took its measure with a steel tape. Then he stepped below, laid out a rectangle on a scrap of 3/4" marine plywood, and hacked it out with a saber saw. Then he ran a 1/2" round-over bit in a router around one perimeter of the four newly cut edges, picked up the sawdust with a one-gallon shop vac, and painted the plywood with quick-drying primer.

The third or fourth time he headed aft to retrieve tools, Tipsy had the galley shipshape. Though the carpet was squishy.

Who says it has to be wrong girl, wrong time, wrong place? Red caught himself wondering.

He reappeared on deck with the scrap of plywood and a five-gallon bucket full of tools, uncoiling a dropcord as he went. Tipsy flashed him a smile from the bridge and held up both hands. Easy as pie, her gesture seemed to say. A skyward glance told him that the weather had reverted to the Caribbean's beatitudinal custom: a bright sun crowning a cobalt sky, cumulo-nimbus parading westward, the odd unthreatening thunderhead, southeasterly swells somewhat less than majestic, stately one might say, maybe thirty seconds apart, parading under ten knots of breeze gusting to fifteen. Air temperature was probably back up to seventy degrees, not yet returned to its customary seventy-five or eighty after the depression of the passing cell. The foredeck had already dried. The rest of the passage promised to be fine indeed. We'll still raise Long Cay before nightfall, Red thought, as he strapped on a pair of knee pads. He knelt stiffly at the hole in the foredeck and tried the painted scrap. It overlapped the hole by about two inches all the way round. That would do for now, and maybe forever. He flipped the scrap over, rounded edges down. He swabbed the deck around the hole with a rag soaked in acetone. Retrieving a caulk gun from the bucket, he followed the hole's perimeter with a fat bead of white adhesive. The caulk gun squeaked like a tern. Completing the circuit he sat back on his calves, his back to the bridge. A little creaky, ain't we, old man, he told himself. I'm a goddamn inch shrunk, from my prime, comparably slower, and three weeks under the wheel of one or another driveaway cars transporting heads and broads coast to coast and back again didn't help. Time was, I could heave an engine up and out of the hold, let alone a transmission. I could catch a punch with the right hand as I was delivering one with the left. No longer. These days I'm set back on me wiles, arrgh. He grimaced. Like that's changed worth a shit. I could be rolling bocce balls in some retirement home if I'd played my cards—card—right. But here I am. Sixty-four with nothing but boatloads of t-shirts and weird people calling my shots from far away. A hole in the boat? No problem. But far away people calling my shots?

Fuck 'em.

He laid a bead of caulk around the perimeter of the painted plywood. Then he twirled two diagonally opposite corners of the plywood between his two middle fingers and dropped it over the caulked wound in the foredeck. Nice placement if he did say so, nearly parallel to the centerline of the boat. With a slight wiggle of the piece he gradually brought all of his weight to bear on the patch, until caulk oozed from its entire perimeter. It would make a good seal.

Now he sat back on his calves again. The lower back hurt and no joke. This lower back thing was one of the reasons he'd sold his beloved *Barbarosso*, a gaff-rigged ketch of some sixty-three feet, because, even though she was set up for it, he could no longer single-hand her. Getting that main gaff aloft was one thing; getting it down in weather was something else. Even the mizzen gaff could be a misery. The last time he'd taken her out alone he'd torqued his back while merely hauling on a jib sheet. He'd brought her in under tremendous pain, pain like he'd never known, way beyond a knife wound or a clout on the head for two examples, or even of that to be recalled from his foot having been caught between a tumblehome and a bullrail. That foot still hurt. The back had become unpredictably unreliable. . . .

But with a woman like Tipsy a man might go sailing again. He pulled a screw gun from the bucket, inserted a combination countersink and pilot bit into its quick-change chuck, and bored a chamfered hole through one corner of the plywood patch. Then he switched bits and loosely anchored the corner with a galvanized 1-1/4" #2 tulip-head Torx screw, not driving it all the way home. Switching bits, he touched up the alignment and sank a pilot hole through the corner diagonally opposite the first one. He changed back to the pilot bit and proceeded to eyeball an evenly-spaced series of chamfered holes around the perimeter of the patch. After he'd vacuumed the dust and chips, he bladed a dab of the adhesive caulk over each hole with a one-inch putty knife.

By now Red's back had stiffened considerably, and various aches were stabbing along the muscles parallel to his spine. He emptied the tools onto the deck, inverted the bucket, and sat down on it.

Teach Tipsy all this stuff, he was thinking. She's a quick study. My knowledge and her natural sagacity, my experience and her young back, my wisdom and the agility of her youth . . .

As he exchanged the counterbore for the Torx bit, he gave a thought to its identical twin, resting these several months at the bottom of the sea some forty or fifty miles north of Havana. Torx bit, your innocuous ilk got me into this pickle in the first place. He thought about it for a moment. I'm no longer sure how I got into this pickle.

Goddamn technology. He triggered the screw gun while grasping the keyless chuck, to make sure the quick-change chuck was tight. Another ouch for the not quite healed palm of his left hand, and is a skipper's sacrifices never done? He pinched four or five screws out of the mouth of their canvas bag. The tip of one of them stung him under the nail of his forefinger, drawing a tiny bead of blood. Sweat dropped off the end of his nose. Hey, man, he reminded himself as he drove a screw into an unscrewed corner of the patch, you could have lived differently. He drove a fourth screw diagonally across the rectangle from the third one. You could have gone to graduate school and got that degree in civil engineering. He snugged down each of the two anchoring screws. You actually went and looked at Clemson University, in Clemson, South Carolina. What a shithole, and, even at so great a distance of years, you shudder to recall it. He drove the fifth screw through the middle of the port-side edge. The year, I don't remember. It was in the twentieth century. A freckle on a noseeum's thorax, historically speaking. He considered the next screw. A time so distant, they didn't even have Torx screws. He drove it. Back then they still used cupped galvanized four-penny nails to hang drywall, for chrissakes. Can you beat that? He drove a screw. They had fluorescent lights, though. Those fluorescent lights I do remember. Row upon row of them, and how they buzzed over grids of all-in-one flip-lid chair-desks, varnish long gone, their metal the color of the type on Death's business card. Steam radiators along the wall below the sills of mullioned windows—it gives a man the willies to recall the scene. But to have lived it? A dodged bullet for sure. Single-glaze windows: cold in winter and hot in summer; dirt-dobbers deceased on the dusty sill; and linoleum floors, brown streaked with green. Walls painted an irreproducible gray, same color as the radiators. But you figured that one out. He started another screw in another countersunk hole. They just took all the five-gallon buckets of leftover paint and poured them into one fifty-five-gallon drum and painted the whole school with the result. The engineering school, anyway. So now, that one spun out. Cammed out, is the proper term; nobody but engineers ever use it. He backed out the screw and pitched it overboard. Saved them a whole lot of money, probably so they could paint the English department pink. Another screw. Maybe they sank the surplus dough into the big bamboo demonstration slide rule hanging over the blackboard. Whole semesters were dedicated to slide rules and their logarithmic scales. Son of a bitch must have been two feet high and ten feet long. Another entire technology blown away by progress. Gone as the glaciers from Glacier National Park. Sailboats remain. Where does that leave you? Screwing. Year in, year out, screwing. Screw or be screwed, and there's your reality principle. Take calculators, for instance. Another spinout, and the Torx tip slipped off the screw head and dug a nice little divot into the deck. Not the plywood patch, but the deck. Luck of the afflicted. Another screw. Teach Tipsy to do this. Technology will probably change before I get around to it. There will never be enough time. It's thoughts like these that slowed my progress to this pretty pass. It was right there. Where? Get this one right. He drove it right. On the bulletin board. A plaque. How do you forget another man's nightmare? Same way you remember it? Good answer, even if it's a question. I got another. Shoot. How do you remember it? He wiped caulk off the Torx tip with a rag. One man's dream is another man's nightmare? He folded the rag over the caulk and swabbed his forehead with the flat of it. Nothing but questions. He dropped the rag and pinched up some screws. Even though the school was deserted, job placement want-ads covered the engineering department's bulletin board, all of them yellowed and desiccated, flyblown and brittle, left over from the previous spring. General Electric. The Navy. IBM. Lockheed. Boeing. FoMoCo. The Georgia Department of Transportation needed two civil engineers. But it was the plaque above the bulletin board. The plaque and the obituary tacked next to it. He drove a screw. Its head sank a quarter of an inch into the plywood. *This Bulletin Board The Gift of Henry C. Greenly: The finest product this school has to offer.* The next screw was a half-inch longer than its mates. He tossed it overboard. The obituary explained how Hank Greenly had retired after dedicating his entire career as a civil engineer to a single eleven-mile stretch of freeway between Wilson, North Carolina and a town called Pittsboro. Hank Greenly shepherded the project from its inception through funding, through the ins and outs of permitting, environmental impact review, drawings, revisions, plancheck, more revisions, Title 19 energy calcs, seismic calcs, wetstamps, submittals and approvals, the evictions, relocations and compensations throughout the drainage and right-of-way, construction, an incompetent subcontractor, bad weather, the accidental maiming of a pan driver, an executive bribery prosecution, a plea copped with no admission of guilt, three cases of snake bite, a rabid skunk that chased a visiting Congressman, rejection of wet fill, of frozen fill, of substandard concrete, the pre-computer wording and triplication of change orders . . . One overpass, four each of on- and off-ramps, a boat ramp, six railroad bridges and two dams the scope of work included, plus eleven miles of four lanes with landscaped medians, all of it built over swamps and quicksand. Every yard of earth had to be removed and replaced with dry fill and compacted. Soup to nuts, it took twenty-four years to complete that project—at which point Hank Greenly retired. That eleven miles of four-lane highway comprised Hank Greenly's entire professional career, and when it was done, he was done. By then he'd outlived his parents, his only sibling, and his wife and kid who were T-boned by a logging truck two miles from Bun Level, North Carolina, while he was attending a marathon weekend contract arbitration in Charlotte. A fisherman noticed Hank one day, a few months after he retired, standing on one of the two dams built, it was rumored, solely to protect the governor's summer home some eighteen miles downstream. Hank was staring down its spillway for no apparent reason. It did have a nice, curvilinear sweep to it, shot in with plum bob and chain long before the advent of the laser theodolite.

Nobody saw him again. His retirement lasted eleven months. In the end a massive coronary killed him in his chair in front of his television. He liked old Westerns, the real oaters. The stress of retirement can't be overestimated, as someone stipulated at the funeral. And it just so happened that Red Means had worked on that project one summer, the year before its completion, three years before he decided not to attend engineering college, or any college at all. June, July, and August Red had worked that job, greasing all the big machinery, fixing flats on motorgraders, retreading dozers, but he had no memory of a Hank or Henry Greenly. It seemed almost impossible that they wouldn't have met at least once. . . .

There's no shortage of disturbing stories, but, Red said to the plywood patch, that was one of the most disturbing I'd heard, up to that point in my callow youth. The legion of bummer stories has been thoroughly checked, cross-indexed and stapled to the inside of the vault of one's brain by the intervening years, of course. But, in the event, a clapped-out pick-up truck couldn't carry him away from South Carolina fast enough. He didn't stop pushing until he ran out of road, three weeks later, at a seawall with about twenty people hanging around waiting for the sun to set. He inquired out the truck window as to what the big deal was. A pretty girl with a brilliant smile, standing barefoot in a sun dress astride a salt-rusted bicycle with no gears and balloon tires told him that, vis-à-vis sunsets, it was all about having a daily routine; she welcomed him to Key West; and she handed him a joint. Her name was Carmen. . . .

"Red?"

He looked up, the brim of his hat occluding a full view of her.

"You all right?"

"Sure," Red assured her. He looked down at the plywood patch. All the screws had been driven. He'd even dragged the dampened butt of the tapered handle of the putty knife around the patch's perimeter, by way of fairing the caulk squeezed out of the tightened joint. All that remained was to flush a dab of caulk over each screw head, let it dry, and repaint it. Tomorrow, maybe.

"Red?"

"What?"

"It's hot out here."

"True story."

"You sure you're okay?" She straddled his lap, facing him. The bucket titled. The putty knife fell from his hand as he caught her.

He squinted. Her complexion was tanning nicely, and she was smiling. "Yeah," he said. "I'm way okay."

"Prove it," she said, and she kissed him.

FORTY-ONE

THEY WRANGLED THE DINGHY INTO THE WATER. IT WAS AN OLD PLYWOOD job, glassed from one end to the other, and its outboard, despite being less than five years old, wouldn't start. After filling the clear morning air with the fumes of uncombusted fuel Red boused the motor off the transom, in order to disencumber themselves of its weight, and cursed it. "I bought this bastard so it would haul my ass around, not so I could haul its ass around," he muttered bitterly, and set about rowing them in.

They were away early but beads of sweat were rolling off Red's face before they'd made a hundred yards. He rested the oars, tied a kerchief around his head, removed his shirt, drank some water and set to pulling again, while Tipsy coated his back and shoulders with sun block. He faced backwards to their direction of travel, exposing his back to the morning sun, and the sweat gleamed on his freckled shoulders. Up front the shark's tooth, its gold culet dangling from its gold chain, swung in and out of the tangle of gray and coppery hair that boiled off his chest.

They were in the lee of the southern tip of Long Cay and protected from the current. But a decent swell had them up and down along the line of their forward progress. Occasionally the oars brought up bundles of tape grass, radiant greens and violets shooting along its lengths. Red periodically shipped the oars to shed it, taking the occasion to rest from his labor. Though his arms were thick and did not shrink from their task, he and Tipsy had remained awake much of the night, poring over Charley's logbook and letters, even going so far as to spill what was left of a glass of rum over the largest-scale chart of Long Cay they'd been able to find in Key West, 1:3,000,000. "Mayaguana Passage," he'd insisted. "No mention of Long Cay or Crooked Island or even the Acklins."

"You'd think I was trying to buy a vibrator at the Vatican," she grumbled.

"You don't need no fucking vibrator," he assured her. "Mayaguana Passage."

As he'd swallowed more rum, Red groused about the comparable scale available on the rather expensive computer chart on his on-board navigation system, which displayed more or less the same data as the paper chart, which was to say, hardly any data at all. This was an out-of-the-way place.

They'd brought along that chart as well as much of the package Red had taken off the wreck of the *Vellela Vellela*, Charley's relevant letters to Tipsy, a hand-held GPS, and the bearing compass. Athwart the dinghy were also a pick, a shovel, posthole diggers, a machete and a bush hook, plus snorkle, fins, mask, with two six-packs of Kalik beer and a gallon of water on ice in a cooler. The second time he took a break from rowing, Red snapped the cap off a bottle with his teeth and spat it into the Caribbean.

"That's the most macho bullshit thing I've seen since George Bush landed on that aircraft carrier," Tipsy observed. "Without a doubt."

Red offered her a sip. She declined. He downed it at one go and flung the bottle skyward. "If I had the shotgun," he growled, "I'd blast that sucker to shards, just like we did your cellphone."

"That was very satisfying." Tipsy admitted. "But I'd still like to know how Quentin is doing."

"You told me he doesn't have a cellphone, (a), and, (b), I'm telling you again that cellphones don't work out here anyway. Sit back and enjoy it. Soon enough, technology will pinch out the silence of wide-open spaces."

"Still, if you were to be blasting beer bottles with a shotgun, every bounty-hunter within twenty miles would know we're here."

"Not to worry." Red wiped his mouth and took up the oars. "Today, we're all by our lonesome. Unless you count ghosts."

"What, no casino?"

"Just the Big Casino."

"Is that the same as Manifest Destiny?"

"Did you know that the Bahama casinos brag of the highest payoff in the world?"

"What's that mean? They let you keep your pants?"

"True story," Red chuckled. He glanced over his shoulder. "Let us review our first instruction."

Tipsy opened *Vellela Vellela*'s logbook to the place marked by a paper clip, already rusted by salt air.

> . . . *don't forget to allow for something like ten years' migration of magnetic variation. Tonight, from this anchorage, I can see the mouth of the creek. Oddly enough,* Vellela *is anchored on the exact back bearing of the vector from the creek to the middle of the entrance to Man of War Channel—277° True. . . .*

The page reflected the glare of the sun with great intensity. Tipsy lifted her eyes from it. Red had carefully set stern and bow anchors so that the bearing to the center of Man of War Channel, as determined by GPS, ran right through the axis of *Tunacide* and the rode of its two anchors. He'd given a lot of scope to the rode of the stern anchor, which lay toward

Long Cay, and buoyed it with a fender. A straight line between it and the stern of the boat accurately reflected the bearing to the mouth of Man of War Channel.

Now Red shipped his oars and fiddled with the hand-held GPS until it had found three satellites and made decisions about where it was. "Hm," he said, peering over his half-lenses. "It's not always this bad, but look at this." He tilted the little screen and shaded it with his hand. "The little dart is us. This wavy line is the northwest curve of Long Cay." He pointed over the bow.

She followed his finger, studied the beach, then studied the screen. "According to this device," she realized aloud, "we are about a hundred yards up on the beach."

"Hard aground. And which direction is that beach, the real beach, over the bow?"

"East, more or less."

"That's correct. And where is it on this screen?"

She looked up. "West?"

"That's what is known in the trade as a degraded position," Red said. "Technology, schmecnology." He switched off the unit, dropped it into the canvas tote bag, followed by his glasses. "But this looks good for a start," he added, backing one oar sufficient to jockey the dinghy onto the vector given by the fender and the swim ladder of *Tunacide*. "Two seventy-seven degrees true, straight back through *Tunacide*, bears directly on Man of War Channel. Plus eight degrees forty-five minutes West variation. Plus ten years times six minutes equals one whole degree's worth of annual increase—correct?"

Tipsy's finger, following the figures through a column of addition on the margin of the chart, arrived at the total. "Two eighty-six."

"Have a look. Hand me that anchor."

She passed along a little salt-rusted ten-pound Danforth with its yellow hank of polypropylene rode, and Red dropped it in the bow behind him. Tipsy took up the yellow bearing compass, and sighted along it.

Sighted along its rubber boss and a notch molded into the compass housing, toward the buoy and the stern of *Tunacide*.

"What's she bear?"

"Two hundred and . . . These marks are two degrees?"

"Five."

"Three hundred and . . ."

"Come on, come on," said Red impatiently.

Tipsy told him to shut up. But each time she lowered the compass to read it, she fouled the result.

"Goddamn it," Red said, "give me that—"

She swiped it out of his reach. "I suppose you hatched out reading compasses."

"And that I did," Red growled. "Arrgh . . ."

"Hold your water. I'll get the hang of it."

"That reminds me." Red stood up in the stern, rocking the dinghy only moderately, unzipped his shorts, and arced a stream of retired Kalik over the side.

"If you did that the other way," Tipsy said, and holding the compass at arm's length, one eye closed and the other squinting, "I could sight right under it."

Red zipped up. "Be just like sailing into St. Louis." He stretched his shoulders and resumed his seat. "What's the goddamn answer?"

"I think it's two eighty-two."

As the boat moved to port, the compass needle moved to starboard. Backing one or another of the oars Red jockeyed them to and fro until Tipsy got the hang of the compass.

"Goddamn it. . . ."

"You got no water to hold," she reminded him. "So relax."

"That reminds me." Red repeated his performance with a fresh bottle of beer. "Damn, that's good." He smacked his lips and heaved the second empty toward *Tunacide*. "I hope we don't run out."

"You've got ten to go."

"Like I said."

"Two eighty-six. We're there."

Red studied *Tunacide*. The white fender, maybe a quarter of a mile to seaward of the dinghy, bobbed up and down in close apposition to the center of *Tunacide's* transom, as if eager to sketch a line there. "So far so good." He lifted both his legs and neatly spun a half-circle on the plywood seat. "Now for the mouth of the creek." He took up the binoculars and, with a glance aft, squared his shoulders toward *Tunacide* and slowly glassed the shoreline of Long Cay. "Too far off," he muttered. He handed Tipsy the binoculars and turned to take up the oars.

When Tipsy lifted her legs to turn forward she nearly upset the boat.

"No woman should ever forget," Red said, regarding her as he rowed, "that her ass is her center of gravity."

"I'm not going to dignify that with an answer."

"Fine. Just don't undignify things by capsizing us."

They rowed another quarter of a mile.

"Well?" Red growled. He was wringing wet, the dew rag was saturated, and the scar in his palm felt like it was on fire. "What could it have taken to bring along a pair of gloves?" he asked nobody in particular.

"Foresight," came the prompt answer. "For some reason," Tipsy added, binoculars to her face. "I can't tell what I'm looking at."

Red cranked the dinghy through a half-circle and dropped the oars. "Gimme." He studied the coastline. "Aha." He handed the binoculars back to her and pointed. "There."

He spun the bow back toward the beach and pulled steady and strong. She corrected him occasionally, but, watching their wake and the bigger boat, Red kept their course remarkably straight. Soon they heard surf. Tipsy lowered the binoculars. Red looked over the gunwale. "There's a little current." He dipped his fingers over the side and tasted them. "Fresh water."

Tipsy smiled. "You think?"

He looked left and right, then laughed. There was beach on either side of them. They had rowed straight into the mouth of the creek. "

"It's a stream. Just like Charley said."

Red frowned. "I think it's too big." He looked over the side. "He said that he and Cedric walked their dingy up it."

"But they had a thousand pounds of chain aboard."

". . . which would swamp this thing. They were still navigable. Still afloat."

"Maybe it was a bigger dinghy?"

"Maybe this is all bullshit," Red replied darkly. He gave the oars a few powerful strokes. "Look over the side. You think you could touch?"

She looked. "No. But it's so hot, I'd love to try."

"Watch the compass." Red continued to row against the mild current of the freshet. The beach turned into brush, the creek narrowed and the brush closed above them. Two hundred yards up the creek, "Whoa," Tipsy said. "Look." She showed him the compass, carefully holding it level. "North used to be that way."

"Boxing." They exchanged glances. "So it's not bullshit." He peered over the side. "That's a lot of fucking chain. It's ten feet deep here. Maybe the tide's in," he added. "What would it have taken to check the tide table? Don't answer that."

The creek had deepened as it narrowed, the vegetation nourished by it now provided shade. Red pulled the dinghy to the south bank and grabbed the branch of a casuarinas to hold the dinghy against the current. The needle of the compass spun, meaningless in its glycerin.

Red thought about it. "After he got off parole Charley saw Cedric exactly once, to the best of my knowledge. It was in Key West. Cedric was living aboard a wreck of a borrowed boat and drinking a fifth of vodka every day."

"That's a bit much," Tipsy acknowledged.

"Even though they'd been friends for a long time, the scene didn't interest Charley. He went back to Miami and found me. I fixed him up with the job in Guadeloupe, and that was it for Charley and Cedric."

"Cedric figures in a lot of letters," Tipsy agreed. "Up to a point."

Red cocked an ear. "That's a Bahamas finch." They listened. "Nice bird." He shifted his grip on the casuarinas. "So my money says, if that really is a trove of chain down there, Cedric and Charley parked it at least twenty years ago, before Charley went to prison."

"So the ten years of annual increase is just there to give us a bearing?"

"Maybe. Or to raise a flag for those in the know." Red looked upstream, then downstream. "Twenty years of hurricanes and erosion." The starboard bow of the dinghy gently touched the north bank. They both looked over the port side. The bottom looked like scoured clay. A couple of feet above it, two little fish pointed upstream, holding their own against the current.

"Sheepshead minnows," Red said. "Good bait."

"Red?" Tipsy asked. "What if you wanted to dig a hole down there, bury something in it, and cover it up?"

Red shook his head. "You'd have to caisson the fucker."

"Which means—?"

"You sink a culvert or an open-ended box—or form it with pilings and a pile driver or, god forbid, a sledgehammer. After you pump it out, you can excavate inside it."

"To keep the water from ruining your every move?"

"Yes. Under the circumstances, it's completely impractical."

"Yes." She looked around. "But Charley was here."

"He described it well enough."

"So they just dumped their chain here and left. In the intervening years . . ."

"Nature covered it up," Red finished for her.

Tipsy slapped her shoulder. "What's that?"

"Noseeums," Red said. "They're one of the reasons nobody lives here anymore."

"Dammit." Tipsy slapped herself again. "How come they aren't eating you?"

"They are eating me."

"Well?" She slapped herself twice.

"Well what?"

"How come you aren't slapping yourself silly?" She slapped herself. "Like I am?"

Red shrugged. "Because I don't give a shit."

"Let go of that bush. Get us out of here."

"What about—"

"Turn loose. Let's go down to the beach and cogitate this over a beer."

"I'm your man." Red released the branch and the dinghy began to drift toward the beach, Red fending off the embankments with an oar. Soon enough, the sounds of mildly breaking surf reached their ears.

The creek broke out of the brush, shoaling as it fanned across the tidal flat. Red beached the dinghy, stacked their tools and supplies ashore, made a lean-to of the little vessel and its oars, its hull towards the sun, so that it threw a little shade.

Tipsy dropped her shorts and halter top to the sand. "I'll be right back." She waded into the creek up to her knees and fell sideways into it. "It's cold!" she gasped when she surfaced. "It's great!"

"Spring-fed," Red said. As if to himself he added, "So maybe the tide is out." He sat down in the shadow of the dinghy and retrieved a beer from the cooler. By the time Tipsy came back ashore, droplets of water running along her goose flesh, Red had exchanged an empty bottle for a full one. He admired her as, facing the sun with her eyes closed, she arched her back and wrung water out of her hair.

"Beer?" He tendered the newly opened bottle.

"Just a sip." She drained half of it. "Damn," she said, lowering the bottle, "that's delicious."

"It won't put you on your ass, either." Red pulled a third bottle from the cooler. "Not so much alcohol. Perfect for the tropics."

"I'll say." She handed over the empty, and he dropped it into the cooler.

"What," she said, "no skeet practice?"

Red frowned. "Hell, no. Look around. This place is pristine. I aim to help keep it that way."

"Unless you count the acid reflux due to slavery," she pointed out.

"That was two hundred years ago. Out there," he pointed at the ocean, "a bottle goes to the bottom and makes a nice home for a hermit crab. Here," he indicated the beach, "it's just unsightly."

Tipsy joined him in the slip of shade. "I never figured you for being so sensitive about ecology."

"You have to excavate a lot of crust," Red agreed.

She took up the waterproof packet and withdrew its various materials. "Waterproofing the logbook I can understand," she said, setting it aside. "Likewise the boat papers, money, passport, which leaves us with these two pages torn from the Ricketts book."

Red considered them. "I'm amazed the mildew didn't get to them a long time ago."

"That aside, why did Charley keep them?"

"Because he named his boat for the creature described by them." Red lifted a shoulder. "Why else?"

As Tipsy read the two pages to herself, Red watched the surf.

"There's a passage you didn't read before."

Red squinted. "You mean that stuff about how it sails?"

"That's it."

Red continued to watch the surf. Tipsy read aloud.

> *The sailing ability of* Vellela *may be demonstrated in a broad shallow pool on the beach. George Mackie, one summer at Dillon Beach, designed an ingeniously simple experiment, using plastic bottle tops for controls (they sailed straight across the pool as good controls should). Computing the angle of arrival of* Vellela *on the opposite side, he found that the "best sailors" could tack as much as 63° to the left of the wind. Thus it would seem that the name "by-the-wind"* Vellela vellela Linnaeus *is a more musical name for this stray from the high seas.*

"Well?" she asked, somewhat gently.

Red raised his bottle to his lips. "Well what?"

"Sixty-three degrees," Tipsy said, "is what."

Red stuck his tongue into the mouth of the upturned bottle, stopping the flow of beer, and blinked.

"Sixty-three degrees," Tipsy repeated.

Red lowered the bottle and stared out to sea. A mile or so out, *Tunacide* rode to her anchors. Even from so far away, he could see a gull perched on the radar mast. The two pages of Ricketts fluttered in the breeze. Red looked at them. He looked far up the beach, where a pair of tall casuarinas leaned away from and back into the invisible air. "What wind conditions did Charley record, those days he was here?"

Tipsy opened the log to the paper clip. "Wind 10-15 knots southeast on day one . . ." She turned a page. "Ditto, day two." She turned a page. "Ditto, day three."

"Pretty standard Bahamian breeze." Red continued to stare. "Southeast," he repeated. "If you were a stickler, that'd be one thirty-five. Left of the wind, Ricketts says?"

Tipsy ran a finger down the printed page. "'. . . as much as sixty-three degrees to the left of the wind.'"

"Tacking," said Red. He knifed his left palm to the southeast. "So your *Vellela Vellela* is sailing into the wind, and tacking sixty-three degrees to the left of it." He tilted the hand. "That would be a starboard tack . . ."

"He said left," Tipsy objected.

"Quiet," Red said. "The tack is named for the side of the boat the wind is coming over. One thirty-five less sixty-three . . ." Red moved the hand counterclockwise. "Seventy-two degrees." The hand stopped. "East northeast."

"Seventy-two degrees," Tipsy repeated.

"True story," Red moved his hand ever so little. "Seventy-eight magnetic."

"Seventy-eight magnetic," Tipsy repeated, as if in wonder. "From where?" She looked past the hand at him.

He looked past his hand at her.

"From the buried chain," they said in unison.

Red stood and turned a half circle until he faced in a direction about halfway between the easterly meander of the little stream, on his right, and the beach on his left.

"But with the so-called boxing of the compass there," Tipsy said, "how do we find the correct direction?"

"Easy," Red said. "You get far enough away from it to establish the back bearing. Like we did with the boat." He squinted. "Seventy-eight plus one-eighty makes 258. Okay, that's the back bearing, and now we're on the north side of the creek. And so the question boils down to, how far do we proceed along this bearing? Or maybe there's another bearing by which we can establish a cocked hat? How about a star fix?" He turned so as to spit down wind. "Maybe we can look forward to the pleasure of blundering around out here in the dead of night."

They cogitated. Red paced down to the tideline and went wading. When he came back he sat down and screwed the butt of his beer bottle into the sand. "Read Charley's entry one more time."

She read it.

"That's got to be it," he said. "You see it?"

"No," she said promptly. "See what?"

"How much rode?"

". . . *so much barnacle-encrusted rode,*" she read.

"That's true," Red said. "But later. What they buried."

She skimmed the script. "'. . . 1,352 pounds of BBB five-eighths chain.' You mean, it's that many feet?"

Red shook his head. "I don't think so. It could be feet, yards, meters, fathoms, even cables. Although," he added, "that many cables would put us well to the east of Mayaguana Island in about 5,000 fathoms of blue water."

"So what are you saying? Thirteen fifty-two is not our number?"

"But why would it all be five-eighths?" Red inquired of the opposite bank of the creek. "How many anchors did he find?"

Tipsy glanced at the page. "A dozen?" She looked up. "What difference does that make?"

"Why would a dozen different anchors all have the same size rode? For that matter, twelve identical anchors wouldn't necessarily have the same size rode."

Tipsy said, annoyed, "I barely know what rode is."

"It's the length of chain or line that keeps your anchor connected to your boat and vice versa," Red said. "One thousand three hundred and fifty-two pounds. I'm supposed to know the answer to that."

"Answer to what?"

"Weight per length of a given size of chain. It's occasionally asked on the hundred-ton license exam. Used to be, anyway. Now all they probably ask you is how many stripes are on the American flag."

"Thirteen," Tipsy replied without a thought. "But we've already decided that Charley had no way to weigh thousands of pounds of chain and no reason to do so."

"The chain is there all right, but he never weighed it, and it doesn't make any difference. He worked backwards and imposed the number."

"Backwards from—?"

"The distance."

"So the actual amount of chain at the bottom of that creek—"

"—is irrelevant."

"Came the dawn," Tipsy nodded thoughtfully. "The birds of awareness are chirping, and I'm starting to believe you."

"I'm supposed to know the answer." Red studied the scar on the palm of his hand. "I'd hate to row all the way back to the boat just to look it up."

"You have a book?"

"I have books plural, and they're full of tables. But let me cogitate on it. Hand me a beer."

"You've got one."

"I want a cold one."

She handed him a cold one.

Red opened it with his teeth, spat the cap into the cooler, and took a long pull.

"Red . . ."

"Close the lid, you're letting calories in, and enjoy the weather."

She closed the lid and let the Bahamas envelope her. Breeze. Purling creek. Surf. A seagull banking over the beach. "Twenty-eight ounces a foot,"

Red said suddenly. "It's actually something like one point seven pounds, which is a little less than twenty-eight ounces, but I'll bet it's close enough for smuggling." He looked at her. "You know how I remember that number?"

"You used to smuggle chain?"

Red shook his head. "No money in chain. But there's twenty-eight ounces in eight-tenths of a kilogram of blow."

Tipsy stared at him. "If only the rest of reality had such a reasonable explanation," she finally said.

"You're onto something with that one. Prepare to calculate." He stood up and walked to a flat stretch of freshly smoothed sand. So the tide is falling, Red noted to himself. Aloud he asked, "One thousand three hundred and fifty-two?"

Tipsy had followed him with the paperwork. "Check."

"Feet." Red dropped to his knees and wrote the number large in the damp sand with his forefinger. "Always put in the units. 1,352 pounds of chain times sixteen ounces per pound . . ." Sand flew. ". . . 21,632. And that's ounces. Now. Divide 21,632 ounces by 28 ounces per foot." Eight yards along the beach from where he started Red announced, "Seven hundred and seventy-two point five seven. Call it 773. Feet."

"Seven seventy-three," she repeated. "Feet."

He sidled left. "Now we divide by three."

"Three?"

"Three feet per yard, otherwise known as one manly stride." He sidled right as the sand flew from his forefinger. "Two fifty-seven point five two. Let's round down this time. Call it 257 yards." He drew a circle around the figure and stood up. "Put on your clothes."

Halfway back up the creek, Tipsy held the dinghy against the current while Red took a bearing. "Okay." He chopped the edge of his hand at an angle over the north bank. "That way."

One hundred yards further up the creek, the compass spun helplessly. Red tossed the little ten-pound anchor into a fork of exposed casuarinas root on the south bank, then paid out its yellow rode as the dinghy fell off to the north bank. Once ashore, after they'd unloaded tools and gear, Red passed the rode stem to stern under the dinghy's two thwart seats, bending a clove hitch around the second one, and backed into the bush paying out rode as he went. Arrived at the bitter end of the rode, he arced back and forth, watching the hand compass while Tipsy made sure the dinghy lay above the trove of chain. When Red was satisfied, he drove the pick a mighty blow into the loam, burying its spade blade to the haft, and belayed the bitter end of the polypropylene to it, observing pedantically, "Three points a straight line make."

"I get it, I get it," Tipsy told him.

"Follow the yellow vector. Don't interrupt unless you see an anaconda."

"You mean they—"

"No, no, I'm teasing. But, isolated as we are, this might be a good place to see an iguana. They get pretty big, two and even three feet. But they're herbivores, so only vegetarians need to worry about them. In fact, they like to eat this plant right here," he pointed. "Black torch, it's called. They like to eat these blolly leaves, too. But people and pigs and dogs like to eat iguanas, so they're getting pretty rare. Keep an eye peeled anyway, because they're cool to see. What was the total yardage?"

"Two fifty-seven."

"Yards. Two fifty-seven less forty for the propylene leaves two seventeen. What was the back bearing?"

"Two fifty-eight."

"Oh yeah. No wonder you can remember it. Excellent. I didn't even notice. Okay, you go on ahead. When you get about fifty yards past the end of the rode, come about and sight me with the compass until you get a bearing of 258 degrees. Be accurate because one or two bearings from now, rode and dinghy will be out of sight. When you make the bearing, I'll pace it off, and don't you move till I get there."

The terrain was sand featuring all kinds of trees, brush, plants, and ants. At one point they had to stop so Red could extract a sand spur from his instep with the needle-nose pliers of his multitool. By the time they got two hundred and seventeen yards along the sevently-eight degree bearing, it was hot as hell, and the colonization of Tipsy's tan by noseeums felt like an early case of poison oak. A trail of sandy footprints disappeared into the trees behind them, and there remained no trace of the dinghy or its yellow rode.

Five bearing transfers from the creek, Red numbered aloud his three final strides and stopped fifteen yards short of her.

They stood stock still and looked at each other. Then, without moving, each began to look around. All anybody could see was the undifferentiated flora of the Bahamas archipelago.

"At least there's some shade in here," Tipsy said at last.

Red stabbed the twin blades of the posthole digger into the sand in front of him. "Spiral an outwards clockwise trail concentric to these handles. I'll go counterclockwise."

"What are we looking for?"

"I have no idea. Anything unusual. A beer bottle. Recently disturbed ground—although that won't help much." He pointed. "There are wild hogs all over these islands, and they root up the place something fierce."

She sidestepped certain prickly-looking plants, then tried to correct the curve of her path, always keeping the posthole digger to her right. The sand recorded their tell-tale footprints. The sun bore down. Avifauna scolded. Forty-five minutes passed.

Red was out of sight when he called her name. When she reached him, about sixty yards northwest of their starting point, the hole was already two feet deep.

"Beach morning glory." He nodded toward a desiccated plant lying upside down a few feet from the hole. "It'd have a real pretty flower if Charley hadn't cut off its roots before he replanted it." He dumped a shovelful of sand beside the hole. "And if it had that flower, we might have spent the rest of the year looking for it." He forced the blade of the shovel into the bottom of the hole with his foot. "Maybe two years." A couple of shovelfuls later, Tipsy realized that she'd been holding her breath. Five or six shovelfuls more, and the blade struck metal.

Tipsy fell to her knees and attempted to clear sand from the bottom of the hole. Red retrieved the dinghy's bailing scoop from the canvas bag and handed it to her. This was a half-gallon plastic milk jug with its top cut away such that its D-handle remained intact; good for water, good for sand.

Within a couple of minutes she had exposed the square, red and blue top of a large biscuit tin. She dug around its perimeter until a few inches of its sides were exposed sufficient to get a purchase, but the box wouldn't budge. Red knelt to the task, and together they rocked it back and forth and lifted handfuls of sand. The tin began to grudgingly rise, until, with a final heave, Tipsy fell backwards with it top down in her lap.

Tipsy stood, handed Red the tin, and brushed away ants and sand with both hands. "*Tante Marie's Extra Fine Tea Biscuits*," he read aloud. "*Don't Take Tea Without Tante Marie*." The container was a foot high and maybe eight inches on a side. Its top had been sealed with duct tape. "Charley liked his tea," Red smiled faintly, "and he was never abroad without a roll of duct tape." He retrieved the multitool from its holster, turned out the knife blade, and offered it to Tipsy handle first, along with the biscuit tin. She accepted them, sat on her heels, lay the tin on its side, and went to work.

It took a little time to slit the tape along all four edges, but when it was done the lid came away easily. Inside the tin, nestled among a number of sheets of paper and several desiccant packages, of the sort to be found in bags of potato chips, lay a small amber vial. Its screw cap, of black plastic, had been sealed with a strip of duct tape half an inch wide.

"The pages missing from the log," she said.

"If so, there should be ten of them," Red remembered. She titled the mouth of the tin so he could see into it. "And they seem to have a lot to say."

Tipsy handed the vial to Red, withdrew the pages and counted ten of them. Indeed, each was covered front and back with Charley's careful script.

Red held the vial to the sunlight that filtered down through the branches overhead. "We meet again, you son of a bitch." He handed the vial to Tipsy, who, after some study, frowned. "Is this a lock of hair?"

"Presidential hair," Red reminded her.

"My brother died for a lock of hair," she said bitterly, "and it didn't even belong to a woman."

"This ain't no *Ivanhoe*," Red reminded her.

She returned the vial. Red tucked it into the multitool's belt holster and secured its Velcro flap.

For no particular reason, Tipsy dropped the empty tin into the hole. "Well," she said, nudging the lid into the hole with her shoe, "I don't know what to say."

"There's nothing to say." Red was suddenly very tired. He scrubbed three days worth of whiskers with the scarred palm. "Not a goddamn thing." This exchange was followed by a long and thoughtful pause, during which each of them became quite conscious of the silence that had fallen between them. Finally, Tipsy folded the knife blade into the multitool and offered it to Red. "Put it in the tote," he suggested. She drew the canvas bag to her side and set the tool on the bottom of it alongside the GPS, the bottles, *Vellela Vellela*'s paperwork, and her pistol. She looked up. "Would you like a beer?"

Red blinked. "Hell, yes. Let's have a beer."

Tipsy handed Red two bottles, one by one, and one by one he snapped off their caps with his teeth and spat the caps at the biscuit tin. One hit its open mouth, the other glanced off its side. He handed her the first bottle and raised his own. "Cheers."

"Cheers," Tipsy agreed faintly. She watched Red take a long pull. "So," she said after he'd lowered the bottle from his lips, "what now?"

"What now?" Red repeated.

She nodded, watching him.

He seemed reluctant to address the question. "What now. . . ." He spread his arms. There might have been a little regret in his tone. Tenderness, even. There might have been a little humor in it, too.

"Now," Red said finally, "I am supposed to kill you."

FORTY-TWO

My Dearest Sister,

Well I finally wrote one. And what's it turn out to be?

A mystery.

Pretty funny.

Of course, a novel's not a mystery unless it gets solved. Or is it? Come on, let's tell the truth: mystery novels mostly get solved, big mysteries occasionally get solved, and some mysteries never get solved—right?

Take relativity, for example. Relativity got solved. Although, in fact, there's a case to be made that relativity is an excellent example of a solution in search of a mystery, a riddle that got solved before anybody knew it was a riddle, a solved mystery that posed—and continues to pose—way more questions than it purported to answer.

But we mere mortals don't have to quibble over such things. Let guys like Schopenhauer—and I don't know why that asshole's name just popped into my head—pose impossible solutions to unanswerable questions. Altogether one prefers Einsteinian-type mysteries. With Einstein at least you can pitch in and figure out some stuff, like the Schwarzschild Radius, for one modest example. Einstein's solution is the solution that keeps on giving. Schopenhauer's solution to the mystery, to put it simply, and why get complicated, is that it will only spoil your morning coffee to realize that the will to live is the only reality, and that this will, which necessitates constant strife, is insatiable, the only sure-fire interest-bearing return to which is constant suffering. Well, suffering, sure, Sic passim. There's a Buddhist aspect to this. Buddhists say that suffering is inseparable from existence but that inward extinction of the self and of worldly desire culminates in a state of spiritual enlightenment beyond both suffering and existence. So there. I'm cribbing from various mildewed tomes here, pages flapping in the winds of my mind despite their and its dampness. But I think that (a) "extinction of the inner self" inflicts more suffering than almost anything you can do on earth (short of "pre-emptive warfare"), (b) pre-emptive suffering is not really what the Buddha was talking about, and (c) I'm not a Buddhist, I'm a Taoist. "When life comes, it is because it is time for it to

*do so. When life goes, this is the natural sequence of events. To accept
with tranquility all things that happen in the fullness of their time, and
to abide in peace with the natural sequence of events, is to be beyond
the disturbing reach of either sorrow or joy. This is the state of those
whom the ancients called "released from bondage," which I crib from
Mr. H.G. Creel's* Chinese Thought. *Throw in a taste of Chuang Tzu, a
predecessor of Lao Tzu, he who bequeathed us the* Tao Te Ching, *and
you got philosophy fit to satisfy Horatio, if not Schopenhauer. Up to a
point, anyway. Not that Horatio ever had the advantage of either of
these two guys. One of the beauties of being at this end of history
instead of the other end, or even midstream, is that out here on the
pointy tip, we got all these myriad selections to go along with our pointy
heads. Call it conspicuous spiritual consumerism.*

*Of course the problem with this line of thought is, a life free of joy
and sorrow isn't all that interesting.*

*So I wrote a mystery, and just to make sure he's freed from bondage,
the author isn't going to stick around for the* dénouement. *Are you
around for it?*

*I'm virtually certain that you will be here for the resolution, for there
were a mite too many clues along the trail for you, yes you, not to suss.
Which reminds me once again to dispose of the previous 276 pages of
this manuscript. Do you note that this is page 279, and that the previous two pages are numbered 277 and 278? Ah hahahaha . . . That's
huge, no? Huge for me, anyway. It started out as a novel but wound up
comprising numerous scenarios or playlisps—that's a good one; enough
of this rum and I'll really be speed-writing with a lisp, the playlisp's the
thing, the* Tempest *is one book I've not managed to hang onto, but this
story, my story, is not so mellow and mature and optimistic. . . .*

Where was I.

The resolution. The finalé. Finalé *implies music. The* dénouement.
Better.

*Yes, he said, stroking the heap of papers like it was an old dog, this
is the novel that became its own dénouement, while, significantly, ceas-
ing to be a novel. Actually, it never cohered as a novel, but it was interesting to write my way through what I hoped to see repeated as human
behavior. As Chuang Tzu queried, "Who is it that has the leisure to
devote himself, with such abandoned glee, to making these things happen?" Me, that's who. Charley!*

*You hear about people burning plays in the kitchen sink, and I myself
once fed an entire draft of this novel into a wood stove, so I'm here to
tell you that, one way or another, it doesn't work. The urge doesn't go*

away. Kafka, on his deathbed, asked Max Brod to burn his collected works. Max said sure. Kafka died—and Max didn't do it. They were best friends! So, do not we know Kafka not only because he failed to make his work go away but also because he was betrayed? Okay, Kafka is an exception. But literature is the story of exceptions. And how does that square with the snuffing of the self? Was it not Philip Whalen, himself a bona fide Zen roshi, who said, "Insist there be a voice, then listen"? Okay, take the next step. Ask yourself: Would you listen to a voice uninformed by suffering?

Burning a useless novel is one thing, but scuttling Vellela Vellela is another cup of rum entirely. And I should scuttle this disgusting little phial along with it. All I know is what snippets Arnauld told me. Snippets? What a chatterbox! Everybody thinks he's just a boat bum, but I wonder if Red knows how much Arnauld knows. Insofar as I got the drift and filled in some blanks, these people for whom Red undertook to trans-ship this genetic material are a bunch of royalists whose nationalist fervor has led them into thinking they can take over the so-called first world with a combination of business as usual and a more or less permanent figurehead. Nothing new there. Arnaud flat-out thought it was a joke. But they figure a genetic leg up on the situation is kind of like taking steroids before the triathlon. Without a doubt, they like it when the fix is in. That's how they think. It's what they believe.

Of course I dove the hull. I dove it the minute I got here. And what did I find? A kilo of blow? Check. The Prez's DNA? Check—though I wasn't supposed to know about that part. And then? A fucking transponder, which nobody told me about. So the question immediately became, who's tracking Vellela Vellela? Red? Arnauld? Some unknown third party? Or—worst thought, best thought—am I the only person in this picture who doesn't know what's going on?

I couldn't just leave the transponder behind. That'd be a dead giveaway. And I presume that as long as it's transmitting from where it's supposed to be transmitting from, things will proceed according to schedule, whatever the schedule is. And if the schedule includes my being intercepted? Well, if I leave the DNA behind, they won't get what they want. Fuck them, and pretty simple. And if they're after the blow? Even simpler, they can have it. I couldn't care less about a kilo of blow.

But consider this: what if I make the trip to Key West intact?

The new plan is as follows. Since I'm being followed I touch land one more time, just like I'm supposed to, but not where I'm supposed to. When I get upstream of Boca Chica Key, if nothing untoward happens between now and then, I'm going to set this transponder adrift, *take a left into Key West, and let the Gulf Stream carry the transponder northeast, towards Boca Chica. The minute I'm off the boat, I'm going to Xerox the log of this trip and post the copy to you. To most eyeballs it will read like garden-variety woolgathering. To yours, however, it will reveal necessary clues and advice, depending upon what happens between now and the time I send it, and it will contain everything you'll need, with some cogitation, to find your way to here, here being Long Cay.*

Next, I'll find Cedric Osawa, because if anybody in Key West knows what to do with a kilo of cocaine, it's Cedric Osawa. Vis-à-vis converting blow into cash, Cedric will know the go-to guy. I'll deal him in for a taste, and Bob's your uncle. Then—back to sea, upon which I'll simply sail into history; or, maybe better, I walk away from Vellela Vellela, *leave her right where she's docked, which should make for a few days of delay at least, while I make like the Tasmanian Tiger and disappear. Why? Because it's time. British Columbia, the Yukon, Alaska, Thailand, the south of France . . . As long as I get my ass and a change of scene out of this deal, I don't care where I go.*

Moreover, icing on the Cake of Gone Charley, I'm going to swallow the anchor, *which is sailor talk for giving up the sea. You heard me. Melville did it. Conrad, too. Why not Charley?*

Except, unlike them, I plan to give up on writing, not start. No more dope smuggling either, and perhaps that goes without saying. I'll never be found. Why? Because I won't be me!

I never took proper care of my sister, Red rode my ass to a life of leisure, now he's fucked me on this deal, and so—this phial is my legacy to the two of you.

No kidding, I'm nervous enough to puke.

And get this: your disposition of it is our legacy to the world. Listen to me. Today, I'm doing a favor for everybody except Red Means and whoever hired him. Altruism is my keel cylinder. Whether or not I went down with my ship no one will ever know. And, excepting the revenge factor, my fate will be irrelevant. If you decide to make your fortune in the meantime, the rest of the world might well get the government it deserves. By the rest of the world, I mean humanity. After that, who knows? Will Nature bat last? Think of us, you and me, as shaving the odds.

Even as I write this, a light bulb ensnarled by monofilament and eel grass is drifting past the starboard side. I used to take that stuff aboard and dispose of it properly. But, long since, there's too much of it to deal with. If you want a portent of the endgame, take a look at pp. 208-213 of Archipelago, *by Susan Middleton and David Littschwagger.*

Man is also Nature, of course, and vice versa, alas. What a mass of contradictions, as Aesop noticed, is the creature we call man, able to blow hot and cold with the same breath. But mostly, his breath stinks.

Fire at sea is a scary thing, but I've considered setting the manuscript alight in a dinghy and casting it off at dawn. What a hell of a way to pass the day, watching the horizon for the smudge pot designed to extinguish the fruit flies of the mind. . . .

You see why I will never get anything published except for my epic Similes and Metaphors To Wince By. *Kind of like* Nixon for Lovers.

That dinghy scenario. Oh, the dreary psychology of it all. Whatever else it may be, however, psychology is not THE TRUE.

Why do I keep indenting?

In the end, apraxia will set in. Or I'll be ground up in the torture chambers of ideology. Writing in lemon juice would be too much. Hysterical, even. But it would smell good. I could use a quill from a seagull. Invisible screed which you warm with an illuminated bulb in order to read. Until which point there will be no more reflecting upon that which one has written. Those journalists who write a story then wrap it by going back to the beginning, as if their lead were a hook they thought up from the git-go, and wrap it up into a neat little package? Not that I disparage the effort, or begrudge the trade its tricks. The history of art is a story of exceptions. Will Windward Passage *be an exception? Am I never to know the ending? It's hard to believe I'll be able to resist watching from afar, but some mysteries are best left unscrutinized. Perhaps* Windward Passage *is one of them.*

And finally to business.

You found this duct-taped into a biscuit tin buried three feet deep at a remote location. Upon a quantity of pages torn from a log book, you have discovered this letter, the final chapter of a late, unlamented novel. I'm more or less relying on the likelihood that, if you, my sister, don't find it, then nobody will, and therefore this letter will never be required to change the world. Or to start a new one. Or to repeat the same old horseshit. Maybe that latter statement is all too obvious.

Whose DNA is this? Arnaud, that fount of info, couldn't tell me. Which probably means that Red doesn't know either. But this tuft may well contain the self-portrait of the future Dauphin/Dauphinette of your basic New World Order. I suppose they can predetermine the sex, too?

Preposterous as it may seem, there are people who are prepared to kill in order to possess this little vial. And they're not all venal—per se, anyway. Some of them actually believe in what they're doing. So the phial is not quite priceless. In any case they have brought to bear considerable resources. Leaving it here and walking away isn't going to work. Take care.

The people you need to deal with—for you have no choice: you must deal with them—aren't asking any questions. Not of you, anyway. They are very powerful. Even if you've gotten this far, perhaps especially if you've gotten this far, you will not long be able to avoid dealing with them. They're probably just around the next corner, waiting for you to lead them to it.

The upside is, with this little vial, you're holding the cards. Winner! Ding ding, ding ding ding. Try to avoid the Pow!

There are bidders all over the place. Citizens of former Iron Curtain countries, for example, of no particular ideology, who are merely looking to get in the middle. Members of certain families, for additional examples, who, reverential or not, recognize this vial's intrinsic potential. I prefer the word phial. It sounds eldritch. Or Jacobian. Of course I'm rambling. I'm pissed off and scared. Focus, Charley, focus.

Then there are the members of the various political parties who would like to substitute the genetic material of a being they feel more . . . not more worthy but . . . more suitable, that's it, more suitable to disinherit the earth. It is The True. Many of these players are not in funds sufficient to bid in this game, of course. Certain among them, not known for their lack of chutzpah, think it should go to them what has the bigger agenda. If you have a big agenda, you take. Why pay money? In the pinch, their philosophy of enterprise and unchecked markets always deserts them.

And then there are the Crazies.

Beware the Crazies, Sis. While they represent your best market opportunity, they will kill you if they don't like the way you're exercising it.

The Crazies go beyond reverence for this project. They fetishize it, they are prepared to establish it as a religious relic. They have already set about laying the foundation for a cult to be centered around a carefully groomed personality. Its destiny is predetermined. Think about it. And don't be making your protestations to me. I didn't set the wheels in motion. I'm just the sociopath who got hold of one of the levers.

I forgot about the Provenance. Not to worry. A little birdie told me that if you have a look at that big Kissinger hagiography (definition: the biography of a saint), published not so long ago, I don't know the title, Man of Vision, something like that, but the genome sequence is every third pair of letters starting from the last page of text, not including endnotes and index, and running back to front through the entire book, not including the prefatory material. Which nevertheless probably makes but a limited contribution to why it reads so badly.

Not to worry, the problem is not whether or not this thing is genuine. The problem is to survive its having come into your possession.

You will find that I've bequeathed you a kind of monkey's paw. You remember that story?

Goddammit. I'm trying to strike the Sunset Tone and having a hard time. After all is said and done, this ain't it. I can't tell you how many times I've embarked on this letter. Two, at least. I only left Rum Cay two days ago, and I only realized I had an extra problem to solve yesterday morning, after I dove the hull. Can you imagine Arnauld sounding me on whether I could loan him a T-handled T-2 Torx wrench? What, the conch thinks I was born yesterday? The minute he asked me, I knew something was up. Mon, mon, I lied, I only noticed that the yard used Torx screws when I called in at St. John's. Been meaning to replace them with Phillips heads but there's been no need. Plus, hell, I can't replace them until I get a Torx driver or bit, but if it's a bit I gotta get an impact wrench, and if it's an impact wrench I gotta get a compressor, a hose, a drop cord, and pretty soon I'd be well and truly lost in the Möbius clusterfuck known as Break Out Another Thousand—you hear what I'm saying?

Arnauld just laughed. Smile, mon, he tells me. I whup sompin' up. Vernacular, they say, should be used only if you are running behind in the polls. If you find this, I'm beyond caring—right? And if you don't find it? Well, I'm preaching to the dark side of the lid of a biscuit tin.

Maybe compulsive revision isn't such a good thing after all. It's held me back all my life. I used to know a piano player. Talented guy, but he could never make it all the way through a tune without stopping, and he'd stop with a curse. He'd play the spoilt passage over and over again. When he'd perfected the recitation to his satisfaction he'd start from the beginning and find some other passage to be dissatisfied about. He'd never get to the end of a tune. Somebody would remind him that Thelonious Monk declared that there's no such thing as a wrong note. Fuck him, my friend would say, Monk was a genius, I'm just a piano player.

You see? Unlike the people who want to get their hands on the contents of this phial, I'm not obsessed with my legacy.

Had I had a little advance warning I could have done this on oilskin or something, some patient medium, *for who can say how long this letter is going to stay buried? It reminds me of the time we buried that*

Pueblo Indian wallet dad brought back from New Mexico. We stuffed it with play money and wrapped it in tinfoil and buried it in the back yard—remember? We used a compass and ma's sewing tape to measure from the hole to a fencepost in one direction and to the apple tree in another direction. My first cocked hat! That backyard is probably a mall by now. A temperance center. A gun shop. I always wondered if somebody dug that wallet up. Maybe a backhoe found it? What would it have been like? Rotted all to hell? Could they tell what it was? Were they surprised or shocked or scared? Did they simply recognize it for a prank by two little kids? Or did the backhoe lift it out of the ground and deposit it into the back of a dump truck, thence and to the landfill, never to be noticed by anybody? That's more like it. Way more like it.

Just like Windward Passage.

Rotted in place. Rotted in peace. Rotted unknown.

And now I see we're nearly to the end of page 295. What a story. I'm looking forward to a fabulous last sail, followed by a serious change of mental and physical scenery. It is The True.

All my love,
Charley

P.S. When they find you—and they will find you—just sell it to them and get out. Take whatever they offer, and go.

P.P.S. If this works, buy yourself a lot of books and a nice boat.

After all, see where books and boats got me?

FORTY-THREE

WHEN TIPSY RETURNED TO SAN FRANCISCO, SHE FOUND A MODIFIED WORLD.

It started with a cursory glance at a *Chronicle* in the cab on the way in from the airport.

Whooooeee, she thought on her second jump from page one, all fucked up and nobody left to sell it to. Except foreign policy based on xenophobia, of course; that hadn't changed.

It continued with a calling card tucked between the edge of her front door and the weather stripping, right beside the doorknob, where a body couldn't miss it.

Vassily Novgorodovich
PetroPozhirat, LLC;
Moscow, London, Havana
Beverly Hills, Guandong, Caracas
33-01-46-09-88-88

This must be the guy, she thought.

The first notice atop the pile of mail announced the severance of her phone service due to nonpayment. It would cost her so much to square the account, so much to reinstate it, including a one-year deposit against this not happening again, and the provider would hold her phone's number for thirty days from the above date, some forty-seven days ago. Not incidentally, she'd have to buy herself a new phone, too.

Next she found a postcard from her landlady.

How about two month's back rent, goddammit?

Among similar notices from PG&E and the water department she discovered, hey, her newly restored driver's license, an astronomical bill from the mandated high-risk automobile insurance pool, and two identical letters from the same law firm, dated a month apart.

Chester, Plowright & Samuels
721 Montgomery St., Suite 903
San Francisco, CA. 94111
415-546-3231

Ms. Teresa Powell
321-A Quintara St.
San Francisco, CA
94116

Dear Ms. Powell:

In regard to the estate of Mr. Quentin Asche, please contact this office
at your earliest convenience.

Sincerely,

Hanford Reach, Esq.

She caught herself reflexively reaching for the phone to call Quentin
and ask him if it were true that he had died.

"That's not going to work for a couple of reasons," she said to the empty
room.

His death wasn't unexpected. Quentin had been ill for a long time. Still,
she'd never allowed herself to imagine life without him.

She turned her back on the rest of the mail and went outside. The nasturtiums appeared to be riotously happy, and a mocking bird perched on
the very top of the fig tree was making all kinds of music. The cushion on
the seat of the Adirondack chair was covered in leaves and dust and city
grime. She turned it over and sat down. Then she cried for a while.

Later she walked an armful of correspondence six blocks to a laundromat and used its change machine and pay phone to call the phone company, PG&E, the insurance company, and her landlady. The woman who
answered the phone at the law firm put Tipsy on hold but came right back
with an appointment in two days' time at ten-thirty in the morning. After
some not-so-cute guy with a wrecker got the Beamer started and put air
in its tires, she drove to her bank on Irving and deposited enough cash to
cover the payables.

San Francisco was having some of that cool weather people who live in
the Avenues know more about than anybody else in the city. She sat in the
Adirondack chair wrapped in a blanket and thought about things. Things
like, is this nice tan I got in the Caribbean going to last long enough to
impress Faulkner? Then she remembered that Faulkner would be long
gone to his boat in the San Blas Islands or Zihuatanejo or some place, and

he'd stay there until late next spring. Not only that, but with Charley dead and no more letters to pick up, she had two less reasons to be seeing Faulkner at all. Quentin dead, meaning nobody to drink with, made four. And then, if she quit drinking entirely, she had five excellent reasons never to darken the door of that bar again.

She could get her political fix from newspapers. Or radio. Or even the internet.

It was as if someone had thrown a switch on the rails in front of her.

She fingered the antique locket at the small of her throat.

All aboard for the bifurcation.

First things first, she paid a visit to the coroner's office on 4th Street. Sure enough, the morgue was sitting on an unclaimed head.

"I need to see it," she told them. The receptionist, who was a deputy sheriff, asked her to wait. After no more than five minutes Jimmy Nix himself appeared. He stripped off a pair of latex gloves, dropped them in a trash can, introduced himself, accepted a folder offered by his receptionist, and ushered his visitor into an elevator that took them three stories down to the deep freeze.

Jimmy Nix donned a fresh pair of latex gloves, retrieved a clear plastic bag from a refrigerated drawer, set it on a stainless steel table, unzipped it, unsheathed the head, and turned it so she could see what was left of the face. Lips, earlobes, and eyes were gone. Some of the nose remained, and that was helpful. A ragged gray tonsure. The pallor was not unlike a color often referred to as IBM gray.

"Was there an earring?" Tipsy asked.

Nix consulted his folder. "We found a circular hoop of gold wire, three-eighths inch in diameter, in the left auditory canal. If you like I can—"

"That's him," Tipsy said with a remarkably firm voice. And she placed her hands on the decrepit tonsure, then picked up the head and embraced it.

"Ahm." The coroner touched a gloved hand to her shoulder. "That's not policy."

Though cold to the touch, it was like holding a skull-sized volume of coral, hollowed by sea creatures. "Give me a minute, can't you?" Tipsy said. "This is my brother."

Jimmy Nix had witnessed many such scenes. He turned aside, ostensibly to set down his papers, but really to give the poor woman a moment before he gently prevailed upon her to relinquish the severed head.

"Okay. Thank you." Tipsy brushed a sleeve while she silently counted to three. Then she asked the coroner if she might borrow a pair of scissors.

Jimmy Nix raised an eyebrow. "May I ask why?"

"I'd like to have a lock of my brother's hair," Tipsy replied in a most reasonable tone,

Jimmy Nix blinked.

"As a keepsake," she added.

Jimmy Nix had a certain reputation, around the department, for being difficult to faze. Now he felt as if his composure were but a little board shack built on quicksand.

"You do believe he's my brother?"

The coroner nodded.

"It's true we weren't all that close. We hadn't seen each other in fifteen or sixteen years." Tipsy opened her hands towards the head on the table. "But he was all the family I had."

Jimmy Nix opened a narrow drawer in a roll-around cabinet and selected a sharp-pointed pair of stainless steel suture scissors.

Tipsy snipped a two-inch lock from just aft of Charley's left auditory canal, and she made sure a few strands came away with their follicles, too. "Thank you very much." She handed the scissors back to Jimmy Nix, finger loops first. "Could I trouble you for an envelope, or maybe a zip-lock bag?"

After he had rezipped the remains into its own bag and returned them to their drawer, she asked for Officer Protone.

Jimmy Nix, whose back was turned as he closed the drawer, grimaced. "Why Protone?"

"He's a cop and I know him. Shouldn't I talk to a cop about this?"

"Do you know another one?" Nix stalled, still not turning to face her.

Tipsy thought a moment. "There was his partner."

"Officer Few," Nix confirmed sadly.

"That's him. Oscar Few. Once you start in on the problem, it's not a difficult name to remember."

"That's true. I'll tell you what." Nix turned around. "Let me get a statement from you and, if I may, a saliva sample."

"A saliva sample? What for?"

"DNA." Nix angled his thumb toward the drawer behind him. "If that's your brother, I can release his remains to you. It'll take about a month."

"Oh. I guess—. Sure. Of course." Then, without thinking about how it might sound, she asked him, "There must be such a thing as having a head cremated—no? Or . . . or should I bury him . . . ?"

The board shack of Jimmy Nix's reputation began to sag. "I . . ." he began. "I'm sure that . . ." He moved a finger toward the entry door. "We maintain a database of crematories and funeral directors. Surely one among them . . ."

Eyes moist, Tipsy shook her head.

Jimmy Nix touched her shoulder. "There's plenty of time to think about that."

"Thank you," she whispered.

Later, gaining the hall, Tipsy ginned up questions. "What happened to my brother? Where did you find him? Did you find the rest of him? And why can't I meet with Officers Protone or Few?"

Jimmy Nix shook his head. "There's never been a body. And even stranger, Miss Powell, it was Officer Protone who found your brother's remains."

"Really? But where? How?"

"In a car. Just the head. Before I can tell you anything else," he added, "I'll have to find out if somebody replaced Protone on this case yet. It's a little . . . cold."

She ignored the hint. "Did Protone realize that was my brother?"

"Not that I ever heard. As far as the file's concerned," Nix held up the file, "he's still John Doe No. 12."

Nix felt it in line with department policy that he make no mention of John Doe Nos. 10 and 13, in case Tipsy knew something the department didn't know, and there seemed no point at all in dragging Laval Williamson into it. At least they knew what happened to Laval, Nix reflected glumly, and who he was. On the other hand, being able to explain only one out of four killings didn't make for such a hot statistic, and he heard about it at every department meeting he attended.

"Doesn't Protone want to talk to me?" Tipsy asked. "I'd certainly like to talk to him."

"He can't." Nix tapped the file against his trouser leg. "You can't."

"But why not?" she persisted.

Clearly agitated, Nix abruptly declared, "Lieutenant Protone is deceased." There, he thought: I am thoroughly fazed.

Tipsy stopped in her tracks. "I beg your pardon?"

Nix, who had turned to precede Tipsy down the hall, now turned to face her. There were no windows in this hallway, but there were many doors. A long series of overhead fluorescent lights led, end to end, down the hall to the elevator. "In the course of finding your brother's remains," Nix told her, "Officer Protone accidentally killed the perpetrator of an entirely separate crime."

"I don't understand. Separate from what?"

"In the course of an arrest." Uncharacteristically upset, Nix shook his head. "He was arresting a petty thief, a smash-and-grab guy. Caught him red-handed. Just some street-level jerkoff." Nix cleared his throat. "Excuse the expression."

"I'm familiar with it."

"A professional street-level jerkoff." Nix's lips tightened. "A guy not worth the trouble. Just a bum. Nobody to get upset about—" Nix marshaled his composure. "Excuse me. That's not what I meant to say. If you learn anything working around here," he pointed the file folder at the door they'd just exited, "it's that when the grim reaper comes to call, everybody's a bum. Some, of course," Nix sucked a tooth, "are more grimily reaped than others. The guy resisted arrest, there was a struggle, Protone accidentally broke the guy's neck." Nix sighed raggedly. "Long story short, pending investigation and resolution of the incident, Protone was put on administrative leave."

"I imagine that's standard procedure."

"It's standard procedure, and it's paid leave."

"When," Tipsy frowned, "did all this happen?"

"Three, four months ago." Nix bit his lip.

Tipsy waited.

"Vince—that's Protone—couldn't handle not working. He just sat around his apartment drinking beer and watching daytime television. A couple of hours at some bar only made things worse. After about two weeks, he shot himself with his service revolver." Nix's eyes got distant. "He was in a laundromat." Now Nix's voice got distant, too. "Vince told me once he never realized how bad divorce could get until he started spending time in laundromats."

Tipsy touched her fingertips to her upper lip. They smelled of formaldehyde. "Oh," she managed to say, as she dropped her hand. "It sounds like he was a friend of yours."

"At one time," Nix nodded, "we owned a bar together." He shook his head. "Vince couldn't handle the proximity to alcohol. Eventually I talked him into selling out to another partner and suggested that he should maybe invest in a bicycle shop or an ice cream parlor, something like that. Anyway, over the past year or so, he was going through bad personal stuff." Nix moved his hands. "The divorce cost him his house, which he grew up in, half his paycheck, and his car. There were no kids. He was pulling double shifts to get a little coin in circulation, but he was doing it so as to be at home as little as possible, too, home being a converted garage way out in the Avenues. A one-room place, if you didn't count the bathroom."

"The Avenues can be a lonely place," Tipsy noted sympathetically.

"He had no ID on him when he topped himself, none of the cops or

paramedics on the scene knew him. . . . I'll tell you something," Nix said
after a pause. "It was no picnic coming into work and finding Vince
Protone on the slab."

"Oh, I'm sorry. I'm so sorry," Tipsy repeated—stupidly, she thought.

"That's okay." Nix took a deep breath and loudly expelled it. "Thanks.
Considering the circumstances, it's kind of you to say as much." He looked
at her. "I'm sorry about your brother. You said you weren't close?"

Tipsy blinked at this. Yes, she had said that. And it was true—yes? She
started to shake her head, but she settled for a little wave of her hand.

"Listen to me," Nix chastised himself. "It was your brother, for chrissakes. I'm sorry."

Tipsy only nodded.

After a moment of uncertainty Nix stepped aside, and Tipsy preceded
him down the hall. The wait for the elevator was interminable. As the
doors finally opened, Tipsy thought to ask, "What about . . ."

Nix entered the car and sagged into a back corner. The doors closed,
and the elevator moved. "Yes?" he said tiredly, raising his eyes to the
numerals above the door.

"What about Officer Few? Did he . . . Did he get a new partner? I'm
sorry," she added hastily. "I don't know how this stuff works."

"Few . . ." Nix looked at her, looked down at his shoes, and shook his
head. "Few went nuts."

"You mean, he was upset?"

"No," Nix replied. "I mean he went nuts." He looked at her. "I mean,
of course Oscar was upset by Protone's death. Very upset. But he was
upset about other stuff. The powers that be had been messing with his
caseload. He was moonlighting, too, doing security work at conventions
and rock concerts, like that, shitty, I mean lousy, excuse me, lousy work
for lousy money. So he was worn out. He was also spending a lot of time
in conspiracy-oriented chat rooms in pursuit of some line of investigation
the brass had pulled him and Protone off of. While he was going through
his divorce Protone was basically AWOL, as far as work went. Oscar tried
to keep the case alive in his spare time, but the whole deal made him
paranoid enough to be overheard talking to himself. They gave him a desk
job but supervisor couldn't keep him off the internet. Then Protone came
back and started humping double shifts just like Oscar was. If they'd been
working together, they probably would have taken turns falling asleep.
But, even though they were a good team, management kept them split up.
Protone kicked about the reassignment, he even went to bat for Oscar,
unasked I might add, and for his trouble he got re-reassigned to Park
Station." The elevator stopped and the doors parted, but Nix ignored

them. "Next thing anybody knew—" Nix caught himself. He tapped the spine of the file against the palm of his empty hand. After a moment he continued, "I guess you could say Protone's suicide was the straw that broke Oscar's back. What I meant when I said he went nuts was that he went nuts, that he came unhinged, that he seemed to lose his mind. Long story short, Oscar Few is no longer with the police force. Oscar Few went . . ." Nix touched the file to his forehead, almost as if he were saluting, then reversed it toward the open doors. ". . . out. . . ."

It developed that putting off calling the number on the business card didn't make any difference. When Tipsy showed up at the lawyer's office the Russian was there, too, waiting for her. She'd never met him, of course. At first she thought he was one of the lawyers.

"Nice trip?" he said, standing up out of a leather chair. He held a Homburg in his left hand.

"Um," said the silver-haired lawyer, standing out of his own chair behind a desk, "This is Mr. Vassily Novgorodovich, and I'm Hanford Reach."

The Russian offered his free hand and inclined his head. "How do you do." Tipsy uncertainly returned the handshake.

Barrister Reach shook her hand in turn, leaning over his desk to do so. "As you no doubt know already," Reach said, waving her into a vacant chair, "Mr. Novgorodovich is the executor of Quentin's will."

Tipsy, who was almost all the way down in the chair, stood up again.

"We've been trying to get in touch with you, Ms. Powell," the Russian pointed out. "We were beginning to get a little worried. But by the look of your lovely tan, perhaps you've merely been on vacation?"

"Yes," Tipsy replied slowly. "My first vacation in . . . quite a number of years." She eased into the chair.

"Oh? How nice for you. And where did you go?"

"The Caribbean," Tipsy said, watching him.

The Russian smiled. "I love the Caribbean."

Barrister Reach cleared his throat. "Since neither of us has ever laid eyes on you before, Ms. Powell, I wonder if you might provide us with a photo ID?"

Tipsy looked at him as if he'd asked a question of a much more personal nature. "Excuse me?"

"It's just a formality." Reach waved a hand and smiled kindly. "We know who you are."

Tipsy produced the freshly restored driver's license. Reach gave it a glance and offered it to the Russian, who waved it away. The lawyer called

in a secretary and handed the license to her. "Three copies, please, nota-
rized and witnessed. Just a formality," he said again, as the secretary left.
"So, Ms. Powell, we meet at last. Quentin spoke of you often over the
years and never with any less than the highest regard." Reach tented his
hands under his chin, then angled them towards her. "I suppose you also
know that you are the sole heir to the estate of Quentin Asche?"

Two hours later, in front of the law firm's offices in the 700 block of
Montgomery Street, the Russian asked Tipsy if she had it on her.

She touched the neck of her sweater, where it covered the locket that
hung over the hollow of her throat. "You're that guy, too?"

"I'm that guy, too."

"It's at my apartment."

"Good," Vassily said.

"We could meet for coffee tomorrow. Say, ten o'clock?"

Vassily smiled.

At her apartment forty-five minutes later, she pulled the necklace with
its locket over her head and handed them to him.

Vassily smiled and shook his head. So she'd had it on her the whole
time. He opened the locket and studied its contents. "Gray." He snapped
the locket shut. "Exactly what *glasnost* did to my hair. Back when I had
hair, that is."

"I thought it was *perestroika*."

"Nope." Vassily dangled the locket off its chain.

"Anyway . . ."

"Yes." Vassily swung the locket onto the palm of his hand. "Nice touch."

"Customs didn't even look at it. By the way?"

"Yes?"

"Whose hair is that, exactly?"

Vassily shook his head. "I have no idea."

"Well, whose hair do you think it is?"

"From what I hear, it belonged to a former American president."

"That's what I hear, too. Which party was the guy from?"

Vassily lifted his hands. "The stress of the highest office turns gray the
hair of everybody who holds it."

"Damn it," Tipsy said. "Wouldn't you like to have some idea of which
side of the street you're working?"

"Look at it this way," Vassily suggested.

"Yes?"

"It isn't Ike's."

Tipsy smiled.

"So." Vassily polished the face of the locket with the ball of his thumb. "There's a balance due."

"Isn't that Red's invoice?"

"I didn't take delivery from Red. Did you get it from Red?"

"You didn't see him on your way in?" Tipsy asked as nonchalantly as possible.

Vassily studied her, then smiled. "That guy's always one step ahead of me. I wonder why?"

"He's younger than you are?"

"Maybe so," Vassily said mildly.

A moment passed. "How much is it?"

"Forty thousand."

Tipsy emitted a low whistle. "The downstroke was another forty?"

Vassily shook his head. "Red liked sixty percent up front."

That tallied. "Sixty thousand."

Vassily nodded.

"For that," she pointed at the locket, "plus the kilo of cocaine?"

Vassily tucked the locket into the pocket of his waistcoat opposite the pocket containing his watch. "I don't know anything about a kilo of cocaine."

"Do you have the balance with you?"

Vassily patted the breast pocket of his overcoat.

"An overcoat's a nice idea in San Francisco," Tipsy said.

Vassily nodded. "Russia, too."

"When's the last time you were in Russia?"

Vassily smiled. "About forty years ago."

Tipsy nodded. "That's the way I feel about San Francisco, too."

Vassily nodded. "I like San Francisco."

"Anyway." After a short silence she repeated it. "Anyway?"

Vassily shrugged. "It's academic."

"What's academic?"

"The forty thousand."

"Why?"

Vassily smiled without mirth. "Now I am supposed to kill you."

"What's the problem? You've got what you came for."

"True story," Vassily said.

This disturbed Tipsy. "Why'd you put it like that?"

"Oh, just to make sure," Vassily replied.

"Of what?"

"Of your . . . intimacy with Red Means."

"Intimacy? You mean, now that you know I hung around Red Means long enough to become familiar with that lousy expression of his, you are entitled to make impudent assumptions?"

Vassily chuckled.

"So how did you pick it up?" she asked him.

Vassily smiled. "I'm a quick study."

"I've got a better idea," she said.

"Shoot."

"Better than that."

"What is it?"

"Give me the money, take the first front door you see, and keep going."

Vassily regarded her. "Did Red Means tell you to tell me that?"

"We consulted on it."

And it wasn't until that moment that Vassily noticed the pineapple shirt draped over a pile of books next to the only comfortable-looking chair in the apartment, several sizes larger and a bit louder than anything Tipsy might care to wear. Altogether a tasteless shirt. Vassily permitted himself a rueful tug at his lower lip. Without Miou Miou to cover his back, he was going to have to get used to wondering if he were becoming senile.

"But first," Tipsy said, interrupting his chain of thought, "perhaps you'd like to tell me how you got to be executor of Quentin's estate."

Vassily shrugged. "Right guy, right time, right place?" He tilted his head inquisitively. "How'd you get to be his heir?"

"I have no idea," she replied frankly.

"Lotta dough," Vassily pointed out. "This time next year, you'll be having tax problems."

"Pretty heads up," Tipsy persisted.

"True story. And this?" He touched the locket through the fabric of his waistcoat pocket.

Tipsy nodded. "Right girl, right time, right place."

Vassily smiled. "Now who's a quick study?"

"I'm beginning to like you."

"Don't," Vassily suggested. "I'm not likable."

"Tell you something?"

"I'm supposed to be telling you something."

She indicated the waistcoat pocket. "You turn that in, the job's over."

"Job's over," Vassily confirmed.

"Then what?"

Vassily smiled. "Maybe I'll take a long trip to the Bahamas."

"Oh?" Tipsy replied mildly. "Weren't you just there?"

"That was outsourced." Vassily shook his head. "I can't handle the jet-lag anymore."

"By you? Outsourced, I mean?"

Vassily's expression gave nothing away. "I had my hands full right here in San Francisco."

"So it's true, then? You turn that in and you're done?"

"Done."

"Any prospects?"

Vassily made no reply.

"How old are you, Vassily?"

"Seventy-three."

"Do you still enjoy this line of work?"

"No," Vassily said, betraying no emotion. "Not any more."

"Not like you used to."

Vassily permitted himself a thin smile. "Not like I used to."

"But you don't know how to do anything else."

Vassily shrugged.

"Chess?" she suggested.

Vassily blew air through his lips.

"It's just that I heard somewhere that Russians are gaga for chess."

"You checked your 401K lately?" Vassily asked.

Tipsy laughed out loud.

"Not only that," Vassily added gloomily, "I own a boat."

Around midnight that same night, about a block downwind from Tipsy's apartment, Mrs. Eloise Kleinzahler interrupted her husband's absorption in a program on the History Channel. Its subject was World War II, the 42nd one-hour installment, and he hadn't missed a single program. "Auggie," she brayed, "you smell that?"

"Smell what?" the old man replied, not taking his eyes off the screen.

"It smells like burning hair."

"Close the fucking window," Mr. Kleinzahler suggested. A line of Tiger tanks rumbled across the fifty-two inch screen, and the snow was flying. As he lifted the fourth Old Overholt, rocks, to his lips, he added, "It's probably that bald transvestite up the street, there, curling his wig. What's the name?"

"Miss Enchantment, when she's singing. Bert Fortunato, when he's carrying the mail." Mr. Kleinzahler knew a great deal about booze and World War II. Mrs. Kleinzahler knew everything there was to know about the neighbors.

"That's it." Old man Kleinzahler rattled the ice in his glass. When the Panzers were storming frozen Europe, he was thinking, the Krauts were all shitfaced on looted cognac. "Miss Enchantment," he said aloud, "curling her wig for karaoke."

VII
At the Edge of the Projection

FORTY-FOUR

INVITED TO TAKE A SEAT WHILE HE WAITED, RED PACED THE FOUR WALLS of the antechamber.

The back wall featured the portal to the inner sanctum. Its analogue peephole escutcheon featured a bas-relief of the chondrophore *Vellela vellela*. Red had despised it from its inception. And learned to respect it. One respects the well-honed blade. Despicably ironic, ironically respectful. "One of the few examples of high seas life that a beachcomber may expect to find." He touched the rubber tip of his walking stick to the plaque. Soon to be extinct, of course. And, though he kept the thought to himself, you'll be better off.

Beginning to the left of the door, after an end table with a holoclock atop a copy of *Chondrophore Journal—All Aboard For Luna!*—a tastefully expensive L couch and chair wrapped through the corner and took up the entire south wall. Above the couch hung an oil portrait of an idealized Red Means. He had a bottle of Kalik beer in one hand, the spoke of a ship's wheel in the other, and wind in his very long coppery hair, into a few strands of which had been braided the pin feather of an albatross. Extinct for sure. Red appeared to be squinting up at the set of his sails; but, as sails and rigging were outside the frame of the picture, he might just as well have been seeing far, far into the future. Or perhaps he was watching a well-honed blade slice his sails to ribbons.

To the right of the portal by which Red had been admitted, the east wall consisted entirely of an electrolyte brume framed on either side by two pilasters, and top and bottom by crown and base moldings.

The brume's pixels seethed with Info. Two crawls, two columnulars, the big picture in the background, and two inset feeds, their resolution so crisp as to make their own crawls, though much tinier, easily legible.

Red's mouth straightened a little. His new-to-him v.6 Quietus reduced the audio to a quantum twitter, much as if it were emanating from an adjacent apartment. He was surprised and pleased that it worked here. The gadget, of the old key chain sort, had cost him 75 shells 50 on a BayFill repo auction, but the sporadic peace of mind provided by the device had been worth the price. Though his physical aging had been proceeding gracefully enough, through a perceptible decrepitude it was true, he was finding his capacity to resist the anxiety induced by Info, any Info, less and less resilient. He'd heard rumors of a Homoremote, a sort of Quietus tuned to cancel any audio emitted by humans; but these devices, if they existed—or, more like it, when they existed—would be beyond expensive.

Incongruously, by Red's lights anyway, the east wall had been left transparent. No one could begrudge this outfit the conservation of space, of course, but while they certainly could afford it, a transparent wall virtually flaunted affluence. And it was a good idea, if only for its view of the recently completed arc of the Transbay Tower Wall, which the east window framed, erect and proud and fully two miles across, from the site of the old ballpark north to Telegraph Hill, as if the two, architecture and window, had been built for each other.

Which, come to consider the various issues involved, Red reflected wearily, might be exactly the case.

It occurred to him to look up. And there it was.

Of course. Although the myriad pixel-brumes on the market made anything possible, the adhesives hadn't been perfected. On a floor, beneath a protective transparency, nothing could be easier. Vertical, on a flat wall, on curved or faceted or undulating walls? No problem. And voxel-based décor structures couldn't be too far from market. But a ceiling pixel fresco evinced the acme of contemporary opulence. Given which, the image wasn't all that surprising. In fact it was obvious. Mandated by the expense, one would think, if only to offset the impression that it was there merely to impress.

A tone sounded. The door in the west wall slid aside, and Red limped through it into a chamber of pure, tasteful affluence, the first evidence of which was no Info to be heard or seen whatsoever. Which was good; his device wouldn't work in here.

"Red, Red, Red."

She didn't get up to embrace him. Things hadn't been like that for a long time.

Red was surrounded on three sides by Bahamian vistas. Blue skies, puffy clouds, casuarinas, mangroves, palm trees, white sand littorals, a beached wooden rowboat, even a ramshackle building or two. It was useless, he knew, to attempt to identify the source of the voice. Not while Security scanned him, anyway.

Now he was queried. Do you like the fountains? Kalik of course. Or that roasted green tea? None? And the sensation of a late Chekhov story. "The Lady with a Dog" perhaps? A melancholic fatality? Very good. And how about the sensation that you are sitting down? Would you rather stand? The selection is permitted.

And so forth. Red let the probes work him over, and why not. He had no choice. But anyway they were top of the line, no more invasive to his tissue than neutrinos to a cinder block. It wasn't like visiting a twentieth-century dentist, say, or plugging in to an older nutritional outlet. Among other ironies, the charade was intended to make him feel at home.

And here she was. Looking not a day older than the day she quit drinking, the better to attempt to guide the boy's fate as perceived by the light of her own. In Detox We Trust. Confident. Not a trace of alcohol, cigarettes, not even the slight scar typical of tel-chip implantation. No significant other, either. Unless you count—

"How's the boy?"

"Didn't you watch the ceiling? He's at the shrine."

"Yes," Red acknowledged with a sigh, "of course I watched the ceiling. Very impressive. How do you get it to stay up there?"

She dismissed this with the usual, "My installers get the big shells."

"Naturally. But what's a ceiling—yours or anybody else's—got to do with the boy?"

"He's going to reproduce. It requires at least the illusion of his physical presence."

More dismissiveness. "Ah," Red nodded. "Of course." He laid the cane across his knees. "Reproduction. I figured that's why you exhumed his gestation lottery."

"It worked once," she shrugged, "and it was expensive to produce. So . . ."

From a grove of bamboo beyond her, the unblinking yellow eyes of a tiger watched him.

Abruptly he looked down. *Was* he sitting down?

"Would you like to see him?"

"Sure," Red lied.

A thirteen-year-old boy dressed in shorts, a sweater vest, sock garters and Buster Brown shoes materialized on one of the beaches. The nimbus surrounding the image was not a Bahamian light.

"Klegan," Red declared tiredly. "My, but how you've grown."

The hologram peered past him. Whether from the boy's lack of recognition, or merely a bad signal, or a signal deliberately offset by Security, Red could not discern. Nor did he care. But the ambiguity reminded him of the old GPS technology. It was a degraded fix. And of course it was deliberate.

The boy would have his enemies. Among other toys.

"Klegan," Tipsy chided the boy. "Don't you want to say hallo to your Uncle Red?"

The boy gave up squinting and shrugged. "Hallo."

It sounded just like *hollow*. "Nice accent," Red noted wryly.

"All that English schooling," Tipsy agreed proudly. "He's a born diplo-mat. Happy new year from Beijing, Klegan."

"Gung hay fat choy, Shushu." As the hologram accompanied the salu-tation with a slight bow, Red could not fail to note the child's *hauteur*, along with the note of effete disdain in his voice. Due to the transmission, no doubt, the axis of the bow appeared to be directed more at the tiger than at Tipsy. The tiger blinked at last. Blinked Red's picture. Or maybe his retina scan.

Shushu my fucking ass, Red glowered sourly. That snot-nosed little bastard is going to be the death of us all. It was a thought he'd thought any number of times before, however, and, in the moment, he raised a pseu-do-avuncular eyebrow. "How many languages does he speak?"

"Only the four. Be punctilious in your observances, Klegan my dear. I'll see you tomorrow morning."

"And in your dreams tonight," the boy said, completing a standard salu-tation. He blew a kiss toward the tiger.

Tipsy returned it anyway. With a sizzle much like that of a torch applied to a nest of tent caterpillars, the image of the boy dispersed.

The noise of a fountain, visible in the garden beyond the wall to Red's left, faded up. Tipsy's desk materialized, a chondrophore escutcheon prominent in its modesty panel. The vertical distance from the center of the escutcheon to the lower edge of the panel, in ratio to that of the dis-tance from the center to the upper edge, would be the Golden Mean.

"He's okay, the boy?" Red asked idly. "What with the radiation and all?"

Tipsy dismissed this. "You can't believe what a kid can handle these days. All that stuff in the outer vestibule you carry around that gadget to shield yourself from?"

"That which otherwise," Red pointed out, "would make the marrow tingle?"

Tipsy dismissed this. "Doesn't phase him at all. He can lie on the floor and work his Chinese syntax with snails cleaning his toes, let alone sixteen channels bleating in the four languages." She beamed. "Perfect concen-tration. Next day his non-sycophantic tutor gives him top marks and advances the subject." Tipsy gazed at the wall to her right. As a woman looking out her office window at a garden fountain, she was absolutely convincing. "If the rest of the kids in his generation are as oblivious to Info as Klegan is, the Department of Info is in trouble."

Red smiled. "But Klegan isn't like the rest of the kids."

Usually such a remark invoked further beaming. But now: "True," Tipsy fretted. "But we—I—have tried to give him every vestige of a normal life."

"If, by normal," Red wrinkled his mouth, "you mean Info night and day, scripted celestial events, biodiversity asymptotic to singularity, plastics indistinguishable from flesh and vice versa, holographical filial piety out the holographic wazoo, and a prearranged marriage on his fourteenth birthday to a trollop three years—"

Tipsy raised a hand, palm out, and Red ceased the litany. Sometimes the probes were a little less subtle than neutrinos. But Red was permanently tired, his resistance was way down, and he would never be able to afford a really comprehensive immune system. Plus, it had been five or six years since he had cared.

Comprehensive was a relative term anyway, he reflected bitterly. Any commercially available comprehension being pre-installed with Ithacan beggars, G-string viruses, arachnidan access ports, and out-and-out government resets by way of entertainment, existential thrills, and total control, the shells weren't really justifiable.

Red contemplated Tipsy. Was even Tipsy above a reset?

Only so long as that kid is on your side, babe.

Just out of curiosity . . . Red stood and limped a circle in front of her desk. Pretending to sort his testicles in the crotch of his trousers, he keyed the v.6 Quietus.

"Red, sit down," he clearly heard her say.

Override. So much for 75 shells 50. Better he had purchased a serotonin smoothie.

Red sat down. At least, he thought wryly, it's good for street-level Info. So far, anyway. Insofar, he adduced, as the Department of Info isn't putting out unadulterated Info. Or . . .

Or insofar as Tipsy hadn't become pure Info herself.

Ah, Red reflected, back to Turing. While I'm all fretful about determining whether I'm talking to a human or a machine, it seems in the meantime to have become trivial for a machine to determine whether or not it's dealing with a human. What brume-vista was laving my stupid face while my back was turned to that more sinister development?

Who am I kidding? It's been a long time since I even so much as heard of an un-sinister development, let alone got laved by one.

Tipsy cleared her throat. In other circumstances this alone, this glancing admission to phlegm, might be considered a signal courtesy, a kind of intimation of humanity.

But these weren't other circumstances.

"Let me help you help me help you," Tipsy said.

"Thanks very much, Tipsy, but I—"

"That was not a suggestion," she suggested curtly.

"Quite," Red consented readily.

"You seek unemployment," Tipsy told him.

"Actually, I—"

"And how is the fishing?"

Red lifted his free hand off the crook of his walking stick and, in the timeless gesture, extended it palm down, parallel to the floor, and waggled it. "Eh," he said. "Feck." Sad to say, however, these days it was true. Not even a globally mandated cessation of all commercial fisheries had brought back the fish.

Tipsy smiled. "Why do you still bother? If you need protein, make a requisition. Every time you come back from the Bahamas, you tell me the fishing has gotten worse."

"It is The True," Red replied.

Tipsy's mouth tightened. "Not a good choice of witticisms, Red," she said, "if wit is what you thought to deploy."

"May I remind you—"

Tipsy lofted a forestalling tridactyl, known throughout the Republics as the ultimate homoremote. "Comprehension doesn't get any more expensive than mine," she reminded him.

Comprehension, thought Red. Now there's a word to be used advisedly. How about we substitute *scripted awareness*?

". . . history," Tipsy finished.

Red blinked. He hadn't registered the beginning of her sentence. Involuntarily, he shook his head, as if to clear it. For some time, he'd often been finding himself on the other side of some undefined gap between whatever she had been telling him and whatever she was presently saying. Oftener and oftener.

"That's the word," she continued. "And you get the credit."

Another one, thought Red. She had always relished the right word. A satirical poet had even rhymed it with relish—lush-embellished hishtorical relish :: condiments for freeee, for you and for sheee—and discovered himself or herself reset without a public trace; subsequently to reappear, no doubt, as a midlevel Infoscriptor in Condor Silversteed's anthem factory. The first thing upon which Red deployed every Quietus he'd ever owned was on that sonofabitch's so-called music.

"It was a close thing," she was saying. "He failed, however, and it was left to Red Means, People's Hero, to cut his way through the Legion of Cedrics and save the day. There is no question. It's in the historical record."

Right, Red thought. And I killed the daemonic Lieutenant Miou Miou by virtue of my clairvoyance in regard to the postchondrophoric storyline.

What about the fact that Red Means had cut off her own brother's head? Surely that must count for something?

"We persevered—"

We, Red inwardly snorted, persevere with the broken record.

"The world needed and deserved my brother's fundamental humanity," she recited, engaging full Auntie mode, "not to mention his various talents. Pertinacity, the facility with tools, the cool head in a crisis—."

"Yes, yes, yes!" Red impatiently blurted. "That's a good one, about the cool head—!" And look what you got, he didn't shout aloud. An illusion of dialogue, nourished by shells and years, with a proper little Caligula. Except he's not so damned little anymore. And now you're going to marry him off? What's that? A late-blooming death wish?

The outburst surprised him at least as much as it surprised her.

"Without you, I never would have gotten in touch with him," she stated simply.

Another argument he'd heard before. In fact it had taken Red only six months, and a casual six months at that, to identify a middle-management blow monkey in the San Francisco office of the Cavalcade of Wonders, and it was but a moment or two later, big-picture-wise, that the barely post-cognitive Klegan was given to understand the nature of his special relationship with a Cavalcade real estate specialist called Tipsy Powell.

Red had counseled her to wait and see. But no.

He never heard about what happened to the blow monkey.

Nobody had.

She insisted that he had pulled off an almost impossible task, and he'd let her go on insisting. It wasn't even worth a laugh. He looked at the tiger. The tiger looked at him.

"He is Klegan," Tipsy continued. "The world needs and deserves him. It was all to the greater good . . ."

How sick he was of that expression.

". . . ours a higher purpose. We—"

"I just want to retire," Red interrupted.

Silence.

Well, now that it's out in the open, blunder onward we must.

"When I see that little endomorph . . ." He pointed his stick at the beachscape volume formerly inhabited by the hologram. "How cunning, how patient, how . . . *triangulating*—"

"How evolved?" Tipsy posited.

How evil, Red thought she might better have said. Delusion upon delusion. Looking that kid in the eye is like looking into the wrong end of a riflescope.

"And, you know, hardly anybody in the world takes exception to the term descendant like you do." She touched her breast and added, rather too meaningfully, "Starting with his dear Auntie."

"Precisely." Red seized on the idea. "To me it's, it's almost the opposite of old-fashioned. It's distasteful, I don't understand it. I've read over six hundred books since our . . ."

"Change of fortune," Tipsy suggested.

". . . and I still don't understand it," Red continued, exasperated, not bothering to remind her that they'd mostly been novels and history, with titles like *The Story of a Life*, and having little or nothing to do with political theory, which had become her specialty after she mastered real estate. Except they did have something to do with it. "Oh, I wish the world well and all that, nothing but the best. But for me, myself, I just don't like what's going on around me anymore, Tipsy. And I don't get your wilful blindness to it. Can your probes suss that?"

She dismissed this with a gesture.

"You can't know what it's like to have attained seventy-nine years of age. But when you do, let me assure you, you will have no more interest in making it to one hundred and nine than I do."

Tipsy almost laughed. "Is that what they're advertising?"

"Ridiculous," Red agreed. "I'm tired. The noise, the images, the onrush of their ubiquity, the knowledge of my part in all this." He indicated the room with the crook of his cane. "I can't sleep. I don't want a job. I can't think. I can't do my job. I just want to fish all day. Since there are no more fish it's the same as doing nothing. Can you understand that?" He swept the cane before him. "Not to mention my reputation. The least slippery of my old acquaintances—of the two or three still alive—sees me coming and puts on the big fade. None of them sticks around long enough to so much as express their contempt! And why? Because they're afraid of you. Not of me. You. . . . And if they do stick around?" He made with a rubber face. "It's pure sycophancy. Nothing more. It makes me sick. You yourself must remember the fear, also known as respect, I formerly struck into the hearts of my clients. Your friend Quentin, for example."

"Venerable Asche, to you," Tipsy stipulated coolly.

"I'd forgotten the Revision," Red said caustically.

"Don't come the acid with me," she suggested, not without menace.

"Getting old isn't for pirates!" Red pogoed the cane off the floor and caught it midshaft in his fist. "He was terrified to take a ride on a boat with me! And now that I'm his age?" Red chuckled without mirth. "I'm terrified to take a ride on a boat with me, too." He was probably the only person in the world who thought this was funny. "If he hadn't died on us, everything would fallen out otherwise. Maybe he'd have talked some sense into you. At any rate you'd have remained broke and maybe by now you'd be nothing but a sniveling drunk in some basement apartment furnished entirely by detective novels—"

Red stopped, then sat back in his chair. That ought to have done it, he thought grimly. As he'd done any number of times before, he slyly eyed the various seams and corners of the room, insofar as they were discernible. Where could she be keeping all those detective novels? Was he, Red, the only one convinced of their existence? Convinced of the necessity of their existence? And the alcohol. There was just a little puffiness around the eyes. . . .

He blinked.

Was he the only apostate left?

Ah so, he bethought himself. Progress. Be careful what you wish for, Red. Old man. . . .

Tipsy appeared to consider his outburst. The fountain sounded like windblown leaves. Red listened. The clatter of palm fronds in a warm breeze, iced Kalik in the shade of the canvas bimini, a siesta in a hammock slung main to mizzen, the hammock that rocks by itself. . . .

And you wake up dead.

Sounds good to me, Red scowled fiercely. Real good.

"I suppose you know that this," Tipsy's gesture encompassed the room, "once belonged to Venerable Asche?"

Of course he knew it. Now where are we going? Red shifted uncomfortably. "It's . . . been a long time, Tipsy," he admitted. "Madame Powell. Handmaiden of Our Future. People's Shero. Mentor to Klegan." He couldn't help himself. As he recited these titles he did not withhold a sneer. Why should he? He had helped this woman make this mess.

Abruptly he sat forward in the chair and changed his tone. "I head back to the islands tomorrow," he announced calmly. "I won't be returning."

"I see," she said, with remarkable equanimity. She did see, he realized. And she didn't care. No more than he did. Tipsy's eyes focused on some middle distance, and the projection of Auntie ceased to be animated.

Uh oh, Red said to himself.

The wall to Red's right abruptly repixelated into a wood-mullioned window of sixteen lites and flaking paint. The sound of the fountain went away, and the sounds of distant traffic filtered into the room, as if through an open window. Among them could be discerned the remote honk of an air horn atop a diesel locomotive, a diesel locomotive decommissioned long ago.

"Venerable Asche treasured this view," said her voice. "All the Info continues to say so."

Then it must be The True, Red thought to himself, and who wouldn't treasure such a view? Or any view at all?

"Look at it," her voice suggested. Its tone bore just a hint of coercion.

Red looked. Half the window stood open, the view was framed by the tops of tall eucalyptus trees. A breeze crepitated their leaves, olive, russet, and a red the color of dried blood. The air was cool and fitful and, introduced from west to east, it actually moved, bearing with it the salt tang of a vast, cold sea. A scrub jay, perched on a branch, scolded a domestic house cat, far below the window sill, as it chased and batted at a monarch butterfly down a long flight of redwood treads laid in dirt beneath windrows of leaves.

Beyond the proscenium formed by the eucalyptuses proceeded a vista of forgotten bucolic sublimity. Down the slope and perhaps two blocks away, the tapered stacks of the Pioneer Soap Factory, a rambling assemblage of yellow wooden buildings, emitted sleepy gouts of steam. Farther out, beyond the flatlands spreading away from the north-facing slope of Potrero Hill, boxcars from all over the continent stood patiently in rows, and a diminutive brakeman in blue and white striped coveralls moved among them, lantern in hand. Beyond the freight yards rose the westernmost suspension tower of the old Bay Bridge, beyond that lifted the steep shoulders of Yerba Buena Island, blushing green in response to the ministrations of the first month of winter rains, and far beyond lifted the tawny hills of Berkeley where, if Red were to peer very carefully, he might discern the cylindrical outcrop of the Lawrence Radiation Laboratory, and beyond that the resolution failed and one could begin to discern the edges and corners of the technology.

By an act of will Red kept his mind just within the outer boundary of this projection.

It was there, Red reflected sheepishly, that Lawrencium was first smashed into existence, only to wink out again, as if wilfully. Three-fifths of a nanosecond, as he recalled. That's as long as Lawrencium ever existed.

Was there really a reset button? He might never know. He waited. The image of Tipsy regarded the middle distance without emotion. It was the only way it had regarded anything for a long time.

"Consider yourself retired," she finally said.

EPILOGUE

HUANDYAI AND CROWDER WENT TO THE CHARLEY TO PETITION PERMISSION to take a walk.

It always unnerved Huandyai to visit a Charley. The eyes followed you no matter what, whether the head spoke or not. He wasn't sure of the technology. Except insofar as it applied to the latest shoes, he knew very little about technology.

Crowder was another story. His shoes were another story too. Crowder's shoes converted from Skate to Shock mode and back again within eight to ten neural bursts. Huandyai's shoes took ages to change modes and, often, they caused him to fall down. He'd discovered that it was a lot safer to leave his shoes set to Manual. But only Closet was slower than Manual.

"What's up, fellas?" the Charley asked.

"I want a new pair of shoes," Huandyai whined.

The head let that one slide. Huandyai knew if he asked it a spurious question again the program would default to Sedition and after that it would take all day to get out of the jam. Parents, Councilors, the ride home deducted from his Social Contract—the works.

Well, not The Works.

Crowder shushed his friend. "He does need new shoes," Crowder said, "but what he really wants is to play hooky and take a field trip to the Headlands."

The head blinked and processed. "Is there some reasonable tie-in with your studies?" it reasonably asked.

Crowder was ready. If it had been up to Huandyai, Crowder would have an office out of which he'd be running the entire School District. "We're doing birds," Crowder said. "Songbirds of California."

The eyes, which had reverted to their normally vigilant scan of Union Square, angled down toward Crowder. "You remember songbirds?" the Charley asked.

Crowder shook his head. There was little percentage in lying to a Charley, as he well knew. "No, sir," he said truthfully. "But a bird was sighted in the Headlands last year and—"

"What species?" the head said.

"Audubon's warbler," Crowder said immediately.

The Charley's eyes blinked twice.

Wow, Huandyai thought, in genuine admiration. That's requesting one big data-sort.

"Beautiful bird," the Charley said finally.

"So they say, Sir," Huandyai replied ingenuously.

The eyes had time to roll Huandyai's way before it announced, "Not seen lately." The eyes rolled back at Crowder. "Last sighting almost . . . nine years ago."

"Hey," Huandyai piped up, "the year I was born."

"Wow," chimed Crowder, in full ingenuous mode. "I didn't realize it had been that long." The head chuckled without mirth. It sounded not unlike an empty soy drum ricocheting down the walls of a fifty-story fume-well. "That's probably two-thirds your current enjoy-by date," the Charley suggested, before adding in a severe tone, "Isn't it, son?"

Crowder, who had been chuckling somewhat tentatively, in order to humor the Charley, agreed with drilled precision, "Point eight one eight, Sir."

"Point nine exactly," Huandyai hastened to put in.

"Actually, sir," Crowder made bold to expand, "Nine divided by eleven is point 818181818, *ad infinitum*. A repeating decimal, like."

"How interesting," the Charley replied, with no interest whatsoever.

I couldn't agree more, Huandyai thought to himself.

Crowder, who knew his History, thought to himself, when I grow up, as go certain algorithms, there's going to be some changes made. But "Yes, Sir," was what he said aloud.

"You seem to have an aptitude for figures," the Charley said, as if musing. "If you were to take up mathematics, what do you think? Theoretical? Or Applied?"

"Applied, Sir," Crowder answered immediately. As ever, not only did he know his History, he knew what to say. "There are never mathematicians sufficient to undertake market analysis."

"Very good," declared the Charley.

"Thank you, Sir."

A moment of pure algorithm passed in silence. "You boys realize there's still no chip service out there in the Headlands," the Charley reminded them patronizingly.

"Yes, Sir," they said in unison.

"Be careful, then. Be sure to take vitamins and fluids before you go, and take some along with you. And sun block."

"Yes, Sir," Crowder replied. After receiving an elbow from his friend, Huandyai obsequiously parroted him. "Thank you, Sir."

The head blinked. "I'll e-ceph your parents."

"Thank you, Sir," Crowder said, not without revealing a trace of uncertainty.

Uh oh, Huandyai thought to himself.

"Hey," said the Charley, opening its eyes, "Your mother disappeared shortly after you were born, and your father is a hepkeite miner."

"That's true, Sir," Crowder replied.

And nobody talks about why, Huandyai added to himself.

"But you can e-ceph him on the moon," Crowder stipulated. "Of course, that will take two point five six seconds, round trip." He traced a circle in the terraturf with his toe. "If he's not down in the mine, that is."

As Crowder knows heckawell his dad is, Huandyai realized.

"You think so?" the head replied somewhat testily, as if they needed reminding that perhaps the single most dangerous thing a kid or anybody else for that matter could do in the entire world would be to tell a Charley something it didn't know. "So who's minding the store?"

Crowder made a face. "Oh, Sir, I got programs out the wazoo, Sir. Don't worry about that."

Now the head merely stared at Crowder. No more blinking. "And you've learned to game the programs sufficiently to play hooky?"

Crowder watched his shoes as if to keep a sharp eye on some visible line between fibbing and lying. There were only certain subtleties a kid could get away with when dealing with a Charley, and none of them had to do with Motherland Security. And as he looked at his shoes, he scowled in Huandyai's direction, for the latter, though almost two years younger, seemed poised to establish distance between them. But Crowder, standing his ground, nodded. Then he mumbled something.

"I can't hear you," the head told him.

This is what the head would have said under any circumstances, as Crowder well knew. But then he mumbled something again.

"I said," repeated the head, its inflection conveying less patience, "I— can't—hear—you."

"I said, Sir, that a kid has to find out where the boundaries are," Crowder enunciated clearly, looking up. "Sir."

Huandyai knew his friend to be a ballsy little heckaheck. It was one of the reasons he liked to hang out with him. But this gambit, or whatever

Crowder thought it was, looked certain to be letting them both in for an official session of Gluteal Ardence. Why couldn't the clown leave well enough alone? All they wanted to do was play hooky and take a walk in the Headlands, for Klegasakes.

They could practically hear silicon making demands on superconductivity. But after what seemed like forever the head came back. Still not taking its eyes off Crowder, it said, "That's pretty good, kid. Has anybody ever suggested that you might have what it takes to be Motherland rocket jock?"

"Really?" Crowder lied.

"I'm marking your card," the Charley told them, with avuncular condescension. "We'll see."

That much, both kids knew, was true.

"Now beat it," the Charley said, with the gruff inflection of sentimental pride.

"Thank you, Sir," the two declared almost simultaneously. And though Crowder's shoes went straight to Skate, and he was across Union Square and heading north against the beam traffic on Powell Street before Huandyai could manual from Park through Trudge and eventually to Canter, he wasn't all that far behind.

The eye in the back of the Charley's head, which the algorithm never bothered to blink, watched them go.

Despite the heat of the day, the ascent to Coyote Ridge from Tennessee Valley presented little challenge to either pair of shoes. Sensing dirt both pairs defaulted to arcane settings approximating Primordial Hike. Crowder's pair had all kinds of Tread modes, in fact it had the latest feature you could get for under five hundred shells, called Fuzzy Jog; and Huandyai's did okay when manualed to any of its mere three Tread settings; but Hike was a crude function on either pair. Still, the ergonomics of both pairs were way ahead of, like, bare feet. You hear what the Info is e-cephing?

Being a habitué of the last library in San Francisco, Crowder had taken the time to browse its vast inventory of paper nautical charts, and eventually noticed the tiny designation of Pirates Cove, just a few miles north of San Francisco in the most hotly contested piece of undeveloped real estate left in Northern California. The chart labeled it the Marin Peninsula; locals called it the Marin Headlands.

The name caught his fancy. A precocious and prodigious reader, Crowder had long since burned through Dewey Decimal Section 910.45, "Voyages and Voyaging," which included a great deal of single-hander literature from the twentieth-century, as well as pirate literature from the centuries preceding, and, so, like many a young lad before him, Crowder had buccaneers and the crack of canvas on his mind.

And thus it came to pass that a day of hooky had been planned. Each boy had charged up his shoes, laid in a supply of sunscreen, and prepared a hearty lunch of vitamins and hydration fluids.

It turned out it was only two miles, as the drone flies, once the beam let them off at the mouth of Tennessee Valley, but almost five miles as the shoes ambulate. The first mile, down the valley to Tennessee Cove, is flat, the next half mile switchbacked up to the ridge, and the next two miles is switchbacks, arroyos, ridgerunning, coyote signs and gopher holes, proving the gopher/coyote homeostasis to be humming right along, and a great deal of poison oak. They never did see an Audubon's warbler—they wouldn't see one if they parked an ever-vigilant Head on the highest point on the ridge and left it there for the next hundred years. Huandyai didn't know it, but Crowder suspected it was so, and the Charley had statistics on its side. But the Charley was programmed to dispense Hope to the citizens whenever it wouldn't cost the Program anything, and, thus, rumors to the effect that maybe the Audubon's warbler wasn't extinct after all were encouraged. Still, since nobody Crowder knew had ever actually seen a bird that wasn't a crow, a seagull, or a pigeon, and despite this evidence that the carrion/garbage homeostasis was humming right along, which you would think might suggest the salubrity of the bird/insect homeostasis, a kid had to wonder.

Sure enough, no sooner than he thought this thought, a turkey vulture lifted over the brow of the edge of the cliff to their left, not ten meters away. Two and a half to three hundred meters below the lip of the cliff, the Pacific seethed restlessly at its base, and while this was not without its intrinsic interest, the appearance of a relatively rare member of *Cathartidae* indicated that there must also be relatively rare dead or dying small mammals hereabouts.

"There used to be lots of them. They sit in trees in the morning with their wings out like this." Crowder held out his arms. "They have to wait for the sun to dry them before they can fly."

"Probably doesn't take nearly so long as it used to," Haundyai muttered, wiping perspiration off the tip of his nose. "They need sun block?"

That was Huandyai all over. He was intimidated by the State, but he took very little for granted. It was one of the reasons Crowder let the kid hang around with him. That, and his shoes were never up to date, even though he had parents. Crowder knew a lot about a lot of things, but he was convinced that if you had parents your shoes would automatically

update. Huandyai had never been able to disabuse Crowder of this prejudice, and Crowder kept Huandyai in his orbit because he was convinced
that sooner or later the kid's shoes would update and he'd be right there
to call him on it.

All of this conveniently ignored the fact that Huandyai's parents, who
held four jobs between them, made too good a living to qualify for the
Social Contract that updated Crowder's shoes automatically.

They landed in Pirates Cove accompanied by a cascade of serpentine
rock and uprooted echeveria plants, and, even though it was already
almost time to head back, allowing for daylight at the end of the round
trip, they were both really glad they'd made the trek. The cove lay at the
base of a cirque-like notch in the tall wall of surf-bashed cliffs that ran
north from Point Bonita, at the northern edge of the Golden Gate, all the
way to Stinson Beach, a matter of some twelve or thirteen kilometers as
the drone patrols. Pirates Cove marked the half-way point. There was no
fresh water there, the climb down to it from atop Coyote Ridge took
about a half hour, and the climb out could take twice as long, depending
on the heat and what kind of shoes you were wearing and the relative profusion of poison oak.

There were all kinds of kelp, driftwood, light bulbs, disposable phones,
shotgun shell waddings, feathers, syringes, and yellow polypropylene line
at the high tide mark, and Huandyai and Crowder took all the time they
needed to explore this stuff. The sea made so much noise around them,
and bounced so much white noise off the cliff faces that surrounded
them on three sides, that a mere ten meter separation gave each of the
boys sufficient mental space to allow them to nearly forget that each of
them wasn't completely alone.

The entire cove was only fifty or sixty meters across, with the Pacific
heaving up and around two big rocks in the mouth of it. The near one
was sufficiently accessible that it looked like maybe you could climb it
when the tide was out. Today, right now, the tide was out. And the chat
cribs warned that lunar mining was adversely affecting the tides—not
today, pal!

"Although," Crowder allowed darkly, "it's true, you know. The calculations are available."

"The Info will set you free," Huandyai parroted happily, apropos of
nothing, as he wrapped an extremely long tendril of bull kelp around the
driftwood palings of a fort he was constructing.

"Who ya trying to keep out over there?" Crowder asked, idling digging
the point of a stick into the black sand beneath some rounded gray stones
at water's edge.

"I'm not," Huandyai answered, half paying attention. "I was thinking this would be a good place for a Charley."

Crowder considered this. "It would almost have to be the size of an adult human's. You ever seen a Charley that small?"

"Nope."

"Thought so. There is one, you know."

"What?" Huandyai wasn't really listening.

"That small."

"Yeah, yeah. At the Shrine." Huandyai squinted. "What's these?"

Crowder blinked a few times while he scanned the sector of rote flashed by his shoes. "They're called *Vellela vellela*, or sailors-by-the-wind."

"Must be your shoes tell you so."

"It must be The True."

"Nice color."

"Yeah." He blinked. "Porphyry. They look fresh. There's some over here dried up. Hey."

"Hey."

"Let's go swimming."

Huandyai looked up at him, then looked at the water. "You mean, without our shoes?"

"Sure. Why not? Besides, you want to walk home in wet shoes? Not to mention," he added contemptuously, "yours would probably short out."

The water was cold, but not as cold as it once was, as Crowder reassured Huandyai. According to Crowder's shoes the water was at slack tide, but, still, they had to be careful, as the surge was deceptively strong. The differential between the water when it heaved up and when it was hove down could be as much as three or four feet, and it could sweep your legs right out from under you.

But oh, it was exhilarating! Neither boy had ever been in water outside a municipal pool, and this was a completely different experience. It was colder for sure, and when Crowder came back onto the beach he consulted his shoes, to discover the water temperature was a mere 65 degrees, warmer than it had ever been, according to the profile his shoes had been sufficiently prescient to flash-load before they walked out of the satellite penumbra, but chilly enough to turn his lips blue.

"That's still plenty cold," Huandyai stuttered through chattering teeth. "Boy." He scrubbed his face with his t-shirt and looked out over the water. "We should come back here once a week."

"We come back out here that often, we'll find out whether there's Audubon's warblers for sure," Crowder said, by way of agreeing with him.

"Is that what we're going to have to tell the Charley every time?"

"Sure. Why not? He'll think we're a coupla budding ornithologists."

"I thought it was botanists that budded."

Huandyai was big on bad puns. That was another reason Crowder let him hang out with him. "That's funny," he declared without mirth. "Hey."

"Hey what?"

"Let's climb that rock."

Huandyai squinted up at it. "Do you think we can?"

"Sure. Why not? First, let's do our vitamins."

Even though Crowder had no parents to speak of, he was disciplined about his health. Maybe, Huandyai reflected, as he swallowed, regurgitated, and swallowed three times, it was because he had no parents.

Crowder waded into the water on the beach side of the rock. Despite being in the lee of the swell, the surge lifted from Crowder's knees all the way up to his shoulders before it fell back down again. Crowder had nerve and was a quick study, too, however. He waved Huandyai over and, with the trusting innocence of a younger brother, Huandyai let Crowder boost him higher than his shoulders, buoyed by the next surge. "There's got to be handholds up there somewhere," he shouted over the clatter of rocks rolling in the surf, with Huandyai's feet on his shoulders. The next surge came up to his chin.

"There's a root. . . ."

"Go for it!"

Huandyai went for it. His weight departed Crowder's shoulders just as the next surge peaked, lifting him almost as high as the younger boy's knees. But Crowder's hands were wet, they found nothing to grasp, and down he went, out of sync. The next swell swept over him. This is no joke, Crowder thought to himself as he surfaced, spouting brine.

Huandyai hadn't given Crowder another thought. He scrambled up the steep slope with a graceful agility he didn't often get a chance to employ. These kinds of adventures were few and far between in these times of forty-eight-week school years and parenting algorithms of vast scope, and so, soon enough, he disappeared over the upper edge of the formation. "Come on!" Huandyai yelled over his shoulder. "You can see Japan from up here!"

Japan must be closer to California now, Crowder thought sardonically, than it once was. The next surge lifted him easily within reach of the root, and when it receded it left him almost entirely out of the water.

Above it for the time being, he thought seriously. Pulling himself up into a rocky declivity, teeming with fat-leafed ice plant and other echeveria, he took a moment to survey the cliff faces that loomed above the cove on three sides. Though the driftwood they'd been scavenging had all pretty much been a mere ten or twenty feet above the present tide line, right at the base of the cliff, by their ripple marks he could see that some high tides, at least, rose three or four feet up the base of the cliffs. The chimney-shaped rock stood off the south end of the beach. The trailhead, which was the only way to reasonably get out of the cove, as the scrub and rock were otherwise poison oak and practically vertical, descended through a dry wash at the north end of the beach, just beyond what his shoes had tutored him to call a century plant or maguey (*agave americana*). But his shoes couldn't tell him hecka at the moment because he didn't have them on. And there, come to focus on it, they were, along with Huandyai's shoes and two sets of clothes, not two meters from the tide line. It used to be five meters. So the tide is incoming. Nice. Maybe he could write an applet for the next generation of shoes, whereby they'll respond to hand signals. We need to rethinking our logist—

"Crowder! Hey, Crowder! Crowder!"

Crowder looked up. Huandyai's bare feet appeared, five or six meters above him, and along with them came a shower of stones and plant material.

"Hey, hey!" Crowder yelled, looking down as the detritus cascaded over his head and shoulders and past him, into the water below. "The heckaheck!"

"Crowder!"

"What!"

"Crowder, Crowder!"

The kid sounded panicky. Was it too high up there? Maybe he'd come face to face with an Audubon's warbler?

Either way, Huandyai kept repeating his friend's name, much as he might have wailed for his departing mother over a baby-minder's prothorax.

And when Crowder had clambered over the rim, he saw why.

"Heckaheck, Crowder." Huandyai was indeed scared. "What the heck." On the verge of tears, but angry too, he looked at Crowder accusingly. "Did you know this was here? Is that why I got up here first?" Crowder shook his head. "No, kid. No . . ."

The skull and what bones he could see or recognize as bones lay scattered across the uneven dome of the rock, interspersed among guano-whitened stones and spiculate succulents. They were picked absolutely clean of flesh, and maybe bleached, too. Crowder wasn't sure, for he'd never seen human bones before. They appeared to be as evenly populated with lichens and guano as the rocks around them, however, so they must have been there for a while.

"That's human," Huandyai asked shakily, "right?"

Here and there, scraps of cloth, some with plants grown right through them, fluttered in the breeze.

"It looks human to me," Crowder said.

"Y-You th-think it's a k-kid?"

"You mean like us?" Crowder crawled past Huandyai and approached the skull. "What difference would that make?"

"I don't know. M-maybe this rock has, uh, preferences."

"You mean, maybe this rock demands a sacrifice from the humans that come here?"

"Yeah. Something like that."

"How do you know he got killed? Maybe he died somewhere else and a turkey vulture brought him here to eat him."

"Y-you gonna touch it?"

"Sure." Crowder sounded more confident than he felt. "Why not?"

"Oh now that's hecka nice," Huandyai said. "Hecka."

"Look at this."

"What's that?"

"It's a watch. I think."

"How do you tell time with it?"

"It used to have arrows that pointed to the numbers. Hands, they called them."

"H-hands? Like this p-p-person used to have?" Huandyai giggled.

A pun in the clutch, yet, Crowder thought. The kid's all right.

"D-Does that mean that that p-part," Huandyai pointed, "is a wrist?"

Crowder dropped the watch.

"Gotcha," Huandyai pronounced incontrovertibly.

"Was not that you," Crowder scowled, "caterwauling but a moment or two ago?"

"Caterwauling?" Huandyai drew himself up to his full one point two meter height, minus the fact that he was kneeling, "I do not caterwaul."

"Maybe it was a recording," Crowder allowed.

"Still," Huandyai allowed back. "You got to admit . . ."

"Unnerving," Crowder kindly supplied, as he rummaged among the rocks and bones.

"True." Huandyai gingerly teased a piece of fabric from beneath a succulent. "What's this?"

Crowder squinted. "Some kind of medallion. Or is it a high denomination—what did they call them?"

"What did they call what?"

"It's the same word as—you know."

"If you know it, I definitely know it."

Huandyai snapped his fingers. "Insignificant public servants."

Crowder frowned. "Coins?"

Huandyai snapped his fingers. "That's it."

"That's true. They outlived their derogatory nickname. It started out as a unit of money. There were lots of them. Many civilizations used them for, heck, a couple thousand years, I guess." He fingered the object. "They called coins change, too. There were expressions like pocket change and chump change, for small or insignificant. People would rattle coins in their pockets when they were bored or distracted."

"This one's kind of big, don't you think?" Huandyai pointed out. "For a pocket, I mean?"

"Must have been worth a lot."

Huandyai made with a regretful expression. "If we had your shoes, we could ask them."

"Oh, hey, that reminds me," Crowder said. He turned and cast a glance down at the beach. "Look."

Huandyai followed the line of sight along which his friend pointed. "Our stuff? Our shoes?"

"They're about, I'd guess, one point five meters from the tide line."

"That was stupid."

"At least one of us noticed," Crowder reminded him pointedly.

"If we take this with us," Huandyai said, "some archeologist is going to have a field day."

"I figure we got about ten minutes," Crowder said, looking down at the beach.

"I guess the skull would be the important part? Despite it's missing the lower jaw?"

Crowder shook his head. "We're naked. We'll never get it back to the beach."

Haundyai frowned. "How long do you think he's been up here?"

Crowder shook his head. "Long enough for the birds to have lost interest in him, I guess. How do you know it's a him, anyway."

"Good question. Can you tell from bones?"

"Maybe if you find the right ones. Or analyze the DNA."

"I'll bet not all of him is here, come to think of it. The weaker scavengers probably flew away with the smaller stuff. Fingers and toes. Like that. Carried it off to all heck and gone. I'll bet the wind blows hecka strong here in the winter, plenty strong enough to carry stuff away."

Huandyai crossed his legs, placed his chin in the palm of one hand, and surveyed the scene. The bone with the dangling watch lay on the ground in front of him, along with the large coin. Watch and coin were heavily corroded, and encrusted with an olive and orange colored mold that must enjoy growing on guano. Call it *scatophitic fungi*. But as he stared at it, thinking nothing in particular, he realized that there was an alphanumeric significance to certain raised parts of the surface of the coin. An embossment, perhaps. He turned his head slightly and was able to make out an eight, a one, and a six, which he read to himself, moving his lips, as was his wont when he read anything. Kind of a big number. Which made sense. It was a big coin. He knew that the ancients always put famous stuff on coins. Emperors and slaughters and dogs and such. He really wanted a dog.

A particularly large swell broke against the seaward face of the rock and its spume lofted higher than the boys' heads, so that airborne droplets twinkled between Huandyai and the late sunlight.

"Wow!" Huandyai displayed the body of his tongue to the spangles and tasted salt.

"Well," Crowder announced from around the other side of the shoulder of the rock, "I found maybe a hand."

"What time is it?" Huandyai said, happily blinking in the dazzle.

Crowder reappeared. "It's like a puzzle." In his cupped palms lay several phalanx and carpal bones amid a flat, warped box.

Huandyai took it up. "What's this?"

"It was next to a whole pile of little bones. There's more around the mouth of a hole." Crowder didn't mention that he'd been afraid to stick his own hand in the hole, and so he hadn't.

The box was some kind of warped plastic. That much they could tell. The UV had been very hard on it. If the plastic had once been transparent, the rays of the sun had clouded it to opacity and raised all sizes of bubbles in it, too. Neither boy had ever seen such a box before.

They took turns handling the box, and they handled it gingerly, at first. But before long Huandyai, who was insatiably curious, had begun to pick at it, thinking maybe he could take it apart. But he didn't have any tools, not even his inch-and-a-half pocket knife, which was as big as a boy his age was allowed to possess. He picked at the box, peered into it, picked at it some more, rapped it against a rock, held it up to the light.

"You know," Crowder said at last, looking over the back side of the rock, "we really need to get out of here." He turned and looked west. The sun had about two hours to go. "And I mean, really out of here. Otherwise, there will be an Incident. If there's an Incident, we'll be in the fourteenth grade before they allow us to come back out here again, and by then we'll be too mature to think it worthwhile. Not to mention, there will be little if any time budgeted for idle adventure."

Huandyai grunted. He held the little rectangular box next to his ear and shook it. "Huh." There was a slot along one of the narrow edges, and for maybe the dozenth time he tried to see into it while he shook the box. "There's something in here," he said, squinting.

"You mean, like a life form?" Crowder said.

Huandyai inverted the box so that the slot was downward and struck it twice against the palm of his hand. Scraps of a thin material the color of cinnamon cascaded out of the slot. He quickly turned the slot away from his hand, but the things didn't seem to be alive any more. Mummified, dried up or desiccated, maybe, but not alive. They were all brownish, angular, and all kinds of different shapes. Many featured a pair of parallel edges. None of them was more two centimeters long, all were virtually weightless, altogether ephemeral, light as air, with a substantial surface area relative to its weight, so that the onshore breeze easily carried them away as they tumbled out of the box, airborne as spider floss. If either of the boys had ever blown the down off a dandelion, he might have compared the effect. But neither of them had ever seen a dandelion. The things scattered through the air above the beach like a hatch of winged insects. And, in fact, a snake doctor appeared, nailed one of the brown entities, let it go, and nailed another.

"Heckaheck!" Huandyai said. "Did you see that?"

"*Corydalus cornutus*," Crowder said. "It doesn't seem to like them." He indicated the little box. "Maybe at one time they were nutritious?"

Huandyai waved the box over his head. More little brown things came out of it, to be carried off by the wind. The snake doctor bore off and away, however, soared over the beach and quickly out of sight. "Yeah," Huandyai said thoughtfully. "Do you think they were that guy's food?"

Crowder shrugged. "Not anymore."

Huandyai closed his hand around the box. "I'm going take it with me. Maybe your shoes will know what it is."

Crowder bit his lip. He didn't want to admit that he was suddenly superstitious, but . . . "Do you think we should disturb this place?" he asked. "Any more than we already have, I mean?"

"Didn't you say there is a bunch of these containers? Or seedpods? Or whatever?"

Crowder nodded. "Yeah. But."

"Nobody will miss just this one," Huandyai suggested, a slight edge of pleading in his voice.